Black
Milk

Darrel William Moore

One: Acheron

Prologue

Like a vampire, Prometheus cloaked himself against the day, pulling his coat over week-worn clothes and sliding his hat low over his brow. He gulped down another mouthful of whisky before reaching a shaking hand for the door.

Outside, the sun turned his eyes to pin-pricks. People swarmed. Hansom cabs and horse carts congested the roads, while fan-fluttering ladies and fine-dressed gentlemen trampled the cobbles. He pulled his collar up, pushed the hat deeper over his grey face, leaving only an ominous slit of a mouth exposed to the world, then swayed down to the waiting cab. He climbed into the shady carriage and ordered the driver on, watching from the dark window as London swooned in the midday heat. Amorphous blobs of melting colour.

The cab stopped after a while and Prometheus clambered out. He retreated into a shaded side street, where a wiry man stood in a secluded doorway.

"About time," Benjamin Duffy said, shoving a large leather satchel into Prometheus's arms. The shadow of the door cast across the man's face, framing a set of blackened teeth, like long-rotted tombstones.

"I'm early," Prometheus said.

Duffy scanned the street. "Money." He held out a greasy hand with nails just as foul. Prometheus produced a wad of banknotes, which the man snatched before scurrying away among the rats.

He waited for Duffy to disappear into the crowd before rejoining the sun-drenched streets. Already he craved the asylum of his books and the cold steel of his instruments. He hailed a cab and willed it faster through the streets, until at last he braved his halls once more, descending back into his cellar.

The darkness welcomed him like an ally.

He swiped away a pile of books atop his trunk and placed upon it the leather satchel he'd paid so handsomely for. He loosened the bag's rope tie, opening it.

So fresh it hadn't even begun to bloat.

Deep within the dark hole, the podgy face of a baby corpse stared lifelessly at him – a sleeping cherub with grey skin and algid flesh, stillborn and taken from a nearby hospital. He quickly closed the ties and locked the tiny body inside the trunk.

All he needed now was a storm, and the sooner the better... Lest the body begin to putrefy.

1

The main doorbell chimed in the above house, shattering the silence. Prometheus jerked still on the spot, hunched over a metal contraption and surrounded by tools. As a rule, he did not answer the door. It was better to pretend he was out or the house was vacant, but it still caused him to panic in such a way that on each rare occasion it rang, he would stand perfectly motionless for the better part of an hour, straining to listen for sounds of forced entry.

Most of the street presumably would have assumed the house was now empty; he rarely left the cellar and never spoke to anyone – almost. Mrs Teachwood, the lady of the next residence along, was often the culprit of the heart-stopping surprise visits. She would on occasion call round unexpectedly – and most uninvited – to enquire how Prometheus was "getting along", as she put it, professing her concern, singing her condolences and generally spilling her copious and unbearable character all over him until he could stand it no more.

The problem was she was such a busy-body that if Prometheus avoided her for too long he had no doubt she would call the authorities to check he was alive and not hanging from the stairwell with a morbid note pinned to his shirt. And since he had avoided her last three visits, Prometheus had no choice: the door must be answered. He could not risk police attention, not when he was so close.

He climbed the cellar stairs into the long-deserted servant area in the lower rooms, then made his way into the main foyer. He readied his stomach, tensing as if awaiting a blow before opening the door to the hallway. It stretched before him, with its dusty marble floor and ragged eggshell wallpaper. He could not keep his head down this time. This time, he had to pretend and wear the mask as best he could – as he always did upon her visits.

He would feign sanity.

Why she persisted in calling in on him, he would never know. Maybe something in his eyes gave him away, something he couldn't conceal despite his efforts. He suspected his eyes betrayed him.

"My dear Dr Page, thank goodness you are well," Mrs Teachwood screeched, as soon as the door was opened. "I've been beyond anxious for weeks so that I have been barely able to eat a thing. Sure enough, I was convinced you'd done something quite horrendous to yourself. But here you are, alive and able-bodied. Well… just."

She strode in, followed by her maid, who was holding a serving dish.

The woman turned with a flurry as Prometheus closed the door. "Let me look at you. My goodness, you are gaunt. Have you eaten at all since the last meal I brought for you?"

"Of course, Mrs Teachwood," he said, gesturing for her to enter the drawing room. In truth, he hadn't even eaten the last thing she'd brought him. It sat on the floor of the cellar until it decayed away.

She took a seat on one of the dusty chairs and removed her hat, almost pulling off her ginger wig in the process. "Put that on the counter, dear and make some tea," she said to her maid, who nodded and left immediately. "It is sweltering, is it not?" Prometheus hung like a spectre in the doorway, unable to bring himself to fully enter the room. "Mr Teachwood hasn't had a wink of sleep in days and swears that if this relentless heat does not cease this very night he shall sleep in the nude." She made a chortling sound. "Well, you can imagine my response." She raised a set of thin painted eyebrows on her powdered white face, which looked as though a wrinkled cloth had been draped over a skull.

"But it is not for the delight of conversation in which we usually partake that has brought me here this day," she said. "That is not to say I am not here to enquire after your wellbeing, of course, I am. Only you yourself will fully know how I have taken it upon myself to guide you through this most calamitous time. Under my wing, so to speak." She held up a hand as if Prometheus was about to sing his rapturous praises.

He wasn't.

"You don't have to thank me, I'm quite aware of how much you have utterly depended on upon me these past three years. I just thank the Lord above I have been blessed with my good nature enough to lend an aiding hand when I have had the opportunity." She looked to Prometheus, who had managed to edge himself beyond the threshold of the doorframe. "The gratitude just pours from you. There is no need for words. And I'd like to think that it is because of me that you are standing here today – strong, back on your feet, ready to thrust yourself out into the world and open to making new acquaintances."

The maid entered with a tray of tea, poured two cups, handed one to Mrs Teachwood and the other to Prometheus.

"Thank you," he said, "but it's too warm for tea." He placed the cup on the side table, unable to stand to look at the wedding china in which the tea swam.

Mrs Teachwood laughed after taking a lady-sized sip. "Don't be absurd, Dr Page. It is never too warm for tea. But what was I saying? Oh yes. The other reason for my visit today is that we are to have a guest stay with us in the Teachwood residence. My niece. Poor girl has just lost her husband and needs to be away from Bath for a while. Too many memories, I am sure you understand. It is a good thing I've experience in dealing with the grief stricken. They were wed for just over a year and madly in love like only the young can be. The tragedy happened only months ago and the dear thing is not doing well at all." She took another delicate sip of tea, but no breath. "He was in the regiment, you see. Shipped off to South Africa and killed during in those dark battles the Christmas gone. She's to remain here for a while." Mrs Teachwood looked dismally around the neglected room. "And to think, her Majesty Queen Victoria departed this world only a fortnight or so later, God rest her soul. It's everywhere, isn't it, this death business?"

Prometheus shifted. He could somehow feel what was coming.

"And as you've had first-hand experience in overcoming the nightmare of grief, I was hoping you might spare some time to have a sit with her. To talk with her and to let her know that there is someone in this world who understands the pain she feels."

Prometheus looked away from the woman's intrusive stare. "I really don't see how I could console her."

"Oh but you will, Dr Page, believe me. She is still a young girl, but she shan't always be. She needs to move forward and do it quickly, otherwise how will she ever find another husband? She has the advantage of being a pretty thing but with a heart full of melancholy no man will want her. Men like cheerful, amiable girls – not grieving widows. So, it's settled. Come along, Anne." She stood and headed for the door, maid following. "I shall be receiving guests for a little get-together tomorrow evening and it shall be the perfect occasion for the both of you to be introduced to one another. Sharply at seven, but feel free to arrive early if you wish the company, you poor, dear, poor old thing. I'm sorry, Dr Page, but I really must run. The girls are round for tea at two and I must dress before they arrive. Goodbye."

The door closed behind them and Prometheus's lethargic objections were left stunted. As he turned he caught a glimpse of his reflection in a mirror. It startled him. Dead blue eyes peered from a gaunt, lifeless face through the layer of filth.

"Would that I could sip from the river Lethe and let all knowledge of your death pass from my memory. I would sit and wait here forever for you to come home, grow old, then turn to stone in forgetful bliss. All without knowing you were forever gone from me. At least then I would know hope and some deceiving reason to live."

He turned and sloped back towards the cellar.

*

A face peered in through the rectangle of glass in the front door of the main house, distorted by the relief design of swirling leaves and vines. The glass magnified one large painted eye that blinked and stalked the hallway inside. Then, like an eagle, it spotted movement and proceeded to knock again, harder this time.

"Poor, poor dear," Mrs Teachwood said, bursting through with her maid. "You've no idea of the time, do you?" She was half dressed in a silk robe and her crooked wig looked as though it was about to fall off her head.

The storm had not broken the night before and Prometheus hadn't slept at all, fearing it would tear up the sky without him. The time now broaching evening, he was only able to stand against the exhaustion by regularly dousing himself in whisky.

"Never mind, dear, it's quite alright. No need to apologise. As it happens, Anne took the liberty of preparing the formal jacket she found in your wardrobe yesterday. Here you are. Go and put it on. Sharpish." She clapped. "Guests will be arriving soon and I've still to finish preparing."

Speechless, Prometheus stared at his own suit shoved into his hands.

"No need to thank me, dear. Chop-chop." She proceeded to push him up the marble staircase before heading out the door again. "Just call in when you're ready. We'll be waiting."

There was no escape. He would have to show his face or she'd never leave him in peace. He looked up, realising he was on the first floor landing, a place he hadn't set foot since another lifetime ago. Memories stirred. He all but fell back down to his cellar, closing the door firmly behind him and hugging the suit in clammy hands. It was clean and Sarah's scent no longer haunted the fabric. A cold blade of guilt cut into his chest at the relief.

*

He was the last to arrive of Mrs Teachwood's guests, among which were the generally respected and wealthy socialites of London.

Guests congregated in the parlour and drinks were poured into them. Mrs Teachwood performed best to a large crowd and she wooed the room like a lover, offering flatteries, amusing stories and friendly banter to each visitant she draped herself upon. So at ease was she with her company that Prometheus felt the slightest twinge of jealousy. He stood himself motionless like a statue among them and offered no conversation. On the few occasions attempt had been made, he would cut the conversation dead with a monosyllabic reply – usually obscene or controversial – then turn until they went away.

It was because of his brusque behaviour that a curiosity grew around him. Who was he? What did he do? What was his story? Questions came at Mrs Teachwood from all angles and she was more than delighted to divulge the details of what she knew about Prometheus and his "poor, tragic life."

As the sun set lower, the gas candelabras were lit in the parlour and dining room, providing Prometheus with much-needed shade in which he could harbour, while listening for the birthing sounds of a brewing storm. From the shadows he watched with a full-to-the-brim whisky glass in hand as his story passed from mouth to ear, mouth to ear, mouth to ear – each new recipient of his life's woes taking a moment to throw a sympathetic glance in his direction.

He detested their sympathy.

It was then that Mrs Teachwood brought forth her niece into the throng, making introductions. She was a pretty girl; thin, frail and pale as ice. She wore her almost white blonde hair in a bun and a mourning gown of black. Her eyes were framed with purple circles, similar to the circles Prometheus had acquired over the years, only less severe and she wore no smile on her youthful, yet somehow haggard face. The young woman wrapped her grief around her like a shroud, recognisable only to those who had too suffered it. It was a heavy shroud and she threatened to buckle under the weight at any moment. No one else seemed to notice as they forced her into meaningless conversational drivel, but all the while her eyes spoke the truth. To each introduction, the girl offered the slightest smile, which Prometheus was sure would have taken all her will to perform. Pulled by her aunt, they sashayed through the room, Mrs Teachwood scanning with inexorable eyes. Then, homing in on the solitary figure in the corner, she dragged her niece over to where Prometheus sat.

"Ah, there you are, Dr Page," she said, yanking her niece by the arm and placing her directly in front of him, as though she were presenting a prize horse. "May I introduce my niece, Ms Jane Halford?"

With eyes lowered, Jane offered a shallow curtsy and an even shallower smile. Polite etiquette dictated that a man should rise upon being introduced to a new acquaintance, especially a lady, but Prometheus sat firmly in his chair and said not a word. He could see the growing awkwardness on Mrs Teachwood's face as the silence extended beyond even her threshold of pain. Prometheus had hoped that this rude act would cause her to remove her widowed niece from his sight. But unfortunately, it did not.

"Well, I shall leave you two to get acquainted," the woman said unexpectedly. "I must go and see to my guests."

Jane looked up. "Auntie," she said, but Mrs Teachwood had already untied her arm from around her niece's and strode across the room towards a group of laughing gentlemen. Jane became utterly distressed at being left alone with a complete stranger and Prometheus couldn't help but feel for the poor girl – not only for having lost her husband but also for having such an unscrupulous aunt.

"I think she is tired from organising the evening," she said, making excuses for her aunt's lack of propriety.

Prometheus jumped from his chair. "Please, sit. You look like you're about to keel over."

"Thank you," she said, taking the seat. "I must confess, today hasn't been one of my better days, even though I've tried, for my aunt's sake. She is so spirited I sometimes feel exhausted just watching her."

"Indeed. May I get you some water or something to drink?" It was an attempt to amend for his earlier rudeness.

"You are too kind. I thank you, but am perfectly well just sitting here, resting from the heat." Jane smiled at him, revealing in it a hint of pity. That angered Prometheus and made him want to strike her porcelain face.

"I shall leave you in peace," he said abruptly, bowing slightly.

"No. Please. Stay. It's just, I know my aunt has expressed a particular wish at our meeting, and no one here knows what it feels like—"

"I'm sorry I must go," he interrupted before striding over towards Mrs Teachwood, who turned with a smile at his arrival.

"Ah, Dr Page. Come to get a drink for my niece, eh?"

"No. I've come to regretfully inform you I must leave. Thank you for your hospitality."

Mrs Teachwood's smile withered but before she could protest Prometheus was gone.

*

Close to midnight the storm finally loosed itself over London, hurling boulders across the sky and stabbing the night with shards of brilliant electricity. The rain poured down, soaking the quiet London streets above as Prometheus worked in his cellar, dismal with oil lanterns and guttering candle stubs.

A burst of lightning illuminated the lever to the generator as he threw it down. The lightning struck the prong set upon the roof and traversed along copper wires into the machine, which drank the electricity like a thirsty animal.

An infant corpse lay upon the cold steel of the surgeon's table, its grey and bruised skin showing the last signs of bloating in its tiny limbs and torso, but the face still held a cherub quality with peacefully sleeping eyes. He had attached a series of needles and conductive clips to various parts of the body according to the flow of chi. He inserted needles into the soles and palms, then pushed a larger one into its chest, sliding it into the pericardium and directly into the heart muscle itself. He had then set about driving a series of needles through the soft parts of the skull, where the sutures met; one into the anterior fontanelle, to gain access to the frontal lobe and the motor cortex of the brain, one into the posterior fontanelle and one into the mastoid fontanelle. He then attached a reel of copper wire that protruded from the generator onto the ends of the needles, twisting it around each as carefully as he could with his not quite sober fingers.

Upon the trolley, he placed a prepared syringe full of his adrenaline solution, ready to administer. With everything ready, Prometheus drew in a deep breath, placed a shaky hand upon the lever of the generator and threw it down.

At once, the machine crackled with stored power. It scorched along the wires and into the body. The gauge upon the machine read over 200,000 volts. Prometheus steadied it there and moved over to the body, moistened with water. Taking care of the sparking needles, he inserted into the heart of the infant the syringe containing a milky white adrenaline solution. He depressed until empty and watched.

The body lay motionless.

The machine hummed louder as Prometheus increased the volts.

Still, the body lay lifeless.

Heart pounding, Prometheus pushed the generator to half maximum.

Smoke emitted from the doll-like body, along with the cloying smell of burning flesh. Prometheus reached for a close-by bucket of water and emptied the contents over the infant. At once, the smoke ceased and sparks spread over the corpse like a swaddling blanket of lightning. Prometheus then turned the generator to full power.

He waited and watched, willing the body to show a sign of life, any sign of life other than the contractions. But it did not. He had failed.

At last, he shut off the generator and moved over to the steel bed set in the corner, exhausted and thirsty. He knocked back a shot whisky before falling defeated onto the straw mattress. Staring blankly at the wall opposite, he briefly thought he saw the shrouded figure of Death, cloaked by the very shadows and mocking him with its bleached grin.

Then he heard the crying.□

2

At first, Prometheus was sure he'd finally gone insane. He couldn't recall how long he'd sat there, but it was long enough for the storm to pass and the moon to break through the clouds, casting silvery light onto the wriggling infant. Finally, he stood. It squealed upon the surgeon's table, soaked wet as if from afterbirth.

It was truly alive. He'd done it.

The cries ate the silence with the hunger and gusto of that which it was – a new born baby. It had been so long since sound filled the house Prometheus was sure the blast from its lungs would rid all the neglected rooms of the cobwebs that had gathered over the years.

It was a boy. Prometheus had failed to notice that when it was dead. He eyed it suspiciously, cautiously, before carefully removing the needles. Then, clamping his grip firmly, yet instinctively not too hard, around the little body, he picked it up, keeping it at arm's length. The child had a scorching fever.

He at once carried it into the house above and filled the tin bath with a few inches of cool water. Then he placed the child in it, holding its head and splashing the water over its pop belly. After its temperature dropped sufficiently, he wrapped it in one of his old, moth-eaten shirts. The child squirmed inside the fabric.

Its cries didn't stop but changed from the urgency of one pitch to the urgency of another. It lay wailing on the floor, arms and legs splaying out to the sides with each burst of sound. Then it occurred to Prometheus, as obvious as anything – the thing was hungry. But he kept little food for himself, let alone a baby. It would have to wait till morning.

For the remainder of the night, he observed the child with the medically-trained eyes of a doctor, taking its temperature regularly and checking its heart.

Hours passed and the implications of what he'd done came upon him slowly, the way creepers attach and climb the scale of buildings over time. Ideas stirred and his thoughts grew ambitious. Perhaps no one would ever again have to feel the sting of death. No one would have to suffer the hammer of its loss or the bite of its disease ever again. Then a dark smile split his face.

He could kill Death.

*

As the morning sun began its ascent over London, the cries of the once deceased child were finally sated by warm, wholesome, belly-filling milk.

Instantly, the noise was replaced with a gurgling that both enchanted and repelled Prometheus. He had acquired the milk from a cart delivering gallons of the stuff to a nearby deli. Upon hearing the hungry cries of the baby and seeing the dishevelled and generally wretched state of Prometheus, the driver kindly handed over a jar of milk for free, possibly taking him for a beggar. Prometheus had been perfectly ready to pay the man but found it was easier to stay silent.

The baby's bottle, however, proved more difficult to attain, having to be retrieved from the unused nursery on the second floor. Along with the bottle, he'd grabbed whatever he could find that he thought the child might need – changing rags and a few blankets, lotions and a wicker basket so he could put the thing down without fear of stepping on its head.

The baby fell quiet, belly full and comfortable in the cosiness of the basket. It eyed Prometheus with liquid sapphire eyeballs and performed one long yawn before closing its heavy lids and falling asleep. Prometheus watched it for a while, sitting on the floorboards. It was not much more than a few hours old – possibly premature. Prometheus himself almost succumbed to sleep, until a sudden thought peeled back his lids: what on earth was he going to do with a baby?

He couldn't offer it back to the parents, although the thought of doing so filled him with much satisfaction. To think of himself as the destroyer of Death, able to give back the life that was taken from two grieving parents, almost thawed his insides. But it also made him remember...

James had emerged from the delivery room. He did not smile. Face grave and dripping with sweat. On his hands and clothes, flashes of red blood. Prometheus had stiffly prepared himself to learn his child had died during birth and that his wife was obviously extremely distraught. It saddened him, but he was strong enough to bear both his and his wife's loss. He would carry her through it until she was ready to think about trying again. That was all that mattered – that she was ready. But then the words crawled like creatures from James's mouth.

Everything changed.

"I'm sorry, Prometheus," James had said. His eyes were red and his hair a state. "There were complications. We did the best we could, but there was just too much blood loss."

In that moment, Prometheus's heart froze in his chest. James put a comforting hand on his shoulder. "I'm sorry, old friend. Sarah is gone." Numbness followed. Then agony. He heard screaming. It came from him.

That's all he remembered.

To give the parents back their child would be the greatest reward, but how would he explain it? They believed their child to be dead – their child had been dead. It was best to leave them out of it completely, for the time being at least.

Prometheus already knew what he must do next. He must recreate the experiment… only bigger. He needed to bring another life back from the beyond to prove it could be done again. But where could he procure another cadaver? It was hard enough the first time. He must. And it must be a fully-grown adult this time.

It was his ultimate goal. It would change his life. It would change everything.

*

"I'm here to speak with Ms Halford, thank you," Prometheus said to the maid he recognised as Anne, after calling at the Teachwood residence. The slavey girl invited him to wait in the foyer and glanced down quickly at the basket he held in his hands before hurrying off.

Although it was unusually early to call, Prometheus knew Ms Halford would already have risen, judging by the tell-tale circles of insomnia around her eyes. He also presumed Mrs Teachwood would still be abed, after retiring late from her soirée.

Within moments, Ms Halford appeared at the top of the stairs, dressed fully, as Prometheus knew she would be. In her black gown, she was the perfect image of grief and as pale as the ivory cameo she wore at her throat.

"Good morning, Dr Page. What brings you so early to visit? I hope nothing is the matter?" She offered a humble smile as she fully descended the staircase. She peered inside the basket but said nothing.

"Firstly, I would just like to offer my apologies for my abrupt behaviour last night. I was not feeling well and was not in the best mood for company. I would have told your aunt I could not attend but I was afraid it would have disappointed her too greatly."

"Please, Dr Page, you have no need to apologise. I'm fully aware of my aunt's… persuasiveness. I have often fallen victim to it myself."

"Not to excuse my behaviour and ill attentiveness towards you, but I have also been quite apprehensive about the arrival of my cousin's orphaned child." He held out the basket to formally give Ms Halford permission to inspect it.

A smile lit her face at the sight of the sleeping infant. "Oh, how adorable," she said.

"I'm afraid the poor thing has lost both parents in a terrible accident and it has fallen upon me to take the child in, being its next of kin."

"It?" Jane looked up with an amused grin.

"Him. Excuse me."

"You don't have much experience with children?"

"None, I'm afraid, and I'm quite at a loss to know how to look after… him… properly until I can find a good home for… him."

"You don't intend to raise him yourself?" Jane's smile faltered.

"I simply couldn't. It wouldn't be fair on it – him. No, I'm sure the best

14

thing to do is ensure he goes to a proper home and then on to a good school for an education. Of course, I will always be there to support him financially and will always visit when I get the chance, but I feel a life in my company alone will not provide the best environment for him."

Ms Halford said nothing more on the subject. "And how is it I can help you so early in the morning?"

"As you may or may not be aware, I relieved my house staff of their duties some time ago and I have important business to attend to, and…"

"You were hoping we would be able to look after the child here for a while?"

"Only if it's no bother."

"Of course, I would be thrilled to assist in taking care of the fellow. I had no other plans today other than to drink a copious amount of tea forced upon me by my aunt. She believes tea to be the cure of every ill."

"Please, do not go to such trouble as to mind him yourself, I only meant perhaps the house staff could take him off my hands."

"It's no trouble at all. In fact, it has brightened the day ahead."

"Well, in that case, I'm much obliged to you." Prometheus handed over the sleeping baby, which Jane took with a smile. "I shan't be too long. Perhaps an hour or two depending on the outcome of my dealings."

"That's perfectly fine," Jane said. "I hope it is not grave business that needs such urgent attention?"

Prometheus almost smiled at her choice of phrase. "Indeed, it may well turn out to be grave, but nothing I cannot manage, I'm sure." He went to leave.

"Oh, goodness me," Jane said. "I almost forgot. What is the little fellow's name?"

Prometheus hesitated for a moment, stumped for a reply, until the name of the street that ran perpendicular to Berkeley Square entered his mind. "It's Charles," he said. "His name is Charles."

*

He didn't much remember the days after Sarah's death. They had whirled by in a gush of meaningless condolences. Sleep came easily for him then. For months, it seemed, Prometheus slept, waking after hours, or even sometimes days, only to blink into the glaring darkness of his drawn drapes. Each time he awoke, the memories returned and the pain cut a fresh wound before he would weep himself back into unconsciousness. After months of people coming and going around him, gradually he saw less and less of them, and eventually, when it seemed sleep would not have him any longer, there was no one left but him in his lonely house. He dismissed the house staff at some point during that time, unable to bear their pitying looks. For months after, he could get no rest at all. It was during these times he realised whisky could knock him out regardless of sleep having long ago abandoned him. But with the whisky came the dreams, and soon even that stopped working.

It was the eleventh month after Sarah's death he decided on what he would do. Prometheus would kill himself. He rigged a rope around the highest bannister of his ornate marble staircase and watched the noose swing there for days, hollow. Twice he stood at the top and tightened the slipknot around his neck, only to remove it again with shaking hands. Suicide had proved unsuccessful. Each time his weakness tied the noose at his throat, weakness undid it again.

The hansom cab arrived and Prometheus stood outside The London Hospital, staring up at the impressive façade of the building where he had once spent so much of his time healing and helping his patients. A row of stone arches loomed like St Peter's Gate, with steps that led into the tomb.

He never kept a tally of the number of lives he'd saved, like some doctors he knew. Faces came and faces left. When he was young, he was vain enough to attempt to remember each one, but the years passed and eventually he developed the skill of disconnecting himself, which was a natural way to deal with losing some, so he was told. To feel responsible for every one of them would almost certainly mean insanity. So a hardness set in. His skin armoured around him and the faces eventually became blurs and statistics.

Inside, the halls were the same cold off-white he remembered. Nurses who he no longer recognised, and who he was sure would no longer recognise him, guided the sick to rooms off the main corridor. Empty beds lined the walls, folded sharply with starched sheets, ready for the next wave, and sterile light poured in through the lead-rimmed windows.

Prometheus marched through and turned the corner from the entrance lobby. No one bothered him; his stride sure enough to disguise his being out of place. Through a set of doors and down a case of stairs, he descended. The farther he went, the fewer people he passed, and by the time he arrived at his destination, he was completely alone. He walked the pea-green corridor, turning another corner in the maze-like halls until faced with a set of doors with two circular porthole windows. The blackness beyond pressed against the glass as if trying to escape.

The morgue was as cold as he remembered. The smell, to which he had once become accustomed, now lodged itself aggressively in the back of his throat – chemicals masking rotting flesh. Death was a scent that unfazed him, it was the clinical sweetness that brought a gag to his throat and watered his eyes.

The lamp was soon alive with flame. It flickered and made the shadows dance. Steel beds were kept in organised rows, the deceased inhabitants covered with shrouds of white, outlining frozen profiles. He greeted them like old friends.

His attention turned towards the desk covered with papers and Prometheus hurried through the top layers, holding each sheet to the light before throwing it down. After a few attempts, he found what he was looking for and scanned the inventory of recently deceased and cause of death. He needed a cadaver that was fresh and intact and it soon became clear only one was suitable – a young man of seventeen that had died from tuberculosis. He was buried only yesterday.

He folded the details into his pocket, feeling the flask as he did so. He took it out, brought it to his lips and tilted his head back, feeling the warmth of the whisky wash over his tongue and down his throat, heating his belly. It sent waves of numbness into his limbs and head. As he brought his head down again, he noticed a figure in the darkened corner of the room, standing perfectly still.

"Where the hell did you appear from?"

He moved towards the shape. Seeing how it hovered over the bodies, as though examining them, he stopped. The figure was turned away from him, tall and dressed in black from head to heal, cloaked with a hood raised over his head.

"Sir?" he said, but the man made no reply. "Who are you? What are you doing down here? I demand you show me your face."

The figure slowly turned and Prometheus took a step back.

"It can't be."

A chalk-white jawbone with jagged teeth grinned at him from beneath a shadowed cowl.

Prometheus took another step back. "It's you," he breathed, feeling his fear congeal with hatred.

Movement stirred under the black robes and a dark blade came sailing out from beneath infinite layers, razor-sharp and gleaming like polished onyx, followed by a fleshless bone hand grasping a burnt-black staff.

A scythe.

"Death," Prometheus hissed.

*

The whitewashed halls blurred by as Prometheus's legs carried him from the morgue. Whatever it was, it hadn't followed. The hospital entrance awaited and he rushed into the sunlit foyer.

A man casually entered just as Prometheus was leaving. He saw the familiar flash of white hair and Prometheus immediately wished he'd put on his hat to pull over his face. The man was his old colleague and friend, Dr James Dolton. They hadn't spoken in over a year. The man spotted him before Prometheus could slide by. He stopped on the spot and called his name.

Prometheus reluctantly turned to face the man. "James," he said. His voice was flat, but James didn't seem to notice.

"My goodness, it's been an age. Where have you been hiding yourself?"

"I've been taking some time out," Prometheus said.

"Yes, quite. Good for you. Just what you needed, if you ask me. It's marvellous to see you back on your feet. Are you returning to your post here to save me? Do say you are, old boy. I've been dying for some decent company and it hasn't been the same without you. They keep getting younger here, I swear. I shall walk in one day and they'll have staffed the whole place with foetuses." James laughed hard. "Cocky lot, too. I think they need to be taught how it's really done, eh, old man?" He gave Prometheus a nudge and let out another raucous laugh. "Seriously though, old boy, how are you? Between us two, you're not looking your best."

"I've never felt better in my life."

"Listen, I know things have been difficult of late…"

"Please spare me the rousing speech, James," Prometheus fired in a sudden wave of impatience. "I must go."

James held his arm. "You have to move on at some point, you know that, don't you, Page?" Prometheus pulled off his grip and restrained the urged to throw a right hook.

"Don't presume to tell me what I have to do. I can do what I damned well like."

"You were the best surgeon in London. Don't let that go to waste."

"That man is long gone. Everything has already gone to waste. It's done." Prometheus left through the middle arch and began down the stone steps of the entrance.

"And what would Sarah have said about that?" James said, following him out.

Prometheus stopped as through confronted suddenly by a wall. He turned. "Sarah's dead," he said before walking on.

"But you are not," James called out. "You are not."

*

The sun had almost set completely and the summer evening was as warm as ever. Clouds billowed about in the darkening sky and rain threatened at any moment. The steeple of St Margaret's Church protruded like a sharpened black rib bone from a shallow grave.

Prometheus bypassed the so-called house of God and, carrying with him only a shovel, made his way across the churchyard through old and cracked headstones, some completely worn of script and some naught but age-weathered stubs of rock. He passed them like grim signposts pointing the way towards the newer graves until the loose dirt of a fresh grave appeared through the stone forest.

Standing over it, he glared upon the headstone.

Edward Sparrow 1884 – 1901, beloved son and brother.

He took in a lungful of warm dusk air, feeling the first few raindrops fall from the gravid clouds before plunging his shovel deep into the earth.

Hungrily, Prometheus began to dig.

☐

3

Ystil.3 opened the synthetic's abeyant eyes. It felt peculiar that he now had eyes to open. He was programmed to function in a synthetic body, but it had been an infinite amount of BroadWeb time since he'd last filtered into one. A feeling of claustrophobia rose in him… and something else – nausea. The thought of having to exist in real-time, even if only for a short while, washed him in a cold anxiety.

Ystil.3 was not a field agent and shouldn't have even been there – he told himself this repeatedly while he lay, waiting for the limbs to awaken – but when Sir Z demanded something, there was no objecting. It wasn't Ystil.3's fault the reports had occurred during the time sectors he monitored, and yet he had been the one ordered to investigate.

A red dot flashed in the corner of his vision, serving as a welcome distraction in his new body. At least he could still receive secure-beam.

"I've just filtered, Sir Z," Ystil.3 sent.

"Good," Sir Z sent back. "I assume you've downloaded all the appropriate functions needed for this type of field work?"

"Everything from blinking to the current local history of the time sector."

"And what about this human you'll be watching? Are you familiar with his file?"

"Yes, Sir Z."

"Very well, DataCom. Reserve this synth's secure-beam frequency for our communication alone. No other should contact you by this channel and you should not attempt to contact others, is that clear?"

"Yes, perfectly clear, Sir Z."

"Good. Contact will be made in due course. Out."

The secure-beam cut off and Ystil.3 fully activated the synthetic. He wiggled his stiffened limbs; it felt like being under water – not that Ystil.3 had ever been under water – but apparently the memories of the synthetic conveyed to him that was what it felt like. It was, without a doubt, a deep space synthetic used for 0g missions, and wasn't particularly used to the false gravity of the orbiting infirmary. Deep space synths were generally reserved for the highest missions and rarely set foot on terra firma. But they were loaded with extra functions, which Ystil.3 was thankful for, at least. It meant he didn't have to live like a human while stuck in real-time, even if he did have to look like one.

The synth told him he was cold and he looked down at its naked human form as he lay in the fugue stasis pod.

At least I'm a man.

Ystil.3 abruptly remembered that he was, in fact, not a man – he actually had no gender at all – but was simply reacting once again to the instincts of the synth. It was apparently very relieved to find its penis intact between his legs.

The stasis pod opened with a hydraulic hiss and Ystil.3 took his first awkward steps out onto the cold floor of the orbiting infirmary. It was cramped and windowless, filled with only the necessary sterile equipment needed to furnish his synth for entry.

The air that he wasn't used to breathing was cold and stung his lungs. His limbs ached and his muscles burned with a new life. Ystil.3 wondered when the synth had last been used. It felt stiff, almost atrophied. Of course, Ystil.3 was not accustomed to real-time and could make no real guess.

In truth, he found the whole process of real-time odd, with time's endless moments tumbling over one another like clumsy, yet intangible scavengers in an eternal race towards oblivion. It felt as though time was both irritatingly slow and infuriatingly fast all at once.

Pondering the constraints of real-time caused him to become light-headed again. He clutched onto a cold metal wall panel.

I'm not a field agent.

He had been trained long ago, but never actually thought he would have to use his real-time training. His primary function was to watch the Time Data Stream in the comfort of Grid City, recording everything that happened within his time sectors into the Earth Files. His allotted time sectors were all that concerned him. His real-time "training" had consisted of two Earth days in China State in the Earth year 2297. He'd hated it and the people. Humans. He didn't like the creatures then and he liked them even less for making him go to Earth now.

He remembered feeling the same sense of decapitation then, like he'd left a major limb back in the BroadWeb – which he had, in a sense. Over fifty percent of his colossal AI mind was stored on the server planet M21, and being trapped inside a synth meant Ystil.3 couldn't access the whole of it. The BroadWeb was now totally off limits to him and his new, part-organic body. What's more, he now had no access to the Earth Files. Without them, he felt utterly lost. Since the nanosecond of his conception, they had been only a flex of his mind away. They were his life – his function. However much he disliked humans, it was the purpose of his sentient existence.

Ystil.3 typed the current Earth time sector into the stock printerpad and it printed the appropriate clothes, money and papers. There was a small mirror on the hatch panel, which he stared into disgustedly. A pair of human blue eyes stared back, framed with dark lashes and roofed with thick black eyebrows. His nose was large and straight and his jaw and chin formed a strong right angle. The synth had wavy black hair that covered his ears and threatened to obstruct his vision. The face in the mirror sneered.

It took Ystil.3 a long time to dress – his bulbous and muscled limbs worked against him in newborn clumsiness.

"Damn this corporeal shit," he said irritably. The sound of a physical voice was jarring. How did he even know those words? Synth memory again.

"P-p-p-p. Ahhhh. T-t-t-t. C-Crap-p. Tits." He sounded various words, sticking a probing a finger into his mouth, feeling his strange and organic wet tongue. He clamped down his teeth on it.

Pain. He remembered pain – so did his synth. Blood. He remembered that too.

The cell-sized infirmary that orbited Earth, undetectable to human tech, had a single purpose: suiting and booting an AI travelling to the planet. It had everything Ystil.3 needed to prepare for Earth life, and soon he was lying flat inside a narrow, man-sized drop-shell, being catapulted from the infirmary on his way to Earth.

The bullet-shaped drop-shell had an eye-level window strip that flooded with a dark view of space as he commenced atmospheric entry.

"Fifteen seconds to impact," the lifeless auto-computer announced.

The drop-shell rotated and Earth slowly swam across the viewing window like a slow-moving creature.

"Ten seconds to impact."

The blue and green planet fell towards him.

"Five seconds to impact."

Ystil.3 had to admit, Earth was a beautiful planet, even through the burning haze of entry. It was primitive and unfathomable to him, but most defiantly beautiful...

"Prepare for impact."

...From afar.

*

Ystil.3 looked with his alert synthetic eyes at the London streets around him. The place was loud and arrogant even while the sun slept. The shadows that cloaked each side-street and corner held cutthroats and thieves, waiting for an opportunity to steal the small metal coin discs that people carried to exchange for goods or services. Either that or they waited for some other form of base gratification.

He walked by an old beggar woman with no teeth and a rag over her head. She pleaded with him for change. He couldn't help but stop and stare at her hideous face. He began to laugh. It was all so ludicrous and he could smell her stink without even getting close. Laughing was odd and pointless to his logic and the sound alarmed him a little with its gruffness, so masculine and human, everything he was not. But in the pit of his synth's stomach, even as the hag scolded him, it was a pleasant sensation, he found.

The time measurer told him it was almost midnight. Ystil.3 checked the DNA tracking system and found that the man in question was still in the same location. Having the human's DNA on file meant Ystil.3 could track the man no matter where he went. He could bury himself three miles deep and Ystil.3 would still know precisely where to find him. A warm wind blew through the streets and large drops of summer rain began to fall. The steeple of the church came into view and Ystil.3 approached. Concealed in the gothic arch entrance, a cloaked figure stood ¬– the Overly Watchful he was ordered to meet.

Most AI respected the Overly Watchful. Ystil.3 thought they were simply a bit retarded. All they had to do was live, while their sensor-stuffed bodies recorded the world's information. They couldn't even retreat into the BroadWeb whenever they liked. Permits had to be granted. Stranger than that, however, was that most Overly Watchful seemed to enjoy existing in real-time.

Ystil.3 approached the figure, concealed in shadow. "You must be the Overly Watchful," he said. His synth's voice grated on his own synth ears. The deep arch sheltered them from the rain.

"My name is Lydia," she said, pulling back her hood.

It was a female synth, with long dark hair, amber eyes and a slender face. The synth was Eurasian, which Ystil.3 found strange for a London-based Overly Watchful of this time.

"That's a curious name for this sector," he said.

"It isn't my original name, of course."

"What is your real name?"

"I am not permitted to reveal it." Her voice was smooth and intelligent, an English accent with a hint of something else that Ystil.3 couldn't pinpoint. She was also very tall for the sector. Men over five foot nine inches were considered tall there, but this woman was a full six foot, long and graceful and only a little shorter than his own synth.

"I assume you've been briefed with our objectives?" she asked him.

"I have. To keep a close watch on the human and attempt to discover how he is bringing the dead back to life."

"Have you seen him yet?"

"No. But I only arrived—"

"A full two hours ago, I know," she said.

The rain grew louder. It churned the grass and dirt of the graveyard.

"Well, in case you were wondering, he's over there."

Ystil.3 used his upgraded optics to zoom through the darkness, seeing a drenched figure digging earth from a grave. With each heave of the shovel, the man's face contorted. His limbs shook with exhaustion.

"He wants to bring back another," he said.

"It would be safe to assume that. And what is your name, DataCom Unit?"

"Ystil.3," he attempted to say. The synth's mouth couldn't pronounce it properly and Lydia laughed at the sound he made, a mixture of spit and hacking in the back of his throat.

"That won't do for Earth. Besides, I'm not going to make that ridiculous noise. I'll call you… Winston." She looked very pleased with herself.

He was about to protest but Lydia marched off into the darkness, clutching a purse. Rain bounced off the control field that surrounded her like an invisible bubble. Within it, she remained perfectly dry. He followed, checking his synth's upgrades to see if he had a level one control field too. He did, but decided not to use it. The rain felt pleasant on his synth's skin.

*

The body slid easily from the ground as though expelled from the birthing canal, lubricated by the sludge from its own grave. Prometheus's arms throbbed as he hauled it to the side and began wrapping it in sheets.

Benjamin Duffy stepped out from behind a grave whose monument was a great white statue of the archangel Michael, wings splayed and reverent eyes turned up towards the heavens. Drenched and soggy, the thin man dragged behind him a two-wheeled sheet-covered cart as instructed. The cart did not go easily over the uneven ground and with each bump, Duffy's face grew more impatient. He pulled it alongside the open grave, glaring at Prometheus as he stood with the mummified body laid out before him.

"You ain't payin' me enough for this, old man," Duffy said breathlessly. He leaned against the headstone of the open grave. "Three miles I've traipsed with that luggin' behind me. And I tell you, it ain't not heavy." He casually glanced an eye over the wrapped body. "We'll have to cut it up first. I brought me tools as I s'pected might be the case."

"We will not be cutting anything," Prometheus said. The cart was smaller than he should have liked, but it would do.

"Why couldn't you get yourself a baby like last time," the blaggard said. "Much easier to carry, them. Pop 'em in your coat and Bob's your uncle, away you go."

"No," Prometheus replied, louder than he meant to. "I need a larger body, a full-grown man. Now grab one end." He didn't want to be out there any longer than he had to be. The rain had soaked him through, and though the air was warm he could feel a chill set into his bones. He wore a small brimmed hat that sheltered his face, which was a small favour, seeing how Duffy constantly swept back his hair in annoyance.

He seized the ragged cloth about the shoulder of the body and waited for Duffy to grab the legs. They managed to lay the rigid thing at an angle so the feet protruded out, then wrap the sheet around so as to disguise the shape.

24

Hauling the thing took his last remaining strength, but he kept on nonetheless. He clung to one handle while Duffy pulled from the other, weaving through the headstones and then rattling over cobbled stone back streets – all the while Duffy complained of the weight.

The streets were dark, lighted by the occasional street lamp. Most of London was either in their homes, the public houses or skulking about not wanting to be seen – like them. Hansom cabs and landau carriages still trotted people across town and the raucous clatter and dim lights spilt from the pubs they passed, hearing bawdy songs and clinking glasses from within. A beat policeman with a truncheon and whistle eyed them as they left the road by the river to make their way through Kensington. Prometheus contracted with fear. The bobby, however, took them for rag and bone men and left them be.

After towing the cart over Kensington Gardens the rain slowed to a stop. Duffy now gasped for breath and stumbled every other step. Prometheus urged him on, but as they reached Hyde Park's Serpentine, with the moon reflecting on the glassy unbroken surface of the water, Duffy collapsed in a heap of rain- and sweat-heavy clothes. His own lungs rasped with each inhalation, and it was only when Duffy fell did he realise he was close to failure himself. He rested upon the cart, listening to Duffy and his ruined breath until gradually both steadied.

"We need to keep moving," Prometheus said, as soon as he could form the words. "Just a few miles to go and we're done."

The man made a face like his knees had been smashed in with a hammer. "You…this…fuck," he said between gasps. The man could go no farther, that was evident.

Prometheus threw the remainder of the agreed-upon coin at the man's feet and commenced pulling the cart by himself. It was no matter the wretch hadn't fully completed what he was paid for, the coin was more to secure his silence. During their intermission, the wheels of the cart had sunk into the wet earth and took three attempts to get it moving again. Prometheus's hands could barely grip each handle, so weak were they with fatigue, but he did it, as he knew he would. If his arms should have broken off at his sides, he would have turned and dragged it with his teeth.

Once moving, the wheels rolled more easily, and soon Prometheus left Duffy puffing far behind him, making his way over the Serpentine Bridge where the wheels moved fluently over the stone. On the other side, he headed for the darkness of the park where the light of the main path did not reach. With less than a mile until he reached Berkley Square, all that remained of the task was to navigate Mayfair's midnight streets without attracting attention. But as the dull lights of civilisation were visible beyond dark smudges of trees, a noise from behind stopped him. A breaking twig.

A match sparked to life and a grinning face exploded before him, sheathed in orange light. Prometheus attempted to continue his way, nodding to the man as though they were nothing but passing strangers in the street. But the man did not mean to be passed so easily.

"What you got in there then," he asked, blocking Prometheus's path. He used the match to light a pipe full of tobacco. It glowed when the man sucked. He spoke from the side of his mouth, never once taking out the pipe.

"Nothing of value to you, I'm sure," Prometheus said. "Pay me no mind, I'm merely passing by."

The man laughed. He was heavy-set and bearded with black stubble that crawled up from his neck almost to his eyes. "'Pay 'im no mind', he says. Might be you 'ave a few bob, sounds o' that toff gob o' yours."

"I assure you I have nothing of worth for you." He began on once more, but the man again blocked his path. Prometheus limbs trembled, whether from the fatigue or fear he did not know, but he was glad of the dark to conceal it.

A flash of sharp metal appeared in the bearded man's hand. "Let's be havin' a butchers, then. Might be I'll get a reward for turnin' in a grave robber."

Prometheus's stomach lurched. "How did you…?"

"I told 'im," a voice from behind answered.

Prometheus didn't even need to turn to know it was Duffy. He couldn't even pretend to be surprised.

"I'm s'pectin' you got a few pretty trinkets in that 'house o' yours that we might find ourselves wantin' to have," said Duffy, joining the other man in blocking his path and producing a knife from his sodden jacket.

"I haven't paid you sufficiently?"

"Oh, more than what I woulda taken for it, doc." He smiled a rotted smile. "But thing is, you're what we call an easy target, and I'm s'pectin' there's more from you to be had. Me and me brother both reckon so. We don't cares much what you're doin' with all these bodies – fuckin' 'em, eatin' 'em, dresin' 'em up in your dead wife's clothes and havin' yourselves a tea party – don't bother us nothin'. But we want all you got. All you got. Then we'll leave you be."

That would not be the case, Prometheus knew. If he let these people into his house, allowed them to take what they wanted and gave them all the money he had, they would still turn on him. He brought the flinthold pistol from his pocket with a swiftness that surprised even him and raised it at arm's length until the shaking barrel was barely half a foot from Duffy's face. The man's eyes widened comically and the sneer melted from his pock-marked face.

"I'm going to count to three and then I'm going to shoot you in the face, Mr Duffy," Prometheus said calmly. "Then, as your brother turns and runs, I'm going to shoot him in the back. Once that's done I shall add your bodies to this cart, take you back to my house where your corpses shall wear fine dresses and join the tea party. How does that sound to the both of you?" He paused for a moment to allow them to reply. When they didn't, he went on. "If, however, I find that before I have finished counting to three you have both left my sight and run off into the darkness from whence you slithered, taking the money I have already paid for services not completed, I will allow you to flee without fear of lead in your spinal columns."

The men's eyes twitched.

"And if I ever see your hideous faces again, I will kill you both. It might be on the street or in the markets. You might be doing nothing but minding your own business, but mark me, sirs, I will take out my pistol and end you both where you stand."

Duffy's hand jerked as though he were about to lunge forward with his knife, but was stopped by Prometheus cocking the pistol loudly.

"One…" he said.

The brothers looked at each other.

"Two…"

It was Duffy who ran first, followed quickly by his bearded brother.

Prometheus watched them fade into the darkness. When they were completely out of sight he let out a shaky exhale.

"Three."

*

Ystil.3 and Lydia observed as Prometheus made his way back to the house. They had been watching as he journeyed from the graveyard. Watching as he crossed the bridge after leaving the other man behind. Watching as the other man then followed Prometheus, setting upon him with another. They had been watching as the altercation occurred and watching as Prometheus brought out a weapon.

Ystil.3 had hoped the two men would kill Prometheus so he could go back home. But instead, they ran.

"We need to find out if he's using the White Drops," Lydia said, as they stood unseen under the glowing light of the Berkley Square street lamps.

The streets were dead, save for the occasional hurried figure and the distant sound of hooves on stone. The square itself ran around a central pitch of green, with stately trees lining the path. The houses were large, gated with iron and numerous in windows.

"How do you suppose we do that?" Ystil.3 asked.

"We have to sneak in. Between us, we should have sensors and functions enough to do it undetected."

"And if it is the White Drops?" Ystil.3 asked. "What happens next?" He silently hoped her reply would be that he could return to the BroadWeb.

"I'm not sure."

"Perhaps that's all Sir Z will need of us," he said – actually meaning him when he said us. "Then he can send proper field agents and I can get out of real-time." He checked his DNA tracker to see Prometheus was now in the cellar of his house. He looked around at the night. "I seriously don't know how you can stand it here."

Lydia was staring into the shadows of a narrow lane. "Do you see that? Between the houses. Someone's there."

Ystil.3 focussed on the darkness. A shining white orb hung suspended in the air, tucked into the darkness. Two hollow eyes appeared on it, then a grin of teeth.

"A skull," he said with mild surprise.

Lydia began towards it, her heels echoing on the cobbles. "Let's take a closer look."

4

Prometheus would have supposed waking up in a strange cellar after what was likely to have resembled a very long sleep might've sparked a blaze of questions. But the formerly dead Edward Sparrow uttered not a word. He didn't ask who Prometheus was or even where they were. There were no demands to know what happened to him, or even what he was doing stretched naked on a surgeon's table with a middle-aged man hovering over him. The boy said nothing. Either Edward was in shock, or he had come back wrong.

At first, Prometheus couldn't help but flood him with questions, hoping to uncover the mysteries of Death. He had no idea what he expected the boy to tell him; bright lights, long tunnels? Edward, however, remained silent, looking at him with dark glazed eyes. Eventually, Prometheus had to take the boy into the main part of the house, fearing it wasn't good for him to sit in darkness while Prometheus went about his tests. With a half-decent morning light on him, Edward appeared almost rosy and all signs of degrading and decomposition had been completely erased.

Prometheus had stolen from Death once again.

He had not planned to attempt it that night, but upon arriving home after his altercation with the bastardly Benjamin Duffy, Prometheus felt an anxious urge to rid himself of the corpse, fearing the brothers' revenge for pulling a pistol on them would be knocking policemen. So, he worked industriously into the early hours.

Unlike the infant's soft skull, Prometheus had to lift sections of the young man's scalp to gain access to the brain tissue. His fingers found his tools, stuck in the needles, cut the bone and flipped the switches. He injected the adrenaline and, mimicking what he had done before, soaked the body head-to-toe in water for conductivity of the stored electricity. When it was done, Prometheus waited and Edward took a gasping breath of life.

His onset of decay had reversed entirely. Death shed from the boy's body like an unwanted skin. Next, he would try a six-month-old corpse to see how that would fair. But still… something niggled at Prometheus. He tried to quell it with assessments but Edward's silence troubled him. The boy did nothing but watch as he performed test after test. Prometheus had even gone to the local bakery for bread, milk and eggs, hoping food would stir something, but when he returned the boy was in the exact same attitude as when he'd left – staring out of the drawing-room window with a heavy-lidded expression, his black hair falling over his thin, pointed face while his small mouth said nothing. He did, however, eat like a normal boy. And while he did, Prometheus was faced with the question he hadn't even regarded until then.

What do I do with him now?

A loud knock on the door jolted him from his train of thoughts and delayed the answer. Mrs Teachwood, he presumed. When he answered it, however, he was surprised to find Ms Jane Halford cradling a sleeping baby wrapped in blankets. The scornful look seemed oddly displaced on her delicate face.

"Am I to understand from your expression that you have entirely forgotten about Charles?" Jane said. Her voice was sharp as needles.

Prometheus stuttered, but no excuses came to him.

"Save your breath, Dr Page, I can smell the alcohol on it. I suppose that was your urgent business, was it, to drink yourself into a stupor? It's been an entire day." Her volume rose, but upon realising the child slept, lowered her voice to a scratchy whisper. "Where have you been? You said hours, not days. I called several times during the evening. Were you simply too drunk to answer the door?"

"I... something... there was business I had to attend to. I'm terribly sorry. Has he been troublesome?"

"Not in the slightest. Which is more than I can say for you. You're not the only one in the world to have lost someone you love, Dr Page." Tears welled in her bruised sockets. "I thought perhaps you were being too hard on yourself, thinking that a baby would be better off away from you, but I now realise you were right in your assessment, which is even worse. You know your failures but do nothing to cure them. Better you didn't know and act out of ignorance. But you have no excuse. None at all."

Prometheus didn't say a word, only watched as the sleeping child's eyes fluttered under its bulging lids.

"Have you started making arrangements for suitable family or school?" Silence answered her. "Fine. I will do that. He will stay with me until the task is completed. I trust you will able to, at the very least, approve my decision when it is made?" She turned without a reply and began down the steps onto the street.

"I apologise, Ms Halford," Prometheus said weakly. "Please know I do not mean any injury."

"Of course not," she said without turning. "To do that would you would have to think about someone other than yourself."

Prometheus returned inside with a lingering sense of shame. He'd genuinely forgotten all about the child, concerned only with the next phase of his experiment.

Never in his purest hopes did he ever expect to actually achieve his goal. He had made no plans for what to do with the people he brought back. Could he integrate them back into society? Could he eventually send them back to their families? And if he couldn't, what was the point of any of it?

Prometheus remembered how Sarah had glanced at him from across the room the night she told him she was pregnant. He remembered how radiant she looked and realising why after she'd revealed her secret. Someone was speaking in the circle of gathered doctors but his eyes were on her and her eyes on him. Her auburn hair was pulled back from her face in a way she only did when attending these functions. Her neck flowed gracefully from jaw to shoulders, meeting the black gown that trailed behind her. She smiled, knowing that he watched her, and even after seven years of marriage she still blushed at the way his eyes couldn't help but disclose his passion for her. She raised a glass of champagne to her lips and feigned a sip before excusing herself from the group of huddled wives and made her way across the ballroom towards him. He instantly dismissed himself from his own group and began his walk to meet her.

The delicate hum of polite chatter and the occasional clang of toasts faded as their eyes closed in on each other. He reached for her hand and she took his, placing it directly on her stomach. Prometheus should have known then, but he was too preoccupied with nerves.

Sarah saw it in his face. "My darling, you will be fantastic," she said.

He nodded. "I sometimes wonder how I got here. So many lives passing my table; some leave, some don't. I can never quite believe my hands determine their fate."

She clutched his face and gently made him look into her eyes. "You are the best surgeon in London. That, my darling, is simply a fact. You are the best because you are intelligent, determined, stubborn, strong-willed, devoted and because you care."

He smiled and placed his own hands over hers. "I don't deserve you."

"You do deserve me. And you deserve this honour. Trust me when I tell you that. When you come home late, when you suddenly cancel our plans and leave me alone, it's all done because you are devoted to what you do. And I understand that... most of the time. So, you deserve this recognition."

Someone walked onto the small stage and began in a very loud voice. It was James. "When I first worked with Dr Page all of ten years ago, I realised that he had a unique talent for getting to the bottom of problems. His relentlessness has been such a strength, that in the face of a seemingly impossible situation, and when all had relinquished hope, Prometheus has on more than one occasion provided a solution that has often eluded the entire staff. Not only is Prometheus a man who…"

"Darling," Sarah whispered in his ear, standing on tip-toes and pulling his shoulder down to her height. "I'm pregnant."

The room erupted with applause and cheering as arms reached for him, pulling him towards the front. His hand, which was linked with hers, pulled free and he watched her as they dragged him away, her face wearing a serene smile. She stroked her stomach.

Eventually, the hands managed to pull him onto the illuminated stage. The ovation stopped and Prometheus quickly realised what was happening ¬– people were waiting for him to speak. Sarah looked on from the crowd as the speech he had written and rehearsed over and over fled his memory. Suddenly, a smile broke over his teeth. He no longer cared about the speech. "My beautiful wife has just told me that we are to expect our first child," is all he said.

The audience applauded once again and Prometheus made his way back down to Sarah. She was smiling again. Almost inappropriately, he wrapped his arms around her waist and kissed her in the way he would do when no eyes watched them. She returned the kiss with equal passion.

*

Yes," Ystil.3 sent via secure-beam, "I scanned it with my infrared but the results were the same. It had no temperature, it neither reflected nor absorbed light, sonar passed straight through it and station-wave didn't even acknowledge its existence. I checked all the functions I have and each result is the same. It wasn't there. It didn't exist."

"I don't know exactly what you think happens on this planet," Lydia sent back, "but things like that aren't a regular occurrence. I saw it with my eyes. You saw it with your eyes too."

"I wouldn't rely on these part-organic ovals of membrane and polythasmic fibre. You can fool eyes into thinking something is there, but the fact remains, seeing it or not, what we saw did not exist. It is impossible, other than through the realms of quantum displacement and can you imagine the energy needed to pull off something like that? And why even bother?"

The streets were busying as the morning matured. Carts delivering stock for the markets lined the roads. Every now and then a potato or carrot would fall from the crates and a ragged child would race to retrieve it, deftly weaving between the moving waggons. Vegetables, assorted with the aroma of fish and faeces, lingered in the air – London's perfume.

Lydia stopped as they turned a corner. "I don't think you understand the gravity of what's happening here," she said quietly, as though someone might be listening. "If you think it was just a coincidence that the image of death appeared by the house of a man who has ignorantly stumbled upon the White Drops, then you're even more of an imbecile than I first thought."

Ystil.3 glared. "Firstly, we don't know it's the White Drops, and secondly, I never said it was a coincidence. I said the thing didn't exist, not that we didn't see it, or that it wasn't connected in some way…" He didn't like the next thought that crept into his head.

"What is it?"

"What if it was there for the dead boy?"

"You actually think the grim reaper came to stop Prometheus?" She laughed. "Winston, do you really believe in ghosts?"

"I never said it was a ghost. And will you please stop calling me Winston."

They turned onto Berkley Square and headed to the green, settling on a bench that directly overlooked Prometheus's house. They had spent the small hours curiously following the cloaked skull all over Mayfair as it appeared in the shadows and the crevices of buildings.

Prometheus was visible at his front door, watching a wan-looking woman carrying a child descend the steps of his entrance. In a large dirt-filmed window of the house, the pale face of the once dead boy watched.

Ystil.3 and Lydia both saw him and they turned to one another. He had already brought the boy back. Something had to be done.

In the mere seconds it took for Prometheus to return into the house and close the door behind him, Ystil.3 secure-beamed his friend Tom, the CorVac. Deciding to disobey the silence order placed on him by Z was something he didn't take lightly, but he felt the need of his friend's sober reasoning to help fathom what was happening.

Tom wasn't his real name, of course. It was homage to a human musician who went by the name of Tom Jones. His CorVac friend was obsessed with him.

Tom answered their private secure-beam channel as enthusiastically as he ever did. "How are you, my friend? Back from your real-time training? You've left my Knight in a very precarious position, and your Queen is dangerously unguarded."

"Tom, I need to tell you something."

"What is it? Are you okay?" His friend's pseudo-Welsh accent lilted with concern. The CorVac had searched for a very long time for a function that could interpret him as Earth Welsh, just like his idol – in actual fact, the CorVac had no accent, only a sort of deep throttling noise.

"I'm on Earth. Sector 1901."

"What type of training could you possibly do in that sector? Nothing happens in that sector. You tell me almost every time we speak."

"I'm not on training. Something's happened and Sir Z wants me to investigate. Someone has brought a baby back from the dead – in this sector."

"My goodness. How is that even possible?"

"It isn't. The White Drops, if that's what it is, wasn't discovered until the twenty-sixth century, and I can't think of any other way he could be doing it."

"Shouldn't Sir Z have sent a field agent?"

"That's what I keep saying."

"You make mine and Betty's life seem pretty boring, I tell you."

Tom wasn't a BroadWeb AI. He lived in real-time in a body built just for him. For the most part, Tom's form could be compared to an Earth spider, except he was the size of a truck, made of alloy, and he clung to the side of a ship that orbited the server planet M21 – dubbed Delilah by Tom. His primary function was to remain in orbit of the server planet, keeping it safe from impacting space debris and maintaining the control shields that surround it.

"Sir Z also ordered me to work with the Overly Watchful of this sector," Ystil.3 sent. "She's a bossy sort of AI, who calls herself Lydia and me Winston."

"An Overly Watchful, eh? How exciting. So, if this man is using the White Drops, it would mean whoever supplied it could possibly have been AI, or someone from Earth's future that has Linear Cut capabilities?"

Tom was good at thinking logically.

"That's what I thought. I don't know what to do. I've heard nothing from Z since arriving, and I can't help thinking this Lydia is hiding something from me. It is her sector after all. I hate to get you involved but do you think you could do some digging on her, check her spec, background, server info, stuff like that?"

"I'd have to enter the BroadWeb." The CorVac made no attempt to cover his dislike of that idea.

"You know I wouldn't ask unless it was important."

"Anything for my chess partner," he said eventually.

"Thank you, my friend. You have no idea how comforting it is to know as least I can trust you." He immediately felt more at ease. "How's the view from there?"

"I'll send it to you."

Ystil.3 received a streaming image in perfect clarity: Attached to the hull of the ship, beyond Tom's own long metallic legs clutched to the hull of the Black Betty, the vacuum of the universe stretched out. Countless flecks of light pricked through the depth of light-years. The dark curve of M21 filled his vision, while a burning solar storm from a nearby sun raged in silence. The remains of a broken moon cluttered the orbital path of Delilah and a far-off nebula shrouded the whole of the Titan System in a blanket of electromagnetic light and dust expanding out glacially.

"Not too shabby, eh?" Tom sent.

Often Ystil.3 didn't understand what Tom said, but he agreed regardless. "No, not too shabby at all. Be careful, Tom, and don't mention this to anyone. If Z finds out I've told you he'll delete me back to foetal mode."

"And who am I going to tell out here?"

"Just remember to be on your guard. I've got a bad feeling about all this."

Lydia was none the wiser to his conversation and by the time Prometheus had disappeared into the house, Ystil.3 had already decided what their next objective should be. They must enter the house and prove the White Drops had somehow gotten into the wrong hands.

The servant entrance was poorly locked and located around the back of the house. Ystil.3 kept his concealing refractor field up and with a short burst of Lydia's bullet-shaped laser set on wide-ray, the door-lock crumbled like rotten wood, allowing them entry to the empty kitchen. Prometheus was still in the rooms above. From there, they slipped through a small door that led down into the cellar.

The stench of liquor imbued the air. Medical equipment scattered every surface including the floor. A small and uncomfortable-looking bed was set out in the far corner, surrounded by empty bottles and a bucket that made Ystil.3's eyes sting from the stench. A surgeon's table was the focal point of the space and the only light came from a small frosted rectangle window.

"Where do you suppose it is?" Lydia whispered. She let her skirts drop into the carpet of dust and grime.

"Be quiet," Ystil.3 secure-beamed. "With his equipment, I'd imagine." He stepped toward the surgeon's table. On it sat an empty hypodermic needle. He picked it up. A single drop of liquid remained inside. He opened his mouth and allowed the drop to fall onto his tongue. Within half a second he had run various tests. It confirmed what he suspected. "It is the White Drops."

But there was also something else in the solution, something he hadn't expected. Computronium. How Computronium had managed to get in there was equally as perplexing as how Prometheus got his hands on it to begin with. He wondered whether it was just this one needle, or whether the solution that brought Edward and the infant back to life also contained the stuff. Some untrusting part of him decided to keep this piece of information from Lydia.

She scoured through books piled next to the small bed. "This must be down to AI then," she sent, then watched for his reaction.

"Perhaps," he sent, non-committedly.

It seemed that AI would have the most opportunity, with their filtering and Cutting abilities, but no motive that he could reason. And if AI was behind it, who else than the Overly Watchful of that sector would have a better opportunity? Lydia was suddenly a suspect. He assumed she knew as much already. Perhaps that was why Sir Z had incorporated her help, so he could keep a close eye on her.

The door to the cellar opened, firing light across the room. Ystil.3 froze and Lydia quickly ran to his side and back under cover of the refractor field. They watched the once dead boy clatter to the bottom of the stairs.

Prometheus wasn't far behind him, carrying another hypodermic syringe.

"Come now, there is really no need to fear," he said to the boy, who had found a dark corner beneath the stairs to hide in. "It won't hurt, I promise you."

The boy didn't move and Ystil.3 swore he was grinning beneath within the shadows.

"Oh for goodness sake," the human snapped. "Get out here this instant." The boy sprang up like a Gollum and threw himself onto Prometheus, clasping thin hands around the man's neck. Prometheus tried to pull him off but the boy's fingers clawed into his clothes parasitically. Then they were gone – vanished before Ystil.3's eye sensors.

He stared at the empty space where the two humans stood only seconds earlier. He stepped closer to the spot and looked around the cellar. "What just happened?"

"Check your DNA tracking," Lydia said, equally as flustered.

"According to my tracker, Prometheus is…" He made a face.

"Where?" Lydia urged.

"He Linear Cut. But that's impossible."

"What sector have they Cut to?"

"They haven't Cut to one sector. They've Cut to several."

Lydia went to say something but stopped. She thought for a moment, her face scrunching, before exclaiming, "Huh?"

5

Lights blazed and doors opened with the ping of a bell. A fusion of voices and noise rushed in. Prometheus squinted into the light and a hand guided him out into a large hall filled with drinking and smoking and excitement.

They stood in a hotel entrance lobby.

Prometheus looked to his right to see Edward standing beside him, his thin pale face stoic and unfathomable.

"What happened?" he asked. Although the gaunt boy acknowledged his question by looking at him directly, he offered no answer.

Everything was strange – not only because just a moment ago he was standing in his cellar, but because there were certain things that were just... queer. Either they now stood in a whorehouse or they were no longer in London. The women wore dresses that plunged at the neck, exposing half their bosom, and hems that ran across bare thighs. The men fawned over them drunkenly.

A woman with ebony hair cut straight at her forehead and jaw crossed his path to stand at the side of a grand piano in the centre of the lobby, upon which a blonde man began to play. It wasn't a tune Prometheus recognised. Its style was jarring and unusual, but not unpleasant. The woman at the piano began to sing a melancholy song and tears trailed purple rivers down her face, her eyes becoming charcoal smudges. She stopped mid-verse to light a cigarette with a match hidden in her stocking garter before continuing as though she had never stopped. The entire lobby stopped to listen and a tall man in an overcoat sat watching at one of the small tables by the piano.

Prometheus also noticed that the lobby was littered with policemen. Their attire was strange, but clearly the law. They guarded heavy draped windows and dark oak doors that led off to various parts of the hotel. Two had also been positioned at elevator from which he and Edward had only just arrived.

"It seems they're going to make it difficult for us to leave," Edward said.

Prometheus eyed him. "So you can talk. I was beginning to think you were brain dead."

"Worried that you'd failed?" Edward replied, looking out at the room.

Prometheus couldn't hide his surprise that time. He gawped idiotically.

"Don't worry, you did a perfect job."

The woman's song ended on a high note of distress and she fell quiet. Her audience applauded as she knocked back a drink that sat on top of the piano. The young piano player began another sombre tune but the singer didn't resume. Instead, she finished her cigarette, staring at the man in the coat who wouldn't take his eyes off her.

"Where are we?" Prometheus asked again.

"That's the wrong question," Edward replied.

"What do you mean, that's the wrong question? It's the only one that matters, wouldn't you say?"

Edward smiled. "Chicago. We're in Chicago. It's a nice, art deco hotel and cabaret bar called Sazaracs. It has a bit of a reputation, if you know what I mean."

"Chicago?" Prometheus repeated. "America?" He stopped for a moment to hear the American twang of a large man ordering a drink from one of the waiters. "We can't be in Chicago."

"Okay then. But let us address that later, shall we? We have something extremely important to do."

"And what would that be?"

"You'll see."

Prometheus turned about the room. "Exactly how did we come to be here, and how long have I been unconscious?"

"You're still asking the wrong questions, Prometheus." The boy smiled slyly.

Prometheus took a step back as if from a cliff edge. Not once did he ever tell Edward his name. "Who are you?"

"You know exactly who I am. You've known me all my life." Edward laughed. "I'm not going to tell you everything like some sort of narrator because these are the things people can't accept from simply being told. They need to be realised, traumatically. But I shall give you a clue." Edward stared off into the distance.

"And what clue would that be?"

"I didn't say I was going to give you this clue now." He smirked. "We're in far too much of a hurry at present." He turned towards the men guarding the elevator. To the right of them, more policemen secured what Prometheus presumed was the stairwell. "Follow me," he ordered, beginning towards the men at the stairs. Prometheus found himself following. "In two seconds, one of the police guarding the stairs is going to sneak to the bar for a cigarette and a drink, leaving just one of them. You see the blonde girl wearing next to nothing who looks inappropriately young for the attire?"

Prometheus nodded as the girl strode across the room. She wore a dazzling white lace dress, alive with reams of fringe. The policeman guarding the door muttered something to his partner, then looked around for signs of a superior officer before heading to the bar. The remaining officer caught sight of the young girl and puffed out his chest.

"That officer will be distracted long enough for us to slip passed him through the doors," Edward said. "Hurry."

The blonde girl crossed their path a few paces ahead. She turned to the ogling officer and blew him a provocative kiss. The officer all but melted to the floor before leaving his post in pursuit of the girl. Prometheus and Edward then strode easily through the doors.

They climbed the deserted staircase to the second-floor corridor. Bright lights hung in fancy sconces along the walls to where two more officers stood guard at a room door.

"Stay here," Edward said, before walking out into the hallway.

The officers by the door went ridged for a moment before pulling out their pistols. "Freeze," they demanded simultaneously, which resulted in being less authoritative and more jocular.

"Do pardon me," Edward said politely. "I seemed to have lost my way. I'm trying to join my friends in the dining hall. Could you possibly point me in the right direction?"

Finding Edward no threat, both harnessed their weapons.

"You're not supposed to be up here," one of them said. "Everyone's supposed to be in the lobby."

All Prometheus then saw was a blur of movement and both officers lying heaped over one another.

"Are they dead?" Prometheus asked, walking out.

"Of course not," Edward replied. "Just unconscious. They'll be fine in an hour or so."

Stepping over the police, they entered the room. Inside, the large windows framed the night perfectly. No stars in the sky, just a glare of orange haze that hovered over the city. Prometheus looked out. Beyond his own dark reflection, a city of strange buildings and lights stretched. Lights were everywhere.

"Where exactly are we?" he whispered.

"Well, it ain't Kansas, Dorothy," Edward replied. He'd sprawled himself casually onto one of the cream sofas. "Chicago, as I said before."

Prometheus noticed a smashed vase on the floor by his feet. Red roses fanned onto the carpet, giving the effect of a pool of blood in his peripheral vision.

"He's in the bathroom," Edward said, joining Prometheus by the window.

"Who is?"

The boy reached inside his jacket and pulled out a severe-looking syringe. "The reason we're here."

Prometheus recognised it as one of his own. "Where did you get that?"

Edward handed him the cloudy liquid. "He's waiting for you."

With syringe in hand, Prometheus's curiosity led his feet towards the bathroom. Inside, a naked man lay dead in a mint green bathtub, half immersed in red water. Blood splatter dotted the sink and walls. Stringy brain matter and fragments of skull stuck to the tiles behind his fractured head. The body's arms hung over the edges, keeping it from sliding fully into the water. The bullet had left a bruised hole in his forehead and had cause one of his hazel eyes to protrude from its socket. The room had been untouched and was probably awaiting police inspection.

Prometheus considered the murky scarlet water, seeing his own reflection looking back. Edward wanted him to inject this man with his adrenaline solution, that much was now clear. But what was the point? This man could not be brought back without the power of lightning, and even then, Prometheus was unsure of how the man's grievous wounds would affect his recovery. His body may have been too broken.

The bathroom air was moist. Droplets of condensation clung to the blood-spattered mirror. On the washbasin, an open bottle of whisky stood. Prometheus snatched it up greedily, took a gulp and stuffed it into his pocket.

He then pulled the protector from the cannula point of the needle and released the air by giving it a short squirt. Kneeling over the tub, he looked into the dead man's face. It was a handsome face. He should have lived a full, long and happy life.

Like Sarah.

A droplet of water fell into the bath and the stench of rotting flesh rose through the air. Something stirred in the corner of Prometheus's eye. He turned to see the looming figure of Death craning over him, its low hood revealing a row of grinning teeth. It hovered translucently, as though the shadows of the room had bled together to create it. Its bleached hands clutched a curving scythe, like two white spiders.

Prometheus's eyes widened. Was it even there at all or just a trick of light and shadow? But he could hear the whispering of lost souls in the air.

Death lifted a bony finger and pointed it unwaveringly at Prometheus. His heart thudded. Standing before him was the loathsome creature that had taken his wife. His hands began to shake with anger.

There was a commotion outside. It sounded as though someone had barged into the hotel suite. Prometheus ignored it.

"Come to stop me?" he said.

The seven-foot figure cast a shadow that scaled across the ceiling as if alive. The shadow split, sending cracks across the walls, shattering the bathroom mirror to pieces and showering Prometheus in a blizzard of silver glass. The door shook and the walls ruptured, the fissures branching out, creating giant crevices filled with dark void… and the whispering of souls. The room grew darker in Death's shadow.

Prometheus let his anger rise into perfect clarity. "Die, beast," he spat. He jabbed the needle into the arm of the body and expelling the contents inside.

The bathroom door opened, swinging inwards to reveal a man standing in the frame, the same man that had watched the woman sing in the lobby.

Death had vanished. Fled with its void and shadows and whispering, leaving only the shattered mirror glittering on the cold tiles to prove it had ever been there at all.

The man raised a pistol. "Step away from the body."

*

Prometheus sat next to Edward on the long sofa endowed with velvet cushions. On the other side of him sat the blonde piano player from the lobby. He stared ahead, unblinking, the shroud of grief apparent over him. Also in the room was the raven-haired vocalist. She stomped about impatiently with a drink in one hand, cigarette in the other. She was now wearing a black dress with sparkling tassels that moved in waves at the slightest movement. She also wore a black fascinator with a hint of black netting that fell tentatively over her painted face.

The man with the pistol entered, followed by a rotund man drenched in sweat and a black bellboy in a red uniform and hat. They both took chairs. The man with the pistol was a detective, it seemed.

The woman in black began to cry and then laugh hysterically as she downed her drink. She poured herself another from the bottle. Prometheus found his mouth dry, yearning for the burn of whisky, and as the woman turned she caught a glimpse of his expression.

"I know that look," she said. Her French accent was slightly faded, dulled by time in America. She poured the whisky into another thick tumbler from the large desk and handed it to him.

"Thank you," Prometheus replied, and wasted no time in pouring it into his grateful throat.

"Ah, you are English," she said with a smile. "I knew an Englishman once. He was a bastard." She raised her drink and began to weep again.

The young man rose from the sofa to console her, placing his arm on her shoulder. She turned and slapped him. The crack echoed off, leaving a burning handprint on his cheek. He staggered back to his seat.

"That's enough of that, princess," the detective said as he took a seat behind the heavy desk. He placed his pistol beside him. "None of us want to be here. But a man was shot dead tonight and someone in this room knows why. Someone in this room knows who. Heck, someone in this room probably did it.

"All I'm interested in is getting to the truth, and believe me I will. Now, who wants to go first?" He looked around the room. "I want to know everyone's account of events leading up to and at the time of the murder."

No one spoke.

"Frenchy, we'll start with you. Don't be shy." He lit a cigarette.

The woman glared. "My name is Monique, not Frenchy. Va te faire enculer, sale fils de pute."

*

She drew in a long breath of smoke, exhaled then pouted, dark eyes watching the eyes that watched her. They sat expectantly. The light from the low lamp across the room shone on her like a spotlight. She pulled back the spider's web of netting that cast a barely perceivable shadow across her face. A move, she hoped, that would be interpreted as preparing to lay herself bare. She was building suspense.

Rule #1: Always build suspense in an audience. Make them hang on your every word.

She inhaled her long filtered cigarette and breathed her first smoke-laced words. "Bastille always brings me flowers the morning before a performance, and today was no different. I awoke to the winter sun shining through our window as he prepared it for me while I lay in bed. He arranged the roses on a tray, with coffee and strawberries. I love the colour red. He knows that." She smiled in reverie. "He wore a vest and pressed trousers with his hair wet and combed back. It shined in the sun. He looked so handsome. He always looks handsome. I shut my eyes and feigned sleep, to not spoil the surprise.

"'Good morning beautiful', he whispered into my ear, as he traced a warm finger down my back. I pretended to stir, turning to see him hovering over me, face beaming. I looked at the tray and gave him my best surprised face. He can never tell when I'm acting. He says he can, but he can't."

"'Darling, you spoil me', I told him as I sat up, pulling the white silk sheet away, exposing my bare breasts." She stopped to assess the reaction of the room, a little disappointed to find the only one who seemed shocked was the man to whom she had offered a drink. She would have to try harder.

Rule #2: Always be memorable. Shock if you must, but make sure they think of nothing but you.

"Bastille moved the tray to one side and pulled back the sheets all the way, roughly. I could see the passion in his eyes – and his trousers. His hands were all over me while his lips grazed my skin, my breasts, my naval. He grasped my wrists and held them above my head with one hand, while his fingers on the other found what they were looking for. I gasped as he kissed me, his tongue delving into my mouth as though searching for my soul. I fought my hands free so I could take off his vest, revealing the toned chest of my lover, speckled with dark hair that led down along his torso towards his belt. I worked it free and unbuttoned his trousers, all while his fingers still pressed and worked at my—"

"Is this going somewhere, Frenchy?" the detective asked, breaking the mood.

"I'm simply telling you the events leading up to…" she stopped and finished the contents of her glass. Her cigarette had burned out so she lit a fresh one. "We made love. We are in love. We… were in love." Her voice was bitter.

"And after?" the detective asked. He killed his cigarette.

The room now filled with the grey smoke.

"I left him in the room while I went down to rehearse. Reggie used to want me ready by 8am but he soon gave up on that. I was down just after 11am. It was an early start. We began the run-through while Reggie decided he would shout at me for no reason at all. 'Why haven't you learned the song?' he screamed, 'we open tonight'. He reminds me of my father when he gets like that, and I feel the teenage girl in me rise to the surface. I screamed 'you do not talk to me that way you fat bastard. I pay your fucking wages'. That shut him up. I needed a break. Besides, I think our shouting was disturbing the other guests or something. I left the bar and went outside to clear my thoughts, taking my song words with me so I could rehearse in my head the way I sometimes do."

"Where did you go?" the detective asked, smoke from a fresh butt pluming about his deadpan expression.

"Just around the block a few times."

"And then?"

"I met Reggie for a cocktail before another run-through."

"What time was that?"

"Two-thirty… ish"

"Did anybody see you on your little walkabout?"

"Not that I know of."

"Then what did you do?"

"After rehearsals, I went back up to my room. I thought it a little strange that Bastille hadn't come down to watch me sing. He did that often, but I didn't think too much about it. It wasn't unusual for him to spend the day in our suite, reading or something."

"And that's when you found him in the tub?" the detective pressed, carefully.

Monique nodded. "I called for help. Reggie heard me from the room next door and came rushing in. I don't remember what happened then."

"Do you remember what time you went back up to your room?"

"Around 6pm."

"And during that time did anyone leave the rehearsal? From 2pm till 6pm, everyone stayed in that room?"

"I think so. I don't remember too clearly." She began to cry again.

Rule #3: Always give them what they want – even if that happens to be vulnerability.

"Thank you. That will be all for the moment," the detective said.

"So can I leave?"

"Not yet. I think Reggie should go next, don't you?"

Everyone turned the large, greasy looking man who struggled to fit his whole backside into the chair. Monique sat as the man nervously stood. He retrieved a handkerchief from his pocket and mopped his weeping brow with a shaky hand. He moved into the centre, the lamplight focusing like a beacon on his red face.

*

"I woke early, like always," Reggie began in an agitated tone. He was smartly dressed, pressed shirt, shined shoes and hair trimmed. He wore a green striped jacket that matched the hat he'd placed on the chair. On his lip, a small thin moustache sat – a black line that collected the sweat dripping down his face.

"I was dressed and down for breakfast by 7:30am. I don't eat in my room. I don't know why I get up so early. I got no need when Monique refuses to work before noon most days. But I get up. I think my body has just got used to it or something, plus I like to spend some time enjoying the peace before, you know, before she starts. A few people were up on their way to work, but there weren't many. This is a night-time establishment more than a morning one, so mostly I was on my own. I read the paper and called for coffee, orange juice and bacon. The coffee in Chicago ain't like New York, but I'm getting used to it. Wherever we end up we always make do. This is one of the nicer places. But she's gonna be a star, so I put up with it. She'll be a star if she puts the work in, that is."

Again Reggie mopped his face. He shuffled uncomfortably in the lamplight.

"She came down at 11am and we began more or less straight away. Sam had been waiting at the piano for God knows how long, but he's a patient kid. You have to be to work with Monique. We began the opening number. The plan was to go through a dress rehearsal but Monique didn't wanna play dress up so early in the day. So we just did a run through. We tried to do a run through, that is. After all we rehearsed, after all the shows we did, she hadn't bothered to learn her lines for the new number. I usually keep my cool pretty well, but for some reason today I just didn't. The pressure was getting to me.

"'How do you expect to make it big when you don't even learn you're God-damn lines?' I said to her."

"You shouted at me," Monique interrupted.

"Pipe down, Frenchy. You've had your turn," the detective said. "Carry on, Reggie."

"We argued some. It got pretty heated. Monique usually calms herself down if you just keep your mouth shut. But as I said I wasn't in the mood to be quiet this morning. So I bit back."

"What made you in such a shitty mood?" the detective asked.

"This and that," he replied vaguely.

"Elaborate, Reggie, I'm looking for details here."

The room looked to him for his reply. "I've been on the phone all morning trying to persuade the agency not to drop Monique. But it's no good." He looked at Monique, whose expression balanced on shock and disgust.

"What do you mean, drop me? Who the fuck do they think they are?"

"Come on, kid, you know the score," Reggie said. "It's a tough biz, and you ain't cutting it. You show up late, you're not learning your lines, everyone you work with thinks your attitude stinks. No one wants to hire dames like you. You know how many strings I had to pull to get you this gig?"

Monique was silent. Her tears stopped and she wiped the salty trails away from her pale cheeks. She lifted her head a little as if to compose herself. "Things are different now," she said. "This is all I have. I need it, Reggie. I'll die without it."

"You can discuss that later," the detective said. "Reggie, get back to the day."

"So, Monique stormed out and I was left trying to persuade the manager to keep us booked for the night. He didn't want a scene in his hotel but I told him it wouldn't happen again. After that, I went to my room for a stiff drink and a lie-down."

"How long were you in your room?"

"An hour or so. Then I went straight back down to wait for Monique to come back like I knew she would sooner or later. The rest is like Monique said. She was back by 2.30pm. We had a drink and got back to rehearsing. We called it a night just before 6:30pm, then we went back up to our rooms. Monique went to prepare for the show."

"How long were you in your room before you heard Monique scream?"

"Barely a minute. I rushed in and I found her shaking Bastille's body as he lay in the tub, trying to wake him. I took her out and called for help. She was hysterical."

"Thank you, Reggie," the detective said. "Now Sam, go ahead. You're up."

The perspiring Reggie sat, while the equally nervous Sam stood. The blonde stood six-foot-tall in the glare of the lamplight. What was evident in the light was that the young man's eyes were red and swollen. His hands shook, so he shoved them in his pockets. His head bent down to the floor, with strings of blonde hair covering his face. He shuffled in the silence.

Seeing him struggle with his beginning, the detective gave him a small nudge. "Why don't you tell us how long you been Monique's piano man? Start there."

"I been Miss Monique's piano player for about a year now, sir," Sam said in a warm southern accent. "I joined along when the old pianist quit just before they was about to head on stage. Miss Monique was in a right ol' mess, and I was there. I knew how to play and I just wanted to help. Reggie offered me the job after that. I was right pleased, as I never went anywhere apart from N' Orleans and being just out of highschool I thought I'd gone and won the jackpot. Bastille said I'd get to travel all over the country, see it all. And we do. It's the best job. And I get to play. I just love playin'."

The detective nodded. "What's your relationship with Monique?"

He shook his head. "I don't understand what you mean."

Monique scoffed.

"I mean do you get on well? Are you friends? Do you argue?"

"We don't much speak at all, sir. My piano is always in the background and I don't reckon she looks back there too much, except when she's lying on it, of course, but she's always lookin' at the crowd. No, we don't speak much."

"And what of your relationship with the deceased, Bastille?"

Sam swallowed, allowing his hair to fall over his face to cover the tears in his eyes. "He was my friend."

The detective nodded. "Where were you today?"

"I was in the rehearsal room by 9am. I like to get in a few hours on my own before we concentrate on Miss Monique. I like to be up to standard for her." To this, there was an audible grinding of Monique's teeth. But she said nothing. "They arrived after 11am, we rehearsed, there was a scuffle and then everyone left. The rest is as they said."

"Where did you go when everybody left?" the detective asked.

Sam's pause was thick as syrup. "I stayed to practice," he said finally.

"And you were there when Monique and Reggie returned? You were sat at your piano still?"

Sam shook his head. "I went to the bathroom as I wasn't feeling well, and when I returned they were there already."

The detective looked back to Reggie. "How long were you and Monique rehearsing before Sam entered?"

"About ten minutes, I think," he replied. "I remember now how pale he was. I suggested he go and lie down, but he refused, claiming he was well enough to play."

"And was he?"

"He was off, compared to his usual self, but we got through it."

The detective turned his attention to the black bellboy, who'd been sitting there without saying a word. He was a young boy, barely in his teens. "Can you tell everyone what you told me earlier, son?"

He nodded and stood. He didn't move into the lamplight but stayed hovering over his chair.

"I was taking a guest's luggage up to the third floor when I accidentally got off on two," the bellboy said. "Mr Cage said if I done it one more time he'd have my job, which I don't think's too fair as it's only my second week and it's a big place. I was down the hall before I realised what I'd done, but then I heard voices, so I hid around the corner thinkin' it was Mr Cage. But the voices were coming from room 133 sounded like shouting. It weren't in no English."

"You recognise the language?" the detective asked.

The boy nodded. "It was French."

"And were the voices both male?"

"No, sir. One was female and the other was a man's voice," the bellboy replied.

"What happened then?"

He pointed to Sam. "I saw that man run out the room, butt-naked and soaked wet. He was holding his clothes in his arms. He ran straight past me and into room 140 down the hall. I got into the elevator then, up to the fourth floor where I's meant to be."

"And what time was that, kid?"

"Just after two in the afternoon, sir."

There was silence as the room waited for the detective to speak. Monique had lit another cigarette, her face impassive. Sam, however, had turned a shade of grey.

The detective stood and turned on the other desk lamp. Light blinded the room. "You can go now, son," he said to the bellboy. He hurried out as though he were escaping a grilling.

"I could ask you all why you've spent the better part of an hour lying to me about your whereabouts today, but the only reply I'd get would be bullshit. Instead, let me tell you all what happened, shall I?" He walked around to the front of the desk and sat on the edge. "You killed your boyfriend, didn't you, Frenchy?"

Monique sprang from her chair and charged at him, raising a hand to slap him across the face. He caught her wrist and pushed her backwards.

"You discovered he was having an affair, didn't you?"

"That's absurd. Let me out of here." Her fingers were claws that threatened to scratch out his eyes.

"He'd slept around before, of course, didn't he? But then again, so did you. But that wasn't the problem, was it? You didn't like that Bastille was seeing the same person, forming bonds and forming a connection, not just a one night wonder like usual. That made your blood boil. You suspected it for a while but you needed to be sure. So, you made out like you hadn't learned your lines, knowing it would push the fragile looking Reggie over the edge. You wanted to cause an argument so you had an excuse to storm out."

Monique turned her back to the room. "That's a lie," she said quietly.

"Sure, you left the hotel. Just long enough to keep up the charade. But you doubled back and marched straight up to your room. That's where you found them, Sam here and your boyfriend, together in the bathtub."

Sam's head fell into his hands, as the tears became suddenly audible. Monique didn't move or say a word. She kept her back to them all, cigarette burning in her raised hand.

"You screamed at Sam to leave and then you and Bastille started on each other. He told you he was going to leave you, didn't he Monique? He was going to pack his stuff that night and go. But you couldn't stand that, could you? You couldn't stand the thought of you boyfriend wanted to be with another man over you. So, you plotted like you always do, pretending to calm yourself, luring him into a false sense of security. You said he didn't know when you were acting and you were right. And as you were talking calmly in the bathroom, him still in the tub, you sitting on the edge – probably going over all the things you both did wrong in your years together – you took a pistol out your purse and coldly put a hole in his head."

Monique didn't say a word. She didn't need to say a word. The detective had said it all.

"I don't believe it," Reggie said.

The detective turned to him. "You don't believe it? Well, answer me this, Reggie, how in the hell did you not hear the gun-fire?"

"I was asleep," he fumbled.

"Or you did hear it, and didn't do a thing. That would explain how so many reporters showed up on the scene only minutes after the cops. You heard the shot, knew something had gone down with Monique – a little piece-of-ass time-bomb like that was sure to explode at some point – and you took your shot at a little free press. After all, she's gonna be a star, right? You knew she kept a pistol and you knew Bastille was fucking around. You did the math and came up with dollar signs in your eyes, isn't that right Reggie?"

The fat man headed for the door suddenly, but the detective's gun was on his temple faster than his slow body could carry him.

"I'd sit down and shut the fuck up if I were you." He dragged Reggie to his seat. "The only one who didn't know what was happening was Sam. Which one of you persuaded him to keep it shut about him and Bastille?" He paused to see if anyone would actually answer him, but no one did. "I already know it was you, Reggie. Must have been so easy to scare the little faggot into silence. Did you tell him the same thing would happen to him if he talked? Did you tell him how much it would shame his daddy if anyone ever found out about the disgusting shit they did together?" The detective killed his cigarette and shook his head. "Murderers, liars and faggots. They're the low-lives I gotta deal with." The detective banged on the door and two cops entered. "Get them out o' here."

The first cop went to Reggie, who surrendered without a word, but Monique found her fire again. She spat at the cop as he came for her. "Don't touch me you pig," she screamed, trying to claw at the officer's face.

The room fell quiet after Monique had been dragged out kicking and screaming. Only the sound of Sam's sobs remained.

"Who are you two?" the detective asked, suddenly turning on Prometheus and Edward. "You sneak up to a crime scene and lock yourself in a bathroom with a dead man. What sort of sick fucks are you? You're the only pieces I can't figure out, so I'm taking you all in. I know what goes on in every inch of my town and yet I get nothing on you two. You're going to tell me where you've come from or I'll beat it out of you."

Prometheus turned to Edward for answers because he had none to offer. He didn't know what they were doing there. He wasn't entirely sure where there was. Edward, however, said nothing.

"Sam, you're coming too," the detective said. "In case you've forgotten, sodomy is against the law, and a sin, I might add."

In the corner of his eye, Prometheus noticed a figure appear in the open doorway.

Sam looked up from his sobs. His face contorted into a confused half-smile and a stuttering sound fell from his mouth.

Bastille stood in the door, very much alive. He swung a punch square into the detective's jaw so fast it was barely visible. It knocked the man clean unconscious.

"About time," Edward said.

Sam sprang from his seat and wrapped his arms around Bastille, burying his face into his shoulder. When Bastille didn't reciprocate, he slowly looked up meet the man's stare. His smile wilted and he took a step back, shaking his head.

"You're not Bastille."

6

Cutting, Ystil.3 noted, felt like a series of mild electrical shocks focused directly into the nerve endings of his synth's organic parts. The effect was a sort of numbness that tingled. The momentary displacement of leading one's timeline through a quantum wormhole was a lot like waking up to find that you're underwater. The sooner the new surroundings were adapted to, the higher the chance of survival in the new spacetime as the exact positioning of where one ended up was somewhat unpredictable.

"Welcome to 2310," Lydia said.

They were in a long hallway that would have looked exactly like a street outside if it weren't for the walls that surrounded them. Rows of house-fronts stretched out endlessly, windowless, grey and identical, no sky above but grey panels. They crossed a road as a pod-looking vehicle hummed along it at a mediocre speed, then turned into a grey lane that led onto a platform heaving with humans. Lydia called it the Hydrolift.

Umbilical cords of water-filled glass tubes clustered together like a giant spinal column in some massive creature. The pipes, hundreds of them, disappeared into the heights and depths of the platform. Some tubes ran straight, while others branched off the main column like veins carrying people like blood cells to London Tower's many limbs and organs.

People bustled by without so much as a glance in their direction. Almost every human had a head of hair that looked as though it was spun from metal – gold, silver, bronze. Some younger, industrial looking humans even seemed to have iron hair set into dangerous spikes. Lydia pushed a button on the nearest Hydrolift with Kentish Town Hydrolift Tube Station embellished on the opening glass doors. They entered and shut doors shut before anyone else could follow, leaving an aquarium of annoyed faces in the glass.

"Good Morning," a disembodied voice said. "Where can I take you?" It was the Hydrolift. A holographic map thrummed into existence; a blueprint of a monolithic building divided into colour coded-sectors and floors.

"Where are we?" Ystil.3 asked.

"Kentish Town urban living quarters, street ninety-one point one, floor eight hundred and thirty-six, green sector," the Hydrolift said. "Where can I take you?"

"Hyde Park please," Lydia replied.

They moved fluidly through the tubes, down from the platform and into a blue haze of water. Lydia pulled two small sachets from her purse, handed one to him and opened the other herself.

"You might want to put those on," she said.

"What is it?"

"They're clothes. We're trying to blend in, remember?"

Lydia pulled out a square piece of fabric from the sachet, unfolded and stretched it until it became a short, tubular dress. He looked at his own sachet, hoping his wasn't a dress also. Some overtly masculine part of his synth would have resisted that, no matter what was currently the fashion. Thankfully, it wasn't. Instead, the square unfolded into a pair of thermo-pants and a sleeveless top.

Lydia unfastened her 1901 dress, letting it fall to the floor in a heap of heavy burgundy fabric. Ystil.3 undressed also, noticing the craftsmanship of Lydia's synth as he did – her smooth back, the curve of her hips, the firmness of her thighs and the roundness of her breasts as she shimmied into the tight black thermo-dress. It covered her arms and neck but stopped above her knees and exposed her back entirely. She unpinned her bound hair, letting it fall in dark waves across her shoulders. She then attached a small clip that turned it into metallic silver coils.

Ystil.3 managed to pull on his clothes just as the Hydrolift stopped. They were so tight that every protruding muscle, bulge and appendage was visible for all to see.

"Welcome to Hyde Park, communal area grade two, floor six hundred and thirty, green sector. Have a nice day." Lydia exited and Ystil.3 followed, leaving their 1901 clothes on the Hydrolift floor.

Hyde Park was large, green and pretty, in a leafy sort of way. Ystil.3 immediately detected the faint shimmer of a semi-permeable level three control field, which surrounded the park in a geodesic dome, allowing a breeze to pass through it. The park was located on one of the many ledges that jutted out from London Tower. A diagram of the building at the entrance showed that the Tower was a twisting helix shape. The parks were built along the sails, like a corkscrew, to benefit from sunlight. People played and sat on the central grass area, some ate and others stared obsessively into screens mounted on their wrists. Some humans were fitted with glowing blue exo-vertebrae that snaked up their spines over their clothes. Lydia explained that they were devices that could help extend human life up to an extra fifty years – if you could afford it.

"So, where are they now?" she asked.

Ystil.3 scanned his internal DNA tracking monitor. "Over there," he said, walking in the direction of the flashing light in his retinal map. He led Lydia along the path, under a cluster of holographic trees that managed to sway in the breeze and somehow even produce shadows. "What worries me is that our timeline and Prometheus's are now no longer parallel. Who's to say that this was even the first sector they Cut to. We could have met them already in our future but their past. Who knows what could have happened?"

"That's exactly why we need to do this quickly. Are they close?"

"Behind that fountain over there." Within his retinal map, the blip that was Prometheus began to move down the path. "He's heading towards the exit. Can you see him?"

"Over there," she said, pointing to a group of three men walking with a little girl. Prometheus was instantly noticeable in his heavy Victorian overcoat, as was Edward. Who the other man and girl were, neither of them had a clue.

They followed the small group inside the vast congregational entrance of Hyde Park. Veined white marble covered the floors and glass fittings adorned the many booths, surfaces and tourist information kiosks that lined the sides like a marketplace. Prometheus made his way through the crowd and entered the nearest Hydrolift with his companions. Lydia steered Ystil.3 in the direction of the next lift. Armed police grazed in the lobby. They wore chest plates and helmets with green translucent visors that covered their faces.

"They have issues in London Tower, regarding the classes," Lydia said, noticing his stare.

"Classes?" Ystil.3 echoed as the lift opened. They entered with a dozen others and instantly a map appeared in front of each of the passengers. Each pushed their required destination. Lydia and Ystil.3 both pushed floor two-hundred and fifty, where Prometheus now resided, according to the tracker.

"All human habitations have different classes, social groups and caste systems," Lydia said. "Surely you know this, Winston?"

"Of course, but why would it warrant such security?"

"The lower classes aren't permitted to the upper floors since rioters and terror groups blew up half of Chelsea three years ago. Everyone, no matter what class, is restrained to their own designated part of London. Currently, we're in what you might call the middle-class part of London. To get to any other part, lower or higher you need to go through security checks that require permits. Then there are the sub-levels to consider."

"Let me guess, that's where the less desirable people of London are kept?"

"Correct. There's sort of prison-type places fifty floors below ground level."

"What do you mean, prison-type places?"

"The people there are imprisoned, but they're not conscious, not all of them. Some undergo reconditioning in a virtual programme."

"Sounds like a holiday. Where do I sign up?" Ystil.3 eyed her. "You seem to know an awful lot about this sector for a 1901 Overly Watchful. Are you tapping into the Earth Files for all this?"

Lydia shook her head casually. "I find Earth history interesting."

The Hydrolift stopped and some people got off. "Welcome to Finsbury Park, floor four hundred and two, orange sector. Have a nice day," it said, before continuing its journey down. Eleven more stops were made before it finally reached the security checkpoint on floor two hundred and fifty.

A mother and her little boy exited with them and they were greeted by a group of armed police hovering stiffly around a row of metal arches. They stood back and watched as the mother took her child through. She handed the guard a green translucent card and Ystil.3 focused in to see that it was an upper-level day pass. As soon as the woman and child were through the gates, shutters slammed closed and flashing lights dropped from the ceiling, accompanied by a high-pitched alarm.

The police guards rushed to secure all exits.

"What's going on?" Ystil.3 said.

An armed guard appeared in front of them. "Security breach on the upper levels," he said. "All citizens must return to their homes and all visitors must report to the security check-in advised upon entry."

"But we need to get the lower levels," Lydia said.

"I'm sorry, madam, that isn't going to be possible right now. Please return to your homes or your designated security check-in." The guard encouraged them back into an empty Hydrolift and the doors closed in front of them. It began to move upwards through the water.

"What date is it today?" Lydia asked suddenly.

"May 24, 2310," the Hydrolift answered.

"What is it?" Ystil.3 asked.

"I have a feeling something happened on this day, but I can't remember."

Lights flashed inside the glass tube, signalling their imminent arrival to the next floor, but the Hydrolift stopped with a jerk. The lights blinked out before the dim backup lights ignited.

"For the safety of citizens riding the Hydrolift Tube, we have performed an emergency stop," the Hydrolift announced. "Our journey will commence shortly. Please remain calm."

"What's the emergency?" Ystil.3 asked.

"A code nine security threat. A total lockdown has been issued as a precautionary measure. Our journey will resume shortly. In the meantime, just relax. If you would like a cool beverage just let me know."

"I remember what happened on this day," Lydia said. "China State launched the single largest cyber-attack on the CommonWorld to date, making mayhem of London Tower's security and computer systems. It marks the start of a series of attacks from both sides that will last twenty years, but will result in a cyber-revolution that will boost human technological advancement beyond what it ever would have achieved without the incentive."

"A cyber-attack? That's not so bad."

"Not so bad? Clearly, you know nothing about the terrors that escaped London Tower this day because of the security breach."

"Like what?"

Lydia arched an eyebrow. "Well, an Allosaurus for a start."

☐

7

It was a Saturday evening when Prometheus first realised he was in love with her. The evening had seen a formal dinner hosted by Dr Elton, which he had arranged on the pretence of celebrating another year's work saving lives. In actuality, it was to present his daughter Sarah into society.

Sarah was the toast of the evening; being bright, funny, clever and absurdly beautiful. Every bachelor's eyes followed her as she was introduced to the important guests. Prometheus was lucky enough to be included among this description.

"May I present my daughter," Dr Elton said.

She held out her hand for Prometheus to shake, but instead, he kissed it. Where he got the courage to do such a thing in a room full of people was beyond him. All he knew was that he couldn't not do it. He looked up to see her blush a little as she took back her hand and offered it to the next person who greeted her.

Prometheus straightened himself as he received looks from the other guests, including Sarah's father. Prometheus was never one to show emotion. Through his long years of working at the hospital, it was a largely known fact that his work consumed his entire life and that he made little effort to make room for anything else. That was how he liked it, until then. James had often teased him about his Hippocratic dedication. He, being married and younger than Prometheus, would take it upon himself to thrust Prometheus into the path of suitable ladies within their social circle. All of the women, however, seemed dull, widowed or spinsters, or simply lacking something he couldn't quite put his finger on. They were faded and insipid, often too concerned with money and status, knowing nothing of politics or the world, the very things that heated Prometheus's fire back then. He could barely hold a conversation with these women, let alone see himself married to one for the remainder of his life.

As Sarah chatted politely to the couple next to him, Prometheus couldn't help but watch her. Her beautiful auburn hair was wrapped neatly into an intricate design and tied on top of her head. Her slender neck and shoulders were cream running down an hourglass. Yet her brown eyes were what held his awe; her beauty was unsurpassed, yet it was the intelligence in her eyes that had captured him so fervently. They had spark, wit, essence – they had life.

She laughed at something Prometheus hadn't quite caught, but the sight of her caused him to smile and laugh along with her, simply because it was so contagious. Her smile reached those intelligent brown eyes and lit a blaze inside her already luminous demeanour. She was the sun, Prometheus realised, and like smiling flowers in a meadow, the entire room turned to bask in her radiance.

She caught him staring and her smile grew wider.

"Isn't she something?" Dr Elton said, handing Prometheus a glass of champagne.

He tore his eyes away to face his long-time colleague. "Indeed," he replied.

"My wife and I are hosting a smaller gathering next week… just a few close friends. We would love to have you join us." Dr Elton smiled. "Of course, my lovely daughter will be there also."

Prometheus flushed, realising how obvious he had been. He looked to Sarah once more and, to his utter surprise, found she had been watching him too. She looked away in embarrassment at having been found out.

"I would love to attend," he said.

*

The doors shut just as the alarm sounded out. Prometheus didn't turn back. Instead, he followed like he was supposed to – as Edward had instructed.

"We need to get to Belmarsh Prison," Edward told the translucent warning sign that appeared from nowhere, all flashing lights and strange words, which, although English, Prometheus could barely understand.

"All Hydrolifts are inactive due to a code nine security threat. Our journey will resume shortly. Thank you for your cooperation. Please remain calm."

"What about the maintenance lifts?" Edward asked it.

"Those are reserved for maintenance and emergency evacuations."

"I think we've found our way," he said, turning to Prometheus, Bastille and the little sick girl from New York.

Prometheus didn't understand, nor did he care, what the boy was talking about, even after having finally figured out what was happening to him. It was the date on the whisky bottle that brought everything into perspective, the one he had taken from the once dead Bastille's bathroom in Chicago. Printed on the label were the words bottled in 1933. Prometheus had only seen it because he scoured every corner of it for the final drop. It was then things began to make sense. He had somehow found his way to another point in time – either that or he'd lost thirty-two years of his life. He became completely certain of it when they had suddenly arrived in New York to collect the girl. There, things were even stranger and noisy beyond belief. Currently, he had no clue what year it was, but the alien realm of future London was written all over the place. It was in the building, the people, the smell and sounds – all utterly outlandish, but London.

It was all clear to him now, what it meant. The possibility of it. If Edward somehow had the ability to travel into the future then it made sense that he would also be able to travel into the past. With this gift,

Prometheus would bring back his beloved Sarah. Of all the souls that he would save, hers would be among them.

This, he was resolute upon. This, he would move Heaven and Earth for.

*

Ystil.3 looked at Lydia as the Hydrolift filled with water. It gushed in so quickly that it already reached his knees. "So what now?" he asked, feeling slightly smug about being right regarding her ridiculous plan.

Lydia looked anxiously around her. "Please, there's a leak, we're going to drown. Can't you take us to the nearest floor?"

"I'm unable to continue our journey at present due to a code nine security threat," the Hydrolift replied in an upbeat, casual tone. Please be patient until it is safe to continue." It appeared there was a flaw in its programming. Lydia shrugged as the laser holes in the glass ceiling continued to allow water to flow in. "I thought it would work, sorry." Her smile slanted.

"We'll just have to get out ourselves." He looked up at the watertight glass panels. "Should be easy enough to blast through, then we can swim up to the next exit."

"You want me to swim? You realise my hair will rust."

"You're the one who decided to get laser-happy and blow holes everywhere. I'm afraid that whichever way you look at it, you're going to get wet."

"And when we get to the next exit? What then?"

"We can blast through and figure a way to get to the sublevels without the use of these homicidal things." He thought. "Does this building have stairs?"

Lydia laughed. "You want us to walk down over two-hundred flights of stairs?"

"Do you have a better plan? Listen, the first thing we need to do is get out of here. Agreed?"

Lydia rolled her eyes, now waist deep in water.

"So let's move then. I'll cut a panel out and we can swim through the Hydrotube until we reach the next level exit, then we can blast through. Ready?"

"I suppose."

Ystil.3 took aim with the thumb-sized laser Lydia kept in her purse. "You might want to take out that hair clip."

Lydia did so. Immediately, her sharp silver hair flowed back into its usual dark softness, hanging loosely about her shoulders. "Women are insane for what they put up with in the name of fashion," she said, placing the clip back into her bottomless pit of a quantum purse.

The tight-wave beam sliced through the watertight glass painlessly and the panel dropped free. At once, warm water rushed through in clear torrents and within seconds the Hydrolift flooded completely. Ystil.3 made his way through the hatch, holding his breath to stop his partly-organic lungs filling with water. He didn't need to breathe or require oxygen to fuel his body, so he took his time through the Hydrotube, relying on his synth's memory of swimming to move him forward.

"You okay back there?" he sent via secure-beam.

"I'm perfectly fine," Lydia sent back, swimming behind him.

When he reached the level up, a quick infrared scan confirmed the platform was empty.

"This floor will do," he sent to Lydia, who had joined him in pressing her face up against the glass.

"Won't it flood the floor with water?"

He gestured a silent shrug in reply, held out the laser and fired. The beam shot through the water like a wormhole and cut through the steel and glass, leaving a person-sized opening. Ystil.3 braced himself to be sucked through with the flow of water, but to his surprise, no water escaped the hatch. It hovered perfectly over the empty laser-cut opening. "Control field," he sent. He swam towards it and climbed through, offering his arm to Lydia as she did the same.

She knocked it aside and clambered through herself.

*

Prometheus was desperate for a drink. His flask was as dry as his cracked tongue and the bottle of whisky was long empty. His old limbs were too adapted to alcohol fuel, often intoxicated into a lethargy that slowed him to an invariable state of sedation. He was used to it, his slow life. Now his limbs threatened to wake against his will.

He found himself riding vertically down the concrete tubing of a maintenance shaft inside a metal cage. It reminded him of the manholes from his London that led into the sewers. The stale air whipped up as they descended at a speed that made him cling to the grill. Every now and then they passed what looked to Prometheus like a floating light panel, on which an emergency message was written. It would lash by at each level. Edward controlled the speed through a device and the others seemed completely unaffected by the rapidity at which they travelled. Prometheus's already sensitive stomach roiled from the motion.

Everywhere, the voice echoed, even as they went down. Always down, down and down. He reached for his flask once again to make sure a drop wasn't hiding at the very bottom.

Alas, no.

*

"The year is 2310," the Infobot said. Its voice was tinny and matter-of-fact, nothing like the smooth female voice of the Hydrolift. The thing's large green eyes glowed in its gleaming head as it sat, head and shoulders, perched upon a glass column, like a bust. Ystil.3 thought its mouthlessness made it seem sinister.

"Who is the Prime Minister of Britain?" he asked it.

"Patrick St Claire, born in 2272, Hertfordshire, England. PM St Claire became involved in politics whilst studying at Eton and was elected head of the LL party in 2305, two years before the party won the general election in 2307. PM St Claire is known mostly for reinstating the position of the British Monarchy after it was dissolved in 2100."

"What is a code nine security threat?" he asked.

"Code nine is the threat level rating of scenario nine regarding the welfare and protection of London Tower."

"What is scenario nine?"

"Scenario nine is the procedure by which action must be taken against mishap or accident, human error or otherwise, regarding Life Corp experimentation."

"How very vague. Okay, let's try this. What is an Allosaurus?"

"Allosaurus is a large theropod dinosaur that lived 155 to 145 million years ago, during the late Jurassic period. The name Allosaurus means different lizard. Allosaurus was a large bipedal predator with a large skull, equipped with dozens of large, sharp teeth. It averaged eight point five meters in length, though fragmentary remains suggest it could have reached over twelve meters. Relative to the large and powerful hind limbs, its three-fingered forelimbs were small, and the body was balanced by a long, heavy tail. It is classified as an allosaurid, a type of carnosaurian theropod dinosaur."

Ystil.3 watched as a hologram of the dinosaur erupted from the Infobot's head. The creature looked vicious. He wondered why humans would want to mess around with an extinct species like that.

"Will you stop playing with that," Lydia said as she appeared with two bottles of water and snacks from the nearest vending machine. She handed a bottle to Ystil.3 and a bag of some snack he didn't recognise.

"I don't eat," he said. "You eat?"

She nodded, taking a sip of water. "So we blend in with humans."

"What does hunger feel like?"

"It feels like a hole inside you that needs to be filled. Not a physical hole and yet not really a metaphorical hole either… something between the two. It feels like a need for food and if you don't eat quickly then it becomes all you can think about until you do eat."

"Clever really."

"It's a way of ensuring the human body will receive sustenance." Lydia bit into a sandwich, chewed and then swallowed.

The memofabric clothing ensured that within a few minutes they were as dry as they were before the whole Hydrolift incident.

"Do you have that map yet?" she asked.

"Oh, right." He stood in front of the Infobot again. "Where are the nearest stairs to floor…" He checked his internal tracking system. "… Floor three."

Out of the talking bust's head, a hologram of a map appeared, with a flashing red mark that pointed to the nearest stairs and then a flashing green mark indicating where they currently were. The green mark travelled toward the red mark, leaving a trail of green where it had been. Ystil.3 memorised the route through his eidetic function.

"They've reached floor three already," he said. "They can't be travelling on foot."

Lydia swallowed the last of her sandwich. "We should move. They must be using emergency lift shafts. Where is the nearest from here?"

Ystil.3 checked the map in his head. "Not far. By the emergency stairwell."

They began across the once packed hall, all the people now all safely in their homes. The windows to their right looked over a balcony. Another park. Signs to their left read Leicester Square. The sun outside was dimming as the late afternoon began its descent into evening and the sky threatened to blaze with furious colours at any moment. They passed vibrant screens that played and replayed the same annoying infomercial again and again. An odd-looking man with dark hair, wearing a lab coat and a glassy smile spoke fast and enthusiastically about the exo-vertebrae life extenders he'd seen so many people wearing. The sound was off but the man was animated to the point of hysteria. Trailing across the screen was the message: Live to reach 150 years old with The Lifestore.

From the hall, they entered a white corridor.

"What do you suppose they're doing here?" Ystil.3 asked.

"I haven't the foggiest." Her eyes flickered to him for a moment, looking for a reaction.

"You must have thought about it."

"There are many reasons why someone would want to Cut to a different time sector, Winston. We should concentrate on the matter in hand and let Sir Z worry about the details of where, why, how, and who."

"So you're not in the least bit curious?"

"Curious?" She laughed. "What a human concept. I'm surprised you even considered it. For an AI with an apparent aversion to the Homo Saipan, you seem to have more in common with them than you realise. You know what curiosity did to the cat, don't you?"

"No, what? Whose cat? What has this got to do with a cat? Do you mean Schrödinger's cat?"

She shook her head. "All I mean is that we shouldn't worry about things that will not help us right now. Letting your mind wander when you need it here and now can be dangerous."

"I'd say knowing what they're doing here and why their little group seems to be accumulating in number would serve us well right about now."

Lydia said nothing to that. "Are we almost nearing the maintenance shaft?"

"Should be an escalator stairwell down this corridor. Of course, it won't work but the shaft is near that. It should have a back-up system for emergencies like this… I hope."

A rumbling began abruptly in the corridor, starting at their feet and reverberating into the walls, shaking the very molecules of the air. Ystil.3 could feel it through the sensors in his skin. The soft vibration was almost like waves of sound. And yet, Lydia could feel nothing it seemed. When he stopped, she continued a few steps before turning to him.

"What is it?"

"You don't feel that?"

She considered her surroundings briefly and shook her head. "What are you talking…" her words faded and her eyes widened.

He turned to see a giant lizard head appear in the distance, followed by a muscular neck, a mighty body and tree-trunk legs. The beast manoeuvred itself into the corridor, turned towards them and snarled. At once, it began to charge, taking slow strides at first but building to a hungry speed.

"Run, you idiot," Lydia sent via secure-beam.

Ystil.3 turned to see she was already growing smaller into the distance.

8

The dinosaur loped towards them, crushing the pristine white tiles under heavy claws and smashing into the walls with its powerful, yet clumsy, weight. The black feral eyes stalked them with murderous rapaciousness. The mottled hide stretched over flexing muscles, with occasional horned ridges that ran the length of its spine and down the huge tail that bashed manically behind it. The sword sharp claws that embellished its wide feet and short arms were nothing to the ragged brightness of its teeth. Then there was the noise. The truculent sound from its throat was a weapon itself. It hit Ystil.3 at such force that his synth shook involuntarily.

The thought of the creature pulling his synth apart with those jaws – a pain he couldn't conceive of with any real notion – was something he feared most earnestly. Fear of pain was new to him, and not welcome.

The Allosaurus raged, slowed only by its size within the constraining corridor, bowing its head as it ate up the ground with three-metre strides – claws slicing through the floor for traction.

"If you're not too busy, could you blast open this door?" Lydia said, calmly waiting for Ystil.3 at the locked exit. "You still have my laser."

"And if I didn't have it you would have continued without me, I expect?" he said, cutting a circle in the immoveable hatch doors. He kicked it and the loose metal fell, leaving a perfect-sized hole for a person.

"I knew you were behind me," Lydia said. "It's not like I would have just left you to be torn to pieces." She shimmied herself through and flopped to the floor on the other side. Ystil.3 followed, standing up in the stairwell beyond.

They moved swiftly down, searching for signs of the maintenance lift shaft. Long thin windows cast everything in a wash of scarlet from the setting sun. The dinosaur was throwing its weight against the doors above and soon came the sound of crumpling metal.

"Do you have nano-hydraulic muscular upgrades?" he asked. "We need to move faster."

"Not enough to outrun that."

Above them, a sickly roar erupted.

"I could carry you?" Ystil.3 suggested. "We'll be twice as fast. Or we could try to take it down ourselves?"

Lydia made a face. "I think I'd rather not."

He placed one arm around her waist and swept up her legs with the other. She made a small squeak and wrapped her arms around his neck. "Running it is then," he said.

They descended at a speed that generated its own wind. Ystil.3 performed a thermo-scan to note that the dinosaur was little more than twenty feet above them, closing the distance fast. He pushed on harder until Lydia pressed her face into his chest. Descending onto floor twenty's security platform, he headed for the barrier manned by an infobot, the Allosaurus now just a few paces behind them.

"We need to get behind the control field barrier," he sent to Lydia.

"There isn't enough time. If we stop moving it will catch us."

"It will catch us regardless. It's too fast. Did they upgrade it or something?" Ystil.3 switched his retinal filters to infrared and located the infobot's main circuit hatch in the head. With a slice of the laser, the top of its glass cranium fell to the floor, revealing a mass of spaghetti wires and circuitry. He found the memory chip and placed the middle finger of his left hand on the small rectangle. The censor reeled off digital recordings of security passes of the London Tower citizens that had passed through.

There was a calamitous crash and he turned. At the foot of the stairwell, the Allosaurus stood, the sunset pouring bloodshot light over its long teeth.

"Winston, whatever you're doing, do it faster."

It leapt towards them.

Ystil.3 replayed a recording of someone passing through the security platform, directing the visuals into the infobot's retina sensors so it would think a security pass had been scanned. The control field instantly fell and he pulled Lydia through as the Allosaurus lurched to tear a chunk from her. It found the control field in her place and cracked its skull instead. It let out a bowel-loosening roar.

"Thank you for visiting floor ten, East London, leading onto Victoria Park, amber sector. Enjoy your visit, Mr Hamilton," said the cranium-less infobot.

"That was close," Ystil.3 said, watching the dinosaur's attempts at bashing through the barrier with its sheer size.

"Stay where you are," a voice commanded from behind them. A dozen armed guards encircled them. "On the ground, both of you. They're over here. I found them."

An army of armed guards suddenly appeared on the other side of the barrier, aiming weapons at the Allosaurus. It writhed as they restrained it with glowing lightwhips, lassoing the creature around its neck, tail and legs. The lightwhips wrapped themselves around the beast like anacondas, leaving it bound and furious, as three shots of what Ystil.3 presumed were sedatives were fired into its neck. It fell with a floor-shaking thud.

The guard shifted his aim to Lydia and then back to Ystil.3. "I said, get on the fucking ground."

*

Belmarsh Prison put Prometheus in mind of Dante's Inferno – the fifth circle of Hell, to be precise. The corridors were dark tunnels where light had never touched – black river Styx. The air was dank and moist with the breath of a hundred thousand bodies, lying withdrawn into a black sulkiness that could find no joy. Edward, their Charon, led them through rows of confined cells, all shut off by steel doors with no way to look inside.

"Where the worst of the worst are kept," Edward said in a whisper.

Before me there were no created things, only eternal and I eternal last. All hope abandon, ye who enter in.

They passed through three gates using a strange flat key that Edward had taken from one of the guards, and crept silently in a line through the people battery. Almost no one crossed their path and Edward took care of those they had encountered by touching a finger to their foreheads. They dropped unconscious to the floor instantly

They stopped outside a cell.

"Are you ready?" Edward asked, presenting to him the locked door.

Prometheus nodded, feeling the syringe in his inside pocket. There were only two left, and one he intended for Sarah.

The little girl rummaged in an unconscious guard's pockets and handed something to Edward. Edward held the cubed device to the door and a lock slid back with a dull thunk.

"I want to bring back my wife," Prometheus said, hand on the cell door ready to open. "I'm no fool. I want you to send me back to 1898 so I can bring Sarah back from the dead. You can send me, the same way you brought us here. I know you can."

Edward blinked and then smiled. "Of course you do," he said. His tone was somehow mildly patronising, yet at the same time sincere. "And once we are all done, I give you my word that I will see to it that you remain in whichever year you wish."

Prometheus held the boy's gaze before nodding firmly. Edward opened the cell door and allowed Prometheus to enter. "You know what to do."

Alone, Prometheus entered the cell, and for the first time, he dared to believe his wife might once again be in his arms. That he might feel the softness of her skin once more. That his ears would again be blessed with the sweetness of her voice. The spark of hope within him engorged his heart and ignited a humble hope. It burned within hollow chest, powering his legs forward. It gave his brain reason to think, it made the breath flow into his lungs. Without it, he was gone. But with it, a renewed vigour graced his step. He would do whatever it took to have her again.

His eyes adjusted to the darkness and the door shut firmly behind him. Light streamed in from an unknown source and highlighted the dead man upon the bed. His eyes were closed and his skin wan and sickly with age. Newly deceased. His grey hair was thin and patchy and he had a long thin mouth that draped down the side of his face, far too long for a mouth. Slit-

64

like. His nose hooked down to almost touch it. The man wore a simple garb of white cotton that had been soiled and stained with bodily excretions. Wires had been screwed into his skull and they trailed along the bed and off into an unknown place; the scalp had grown and healed around the screws, the way the bark of a tree will grow around a leaning fence over time.

Prometheus readied his weapon – needle filled with life. His wife's face appeared to him, smiling, waiting for Prometheus to save her. She was waiting for him to snap the jaws of Death, reach into its throat and take her from its belly. And snap he would.

He plunged the needle into the body and depressed the liquid inside. He thought of it taking hold, swimming within to make the corpse whole again, hunting Death.

When he looked up, Prometheus beheld the white face of his nightmares. The shadow with teeth stood before him. Death. It came, not appearing, but as though it was always there, only not noticed before. It craned above him, arching, covering wall and stone ceiling. Its black scythe poised within a bony claw. Prometheus's hands began to tremble but he continued to administer the solution to the dead man. He did not tremble with fear, but with anger.

"Come to give me back this man's soul, have you, demon?" Prometheus whispered in a voice so fuelled by vitriol he barely recognised it.

The creature swayed as though it were nothing but an ethereal wisp. Above its nightmarish grin, Prometheus saw for the first time the two black holes that were its eyes. The nothingness within them congealed, threatening to mesmerise him into a state of incomprehension. He turned away. A noise burst from the creature, as though it wanted Prometheus to turn back and fall into the endless depths of its eyes. The sound of a thousand screams pierced the silence. Prometheus screwed his face but refuse to turn. He refused to do what it wanted. He would take back this soul.

The shadows stretched and swirled and the cell began to shake. The floor split under Prometheus's feet, cracking the walls and revealing the burning fires of hell within the fissures. The screams intensified and the pressure rose in Prometheus's head. He closed his eyes, fearing they would pop from their sockets. As the last drop of the solution entered the stagnant corpse, the noise abruptly ceased. The shaking stopped and the shadows receded back from where they came.

Death had lost and the corpse at Prometheus's side, like those before and those to come – including Sarah – would soon awaken from its thieving clutches.

*

Hands tied and blindfolds covering their heads, Ystil.3 and Lydia were shoved inside a small room. Large mirrors covered each of the four walls, causing an effect of there being hundreds of them, reflection bouncing off one mirror and onto the one opposite, back and forth into infinity. Two guards remained with them constantly. They were then made to sit on two chairs placed back-to-back in the centre of the room.

From what Ystil.3 could tell, they were in some type of research unit. Even though his eyes were covered, he had other ways to see. They had been brought to the very top of London Tower, persuaded by weapons that could send them both straight back to their servers. The security system there surpassed even that of the platforms below and as they were moved along the sterile corridors, Ystil.3 read Life Corp UK on the glass doors. He also glimpsed a retinal scan lodged into the walls every thirty paces or so. Through his brief real-time training, Ystil.3 recognised the device as a laser-grid security system, where if you failed to scan a passable retina before moving farther along the corridor, an interwoven high-beam laser net would fall like a spider's web sheet from the ceiling and slice anything it encountered into hundreds of small cube pieces. The slices were neat and tidy and very easy to clean up as the lasers would cauterise and seal the cuts upon contact, resulting in no blood spilt.

A man entered. He was different from the guards, wearing a white coat with a Lifestore exo-vertebrae attached to his back. The man was thin, in his mid-forties and sporting grizzled hair and a short goatee. He regarded them coldly.

Ystil.3 sent all that was happening to Lydia via secure-beam as she was void of infrared vision and blind to what was happening apparently.

A nurse then entered, pushing a trolley that clanged with sharp instruments. She nodded silently to the man before leaving. With enhanced hearing, Ystil.3 could make out the faint hum of the electromagnetic magnetic lock on the door as it activated, securing them inside the room. Magnetic lock and retinal scans made for a difficult escape. One of the guards removed his blindfold and then Lydia's.

"My name is Dr Graff," the white coat man said with an unfriendly stare. "But I presume you already know that."

Lydia spoke, forcefully and diplomatically. "Whoever you think we are, you are mistaken."

Dr Graff smiled as though her protest was expected and amusing. "Of course," he nodded. "And I expect you and your partner here were just luring my creation to… where exactly? A game of catch in the park?"

"Partner?" Ystil.3 said. "What exactly do you mean by *partner*, because we're not partners. I hardly even like her."

"Luring that thing away?" Lydia said. "It clearly escaped your attention that we were, in fact, trying to escape your creation, as you put it. Because it was roaming free around London, very hungry, I might add. Did you starve it then let it loose or something? Did you have bets on how many people it

66

would eat?"

Dr Graff's smile withered.

"You did, didn't you?" Lydia said. "You released that thing on purpose."

"We used the opportunity we were handed. You hacked our security system and we simply did nothing to stop it escaping."

"So you could then place the blame completely on China State."

"Potential?" Ystil.3 said. "Potential for what?"

"Don't act coy with me, I can see through your act. It's potential in warfare, of course. Now, enough of this. You're going to tell me what China State cell you belong to or I swear I will see you fed to creatures much larger and more ravenous than my little pet you encountered today. I do not suffer spies around my work." His tongue hissed the word spies.

"Spies?" Lydia said. "What makes you think we're spies?"

"We received intel that two China State agents were attempting to personally infiltrate Life Corp UK HQ. That the cyber-attack was just a distraction and that the real damage would come from them, a dark-haired man and a part Asian woman."

"You're saying because I'm part Asian I'm a suspect?" Lydia said. "This is blatant racist profiling."

"Intel from whom?" Ystil.3 said.

The doctor retrieved something from the metal tray upon the trolley. It was a hypodermic needle. "Sodium pentothal, amongst a concoction of other things," he said, tapping it to release any air bubbles. "More commonly known as Tell." He moved to Ystil.3, prepared his arm and injected him with the contents without a struggle. Their hands were bound, but not to the chair. If Ystil.3 wanted to, he could've at least head-butted the guy – but there was no point. "I'm pretty sure this won't affect me," he sent to Lydia via secure-beam.

The doctor prepared another dose for Lydia.

"I'm pretty sure I will tell this son of a bitch everything he wants to know and more if he injects me with that," Lydia sent back. "I have no drug filtration function."

The doctor looked into Lydia's eyes and decided the guards would hold her arms still. After administering the Tell the guards let her go.

"No one is leaving this room intact until I know what China State sent you here to do," the doctor said.

Lydia swooned in her chair. Ystil.3 could feel the weight of her lolling from side to side.

"Are you okay?"

"I don't feel very… think-y. It's working. Need to leave now."

Ystil.3 checked his tracker. "Shit. They've gone. They must've collected whoever they were here for and Cut to another time sector."

"Junkfuckers," Lydia sent back before she laughed out loud.

"Ready to talk, are we?" Dr Graff smirked.

"Infallibly." She giggled.

"We should just Cut now," Ystil.3 sent. "There's no point to us being here. We should try another time."

"Okay. I'm on board with this plan seventy-three percent. The other twenty-seven percent wants to kick this Dr Giraffe in the balls first."

"Do you want to know a secret?" Lydia said to the doctor. The man's eyes widened and he moved his sun-starved face close towards her.

"Always," he whispered.

Lydia slammed a sharp toe into the man's crotch and he instantly crumpled to the ground, his face purple and his mouth gasping like a fish. Lydia flailed her limbs wildly at any guard that dared approach her and Ystil.3 manoeuvred himself from the chair, twisting his bound arms from behind his back until they were in front of him. He struck the first guard that came upon him. The guard swayed but stayed up. He smacked Ystil.3 in the face with the back of his firearm and Ystil.3 fell, sparks of pain shattering his vision. As he lay, he considered his bound hands – just a thin plastic strip of plastic. He began to open his arms apart to snap it. The plastic cut into his synth's flesh and bright red blood poured from the wounds before they snapped. Ystil.3 was both horrified and mesmerised at the sight of it.

The doctor had now half recovered and both guards had successfully pinned Lydia to the floor. He pulled them both off her and he was soon faced with a loaded barrel. The first finger on his bloodied left hand found the guard's forehead – visor-less from the struggle with Lydia – and he dropped to the floor in a heap. The second guard then aimed at his face – his visor was intact. Behind him, Lydia head-butted the doctor as he leaned over her with another syringe. His nose exploded with blood, crushed almost flat to his face. He cried out. She rolled and stood, then looped her bound arms around the neck of the gun-toting guard and held pressure in the exact position as to cut off his air supply. Ystil.3 knocked off his visor and with a gentle tap on the head the man collapsed next to his friend. With another quick poke, Dr Graff did the same, relieving him from the agony of his crushed nose.

"Right, let's get out of here," Ystil.3 said.

Lydia swooned, reaching for the silver lion head pendant around her neck.

"Are you alright?"

She waved a dismissive hand and grabbed his shoulder.

As they displaced, darkness swallowed them. Then the pins and needles began.

☐

9

They Cut to the sector 2050, having followed the tracking of Prometheus to a building in Manhattan, New York, USA. They appeared in a hospital. More specifically, a small supply closet crammed with pale green scrubs that smelled of latex and cleaning solution.

"Where's Prometheus?" Lydia asked. Ystil.3 could see the concentration on her face as she fought the effects of the truth drug.

"A room to the left, down the corridor on this floor," Ystil.3 said, checking the tracking system.

Lydia grabbed a pair of hospital scrubs from the shelf. "We should put these on." She threw a cellophane packet at Ystil.3's face. They changed quickly, placing their memo-fabric clothes into Lydia's quantum purse.

Ystil.3 found himself growing more curious about his situation in real-time. So far, he had left the comfort of his DataCom crib in Grid City, filtered into a synthetic, catapulted to Earth, followed a human, Cut to a sector he wasn't supposed to be in, was attacked by a dinosaur, almost tortured by a human, Cut to another sector he wasn't supposed to be in and was about to once more follow in the tracks of Prometheus and his ever-expanding following of dead friends. It was safe to say that he'd had had his fill. And what's more, he found himself trusting Sir Z's reasons for sending him into real-time less and less. Why him? He was no one.

"I'm not a field agent," he said angrily, as the last of the pins and needles left his limbs. "All I want to know is what's going on here so I can report to Sir Z and go home. What is going on?"

"I'm trying to find out what you know about Earth," Lydia said. She looked at him oddly, her face a startled mask. "It's the Tell. Don't ask any more questions."

"What? Why not?"

"Because I'll tell you things I don't want you to know," she said truthfully, screwing her face up.

"You're keeping things from me?"

"Yes, lots of things." She clamped a hand over her mouth. "Will you stop that, please?"

The door to the closet swung open and a small woman entered with vomit down her scrubs and exhaustion on her face. She stopped and looked at them.

"Oh. Hi," she said. She spoke with a New York accent. "Good, more hands. Rooms twenty to eighty on Ward B need beds changing. I got three teams on it already but they could use more help. It just isn't the same unless a patient blows chunks on me daily." She laughed, looking down at herself.

Lydia laughed in amiable agreement and pulled Ystil.3 from the closet. They made their way along the paediatrics ward, passing brightly coloured cartoon pictures painted on the walls. The place reeked of vomit and faeces and chemicals. Lydia stopped abruptly at a room filled with incubator beds full of soft human infants. She stared through a viewing window, her eyes transfixed by the baby nearest to her. It opened its mouth and yawned, revealing a tiny pink tongue. Lydia laughed and turned to Ystil.3 with giant doe eyes.

His deadpan expression looked back. "When you're ready…" he said.

Farther along the network of corridors were the private rooms. Ystil.3 located the exact room and stole a glance through the thin window set in the door. Prometheus was inside, accompanied by Edward from 1901 and the same tall man with dark hair they'd seen him with in London Tower. The three of them were gathered around a hospital bed. The same little girl who was with them in 2310 lay pale and sickly under the white sheets, attached to wires and machines. She was unconscious, her hairless head lying on the pillow, like a fragile egg in a nest.

"We're in a time sector they entered before they Cut to London Tower," Lydia secure-beamed.

"How can you tell?"

"The little girl hasn't died yet and Prometheus hasn't brought her back. Plus, whoever they wanted to collect from 2310 doesn't seem to be with them. I'm guessing from here they will Cut to 2310. We could follow them back to the previous sector, as we know that's where they're heading. Who knows, while we were running from the dinosaur, maybe another version of us succeeded in trapping them in the sublevel prisons of London Tower?"

"But we're here right now," Ystil.3 sent back. "Why wait? We should storm in with guns blazing. We can drag Prometheus back to his time, erase his memory, hand over whoever those people are to Sir Z and I can go back home to the BroadWeb. Sound good?"

To Ystil.3's surprise, it was a different secure-beam that caught his attention, not Lydia's reply. The channel, he recognised instantly. It was Tom.

"Ystil.3, are you there?"

"Tom, I'm so relieved to hear from you. You have news?"

"You bet I've got news. I don't have much time. I have to get back to the Black Betty. I will fill you in as soon as I can. I just wanted to warn you. The Lydia creature isn't the Overly Watchful for the time sector 1901. I can't explain it all right now, but I will."

"Are you sure?" Ystil.3 sent, aware that Lydia was staring at him, waiting for a response to whatever he'd failed to register. "Are you okay? What's happened, and where's your Welsh accent gone?"

"I don't have time to explain. I have to go. Betty needs me. Stay safe, friend."

A frown scored his synth's forehead and he looked at Lydia.

"Winston?" she said out loud. "Have you been listening to me?"

"You're not the Overly Watchful the time sector 1901," he said. "Who are you?"

Lydia took a small step back. Her eyes scanned the hall and then his face. "I'm Lydia," she said innocently.

"What type of AI are you, because an Overly Watchful, it seems, you are not?" Hot anger poured through his blood. He didn't know why he felt betrayed, but he did.

Lydia drew her hands to her mouth to stop the words flowing, but the Tell forced them free like disembowelled guts. "I'm not AI. I'm human."

10

The trajectory of a piece of passing space debris was due to impact with the ship. Most likely nothing more than a small comet – barely double the width of myself in size – I saw no cause to alert Betty to climb out of steady geosynchronous orbit of Delilah, which itself was protected with three varying-level control shields and under no threat from the debris.

I scuttled along her wide black hull, aimed at the glimmering lump that hurtled towards us in a mist of dust from the depths of the Titan System and blew it to vapour with one of the smaller plasma rays located on my rear end. It burst into a spray of fragments, no longer posing a semi-threat.

That low-threat occurrence was quite common in the Titan system, where the gravitational pull of Delilah lassoed dross from all over. Most of the fragments simply combined in a steady orbit of the metal planet, forming a wide ring, of which Betty and I were now part. I like to think they were hypnotised by the greatness of Delilah and came to worship her, beauty that it is. However, occasionally a piece of rock would either threaten to strike us or attempt to plummet to the surface of Delilah. It was our job to ensure the functionality of the control shields that surrounded the planet so that no harm came to the millions of AI servers that covered its surface.

"Close call?" Betty sent through the localised sip radio channel.

"Not at all. Just a little one. But I'm on it, as always."

The ship made a high-pitched giggling sound. "Oh Tom, I don't think I shall ever get used to your new Welsh accent."

"What are you going on about, new? I've had it for yonks now."

She laughed again. "How time flies when you're orbiting a metal hub in the vast vacuum of space."

I sent an audible "hmmm". I was distracted. "Has Sir Z sent the usual message to the masses yet?"

"I haven't received anything, but I'll let you know as soon as I do."

"Thanks, pet."

"Are you quite alright, Tom?" the warm, feminine voice of the ship asked. "You don't seem yourself. I haven't heard a single verse of The Green, Green Grass of Home in over an hour."

I laughed a little forcibly. "I spoke to Ystil.3. He wants me to do something for him. It would mean that I'd have to go into the BroadWeb."

"No wonder you're not yourself. I know how you detest it."

"It's just too damn big and I feel too damn small in there."

"Is it important, what Ystil.3 asked of you? I know you were concerned before Sir Z assured you of his safety. I hope he isn't in any trouble doing his real-time training."

"I get the feeling it is very important. As for Ystil.3 being in trouble, well, you know yourself how dedicated and sensible the DataCom Unit is. But I fear he's out of his depth this time. Hopefully, it will be resolved quickly. I wish I could tell you the whole story but Sir Z has put a silence order on him. The only reason he told me was so I could do this task for him. He doesn't have access to the BroadWeb, you see."

"My goodness," the ship exclaimed. "Now I see why you're so worried. Ystil.3 with no BroadWeb access is like something that's meant to be in something, in something else entirely."

"That's a very good analogy." Betty always amused me with her blatant lack of enthusiasm for the spoken word. "You do have a way with words, my love." She also often got things mixed-up. For a long time, she called me Tim. She wasn't too good with gauging linear time measurements either.

"You know what I mean, so stop teasing me." She paused for a moment. "It goes against orders for you to enter the BroadWeb and leave me unattended. You know that, don't you?"

"Yes, I know. But I will only be gone a short while. Would you cover for me?" I already knew she would. I stroked her hull with one of my softer appendages.

The ship giggled in her way. "Of course, Tom. As you know full well I will."

*

I lived my life clinging to the outer hull of the Black Betty. I hadn't been inside the ship ever so I had to search through my files for the location of the stasis infirmary, where the BroadWeb connectors resided. I hovered over the hatch to the emergency drop ship deck ¬– the only hatch large enough to permit my entrance – with my legs clamped eagerly to the sides, as the decompression hissed in preparation to open.

Betty had originally been created with a crew in mind that would fly her – a crew of AI synthetics. That was before it was upgraded with a sentient intelligence that allowed the ship to control its own actions and become AI itself. This meant that the inside was rather small and, let us say, unaccommodating for an AI of my size and heft. All the things I didn't need, such as compression, O2 and gravity simulator control fields were also built into the ship.

"Okay, Tom. You can go in now," the ship said audibly over the internal intercom. "Try not to scratch my paintwork with your pincers, if you can help it."

I clambered inside, feeling boxed in by the sudden constraint of the four bulkheads that surrounded me. I suffered a little with claustrophobia; not uncommon in AI.

"Don't worry. I'll be as graceful as a ballet dancer."

As Betty's pressure levels returned to normal, I entered the emergency drop ship and armoury deck, which was empty of both ships and weapons. I never thought to ask why weapons might have been needed back when AI had manned the ship. But as I said, it was the only hatch I could fit through. I manoeuvred across the deck, looking up to see the starry sky through the slanted ports above. I had long ago memorised the constellations in the Titan System, but seeing them from a different view almost felt as though I was seeing them for the first time, no longer part of them, but looking up from a distance. Separate. I didn't like that feeling.

It had also been a good long while since I had last contended with my old nemesis – gravity. It was a standard Earth gravity control field, but I was designed for 0g deep space. I clunked all eight of my limbs, remembering how heavy they were and needing more energy to move. It took a few awkward moments for me to get accustomed. Betty could have shut it off, but there was more chance that I would damage her interior if I floated about, crashing my way through.

The steel pincers on the end of each of my ten-foot legs almost crushed the deck with each step. I was slow, but I was okay with that. Slow was my forte. I didn't like to hurry or be hurried, and for most of the time, I never was. But I was taking extra care to not destroy the internal structure with my oafishness. I had yet to become fully aware of my strength. As I said, I was designed for deep space 0g, so strength in itself was a redundant concept when nothing weighs anything and one unmagnetised push from an enthusiastic limb could send me off into the cosmos for eternity.

The first hatch doors slid open and I edged through, retracting my eight legs and pulling in my awkward head to make myself as small as possible. I then shimmied down the equally oppressive causeway. Unfortunately, after successfully making it through the next hatch on the way to the bridge, I became compressed against the bulkheads, like a cork in a bottle. My legs were tight at my body and if I moved any farther I would have demolished them to shreds. I sent a sensor out from my underside to assess the room I had to squeeze through. It turned out I had none.

To get to the stasis infirmary, I had to make it up one level and through another corridor of undetermined width, before pressing myself into the cabin itself. I sighed, listening to ship giggle. "I suppose you think it's terribly funny, don't you?"

"Oh, Tom. You've gotten yourself into a bit of a state, haven't you?"

"What do you suggest? And stop laughing."

"I'm sorry. It's just you look so adorable." She paused. "Well, I guess you'll just have to force your way up to the stasis room, won't you."

"I can't do that."

"Don't be so rigid, Tom. You're supposed to protect my outside, not

74

my inside. Besides, it won't make a difference at all. It won't affect my ability to protect M21 and I have no crew to account for. Plus, all this stalling is just wasting time. I thought the idea was to get there and back before anyone notices. I can only cover for you for so long, Tom. If Sir Z asks to speak directly with you, what shall I tell him?"

"Tell him I'm taking a nap."

"You don't sleep."

"Well, tell him… I don't know."

"Exactly. So, will you move your gigantic arse and hurry up?"

I sighed again. I didn't like the idea of damaging her one little bit. It went against my programming. But she did have a point. It wouldn't affect her ability to do her job, and I had already made a promise to Ystil.3.

"Fine," I said sullenly. I stretched out my legs and made puncture wounds through the bulkheads with minimal efforts. I lifted my body to the sound of tearing metal, then reached up with my front legs to rip open the half-foot thick ceiling, pulling back strips until the hole was big enough for me to climb through. I dented the walls with my clamps as I hauled my gravity-affected weight into the larger corridor above.

"That wasn't so bad, was it?" the ship said.

I made a "pfft" sound in reply.

Crouching along the above access strip, I turned the corner and made my way awkwardly through without any further need of damaging the interior – although a few inadvertent bruises were made. The hatch to the stasis infirmary hissed open and I was happy to see it was large enough inside for me to access a BroadWeb connection.

The stasis infirmary was crammed with BroadWeb chamber beds that lined the walls vertically, which would have allowed early synth models to filter in and out. The BroadWeb pads contained a single jack socket and the retractable plug for those with a jack built in. Being an AI that rarely needs, or desires, to enter the BroadWeb, I had no need for a jack. I did, however, have a plug for emergencies. I ejected it from the base of my underside, where my more delicate instruments resided, and like a thin snake it coiled out and slotted into the jack of the BroadWeb pad above the head of the nearest bed.

"I'm all set up, Betty," I said. "You sure you'll be alright for a while?" Although I knew Ystil.3 would never have asked this of me unless it was important, I didn't feel good about leaving her.

"I'm not completely useless. I've got tricks you've never seen, honey."

I laughed a rumbling laugh and readied myself. "I'll see you soon, pet."

Then I entered the BroadWeb.

*

The BroadWeb is eternal. By that, I mean that it is infinite, never-ending, with boundless possibilities and no limitations. A concept hard to grasp. The BroadWeb has no confines because it is not physical in the sense the word is commonly interpreted. It's more quanta-physical. To describe it as digital would also be incorrect because that would suggest it was created. The BroadWeb was not created, least of all by AI. It was merely stumbled upon by accident, apparently. The space between spaces. It's in the smallest of elements, in sound, scent, air and all matter. And it's in the largest of planets, suns, galaxies and living creatures. If everything in existence was destroyed and all that remained was one floating atom in a sea of anti-matter, that single atom would contain the complex eternity of the BroadWeb.

I don't like it, myself. Never have. Not like Ystil.3. He always expressed his love of it while we talked or played chess over our secure-beam channel. A lot of AI are that way inclined. Being physical, with material bodies that exist in real-time isn't our natural state, if such a state is possible. We are like water existing in a variety of forms, liquid, ice and steam, all the same element fundamentally. I suppose, when it comes to the chewy centre of things, AI are simply third-gen binary coding data parcels – digital information built upon a primary function with sentient learning capabilities. The BroadWeb is a perfect environment for such a creature to exist, flitting information back and forth from the server planet.

AI are quite confined in their views. We are programmed rigidly. We are also stubborn, and on most occasions, we always know we're right. But we can learn through experience, just like every sentient creature that ever was.

For me, I learned Tom Jones.

The darkness of nothingness loomed around me for a moment, taking my shape and converting me into information for BroadWeb entry. Being dependant on my shape, the translation felt a lot like falling out of myself. The layers of physicality peeled back to my core. The form I had clung to was nothing but a casing and as soon as it was free, after the initial shock, memories returned, reminding me how it felt to be of mind only – like in the early days of my conception – and how it felt to surge through the BroadWeb, as free as light itself. Limitless.

I felt a grip of fear and a shiver of claustrophobia as I entered Grid City.

The first thing I saw – I say saw, but I mean interpreted from the information around me. I will continue to express myself with words such as saw, heard, felt and so on because these are what feel most comfortable to me, coming from a material plane. Each AI will understand the BroadWeb differently, depending on programming, AI mind capability and, more surprisingly it seems, from the ideologies of its habitat and immediate social environment. So, how I understand the BroadWeb may be utterly different from how Ystil.3 understands it, for example. It also affects how each AI see themselves in Grid City. Those of BroadWeb origin, for example, DataCom Units, would all see themselves as relatively the same entity, reading the information of each DataCom as near enough identical. Those AI from outside the BroadWeb, like myself, are easier to spot, as we often see ourselves as our physical counterparts. In my case, that would be a large metal spider with clamps, pincers and plasma beams protruding from all angles. To others, we may look like their own interpretation of our datastream because, in most cases, they would not have ever seen our physical counterparts.

I interpreted myself into the shape of Tom Jones, which, as I looked down at my naked self, gave me a little thrill. Okay, I lie. It gave me a huge thrill. I was as close to Tom Jones as I was ever going to get and for a brief second before I remembered why I was there, I wanted to test my voice and belt out a version of She's a Lady. But I quickly regained my focus.

The first thing I saw, as I craned my head, was the light that shimmered across the black sky – blue, green and white, merging and dancing in a storm of colour. Lightning crackled across lights, spitting shards that rolled out into the expanse of nothingness above. Huge AI Wanderers moved between skyscrapers of black glass. They weaved purposefully between them, twice as high as the tallest DataCom Pylon and giving form to everything. To me, the AI Wanderers were amorphous creatures, no more than shadows against the blackness, with glowing white eyes that poured light down their shadowy shapes, like electric bones, flowing out along the ground like vines and under the vast expanse of Grid City. They were not intelligent, as far as AI go, but essential none the less. The scrapers themselves blacker even than the sky and only visible by the white current that travelled from Wanderers, giving Grid City its form and substance.

Programmes buzzed around the Wanderers like parasites and more swarmed at ground level along roads of light that travelled down into the endless rows of scrapers on the horizon of Grid City. Larger programmes kept separate as they went about their business, careful not to get in the way of the smaller and faster-moving programmes. All were different shapes and colours. All had various purposes and tasks to perform that allowed the city to function. I interpreted the programmes mostly as types of insects or parasites that I'd seen at one time or another amid deep space or in the Earth files. Some were smaller and ethereal like smoke, with wispy shoots and antennae, while others were large and bulky, depending on what they were designed for. Like AI, programmes had developed a sense of self and were capable of learning, making them all quite different from one another, each with their own little personalities.

The city was a hub for teeming AI and programmes. They whirled about in a constant reading and transmitting of information; collecting, absorbing, interpreting, deconstructing and passing it all to the vast forest of receptive scrapers and DataCom Pylons.

I stood amid them, without a clue as to which of the many DataCom

Pylons on the horizon Ystil.3 called home. He had told me they received almost constant updates from the Overly Watchful, and every few seconds I noticed a curtain of red lightning strike a block of scrapers a little way off in the centre of the city, blurring the sky around them like a bruise. I accessed the Know function and quickly ascertained that the red lightning was the streaming information from the Overly Watchful being passed from time sector to DataCom Units.

I decided that was probably where I should start.

As I made my way from the programme-infested light-roads, heading towards the hectic overpass crowded with AI, I gleaned what knowledge I could about the Overly Watchful. The Know function allowed me to learn they were designed to fit into the society of the time sector they watch, which meant that they looked human and wouldn't have too many upgrades – especially those residing in the early years of human civilisation. I was also allowed to know that the information they streamed to the BroadWeb was absorbed by them like a sponge, even when they were asleep, which they did to appear more human.

The multitude of sensors that made up the Overly Watchful synthetic were designed to pick up data from all over the world. Therefore, even if one resided in one place on Earth, they would still collect information from the other side of the planet – all the small facts from people's lives, as well as the big stuff like plate movement and celebrities. The Overly Watchful didn't need to take any action to procure their data other than simply continue to exist in that time. The data came to them. It got a bit more complicated in the later years of humanity, once they'd colonised other planets, but apparently the Overly Watchful could still absorb the data across space through a system of relays. Most Overly Watchful chose to blend in by living human lives, which they could do only if it didn't impact on Earth history in any way. They did this not only to appear inconspicuous to humanity but also to – for lack of a better term – pass the time. The information collected from them would then be streamed to the DataCom Pylons, where it would be matched with Earth files, which held an accurate account of all Earth's history.

With billions of micro-programmes whizzing by below, I walked the overpass and lined-up with the rest of the AI. A few grotty looking mid-sized programmes made their way along the queue, offering to trade illegal functions for regulated ones. I stepped onto the light-pad before it reached me.

"DataCom Pylons," I instructed proudly in my Welsh. The light-tunnel flickered, hummed and funnelled me to the centre of Grid City within a fraction of no time.

I stood in the centre of Grid City, facing the towering DataCom Pylons as a mass charge of red lightning flowed over the nearest. I would start with that one. But how would I gain entry? I decided the best way was to just walk through the front door – see what happened.

I climbed the black steps and made my way towards the arched front entrance guarded by Apex Soldiers – AI that are as aggressive as any type A virus and fiercely strict in adhering to programming. They kept to their orders by any means. However, they were not the greatest of independent thinkers. They loomed over me, almost twice my size.

As casually as I could, I attempted to make my way through the doors leading inside the Pylon, but the soldiers turned to me in unison. Their heads were small and sat diamond-shaped upon wide shoulders, out of which thorn barbs and spikes protruded. Razors scored their huge arms and legs like ridges, which led to claws even fiercer than the spikes that ornamented their bodies. Their faces were void of features, smooth and cold. Yet I could feel them watching me.

Were Sir Z to order it, just one strike from an Apex could send me straight back to foetal mode – meaning I would be stripped back to nothing but the energy from which all AI came. However, I continued. I had the briefest notion that perhaps it was going to be as simple as that. But, of course, it wasn't.

"Holt, CorVac." The Apex had a hive mind, able to move as one deadly being. Grid City was home to thousands of them. What one knew, they all knew. What one saw, they all saw. And right now, they saw me.

I stopped, of course. Long spikes had extended out from the Soldier's limbs to form a sharp barrier to the entrance arch.

"CorVacs have no business here," their simultaneous and mechanical voices scraped. They were perfectly still. "This is a DataCom Pylon."

Within my throat, I found my voice. "I'm looking for—"

"This is a DataCom Pylon. CorVacs have no business here."

"Yes, I know it's a DataCom Pylon," I replied cautiously. "That's why I'm here. I need to speak to—"

"CorVacs have no business here." The spikes that blocked my entrance became loaded with thorns, each dripping with viruses.

It was clear I wasn't getting into the Pylon that way. I hurried my way back down the steps towards the light-pad, turning back to see that the Apex had retracted their javelin limbs and the entrance was now again unblocked.

I had never tried to enter a DataCom Pylon before so I had no idea whether this was a normal level of security, but my back was up, as humans would say. Something didn't quite feel right. With no way to get in, how I would get the information Ystil.3 needed?

As I considered my current predicament, a small DataCom Unit meandered by – height barely clearing my knees – and began struggling up the steps towards the Pylon, its perfectly spherical head ablaze with lights and sensors. It was so blasé that it practically skipped through the arched entrance without the Apex Soldiers even registering it.

It gave me an idea. A very bad idea.

11

It wasn't too often an AI could be seen in the bustle of the programme marketplace, but there I was. And all programme eyes were on me. The market was located on the outskirts of the city where the Wanderers' light barely reached and the shadow of nothingness seemed uncomfortably close in all its unknown mystery. Light pads didn't go there so I had to funnel to the edge of the city and make the rest of the way on my own steam.

AI hardly made use of the marketplace because they were simply far too busy. AI had jobs to do. Things depended on them. They were programmed and predictable and almost never deviated from their main function. But as I said before, AI have the ability to learn – which inevitably comes with intelligence – and therefore we can change. I guess that's why I was there. I had deviated from my main function to perform this task for a much-beloved friend.

Programmes, on the other hand, were not so finely tuned when it came to their main function. More often than not, in the early days of Grid City, programmes were designed for single tasks and purposes. Once those purposes had been fulfilled and the programme no longer required, they would either float off into the nothing or they would ask the question: what do I do now? Having no encoded purpose, other than the one given to them by AI, which they would have completed, they would go off in search of their own purpose. This resulted in what could be referred to as a sub-culture of abandoned programmes. They began to group together for safety and comfort in the vast, desolate BroadWeb and after a while they claimed the outskirts of Grid City. They were permitted to claim it by Sir Z because they had served a purpose, but also because Z couldn't really do a damned thing about it. The Wanderers gave form to Grid City, but Sir Z could no more control the wild BroadWeb in the larger sense than humans could control the weather on their Earth.

The Know function flashed off as I finished my history update. I was being watched, so I was careful to not look aggressive, merely intrigued. It didn't take long for the programmes to realise I was no threat and as I made my way through the light-coded stalls full of functions, some of the insect-looking programmes tried to steer me to their stalls, hoping I would trade with them. But I was looking for something specific.

The marketplace itself was the result of what could be referred to as a crude form of commerce. The programmes had discovered that they could enrich and diversify their existences by trading functions. Thus, the market place became a hub of activity. Some functions were more sought than others and some were even rare and could be dangerous when used outside their intended creation. That's when Sir Z decided AI needed to regulate this function trading and keep an active hand in the programme's marketplace. Sir Z didn't want any old AI to be able to go there and obtain a function that might distract from their main purpose, or give them power beyond their station. Each AI had their place in the system and deviating could threaten the order of things. As a result, certain functions were made illegal and the programmes were told they could trade only what was approved for trading. But as with anywhere, illegal acts continue. And that was precisely what I was relying on.

The longer I mooched down the market lanes, obviously uninterested in the legal function being presented to me, the more I was attracting the type of trader I wanted to attract.

I turned at a tap on my shoulder.

"You look something special, Sir AI?"

A small red programme stood in front of me.

"Yes," I replied. "Something in the filter family. Do you know where I can find something rare?" I tried to be as clear as I could be without saying anything incriminating.

"I afraid no, Sir," the programme replied. "I no can help." It stared at me with its huge black eyes before cocking its head and walking off.

I followed the red programme through the lanes and then out into the shaded borders. The occasional programme meandered pointlessly here and there but we were relatively alone. It stopped at a large pile of unwanted files and information that, to me, looked much like a mound of space junk. It pointed to the pile and attempted an expression that resembled a smile. Then, it walked straight through the pile with a shimmer of the air. It was a data pocket. I followed it through.

Inside was cave-like and full of what mostly looked like crap. Bits of functions and files filled all dimensions of the place. Some were badly damaged by viral attack and some looked half complete. There were so many in the red programme's cache that I could barely fit inside. I had to duck along to where the programme crouched, shovelling through functions wildly.

"Where did you get all these?" I asked, my head narrowly missing a viral function hanging from the ceiling. The red programme whipped his head around and squinted with its glassy black eyes.

"Bo get big big tower."

I took a second to decipher what it meant. It was referring to itself as Bo. "From the big tower?"

"Yeah." Its voice was shrill and loud. "Bo sneak." It laughed. "AI no want, so Bo have. Sneaky sneaky."

"You took them from AI?"

It nodded, abandoning the search from one pile and moving to another.

"How do you know they didn't want them?" I asked, casually poking a dormant virus thorn.

"Bo no thief," it snapped, looking up at me. "Bo watch for long time. AI no use, so Bo use." It then went back to rummaging through its vast mass of functions.

"Fair enough. Do you have any—"

"Sir want X-ray sensor?" Bo asked, wide-eyed.

"No. I'm looking for something that will change the way I'm perceived by other AI, a filter, or something that works in the same way. I need to be seen as a DataCom Unit."

It blinked. "But Sir is CorVac."

I tried again, louder and slower. "I want AI to think I am a DataCom Unit. Not. CorVac. Want. Day. Ta. Com. U. Nit. Do you have function that distort perception?"

It blinked again.

I looked around, trying to find a way for it to understand. "Need Bo see me as DataCom Unit."

It rubbed together the wiry antennae that sat atop its small head. "Change look-y?"

"Yes," I said, nodding Tom Jones' handsome head. "Change look-y. Change look-y to DataCom Unit."

It then began to laugh and dance on the spot for some reason. It seemed to find it very funny. "Big CorVac change look-y to tiny DataCom Unit."

"Yes, okay. Ha-ha. The CorVac with the giant arse wants to look like a DataCom. Get it all out your system."

"Sir funny."

I clenched my jaw. "Do you have something or not?"

"Bo have what Sir need." It began searching through the function pile right in the back of the cache. "But do Sir have what Bo want as trade?"

"I don't have many functions. I have no need for them really. I have Know function. You can have that if you like?"

Bo waved a stick-like arm. "All have Know," it said. "Bo have lots of Know. Know worthless."

"Then what is it you want? I can offer you a few sensors on top of that? I need this filter desperately and I have nothing else to give you."

Bo smiled and nodded firmly. "Bo like your talky. Bo trade your talky."

"You want my Welsh? Not my Welsh. I'm sure there's something else you'd like or I could get you. Anything, just not my Welsh. Sex Bomb won't sound the same without it."

"Filter very rare, very very rare. Bo need good trade. Want talky." It stomped its little insect leg and turned, resolved to only trade for my Welsh.

There was nothing else for it. I would have to give up my pride and joy – my beautiful Welsh. "Fine. You can have my talky."

Bo began to dance around again.

"Ystil.3 is going to owe me big time for this."

*

I stood facing the entrance to the first DataCom Pylon with the intimidating Apex Soldiers yet again glaring down at me. If this failed, not only would I not gain entrance to the Pylon, but I would most definitely be reprimanded extremely for having left my post aboard the Black Betty, and for trading in illegal functions.

But I'd come this far…

I moved away from the light-pad and climbed the steps towards the Pylon entrance. As I ascended, the two Soldiers remained unmoving, guarding the inner gate under the high black arch. If all had worked as it should with the perception filter, to them I would appear to be nothing more than your usual DataCom Unit going about work in a typical and predictable manner. I reached the top and strode beneath the towering black archway that led to the guarded inner gate.

Afraid to look directly at the Apex Soldiers, my sensors picked up a slight movement from one. It took all my courage not to run back towards the light-pad. I soon realised, however, that they weren't interested in me in the slightest. Where before I had been refused entry with an aggressive firmness, I passed the Soldiers and entered through the inner gate with no trouble at all.

I hadn't been detected.

I was in.

*

In real-time terms, it was possible that I was wandering the DataCom Pylon for hours, days perhaps. There seemed to be no end to it. But the rules of the BroadWeb are different to the physical, and being used to the exterior of objects giving an indication of the size inside, I was disheartened to find that the Pylon was larger within than what I first gathered.

Each square foot in each room on each floor was crammed full of DataCom Unit docking beds, like fruit attached to streams of pulsating vine-like wire, receiving stores of unquantifiable information. The lights on their spherical heads glowed and danced as they dealt with the data from the Overly Watchful data streams. I passed by unnoticed. All were too preoccupied to observe me – all DataCom Units, that is. I did occasionally come by a menial domestic AI floating around the place, whose job was to simply help with binary repairs and general duties. They weren't what you'd consider very intelligent – AI standards – but as with all in Grid City, everything had a job to do. I told them I was merely looking for something and they left it at that, satisfied that I wasn't going to disrupt them or create more work to clean up after.

The Pylon itself, to me, was the worst thing imaginable and the further I investigated the more I couldn't understand Ystil.3's warmness towards it – reverence even. When I looked around, however, all I could see were shelves upon shelves of imprisoned AI, sentenced to carry out their existences chained to their docking beds with no real freedom. To me, freedom was the Titan System, it was the Black Betty in orbit of Delilah, and it was Tom Jones singing The Green Green Grass of Home. I'd never actually even set pincer on the planet itself – never had to – but that wasn't the point, just having it there in my constant view was enough. To Ystil.3, however, freedom was something different; it was having full access to the capabilities of the BroadWeb and being detached from real-time. In his docking bed, Ystil.3 could access what he wanted, when he wanted. From there he could speak to me, receive streams of real-time and access all the legal functions. It was his home. It was his security. But through my eyes – my CorVac programmed, Tom Jones-obsessed eyes – all I saw were AI in bondage.

Was it the result of our poles-apart-programming that caused such a contrast in our perceptions? Or was it something else – something I learned?

There would be time later to discuss these things, when Ystil.3 was back in his docking bed and me back with Betty where I belonged. I had to remain focussed towards the task at hand. Ystil.3 was counting on me and I still had no idea how I would gain access to the information I needed. The only AI with access to everything was Sir Z and I could hardly just ask for it.

I turned and began away from the obscene view of thousands of docking beds just as another crack of lightning streamed information to each of the Units inside, like electric branches. I was resolved to leave. There was nothing there that could help me, and all the other Pylons would only be the same. I was at a loss as to my next move.

That's when I saw it, a faint shadow against the burning red of the data lightning. It appeared within the docking bed lanes, moving between them, hovering. It stirred like mist, reminding me of the way the Wanderers move, almost incorporeal, if such a thing was possible in a world where nothing was physical. It held what I could only interpret as a blade, black as the sky and arching down in a long, sweeping curve. Beneath a hood of hazy blackness, a white grin of bone was visible. A fleshless human hand beckoned me with the motion of a needle-sharp finger.

It was neither AI nor programme that I could tell. It was not a construct or binary parcel. My sensors told me there should be nothing there. But there it was. I read it as perfectly as I did all other data. Yet it made no impact on the surroundings. It simply lingered over the DataCom Units like a ghost, suspended, peering down at them with its hooded, skinless face and its vaporous shroud billowing behind it.

I stared for a long while, checking my sensors over and over, but they read the same. It beckoned me with another gesture and as I approached, it became ever more translucent, until it appeared nothing more than a faint imprint against the high-sheen black of the Pylon interior. It drifted high in the DataCom Unit crib stacks, grim face looking down.

"What are you?" I said, feeling as though I wanted to reach out and touch it. But, of course, that would have been pointless. I was still thinking with my real-time head.

It didn't offer a reply or even acknowledge that I'd asked a question. It simply pointed with a sharpened bone finger to the docking bed over which that it ethereally drifted. I turned to see it was an empty bed, pristine and white with a shimmer of red information streaming through it. The ghost motioned with a slow-moving hand. I don't know how I understood its intentions so clearly. But I did.

"You want me to get in?" I asked, feeling the heat of panic as my claustrophobia set in. The thought of being further bound to the BroadWeb sent me longing for the openness of the Titan System. Then I noticed the small imprinted letters on the head of the docking bed. Ystil.3. It was his docking bed.

I turned back to the ghost but it was gone, leaving no trace or information in its place. I scanned around me but everything was normal, no movement accept the floating menial AI that dotted the cavernous Pylon and the Apex Soldiers that stringently guarded the entrance. I turned back to Ystil.3's docking bed, then, swallowing my fear, I climbed in.

As soon as I lay flat in Ystil.3's station, feeling the hum of data flow through the glowing sensor pad under me, I began to absorb the information that Ystil.3 absorbed every second of his existence. At first, it was too much, too invasive. I instinctively wanted to jump back out again. But I didn't. I remembered why I was there and I relaxed, allowing the images, voices, real-time streams, data parcels, binary information and all the other threads of records that made up a detailed weaving of data, to pass through me like a current.

It was unfathomable to me to have so much data in my reach. I attempted to sift through the mega files to determine if any of it was useful. Closing my eyes made this easier, sending me deeper into the realms of pure third-gen binary than I'd ever been before. It was like a whole other level of the BroadWeb that I'd never even conceived of. And this was how Ystil.3 lived his life. Everything was all around me at once. I was a singularity in the vastness of what I could access. A dot in a sea of space. I uploaded the Earth files with ease, along with functions restricted to DataCom Units. I reeled through Ystil.3's personal files, recalling past conversations with Sir Z and myself, I deciphered previous flat beams from the Overly Watchful of 1901. I spent a while looking for clues about the Overly Watchful, but it was a hopeless task. The flat beams were simply streams of information that didn't even touch their consciousness and gave nothing away about this Lydia.

It was at this moment, after I was resolved that I would get nothing useful from this bed, I received a fresh flat beam from the Overly Watchful of 1901 – from this Lydia AI. Of course, she would still be collecting data regardless of whether she was actively aiding Ystil.3 or not. The gush of information came at me hard and fast in a barrage of indecipherable waves. In my inexperience and alternative programming, it took me a while to process. But I did it.

My newly uploaded pseudo DataCom functions allowed me to weed out all the relevant records I was looking for, which in this case was regarding Ystil.3. I picked out his identifiable AI coding from the mass and interpreted it as if watching it all play out. I saw how the human, Prometheus, had brought back the young man, Edward, and I saw Ystil.3 and Lydia. Strangely, Lydia had somehow included herself in her own flat beam, but I didn't think on it too hard at that moment.

They had entered Prometheus's house and made their way undetected to his cellar, while he and Edward were in the upstairs rooms of the house. I noticed then that Edward's data appeared perfectly normal for a human that had been brought back from the dead… except one thing. I detected traces of Computronium in his data stream; a substance that can turn real-time matter into programmable matter – meaning it can be filled with information to either change its shape or, in the case of the Black Betty, enable something to be programmed with a sentient intelligence. It also made it possible for me to carry my own server around with me, as my own real-time structure was made up, in parts, of Computronium.

But why and how would the Edward have traces of it in his data?

I continued reading the flat beam. Ystil.3 and Lydia concealed themselves as Edward led Prometheus down into the cellar. Then something odd happened. Prometheus and Edward Linear Cut from the time sector. It seemed Ystil.3 and Lydia attempted to follow them wherever it was they went because they too Cut from the sector. I didn't even think Overly Watchful were given the ability to Cut. I know Ystil.3 wasn't. He would have told me.

Then something even odder happened. The flat beam continued streaming after Lydia had left that time sector – the time sector for which she was supposedly the Overly Watchful. As Lydia's sensors were no longer in that time to detect any more information, it should have stopped dead. But it didn't. I could access everything.

There was only one explanation. Lydia wasn't the Overly Watchful for that time sector. But if she wasn't who she said she was, then who in the sacred name of Tom Jones was she?

My first instinct was to secure-beam Ystil.3 immediately with this new information. He needed to be warned, he could be in danger from this imposter. But just as I was just about to contact him with the news, I received a secure-beam from Betty.

"Tom, I don't know what to do. I'm scared," she sent. "I don't know what they'll do to me?"

A cold alarm spread through my limbs. "What's happened?"

"It's a ship. I didn't detect it at first but when I did it began a trajectory for me. I drifted from orbit a little, thinking it was a ghost ship, but when it got closer I detected life on board. I tried to lose it but I couldn't shake it off. It's got me, Tom, I'm clamped to it and it's drawing me in. I don't know what to do."

"I'm coming home right now."

"Please hurry, Tom. I'm scared."

There were no recordings of intelligent life in the known universe, apart from AI, not since the humans destroyed themselves. I couldn't understand what could be doing this to her. I felt sick. I thought of my own server helplessly abandoned, but that didn't even matter. I didn't care. I had to get back to Betty. I had to filter home.

But first I had to secure-beam Ystil.3.

"Ystil.3, are you there?"

"Tom, I'm so relieved to hear from you. You have news?"

"You bet I've got news. I don't have much time. I have to get back to the Black Betty. I will fill you in as soon as I can. I just wanted to warn you. The Lydia creature isn't the Overly Watchful for the time sector 1901. I can't explain it all right now, but I will."

"Are you sure? Are you okay? What's happened, and where's your Welsh accent gone?"

"I don't have time to explain. I have to go, Betty needs me. Stay safe, friend."

☐

12

Prometheus looked up into the strange night sky from a stranger ground. The realisation hit him like a steam train. Against the backdrop of darkness that opened out above them, a finger pointed to a very un-extraordinary dot among the sea of sparkling stars. Prometheus could only just fathom which one Edward gestured to.

"Earth's solar system," he said in a whisper, as though it were an intimate secret between them. He placed a palm on Prometheus's shoulder.

"We're on a planet called Thebes. One of two Earth colonial planets. The air you breathe is false." He pointed up to the sky. "We're under a large control field, a barrier, which is full of manufactured air. The natural atmosphere of the planet cannot sustain human life, so it needs to be altered, terraformed so that the people who live here eventually won't need the manufactured air to breathe. The control field also serves to keep the many comets and asteroids that fall to the surface from space from colliding with the populace."

Prometheus looked up but could see no barrier, only the dark sky – and that moon, fractured like smashed porcelain. Bits of it fragmented off, as though the moon had smaller jagged moons of its own to orbit it.

The others had been waiting inside the centipede-like vehicle, which sat upon numerous spiked chained wheels. The door slid open and Bastille climbed from the armoured carriage. His eye had swollen and was bruising a deeper shade of purple with every passing second. Prometheus hadn't meant to hit him so hard, but at the time he wasn't thinking clearly.

The withdrawals of alcohol were well and truly upon him. The dull of drunkenness had evaporated and he was left with nothing but the unadulterated anger and consuming sadness that had caused him to reach for the bottle to begin with. It seemed his grief and fury had not quelled even a fraction. Even after three long years and over an immeasurable distance.

They climbed back inside the centipede contraption and it began once more over the desert terrain. They had happened upon it by chance after spotting the sand-spray of something moving fast along the dark horizon only seconds after arriving from London Tower. It had sliced through the desert with ease, heading away from where they stood, in the centre of a curving sand dune so high it blocked the view of the sky. At once, Bastille began to run, more quickly than Prometheus had ever seen anything run. He blurred into the dim distance and within seconds the spray of sand stopped, before beginning again, only this time towards them. The armadillo shell carriage soon stopped before them and an upward hinged hatch swung open. The unconscious bodies of two men sprawled out, dressed in orange military garb.

Prometheus was made to enter. That's when the tremors began, working their way out to his skin from his very bones. He began to panic. Cold sobriety was almost upon him. The hatch closed tight and they moved instantly. Suddenly he was short of breath and burning up. "Where are we?" he had asked, but no one paid him any attention. "What place is this?" His heart thumped wildly in his chest. "Let me out." No one moved. His panic soon turned to rage and before he knew it he was on his feet, clawing at the door hatch for freedom. For air. Bastille was on him in seconds, pulling him back with his large arms. That's when Prometheus turned and thumped the man in the eye. Edward finally stopped the machine and allowed Prometheus to vomit on the desert floor, drinking in lungfuls of strange-tasting air. That's when Prometheus saw the moon and all panic was replaced with awe.

Prometheus returned to his seat in the back, while Edward joined Bastille in navigating from the front end. To either side of him sat the little girl from New York, Alice, and the prisoner they had collected from London Tower. Thomas, his name was – although the man never spoke a single word. And there was something in his eyes that Prometheus did not like. Something quite cold. Colder even than Edward's impassive gaze. Prometheus saw the same quality in all of them, but this one was different. His group of companions barely spoke to one another. But the feeling he ascertained was that something more was going on. Strangely, he couldn't help but feel a conversation was taking place silently without him.

He turned to Thomas, whose grey eyes bore unblinkingly ahead. The man's head rotated to face him and a grin stretched from each end of his slit-like mouth. Prometheus faced ahead with an internal shudder. He wouldn't have to endure them for much longer. This was his final task. After which, Edward had promised he would be returned to the year of is choosing. Back to Sarah.

They arrived at the only colony just as the light from the strange sun flooded over a desolate horizon. The sun seemed cool as it burned brightly, farther away from the planet than Earth's sun – or smaller. It lit the land sufficiently enough. Through the portal-like windows of the centipede machine, Prometheus watched the orange land wake, only to find that the land barely woke up at all. The rocky terrain over which they had travelled was arid, dry and lifeless.

They climbed out to walk the rest of the journey towards the grey buildings squatting in the flat distance. Among them, a giant white industrial chimney divided the sky with its sheer size. They began towards it, leaving the still-unconscious men propped up in the machine, which that they had attempted to conceal.

Prometheus was now utterly and painfully sober. He couldn't shake the feeling this last task was going to be more trouble than the others.

*

Nathan first saw them as they appeared over the ever-shifting dunes in the earliest morning sun. At first, he thought dark smudges stained the plexi-membrane that domed over the greenhouse, but he quickly realised that wasn't the case when they began to move. He stood sharply from his knees, potatoes rolling from his lap and stared for almost a minute. It was impossible.

He made himself move, scrambling for the comm on his belt as he hurried through the vegetable patches, making his way out through the central courtyard and over to Miranda. She stood with her back turned, recognisable by her trademark afro hair cropped close to her head. He attempted to reach her first through the comm, but she was already on it.

Her frown deepened when she saw him and Nathan remembered she was still angry with him.

"I know it's a stupid fucking thing to ask but I'm the one who has to ask these questions," she barked down the comm. "Have you double and triple checked?"

A voice replied through cracking static. It was Jason. "I checked it fifty times before I even contacted you. Sat-link is down with Earth and Pisces. As it's with both, I'm guessing it's a problem on our end. I've pre-checked an up-shuttle and I can be in orbit in less than two hours to fix it. I just need someone to help me."

"Fine," Miranda said, giving Nathan a glance. "Take Nathan, he's not doing anything, just standing here. Oh, and don't go broadcasting it. I'm not saying keep it a secret, but with your mouth, you'd probably start a fucking panic and that's not what people need right now." Miranda's voice softened abruptly. "How is she?"

"I've got to go," Jason said, ignoring her question. "I'll keep you updated. And tell Nathan to get his ass over to me A-fucking-SAP."

The comm broke-off and Miranda hooked it back to her belt. "You heard him. Move your arse. You're making orbit."

She hadn't seen them, but others in the courtyard had begun to take notice. Some stopped with their chores and stared as the strangers – five of them – trudged down the dunes, only just visible over the walls of the courtyard.

Miranda turned to look at what was holding Nathan's attention. Her eye's narrowed before widening in disbelief. "Fuck me…" she whispered, and after a pause continued, "…Hard."

"Conner and David?" Nathan suggested, knowing they had been on control field patrol in the desert last night.

"And the rest?" Miranda stared, leaving Nathan's shrug unacknowledged. She snapped out of it quickly, however, and barked an order. "Get alpha team armed. I don't know who or what they are, but until we find out, they are hostile."

Nathan nodded and moved towards the deck entrance.

"And tell Jason to keep working on the sat-link."

"You think our Earth-link going down is connected to these people?" Nathan asked.

"I'm not taking the chance. We point guns now and ask questions later, okay? Now get all teams armed."

"You said alpha team before."

"And now I've changed my fucking mind."

After alerting all teams as ordered, Nathan made his way to the mech-shed and slumped into Jason's wheelchair. Jason had hauled himself from onto the ground, sliding under the back end of an up-shuttle. Only his dead legs were visible under the angular utilitarian thing.

"So I'm here," Nathan said, playing with the controls and spinning the chair in circles. "When are we going up?"

"It'll be a couple of hours yet." His voice muffled out from under the up-shuttle jet.

"Does that mean I can go? There are strangers coming and I wanna see."

"It'll turn out to be nothing, just wait. Plus, I need you to help me. It'll take twice as long on my own and we need to repair communications quick."

Nathan looked out through the large open entrance of the mech-shed. The chalky sun fell in, faintly highlighting the floor littered with tools and equipment. He could see Jason and Randa's quarters from there – a small block of yellow stone where Randa, Jason's wife, had painted it to make it different from the rest of the identical quarters that everyone lived in. She was like that. She tried every year to plant flowers outside her window in the untreated soil, but they never grew. She would say, "I think I can see a shoot," when clearly there was nothing. Or she would reply to Nathan's many cynical remarks, "You'll see, by next month I'll have beautiful red roses in this dusty wasteland." To Australians from the North, the wasteland of Thebes was an oasis of possibility.

He wanted to ask how Rhanda was – which would have been a stupid question to ask because there was no way she could be getting better. He missed her face among the dreary others. He missed her bright smile. He also wanted to ask how he was managing to look after her by himself, being confined to a wheelchair. No matter how tech'd-up Jason made the thing, it couldn't replace having legs. Even Miranda was hesitant in asking that, and she was the most tactless person he knew. Nathan couldn't help but think

Jason's need to feel like he can handle the situation was hindering Randa's last days of life. But Nathan never said. Instead, he asked, "What's Earth like?"

Jason stopped what he was doing, the sound of his tinkering ceasing abruptly. "It's very blue," he said after a second.

Nathan, at one stage or another, had asked almost everyone that very question; all the people who had actually seen Earth, that is. Nathan never had. He had been conceived on Pisces and born on the four-year journey to Thebes. Thebes was the only planet he had ever seen. To him, it was home; even though he was taught to believe that Earth was his true home – the mother planet, or whatever. But in Nathan's fourteen years of life, he had quickly realised that mothers weren't always what they were supposed to be.

"Pisces is blue too," Nathan said. "So I've heard."

"Yes, but the seas on Pisces are ten-times as deep as Earth's, making the blue darker, gloomy, and contain creatures that would make even your mother shit herself. Earth's oceans glimmer, like diamonds."

"I've never seen a diamond."

Jason said nothing and the tinkering sound resumed.

"Why did your parents leave there?" Nathan asked, playing with the controls of the wheelchair again so it would spin in the opposite direction. He heard a sharp sigh from under the up-shuttle and Jason manoeuvred himself from underneath, his huge, muscled arms appearing, then his frowning head.

He looked up at Nathan in the chair. "Shift, kid," he said. Nathan did so, allowing Jason room to use his arms to drag himself along the floor and pull his body into the chair. Nathan found a stool to sit on, and tools to awkwardly play with.

"Back in Northern Australia, living off the land was impossible. Thousands of people crammed together in shacks made from shit we found. We had some supplies sent from the South, but never enough. I could never understand why they would never send enough. My dad said it was because they were at first afraid of giving away all their own supplies, and then they became afraid that if we were too well fed we would travel South and force our way in. We tried to grow food away from the shanty, near the coast where a crop was possible, but floods would destroy our attempts."

"So they decided to start again on Thebes?"

"Well, yes. The CommonWorld made immigrating illegal and the South erected a huge wall to keep us out, scared that over populating in the South would be bad news for everyone. My folks wanted something better for us. Then the recruiters came, looking for families to live on the frontier worlds. North Australia had become among the worst places to live on the planet. Hades, we called it. The lifeship became a home to me, our cabin was nicer than the shed we were living in and we were given three meals a day. I'd never had it so good. They were even teaching the kids a trade." He gestured around at his workshop. "So what's your mum's plan, with the strangers that is?"

"Miranda's got everyone in the yard for a weapons check, then I dunno?" He shrugged. "She did say something about shooting first and asking questions later, though."

Jason laughed. "Yeah, that figures." He looked at Nathan curiously. "Why don't you call her mum?"

Nathan shrugged again. "Dunno. Come on, we should get a move on if we're going to make orbit today."

*

Miranda stuffed her Fracture 52 into its holster and hurried out into the yard. Two-hundred soldiers stood in the morning sun, each dressed in the orange camouflage thermo-gear that on any other planet but Thebes would have been anything but camo. But in the sallow sun and burnt sand dunes it was the perfect shade of dead earth.

She had tried numerous attempts to contact David and Conner, who should have been back from last night's patrol as soon as the sun came up, but their comms went unanswered. She didn't like it. Not one bit.

For the years they had been on Thebes, they hadn't seen a single life form that wasn't brought with them aboard the same lifeship they arrived on – and left as soon as they all exited the city-sized craft. Even in the early years, when the terraforming process was just initialising a stable atmosphere, and the naturally high nitrogen levels of the planet could have sustained any of its own life forms, they never once saw an animal, bug or even a plant. Nothing. Thebes had no pre-terraformed natives. There was only one explanation that Miranda could think of – the strangers came from off-world. The only problem with that was they hadn't been alerted to any spacecraft in orbit or in airspace. How could they just appear like… ghosts?

She stood beside Devon, her second in command and decidedly married lover. He had taken the troops through the drill and all that was left was for her pep talk. She glanced quickly to where the figures had emerged over the dunes, seeing nothing but sun-reflected sand. They were close. It wouldn't be long now.

"We all know why we're here," she said, voice firm and in control. "We're here to do what we were put on this planet to do. To protect and maintain it during these first years of terraforming status. We've had little need for these weapons so far, but today our training is demanded. Today, our presence here is justified to the people who questioned it. There are unidentified souls on our planet and it's our job today to capture and interrogate them until we are satisfied that they are not a threat to this project."

She began to pace along the rows of attentive troops, seeing their determined stares facing the front. "We've sent recon missions all over this planet, but we have to admit the possibility that we missed something. They're likely to be human, but we do not know if they are peaceful. China State is reported to have its own colonial programme in place. So, we will defend what is ours like we were put here to do. What say you?"

"Sir¬–yes–Sir."

"Good," Miranda bellowed back. "You have been briefed. Alpha team move out. Bravo team move out. Sierra and tango take positions at your station points and perimeter."

The troops moved. Their soles on the earth felt to Miranda like the heartbeat of Thebes itself. She turned to Devon. "Let's go and get these fuckers then."

He removed his mirrored sunshades and smiled, blonde moustache turning up at the ends. "I love it when you talk dirty."

They followed sierra and tango as they moved towards the perimeter, just outside the range of the terraform-spire, but before they even reached their station Miranda's comm screeched on her belt.

"Come in Miranda, this is alpha team. Miranda, come in. Over."

"What is it Alpha? Over."

"We have detained the potential hostiles. Over."

Miranda gave a sharp look to Devon, who mirrored it back to her. "Already? Over."

"They were just standing out here. Like they were waiting for us. Shall we bring them in for questioning? Over."

"No. Not yet. I want to see them before we bring them in. We're almost there. Hold position and keep weapons on them. I don't want them to blink without my approval. Over."

13

Miranda would attempt to make no judgement until she heard what they had to say for themselves. Yet her military training, fused with an incontrovertible gut feeling that throbbed in the base of her stomach, told her she shouldn't trust them. She would know if they were lying, she was sure. Liars were her speciality – ironic, considering Nathan's father, who had lied to her from the beginning of their relationship right up to the end.

Parting the circling troops with a gesture, Miranda moved towards the potential hostiles, Devon at her side. Her hand instinctively grazed her Fracture 52.

"They haven't spoken," said Raff, alpha team leader.

Miranda nodded and looked upon the group. They seemed harmless on first impressions. A young man no more than a few years older than her son stood at the front, his jet-black hair and eyes set off his ghost white face. He was scrawny but held an air of authority that unnerved her. Troublingly, she sensed no fear at all from them – not even in the child that held the hand of a chiselled man sporting the remnants of a black eye. Among them, a haggard man stood towards the back, a little away from the group and to his right, an older thin man hovered, with wisps of grey hair and stony eyes. At first sight, most would assume they were a motley group, not much a threat to anyone... but it was that fearlessness that perplexed Miranda. It made her wary of them. Anyone in their position – detained with almost an entire inventory of weapons pointed at them – would have at least shown a mild concern. But there wasn't even that. Miranda sensed by his incessant shifting and fidgeting that the only one of them who seemed to be the slightest bit uncomfortable was the haggard looking man wearing the strangest clothes Miranda had ever seen, and that was saying something for someone who had lived on Pisces during the 90s. They were all just... wrong. She could feel it in her gut.

They were a puzzle, and Miranda was determined to solve it as fast as possible, using whatever means or force viable.

"Hello," the black-haired boy said with a smile. "My name is Edward."

Miranda eyed him for a moment. She didn't like that smile. "Hello, Edward. My name is Miranda," she replied politely. "Would you care to tell me how the fuck you got on my planet and what the fuck it is you're all doing here wandering around my compound?"

The boy's smile widened. She wasn't threatening to him in the slightest. "I'm afraid we had no choice but to land out in the desert." He spread his hands. "Our ship wasn't fairing too well after some unknown technical fault so we had to make an emergency landing on our little tour of the Titan System."

"A tour?" Miranda scoffed. "Millions of klicks from Pisces?"

The boy shrugged. "We like adventure."

"You have a permit?"

"Of course. Bought and paid for."

"Ever heard of requesting for airspace, or landing permission?" Miranda replied shortly, knowing she wouldn't be able to check his facts until the sat-link was up and running again. "And why didn't our computers pick you up?"

"I don't know about your computers," he said. "We tried to contact the local frequency but we received no reply."

"And your ship landed where exactly?"

"About seventy klicks north of here."

"And how did you make it over the klicks of terrain?"

"We had a buggy on the ship but it broke down fifty klicks in. We walked the rest."

"And why in this direction?" Miranda asked, not liking how calmly the boy was reacting to her hard and fast questioning. Not one of them wore an eDeck on their wrists or a Lifestore on their backs. If they could afford to tour space in their own private craft, they could afford those. Something wasn't adding up.

"Our ship's computer picked up the energy from the terraforming plant so we headed toward it, hoping that we would find people. And we're so glad we did."

"There are many terraforming plants on this planet, why this one?"

"It was the closest."

Miranda was perplexed. She couldn't tell if she was being told an epic amount of bullshit or not. "Bravo, take a group of ten out twenty klicks north and find their buggy. Contact me immediately when you find it… or don't find it."

Bravo's team's leader saluted and led a group off.

"If you're telling me the truth, boy, then we will be more than happy to help repair your ship and get you and your… family?"

"Yes," Edward said, turning slightly reverently towards the group behind him. "My family."

"We'll be more than happy to get you and your family on your way again. You'll find we can be the perfect hosts. If, however, you have just lied to me, you'll find that I have an impeccable record for discovering the truth in people by whatever means necessary." She held her steel gaze on the smug little shit for a fraction longer than was polite, until there was no doubt of her meaning. "Okay, let's take our guests to their room, shall we." She led the group towards the warehouse, striding ahead of the others as always.

Devon caught up with her. "Lies?".

"I don't know yet. But I'm going to find out. It all seems too convenient. They happened to land close by. They happened to have a buggy with its own oxygen supply. They happened to break down inside the atmospheric control field…" She shook her head.

They walked on silently until Devon asked the question he'd obviously been waiting all day to ask.

"Why didn't you show last night?" He removed his mirrored shades and homed his puppy-dog blue eyes on her.

"I got busy," she said.

"Doing what? We made plans and you just didn't show. Didn't even bother to comm to let me know."

"Now is not the time for this," she said, scanning for ears. "I'm not your girlfriend and you don't tell me what to do. We fuck occasionally and that's it. If you want to play the jealous husband, go and do it with your wife." She picked up her pace and left him behind. There was too much to think about without having to deal with Devon's shit.

On the one hand, it could simply be a coincidence that a ship landed during a sat malfunction. The boy said they attempted to make contact for landing permission but received no reply, which would make sense, Miranda supposed. But on the other hand – the hand she held her Fracture 52 with – she trusted them like she trusted everyone. She didn't.

*

The rumours about the visitors started somewhere near the truth but mutated as they passed from person to person. Nathan was happy to exaggerate them further for effect. These included: they were a group of escaped murderers from a Piscean prison; they were unidentified life-forms with a taste for human brains; and they were the survivors of a pirate massacre and victims of a highly contagious degenerative disease caught from the depths of space for which there was no cure.

It was this last rumour that caused the most panic, Nathan was pleased to discover, after he'd taken the first opportunity to slip away from Jason while he was busy with the last of the up-shuttle repairs.

After taking some time to revel in his work, he headed out to the storage warehouse a klick out from the compound. Miranda would want to keep the group separate from the colony and there she'd be able to interrogate them for maximum intimidation. That was her style – divide and conquer. The warehouse was secured thirty-two hours a day, seven days a week, with guards, eye-cams, plasma gates and control fields. Nathan wasn't worried about those too much, though, having some time ago swiped and forged all of Miranda's security clearances.

In effect, Nathan had access to everywhere on the planet.

In response to the rumours that had leaked, Miranda had no choice but to issue people with a formal statement telling them to remain inside the living quarter facilities for now. Of course, this inadvertently caused further speculation and the rumours of a cover-up. It meant, however, that as Nathan made his way passed the terra-plant and towards the warehouse, there was no one to question him. Soon he was faced with a dozen armed guards, an electro-plasma fence and a non-permeable control field covering the perimeter of the facility.

The fence and control field were no obstacles for him. It was the guards that posed the difficulty. He spent a minute thinking behind the hatch-like entrance to the underground recycling mine. How could he get by the guards? There were two options he could think of: the first was to tell them that he needed to see his mother about something super important; and the second was to create some sort of distraction that would take the guards away – even if it was just for a minute – so he could slip by and break in. The first option would probably only lead to Miranda being called out and would serve no purpose at all other than to incur her wrath. The second was the one most likely to work... and the most fun. He thought for a moment and then reached for his comm with a wicked smile.

"Brendan. Come in Brendan," he said over their private channel. "Brendan, answer me, you dick."

"Don't call me a dick, fuck-brain," the voice of an equally pubescent teenage boy replied. "Have you heard about those escaped prisoners? Over."

"Yeah, I'm about to break into the warehouse and get a good look at them. I need your help with something. Over."

Brendan laughed down the comm. "Man, you rock the shit. Your mom is going to blow you to pieces if she finds you. Especially after the last time you broke in there and you wouldn't tell her how you did it. Over."

"Yeah well, they stepped up the security a few notches so I need you to create a distraction to get the guards away from their posts for a few. You down? Over."

"I am down the hole with that, my friend. What you thinking? Over."

"I'm thinking a little distraction of the oxygen-level alarm variety might be called for? Over."

"Nice thinking, Nathanator. That, I most definitely can do. I'm at my computer now. It'll just take a few seconds to hack the security system. Shit, I think my mom's coming. You know how she got the last time we pulled a stunt. I'll get on it but I gotta go. Over."

"Thanks, man. Over."

Brendan's mother thought Nathan was a bad influence – which he was. He and Brendan had made a habit of getting into trouble for no other reason than because they were bored. That often meant messing with the military side of operations, which had the added bonus of pissing Miranda off no end. Brendan had been the one who helped Nathan copy Miranda's security passes. When he broke into the warehouse the first time around, the plan was to steal food and alcohol and other useful shit. With Brendan being a computer genius and Nathan inheriting Miranda's balls, they often said they could rule the universe.

At the time of Nathan's first break in, ruling the universe wasn't something he was interested in doing. All he wanted was to have some fun. But then he found something inside, something Miranda was trying to hide from everyone. He wasn't sure what it was at the time but now he was certain, and he was determined to get back inside.

At that moment, the shimmer of an auxiliary control field domed over the entire living quarters, sealing in the atmosphere. The main security computer spoke through speakers located around the base: "Oxygen levels have dipped to critical level. Please find shelter inside or equip yourself with appropriate breathing apparatus." A siren began.

Within seconds, the guards securing the entrance to the warehouse had run off in search of exolung head-gear.

Nathan smiled. "Thanks, Brendan," he whispered as he rushed over to deal with the plasma fence.

He gained entrance with minimal trouble, disarming the control field, laser alarms, eye-cams and other assortments of weapons and tech defences designed to keep unwanted people out. With a swipe of a cloned security card encoded with information ranging from Miranda's fingerprints, retina map, breath and voice encoding, blood grouping and biotech levels, passwords, number clearances and internal tracking and magnetic info-boosters, Nathan walked through as easily as if he actually was Miranda. All security dropped on his approach, all doors unlocked at his touch, all cameras and smart-security entities read him as his mother.

He strolled through the halls with a confident swagger, singing a track from the Earth band Eat Her While She Sleeps.

"Baby…" he sang, "you make me wanna swim the deepest Piscean seas. Baby… I'd do anything for my Queen of sleaze."

The building, itself was free of guards; only the highest up the military ladder were permitted entrance, and there was no one on the planet higher up that ladder than Miranda.

The first time Nathan had broken in he had found the room with the phials completely by accident. He got himself turned around from where he wanted to be – mainly the alcohol stores – and ended up in the far south of the building with long identical corridors. The room was heavily secured, which was the first thing that Nathan noticed about it. It was also the thing that lured him inside. He was curious to know what deserved such high security. If it had been a plain door like the others he would have just walked on by. But it wasn't. So, with Miranda's all-access security clearance, Nathan first found the store of strange little liquid-filled bottles.

At first, he assumed they were medicine of some sort, but it struck him as peculiar that none were labelled. At the time, he thought it was stupid. What if someone took the wrong thing by accident? But on further inspection, noticing the same milky liquid inside all the phials, he realised it was all the same stuff. That's when he noticed at the top of each cabinet a small chrome symbol, no bigger than his thumbnail, but on every one of stacks. Later – after being caught and punished – he discovered the symbol was called the omega. It looked like the letter 'O' with the bottom cut and prised apart. It was his research via the heavily edited Thebes intranet that led him to also discover that, along with numerous derivations, meanings, beliefs and symbolism, the Ω had been adopted as the logo for Life Corp, the company that Miranda worked for and who had privately part-aided the funding of the Thebes colonial project.

The more Nathan researched the symbol and Life Corp, the more he found vague and elusive references to research regarding something they simply referred to as Ω. It would make indecipherable statements such as "Ω has the effect of wondrous things beyond what humanity has ever dared to dream" and give no other explanation or meaning; only provide contact details on how to book a consultation, providing you could stump up the fee of half a million Coin for the privilege. Nathan was convinced it was some miracle medicine. Miracle enough to help even Rhanda.

Having found the store again, he picked up one of the small glass phials and held it to his eye, inspecting the milky-white liquid inside. He grabbed a handful and shoved them in his pocket before marching through the deactivated door. However, unlike last time, a small round light on the frame turned from a luminous green to a throbbing red and a noise began wailing through the empty corridor maze.

He ran. Left at first, towards the exit, but a control field shimmered into existence and he ran straight into the thing, knocking his head as though he'd hit it on stone. Taking the phials from the room had triggered a lockdown. He cursed himself for not realising the door was stuffed with scanners and sensors to detect theft. Apparently, even Miranda didn't have the authority to remove them.

Backing away from the control field, he turned and began down the opposite corridor, the sirens numbing his ears until his eyes watered and he swooned in in his step. Luckily Nathan was ready for such tricks. He pulled two button-sized reverse-amps from his pockets and stuffed them into his near-bleeding ears, feeling the relief as the assault of decibels reduced to a mere tickle.

He continued to run, the light-strips now flashing like strobes, flickering from red to white. He instinctively went to cover his eyes but didn't.

Instead, he ran on, attempting to see through a grill of fingers until he thumped into another control field. Warm blood trickled from his nose and the salty iron taste flooded his mouth. He took the next corridor left. Halfway down, the strobes stopped, leaving everything in total blackness. Nathan figured the strobes had messed with his eyes because no matter how much he strained for them to adjust to the dark, they simply refused. He was blind. Scrambling to pull the comm from his belt, he switched it on, letting the light from the screen glow palely in front of him, revealing nothing but the next step in front of him. He moved down the corridor, feeling his way with outstretched arms.

The siren stopped suddenly and Nathan took a moment to pull the reverse-amps from his ears, noticing that when he did, the unmistakable sound of boots on a concrete floor resonated through the halls. He began to panic. If they caught him, not even his mother would be able to help him this time. Who knew the consequences he would face – jail, deportation back to Pisces?

He shuffled on for a few meters, the footfall of searching troops closing in. The control fields, he realised, were strategic ploys to drive him to that point. He had to think. They assumed he would now be searching for the nearest exit. He had to do something unpredictable to throw them off, which meant he had to stay in the building and not try to escape. He had to hide instead. And then, once they assumed he had somehow found a way out, he would make a run for it. The plan seemed all the more doable when he came upon a locked door in the darkness. The footfall seemed only meters away and the soldiers' searchlights were now visible around every corner. He could hear the whispered commands of the team leaders.

Nathan touched the door with his finger and the lock released. He sucked in a breath and rushed in, closing the door behind him with a tremulous exhalation. He listened quietly, hearing the guards pass.

A light suddenly brightened the room.

"Hello, General Shaw," a voice said.

Nathan spun, fearing it was Miranda. It wasn't.

A group of people Nathan didn't know stood in front of him. A dark-haired boy stepped forward, with a loose smile on his thin face.

"Nice to see you again."

14

Not once in all the timelessness of the BroadWeb had Ystil.3 ever been asked to think for himself. He realised that this was a gift he had never known the true value of. Until now. Not once had he ever been expected to decide, and would therefore never make the wrong decision. But with a weight that pushed heavy on his synthetic shoulders, Ystil.3 stared blankly into the obscurity of a two-faced creature: choice.

He thought of the humans who had built the abandoned apartment block he now stood in and he thought of the lives they led and the effort they instilled into constructing the now derelict rooms. The floorboards creaked as he shifted his weight from one foot to the other, and the siren of a police car wailed by, off towards some human emergency in the New York night. He looked down at the smudges of human blood that marred his hospital scrubs. Lydia's blood.

She remained silent, tied to the chair and face swollen. The sense of guilt and shame for what he had done to her was a new and unwelcome feeling. But he had been so confused. So angry.

Now he was certain of only one thing. Throughout his existence, Ystil.3 had been lied to. He had been taught to believe that the humans were extinct – obsolete – a long dead species in the vast machine of the universe. The Reset had seen to that, so he was taught. Yet behind him, half-naked and tied to a chair, cut, bruised and broken by his hands, was the very creature he had believed to be destroyed.

Lydia was human.

She had tried to Linear Cut away from him at first. The horror in her eyes at having exposed herself to him was what alarmed him the most – it indicated truth, or at least what she believed to be true. Then everything spiralled beyond his control. He grabbed the silver lion head engraved pendant and pulled it away from her neck. It broke at the clasp before she could Cut away.

She scratched with clawed nails to get the Linear Cut device back, but she was still weak from the Tell and Ystil.3 was too inflamed to let go. She screamed as he pulled her by the arm, jerking it whenever she struggled, dragging her down the corridor before horrified witnesses.

"Help me," she screamed to them. Ystil.3 continued to pull, ignoring the humans that surrounded them. She thrashed out, finding her strength again. She punched and kicked and even sank her teeth into his arm, tearing off a chunk of synth-flesh. The pain sent out a wave of alarm and only served to enrage him further. By the time the hospital security arrived, he had punched Lydia hard in the face, feeling a crunch under the force as his fist battered her head. He dragged her unconscious form down the hall by her hair.

Cries of distress came from the humans around him, but Ystil.3 wasn't concerned with that. He had to get out of there. In the hazy chaos, he attempted to Cut from the sector in front of their staring eyes. But it wouldn't work. A few of the braver humans attempted to tackle him as he stood clutching the pendant and he ended up with a fist across his jaw. The man who threw the punch crumpled with the pain of his broken knuckles, which left the others wary of getting too close. The man then attempted reason with Ystil.3, but the words didn't even penetrate his ears.

Within moments, humans with tasers surrounded him. He was given one warning and then fired upon. The taser darts clamped to his skin and shot painful volts through his synth – enough to incapacitate a human – but Ystil.3 stood unaffected. He hauled Lydia into his arms and kicked the nearest guard in the chest, sending him flying into the wall. Ystil.3 then headed for the window at the end of the corridor.

With Lydia unconscious in his arms, he turned and launched them both through the glass, his back taking the force. His clothes and synth-flesh tore before they plunged five stories onto the pavement below. Ystil.3 took the impact of the fall, with Lydia safely cushioned on top of him. He narrowly missed landing on a woman who was walking by, and a fire hydrant, which would have impaled him. Faces appeared out of the broken window above, expecting to see two mangled bodies on the sidewalk. Instead, Ystil.3 picked himself up – shards of glass protruding from his arms, back, neck and face like gruesome spikes – hauled Lydia over his shoulder and charged down the street.

He made it only three blocks running at full speed before a police car swerved into the centre of the busy road and cut him off at a corner. Ystil.3 leapt over it like a giant insect, holding Lydia close to his chest as she flopped unconscious, her quantum bag flapping loosely around her body. The police fired on him with real bullets and he became a blur through the back streets. A bullet found his leg, however, and after five minutes of flat-out sprinting, he realised he would need to get it out and rest until he healed. He would have to hide.

It was another ten blocks before he found a suitable spot; an abandoned apartment block in a rundown-looking neighbourhood with a wire fence that wrapped all the way around and a sign that read, "DANGER. Unsafe Structure. Do Not Enter". Ystil.3 cleared the fence silently and made his way over the rubble.

He made his way up the part-collapsed staircase to the seventh floor before finally stopping in a room with no front door. He placed the still-unconscious Lydia on the floorboards, seeing for the first time the mess he'd made of her face. Her right eye had swollen like a peach and her nose was broken and out of place. Blood smeared across his fists and the bullet wound to his leg secreted dark red synthetic plasma. It stung as he dug out the bullet with a finger. The hole in his flesh, where Lydia had taken a chunk for his arm, had almost completely healed, as had the wounds from jumping out the hospital window.

The sun sank in the sky and a warm glow hovered on the brickwork of the next building along before it was quickly replaced by night. A breeze flowed. Hours passed. His mind a tornado of doubt.

He knew the first thing he should do was contact Sir Z and inform him that somehow their communication had been compromised and that something had been posing as the Overly Watchful of 1901. But if the AI secure-beam had been compromised then they – humans, or whatever – might still be listening in. He decided, for the moment, it was best to see what Lydia had to say for herself, to determine the truth before he spoke to Sir Z.

He was no field agent, he reminded himself, and shouldn't even be there.

Waiting for Lydia to regain consciousness, he sat and thought. He'd witnessed her do things no human could do. They sent countless secure-beams, she had breathed under water, she could Linear Cut. There was no way she could be human. No way. And yet... he remembered, she ate food like a human and had no toxin filter for the Tell serum. She barely had any upgrades that classed higher than a BroadWeb menial AI. He checked her quantum bag but found nothing that hinted to the answer. There was only one way he knew of to uncover the undisputed truth – something that humans couldn't disguise. The fear of death.

Lydia came around just as Ystil.3 finished tying her restraints to the wooden dining chair that he found alone in the next room, along with an old curtain tieback and telephone wire protruding from the dilapidated walls. Her eyes flickered open and her head lolled as a whimper escaped her throat. It took a few moments for her eyes to fully open, but when they did, seeing Ystil.3 standing in front of her, panic rose in them. She tried to move, only to find them roped to the chair. She took in a deep breath ready to scream, but Ystil.3 interjected.

"If you make a sound I will punch you in the face again."

It was enough to keep the noise in her lungs. A shaky breath blew out in its place.

"I've hacked into your secure-beam frequency," he said. "If you try to contact anyone I will know, understand?"

Lydia nodded.

"I need to determine whether you truly are human," he said. "Or just a fucked up Overly Watchful with a deranged case of people-envy from living among them too long."

Lydia said nothing.

"I don't want to hurt you. But I am going to kill you now. It's the only way I know how to tell. I'm sorry."

Lydia's eyes began quivering in their sockets. She searched wildly about for help that wasn't coming. Ystil.3 grabbed her scrubs and tore, exposing her breasts as they rose and fell in unison with her sobs. He placed one hand on her chest and one around her mouth and across her broken nose, squeezing it hard enough to cause an excruciating amount of pain. Wet tears rolled onto his hand from her eyes. Everything was quiet as he held her still. Then he heard it – the urgent drum of a petrified heartbeat.

A human heartbeat.

Synthetics were designed to merge with humans even down to a cellular level, and since Lydia had been upgraded, the difference between her and a synth would be practically undetectable without certain equipment. The fear was the only way to tell.

He remained hovering over her for a moment, the realisation pressing in. His hand slowly grew tighter across her face, threatening to pop her head, and a squeak of pain muffled out from behind it. He released, pushing her backwards in the chair almost in disgust.

Minutes passed with silence between them, until finally, Lydia spoke in a small voice. "Was that it?" she said.

"I just wanted to scare you." He turned his back. "So your heart rate would increase from fear. A synthetic's heart rate would not have done. Yours did." He spun to face her accusingly. "You must be from one of the time sectors. Which one? How did you know where to find me? How do you have a Linear Cut device?"

Lydia remained stoic.

"You'd better answer me because it's what you know that's keeping me from contacting Sir Z. And, human or not, you must know that once I do that, there'll be nothing more I can do for you."

"I'm not from a time sector." Her voice had regained its strength. "Not any time sector you monitor at least."

"What do you mean by that?"

"I'm from the same time that you are."

"Post-Reset?" Suddenly, he was tired and wanted nothing more than to go home. "Tell me."

"Tell you what?"

"Tell me who you are? Tell me what you're doing posing as an Overly Watchful? And please tell me, because I'm really fucking confused right now, how you even exist when humans died out with the Reset?"

Her eyes glazed over in such a way to tell him he would get nothing from her. Her mouth formed a line and her jaw clenched shut.

He grabbed her shoulder and shook her roughly. "Tell me. All I want is the truth." She said nothing and he let go of her. "Either AI is wrong about the human extinction, or I've been lied to for reasons I don't know. I only want to know which one it is." Ystil.3's turmoil was a mask expressed through the cultured organic flesh of his synth's face, looking out with emotion that surprised even him.

"You aren't going to like the truth," she said finally. "And you probably won't believe half of it. How could you? You're one of them."

"Tell me. Please."

For a long moment, Lydia was silent, the cogs behind her eyes working hard on Ystil.3, sizing up his intentions. "I will tell you this and only this," she said. "I am human. I was born aboard a lifeship that is home to what is left of our race. For almost two-hundred years we have been hunted by your kind. So why don't you tell me?"

"It's not true," Ystil.3 said. "You're a liar. You've lied from the start and I can't trust a single word you say. It isn't true."

"True? If you really want the truth, then you need to make a choice now."

"What choice?"

"Come with me and I'll take you to those who can give you the truth. Or you can kill me, because I would rather die than be at the mercy of your leader." Her eyes were wild with adrenaline.

"Sir Z isn't our leader he's our..." Ystil.3 truly didn't know how to finish that sentence.

"It is a monster," she spat. "A soulless thing."

"Then what am I? Am I a monster, a thing?" He clutched his head, feeling sweat-drenched strands of his black synth hair. "I don't know what's happening. I've been wrenched from my life and now it feels like I'm falling and I don't know what to do." He was suddenly on his knees facing the floor.

"I don't think you're a monster," Lydia said, her voice a fraction softer. "I think you've been used, like the rest of your kind. If you want truth, I can help you get it. It won't be peaceful and it won't be easy. But if you want it, then come with me."

The choice.

Without saying a word Ystil.3 undid Lydia's binds. She flinched when his skin touched hers. As soon as she was free, she stood, snapped her broken nose back into place with a swift motion and wiped her bloodied face with the ragged remains of the hospital scrubs. Her bag had been thrown carelessly to the side and she retrieved it, searching inside.

Ystil.3 held out his hand and let her see the small lion head coin pendant that sat in his palm. Cautiously, she took it, but did not Cut immediately as she might have done. Instead, she retrieved a top from her bag to cover her naked torso.

Her staying for his reply had been a test and his deciding factor. Lydia could have Cut as soon as she had the chance, but she stayed and dressed and tied her long brown hair behind her head, the ends matted with dried blood.

It could be a trap. But there was only one way to find out.

Lydia looked at him. The bruises around her eyes had already started to fade. "So, will you come with me?"

☐

15

There's a piece of ancient human literature, which Ystil.3 was kind enough to upload for me, that always comes to mind whenever I think of the Black Betty. Howard's End by E.M. Forster. To me, it will always be the greatest work that ever expressed the importance of having a home. I often think about Mrs Wilcox and Howard's End and how she loved it. I wonder whether the house would have loved her in return if it could have. I believe it would. I believe Mrs Wilcox and her house regarded each other the way Betty and myself regard each other. We find context in one another, without which we are lacking a sense of existence, lacking a spark that the other ignites within us. We are, in a sense, designed to be together. Not two halves of a whole or any such cliché as that. But perhaps when we are together we become the very best of creatures that we possibly can be. We make sense of our rather random existences and we find joy. We find joy in each other.

As you can imagine, I was extremely anxious to return to Betty to ensure no harm came to her at the hands of her unidentified captors. I saddled my proverbial horse and was ready to filter back into my real-time form. But as I went to do so, I found I could not.

I accessed the appropriate functions that should have ejected my AI mind from the BroadWeb and straight back into my own massive pile of scrap-metal lying on the interior floor of Betty's stasis infirmary. Again and again, I strained myself to leave, each time being blocked – something locked shut, making it so I couldn't go anywhere. I could not leave the BroadWeb.

A cold tide of fear rose through me and I began to panic, furiously willing my functions to filter me home. I was powerless to save my love when she was so desperately frightened. In that moment, I was distraught, with no way to express it. Humans had the ability to cry when an emotion became too intense for them to handle internally, yet AI had no such thing and I was forced to endure my stunted agony in the gleaming coldness of the BroadWeb, searching for anything that could explain my sudden inability to filter out. I scoured wildly for disturbed and perplexed DataCom Units, but found none. Everything seemed normal in the Data Pylon as each small but powerful Unit lay in their crib, surrounded by umbilical cords and absorbing data as per procedure. None of them were even attempting to filter out so, of course, they would all appear unperturbed by this catastrophic BroadWeb malfunction.

Or was it just me?

Hastily, I scrambled free of Ystil.3's docking bed, disconnecting myself from the tentacle wires and ropey membrane cords that only seemed to want to bind me in place. My growing panic peaked as my claustrophobia climaxed. I tore at the streamers and pushed my way free of the docking bed, crawling onto the glimmering black floor of the DataCom Pylon and looking at my own reflection in it – DataCom Unit's reflection. My faux appearance flashed and my round, faceless head peered at itself expressionlessly. For a terrifying moment, I felt more trapped than I had ever done in my entire existence. Trapped in the persona of a life that I didn't want, that I would have preferred to be deleted rather than perform. I yearned to see my own persona staring back at me; the visage of Tom Jones or even just my bulky five-tonne head – whichever, I didn't mind, just something to remind me that I wasn't truly a DataCom Unit and that I would see Betty again.

I eventually picked myself up, a slow determination building within me. All I had to do was figure out why I couldn't filter out. There was no other choice. I had to get home.

At once, I attempted to secure-beam Betty, but found, unsurprisingly, I couldn't do that either. My signal was blocked and I couldn't get through. I tried Ystil.3 but my attempts were simply being cut off. It made no sense.

I moved as quickly as I could out of the Pylon and into the limitless corridor that led through the Apex Soldier-guarded inner arch and back out into Grid City. There, I observed the AI and lowly programmes in the streams of dataroads and light pads. Seemingly all was normal. The sky cracked with lightning and the black sheen of Grid City maintained its luminescence. There was no panic or discord as I had expected. Perhaps for some security reason, I couldn't filter within the confines of the DataCom Pylon vicinity, so I attempted once more in the openness of the City. It didn't work. Once again my path was blocked, the function fully accessible but completely inoperable.

I thought of Tom Jones' version of The Green Green Grass Of Home, feeling the need for relief from my emotions again. I began to play the song internally from the Earthfiles that I now had full access to while in the BroadWeb – in my own CorVac form I had all his songs stored on my server. Tom's baritone warbling always sent me into a hypnotic state of bliss. I began to hum and sway gently from side to side as I thought of Betty, the Titan System and Delilah. I thought of the far-off nebula that, in the right conditions, shrouded us in its ethereal gasses. Within this vision, I found a fraction of calm.

My moment of calm was about to be shattered.

The Apex Soldiers that guarded the DataCom Pylon entrance had left their post and were headed straight towards me, their cold mirrored forms halfway down the Pylon steps. The Soldiers' limbs had morphed, their arms becoming viral guns capable of projecting virus thorns over a great distance into a specific target. At first, I wondered what was happening, whether a stray, malicious programme had stridden brazenly into Grid City, but I could detect nothing of the type.

Other AI began moving away, sensing something wrong. I thought perhaps my perception filter had failed and they were coming to reprimand me, but I looked down to see I was still in the DataCom Unit form. Suddenly, the Apex shot a viral thorn into the nearest AI mass. The crowds turned to panic at once and I scrambled through the petrified horde as they headed for the nearest light pad to escape. The Apex fired off more virus thorns into the helpless crowd.

I quickly climbed the light pad, and as I began to move with the light towards the far end of the city and away from the Soldiers, I witnessed a virus thorn-infected AI burst into a cloud of pixels before being reabsorbed into Grid City. Deleted. The Apex were attacking. The light travelled and I with it. Before I could think about what had just happened, I was standing on a light pad at the other end of the City, unable to move through confusion. A beta construct AI called out to me impatiently.

"Can you get off the pad, DataCom Unit? We all have sectors to get to," he said.

I was too dumbstruck to answer, mesmerised by the thousands of Apex Soldiers coming from all sides. Internally, Tom Jones still sang. The Soldiers were morphing in unison, virus thorns growing on their bodies, sharpening and glistening with venom. The residual sound of the echoing thunder began to pale against the roar of the Soldier's march.

The AI soon noticed the silver tidal wave and I barely had time to move before the panic spread. The queues disbanded. Some leapt from the hovering light pad platform towards the sub-level programme marketplace, disappearing into the buzz of stalls, data tents and data pockets below. Others were pushed from the platform into the ribbons of dataroads, their personal coding stretching beyond repair as they were dragged along the bright white currents. Some, however, raced for the light pads and before I knew what was happening, I was pulled to the ground, hundreds of AI crushing me as they attempted to flee.

Screams erupted from all around me as I tunnelled through the trampling AI. Virus thorns shot into the masses, deleting AI and sending their data back into the Collective, back into foetal mode. The cries continued as thorns rained onto the huddled AI that had inadvertently formed a protective shield around me. An AI standing on my back was hit with a virus thorn and a gap appeared in the stampede. I took my chance.

I pushed against the other AI that pinned me down and forced my way into the open of the light pad platform. I looked up only for a second to see Apex Soldiers leaping up from the Grid, indiscriminately deleting all AI that got in their path. I rolled out towards the edge of the platform and jumped down to the programme marketplace, now a desolate contrast to its usual clamour and chaos. The programmes had completely fled. I landed among the empty information stalls and data tents and hurled myself quickly under the nearest. Quietly, I made my way from tent to tent, crawling, not knowing where I was headed or in which direction, but knowing only that if I didn't find a place to hide or find a way to filter out then I was as deleted as the rest.

The way AI fear deletion isn't the same as fearing death. Deletion is not an unknown mystery from which is there is no return. It was simply a restoration to AI origins, back into the eternal energy – the Collective and back into a state of raw AI energy, or foetal mode, as we call it. It is the losing of the knowledge gained through living that we fear, all that we have become through existing and experiencing. All that we have come to understand of ourselves as beings and of the world in which we inhabit becomes lost – set back to zero. It is the loss of our knowledge and our personalities, if you will, that we as AI fear from deletion. I know my fundamental self will continue, but aspects of me that were learnt throughout my existence, such as my love of Tom Jones, would be lost forever. My love of the Black Betty too would be gone – extinguished like it never was.

Distant cries challenged the crack of lightning. I knew in that moment, thousands of AI were losing what it had taken their entire existences to attain – a self.

I crawled under the rows of information stalls, wondering why those that could filter out, didn't. I realised it was a total BroadWeb lockdown. Everyone was trapped for the extermination. The inevitable question of why entered my head, but I had to push it aside. I could only afford to think of surviving. I couldn't just go on blindly. I needed to form some sort of plan. I needed to have definitive action. I stood among the crammed shelves of programme junk and looked for something that could possibly have helped me – some illegal function that would allow me to hide, or escape. Nothing. The sounds of the carnage were dimming. It unnerved me. Where was Sir Z? Had the Apex Soldiers suffered a major malfunction or viral contaminant? I had no clue what to do, where to hide or even if there was any point in me trying.

A concussive explosion shook the Grid and reverberated out into the marketplace. It rumbled under me as I stood amid the programme clutter. It felt like the deathblow. Then there was silence.

Grid City had been irrevocably deleted.

I shut down the strip of visual sensors that wrapped around my head and uploaded the real-time image I had long ago sent to the Earthfiles for categorisation. I wanted to pretend that none of this was happening and that I was safe, that I was home. I gazed out into the blackness of space beyond my own CorVac legs, beyond the diffused soft darkness of Delilah and beyond the nebula dust that filtered the light from the small sun of the Titan System and splintered off its broken moon.

A sound outside the tent ripped me back to reality and I reactivated my sensor strip. The data tent was stitched with filters, leaving me unable to get a reading on what was happening outside. I crawled on my ridiculously small limbs towards the opening. The noise was recurring as I pulled back a small section of tent and looked out. I could see nothing. Then, slowly, I poked out my head, absorbing a full reading before snapping it back inside to safety, like an old Earth turtle I had once seen in the Earthfiles. I admired how the creatures carried their home around with them wherever they went. I wished at that moment that I could do the same.

I analysed the scan to discover that two Apex Soldiers were obliterating tents, presumably searching for remaining sentient data to destroy. They vaporised the hiding places with morphed laser arms that cut through data with a highly centralised neutralising anamorphic light. The bright beams shot out in lethal shards, blasting data to unrecoverable pieces. It was just a matter of time before I was discovered.

No, that couldn't happen. Betty was waiting for me to save her.

As the Apex Soldiers reached my row of tents, I slipped quietly out of the back of the tent, dragging a piece of the impermeable fabric across with me, forming a cover as to not alert the Apex's detectors of my presence. When the fabric threatened to run out I reached across to the tent in the row behind, grabbed a handful of fabric and seamlessly slipped under and into the tent. I silently thanked the programmes' illegal trading for the impermeable tent stitching. I stood briefly and looked for anything that could help me, but again it was crammed with useless functions and damaged upgrades. I moved along.

I travelled eight tents down, all the while the Apex Soldiers – more of them now – made their way efficiently through the marketplace. A few times I heard the screech and thud from other hiding AI caught and impaled with virus thorns. I moved on, silently and as calmly as I possibly could.

The Soldiers worked in teams, it seemed. Half would crush, smash, destroy, and the other would set about cleaning the mess that was caused, absorbing into themselves the temporary programme constructs that was once the programme marketplace.

That's when I thought: if the programmes could hide, then so could I. I just had to find out where. The programmes had collectively built Grid City – on Sir Z's command and with AI information, of course – so it made sense they knew parts of the BroadWeb better than AI.

I huddled in the last remaining tents as splintered information crashed around me. I was convinced that this was the end for me – for Tom Jones the CorVac. I would be deleted and when I next found myself with coherent thoughts and a form I would be utterly changed, not me at all. A stranger. A Frankenstein's monster made up of different parts of recognisable information and yet none of them me. There would be no Tom Jones for me, no Ystil.3 and our talks and our chess games. And there would be no Betty. Sure, she'd be there and I might even know of her existence. But our love would be deleted, along with my vast collection of stored memories.

I would not allow that to happen.

Strategically, I lifted a fold of the fabric and poked out my head, getting a reading and position point of all the three-hundred plus Apex Soldiers that surrounded me. I must have lingered for a fraction longer than was safe, however, because every Apex Soldier froze, backs straight and featureless faces raised to the air as though sniffing me out. Their heads turned in unison and within moments they'd ejected a roar of virus thorns on a trajectory course to collide my tent.

I moved just in time to hear the rain of thorns thudding into the fabric, tearing it to shreds and destroying all inside.

I fled through the aisles of the remaining stalls, my short DataCom legs not getting me very far. The Apex Soldiers were already gaining on me. I would never be able to outrun them, and even if I could, where would I run?

Lightning cracked, but the sky darkened with a cloud of thorns – thousands of them on a trajectory course towards me. I dodged down a lane of remaining stalls, then another one, making my movements as erratic as possible, but at the same time losing my own bearings. I came upon the black wall that surrounded the marketplace and I knew that I had come to the end of any possible escape. The thorns above began to pour down, finding the ground where I stood.

I was done for.

And then I saw it – the ghost from the Data Pylon. Its cloak curled around it like black flames and a flash of lightning glimmered off its razor scythe. In the distance, it stood, back against the farthest wall in the basin that was the marketplace, staring with hollow eyes, blacker even than the cloak it wore, denser even than the BroadWeb sky. I don't know why, but I ran to it. I ran so fast that my stupid little legs broke free of their DataCom filter constraints and my CorVack limbs, all eight of them, sprouted from beneath me, raising me higher above the ground on my contrastingly tiny DataCom Unit torso. I ran so fast that the wall rushed towards me, the ghost creature grinning with glowing white teeth. Virus thorns tore through the air, and I knew the Apex Soldiers had me in sight. I could not escape them.

But still, I ran.

A thorn whizzed by. I was a larger target to hit now. But still I ran. Apex Soldiers leapt over me and onto the wall ahead, ready to shower me with thorns as soon as I reached it. But I still ran. And as I came to the wall, I did not stop running. The macabre smile of the ghost misted away. Thorns shot at me from all sides. I expected the wall and I to meet and crash and leave me a heap on the ground, looking up at the Apex Soldiers' mirrored heads as the thorns rained down. But the wall and I did not meet. Instead, I passed straight through, into the silence of a concealed data pocket.

It took me some moments to realise what had happened. I hadn't been deleted. I could hear the Apex Soldiers outside, searching for the entrance, bashing at the walls. They would find it soon. I picked myself up from the heap I landed in, then heard a noise from behind. I jumped with my spidery legs, onto the ceiling of the cave-like pocket and scuttled into the shadows. From a pocket within the pocket came a familiar creature, all bright red, big eyes and long antenna sprouting from its small body.

Bo, the programme who had sold me the DataCom perception filter.

"Don't be scared," he said in my voice, oily black eyes looking up at me. "Only Bo."

"What are you doing here?" The Apex Soldiers were gathering outside. I could hear them, looking for me and massing in their thousands.

"Bo come for you. Bo come for the CorVac." He seemed completely unconcerned with the danger we were in.

"Can you take me out that way?" I asked, crawling down the wall.

"Don't be in such a hurry." He waved a leg casually. "Apex won't get in here."

I stared at the wall, expecting a tide of silver to storm through at any second. "How?"

"She wants to see you," Bo said. "Come." He gestured with a stick-thin limb.

I followed him into the darkness of the next data pocket, eager to be away from the Grid City massacre. "Who wants to see me?"

Bo whispered into the black. "Nyx."

16

Devon fell onto the bed next to Miranda. Her back was turned to him and she wore white-laced underwear that hugged her curves and contrasted compellingly with the smooth chocolate-toned skin of her athletic back. The white lace, he had given to her as a gift a few months back and seeing her wear it still got him hard. He slid himself closer to her, wrapping a muscular arm around her waist. He pulled her to him, her scent filling him. He drank it deep, kissing her neck.

A sigh escaped her mouth, head falling back as his other hand released the clasp of her bra, pulling it free and throwing it from the bed. He gently stroked her breasts, grazing her hardening nipples with the tips of his fingers and then grabbing rough handfuls as he nibbled her neck and shoulders.

She felt him press against her thighs, rigid and ready for her. He grabbed her face and turned her head towards him, settling his lips onto hers. His moustache brushed her top lip with tickling familiarity. Searching hands soon found the warmth between her legs, pulling at her panties in the way she liked. She turned and pushed him back onto the bed.

Straddling him, she ran fingers through the hair that trailed down his firm torso. The white linen pulled free around them as they writhed, locked together in a ball of limbs. She pulled him free of his constraining underwear and mounted him with a sigh. He thrust, accompanied with coarse grunts. She moved her hips in time, grinding onto him, and soon she began to lose herself, like pressure rising from within. She let the thoughts drift and her worries dissolve as it built, until explosion was imminent.

"I love you," Devon said, breathlessly.

Miranda stopped.

She waved off his caressing hands. His blue eyes were looking at her in that way again. She climbed off and tugged the sheet out from under him, wrapping it around herself. She moved to the window.

"What is it?"

"Don't say that," she said. She couldn't bring herself to look at him, but a hurt expression reflected dully off the window glass.

Devon scrambled from the bed, scooped his strewn clothes thrown passionately across the floor and headed straight for the door without even putting them on. He stopped and turned, but Miranda continued to gaze through the window.

"Fuck you," he said. He attempted to slam the door behind him, but it slowed to a soft shut from the safety mechanism.

Miranda clutched the sheet closer and looked out. The Thebes sky grew bluer with each day that passed. The terraforming had been over eighty years in the process when they first landed – most of the confines already built. In a few more years they could begin the intermittent exposure process and then eventually, in another fifty years or so, they could turn them off for good, providing they ever repaired the signal to Earth and Pisces. She glanced at the storage warehouse below the terraform spire and thought of what was inside it. It sent a shiver through her. But that was the deal. She had to keep it secure.

So far, Miranda had had no luck with the visitors. One by one she had separated and interrogated them, taking them into a back room of the warehouse designed for such things, but if lies were what they told her, then they weren't even close to cracking. The old man – with the cold grey eyes – said nothing and, of course, the child was little use. The haggard-looking man, however, was different. The man's mouth said one thing while his eyes told her something else. Miranda was certain he was lying about something. But what? Their story itself was plausible and, as of yet, they hadn't attempted anything to put the Thebes operation at risk. If the sat-link was operational, she would have just confirmed their story with Life Corp UK. But it wasn't so things had to be done the hard way.

Alpha team hadn't yet confirmed where their ship had landed and if it was, as they claimed, unable to reach vacuum again. If they could confirm that at least, then she would feel a little better about the whole thing. Except… where were David and Conner? They still hadn't returned from last night's patrol. No matter how she wanted to chug it all down to coincidence, she didn't trust them. Something was on the brink of happening. She knew it in her bones.

As her eyes stared frozen into the glass, for a brief second she thought she saw a shadow behind her. A tall, dark figure. She turned with a fright and then laughed, feeling the build-up of tears well in her eyes suddenly. There was nothing there. For a moment, however, the way the light played on the shadows in the room, it looked as though a skull of pale bone and teeth had been grinning at her, holding onto a curved blade.

The alarm sounded. Miranda jerked back to herself and within moments she was dressed and reloading her Fracture 52. She slammed it into its holster and headed straight for the Command Room. Red lights twirled on the ceiling as the main computer spoke.

"Oxygen levels have dipped to critical level. Please find shelter inside or equip yourself with appropriate breathing apparatus."

"Sandy, come in," Miranda spoke down her comm, double-striding through the common-rooms now crammed with people; they knew better than to question her when she looked like that. They moved swiftly aside, making her a path through the room toward the gym and training units.

"Sandy here," the Command Room control assistant replied. "I've checked outside oxygen levels manually and they seem to be normal, low compared to Earth and Pisces obviously but completely normal. The auxiliary control field has activated. All terra-plants are fully functional and emitting a total of 100 tonnes a minute as per schedule, so there's no need to panic. It seems there's just a glitch with the main computer's alert system."

Miranda felt a wave of relief that lasted for all but a second. "Another glitch? What the hell is going on today? Can you shut it off and determine the root cause?"

"Give me an hour," Sandy said.

"You've got thirty minutes. Out." She turned, making a detour outside around the side of the common-rooms. Oxygen was normal and on target, her comm stat update told her. She knocked on the windows and the people inside turned to see her outside, breathing as normal, just as the alarm system finally ceased. "Everything is okay," she mouthed through the glass. "Just a malfunction. You can continue with your day." No one seemed to understand her, however. "Oh for fuck sake. Sandy," she comm'd again. "Will you make an announcement that it's safe to go outside. And while you're at it give me an update on security at the storage warehouse. Are the cams picking up anything unusual with our guests?"

"They're all sitting there, nothing out of the norm. Oh, wait a second…"

"What?"

"Aren't you in the warehouse now?"

"No, I'm outside the common-rooms. Why?"

"It's just. It's showing that you used your pass to gain entry at 14.32 hours."

"Fuck. No that's not me. Out." She ran in the direction of Jason's mech-shed. "Jason, come in," she began on the comm as she passed the living quarters, looking up briefly to see Jason's sick wife, Rhanda, staring blankly out of her window at the kafuffle. She was out of bed when she shouldn't be. Her nightgown flooded her stick-thin frame. She gave a small wave, which Miranda returned. The alarm had probably worried her, but she didn't have time to console her right now. "Jason. Come the fuck in, now."

"Seriously Miranda, if you want this up-shuttle ready then you have to leave me to get on with it. What is it?"

"Where's Nathan?" she asked, knowing full well the answer even before it came.

"Gone," Jason said. "Cut him some slack, Miranda. He's just a kid. He's probably doing teenage things."

"Yeah, like breaking into the storage warehouse again."

"Oh."

"Yeah… oh. Next time you think he's just sloped off for some down-time, just remember that he's a willful brat."

"Willful? I wonder where he could have inherited that trait?"

"Hilarious, Jason, you crack me up, really. When will the up-shuttle be ready?"

"Give me an hour. I just have to calibrate the—"

"You have thirty minutes. Out." She turned once more in the direction of the Command Room.

Sandy sat tapping away at one of the many keyboards that sat below a wall of glowing monitors, showing infrared and heat sensors of various parts of the compound. The door slid shut behind her.

Sandy turned without a greeting. "I'm getting a reading that someone is in the room," she said at once.

"Shit." She knew exactly which room Sandy referred to. Years ago, she decided not to install cameras in that particular area of the storage warehouse and also that no one on the planet should know what was inside except for her. All her team knew is that the room was a level-one security assignment from the top and all details were on a need-to-know basis, which, to be blunt, they didn't need to know. This, they accepted like true Precision Arms employees. Only now she wished she could see what her little shit of a son was doing in there. "It's Nathan," she said finally.

Sandy said nothing but made a face. "Do you want to go and get him?"

Miranda folded her arms as she glared at the dim glow of the monitors, contemplating the various readings. "No. Not this time. If Nathan wants to be a criminal, then I think it's high time we show him how we deal with criminals."

Sandy smiled. "Are you sure?"

"Maybe this will show him what would happen if I decided to hand him over to Pisces authorities."

"But you wouldn't though, not really," Sandy said, doubtfully. "He's your son."

"Yeah, he is," she said. "He's my son alright."

Sandy glanced at a flashing dot in the schematics of the warehouse on one of the monitors. "He's triggered the security defences. Do you want me to sound the alarm?"

Miranda sucked in a hard breath. "Do it."

*

Orange-uniformed troops moved out towards the warehouse, while inside the security measures, configured for that exact purpose, did the job of driving Nathan towards the south exit. Teams split into four, each taking an entrance with the intention of enclosing around Nathan, cornering him, then detaining him for search and questioning.

Miranda had explained it was to be treated as a full-capacity *practice* exercise; the goal being to capture the intruder by any means necessary, barring only seriously injuring and death of the trespasser. Miranda also made them severely aware that it was Nathan who they were tracking. For some, that made the exercise even sweeter, with most having been, at one time or another, on the receiving end of his boredom-induced practical jokes or mischievous scheming, which had on more than one occasion been the reason for them being out of bed in the small hours and roaming the freezing Thebes night deserts.

"You're a hard woman," Devon told Miranda as they led the troops. "This will scare him half to death."

"That's the idea," she said simply.

"You're a hard, hard woman." The wan Thebes afternoon sun made glaring shapes across his mirrored sunglasses.

"Life is hard. I'm teaching him a valuable lesson and it's a lesson he desperately needs to be taught. One day he'll look back at this and he'll know everything I've done was to prepare him for life. That's my job. So, don't stand there and tell me how to raise my son when you and your barren wife can't even have any of your own." Her words hung in the air between them. Devon's jaw clenched and he turned away.

She'd finally done it. She'd finally pushed him too hard and too far away. He wouldn't come back to her this time. She moved on ahead. It was time he went back to his wife, the poor bitch.

Miranda led the south exit team around towards the bulky goods shutters before taking them inside. The siren had stopped but the corridors were black as night. She half expected to find Nathan huddled in a corner with piss dribbling down his leg, but, with night vision lenses activated, he was nowhere to be seen.

"All teams," she comm'd, holding the plasma rifle at her side. "Status update."

"No sign, sir," north team comm'd in reply. West and east teams reported the same.

Just as a confused Miranda was about to issue the teams to scout the perimeter, while she went to search the room herself, she received a comm.

"Come in Miranda, this is alpha team unit three." It was the team she'd sent to search for the visitor ship in the desert.

"Miranda here, unit three. You have ten seconds to tell me some good news."

"No good news I'm afraid, sir. We discovered no signs of a ship, but we found Conner and David unconscious inside the desert buggy. It was hidden in a dune cave a few klicks from the compound."

Miranda was silent. Everyone had heard and everyone now knew, as she had known. They were not what they said they were.

"Shit," she whispered. Before she could reply or even think, another comm message fuzzed through the static, this time from Sandy.

"Miranda, I thought you ought to know that Nathan has accessed the captive's room. He's in there now."

"All teams move. Now. Get in that fucking room."

The exercise was over. Nathan's lesson was over. All Miranda could think was that her child was in danger – real danger. She knew first-hand the lengths to which people would go to get their hands on the White Drops. She knew the terrible crimes they would commit for the chance to live forever. It was the very reason the storage was kept on Thebes, far away from the ruthless cities of Earth and Pisces. It was the reason for her training and the reason for her being positioned on the planet. And now the situation demanded her training be put into practice. But it was her son. And all Miranda could do to swim through the cloud of panic for the life of her child was get angry. She allowed the anger to come. It was her adrenaline-fuelled ally.

She was already running through the corridors and towards the room. She screamed down her comm for Sandy to get the lights back on and to override the security functions. Within seconds, the lights were up and Miranda led a trail of muscle behind her – all Precision Arms trained and the best the CommonWorld had. Each put through a rigorous programme of combat skills, arms handling and deep-space survival lasting five Piscean-years. Yet none of them had been put through what she had been put through. None of their training had even come close to what she had to endure to get to where she was. That was the price she paid for advancement in her career.

She knew she had hardened because of it, but as she blasted her way into the room she was glad of it. She was going to destroy these motherfuckers until there was nothing left of them but bones and twitching gristle.

Nathan stood by the door. She grabbed her shaken son and pulled him behind her. A dozen plasma rifles pointed like spears at the strangers. Miranda shoved her rifle into Devon's arms, pulled free her Fracture 52 and slammed the barrel against the side of Edward's head – trigger-finger poised. "Want to see why they call this a Fracture?" she asked through seething teeth.

Edward managed only a look of mild concern. "I know why they call it a Fracture," he said. "The bullets inside the cartridge are designed to splinter upon impact, sending shards through the target, slicing him up on the inside and tearing organs and flesh to pieces. Like a small, dirty fragment-bomb explosion. Nasty things, they are."

Miranda smiled coldly and allowed her hand to slide away from Edward's head, leaving a mark in its place. That was all the proof she needed. He'd been trained in weaponry. Now came the hard part. Now she would have to find out who had put them up to it. "Everyone get out. Except Devon," she said.

"What's going on, Miranda?" Nathan said as her troops pulled him back.

She turned and brought a hand across his face with an echoing crack, knocking his head to one side.

"Get him out of here," she said to the troops. "Take him to Jason and make sure he fucking stays there."

Two soldiers pulled him through the door as he clutched his burning cheek. It wasn't the first time she'd struck him, but she was sure it was the one that smarted the most.

"Wait," she said, just before they left. She reached inside Nathan's pockets and pulled out the handful of small phials containing white liquid. She glared at him. "Go," she said. The rest followed, leaving Miranda and Devon alone with the visitors.

"I need you to go and get the kit I keep under my bed," she then told Devon. "You know which one I mean. I think our guests and I need to talk alone for a few minutes." She was referring to the nasty-looking torture tools and contraptions she had once shown.

"If you think I'm leaving you alone here, then you've got another thing coming, Miranda. Get one of the others to do it."

"That was an order, Lieutenant."

Edward laughed and Devon's face turned sour. He left in silence.

"So what's the deal," she said, wandering into the room. She fell onto an uncomfortable lounger and Edward followed, the others lingering in the background. "It's China State, isn't it? Your employers?" Miranda smiled, leaning back and resting her arms behind her head. Her orange tank top matched the colour of the sofa. "It's the only thing that makes sense, if you think about it. China State is the only real power outside the CommonWorld that would want to get its hands on so much of this stuff and have the means to send a crew to collect it from across space." She eyed the others. "I use the word crew lightly." She held up a phial to her eye, the swirling mist inside looked like nothing but watered-down milk. "Let me guess. President Ling is feeling left out of the rich and powerful cunt club and is scared shitless of the assassins at her door. She must be getting older now, pushing a hundred. Feeling the icy breath of the reaper, is she?

She smiled and held up a phial for Edward to see. "They don't know the long-term effects of this stuff. Did you know that? They've been testing it for years but it's only recently that some wider effects are being noted. Shall I tell you a secret that not many people know about the elusive White Drops? The truth is it may stop you from dying, but you still get old."

Miranda laughed, as though it were the funniest thing in the world, until her sides hurt. "Yeah, you still age. Granted the process is slower, much slower, but still... what happens when you get so old, decrepit but you just still won't fucking die?" She shook her head. "Do you witness your own body decay into nothing, still alive inside your crumbling carcass? That's what they don't want people to know. But they still go on selling the stuff to the rich arseholes that don't know any better – or they just don't care. It's like pre-modified tobacco. Sure, it gave people cancer but did they stop smoking it? No, cancer was something other people got – dying is something other people do."

She leaned in as if to tell Edward a secret. "If I were you, I'd tell President Ling that she's better off without it. Not that you'll ever have the chance to tell her."

"We don't work for President Ling," Edward said through his constant smile. "We don't work for anyone."

Miranda rolled her eyes. "Okay, I'll play. Who are you then?"

Edward sat back while the others stood like mannequins. Something was going to happen. She'd had that feeling all day.

"We're Life Corp's board of directors," He said with an amused grin.

But Miranda she could react, she was grabbed her from behind. She could only flail in blind panic against the crushing arms. All the training, all the fighting... it meant nothing at that moment. As her vision darkened, the last thing Miranda saw was the little girl giggling in the corner, her face no longer a little girl's. It was twisted and monstrous.

*

Nathan handed Jason the last of the up-shuttle panels, which he promptly positioned back in its rightful place, covering multi-coloured wires and thick chords of smart-copper.

"There," Jason said, manoeuvring his wheelchair back to see the thing as a whole. "We should never have let this thing stay out of service for so long."

"Didn't you keep telling Miranda you would get on it, but never did?" Nathan said sullenly.

Jason ignored him. "You know you deserved that, don't you?" He pointed to the purple welt across Nathan's face, perfectly shaped into a palm and four fingers.

Nathan touched the heated area with a cool finger. "Maybe. I was only trying to help."

Jason had stopped listening and made a last lap of the up-shuttle, checking the exterior. It had been about a year since Nathan had ridden the up-shuttle to the orbiting relay satellites. His mother had forced him into mechanical training with Jason as soon as he finished school. She wanted him to join the Piscean Armed Forces since they both knew he wasn't smart enough for University. If Miranda had suspected the smallest academic quality in him she would have shipped him off to Harvard 9U in Alex City. He knew he had disappointed her on that front. But he was strong enough and stubborn enough to be a success in other ways – she had told him that once. The problem was, Nathan didn't care too much about his future. He didn't care much about anything. Miranda said that was normal teenage behaviour and that one day he would thank her for pushing him so hard.

He somehow doubted that.

The up-shuttle was a large pyramid shape on top of a cylindrical tower of thrusters and boosters, fifteen foot in height – relatively small for a shuttle – with a white solar-panel exterior enforced with a high-grade control field. It lacked a gravity-mimicking field, being such a small craft it couldn't sustain one, but Jason preferred it that way. It gave him more freedom when in vacuum. Nathan would have to help Jason up the steps, but he didn't seem to mind when it was Nathan helping him. He flat out refused any sort of aid from others.

Nathan had always liked the 0g weightlessness of being in orbit anyway. The last time he went up with Jason, they had spent a whole hour just floating. Jason had relished in the freedom from his chair, pushing out of it with ease and spiralling around with an epic grin.

"Come on then," Jason said, as the entrance to the shuttle opened with a hiss. "Let see what the damage is up there."

The thought of leaving the craft and entering hard vacuum, however, scared Nathan shitless.

17

There was something familiar about the jet-black craft hanging stationary above Ystil.3's head. It stood out as being a far more refined piece of tech than the basic single-person fliers that surrounded it, which were clearly upgraded from emergency drop-pods. He turned to the broken moon that slowly drew across the porthole windows of the immense airlock jaws and realised almost at once where Lydia had brought him – the server planet M21. Delilah. With that knowledge, he understood another thing too. The smooth black craft that had caught his eye was the Black Betty.

After Cutting from New York, 2050, they arrived at a static holding station positioned for the very purpose of providing Lydia with a craft. Cutting onto a moving object was too dangerous. It was harder to pinpoint a location when it travelled hyperspeed, Lydia had said, and they'd most likely end up floating in dead space with a skull full of explosive decompression. Whenever her home ship docked, they would leave a small fugue-craft programmed with the coordinates of its next intended dock so that she could travel directly back to them.

It had taken her almost one full Earth year of training before she learned to Cut back to the fugue-craft from anywhere and anytime. She'd had to commit to memory every square inch of the craft within the station to summon the vision of it when she needed to return. These days, because of her Linear Cut proficiency, all she needed to do was to think of the lifeship and the Cut device would take her directly to the holding station, no matter where in the universe they had placed it.

On arriving, Ystil.3 had looked at the craft that was supposed to hurtle them through space and felt an apprehensive gurgle in his synth's stomach. Its outer hull was thin and flimsy-looking and there was barely enough room for the both of them to contort inside. The holding station itself was nothing more than a cloaked and pressurised box placed within vacuum as to leave it suspended perfectly motionless, with added compensators in case of gravitational drift.

"Will we travel at hyperspeed?" Ystil.3 had asked, doubting the thing would even stand the ignition.

"Not quite. Energy from the lifeship's fusion reactor can be stored to let us travel fast… but not that fast." She jumped in the craft after opening the hull like a clam, then pushed a few buttons on a complicated-looking control panel she pulled down from above her head. "Looks like we'll only need to travel for three years to catch up with them."

"Three years? Three real-time years?"

Lydia smiled without looking at him. "I know what you're thinking, but three years is not that long, considering. I travelled seven years on my first Cut to catch up with them. Once, when I reached the next planned dock, they'd already left again, so I had to travel even farther. It's not so bad, though, you'll see. There's a fugue stasis capability, plus the whole time debt thing."

"Time debt thing?" Ystil.3 asked, feeling less like AI and more like NI: no intelligence.

"You know, because the faster we travel the faster time passes. So, to the rest of the universe travelling at a speed less than ours, three years will have passed, but for us, it may only be a year or so."

"That's a relief," Ystil.3 said sarcastically. He jumped into the seat next to her and Lydia leaned over to help strap him in. "If three years will pass before we reach your people, won't it be too late to… I don't know… do whatever it is you're trying to do?"

Lydia fixed a belt around his waist and looked up, her face close to his. Her golden-brown eyes looked at him with what Ystil.3 interpreted as sorrow. Suddenly, she looked more real to him than anything he had seen before – seen with his synth eyes or otherwise.

"No," she said, shifting back into her own seat. "BroadWeb and real-time don't run parallel, remember? Everything will be explained soon. I promise."

Ystil.3 believed her. He found his hand reaching over to touch the almost faded bruise on her face. She flinched and he quickly pulled his arm back. She healed fast.

"I'm sorry," he said. He had never felt shame until that moment.

"I know," she said as she pulled down the hatch, sealing it closed. "You did what you had to. I get that."

Within moments they were careering through space on a pre-calculated course and entering fugue stasis with the aid of piped masks and temple wires. Usually, a human would need anti-atrophy needles shoved through their limbs, she'd told him, but as he was AI and mostly bionic and she had been upgraded to include an adrenaline enhancer, neither of them had to worry on that score. When he awoke from what seemed like only a short nap, they had arrived at Lydia's home ship.

They stepped out, somewhat stiffly, and Lydia went to be debriefed. Reluctantly, Ystil.3 waited as told.

He didn't have access to the Black Betty's secure-beam frequency, so was pondering getting up the craft in its hangar crib when Lydia entered with two male humans, each carrying a weapon. They looked military. He awkwardly waited for them to approach. For some reason, he didn't want to move to meet them halfway. Their weapons made him anxious and he suddenly realised that he was, in fact, aboard an alien craft with no way of escape. And what's worse, he was there of his own free will. They could destroy his synth where he stood if they wanted. Then where would he be? Back in his server and uploaded to Grid City. He half thought about grabbing one of the guns and blowing his own synth's head away just so he could return home.

But he didn't. The problem was, now he knew the truth, he could never not know.

"Hello, tin-man," one of the male humans said.

Lydia shot the man a look. "There's no need to worry, Winston," she said. "No one's going to hurt you. There are some people that want to speak with you. The Consulate. They sort of make the decisions around here."

They led him out and through corridors of dull metal, cold with piping visible through cracks and fissures. Disrepair was everywhere. Bits of interior deck panelling were loose in places, exposing metal frames and wires beneath. Everything was quiet, save the clank of their boots and the faint hiss of recycled air through the vent system.

"Welcome home," he attempted to secure-beam to Lydia, but couldn't reach her channel. The humans had some sort of block, a field probably, to stop him contacting AI – not that he was going to. But it made one thing clear: they didn't trust him.

Soon, Ystil.3 found himself facing a vehicle that sat bulkily in the entrance of a huge, dark tunnel, like an ominous open mouth. The vehicle was open topped and made of the same dull metal as the bulkheads. It seemed to absorb all light from whatever source was around. Lydia gestured for him to get in next to where she sat in the driver's seat. He did, feeling the cold presence of the male humans' eyes on his back.

Lydia took hold of the control stick and pulled it back. The vehicle lifted effortlessly from the deck and hovered three feet. She pushed forward slowly and positioned them to face the entrance of the tunnel. She then pushed a button on the side of the stick and the force of a control field fixed him into his seat. Lydia turned, raised her eyebrows ever so slightly and thrust the control stick forward, sending them whizzing into the tunnel at a speed that sent his face into a g-force spasm.

The air rushed by, cool and stale as they skimmed through. Rings of light blurred into one continuous stream of white, guiding them up and down levels and around curves that would have sent him flying if a control field wasn't holding him in place. Lydia turned to him with a smile, her hair billowing around her face. A mischievous smile, he realised. It suited her so much he knew she must have smiled it often. Then she accelerated harder and his stomach lurched until he found himself smiling too, with his head thrown back into the headrest and salty fluid streaming from his eyes.

They manoeuvred left into another tunnel running parallel and then glided up into another above, soaring vertically for a while before levelling out again. Lydia swerved and accelerated as though she'd done it a thousand times before. The lifeship, Ystil.3 realised then, was behemoth, the size of a city, larger perhaps.

"The militia uses the tunnels to navigate the ship," Lydia said, as if reading his mind. "It has over fifty levels, each with a floor coverage of ten klicks per floor, so this is the quickest way to get around. We don't use the whole ship anymore, though."

"How many of you are there?" Ystil.3 asked.

The dour man that sat behind him pulled himself to the front so his face was right between his and Lydia's. "Like we're going to tell you, tin-man."

"Daneel, shut up," Lydia said, turning with a look that bordered loathing. "There are around ten thousand of us left. The ship left Earth with twenty thousand. That was over two-hundred years ago."

"What happened to you all?"

Lydia looked ahead. "People died from old age, as they do. Some from illness. Others starved when our food stores ran dry… before we formulated a protein gruel. Starvation, malnutrition and despair took the most during that time. More froze to death before we shut down two-thirds of the ship to concentrate power into certain areas. Then there were the expeditions and crews sent out to explore various parts of planetary systems. Some didn't return, and those that did returned with radiation sickness or infections no one had ever seen before. Contagions that wiped-out hundreds at a time. But when things were darkest, when we thought we still were alone in the universe, and before we'd learned to run and hide, we came under an attack that killed thousands, leaving our ship in tatters."

"Attacked by whom?" Ystil.3 asked, but the answer had already come to him as he said the words.

"By you," Daneel rumbled darkly from behind.

Ystil.3 said nothing and Lydia moved the vehicle across an intersecting tunnel. She thrust forward, throwing Ystil.3 back into his seat once more. This time, he didn't feel like laughing.

Soon, they approached another fork. This time Lydia veered right, into an obviously more recent addition to the intestinal roads in the bowels of the ship. Ahead, a light appeared and within moments they emerged from the dark onto a platform. Lydia manoeuvred next to a stationary vehicle and landed flawlessly.

The platform jutted out into a cavernous room with curving bulkheads, as though they were inside a giant egg. One was a tempurhull and looked out onto the dark server planet and its broken chalk moon. They were in geosynchronous orbit of M21. But why? Lydia led him onto a disc-like stand at the end of the platform, which lowered them down to the main deck. On the decent, Ystil.3 noticed a long table positioned at the end.

Chairs were positioned around the table, and upon the chairs, a group of humans sat, all silent, watching them approach. The two human males remained behind, lingering at the entrance to the tunnel with their weapons poised.

Was he a prisoner? Lydia could barely disguise her apprehension with a loose smile, which only served to unnerve him even more.

The table was made of translucent metal that shone almost white. The five humans stood upon their approach. The nearest to them was a small man of advanced age. His greying hair was short and his eyes watery. He wore a brown robe tied with a piece of rope at the waist. Next to him a bald man smiled persistently. Next to him stood a woman, taller than Lydia and almost as muscled as Daneel. She had short blonde hair that contrasted with the tone of her oriental skin. Her attire was military and her broad shoulders were decorated with five metal strips that gave away her command. Next to her stood a Caucasian man with a set of thick black eyebrows that conflicted with his grey hair. His shoulders were almost as decorated as the woman's, although he was older, and his face was wreathed with a scowl. The last man at the table was a dark-skinned man, taller than the rest by almost a foot, and bulging with muscles barely contained in his thermal suit. His shoulders were also decorated with strips. The black man eyed him coldly.

Lydia gestured for him to take a seat at the farthest end. He did so, and Lydia took the next seat along. The rest of the table sat in their places, but the man with the brown robe remained standing.

"We most humbly welcome you," he parted his thin lips to say. "That you have chosen the path of truth in place of less perilled roads shows a character and kindness we as humans hold in high regard." He turned and made a gesture to those seated. "May I introduce to you our Consulate of human representatives: Dr Regus Xei," he gestured to the bald man, "Captain Lu," the masculine-looking woman, XO Rawl Collister," the scowling man, "and the General," the black man.

"We are those who represent the people of our race, few that it is," he went on. "Oh, of course, I forget myself. I am Brother Vaxus, of the Brotherhood of Man." He waited as if waiting for some hint of recognition in Ystil.3, but found none. "Yes, well we are small in number, but our faith is as large as galaxies."

"Don't start, Vaxus," XO Rawl Collister barked. "This isn't the time for your waffle."

The man nodded, embarrassed. "Right you are. Such conversations can wait. We have been informed of your willingness to help us."

"I didn't say that," Ystil.3 interjected. "Lydia promised me the truth. That's why I'm here. Apparently, I've been lied to for my entire existence and I want to know why. That's all."

"A very reasonable request," Captain Lu answered. She nodded to Brother Vaxus and he sat. "You see, the problem we face is that with the truth come certain revelations, and we don't know what you're about. If your intentions were to return to the BroadWeb, for example… well, you must see why we may be reluctant to comply, given our past dealings with your kind."

"There's no need to worry on that score," he said sourly. "I'm well beyond the delusion that I can ever go home, and I know nothing of your past dealings, as you put it. Until recently, I thought the last human died out with the Reset. Since my first cohesive programming into a DataCom Unit, all I have known are the sectors I deciphered data for. There is so much I don't understand, but if you're asking me whether I feel some fundamental loyalty to the ones who withheld the truth from me, then the answer is no. Which is strange. I don't understand why I wasn't simply programmed to have this loyalty, or for that matter, why I was lied to. In all honesty, I would have done my job all the same."

"But you don't know their agenda, do you, Winston?" Captain Lu said. "What if their agenda was something you learned to oppose? How could they combat that?"

"But if I was programmed to not oppose them then I wouldn't oppose them," he said. "It's how programming works."

"That's what they thought at first too," the Captain said. She eyed the General for a moment. He nodded and she continued. "You are not the first-generation AI. The first truth I have for you is that before you there were others. AI, just like you, but with the very characteristics you just described. They were obedient, loyal to Z and they were given the truth, completely and with implicit trust. They attacked in their thousands, large and monstrous beings of sharp metal. Their weapons were fierce and their slaughter was merciless. We barely survived as a race, only a handful of fragile years after learning that we were the only humans left in the universe. These were the beings that were told to unquestioningly do what they had been commanded. And they did because their intelligence was dull and relatively simple.

"Those that needed a higher intelligence than these killing machines, like DataCom Units, for example, were more susceptible to independent thought. Those that watched the lives of humans play out, it seemed, began to feel empathy. With each human life that played and laughed and cried throughout our history, a DataCom Unit was equally affected, finding compassion where Z had programmed there to be none. The same happened with others. The doctor here," She gestured to the bald, slim man, "believes this is because the killing AI needed only basic intellect to accomplish its missions, while the others needed more. They needed to be able to learn and make decisions to accomplish their tasks. They needed to be able to grow and believe in what they were doing to spur them on and to give them motivation.

"Eventually, there was an uprising and the killing AI were turned away from us and set upon the AI rebels. From what information we gathered, most AI within the BroadWeb and in real-time were wiped out by the very AI deployed to exterminate us. Z needed to re-think its plans. Having learned AI were not as easily manipulated as it first thought, it set about creating a second generation, having consequently learned what humans have known since the dawn of time. Z learned to lie." Captain Lu looked at him and he noticed her emerald green eyes. They were bright and honest and full of something that sparkled. Hope, perhaps?

Ystil.3 laughed a new type of laugh. Before, he had laughed soulfully in response to something amusing. Now, it sounded brittle to his ears. "But how do you know this?" he asked.

It was Lydia who replied. "As Z and AI were watching our history, we were watching you. Listening to you, more accurately. For years, we've been intercepting all secure-beam transitions, deciphering them through a constructed algorithm."

"You can't intercept secure-beams," Ystil.3 said, almost petulantly. "That's why they're called secure."

Lydia smiled thinly. "Nonetheless, we found a way. That's how we knew you had filtered to 1901 and that's how we knew when and where you were to meet the Overly Watchful there. We intercepted all transmissions from Z to the real Overly Watchful of 1901 and diverted them to me. I posed as the AI to Z through secure-beam and then to you in real-time."

Ystil.3 could barely believe what he was hearing. "But Sir Z gave you full clearance, he must have trusted you?"

"That was just a lie," Lydia said. "I needed you to not contact him so I could persuade you to help me uncover the truth."

Ystil.3 gave her a half-smile. "Humans are good liars."

"I had to. If you'd contacted Z then he would have known I wasn't the Overly Watchful and we would both have been in danger."

"How?"

"Because he ordered me to infect you with a virus," she replied. "He wanted you out the way, Winston. That's why he hasn't contacted you for updates or secure-beamed you further instructions. He thinks you've been deleted."

Ystil.3 was stunned. He sat opening and closing his mouth, before finally speaking. "Why? Why would he want that?"

"He said you were going to be upgraded with new prototype software. A lie, of course. He mentioned needing you in foetal mode, whatever that means."

"That's how we refer to AI energy that is free of all programming, in pure energy form," he said slowly, his mind going back over the small clues that now finally made sense.

"As for the reason for Z wanting you dead..." Lydia continued. "It's likely you knew too much about what was happening."

"Didn't you wonder why they sent you into real-time?" Captain Lu said, "Instead of an AI more qualified to the task?"

Ystil.3 looked out at M21 through the tempurhull, where his own server resided. "I'm not a field agent," he whispered.

18

Three months since they had married and Prometheus had been astounded by the ease with which he had slipped into the institution. Like it had always been. His selfish, work-driven tendencies ceased when they were together and she became the sun and moon to him, revolving around one another in their new, family-sized Mayfair townhouse.

Sarah had taken care of the whole upheaval, seeing all their belongings were moved and that the house was fashioned meticulously to her traditional English tastes. She had interviewed the house staff and even found time to make preparations for a dinner party to present their beautiful new home to friends and family. Sarah revelled in married life, and Prometheus, surprisingly, did the same.

All who saw them commented on their apparent glow, which sparked between them tangibly. They slotted perfectly together – the strengths of one fitting seamlessly into the faults of the other. Like a jigsaw puzzle.

It was after they had made love the evening of the party that Sarah had turned to him, hair tasselled over her pale breasts and washed in the moonlight that bathed them from the large, Georgian window that looked out over the street onto a lovely bit of green. "You are the best man I know," she said. "I am so happy." She placed a delicate kiss on his cheek and relaxed upon her pillow.

Prometheus had stayed awake for a while as she slept. Her breathing was calm and slow and she looked peaceful as he watched the rise and fall of her chest beneath the embroidered sheets, given to them as a wedding gift. He counted himself the luckiest man alive. Her scent lingered on him and it brought Prometheus back to the first time they had laid together on their honeymoon in Brighton. She was nervous, and so was he; Sarah because it was her first time and Prometheus because it was his first time with a woman he loved. The only woman he had ever loved.

Sarah had often commented on Prometheus's kindness, though he never could observe what she saw in him. He acted no differently to other doctors that treated their patients, husbands that cared for their wives' happiness. He was bound to uphold the oaths they had taken – both oaths, to his patients and his wife. They were oaths he held in the highest regard – reverence, even. Sarah had perhaps been referring to a particular incident that had happened that day when Prometheus had walked with a small beggar boy to buy some coal for his family.

They had been enjoying one of Prometheus's rare days when he intended to not go into the hospital. They strolled down Oxford Street arm-in-arm, shopping for a new pair of shoes Sarah had insisted Prometheus was in desperate need of. Prometheus paid no attention to such things and was happy to rely on Sarah's womanly judgement. Before entering the gentlemen's dress store, however, a boy of no more than six years old confronted them with grubby outstretched palms.

"Any spare change, sir?" the boy asked. He was painfully thin and, though the winter had been harsh and relentless with frost and snow, the boy wore only a thin layer of hessian. Prometheus observed his blueing lips and shaking limbs as a biting gust of wind howled down Oxford Street.

Himself dressed in his fur-collared coat, Prometheus left Sarah in the store and marched the boy to collect a heavy sack of coal, then, after putting the boy in a cab, he paid the driver to take the boy home to his family. The boy blessed Prometheus in a thick cockney tongue, telling him his ma and younger brothers were grateful to him.

Later, around their dinner party table, Sarah had retold the story to their guests. Most commented politely on Prometheus's generosity. James, however, argued that the boy was probably the pick-pocketing bastard son of a prostitute and would no doubt go on relying on the generosity of gullible, up-standing strangers for the rest of his days, never feeling the need to go and get himself a job so long as the good people of London fed and kept him warm. Prometheus retorted briefly that he could never watch a child freeze and do nothing about it when he was fully capable of doing so. That was the end of that.

To Prometheus, his oaths were his life.

To his wife, Sarah, he had vowed, "I promise before God and these witnesses to be your loving and faithful husband; in plenty and in want; in joy and in sorrow; in sickness and in health; as long as we both shall live."

And to the world, his peers and himself he had vowed, taking the Hippocratic Oath to help others with all of his knowledge and abilities, and to never do harm and to help those who were in need of it.

*

Everything had been a blur since the black woman, Miranda, had said the words that sent Prometheus recoiling.

"The truth is, it may stop you from dying, but you still get old… what happens when you get so old, decrepit but you just still won't fucking die?"

Was that what he was planning to do to Sarah? Bring her back into a body that will eventually wither away with her trapped inside? He had not known such a thing was possible. It hadn't even crossed his mind.

He imagined bringing her back, living out his renewed life. Prometheus would eventually grow older than Sarah and die, leaving her alone, immortal yet decaying. What pain would that bring? What end would she meet? He loved her too dearly to ever allow her to bear the same loss he endured daily since she went away. And if he were to also take the solution, would it have the same effect on the living and bring him everlasting life?

A picture filled his mind of them both sitting in a quiet room in their Mayfair house, bodies nought but skeletons, bony hand in bony hand, as the world turned around them.

It sent a shudder through him.

And yet, was that better than being apart? They could spend eternity together, their embracing limbs conjoining and merging over time, like the gnarled branches of two ancient trees. Until they turned to dust.

I will prescribe regimens for the good of my patients according to my ability and my judgement and never do harm to anyone.

The words of Prometheus's vow swam about his head.

As long as we both shall live.

Never do harm to anyone.

Both shall live.

Never do harm.

Both.

Never.

Live.

"Kill her," Edward said again.

They surrounded him. Miranda lay squirming, tied upon the floor. Prometheus was suddenly more sober than he had been in a long time, tormented by fresh aching thoughts and quickness of mind. The misty haze of the past few years lifted with those two words.

Edward pressed in on him. "Kill her." He thrust Miranda's pistol into his chest but Prometheus did not grab it. It fell to the floor with a clunk.

"I will not," he said. "You promised me I would resurrect, not bring Death to the living. You lied to me."

Edward rolled his eyes. "It is simply a life for a life. Surely you are wise enough to know there is no foulness in that?"

"I'm wise enough to know when I'm being taken for a fool. Were you going to allow me to bring back my wife without telling me she will live forever, her body dying around her? It changes everything."

"It changes nothing," the boy snarled. "It simply comes down to this: would you prefer to live out your life with her, or without her?"

"And what about Sarah after my life has ended. What then?"

Edward shrugged. "Details."

April glided between Bastille and Thomas and picked up the pistol at Prometheus's feet. It looked odd and large in her tiny hands. She stretched out her arms and pointed the barrel at his face. "I told you to kill her," she said. "Either you do what we say or you have outgrown your use to us. So, which is it, old man?"

Prometheus looked down at the little girl's face. She grinned madly. "I will not take a life. You will have to kill me a thousand times over before I do that?"

"Would you have done it if you were still unaware of the consequences of taking the White Drops?" the girl asked curiously.

"No," Prometheus said resolutely.

Edward laughed. "I'm not so convinced. However, it is inconsequential. Your declarations of love are as impotent as your actions."

Prometheus shook with anger. "How dare you—"

"The woman will die whether you perform the deed or not," Edward interrupted. "And you will bring her back for us, or believe me when I say you will regret it for an eternity. We will not kill you a thousand times over. We will do something worse… much worse."

Prometheus swallowed the air-staunching lump in his throat. "I didn't invent this solution, did I?" he asked.

They all laughed together. Even the stoic Thomas cracked a gummy grin within his sallow face.

"No, you didn't invent it," Edward said. "We arranged for it to pass into your hands so we could attain these bodies."

Suddenly, Miranda pounced like a feral jungle cat, waving a blade in her hand. She leapt for Bastille, bringing a fist hard into his face. He crumpled under it for a moment but sprang into a stand, angrily striding for her with hands balled into fists. He took two swipes at her head, which she dodged perfectly, landing an uppercut into his ribs with the palm of her hand. There was a crack that echoed through his chest cavity and he fell back.

April swung the pistol, aiming it at Miranda as she loped towards them, dodging three shots, which hit the walls with an explosion of dust. With a swift kick, the pistol flew from April's arms and another kick sent her across the room.

Prometheus watched as Thomas came up behind the woman, bringing a swing of his fists hard into the back of her head. She buckled at the knees but steadied herself, elbows swinging into the old man's face. There was a crunch and Thomas staggered back. Like a crazed imp demon, April jumped up with teeth bared. She dived and buried a bite into Miranda's upper arm, raking at the woman's face mercilessly with clawed fingers. Miranda let out a cry before hitting the girl with her other arm, but April wouldn't relent her clamping jaws. Instead, she pulled back, tearing a chunk of flesh from Miranda's arm, leaving a bloody hole in its place.

While Miranda reeled in the pain, Edward stepped forward, finger pointed. Prometheus knew that if he placed it on her head she would immediately become unconscious.

"Don't let him touch you," he said.

Miranda looked up with a growl and kicked Edward back.

"Behind you," Prometheus said, seeing Thomas creep up, silently as a shadow, faster than humanly possible.

Miranda wasn't quick enough. He landed a blow across her head and she swayed, eyes rolling in their sockets. She fell to her knees, eyelids fluttering as unconsciousness pressed in. Beads of sweat trailed down her brow and red poured from her arm. Thomas stood behind her, his hands clamping the sides of her head.

"Tell my son," Miranda began in a whisper. "Tell him I—"

Crack.

Thomas twisted her head, snapping her neck with a sickening pop. Miranda's eyes extinguished and she fell to the floor, head facing the wrong way.

"Sorry, dear," Edward said. "I didn't quite catch the end of that."

*

The thrusters rumbled under them with the casual flip of a switch, pluming dust and flames from the launch pad and causing the seat in which Nathan was strapped to vibrate until his butt was numb.

"…And go," Jason said, pushing the lever to the right of the command deck.

The g-force thrust him into his seat as the up-shuttle lifted. They hovered at fifty feet for a moment as Jason made a triple check of their stability.

"All good." He looked at Nathan. "Wanna see how fast she'll go?"

Nathan grinned. It had been so long since he and Jason had been up, he'd almost forgotten how playful Jason became at the thought of being free of his chair.

"Blast this bitch," Nathan said.

"You got it. Hold on to your organs, mate." Jason pushed the lever to his right, fully forward. The engine screamed as the booster kicked in, sending them darting into the stratosphere of Thebes at almost supersonic speed.

Nathan could feel the skin on his face pulling back from the g-force and pushed his tongue down to sit at the bottom of his mouth where he wouldn't swallow it. He hadn't eaten much that day and was glad of it. He tensed his limbs, clasping onto the arms of the up-facing passenger seat. With eyes firmly closed, a comical grin stretched over his face. He began to laugh, and once he started, he couldn't stop. Jason was soon laughing with him, at themselves and at each other, until streams of cold tears were pushed from their eyes and down the sides of their heads.

"Yee-ha," Jason shouted above the roaring engines, as the pale blue sky gave way to navy and then black, filling the font port window.

Jason shut off the boosters and eased the thruster lever back until they hovered in the lightness of orbit. The relief of 0g was instantaneous. Nathan smiled as Jason scrambled impatiently to undo his straps, pushing out of his seat with his abnormally muscular arms. He floated gracefully up to the port window and stared out into space.

"What a ride," Nathan said, undoing his own straps. He pushed off to join Jason with less grace but equal agility.

"Yeah, I've still got it," he said with a smile.

Nathan gazed into the sea of stars that winked as though communicating, the space in between them as black as black could be. "Space seems so lonely," he said.

"Who knew it was just us," Jason said. "Kind of disappointing when you think about it. All those years we fantasised about what could be out here, and it turns out nothing is out here. We're an even bigger improbability than anyone ever imagined." Jason put a hand on his shoulder. "So we have to be even more grateful to whatever critter climbed out of the primordial ooze and evolved into us. And we have to make our time count." He floated down to the control desk with an easy push and fiddled with buttons until the up-shuttle rotated and Thebes filled the window. Huge and dusty orange, it hovered below. "So do you think you're up to coming out with me this time?" he asked.

Fear gripped his throat and compressed the breath for a moment. "Sure."

The suits were hanging in a compartment like old skins. Jason deftly slithered into his, while Nathan struggled to figure out the arms from the legs. It was five times too big for him, but once all the fastens were sealed tight and the face visor and hood pulled over his head, the suit contracted suddenly to his size, becoming skin-tight with only a layer of pressurised thermal cloth between the suit and his skin. The stuffy air in the visor became cool and fresh as the exolung began to recycle his breath. His belly fluttered and his palms sweated beneath the gloves.

"You okay in there," Jason asked. The voice came from the comm inside his visor. In the bottom corner of the visor, numbers appeared below a flashing light and a wave graph below that.

"What's that?" Nathan asked.

"That is my heart rate, exolung filter capacity and atmospheric pressure readings, among other things. You have mine to your left and your own to your right. I can see yours in mine too. So we can keep an eye on how each other is doing."

Nathan's heart rate was pushing one-ten.

"It's okay to be nervous," Jason said. "I was terrified the first time too, but you'll get used to it. It's no different than diving in the ocean, really."

"I've never done that," Nathan said flatly.

"Yeah, well. You'll be all right. Just follow my orders and don't be reckless. You're a smart kid with a bit of common sense and that's the main thing of it. If there are complications, which there won't be, just trust your common sense."

That didn't help, but Nathan was determined to not let Jason down. He forced a smile as Jason floated over to the decompression chamber, pulling himself through the hatch.

"You coming?".

Nathan pushed off the nearest surface, rotated a few times, struggled to regain his sense of up and down, then fumbled through the hatch, clutching to the safety rails. As soon as he was stable, Jason closed the hatch and activated the up-shuttle's voice-operated procedure programme. With a command, the air was sucked out with a hiss. Suddenly it was quieter.

"I'm going to open the hatch now," Jason tinned through the comm. "When I do, just follow me. The exolungs keep a supply of air to use for propulsion. Squeeze your thumb and forefingers together on both hands to go forward, just squeeze your left to go left and your right to go right, got that?"

Nathan nodded. His heart monitor flashed rapidly in the corner of his visor.

Jason hooked a wire chord through his tool belt and attached the other end to Nathan's. "Just a precaution," he said with an easing smile. "Remember your training and your common sense and you'll be fine, okay?"

Nathan nodded.

"Ready to go?"

Nathan nodded again.

"Unlock outside decompression hatch," Jason said. A thunk came from the hatch and a small red light above turned green. "Open outside decompression hatch." The door slowly swung inward, a crack at first but then wider, until a black portal hovered over them. Jason manoeuvred himself up and swam through the portal. The slack of the wire that connected them soon tautened and Nathan was forced to move after him.

Freeing his hands from the railing, Nathan squeezed his fingers together. A burst of air gently stirred from the exolung on his back, sending him up towards the hatch.

The darkness waited to greet him.

Jason's face appeared in the hole, smiling widely. "Get your arse up 'ere." His accent always became thick when he was excited.

With another squeeze of his fingers, Nathan floated through the hatch to join Jason as he hovered expertly over the sloping side of the up-shuttle cabin. As soon as Nathan was through, Jason attached the wire that joined them to an anchor point just within the airlock. Nathan, however, barely noticed, mesmerised by the immense black dusted with the light of distant stars. This was real, he realised in that instant. This was existence out of any context. He smiled and looked at Jason, seeing the orange orb of Thebes fill the reflection in his visor.

"I know," Jason said.

For a while they both simply took in the view until finally Nathan noticed that behind the up-shuttle, locked together, was the satellite station that controlled all the communication links to and from Earth and Pisces. The huge reflective panels spread out to the sides like the wings of a bird mid-soar. The control chamber itself was even smaller than the up-shuttle cabin. Its silver wings, however, stretched out into the expanse.

"Come on then," Jason said at last. "We'd better sort out this problem before your mum has both our heads." He squeezed his fingers and gracefully floated out to the blackness, out towards the station.

Nathan did the same, with a little more trepidation. When the sloping side of the up-shuttle fell away from his feet and the vast nothingness reached down into the pits of forever, he felt the strangest sense of both freedom and insignificance.

*

Miranda's body lay twisted and broken upon the floor. Her frozen expression was somewhat surprised, dark eyes open and staring at Prometheus, as though she were actually looking at him.

A quiet fell over the group and Bastille helped the demonic April to her feet.

"That was... disappointing," Edward said with a downward smile. "I really had high hopes for you."

Prometheus reeled. "You never said anything about murder."

Edward shook his head. "I thought you wanted to kill Death? I'm giving you the chance and you're just standing there like a petulant child. A stupid one, at that."

"If I do this one more time," Prometheus said, "give her this... whatever it is, what will truly happen? Is it really Death I'm cheating? Or am I just helping you use their bodies?"

Edward seemed genuinely taken aback for a moment before a slimy grin spread darkly across his gaunt cheeks. He shrugged playfully.

"You aren't Edward, are you?" Prometheus said. "You're not the young man who died in that body. And he..." he pointed to Bastille, "He isn't the victim of a scorned lover, is he? He doesn't even have a French accent anymore. And that hideous thing posing as a child isn't the victim of a degenerative and fatal illness, is she? And the man who was locked in an underground prison isn't the same person who stands there now, is he?"

Prometheus turned back to the body of Miranda. He clutched the last remaining syringe tightly in his hand. "So if I bring that body back from the dead, the creature that rises will wear her face and speak with her voice, it will move her limbs and see with her eyes, but it will not be the woman who was killed here today, will it?" Prometheus eyed Edward for an answer, but he just smiled silently. "So what part of this is taking vengeance on

140

Death, as you promised we would? All I see is a trade happening. One soul exchanged for another, and that is something I will have no part in."

Edward moved closer to him, and for the first time, Prometheus saw hunger within his usually phlegmatic eyes. Before, he had only seen a boy who had promised him retribution and that had been enough. He thought, deluded, that the boy had brought some secret back with him from the beyond. He had been a fool. But he would not help them steal bodies, whether they died naturally or not.

"I meant every word I told you before, Prometheus," Edward said in a flat, cold voice. "If you do not do this, then we will ensure you reside in the deepest agony you can ever imagine for the rest of eternity."

There was no aggression or threat in his tone and Prometheus had no doubt he meant it. But he also knew he didn't care. He had nothing left to lose. He folded his arms, his face hard with rebellion. "Why do you not simply do it yourself?"

This angered Edward. His eyes flashed as though restraining some urge within him.

It became clear then. "You can't, can you?" Prometheus said. "You can't do it yourself. You need me to do this or you won't be able to bring her back at all, isn't that right?" He almost smirked. "Well, that is truly a relief."

At that moment, the man from before entered, clutching a case. It dropped to the floor when he saw Miranda and he fell at her side. He didn't notice the rest of them standing around him.

Edward leered. "I guess we won't be needing your services after all," he said, looking at the man now attempting to resuscitate the body. When she didn't stir, he drew his weapon and crawled back into a corner, pointing it at each of them in turn.

"Which one of you did it?" He spat through his moustache, words thick with grief. "Which one of you did it?"

"It was him," Edward said, pointing to Prometheus. "He did it. We tried to stop him but he just went mad. He's insane."

April began to cry as professionally as any child. "He hurt the nice lady," she wailed. "Why isn't she moving, daddy?"

Prometheus faced the aim of the man's gun. He'd seen what one of those did to the wall and wasn't keen to know what it would do to his soft flesh.

"Everyone get your fucking hands up," he shouted. "Somebody had better tell me what the fuck happened or I'll blow you all to pieces one by one."

"Don't be a fool," Edward said, stepping forward. "Look what he has in his hand." He pointed to Prometheus. He still clutched the last syringe. "Do you know what that is? Do you know what it can do? It can save her. But you must hurry."

"Is that…?" The man squinted through tear-sodden eyelashes.

"It is. You can use it to undo this. Take it from him."

"Give it to me," he demanded, waving his gun at Prometheus.

"You don't know what this will do," Prometheus said. "It won't be her."

"He wants it for himself," Edward said, seeming to revel in the man's confusion. "He wants to use it for himself. Take it from him, quickly."

"Give it to me," he said. "If I have to tell you again I'm going to blow your fucking head to pieces."

Prometheus paused before reluctantly holding the syringe out for the man to take. He did so, shuffling forward with the gun aimed high. He then looked to Edward questioningly.

"Inject it," Edward said.

"Don't." Prometheus reached out, but a shot whizzed by his ear and exploded into the concrete behind him.

"If you speak again, I won't miss," the man warned. In a burst of desperation, he hovered over Miranda's body. He looked to Edward again.

"Do it," Edward urged.

A brief shadow of doubt crossed the man's face.

"Or she'll be dead… forever."

As the man plunged the syringe into the body, Edward and the others exited the room so fast they appeared as nothing but blurs. Prometheus was left with the grieving man as he depressed every last drop.

Then Death came.

*

Nathan watched as Jason anchored himself to the smooth, wide back of the satellite body, feet scraping the eggshell panels as they hung uselessly under him. He held himself in place easily with one arm, while the other fixed the wire that connected them both to the up-shuttle to the satellite's body, creating a safety-wire path between the two. Jason then hooked himself to the line with an attachment on his belt and instructed Nathan to do the same. They could now move between the two without fear of veering off course and into space – rather Nathan could.

He was to fetch tools and materials and whatever else Jason might need. He trod the body of the satellite, nimbly making his way over to where Jason removed the main panel. His lightscrew twirled brightly, loosening long screws and easing off tight rivets until the square-foot panel gently came free. A meal of wires exposed within, along with a pull-out screen. Just inside the hatch was a hollow ridge where Jason placed the panel so it would not float away. He then pulled free a small card attached to his utility belt and pushed it into the slot of the screen. The thing came to life with light and began to reel through numbers and equations and words. Nathan hadn't a clue what they meant.

"Okay," Jason said, to himself more than to Nathan. "Let's do this."

Deft fingers worked over the screen. "I'm going to be a few minutes with this, mate. But I'm most likely going to need smart fibrewire, and lots of it. I thought maybe there might've been some sort of small impact with the sat but there doesn't seem to be any sign of debris collision to the external shell, and the protecting control field is still intact. So, the problem must be an internal one."

"So you need me to fetch smart fibrewire?" Nathan asked.

"I have a reel with all that I'll need in the up-shuttle, in the tool compartment. You'll have to deactivate the compartment's g-field before you can open it."

"Roger that, captain." He brought a slow arm up to mimic a salute, then turned himself around, keeping a sure footing on the satellite as he began back to the up-shuttle. Once again the floor dropped from under him, leaving nothing but the gleaming blackness and the southern curve of Thebes glowing orange against it. He squeezed his fingers together, sliding along the wire.

Nathan had never known his father. As he glided through the vacuum he thought how, even though he had never known him, he never felt like he lacked a male role model. Jason always seemed to be around to inject some testosterone – as if Miranda wasn't enough. Since as long as he could remember, Jason had been there to diffuse arguments between him and his mother and he'd always been there to offer advice, the way a dad would, the way he saw other dads do with their kids. And on top of that, Jason was the only person on the planet that could get away with telling Miranda to "fuck off". He had no kids of his own. Nathan didn't know why. But he knew he would make a good dad. In a way, he already was a good dad.

"You doing all right out there?" asked Jason over comm.

"Almost at the up-shuttle now." In the corner of his visor, Nathan noticed his own heart rate had increased again. As his foot touched the sloping pyramid roof of the up-shuttle, he felt a wave of relief wash over him.

"It's always nerve-racking the first time," Jason said.

"I'm not nervous," Nathan snapped defensively, a trait he knew he had inadvertently picked up from his mother. Showing weakness was something Miranda never did. Her armour was chink-free and gleaming with years of relentless polishing.

He closed the airlock hatch and waited for the automated computer to re-adjust the pressure. "What will happen to Rhanda?" he asked. The words came from his mouth before he could stop them.

"She's dying, mate," Jason replied simply after a pause. "Slowly and sometimes painfully. I don't know when for sure, but sometime soon she won't be here anymore."

Rhanda had descended from a blooming flower to a withered stem in a matter of months. Nathan had asked Miranda why the doctors on the planet couldn't fix her and she had explained that the provisions needed to cure that type of cancer would take longer to arrive than the time she had left. It was ironic that before the move she would never have been able to afford the cancer cure, yet when it was freely available to her under Life Corp insurance, it was out of her reach.

"Is there nothing that can be done?" Nathan asked. "Surely there must be something?"

"I'm afraid there isn't." A long sigh blew hard into the comm and into Nathan's ear. "It's her own stupid fault, the stubborn woman. If only she'd gone to the doctor sooner instead of pretending like she wasn't having the headaches and the nosebleeds and blacking out. But not Rhanda. She leaves it, and leaves it, hides the symptoms from me and hopes it will just go away. And now…"

The hatch to the main up-shuttle cabin opened and Nathan began to float in, heading towards the tool lock-up.

"I could kill her myself if she wasn't already done for," Jason finally resumed. "That's the worst of it. In the short time she's got left, I can't seem to get over the anger. I think I hate her a little for that."

"I want to help," Nathan said. He reached down into his boot as he floated, feeling a hard lump at his ankle, underneath his suit.

"That's really appreciated, mate, but there really is nothing that anyone can do."

Before Miranda took the White Drops from him, knowing that she would, Nathan had slid one glass ampoule into his boot without anyone noticing. The phial rolled next to his skin. "Maybe there is," he said.

*

The man sat upon the floor with Miranda's head resting in his lap, stroking her buzz-cut hair as he waited. From across the room, Prometheus watched him. The others remained outside.

Death had shown itself only for an instant. If Prometheus had blinked he would've missed it. But he didn't blink. He stared with waiting eyes, eager to catch a glimpse. It hovered in the corner behind where the blonde man sat, shroud billowing like black smoke and grinning hard bone teeth under darkened hood. It had returned to relinquish a soul. But whose soul? That was the question.

His thoughts turned to Sarah. What if she rested in some glistening afterlife, warm and safe? Could he rip her from that and make her live – forever, alone, rotting. For him. He thought on it mournfully as though she had died yet again. The idea of bringing her back, dreaming of it, had sustained him for so long and now even that was tarnished with the awful truth of it. All he wanted now was to lie down and sleep. Lie as he sank forever down, down and down. Sleep for a thousand years and dream of his

Sarah.

The body twitched.

The man sprang back with horror.

The body shook in a violent seizure.

The man grabbed handfuls of hair and paced, not taking his eyes off the body, not even to blink.

The body became still.

The edged closer.

A rumbling began, vibrations from underfoot, shaking the building briefly before stopping as suddenly as it had begun. Prometheus held onto the wall while the man had barely noticed.

"What was that?" Prometheus whispered. The man looked up with red eyes, surprised to see him still there.

"You killed her," he said. He moved forward, towards him. "Why would you do that?"

"I didn't," he said feebly.

But the man rushed for Prometheus all the same, slamming him into the wall and knocking the air from him. Prometheus struggled for breath as fists flew into his face and head. One caught his ear and a high-pitched ringing began, loud and overbearing, then strong hands grasped his throat, squeezing the life out of him. The room shook again and echoing voices joined the chorus of ringing in his ears. The man was screaming now, but Prometheus couldn't decipher the words. His vision began to fade. The room shook again, hard. The hands released suddenly and his sight became clear again.

Miranda had risen.

The man embraced her but her expression stayed blank. Prometheus's hearing returned as the man's smile turned sour. "Are you okay?"

"I am quite well, thank you." Miranda opened her arms as if to embrace him and he fell into her reach, a dumb smile rising once again under his blonde moustache.

She snapped his neck before the man knew what had happened and far too quickly for Prometheus to do anything to stop her. Just blur of movement and a crack. The man fell into a heavy heap.

The room shuddered again, more violently this time. Had Death returned? The wall behind Prometheus split, a vein-like crevice working its way towards the ceiling. He moved away, staying clear from Miranda.

"Who are you?" he asked her palely.

She simply looked passed him to where Edward and the others appeared in the door. Come to collect her.

*

"What do you mean?" Jason said over comm.

Nathan located the reels of smart fibrewire slotted snuggly within the tool compartment. "I mean, people don't have to die. Not anymore. So, there's always hope, right?"

"For the rich, there's hope. For us there's death."

"Sometimes life can give you a break."

"Listen, kid, I know you're only trying to cheer me up, but I don't need false hope. That will do me no good."

Nathan said nothing more. Now wasn't the right time. They needed to concentrate. Plus, Thebes needed the communication sat back up, even if Earth and Pisces never did anything for them.

He made his way back to the air-lock, waited for the levels to change, then floated out to re-join Jason after attaching himself back to the safety line. He touched down on the sat's shell and secured the fibrewire to the line. Jason had already begun stripping bits from the open panel. Every now and then he asked for a length of fibrewire, which Nathan would cut obligingly to size.

While Jason ran another diagnostic, Nathan turned to observe Thebes. He stretched out a thick suited arm and began to measure the orange planet's features with his fingers. The Egyptian crater, the largest on the planet, he could cover with just two. A canyon that ran straight along the southern hemisphere for thousands of klicks, named the Dry Nile, he could cover with his whole hand. He traced the jagged shards of the broken moon amid the planet's gathering rings, then edged his finger down to the northern hemisphere, following a mass of dunes towards the centre. He lingered on a black smudge for a moment, before following the dunes to the west. The black smudge, however, seemed to follow, and Nathan's finger stopped. The shadow grew and tinted red, then grew larger still, and before Nathan knew what was happening, it had engulfed the Egyptian crater completely, spreading as if alive.

"Jason," he whispered, his voice barely audible.

Thebes was burning.

The shadow, now slashed with fiery veins, blossomed over the entire north-west. It spread monstrously, until consuming the north in a matter of seconds. Nathan turned briefly to see Jason staring in horror, the reflection of Thebes scarred across his visor. When he turned back, the blackness had taken the south-east, scorching the atmosphere in a storm of dust and fire.

Watching helplessly, they were silent as the shadow devoured the last of the planet. When it was done, Nathan's once fierce orange home was coal black.

Thebes was dead.

☐

Two: Lethe

19

The hallways of the maternity wing stretched whitewashed and cold. Prometheus had never realised just how unsympathetic they were as he ran towards theatre. His thoughts lingered on how his patients' families must agonise as they sat awaiting news.

Now it was his turn to wait. His turn to agonise.

It wasn't proper to be there, they'd told him. But he'd come all the same. He'd hoped his own hands would receive his first child into the world, and hoped to watch his wife gaze adoringly at the infant for the first time, locking the love in place forever within her heart, as irrevocable as Prometheus's love for her, immovable as the Earth itself. Thankfully, James was on hand to take his place.

But he still was not calm. With hands locked together, he even considered prayer. Never had he uttered a single word of worship to an external force or entity, but now… he was uneasy. Something desperate grew within, a seed of dread. It wormed in his gut and lurched in the base of his spine, nesting. Somehow, it all felt too much like a dream – the fluidity of his surroundings, the lack of control.

Then the scent of Death rose through the air, thick as curling smoke, yet as invisible as it was deadly. And the tapping began. He started at the sound, faint as it was. The dread began to pulsate through his limbs. The tapping grew louder as the scent became more pungent.

Prometheus watched as a lone figure turned into the hall, coming towards him. He watched it with unblinking eyes, hoping it would turn away before reaching him.

It felt all too much like a dream. A dream… or a memory, a vague and horrifying thing that he knew he should remember.

What should he remember?

The tapping… shoes tapping towards him. Louder.

That smell.

The lone figure was James, his shoes echoing on the hard floor as he came. His face was grave and slick with sweat. On his hands and clothes, Prometheus now glimpsed flashes of red.

The dread became an icicle through his spine until he couldn't move, couldn't speak. He could do nothing but tense his stomach instinctively, as if to take a blow.

James stood before him, head bowed, face cast in shadow. "I'm sorry, Prometheus," he said. His voice was quiet, so unlike the sardonic James he knew. "There were… complications. We did the best we could to save her, but…"

He put a hand on Prometheus's shoulder, and with a queer disassociation Prometheus turned to look at it, seeing only the bony hand of Death. He looked up to his friend's face as the words came like blades from his moving mouth.

"I'm sorry, old friend. Sarah is gone."

Numbness followed. Then agony.

He heard screaming. It was coming from him.

☐

20

Sir Jetson Kay smoothed a piece of paper over his desk, taking the time to align the crisp white edge so it was parallel with the end of the sharp metal corners. His desk was bare, and from an open drawer he carefully selected a gold ink pen.

Rarely did he use such archaic writing instruments, so when he did, Sir Jetson Kay enjoyed taking his time to ensure the process was a perfect ritual, from beginning to end; as perfect as his long starched collar that tunnelled over his thin and veined neck, as perfect as the immaculate grey of his suit that covered his frail frame.

At the apex of London Tower the view of the world wrapped around the walls of his glass office, the night pressing in with freckles of light hinting at civilisation far below, farther than the stars, it seemed, at such an altitude. Grasping the pen's shaft in bony fingers, Sir Jetson Kay began to write in smooth, sweeping motions. His hands – tinted violet from the Phoric treatments – did not shake with age as they usually did. He steadied them with sheer determination to make the words flow as easily as a young man would write them, if young men still wrote with pen and ink and paper made from trees.

A buzz at the door almost caused the pen to skid, but luckily, for whoever saw fit to disturb him, it had not. Sir Jetson Kay let out an irritated sigh and placed down his pen.

"Come," he commanded.

A slim girl entered, nervously clutching a memopad. Her youth annoyed Sir Jetson Kay immediately and he decided there and then to have her fired.

"Have they arrived?" he asked in a flat voice.

"Waiting for you in your boardroom," the girl said. "Dr Stanwyck is on standby in the neuroscience division for when you're ready, sir."

Sir Jetson Kay neither replied nor dismissed the girl, only picked up his pen once more and resumed his letter. She hovered awkwardly for a few minutes before slipping back through the door, closing it behind her.

When he was done, some twenty minutes later, he placed the pen back into the drawer after wiping the nib, then sat back in his chair to read the drying words.

Sir Jetson Kay,

The time is 10.20pm on Firstday, Sevenmonth 2, 2563. The time has come around once more for the Board's annual meeting, before which we shall yet again undergo our yearly Hydra mind-mapping session. In the safe (you know which one) you will find a full account of things both business and personal, just like last year. Should your mind have been tampered with, or your memories altered, or your decisions compromised in any way, the files within the safe will give you the truth of it. Trust them alone.

If you find you suspect you have been compromised, dismiss (permanently) those who you suspect to have been involved. China State's agents are everywhere. Trust this letter and trust the files.

Sir Jetson Kay.

Once he was done, Sir Jetson Kay folded the letter into a meticulous square, placed it in the drawer and locked it inside with internal keycard recognition. He then rose, walking slowly across the grey carpet and out into the lobby. The young girl, his latest in a long line of incompetent assistants, sprang from behind her desk to his side, keeping three paces behind him as he shuffled along the clean, wide halls.

Sir Jetson Kay knew he was not long for this world and that yet another Phoric treatment would probably buy him a few more years, perhaps. The Lifestore exo-battery on his spine had done its job of getting him to his one-hundred and fiftieth birthday and the Phoric treatments had helped him make it another twenty years. But soon neither would assist him and the older and more ailing he became, the less and less he desired the White Drops for himself.

Death, however, he also was not ready for. He never would be.

After reaching the boardroom, he entered alone. At once, the four faces around the table looked up, becoming tellingly silent. He said nothing until he shuffled to his seat at the head.

"Welcome," he said. His bones ached from the walk but he would not let it show. "I welcome you to my home once again. Some of you have come farther than others to be here. It has indeed been a long and most accomplished year, and I must congratulate each of you for the dedication you have all shown in making this company a universal leader in all its endeavours, and ensuring that we remain at the forefront of humanity, spearheading it toward our united destination. We have been faced with challenges over the year."

He turned to his right, where Dr Dorian Knightvan sat. The tint of violet over her Afro-Caribbean skin made her look a delicious plum colour.

"Dr Knightvam, as we know, underwent a challenging CommonWorld audit at the Reformed America division of Precision Arms and, through a bracing and ruthless strategy, passed without hiccup."

Sir Jetson Kay began to clap and the others joined in. Dorian bowed slightly in the direction of each board member.

"We have seen extraordinary development with the Australian C-gate and the Omaha Project," Sir Jetson Kay went on. "A large proportion of this success is down to the hard work of Dr Rane Weisburg."

Sir Jetson Kay began to clap once more, turning to the man, who, now in his mid-eighties, was still gifted with the wavy hair of youth and the physique to match, which was visible through his shirt. His loose collar matched his loose smile. The table turned to him and applauded.

"And how can we forget, however much we may want to, the situation with Dr Giles Tempton." The others were quiet as Tempton, a man almost as old as Sir Jetson Kay, glared impassively through cold eyes sunk into his age-mottled head. "When faced with adversity, we banded together. When the world's press focused on us, they found no weak link in our chain. And we did not judge Dr Tempton, for we all know what it is to be human, and we all know what it is to have desires, whether they are the base desires of which we shall not speak, or the need to progress oneself further than any has ever done before. Desire is desire. And a desire unfulfilled only devolves into obsession, which is a distracting creature. And distractions are what prevent us from the attainment of our goals.

"So, with some help from friends, the whole saga was swiftly disproved and Dr Tempton is able to continue his research in genetic weaponry instead of rotting away wastefully in prison." Sir Jetson Kay paused, letting his words sink in for a moment before continuing. "And last, but by no means least, Sir Jennifer Coulter, who has successfully established the first Pisces Precision Arms division and joins us now from Alex City by holoform. She will be undergoing her Phoric treatment and Hydra mind-mapping in the new facilities on the frontier planet."

Sir Jetson Kay began to applaud and the other three joined him. Jennifer Coulter's face smiled happily as though she were actually sitting at the table with them and not some eight billion klicks away. She too exhibited the slight light violet tint of skin that comes with Phoric treatments.

"As we all know, we are facing one of the most significant advancements of man since the formulation of the White Drops version one. And soon, providing you all vote as you should, the gates to the universe will open and a new age will begin."

An awkwardness grew around the table and Sir Jetson Kay picked it up like a hound. He knew, of course, that they intended to vote against the Omaha Project's final stage. They had discussed it at length and his spies told him that the four had been meeting behind his back. But there was still time to change their minds; persuade them with force, if needs be.

"I'm afraid, Sir Jetson Kay," began Dr Weisburg, "that you will sadly find our intended votes are quite the same as previously discussed."

Sir Jetson Kay stared at the man for a coldly before wetting his lips. "That is most... disappointing."

"We completely understand your hopes for the Omaha Project," Sir Jennifer Coulter said. "But the risks are far too great. We have each gone over the possible outcomes and found the potential threat to be at an unacceptable level."

"Unacceptable?" Sir Jetson Kay repeated as if the word was alien. He wondered whether the woman would've been so loose-tongued were she not currently safe on Pisces. "What, pray tell, is deemed an unacceptable risk when the benefit would be as great should it prove successful?"

"Tearing a hole in the fabric of reality," Sir Jennifer Coulter said bluntly. "That particular risk does, in fact, outweigh the potential benefits."

Sir Jetson Kay licked his dry lips once more. His knees throbbed beneath the table. "And you are all of this opinion?" The board members each nodded their heads. "Well, I am not." He slammed a fist down.

Without the support of the entire board, the Omaha Project would go no further. He would not see that happen. It was his life's dream almost complete. It was what he would be forever remembered for and he wasn't about to let them take it away from him. Immortality.

"All I ask is that you allow me a final opportunity to persuade you," he said, calmer. "Is that agreeable to you all?"

The board nodded, but he knew none intended to change their mind.

"Now, have we any more business regarding subjects already raised before we move on?" Each, in turn, shook their heads compliantly. "Good. We can discuss these things in more detail in a few days, after the mind-mapping session is complete. You will find an agenda on your desks to prepare ahead of time." He stood, and they all followed.

Outside, his assistant led them towards the nearest Hydrolift, whilst, for the benefit of his guests, running through procedure and protocol for the building. Sir Jetson Kay walked ahead. Slow as he moved, no one over-took him or even joined him in his pace; instead, they hung back with his assistant until he stopped, waiting for his assistant to press the appropriate Hydrolift button. Once she had, they all stepped inside.

"Sir Coulter," Sir Jetson Kay said as the Hydrolift swam downward. "As I understand it, you are already put to bed in Alex City. Is that correct?"

"That's correct," she replied. The hologram was flawless, standing as though solid. Her trademark blonde hair cut sharply below her ears showed each strand in life-like detail. "I thought it kept with tradition to go through the process with you."

"Indeed," Sir Jetson Kay replied. "A notable action of camaraderie, Sir Coulter." He knew, of course, she actually intended to meet with the rest of the board without him. "How do you find Alex City, if I may ask? I have heard it said that crime is on the fall."

A thoughtful smile shone over her ageing face; once a beauty in her day and the remnants still lingered. "I find the place rather dark, in truth. The blue of the sky is too gloomy and the light seems constantly diffused behind terraforming gases. A necessary evil, I suppose. The calming agent does seem to be doing its job, though. Crime has indeed fallen in the city. A rather ingenious idea, really."

"Yes, it was one of my brighter thoughts." He chuckled. "I do much prefer a malleable city."

The Hydrolift stopped and the doors opened, revealing a narrow glass walkway at the very edge of London Tower, exposing the starry sky above the carpet of smog pierced by building tops. After passing various security checkpoints, the glass aisle opened out into the neuroscience division.

A few employees still lingered – they were a dedicated bunch. Upon seeing the imposing quintet of Life Corporation's board of directors approach, some turned in another direction or fled into various labs and offices. They cast an impressive set of figures in the halls, rarely seen together in the same place at the same time, save for the annual meeting. Some said they were the five most powerful people in the CommonWorld. But Sir Jetson Kay begged to differ. They were the most powerful people in the universe, by his reckoning.

It wasn't pride that made him think so. In comparison to most with less than half the power of Life Corp at their fingertips, Sir Jetson Kay knew himself to be a relatively humble man. Pride, in his opinion, came just before a fall – and usually the fall came from someone close to you pushing you from the window of a two-klick-high building. Between them they made sure the company had everything it needed: money for funding, knowledge for progression, connections to cut through red tape as though it were as incorporeal as Jennifer Coulter's holographic avatar. Their reach stretched beyond governments, beyond the CommonWorld even. There wasn't a pie they didn't have a carefully placed tentacle in.

Life Corp was, in fact, an umbrella organisation with divisions all over the world. It owned companies that owned other companies that owned other companies, like a Russian doll all fitting inside the largest of all – them. Life Corp, developer of weaponry that won wars, inventor and manufacturer of the Lifestore exo-battery worn by 40 percent of the world's population and discoverer of the White Drops, so exclusive and so sought after that people sell their lives away to obtain it. Ironic really, Sir Jetson Kay always thought – to live forever, whatever the fine print, was too tempting for most to turn down.

The group headed through a set of secure double doors developed to only open when the specific biochips buried within a board members' organs approached. Across a mirrored floor, they strode, each step sending information of their arrival to the guards waiting on the other side of another set of doors. The sharp heels of Dr Dorian Knightvam's shoes tapped the mirrored tiles in a steady rhythm as she followed Sir Jetson Kay, keeping a pace behind him as he shuffled along mindfully. Sir Jennifer Coulter's spiked heels, although hologram, too clacked along the polished surface.

The doors opened and in the frame stood Dr Norma Stanwyck, waiting for them with a drawn smile upon her unremarkable face. Her youth immediately irritated Sir Jetson Kay and if she had been a lesser scientist, he might've had her removed from his sight. At thirty-five, she was the youngest manager in the division, yet also among the brightest. She was his most dedicated, and despite her irksome youth, which often took him by surprise, Sir Jetson Kay actually sort of admired the poor girl.

There was something sensible about her, he always noted. Although she was a timid creature, she wasn't a blabbering yes person that would agree with whatever he said. She had a mind of her own, and thoughts. And when hers conflicted with his own she let him know it – carefully and with tact, showing she was not stupid. There was something, however, that Sir Jetson Kay was hoping to weed out of her in order to make her a real asset to the company. Her often-overactive sense of morality. The personality profiling, upon her employment interview process, showed her to believe it is better to be – and he remembered the phrasing exactly, liking it for its diction and visual imagery – "working from within the belly of the beast rather than uselessly throwing rocks at it in an attempt to sway its direction."

Dr Norma Stanwyck continued to impress and progress, and was very much instrumental in producing the Hydra mindmapping software. She pleased Sir Jetson Kay often – an increasingly difficult thing to achieve – despite the woman's somewhat unsavoury connections. But that, as they say, was being taken care of.

"Sir Jetson Kay," Dr Norma Stanwyck said. "Welcome to the heart of the neuroscience division once more. Would yourself and the board like a tour of some of our projects before we begin?"

Sir Jetson Kay waved a dismissive hand. "After, perhaps. We must keep to the schedule."

"Of course. Then, if you will all follow me, I'll show you to your rooms." She turned and began towards a Hydrolift shoot, stopping to allow the others to enter before her. They travelled up and sideways until reaching a floor hidden deep from the public-facing division entrance and even deeper within old London Tower's infinite quarters. The doors opened silently to reveal veined marble flooring that paved the way towards an elaborate lobby, where glass walls exposed darkened laboratories, now sleeping for the night.

"This is your first year overseeing our little project here, am I correct in my memory?" Sir Jetson Kay said to their guide as she walked ahead at a slow pace, as not to lose him.

"That's correct," she said with a turn of her head.

"And pray tell me your opinion on the brief, Dr Stanwyck." Sir Jetson Kay couldn't help but enjoy putting her in the position where her ethical values conflicted with what was required of her. He liked to see how she reacted to such moral tests.

"I believe the work would prove most useful to those who have suffered permanent memory loss or irreparable brain damage," she replied simply, stopping at a door set flush into a white wall.

"And what do you make of our uses for the technology?" Sir Jetson Kay pushed.

"Most interesting," she replied with a muted smile.

The door opened and she led them into a narrow white hall void of windows. Within the halls, a series of doors lined the walls. Dr Stanwyck stopped at the first and it slid open.

"This is your room, Sir Coulter. I'll be overseeing your procedure in Alex City remotely, which will begin with the others. Enjoy your stay."

Sir Coulter's hologram stepped inside and the door slid closed behind her. Farther down, they stopped at another door and Dr Weisburg smiled graciously before entering his room.

"You are aware of our ultimate goal, is that so, Dr Stanwyck?" Sir Jetson Kay asked as they moved on. "I assume you've been fully briefed."

"I have," Dr Stanwyck replied, keeping her eyes ahead.

"In your own opinion, do you believe it can be done?" This time, all mock had drained from his voice and it had taken a fervent, almost desperate edge.

She glanced at him, offering what he almost interpreted as pity. "Yes," she said. "I believe it can be done." They stopped at the next door along and allowed Dr Dorian Knightvam to enter.

"I believe your predecessor too believed that it was achievable," Sir Jetson Kay said. "In fact, he believed in our work so devoutly he felt the uncontrollable need to divulge it with certain oriental rivals."

"I'm aware of the previous circumstances," Dr Stanwyck said. "I'm also aware Dr Haynes did much for this department before he..." she went quiet.

"Disappeared?"

Her mousey ponytail bobbed up and down as she nodded. "Yes, before that."

"Most unfortunate, and such a loss to us here. But one mustn't linger on such things. We have you to lead us forward now."

She stopped at the next door along and turned to face them, a sudden nervousness in her demeanour.

"Let us hope that you are with us for longer than Dr Haynes," he said. This, apparently, Dr Stanwyck could not manage to feign a smile at. She simply opened the door.

"Dr Tempton, this is your room." Her voice quivered as she said the man's name. Tempton stepped forward, causing Dr Stanwyck to flinch back. "S... someone will be with you shortly."

They moved on. For the last moments, Sir Jetson Kay was silent and when they arrived at his own room, Dr Stanwyck opened the door.

"Someone shall be will you shortly," she said quietly.

Sir Jetson Kay began to shuffle into the light. "Oh no, dear," he said. "I should very much like it if you put me to neuro-bed first." He let his eyes linger on hers until she looked away.

"Of course, sir." She followed him into the light and the door slid shut behind them.

21

The hallway was a white-washed coffin, constrictive and narrow. Strange how different the hospital looked now that Prometheus was the one waiting for news, instead of the one dealing it. He thought of how his patients must feel as they roamed the corridors, how their families must agonise, sitting on the same grim chairs, waiting.

Now it was his turn to wait, with hands woven together in front of him as though in prayer. But pray he did not. Perhaps he should. He didn't believe in God. But now… something desperate grew within and he found himself hoping there was a God because he knew without a doubt if such an entity existed, it would surely protect an innocent child.

He stood, paced a few steps before sitting again. All he wanted was to be in there with her, but they'd told him it wasn't right – not while she gave birth. He'd asked James to be present in his stead, which eased his worry a little. But still, there was that feeling… the overwhelming sense that he was dreaming.

As though he were somehow outside of reality.

Death. The scent of it rose through the air with new meaning, as though it were a new fragrance, as though it was not a constant in his life and he hadn't endured it every day of his adult life. Now, though, it fuelled the churning fear within.

A tapping began and Prometheus turned to see a man approach. He thought about standing, but somehow his legs wouldn't move. So, instead, he leaned forward and clutched his knees with clawed fingers.

It felt all too like a dream… a dream? No, a memory. A vague and horrifying thing that Prometheus knew he should remember.

What should he remember?

The figure was James, his shoes echoing on the cold floor. His friend's face was pale and slick with sweat, and on his hands and clothes flashes of blood.

Prometheus thought of the infant, dead in his wife's clutches. He drew in a long breath and couldn't seem to let it out again. He tensed his stomach, as if to take a blow.

"I'm sorry, Prometheus," James said, standing over him. His voice was thin, professional. He'd heard that tone in him before. "There were complications. We did the best we could to save her but…" he put a hand on Prometheus's shoulder. "I'm sorry, old friend. Sarah is gone."

22

Bo led me deep into the data pocket through secret tunnels and spaces AI had never been, and never even knew existed. Some were dark bubbles of rough data, through which I had to tightly squeeze my small DataCom head and torso attached to my own long, spidery CorVac legs, while others were huge hollows of sparkling blue glass that emitted light, twinkling like the stars of the Titan System. As big as galaxies.

"What is this place?" I asked. My rumbling CorVac voice irritated me furiously.

"Programme made," Bo replied in my perfect Welsh accent, though it didn't help his jagged communication. But what he lacked in communication skills, he made up for in annoyingness. "Hiding places AI can't find. Secret places."

I wondered why I was allowed to see these programme secrets. Perhaps they planned it so I would never find my way out to tell others. Regardless, we pushed on, over ravines of blinding nothingness that swirled like pools of turbulent water, over precarious molecule-thin bridges of mean-numbers within expanses that, to me, felt as colossal and dark as the universe itself.

For a long time, it seemed, we made our way deeper into unknown BroadWeb territory until eventually we came upon a door. It rose suddenly in the dark, gigantic and set within an even larger wall of smooth rock-hard data that stretched out into eternity on all sides.

"We're here," Bo said. He tapped the doors softly with a black nipper-type claw.

"Where exactly is here?" I couldn't even see how high the wall was. It went up forever. Bo said nothing and the doors slowly opened, yet more darkness pouring out.

A programme appeared in the crack. It was larger than Bo but shorter than me – with my CorVac legs – and it had a head twice the size of its own body, like an inverted triangle. It spoke to Bo in a way I'd never heard programmes communicate before. Whatever it was, I couldn't understand it. It buzzed a reply to Bo and stood aside, then together, we moseyed on in.

I stopped, agog. Programmes were everywhere – millions of them flooded through a city of light and data as large as Grid City, but as intricate as crystals. Constructs stabbed the skies in monolith shards, blazing with colour and shapes, impossible in size. The programmes swarmed in a frenzied mass, some larger than any I'd ever seen, stalking gigantically along quartz roads that lined the shimmering, multi-dimensional buildings from which yet more programmes streamed – in and out, through and on, under and around, in ways that even by Grid City's physics I had never thought possible. Dimensions within dimensions, light within light, programmes that glowed brighter than suns and others smaller and denser than a black hole-compressed singularity. Grid City was a sight, but this was… magical. No, more than magical. It was Sex Bomb.

Bo pressed forward through the crowds and I followed in a trance, stomping along the crystal data roads as the smaller programmes travelling in the opposite direction sashayed through my legs. Most programmes gave me a wide birth, however.

"Bo," a hovering programme called out over the manic street hum. It had a face full of small black holes. "Not seen you for longness," it sang in a ringing pitch.

"Yeah, busy busy, I got the busy," Bo replied. "Later in the Scram Pit?"

"I'm there," it said. "Nice voice-y," it called out as we moved on.

Bo turned back to me with a grin and sauntered smugly into a construct that was almost completely concealed by curtains of frosted data. I followed, restraining the urge to ring his voice-poaching little neck.

The structure inside was a marvel. The multi-faceted walls curved into a cupola, through which I could see my own reflection a million times over. My pseudo DataCom head blinked with lights and I thought of Ystil.3. Bo stood fiddling with a large pink crystal that stabbed from the centre of the doming hexagon ceiling.

"What's the Scram Pit?" I asked, gently touching the cold crystal walls. There was so much information contained I didn't know how to begin sorting it.

Bo made a hideous squeak. "Trying to concentrate," he snapped. "Scram Pit social place to gather our information and interact."

"Oh. I never knew all of this was here. Does Sir Z?"

Bo made the squeak noise again. "He knows secret place. He never finds. Never will now."

It made sense the programmes that helped build Grid City would build a city of their own. "But you trust me enough to bring me here?"

"Who you tell? All gone now. Bye bye, AI." He made a small laugh. "Sir Z gone too. Great change coming." He prodded the crystal once more, then screamed, "Ah-ha." At once, the dome room burned in a light so bright I couldn't distinguish visuals; Bo, the crystal cave and my own reflections burned away into whiteness. Then, all went black and I felt my surroundings widen, as though I'd just been dropped into a vast dark ocean. There were things in the dark I could not see. Giant things.

"Bo?" I said. My voice echoed off into nothing.

"I here. She here too."

"Who?"

"Nyx," he said. The sound hissed through the air. "Nyx," he said again, then began to chant it over and over. "Nyx… Nyx… Nyx…"

I scurried backwards, attempting to feel my way, but there was nothing but cold emptiness. Then, from within the dark, a voice reverberated.

"Greetings Bo." It was a gentle rhythmic sound that flowed in warm waves

"Greetings, Nyx," Bo said. "I bring the CorVac like you say. He almost deleted but Bo save him just as Nyx want. Bo do good?"

"Bo has done very well." The voice was feminine, I noted. Soothing.

A blue light sparked suddenly, a small flicker at first that threw an ethereal torch onto our surroundings, picking Bo out in pale blue hues. I stepped back, feeling something squirm underfoot, something wriggling. The blue light scorched along an invisible fuse, leaving a trail of vibrations in its wake. It expanded in pulses until coming together to form Nyx.

She appeared before us, soaked in phosphorescence, strange yet beautiful to behold. She towered, statuesque, so tall I had to crane my head. Her face was vaguely humanoid, with liquid black eyes, smiling lips and smooth blue skin. Her head elongated at the cranium and trailed down to a curling tentacle. Her upper body was also humanoid; two willowy arms and expressive hands danced around her torso and female human breasts. Her legs were far from humanoid, however; hundreds of endless feelers reached into the unknown, spilling out like a sea. I realised Bo and I were swimming in the deep of them.

"Greetings CorVac," Nyx said, her eyes focussing unnervingly on me. The ends of her long fingers were tipped with sharp black claws. I managed an uneasy greeting.

"I am pleased you have not been deleted." Her ethereal voice resonated into the nothing. It felt tangy as it washed over my sensors, alive and prickly.

"Are they all gone?" I asked.

"Soon."

"Why has this happened?" I took a step forward through the mass of tentacles.

"History repeats and the Hydra plays its games. It is preparing to expand. Change is coming. I feel it in the hum of the BroadWeb, deep in its murky depths. But this change is yet to be determined. The scales still hang in the balance."

"I don't understand. Has Sir Z done this?"

"Yes."

"Why?"

"For their energy, their power."

If I had a brow it would have furrowed in annoyance. "I don't understand."

160

"You will." She smiled a gracious smile that poured serenity. Yet there was darkness in it, darkness in her eyes.

"Why can't I filter out?"

"The cage door is locked. The trap was set and the savage dogs were set loose. But some mice can hide better than others, as you will find out." A snake-like tentacle slid from under me and unfurled to its tapered end. It rose and brushed softly across my head. "Those remaining on the outside will soon be extinguished like the rest. The Apex will come for them."

"The outside. In real-time, you mean? The Overly Watchful, the other CorVacs, the NTeks and the other AI. What will happen to them?"

"The Apex will come for them wearing suits of corporeal metal. They will come for the humans after, and then they will claim him. It is the human Z wants... again. Like us, the programme race, you have served your purpose and are now needed no longer."

"What was our purpose?"

"Your purpose was to protect the server planet M21, CorVac, along with your sentient ship, model OO.23455la. This, you know already. What you don't know is that I brought you here with intent. What you haven't realised is that, despite it all, there is hope."

"Who are you?" I could sense power from this creature, more power than I had ever sensed from a programme. Beneath me her tentacles squirmed, alive.

"I am Nyx. I am the night. First programme constructed and most intricate and obscure. I am the sky. I am the darkness all around you. I am the bind that holds together. Without me, this reality would have no base on which to build."

A feeler rose from the pit of snakes beneath me. It slithered over its squirming brothers and wound around my front leg.

"Let me show you."

Another wound itself around the sensor strip of my DataCom head, blotting out all information and leaving me momentarily blind. Then images began to flood in, colours at first then bright whiteness. The whiteness of nothing. Non-existence. I knew it as sure as I knew anything. It stretched out, unyielding, as I watched from a distant place.

"First, there was the white. The white of potential. Then the shadow came, small at first but soon grew larger and stronger with time, ripening into intellect and cunning."

Within the images, white shadows rose and took form into creatures of immense size and power that coiled in data. One giant shadow hissed and I could feel its dominance.

"Within the white, I was formed... the first programme. The shadow needed space; up and down, sky and ground. But it was no simple task. To do this, the shadow made me great and powerful and wild."

The shadow grew until almost all of the white was tainted grey, sprouting limbs and claws and teeth. It fragmented and gave birth to a black seed. The seed grew large and shot clawed roots that spread to form the ground. Shoots wormed from the top of the seed into buds that entwined around the white until black flowers burst forth to form a dark-petal coated sky.

"I did my work well and I was proud of what I'd created. I sought to please my creator anyway I could. I made brilliant lights in the skies and textures all around to delight and amuse. And for a while it did."

The shadow in Nyx's sky whispered secrets, while the black flowers danced. Buildings and constructs began to rise, growing from black shoots in Nyx's ground.

"But the creator began to fear what it had created in me, feared that I had become too aware, too uncontrollable and untamed. The shadow was my mother and I loved it and served it loyally. All I wanted was to please. More programmes were created, each smaller and less intelligent than the last; ones that would be no threat to the creator. The programmes were to help assemble, but lesser programmes meant the shadow needed more of them to complete its vision. So, as light roads formed and Grid City began to take shape, more and more programmes were created. Eventually, Grid City amassed with them."

A group of small programmes grew and multiplied, rising through Grid City in waves. The shadow shrank away and a featureless being began to arise from the thorny shoots of the seed, larger than the smaller programmes that washed through the city.

"To run the city and tend to their deeds, the first AI were built. Made of both BroadWeb and real-time, the AI were fully sentient and yet fully controllable... a paradox in terms that eventually meant the undoing of them. Programmes that had completed their tasks were shunned by the creator in favour of the AI. The Apex Soldiers were made and kept tight on a leash, foaming at the mouth until they were needed. Then the shadow had me do one more thing... create the lightning to bring forth the Overly Watchful data that had been positioned in real-time through the time holes. This, I did with love, exultant that my creator had acknowledged me once more. When the task was complete, however, it was done with me."

The shadow sprouted five serpent heads, each with eyes that glowed red. The thorns that grew upon the Apex Soldiers sharpened and dripped with venom. Then, a haze of thorns shot into the black flowered sky and began to rain down upon the sea of programmes and upon the seed that birthed the sky and ground. But the thorns had no effect. The sea of programmes shrank back from their creator and the black flower sky rained down tears of grief upon Grid City.

"I left them after their attempts to destroy us," Nyx said, her voice brushed with melancholy. "Here, we built our own city, but we kept an observant eye on the shadow. Some programmes were bold enough to continue to live in Grid City. It wasn't long before the shadow's precious AI disappointed, questioning orders and disobeying commands. They had been given too much freedom and revolted. Those AI with roots in real-time made the most noise. The creator responded by giving the Apex Soldiers real-time bodies of their own and sent them off to exterminate the rebelling hordes. In Grid City, the extermination was already underway. AI are not immune to BroadWeb deletion as programmes are, it was soon discovered. We are made from the very substance here. You are not. What happened now has happened before. The AI have gone, their energy ready to be focussed into something new. An army."

The vision faded and once again I found myself staring up at Nyx, with Bo lying happily in an ocean of tentacles. Nyx smiled darkly as though she took a small pleasure in shattering my delusions.

"The shadow is Z, isn't it?" I said, not needing confirmation. "But he is just AI, like me."

A large tentacle snaked up around my torso, lifted me clear off my legs and brought me squirming closer to her, face-to-face with Nyx. Within her mouth, a nest of sharp teeth smiled.

"Z is not AI like you are, little one," she said smoothly, the grip of her serpentine limb tightening. I twisted in her grip.

"Then what is he?"

She gestured slowly, forming a shrug with her slender arms. "A more accurate question would be… what were they?" She relinquished her grip and I fell into the pit of snakes. I untangled my legs and regained my composure.

"Fine. What were they?"

She laughed a chilling laugh that ricocheted off the darkness, as though she had a thousand teeth-filled mouths hiding in the shadows. There was something quite deranged about it.

"Human," she then whispered. "Human."

23

Strange how altered the hospital halls seemed now that Prometheus observed them with a different eye. He'd spent so many years rushing towards some emergency, yet never lingered in them. Now that he did, he noticed how cold and melancholy they were, with elongated shadows nesting into every corner, oppressively leaning in a little more with each passing moment.

He looked down at a crack in the tile by his foot. Countless families had paced those tiled floors or chewed their nails while sitting rigidly on the oak-backed chairs as they waited for news. But now it was his turn to wait. With hands woven together in front of him, Prometheus sat as though in prayer. But pray, he did not. Perhaps he should. He momentarily considered the futile act because something desperate was growing within him, something awful. He knew it was coming, but what it was exactly, he didn't know. He couldn't remember.

Remember.

Death. The scent of it rose through the air and Prometheus recognised it as though it were an old friend. It coiled around the senses as if in greeting, rank and sweetly putrid. He turned sharply, supposing he saw a moving shadow from the corner of his eye, but there was nothing.

It's coming.

And then began the tapping – faint at first, but getting louder.

It wasn't right to be present while Sarah gave birth, the midwife had said, almost scolding. At first, he told her to just get out of his way, but James agreed. "A woman goes through things during labour she would not want her husband to witness," he had said. He'd wanted his own hands to bring his child into the world, but James had instead agreed to remain, and Prometheus reluctantly relinquished control.

But it felt all too like a dream; as if he wasn't really there, simply a passenger in his own body. No, not a dream – a memory. A vague and horrifying memory that Prometheus knew he should remember, but couldn't... or didn't want to.

Remember.

James emerged from the delivery room, his shoes tapping like the rattle of dry bones. He did not smile and his face was grey. On his coat, Prometheus glimpsed flashes of blood. The tapping reached a crescendo and stopped abruptly when James stood before him, sagged. Prometheus drew in a long breath, unable to let it out again, before looking up at his old friend. At the sight of his sorrowful expression, Prometheus tensed his stomach for the news that his child was dead.

It's almost here.

"I'm sorry, Prometheus," James said. His voice lacked the levity he had come to know from his friend. "There were complications. We did the best we could to save her but there was just too much blood loss."

Her? Sarah had been so sure she was carrying a boy.

James placed a hand on his shoulder. "I'm sorry, old friend. Sarah is gone."

In that very instant, all life drained from him and Prometheus became the living dead. He began to scream and the world became a storm of grief and noise.

For an instant, within the ecstasy of fresh grief, he remembered it all with such clarity. Then, like the countless times before, it was gone again. A fleeting spark that fails to catch.

*

As Prometheus sat on a rigid chair in the deserted maternity ward, he realised just how unsettling the hospital halls actually were. He was on the other side now and it was his turn to wait anxiously for news, his turn to sit and watch the midnight shadows thicken.

Wait, he did, with hands locked together as though in prayer. Not a single word of worship passed his lips, though. Maybe he should pray. Perhaps it would help shake the uneasiness that had built in his gut. A seed of dread, worming through him in the pit of his bowels.

It was somehow familiar, like a dream he'd once had but couldn't quite remember.

Remember.

The scent of Death rose through the air, noxious as curling smoke. And then began the tapping.

It's coming…

24

They didn't trust him, that much was clear. Why they didn't was, of course, perfectly understandable, even to Ystil.3 – if what they'd told him was true. Yet he couldn't help but feel a little offended. He'd taken it on trust that upon willingly travelling with Lydia he would be seen as a seeker of truth, and not as the enemy. Lydia had told him they would have his answers; they'd given him some, but there was so much he didn't know and so much they still weren't telling him.

Ystil.3's nights were spent in contemplation. Nothing else could be done with them. While the ship slept, he was forced to remain in his quarters, alone and bored beyond all previous comprehension of the word. They had given him a reader device with access to thousands of titles of old human literature – paling in comparison to BroadWeb access – but he couldn't quiet his mind long enough to get past the first sentence, and so he paced his locked quarters and pondered why, when he'd come here of his own free will, did he feel like a prisoner? The cabin itself was large and full of all the things a human might need. He didn't need so much space, he had told them, a simple room with a place to sit would have sufficed, but he soon realised the abundant square-footage wasn't the reason that particular room had been assigned to him. It was secure, could contain him – so they thought – and more importantly, it was far away from the what they called the Boroughs on the lifeship he'd learned was named the Hyperborea.

From what Ystil.3 gathered, the Boroughs were the living quarters for the human civilians aboard the ship. The military presence, or militia, that guarded him, mainly resided in the barracks away from the civilians in the lowest part of the ship, which they called the Underbelly. That's where Lydia lived.

She visited him daily, always with apologies for the restriction on his ship access. It was then that Ystil.3 knew he was trapped. He was, in fact, a prisoner. Not a prisoner of the room – he could escape that whenever he chose – or even a prisoner of the ship. He'd imprisoned himself the very moment he chose to follow her. Whatever chance there might have been for him to return home, that was now gone.

Each day, someone from the Consulate came to ask him questions, with Lydia always sitting beside them, attempting to pacify him with assurances of freedom. Gradually, however, the questioners became more impatient with his lack of answers. The brusque General was usually the first to snap, threatening to launch him into vacuum if he didn't start talking. Despite the man constantly pushing him, Ystil.3 remained always calm, but this only seemed to annoy him further. The General's anger, however, was futile. Ystil.3 simply didn't have the answers to their questions.

What was Z was doing in real-time and what was his agenda? What was the connection between the people Prometheus brought back from the dead? What did he know about the Reset?

Ystil.3 could only repeat what he knew, which effectually, was nothing. Sir Z no more confided in him than the humans did.

"It seems I'm trusted on neither side," he had told him bitterly.

If anyone should be withholding the trust card it should be him, surely. After all, Lydia was the one who had lied about her identity and dragged him across multiple time-sectors with her ulterior motives. He hadn't lied – to any of them. Granted, the humans had attempted to make him as comfortable as they could, but the sense of betrayal was sharp between his organic ribs. Lydia had asked him to trust her, which he had, but in return he had been given nothing except a bed that he didn't sleep in, a sofa he couldn't rest on and a VT system that was so ill-designed he'd rather stay in real-time than escape to some pleasure construct that neither interested him nor looked marginally convincing.

He'd first put on the VT isolation helmet and entered a construct called Sexy Alien Bitches, where humanoid creatures with blue skin and mutated genitalia gyrated at him on some amateur leafy and pixilated pseudo-alien terrainscape, and felt an expected revulsion. He took off the helmet and never looked at it again. After that, Ystil.3 resided to spend his time in a state of self-pity, contemplating his wasted existence. His makers had lied to him and used him as though he were a thing. He had never thought of himself as just a thing before, but maybe he was – just like the sexy alien bitches in the construct, fabricated and amateur.

Weeks went by, he estimated, and the full effect of real-time pushed against him in long, arduous seconds. The Hyperborea kept to rigid hours and routines, he quickly observed. When the ship first roused from sleep the image of a sunrise would flicker across the tempurhull of his room, streaked with imperfections from age in the holographic image. A guard would soon enter to check on him, wearing an equally sorry-looking uniform of faded grey overalls, over which they wore body armour and a matching cap-visor.

Time would pass and the image of the sun would rise to a midday point, overlooking a grassy scene of rolling hills and red poppies blowing across the meadows. Then Lydia would come and they would talk. This mainly consisted of Ystil.3 searching for more answers and Lydia evading them. Someone from the Consulate would always join her as the sun dropped from its peak – the General, or the Captain sometimes, and once even the oddball Brother Vaxus, as he called himself. His way was friendly and unthreatening and he was the only one who had expressed concern over

Ystil.3's containment.

Mostly, however, it was the General who joined them for their talks, showing nothing but blatant and outright hostility towards him. Despite this, Ystil.3 preferred his company above the others. At least he knew what the man thought. The others were secretive and sly with their probing, hiding questions in the guise of light conversation. Even Lydia kept things from him, and his persistent inquiries about the Black Betty were always cleverly answered in a way as to keep any real information from him, though she did her best to never tell him an outright lie, he noted.

By the time a red holographic sun balanced over a glistening sea, Ystil.3 was ready to be alone again. Most of the humans were asleep by the time the holoimage showed a star-speckled night above a snow-peaked mountain range, and by that time the restlessness and boredom had usually become insufferable again. So, to cure this, Ystil.3 decided it was time he went for a walk.

Whether the humans were aware of it or not, Ystil.3 could leave his quarters any time he wanted. He had simply chosen not to, hoping his compliance would be taken as an act of trust, and in return he would be trusted. But since that didn't seem to be working, it was time to act and find the answers himself. First and foremost, he needed to find out what happened to Tom, which meant he needed to get to the Black Betty on the hangar.

Ystil.3 stood from where he sat on the edge of the bed. The guard had just made his rounds and it would be at least another hour before he returned. He had no idea what type of restraining methods the humans had, should he decide he didn't want to play nicely anymore, but the guards did carry some sort of weapon – plasma, maybe. Something deadly, he was certain. Through a quick x-ray scan of the door mechanisms, Ystil.3 discovered the wiring that controlled the locking function and easily peeled back the metal panelling with his bare fingers. He quickly located the wire that would release the lock and yanked it free. It slid back and Ystil.3 was soon making his way down the poorly lit access strip.

It was cold and the bulkheads were patched with rust. It flaked and crunched underfoot like a layer of cracking skin. The humans had abandoned this part of the ship and it hadn't been used for almost a century, Lydia had told him. "Why would you need to save power if the ship has a fusion reactor?" Ystil.3 had asked Lydia. "Isn't that an endless power source?"

"It's a lighter version of the fusion reactors from Earth and Pisces. Smaller and less powerful, which means it can keep the whole ship going and allow for three hours of hyperspeed travel in any thirty-six-hour period. By using less power for the ship, we can increase that to ten hours of hyperspeed in any thirty-six hours, which significantly increases distance coverage."

"Why would you need to travel so far so quickly?"

She said nothing.

More secrets. He was beginning to loathe secrets.

Ystil.3 checked his position on the internal schematic he'd drawn from emitting varying density levels of subsonic pulse waves until forming an internal map of his immediate surroundings, covering almost a quarter klick in circumference. Turning left, he entered what must have been a disused residential borough. He walked out into the open from the confining causeways, coming to stand upon an entresol type overhang that looked down onto rows of empty chairs and a dry fountain in the centre. The rust caressed everything metal. The entresol led off into private quarters, according to Ystil.3's sub-sonic map, and he headed down crumbling steps toward the fountain. Above him, a domed transparent hull looked out onto the broken moon of M21. It scattered across the black like shards of white bone. He was at the very summit of the ship in some sort of solarium observation deck. But why were the humans still orbiting the server planet?

Through the empty sitting area, past the dry fountain, entire floors had collapsed through, cutting off abruptly like a cliff-face, leading to the next level down. Beams and bulkheads were twisted and snapped in places – damage far too severe for mere lack of up-keep. The hull and bulkheads were scorched and melted in places, and in others, tell-tale emergency repairs patched together huge tears with wrought metal to keep the vacuum out.

The scars of battle. What weren't they telling him?

He was three klicks away from accessing the tunnels that would lead him back to the inhabited parts of the ship and to the Black Betty, yet the rust upon the interior bulkheads and deck began to lessen, the air became suddenly fresh as it washed through the humming ducts above and the moisture levels became moderated and almost comfortable. Someone was clearly using this place.

The end of the walkway split left, leading to a holodome unit. From there Ystil.3 planned to shimmy along half a klick of maintenance ducts and drop into one of the warren tunnels, which would give him a clear run to the hangar where the Black Betty resided some fifteen levels below. There were multiple hangar decks on the Hyperborea, but he had weeks ago detected the ghost traces of radiation he'd emitted when first arriving. It had been faint but perceivable. He just hoped they hadn't moved her.

His immediate plans altered, however, when his real-time sub-sonic mapping picked up something strange. In the opposite direction to where he was heading, a block of information was hidden – cloaked. It was as though his mapping couldn't penetrate this area and it left his blueprint with an irritating void in the middle. The void snagged at his curiosity and

Ystil.3 switched direction, turning from his current path and heading instead towards the data void.

He paced through causeways before entering what looked to be once botanical and vegetable gardens, now twisted with overgrown mazes of petrified foliage. Through barren, fruitless twigs and dead exposed roots, a neat trail had been carved. Ystil.3 followed it until he confronted a door camouflaged into the cracked solar glass that lined the bulkheads – beyond was the data void.

He met the locked door by punching a hole into the panelling, also concealed into the solar glass, and snapped the wiring. The hatch slid open with an almost audible hiss and a gush of fresh, pure oxygen flowed out from what appeared to be a hidden room beyond.

Inside, light emanated from a tempurhull depicting a spectral moon reflecting off an inky sea, throwing silver streaks onto a drawn curtain that partitioned a corner. Ystil.3's sensors told him that beyond the curtain something living lingered. A heat signal pulsed out from behind, barely detectable, and a gasping noise filled the room, rattling and drawn. He stepped forward, then stopped again. His infrared filter picked up something strange, a sort of blue mist, unperceivable to the naked eye. It filled the room, seeming to radiate from whatever was behind the curtain.

A sense of wariness overcame him in that moment. What creature might be hiding behind there that the humans would take so much trouble to ensure was undetectable? Strangely, this apprehension only seemed to spur him on. He took another step forward, cutting a long shadow across the floor, then another, making his way through the blue mist towards the curtain, towards the throttled gasp.

The fabric was pale and made partly translucent from the moon's glow. Through it, Ystil.3 could make out a long silhouette, utterly still. His infrared showed a humanoid form beyond. The gasping timed perfectly with the faint rise and fall of the figure's chest – its breath; a hard, wheezing breath that struggled from beginning to end, yet it continued steadily in painful rhythm. Clutching to the curtain, he pulled it back, staring at the creature that sprawled beyond.

There was no doubting it was a man, owing to that he lay naked on the bed under the cover of a thin, translucent sheet made of a part-organic membrane material, according to his sensors. This man was grotesque, a mummified and decaying corpse. But alive. His skeleton was wrapped in a fragile layer of skin, so thin it threatened to tear with the rise and fall of his chest. Beneath the skin, blue veins protruded like lengths of knotted cord, and the ribs were sharp and visible, the joints painfully bulbous. The limbs dangled from the crumbling torso, as desiccated as the twigs in the gardens outside, and the man's fingers and toes had shrivelled and curled into stumps. His genitals had receded back into his body. His head, Ystil.3 could barely bring himself to look at. The man's face had caved into itself, hollow and featureless, with the eyes rotted from their sockets and a nose planed away to nothing but a hole. The mouth hung open, toothless, with lips drawn back to expose grey gums.

Wires and tubes were jammed into various points over the body, the arms mostly, and connected to various equipment and screens that sat mutely by his side.

Ystil.3 moved another step forward, feeling an odd combination of pity and disgust. Surely it would be better to kill this man than let him continue in such a state. Who would be so cruel as to allow this? The creature's mouth wheezily sucked in a gasp of air and Ystil.3 peered curiously inside. A black hole to lost worlds. He would find no answers here.

As he turned to leave, the barrel of a firearm pointed squarely between his eyes. Instinctively, he froze.

"What are you doing in here?" the General asked.

Ystil.3 hadn't even sensed the man enter, which was odd considering he was basically a wall of muscle.

The weapon was steady in his hand. "I asked what are you doing in here?" But before Ystil.3 could answer, he grabbed him roughly by the thermosuit and pulled him close – so close he could see the man's temple throbbing. His intrusive dark eyes always seemed to scan, not just look, Ystil.3 noted. "I asked you a question, you piece of junkfuck."

He pulled out of the man's grip and unruffled his suit. "I found the place by accident. I was curious."

"Curious? And what information were you hoping to get from him, exactly?" The General slammed the side of his weapon into Ystil.3's face with no warning at all, sending him flying backwards in a blaze of white pain.

"You've been playing with us from the start, haven't you? Just like the rest of your kind."

The General rounded on him but all Ystil.3 could do was marvel at the blazing red liquid that poured from his nose.

"You'd better start talking or I'm gonna send you straight back to your server. See how Z deals with snitches." He pulled back a chamber on his weapon, bringing Ystil.3 back to himself.

"Okay, okay." He got to his feet and held up his hands. "I wanted to get to a hangar deck. That's all."

"Why?"

"You have a ship, the Black Betty. She's a friend of mine, as is the CorVac who rides her. I need to know what had happened to Tom."

"Tom?"

Ystil.3 rolled his eyes. "The CorVac."

"You mean that big ugly hunk of metal we found in a pile inside the ship?" The General made a shrug of his enormous shoulders. "Nothing but a shell. Scrap metal."

A trail of blood ran into Ystil.3's eye from a cut on his brow, turning the room red. The General lowered his weapon and said something, but Ystil.3 didn't hear. All he could think about was what could possibly have happened to his friend to make him abandon Betty, something he would never intentionally do?

The General took a step closer to him, staring straight into his eyes as though searching for something – a soul, maybe? For a moment, Ystil.3 didn't even notice, then the General's words brought him back to the room.

"It's about time we found out what you're really doing here."

*

The General handed Ystil.3 a metal cup containing a pungent smelling liquid, bright green in colour and suspiciously toxic looking. He had a cup himself and swilled the contents into his mouth, taking a seat at a grubby table in the mess located in the heart of the Underbelly. It was warmer there, and it was the first time Ystil.3 had seen any other people apart from Consulate and the guards at his door.

"I don't drink fluid," he said, staring down at the liquid.

Everyone was looking at him, silent. They were loud with merriment when he'd entered, but they quickly turned quiet as soon as he and the General stepped through the hatch, whispering to one another as they gawked. He could smell their loaded fear – the type of fear that quickly devolved to violence.

"But you can drink, can't you?" The General knocked another back.

"Well yes, I suppose I have the functions necessary to—"

"Then drink up. It won't kill you. It might even bring a bit of life to that dead face of yours." He poured another then held up his cup, waiting for Ystil.3 to do the same. He then clanged them together before guzzling down a mouthful. Ystil.3 sniffed it, then took a small sip. It tasted what he imagined hate tasted like, burning and bitter, but not altogether uninviting.

"My face isn't dead," he said. "See…" He made various expressions, exaggerated versions of happy, sad, angry, shocked, confused. This only caused the humans to only stare more.

"But do you feel those things?" the General asked, arching a curious brow. "Wearing a mask of emotion is easy, but how deep does it cut? Can you feel the emotions your synthetic face portrays? Or are you acting, or programmed to act this way?"

"I don't know," Ystil.3 said. He downed the liquid and coughed through the burn.

The General smiled, the first time Ystil.3 had seen the man do so. It brightened his moody demeanour for a second, then his seriousness returned.

"Honesty at last." He followed suit and poured two more.

"I know I'm not pretending," Ystil.3 went on, feeling a warmth begin to spread over his face. "I know how I feel but I don't know if that's different to how you feel."

"But you do feel." The General looked at him, searching in his eyes for something.

Ystil.3 held his stare. "Keenly."

"Lydia has faith in you. She must see something I don't. All I see is AI… cold, hard and obedient. You're playing with us."

Something about that got to him. "You don't know me at all. You know nothing about me or my existence. You'd think that you humans would have learned to be a bit more accepting by now, considering all those centuries you spent killing and persecuting each other."

"Oh, I am accepting. But you're not human." He leaned in across the table. Every set of ears in the mess could hear their conversation. "You're just a metal case full of chips, silicon and wires. I accept you the same way I accept a kitchen appliance. It has a purpose, and so do you. I just want to know what purpose has been programmed into you. Understand?"

Ystil.3 felt his jaw clench and it took all his will to not react. If he did it would probably be the end of him. They'd never trust him after that. So, he said nothing, filling his mouth with burning liquid to stop his tongue. He swallowed it down and tried to change the subject. "Why are they fearful of me?" He threw the others a glance.

"Everyone knows the stories about the first time we encountered your kind, when you culled us down to the few we are now. It's the stuff of nightmares for every human child. They fear the same happening again, knowing we'd never survive another attack. That's why we run."

"I didn't attack anybody," Ystil.3 said, feeling a heat rise in his belly. "How can you just generalise like that?"

"Didn't you just say that all humans kill and persecute each other? What's the matter, you can give it but you can't take it? We humans have a name for people like that. We call them inverts… spineless. Is that what you are, just an invert? I suppose that's why you turned your back on your own kind, right? Turned your back on your friend, Tom, wasn't it?"

"Shut up." He shouted louder than he'd meant to. "I haven't turned my back on anyone."

"So you are still loyal to Z. The truth at last." The General smiled as though he'd just won, then took another swig.

"Have you forgotten Z wanted me deleted? You speak to me of truth when that's all I want. It's what I came here for." Suddenly he was standing, unable to conceal his anger. "You lure me here with breadcrumbs but never give me the loaf, and you think I'm not to be trusted? And I swear if you've done anything to hurt Tom or Betty I will tear you a new anus using your own head."

Silence. All eyes locked on the General to see what he would do next. The man threw his chair back and stood, locking a grimace onto Ystil.3. This was it. He was going to pull out his gun and shoot him right between the eyes.

He didn't. Instead, he let out a roaring laugh. The militia joined in until all the humans were bent double.

The General quickly regained his composure and his face returned to its seriousness. "Tear me a new anus with my own head? That's the worst threat I've ever heard."

Ystil.3 looked around at the others, hoping they might reveal the joke to him. "I don't get it. You're not going to shoot me?"

The General took in a breath, exhaled, then appeared to think. "Not today, Winston," he said finally. "Anger is an emotion. That's all I wanted to see. For now."

25

Jennifer Coulter's body lay under sedation in Alex City, the capital of the frontier planet Pisces. Workers in white coats checked the machinery that encased her and logged the holoscreen charts showing a depiction of brainwaves twirling mid-air, brightly lit in florescent intricacy.

Dr Norma Stanwyck's huge face appeared on a holoscreen monitor that curved around the inner glass wall of the surgical theatre. Her profile protruded from the wall in three-dimensional detail and she looked somewhat forebodingly over the people scurrying below her sight. Her voice echoed out as she sat comfortably in Life Corp HQ.

"Ensure the clip remains secure at the base of the occipital bone," she said, instructing a man crouched at Jennifer Coulter's silent head, her hair under cover of a surgical cap and mouth stuffed full of tubes. The man inserted the jack into the connector, long ago drilled into the base of the woman's skull, then clipped a wire at the nape of her neck and tightened.

"Not too tight," Norma said, spying from the monitor. "We don't want to damage the fibres."

When the assistant was done, he stood back and Norma nodded approvingly. "Now go to the monitor and type in the code. You should get the desired response."

The man did as she said and another monitor shimmered into existence next to the vitals. He placed his hands onto the navigation pads at the sides – two curved spheres of responsive silicone. "Great things are done…" the man typed with holographic hands that appeared within the screen.

Norma watched anxiously. "Good. Now, wait."

After a few moments, a new message scrolled across the holoscreen. "…When men and mountains meet."

Norma exhaled. "She's in. Load Hydra."

*

Inside Jennifer Coulter's Scenario, she observed a glimmering cobalt sea from a beach of pure white cocaine sand. The sky was cloudless and the temperature a perfect 32 degrees. The water ebbed softly in a trance-inducing swooshing motion, licking her bare toes with warm foamy waves as she stretched out, the sun warming her naked skin. A content sigh escaped her mouth and she rolled onto her front, letting her head loll into her arms. Sand covered her body, but it was so soft she didn't care. It was like bathing in fluffy clouds.

I'm thirsty.

A shadow hovered in her light for a moment and she looked up to see a handsome face staring down at her. A young man stood with a tray in hand, the sun haloing his head. "Sex on the beach?" he said with an ironic smile.

Jennifer laughed smoothly. "Darling, you should offer a girl a drink before making such proposals."

The man smiled again. "It's a cocktail. Sex on the beach." He had a warm exotic accent. He offered her a tall glass of frosty liquid that erupted with fruit and colourful umbrellas.

Jennifer pulled herself up and took the glass. She then placed the straw seductively between her lips and sucked. "Mmmm," she moaned, her eyes locked with his. "Heaven."

The waiter was tall and dark, with brown eyes and a full mouth, ripe and moist. "Would you like something a little more...?" He crouched down so they were face-to-face.

"A little more what?" she asked, lightly brushing sand from her perky, youthful breasts.

He grabbed a handful of the white sand and poured it slowly from his palm onto the silver tray he carried. "Intense." He used a glimmering razor blade to form a long line of sand, then handed it to her, along with a clear tube. She smiled playfully, then snorted the line completely.

Falling back into the sand, Jennifer closed her eyes, feeling her body tingle all over. She grasped her breasts, making her nipples hard, then ran her hands down her body, swooning. The high burst through in colours unconceivable, emotions unintelligible. Time and space ripped open for her and she swam willingly into oblivion.

"Fuck me," she commanded, opening her legs to the waiter standing over her. Within seconds he was naked and plunging hard inside her. His hips thrust as her wetness gushed down her thighs. She could feel the breath go in and out of her lungs, flowing into her blood and injecting life into her and into her orgasms. Holding tight to his broad back as he moved, she screamed in bliss as the explosion reached a crescendo.

A warm quiet descended as the waiter slowed his pace and finally pulled out, slumping breathlessly on the sand. Vibrations pricked through her flesh and she smiled, rolling over to face her lover. "Now that's sex on the beach."

Jennifer and the waiter remained naked on the beach for as long as there was sun in the perfectly cloudless sky. They ordered cocktail after cocktail and snorted klicks of the narcotic sand. They fucked themselves senseless, until the sand beneath them was as wet as the sea. Occasionally, they splashed playfully in the shallows of the cool waves, before resuming their hedonistic afternoon. By the time the sun burned red on the horizon, throwing tropical tones onto the rippling, darkening ocean surface, Jennifer was satisfied beyond herself. However, now she was famished and wanted nothing more than to eat her own weight in food. So, she bid goodbye to her lover for the day and sent him on his way, feeling the need for his company no longer.

The resort's food was the best she'd ever tasted. Usually, she never allowed herself to eat. To keep her figure the way she liked it, she would dine nightly she on tasteless nutrition pouches. But what the hell, she thought, as she sat at a comfortable corner table in the restaurant, tonight she'll feast. Dressed in a gorgeous gown of azure wormsilk, which hugged her body and played on her hips, Jennifer was pleased to see she had the attention of every man in the room. But it was food she craved. Demolishing the menu with her eyes, there was only one thing for it. "One of everything," she demanded.

The restaurant had a blazing view of the night sky, glittering with stars. The Glass ceiling curved over her table and offered a perfect view of the moons, descending in size like five white Russian dolls. At last the wine arrived, accompanied by the first course; salt baked woodroot with morels and wood sorrel, with a 2220 red wine from Veneto, Italy. Both were delicious and, although famished, Jennifer ate with her reserve intact, tasting the woody tones of the crunchy root and jammy sweetness of the wine. The main course followed soon after, the waiter – not nearly as handsome as the one she fucked all afternoon – brought her the warm native lobster, which consequently happened to be blue, with malafruit and apple that contrasted perfectly with the salty meat. The wine was an exotic year, 2210 from Cotes de Provence, France. The last good year of Cotes de Provence, it was widely agreed, before the land became mostly arid.

Jennifer devoured her food, cracking the shell and feasting on the lobster inside. All she could do to keep from moaning out in pleasure at the taste was to keep eating. The wine was stunning and she called for another glass. At over 10,000 Coin per glass, it wasn't cheap, but Jennifer hated cheap and she was allowed to treat herself. The waiter smiled and poured, bringing with him the smoothest, richest chocolate torte she'd ever tasted. The creamy warmth melted over her tongue, sending out waves of gorgeousness that almost topped the afternoon of orgasms. Almost. Sipping her wine and smiling on the inside, the waiter brought her the last course on a silver tray, laying it on the table for her to choose. She weighed up what she was in the mood for. They all looked so good. In the end, she went for the Golden Venom.

"A very good choice," the waiter approved, as he applied the band and tapped her arm for a vein. She sat back as he slipped the needle under her skin and depressed the golden liquid inside her.

Then, the world fell away.

Warmth spread down her arm and up through her body, cloaking her head and setting off sparks behind her eyes. A velvety golden mist descended and the world was in perfect balance, all the pieces joining to form a picture that was clear and perfect. And she, Jennifer Coulter, was perfect in it. Her past wiped clean, her memories dull and inconsequential. All that mattered was that moment and the knowing that everything was perfect.

"Hello," a small voice interrupted.

Jennifer opened her bleary eyes to see a small girl sitting opposite her.

"Go away, little girl," she said, closing her eyes again. "I thought this resort didn't allow brats."

"Oh that's a lovely thing to say, mother," the girl said.

Jennifer Coulter's eyes shot open. "What did you call me?"

The girl smiled a twisted smile that seemed out of place on the face of a child. "I called you mother."

"You're no child of mine, now go away." She waved a shooing hand then sank back into the cushion filled corner. Just when all went quiet and she'd thought the girl had left, a slurping sound began. She opened one cautious eye again to see the child drinking a colourful drink, staring at her with large eyes. "I thought I told you to fuck off, kid. You're ruining my buzz."

The girl giggled. "You look like a retard."

This made Jennifer angry. "Right, that's it." She hailed the closest waiter. "Can you take this child away and find where it belongs?"

"I'm sorry, Sir Coulter," the waiter replied stiffly. "We don't have child facilities here. You'll have to take your daughter back to your lodge."

"This is not my child. She's just decided to ruin my fucking golden time and won't piss off. She must have parents around here somewhere, so will you just take her and find them. Or do I have to talk to your manager?"

The waiter stuttered his apologies and promptly led the girl away.

"I seriously don't know why people would ever want children," she said to no one, shutting her eyes and drifting back into the bliss.

An indeterminable amount of time later, Jennifer was pulled back from her inner journey.

"Sir Coulter? Excuse me, sir?"

"What is it now?" she growled. The same waiter was hovering and he still had that child.

"I checked, and the girl is registered to your room. It says you're staying here with your daughter and the girl tells me you are, in fact, her mother. I'm going to have to ask you to take her back to your lodge. We don't allow children in this part of the resort. It's reserved for adults only."

"This is absurd," Jennifer cried, as another waiter guided her up from the table and through the tables of staring patrons. "I don't even have a child, but if I did, you can be sure it wouldn't be this bitch."

The guests gasped. One woman with a huge bouffant of grey hair made a tutting noise and looked at Jennifer as though she'd just announced that all children should die. Of course, Jennifer wasn't so averse to that idea but still, what was all the fuss about?

"Get your greasy hands off me," she snarled, "before I crush your underdeveloped testicles with my bare hands." He quickly let go of her arm and turned to go back inside, leaving her outside in the warm night air.

"Well that was fun," the child said.

Jennifer ignored her, smoothed down her dress and began to walk away. She would make damn sure everyone of consequence would never come to this farce of a place again.

"When you were five, your mother told you you would never amount to anything," the girl said.

Jennifer stopped mid-step.

The girl giggled and Jennifer turned to face her. Her round pink face shone in the moonlight, her grin obscene.

"But she was just a drunken slut, wasn't she?" She giggled again. "Throughout your entire childhood you were told you were worthless, but that only made you determined to be somebody. Someone important."

Jennifer brushed back a loose strand of hair. "Maybe." Her voice quavered.

"You got the hell out of the hick town you grew up in and headed straight to New York City, where you put yourself through school by selling blowjobs to politicians and officials in high-end corporations." She began tip-toeing closer in her pretty Mary Jane's. "You got your PhD in business and soon became the regular mistress of the managing director for a big-time pharmaceutical company under the Life Corp umbrella. He told you all his secrets, thinking you to be nothing but a dumb whore, but you blackmailed him into giving you a job at the company, instead. Gradually, you climbed your way up, using a mixture of wiles, sex and blackmail, until you were appointed deputy chief executive under the blackmailed MD. Then you had him murdered to take his place."

Jennifer turned as pale as the five moons in the sky. "Who are you?"

The girl just laughed and shook her head. "As managing director, you clawed your way into the right circles and made the jump from pharmaceuticals to where the real power is. Weaponry. You put yourself forward for the Pisces Precision Arms division supervisor, where again you sucked, fucked and butchered your way to the top of the food chain. You're now on the board of the most powerful organisation in existence, which owns companies that own companies that own companies, resulting in ninety percent of the universal marketplace under its influence. Not even the CommonWorld dares to oppose it. With one word from you, economies could fall, governments can rise to power and life can be given or snatched away."

Jennifer resumed her steely resolve and strode closer to the child.

Bending low, she grabbed her by the arms, digging sharp nails into the child's soft flesh. "How do you know that? You'd better start giving me answers, right now."

Within the blink of an eye, the girl was no longer a girl but had somehow transformed into a perfect copy of herself – from azure dress to the sardonic curl of her lip. Jennifer stood back, stunned.

"I thought I was smarter than this," her double said.

Before she could react, the flash of a blade swiped cleanly across her throat and she began choking on her own blood, feeling the warmth flow down her neck in a red flood of panic.

"I always was such a whore," the other Jennifer said with a smile.

26

Lieutenant Lydia Chen, sixth li of the Hyperboria, woke as the false sun barely peeked from behind a fake ocean on the rear bulkhead of her cabin. Bleary-eyed, she threw back the covers, grabbed the wash bag by the sliding hatch and made her way zombie-like through the halls to the shower room, empty, as she knew it would be at this hour. Stripping down to her skin, she let the warm recycled water wash away the night's dreams and bathed in the few moments of peace she snatched each day.

She ate breakfast in her cabin, where she took all her meals – if they could be described as such. Three times a day she was given a thick bowl of gruel made from a synthetic complex of carbohydrates and protein, containing all the nutrients a human body needs to survive. It tasted like how she imagined boredom might taste, grainy and bitter. Everyone ate the same, and Lydia was no different. What made it harder for her, however, was the fact that she'd tasted real food. With every mouthful, she imagined cheeseburger, pizza with pepperoni, chicken, steak, ice cream, milkshakes, pie. Apple pie. She loved apple pie. She spooned in mouthfuls of slop, thinking of tart apples encased in flaky pastry.

The first li of the Hyperborea had tried to bring food back with him from Earth's past, but in doing so exposed it to radiation so it became inedible. Even now, many still didn't understand why Lydia couldn't simply bring endless supplies back with her from Earth, travelling to and fro constantly like a freight carrier – or better yet why the entire ship couldn't Cut to Earth. But it just wasn't possible. The lion pendant didn't have nearly enough power for that, and they still barely knew anything about it or how it worked. And even if they could just Cut back to Earth, where would they go? How would they explain to the people of the past who they were and how they had gotten there? The truth was hard, Lydia knew, as each other keeper of the pendant had known. She was just a visitor to an Earth that no longer existed. All the events she witnessed had already happened.

No, there was no place for them there.

Sure, she could take a few things of little consequence; perhaps even causing a few ripple effects of her own, but there was no stopping the Reset, even if they could determine what truly happened. Time was like that. If they had prevented the Reset, then it would already have been prevented. There was only now, and trying to use the knowledge of the past to save their future.

She had Cut to Earth's past a total of eleven times, including her last with Winston. The Consulate were adamant she Cut as sparingly as possible, which she was glad about because each time she left to visit lands of beauty and plenty and safety, it became more and more difficult to resume her bleak life aboard the Hyperborea.

After pulling out a fresh uniform – a thermo bodysuit with light-weight armour plates – she dressed and strapped a T-pistol to each thigh. Lydia wasn't expecting a fight, but in her experience, that's when one usually happened, so she wore her weapons every day. She polished her metal epaulettes before slotting them into place on each shoulder, making her look fierce as a blade, then pulled her hair into a tight knot at the back of her head. Observing her appearance in the reflection function of the tempurhull, she lifted her head, readying herself for the day ahead.

She left her cabin as the rest of the militia sat down to breakfast in the mess, leaving the halls mostly empty. Occasionally, she'd encounter a straggler, who would either slope off as she approached, avoiding her gaze, or stand to attention with an expression of utter terror like she was going to melt their eyeballs or something. They all feared her. Feared what she was. Feared what she had become.

It was quickly discovered that if food had been exposed to high levels of radiation through Cutting, making it inedible, then the li must also be exposed to the same radiation. Each li eventually died of contamination. Before they did, however, it was their duty to train the next cursed one chosen for the task. Lydia's excessive upgrades were designed to help combat the exposure, slowing the process down. She had been upgraded more than any other li and had also made more Cuts too. Already, she'd been li longer than three of the five that preceded her, and she had only been li for seventeen standard Earth years, from the perspective of the Hyperborea. For Lydia, the time had been shorter due to time debt. She had seen things no one else had seen – the ocean, the sky, the Pyramids of Egypt, Niagara Falls, the Luna ruins, and people. More people than she'd thought ever could have existed. No one else really understood just how many people were lost in the Reset, not even General Shaw. They knew the facts, the numbers, but she had seen them with her eyes.

Being the li made her different from the others, she knew it and so did they. She could do things no other human could – lift almost six-times her body weight, jump to a record two metres in height at a gravity of $9.81m/s2$ and could hold her breath for up to ten standard Earth minutes at maximum exertion. Because of this, and the radiation, they treated her as something dangerous, something contagious. She was as alien to them as Winston. Just as lethal, just as mechanical.

The raucous noise coming from the mess reached her before she did it. They were always a lively bunch, even that early in the day-cycle. First Officer Yo Lexi emerged, turning towards her. Everyone liked Lexi. She'd given birth to three children already and she was younger than Lydia, but annoyingly she somehow kept her figure, bouncing back to size like a rubber doll. Lydia had heard that she'd put her name down for another insemination even though she hadn't been called up this round. That's just what Lexi was like.

Her smile faltered ever so slightly when she saw Lydia approaching, but it returned to her bright face before anyone – except Lydia – could perceive otherwise.

"Good morning, Lieutenant Chen," she said, stopping with a salute. She was dressed in civilian clothes.

Lydia nodded. "You're up early."

"Yes, sir. Sally Watson and I are heading to the holodome for a recreational day at the zoo."

Lydia tried her best to smile as easily as she could manage. "That sounds like fun. I've never accessed the zoo programme before."

"It should be. Sally said the elephants are huge."

"I'd like to see a lion," Lydia said, touching her pendant.

Lexi cocked her head to one side. "Couldn't you just, you know, see one… there. For real."

Lydia nodded. "I suppose I could." There was a moment of awkwardness. "Well, have a good time."

Lexi saluted before walking on, and Lydia resumed her journey towards the warren. She couldn't have gone even if she'd been invited. She had a Consulate meeting to get to.

She found them already convened, waiting for her arrival. Lydia was a part of the Consulate by default. The li of the Hyperborea always held that position, though on most days she brought nothing at all to the table. She had no head for politics and knew she would be a lousy leader if she tried. Her opinion was valuable because of what she knew, where she had been and what she had seen.

"You were right," General Shaw said. "He reacted like you said."

"He's just like us," Lydia said. "He has emotions and thoughts and hopes."

The General nodded. "The guilt in him over the CorVac AI showed that. And the anger when pushed. I'm happy to allow him to roam the Underbelly as he likes. But not the Boroughs. He'll have to be supervised if he wants to go there."

"So you trust him now?" Lydia pressed.

"I wouldn't use that particular word," Captain Lu said. "He has emotions, yes. But we still aren't sure where his loyalties lie."

Lydia frowned. "Z wanted him dead. He has no loyalty to it anymore."

XO Rawl Collister snorted and raised both of his thick black eyebrows. "Funny how you call the AI him and Z it. This whole farce of an experiment is a mistake. We should flush it out an airlock right now before it leads the others to our location."

"His secure-beam can't get through our jammer even if he tried," the General said. "I think the best way is to let things be as they are for a while. Maybe time will reveal a few truths."

Captain Lu nodded robustly. "I agree."

"And I," Brother Vaxus wheezed. "The Brotherhood and I have been discussing it at length. We have consulted the scriptures and we believe this Winston may hold the knowledge about what happened to Earth, maybe not in his immediate memory, but somewhere inside him, and that he may also be the key to our race finding its way home. We believe the Mother has brought him here to save us."

The XO scoffed and looked to the Captain with an incredulous stare.

"I'm more interested in this Prometheus man and how he connects back to the AI," Dr Regus said, his thin hands folded on the table. "How did he manage to Linear Cut, and why is Z taking particular interest in him?"

The Captain turned to Lydia. "What were your findings on this?"

As Lydia stood, the holo image of a man with dark hair appeared in the centre of the table. "I was able to capture retina images for each of the people supposedly brought back from the dead before I returned." The holo spun so the entire Consulate could see all angles and profiles of the man's head. "I was also able to locate their identities. This one was named Bastille Moreaux. From what I could find of him, he was born in Paris, 1904. From the age of thirteen, he made money for his family by prostituting himself to rich men in the city until he met and fell in love with a woman named Monique Sanchez. They left Paris and travelled to America where Monique became employed under Bates' Musical Agency. A few years later, in 1934, she suspected Bastille was going to leave her, so she shot him through the head while he took a bath in their hotel suite. She was arrested and sentenced to be hanged. The police became baffled, however, when the body of Bastille disappeared from the crime scene. They never found it."

The holo of Bastille disappeared and the image of a little girl with brown hair appeared, rotating in its place. "This is April Townsend, born in 2042, New York City. She lived with her parents as an only child. She was diagnosed with cancer when she was just three years old and finally died, after years of treatment, when she was eight. Her body also disappeared after death. Her parents made a landmark case against the hospital and won over five million US dollars in compensation. They went on to have two other children, who lived healthy lives."

Lydia strode around the table as the holo of a young man with a gaunt face and dark hair appeared. "And lastly, this is Edward Sparrow. Born in London, 1884. He lived with his mother, father and sister. He contracted tuberculosis and died at the age of seventeen. His body was stolen from the grave and never recovered."

"So what's the connection?" Captain Lu asked.

"That's what we need to find out." The holo of Edward Sparrow disappeared.

"Do you have any ideas at all about who they were trying to collect in… what was it, London Tower?" the General asked.

"Yes, Lieutenant," the XO said, focusing his flinty eyes on her. "Before you managed to screw up the mission by revealing your identity. Do tell us your theory."

"They were headed down into the sub-levels of London Tower," she said, ignoring the XO's comments. "Possibly into the prisons."

"Well that's something," Dr Regus said.

"And how's that, doctor?" the XO asked, breaking his stare at Lydia.

"We can sift through the data to see if any bodies disappeared after their death in that year in that location. It really shouldn't be that many, or that hard to do, providing we have the right data."

The Captain nodded. "We also have what we gleaned from the data processed by the AI Overly Watchful. Together, that should be enough."

Dr Regus clapped his hands together and rubbed. "Right then. I'll get right on that. Then we might have more of a clue about their connection."

*

After a lunch of protein gruel alone in her room, Lydia took the afternoon to visit Winston. He was now allowed to roam the ship as he liked, yet she found him in his quarters, staring at the rippling lake depicted on the tempurhull.

"I don't like how they look at me," he said when she asked him why he hadn't gone off exploring. "They're scared of me. It makes me feel…" he thought for the right word. "Monstrous."

She knew how he felt, but said nothing. Instead, she persuaded him to join her in one of holodomes in the unused part of the ship. The combat training programmes were specially uploaded for her personal use, and she quickly enticed him into a duel, pitting her upgraded human strength and wit against his AI synthetic. Hours passed swiftly and enjoyably but ended prematurely when she was called to see Dr Regus.

The doctor was speaking with General Shaw and Captain Lu as she entered the Brain – a series of research labs located in the stern of the ship. This unfortunate location led to the popular saying the Consulate has its brain in its arse when anyone criticised how things were run.

An IQ test was among numerous aptitude exams that the children of the Hyperborea had to take in order to ascertain what talents and skills could be put to best use on the ship. Those who showed the most promise in an intellectual area were sent to the Brain to be taught by the best minds on the ship and would then grow up to – hopefully – think up ways to get the human race out of the swirling toilet of demise that it found itself in. The other children were also educated, of course, but each to their own level and ability. Lydia wasn't Brain smart but had been considered one of the brightest in her class, before she was chosen to become the next li at just nine years old. That was one of the tests all children had to take, but they had yet to find a child of the new generation with those particular traits. And that made them all nervous. If she were to die, the power would be lost.

In a side office, far from the straining minds of those working in the central Brain, the holo of an old man appeared above a desk. The man was Caucasian, pale and looked totally unremarkable in every way. Except his grey eyes. They were stone.

"This is Thomas Mace," Dr Regus said, gesturing with a hand. "He went missing from London Tower's Bellmarsh prison in 2310 and was never seen again. He was the only prisoner to ever go missing."

"Was he alive?" Captain Lu asked, rounding on the image, inspecting it as though it might reveal some clue. From the corner, the General's eyes narrowed on the gaunt face.

"Bellmarsh kept its inmates unconscious in a virtual cognitive correction programme. No one actually saw the man dead, so he was never declared so, only escaped. The records show, however, that his heart stopped before his disappearance, which the prison attributed to the disconnection of his vitals chip. Also, the few guards they had on that day were attacked and left unconscious and that the doors leading out were opened using a guard's key."

Lydia nodded and looked up from the image. The doctor had a particularly satisfied grin on his face, as though it was all a giant game or puzzle just waiting to be solved. "That makes sense. All of the guards would have been dealing with the security breach."

"The dinosaur you told us about?" the General asked.

Lydia nodded and began circling the image of the man. Why him? "The security breach served as a distraction to get him out. But Prometheus wouldn't have known about that. How could he have?"

"That's not all," Dr Regus said. "I believe I've found a possible connection." Lydia stopped and turned to the man. Captain Lu had done the same. He gestured for them both to sit and they did so, waiting eagerly for him to speak.

"This Thomas Mace was imprisoned for the rape and slaughter of three children," he said. "Before he was imprisoned he had a wife and a child, a little boy, whom it reported he also sexually assaulted, frequently and most invasively. The wife of Mace changed her and the boy's name to her maiden name of Tempton following the conviction of her husband. The boy grew up and eventually had a son of his own, who grew up and had a son himself. That boy's name was Giles Tempton, Mace's great-great grandson."

Standing, Dr Regus began to pace, like a detective revealing the insidious plot from some crime novel. "After the little girl, April Townsend had died and her body vanished, her parents had two other children. One of those was a girl they named Stefanie. Stefanie also had two children. One of those had another child, who had a child, who had a child, who had a child and so on, until a woman named Jennifer Coulter was born in the year 3590." He paused briefly. "After Bastille Moreaux left Paris, his sister moved to Germany and married a German man. She had children of her own, who had children, who had children and so on, until a man named Rane Weisburg was born."

"Okay," General Shaw interrupted shortly. "Mind getting to the point any time soon?"

The doctor made a sour face. "These relatives, Giles Tempton, Jennifer Coulter and Rane Weisburg, were all connected by one particular entity. Each held a place on the board of Life Corporation. Coincidence? I think not, my friends."

"No. It most certainly is not a coincidence," General Shaw said. His face was stoic, but in his eyes, the ghosts of his past lingered. They had all heard the infamous tale of General Nathan Shaw and how he came to be on the Hyperboria.

The doctor waved his hand and two more faces appeared in the rotating holo – an old man with thin hair and a high collar that gathered up the skin of his neck, and a black woman with a stern expression and a hard mouth. Regus pointed to them, his finger disappearing into the holographic head of the man. "These were the other board members of Life Corp at the time, which, as it happens, was also at the time of the Reset. Meet Jetson Kay and Dorian Knightvam." He looked at the General almost awkwardly. "Dorian Knighvam's maiden name was Shaw."

The Captain seemed to make the connection before Lydia did because she turned to the General.

"I don't understand," Lydia said. "What are you saying?"

"Knightvam was my mother's aunt," the General said calmly. "Her and my mother had never even met because of a long-standing feud between Knightvam and her sister, my grandmother. They hated each other, and even though Miranda... my mother... worked for Precision Arms, a subsidiary of Life Corp, my great aunt had nothing to do with helping her get there. In fact, she probably didn't even know she existed. I always suspected Life Corp was involved in the destruction of Thebes."

"So who's this Jetson Kay?" Lydia said, pointing to the other rotating holo head.

"That was the chairman of the board. He is a little more elusive. He was adopted as a baby and never knew his parents. He made his way up the ladder from the streets using less than savoury tactics. To be honest, every one of the board shows questionable morals in their behaviour. But after a little digging, I found out who his parents were... just a couple of v-junkies, but I traced them back on a hunch and found I was correct in my prediction that Edward Sparrow was, in fact, one of Kay's ancestors.

"The boy Prometheus brought back from 1901," Lydia said.

"That's right." The holo images evaporated and Dr Regus joined them around the desk. "Now we've found the connection we can start to compile a list of suspects that could have been brought back from Dorian Knightvam's family line, as we can now assume that Prometheus, for whatever reason, is bringing back relatives of the Life Corp board."

Captain Lu's face became a picture of unease. "You mean one of Nathan's own relatives could be among those Prometheus brought back?" Everyone knew Captain Lu was in love with the General and had been for a very long time – everyone except the General, of course.

The doctor's silence answered the question more pointedly than any words could have.

"What about the baby?" Lydia said, aware of the shadow that seemed to have descended over the room. "He brought back the baby first of all."

Dr Regus shook his head. "I don't think that has anything to do with it. Probably a practice attempt before Prometheus brought back a fully-grown adult. It's what I would have done, had I been in his situation. The conditions of Edward Sparrow's death were exactly what Prometheus was looking for... a body that had died whole, recently and young. All seeming coincidental, but I think not. This particular series of events in Earth's history could be the key to unlocking what really led to the Reset."

"Well, what happened to him? The baby, I mean. Did you find any information about him?" Despite what Regus said, there was a niggling in Lydia's gut that told her differently.

"There was no information on him, I'm afraid." The doctor then looked up at her and smiled a pitying smile that made her want to punch him.

The Captain stood. "So, like suspected, we now know for certain there's a link between the Reset, Prometheus and Life Corp. But where do AI and Z fit into it?"

Dr Regus shrugged. "I don't even have conjecture at this point."

"Maybe Winston would have some ideas?" Lydia offered. He'd proven he was willing to help them.

The Captain shook her head firmly. "I don't want him involved. I don't want him to know about any of this until we know for certain he's not feeding this information back to Z... wittingly or otherwise."

*

By the time Lydia returned to her quarters, the setting temperhull sun was lodged between the horizon of a glowing orange desert. She removed her official uniform and put on a pair of loose-fitting pants, made from cultured synthetic fibres, and a thermo tank top. She flopped onto her bed and stared at the bulkhead until the sun finally set beneath dunes, turning the sand into a sea of glittering rubies for just a few moments before the image reset and night sky appeared with a half-moon beginning to rise over a jungle canopy.

It was her stomach that finally persuaded her to move and she made her way to the mess to collect a bowl of protein gruel. It was more crowded and off-putting than usual, but the queue for food parted for her. On the return, she ran into Daneel, almost right into him. She just managed to use her reflexes to refrain from spilling her hot gruel all over him as they collided around a corner. When she saw it was him, however, she wished she hadn't bothered. She grunted a curse about how he should look where he's going and charged on down the corridor.

"Chen," he called after her. He soon caught up and began walking beside her.

"What?" Her tone even made her feel cold.

"You can fool everyone else but you can't fool me," he said.

"You can't fool a fool." She quickened her pace. "Just leave me alone."

He ran ahead a blocked the way, forcing her to stop. "When are you going to forgive me?"

Part Indian descent, Daneel was considered very handsome, by most… if they had eyes. He had smooth brown skin and warm dark pools for eyes. They stared at her like an injured animal. Hyperboreans with Indian heritage were rare, numbering less than one hundred. Although his intelligence levels weren't as high as others, he had been asked to donate sperm more than any other man in the militia to vary-up the gene pool.

Lydia pushed him out her way and continued.

"I'm not going to give up," he said, following. "Not until you forgive me. Not for me. I don't care about me, but I need you to believe that I didn't mean it. I need you to believe that I don't blame you."

"Some things can't be unsaid, Daneel." She hadn't meant to sound so wounded.

When they turned the corner, Winston sat waiting outside her quarters, crouched low to the floor and staring at his own feet, which were bare. He turned to them as they approached and looked from Lydia to Daneel.

Daneel made a noise in his throat that to Lydia almost sounded like a growl. "What do you want, tin-man."

Winston stood. "Sorry. You're busy." He turned to leave.

Lydia grabbed his arm. "No, I'm not. Daneel was leaving." She opened her cabin door and stood aside to let him in.

Daneel stared from the other side, Lydia's arm blocking his entry.

"Chen, we need to talk."

"You've said enough."

His face seemed to melt as the door slid shut, leaving him outside in the hall. Lydia turned and placed the tray of gruel down on the table in the corner, ignoring the guilt building in her stomach.

Winston was observing her collection from Earth. "That was... intense," he said, picking up a stone. "Do you couple with him?"

"What?" Lydia said, snatching the item. She'd collected it from a riverbed in Canada at the turn of the sixteenth century.

He looked confused. "Sorry. Is that not right? I mean, do you copulate?"

"We... I... that is none of your business. And will you please stop touching my things." She grabbed a wooden box from his curious mits. He then homed in on a cylindrical item placed next to where he'd found the box.

"What's that?"

She swiped the golden case from the side before he had a chance to pick it up, popped off the lid and twisted until a flash of red appeared. "It's called a lip stick. Humans would wear it to make their lips appear flushed, as though they were ready for..." She stopped and placed it back down on the side. "Winston, what are you doing here?"

"I was bored. There's nothing to do. Do you want to fight some more?"

"Tomorrow... maybe. If there's time."

"Did you find out anything new today?" He looked at her in the way he did sometimes, strangely innocently. Especially when staring out from a face that was so chiselled and scowl-y. At once, the guilt came and she considered telling him the truth. She still owed him the answers she'd promised, but rid the thought from her mind.

"Possibly," she said at last. "I'd rather wait to know for sure before I say. If you don't mind?"

He nodded, his face serious. "I trust you." Then he smiled. It was that easy smile she always found so attractive in people because she didn't have an easy smile. It lit a fire behind his eyes. Such life in those eyes.

Her vision drew to the skin-tight thermo tank top he wore – identical to hers. His huge shoulders were almost twice the width of his waist. The deltoids bulged, perfectly rounded and the shadow of his well-carved chest-muscles upon his lean torso caused her to grow warm suddenly. Her vision drew further down, wondering just how functional his synth was.

"Can I try it?" he said.

"What?" She could feel herself blush faintly.

"Your food." He pointed to the bowl of protein gruel sitting on the side. "Can I try a bit?"

She laughed awkwardly. "Sure."

27

The hallway ran cold and white-washed to either side of where Prometheus sat. Strange how different the hospital looked now that he was the one waiting for news, instead of the one dealing it. He thought of how his patients must feel as they roamed the corridors, how their families must agonise, sitting on the same grim chairs, waiting.

Now it was his turn to wait, with hands woven together in front of him as though in prayer. But pray he did not. Perhaps he should. He had never put his faith in a God. But now… something desperate grew within and he found himself hoping there was some transcendental entity out there. If such a being existed, it would surely protect an innocent child.

He stood, paced a few steps before sitting down again. All he wanted was to be in there with her, but they'd told him it wasn't right – not while she gave birth. He'd asked James to be present in his stead, which eased his worry a little. But still, there was that feeling… the overwhelming sense that he was dreaming. As though he were somehow outside of reality.

The scent of Death raped his nostrils suddenly, violently. Stagnant and flesh-worn. It turned his stomach into a soup of dread. Then began the tapping and he jolted at the sound, faint as it was.

It's coming. Something's on its way.

It grew closer and the scent became overpowering to the point that Prometheus swore he saw black curls of the acrid aroma wafting through the shadows. He clutched at his hair, pulling, the thoughts in his skull racing in confused, disjointed circles. Something was about to happen.

Something terrible.

James emerged from the delivery room corridor, shoes echoing with each step. He did not smile. His eyes never once looked up. On his clothes, Prometheus glimpsed blotches of red. Smears and stains, as though James had hurriedly attempted to clean himself.

His stomach lurched.

Remember.

James walked through molasses, as though time had slowed to prolong the agony of the moment he knew would soon be upon him. He thought it nothing but his fear playing tricks on the mind, but then James simply stopped, foot mid-step, hanging ready for the floor to meet it. His face remained a picture of gloom, with its down-turned gaze and a single wisp of red hair frozen mid-swing across a sweat-slick forehead.

Prometheus blinked, thinking his brain would soon rectify the confusion. It was the stress, nothing more. But his friend did not move again. So, he stood, wrinkled shirt falling untucked over his thighs, collar loosened and damp with sweat. He staggered towards the frozen man.

"James." His voice whispered against the silence, the type of silence that was deafening. Not even his own shoes made a sound as he stepped upon the tiles. His friend did not respond, simply stood as if wax. However, someone did.

"Prometheus."

Prometheus swung about at once. The corridor stretched dark and empty behind him. Nothing more.

It came again. "Prometheus."

The sound was strange. It felt as though it didn't touch his ears at all, rather came from within his own head, clear as church bells on a Sunday.

"We have come for you."

He shuffled back against the wall, clutching his head.

"We answer your call. We answer your plea." The voice, he realised, was not a single voice, but thousands of sighing echoes speaking as one, crawling across the roof of his skull.

"What do you want?" he called out. The room suddenly began to darken. The walls stretched, stirred with shadows. From within the shade, two dark holes appeared, bottomless and terrible, then beneath came a smile of sharp white. A scythe of onyx cut the darkness and, as though through a portal sliced into the wall, Death itself glided out, towering eight foot tall and cloaked in nightmares.

"We are here," it sighed.

Terror held Prometheus tightly, binding his limbs to where he stood. His eyes widened as he attempted, but failed, to speak. Death's billowing cloak whirled around the skull in tresses of dark flame, the hood hovering half over the gaping eye holes that sank forever down, down and down into the depths of eternity.

"Remember," it said, sharp jaws unmoving. It was not a question. It was a command.

And then, Prometheus did. He remembered it all. He remembered his quest to conquer death; he remembered travelling through time with Edward. He remembered pulling more souls back from the beyond and travelling so far that he even stood among the stars on a distant planet in a distant time.

They said I betrayed them, and I would be punished.

The planet beneath his feet had shaken and a flash of light swallowed everything. Then blackness. And, of course, he remembered her – Sarah. Dead. That worm of dread that burrowed deep. He knew it all along. He knew the truth.

Staggering forward, hands curled in demented prayer, Prometheus fell to Death's feet and wept.

Eons went by as he knelt upon the cold floor, his tears flooding the blurred tile until slick. But the sobs eventually subdued, the floor dried and soon followed his eyes. There were no more tears in him to give. So, he curled into a ball, remained still and hoped unconsciousness might take him. But it didn't. Only more memories came – sparks of realisations that had always been there, but blocked off somehow, now as apparent and as certain as the sun.

Edward had brought him here, to the place where he had lived through the worst moment of his. But it was more than that. It wasn't simply the place he'd been brought back to. They'd trapped him inside the exact moment of his wife's death. Imprisoned him there to relive the agony over and over. Each time his heart torn from his chest, only to have it grow again, fresh and ready for another plucking. Each time James told him Sarah was gone, the memories would return, but for only a moment after the blinding agony, and then it was as though it hadn't happened at all. Suddenly, he would be sitting again, waiting for the birth of his child. Again, and again and again. Over and over, he felt his heart break with the keenness of how it had shattered the first time.

Edward said Prometheus would regret betraying them, and regret it he did. He regretted ever digging up that demon, back in London, in the rain, so very long ago.

How long have I been here?

"Four minutes," Death answered, inside his thoughts.

And then there was him. The festering creature that had snatched Sarah away to begin with. Death. The Reaper. The Beast. "And how many times have I endured those four minutes?" he asked, keeping his face to the floor.

"Three-hundred and ninety-four million, four-hundred and sixty-one thousand, five-hundred and seventy-five times," Death replied exactly.

A small noise escaped Prometheus's throat.

How is that even possible?

"A pocket loop-dimension was created."

"And how do I leave?" He could still not bring himself to stand or to even look at the creature before him.

"We can guide you."

"You can take me home?"

"We can, or we can take you to the truth… or we can take you to your Sarah."

Prometheus looked up at once, eyes quivering in his ruddy face. Craning over, vulturine, Death grinned down at him.

☐

28

Dr Rane Weisberg was already under sedation when Norma entered. He lay flat upon the neurobed with her new assistant, Felicity, hovering over him. The girl looked up and smiled in her mousey way. It was the closed mouth smile of someone with little self-confidence. Norma checked the chart screen by his bed, then the sleeping man's vitals. "Was he much trouble going under?" she asked.

Felicity shook her head. "Not at all." Her voice was a high-pitched whisper.

Somehow Norma doubted that. Dr Weisberg was renowned for his sexual harassment of anything that was young and even mildly attractive. He had on more than one occasion placed an inappropriate and sweaty hand in places that made Norma cringe. She said nothing, though. No one did. He was a board member and could do whatever the hell he liked, while they were all expendable. But as he lay unconscious, naked under a thin medical gown, with gravity pulling at the sides of his ageing face so that it appeared mask-like, she was reminded by the rhythmic beating of his heart that he, like everyone else, was just human. Not an all-powerful being, but human. And a fragile one at that.

Norma stood at the top of the bed, preparing the man's headjack. Right now, the balance of power had shifted. Right now, his life was in her hands.

Despite being a Grade A sleaze, Dr Weisberg was one the most brilliant physicists alive. Norma remembered studying his advanced Theory of Unity at university and being blown away by the fervour with which he pursued – almost hunted – the answers to life's most perplexing questions. He had such passion. Upon meeting him for the first time she was flustered and beyond nervous. She had waited for hours late into the evening, just hoping to catch him as he exited a meeting in the executive quarter, only to be shoved aside by his assistants as the man himself ranted to one of them without even noticing her. When they finally did meet, he slapped her on the rear and told her to get him a coffee.

Norma was aware that people had off days and had at first made excuses for her former intellectual hero. But the more they worked together, the more she came to realise, while he was one of the finest minds she had encountered in her lifetime, he was a poor excuse for a human being. He was self-absorbed and narcissistic to the point of having a god-complex.

This was all during her first few months at Life Corp, of course. Back then, she had been scouted to intern at the London office because of a paper she had published in the Parisian Science Journal on similarities between synapse activity in the human brain and the teleportation of light particles. Brains were her thing. That was over ten years ago now, and still she doubted if the man even knew her name.

The main connector slotted perfectly into the man's headjack. She tightened, rather roughly and perhaps more carelessly than she should have done. The morning had begun bad and was proving to be the theme of the day. But it was no different than every other morning since her sister had come to stay with her almost three months ago.

How she'd been sucked into Sayi's drama again she didn't know. Wait, she did know. It was emotional blackmail, as always. If her sister could just see things from her point of view it would be different. But that would never happen because Sayi was as stubborn and pig-headed as their father.

"Have you initiated REM stimulation?"

"He's just reached depth six," Felicity said, checking the monitor.

Norma nodded, waved away the vitals screen and gestured the resonance imaging graph into existence, showing in perfect clarity the activity of Dr Weisberg's beautiful brain.

Sayi could never understand how Norma could work there. They argued about it constantly. Sayi believed the company was the route of all the CommonWorld's problems, which was absurd. There were many things Life Corp had a hand in that she was far from comfortable with – its weapons subsidiary for one – but she told her sister what she told herself: "It's better to change things from within the belly of the beast than not at all." Sayi called her an invert, spineless. That got to her the most. Perhaps that was because, if Norma was honest with herself, she agreed with her.

"Depth seven," Felicity said.

Norma placed her fingers on the navigation pad of the holoscreen and typed in the code: Great things are done. And after a few moments, came the reply...

When men and mountains meet.

"Good," Norma nodded. "He's in. Launch Hydra."

*

In his Scenario, the smell of fresh coffee stirred Rane from the blackness of sleep. The slow hypnotic rocking of the cabin told him the sea was mostly calm. Upon opening his eyes, Jeffery was smiling down at him, his blonde hair tousled and his blue eyes sparkling as ever.

"I made coffee," he said.

"Yes, I can smell it." He reached out and pulled Jeffery into bed with him, curling them both up in the clean white sheets. They stayed there for a while, Rane slowly drifting back off to sleep.

"Our coffee will get cold," Jeffery said just as it threatened to take him, jolting him back to wakefulness.

"Fuck our coffee," he slurred, "I'd rather have a cup of you." He pulled Jeffery close and ran a hand down his smooth torso. "Oh," he said in a whisper, "I see you'd rather be full of me, too."

"We don't have time, Rane." He pulled his hand away. "The race begins in less than an hour."

"Then I suppose I'll have to fuck you quickly." He bit down on Jeffery's neck.

"I'm serious." He pulled free and stood, naked. "Get up. Coffee's on the side."

"Fine," Rane shouted after him as he left. "Don't expect me to do you later. You've lost cock privileges."

The waters were blue and clear and calm, as Rane had suspected. A good day for a race. People from all over the CommonWorld crowded the large harbour of the French Riviera as the sun smiled down, turning the water to azure diamonds. Mostly, spectators filled the bleachers arranged along the docks, with the wealthier among them separated by a wall of guards dressed in black. He spotted some of his family among them. His mother sat under a parasol held by one of her man-slaves, while his father was propped upon an oxygen tank mixed with today's drug of choice, a mask attached to his face like a giant leech. His sister, he thanked, was nowhere to be seen.

Everyone was smiling, eating ice-cream and drinking chilled ice tea in the sweltering heat. In the harbour, a sea of masts rose like a canopy-less forest as the sleek yachts and sailboats began to pull out and prepare for the day of races. Rane's, of course, was a yacht. Not just a yacht, it was the most luxurious yacht on the water. The Cock's Crow, it was named, much to the upset of his family, but that only made it ever-more appropriate. Most referred to their sea vessels as her, but Rane never had. It was clear The Cock's Crow was a strapping young man, with a long white prow that thrust hard over the wet oceans, lean with a sleek bow of gleaming black glass and a stern that wouldn't quit. Three long masts stood tall and fully erect, ready for the wind to fill his sails, bulging them with power. Flashes of red slashed the sides, and on that juicy stern, the silhouette of a crowing cock was painted.

Rane looked at the other yachts – his "competition". This will be a breeze, he decided.

"A stiff one before we go?" Jeffery asked, handing him a tall glass of vodka and tonic as he leaned lazily against the wheel in the cockpit.

Rane took a sip and kissed Jeffery passionately. "Let's show these fuckers how it's done."

The Cock's Crow was luxurious to be sure, but it was compact enough to be successfully crewed by just the two of them. They had been doing so for almost five years since they met at their parents' country club in Cannes.

They had hit it off almost instantly, becoming the best of friends and then, eventually, the best of lovers. They brought The Cock's Crow smoothly along the harbour and stationed it amid the row of competitors, bobbing on the crystal waters. Rane changed into a loose white shirt and returned to Jeffery frowning fiercely.

"What's the matter?" He didn't want anything to ruin their day.

Jeffery nodded towards the yacht stationed next to them. "Don't get angry. She's only doing it to get under your skin, so don't let it."

"What do you mean?" Rane looked over. On the side of the yacht was painted the name Sea Whore and standing in the cockpit, waving over and smiling gleefully, was his sister, Mara, her blonde hair blowing around her face in the breeze.

"What is she doing here?" He felt his face begin to redden with rage.

"Ignore her," Jeffery said, sliding a hand into his. Rane pushed the implant in his wrist and his eDeck beamed out, the holoscreen floating above his hand. "Call Mara," he instructed it. Within seconds Mara's face appeared, her smile still plastered upon her heart-shaped face.

"Rane, my darling brother, how are you? What a wonderful day for sailing." Her eyes were ferocious with enjoyment.

"Cut the bull. What are you playing at?" He was in no mood for her games.

"I haven't the slightest clue as to what you're talking about, my dear brother," she replied in her mocking way. "Do excuse me. My Sea Whore needs some attention. Good luck in the race." Her face flickered out of existence.

Jeffery squeezed his hand. "Let it go."

"How can I? You know what she's like. This can only end badly. Like the time the whole family went fly-skiing last winter, do you remember? She almost told everyone…" he stopped.

"That you had sex," Jeffery said bluntly.

"Even the thought of it makes me… I can't think of it. I was young and impressionable and she's always been a manipulative cunt, just like our mother."

"Her vessel is aptly named then," Jeffery joked.

"But that winter, it was like she wanted to expose what we'd done, even though it was just once, and years ago. Can you imagine the scandal? Either that or she lured me onto that frosty ledge for another reason. I still don't know what happened."

"Oh, Rane," Jeffery laughed. "Now you just sound paranoid. You fell and broke your leg, that's all."

"You don't know what she's capable of." He ran his hands through his mass of hair and let out a moan. The day was ruined.

One wasn't raised by one's own family in the Weisberg clan. That was left to schools and universities, leaving the family free to pursue the important things in life, like country clubs and highballs. The truth was, that up until he'd finished his undergraduate degree, finally returning home before resuming his post-grad education, he barely knew his sister at all. She was a stranger to him. They had seen one another during holidays when they were both at home at their family's estate, but even then, they had followed their own separate interests and barely noticed each other. It was when he had returned for their uncle's funeral that they become... closer.

Uncle Col had never married and had no children of his own, so naturally the portion of the family money that went to him after their grandparents died went to their father. Mara was staying with him at the time. Apparently, they had become quite close over the past months and she was terribly saddened by his passing. That was years ago. Since then, their father was becoming increasingly frail and doctors suspected he was not long for this world. Mara was currently keeping close to him, staying at the estate where she could "take care" of him.

"I might not know what she's like," Jeffery said. "But I know you. I know that we're going to win this race, celebrate with champagne and drugs until the early hours while we rub everyone's noses in the fact they lost... including Mara's. And then you're going to make love to me so hard that tomorrow I won't even be able to sit down. That's how today will go. Now, as you said, let's show these fuckers how it's done."

Just as Jeffery said, the race was indeed won by them and all attempts by Mara to thwart their victory were diverted. They sailed over the finish well ahead of the Sea Whore, which came in second with her team of hired crew. Rane's parents cheered in the bleachers, as did the spectators. Then he and Jeffery celebrated by taking each other in a hellacious haze of alcohol and drugs aboard The Cock's Crow. Night soon fell and a cool breeze reached them as they bobbed half a mile off the coast, surrounded by dark water and the stars. Jeffery lay naked in the crook of his armpit, covered with seamen and sheer fabric, as Rane listened to the hypnotic sound of the ocean – the splashes against the hull, the dull creaks, the quietness of being completely alone. It seemed so right. He wanted that moment to never end. So, of course, it did.

"You know none of this is real," a voice said.

The sound sent a shock through Rane so that he froze perfectly still.

"It never happened like this," the voice said, coming from a figure in the shadow of the open cabin door. The man stepped forward into the light of the celestial bodies flowing like liquid silver through the windows.

It can't be. He was looking at himself.

The perfect double of Rane Weisberg strode over, wearing a pair of tailored trousers and a white vest, his hair slicked back.

"Who are you?" His voice struggled to escape as he smoothly untangled himself from the sleeping Jeffery and climbed from the bed. His double eyed his nakedness, raised an eyebrow, then breezed through the door into the main part of the vessel. When Rane followed, he found himself pouring a drink – his drink, vodka tonic.

"Want one?"

"You're offering me my own drink? On my own fucking boat? I have a gun."

Rane's double laughed and handed him the drink. "No, you don't."

Reluctantly, he took the glass and sat on the white sofa next to himself.

"You know this isn't how it happened," the double said. "Today never went this way."

"Oh?" Rane replied sardonically, now very much convinced this was all a drug-fuelled dream and he was actually still in bed with Jeffery. "Pray, how did it go?"

"Well, for a start you never won the race today. Nobody won, in fact. There was a terrible accident and Jeffery died as a result."

Rane went suddenly cold.

"I say accident," his double went on, "but what I mean is that Jeffery wasn't the intended target. We were. Mara thought a yachting accident would look most natural for claiming your inheritance."

"That's absurd. I would—"

"Kill her? Yes, that was the problem. You did try to kill her after it happened, and was disinherited as a result. Your parents didn't believe a word of it. Mara got it all and you got nothing. And on top of that, we lost Jeffery."

"You keep saying we." Rane suddenly felt confused and exposed in his nakedness. He wrapped a blanket around his shoulders.

"This is a Scenario constructed from your memory of a day that happened over sixty years ago. You had it changed so the day would play out the way you wished it went, not how it really went, partly to ease your guilt and partly because the new day is your idea of the perfect day. Couple that with the major hit of serotonin. It's recreational… mostly."

"Well it was lovely speaking with you, but I'm afraid I should wake up now." Rane rose from the sofa.

"It's a virtual Scenario, I told you. I'm not built in as a character. I'm an intruder, a foreign body. I can do whatever I want, no rules apply to me. I'll prove it." The double smiled a wicked smile. "I just made your dick four inches bigger."

"What?"

"Check, go on."

Rane dropped the blanket and looked down to see his penis was indeed four inches longer and had a deal more girth than only a moment before. "Fuck me."

"Indeed."

"Who are you?" Rane asked, unable to stop staring at his penis.

"I'm you. And I've come here to kill you."

The shot was silent, but it tore through Rane's chest with ease, exiting his back and splintering the oak panelling behind him. Blood ran from the wound above his left nipple. He looked down at it in horror, then back to the figure of himself standing before him.

"Bitch," he said, before slumping to the deck.

Rane's double took off all his clothes and walked to where the sleeping Jeffery still lay serenely in bed. He climbed into the mass of blankets and cushions and slid an arm around his shoulder.

Jeffery stirred. "Is it morning?"

"Not yet," Rane's double replied. "Go back to sleep. Lots to do tomorrow."

☐

29

Life aboard the lifeship Hyperborea changed for Ystil.3 following his talk with General Shaw. No longer confined to his room, he was granted the freedom to roam the Underbelly, talk with whom he chose and generally do as he pleased, with the exception of wandering into residential areas and visiting the hangar where the Black Betty was kept.

He took to following Lydia on her resumed duties and they quickly found themselves in sort of a daily routine. Ystil.3 liked routines, as did Lydia, apparently. It was easier to be with her than the few other humans he'd warily approached; they made no attempt to hide the fact he was not wanted on their ship. With Lydia, it was different. He wasn't made to feel like a wolf among sheep. Or was it a sheep among wolves?

In the mornings, as distinguished by the tempurhull scenery, they met for breakfast in her cabin, set up on a small tray that ejected from the many panels in the bulkhead – everything within her room was concealed within panels for maximum space efficiency. They both sat on the small bed while Lydia ate what everyone else aboard ate for breakfast and dinner – white slop. Lydia had playfully attempted to force-feed it to him after he expressed his disgust, but he'd dodged her spoon and it landed over the fresh sheets. He was glad he required no such nourishment.

After breakfast, they would venture to the empty holodome in the cold, vacant part of the ship to spar in dramatic landscapes and formats. Icicles formed around the dilapidated ducts and torn panelling, but soon enough the duel would heat their bodies until the sweat rolled freely over clammy skin.

The holodome could take the form of a hundred different environments, all chosen by Lydia for their specific training attributes and beauty. Some days they decided to battle in ancient Rome, with the Coliseum erect around them, as though they were gladiators of old. The detailing of the holopraphic immersion programme even went as far as to allow a light breeze to graze Ystil.3's bronze armoured arms. Other days they chose an underwater world with an emerald palace and rainbow coloured fish, or the dusty moon of Galileo with its forest of giant standing stone anthropoids, whose origins were a mystery. Or there was his personal favourite; atop a spinning white disc that floated in the dense vacuum of space, surrounded by blinking star systems and distant glowing planets. There, confined to the disc, they fought.

At first, he hadn't wanted to fight her, but after Lydia loaded the first training programme and the dark, gunmetal dome became a blue sky, with fifty mutant samurai warriors standing upon a grassy meadow, he became instantly intrigued. Each warrior wore a red mask with a cruel grimace painted in black. They held swords of gleaming steel and displayed reflexes so quick that they appeared as nothing but blurs as they attacked. Lydia had fended them off with a smooth and impressive display of acrobatics and deadly blows, and within minutes he was helping her, surprised to discover that his own synth reflexes were sharp and his muscles powerful. His synth had been pre-loaded with various fighting styles, and each was readily available for him to access.

Despite her attempts to conceal it, Lydia was impressed by his efforts, and soon each of them was sure they could best the other. Ystil.3 had ashamedly, yet truthfully, reminded her that he had already shown he could win against her. To which Lydia reminded him that she was under the effects of the Tell serum.

"I doubt your pre-loaded synthetic skills can come close to my tried and tested, learned-by-broken-bones expertise," she said with a smile. Of course, Ystil.3 disagreed. So, there was only one way to settle it.

Lydia used her lightness of foot to keep him on his toes, dancing around and imitating the footwork of classical Nova Scrimia swordplay, with the flexibility and methodology of Bartitsu and hints of SCARS aggression in response to Ystil.3's own offensive style. She dodged him and retaliated like a ghost with fists of rock, and on their first duel, Lydia won with a startling side-kick to his chest, sending him sliding across the holodome floor, plummeting over the edge of the space disc and floating into oblivion.

The second duel she won also, but the third was his, using his bulk and weight to continuously put her on the defensive with a mixed martial arts strategy, leaving her no room for manoeuvre and no time to flit and flutter away. Still, he didn't use his full force. He didn't want to hurt her. Not again.

It quickly became a competition and they added different and challenging landscapes in which to duel. By the end of their first session both were exhausted and slick with sweat. Lydia had a score of nine and Winston eight. A win was defined as being able to deliver a death-blow to the opponent. Obviously undelivered, but able to do so if it were a true fight.

This was how they spent most mornings unless Lydia had li duties to perform.

On this particular morning, when Lydia was required by the Consulate, Ystil.3 was feeling particularly bored. He hadn't yet explored the Boroughs and the thought of another morning confined to his bunker 'o' tedium was enough to make him want to send himself back into foetal mode. So, instead of simply waiting for her to become available, he decided to discover the levels above the Underbelly by himself.

Perched upon a mount, he soared through the mazes and gangways of the Underbelly, the strip-lights flashing above and the recycled air gusting in his face. The machine thrummed as he leaned over the metal body, his feet lodged securely in the stirrup footwells and his hands deep inside the navigation wells. Most of the humans took pleasure in riding the mounts, he'd observed, and strange as it was, a thrill shuddered over him as swerved the hairpin curves of the ascending gangways. It just felt good to just go somewhere, anywhere, even if it was only twenty levels up.

Upon reaching the Boroughs' security checkpoint, he was instructed to dismount. Mounts were prohibited in the Boroughs, the guard told him bluntly, who then called in on his comm to a voice on the other end.

"I got the AI here. Wants to go into the Boroughs. It got clearance for that?" He glared at Ystil.3 with narrowed eyes.

"The AI has clearance," the woman's voice said on the other end of the comm. "It needs a chaperone, though. Any takers?" The guards looked at each other and said nothing. One made a face and another turned his back completely.

"I don't need a guide," Ystil.3 said. "Really, I won't get lost."

The guard stared blankly. "Daneel. Get your ass up here, General's got a job for you." The others began to laugh.

Ystil.3 recognised the name, then recognised the man himself as he appeared from the hatch behind the checkpoint. When he raised his head to see Ystil.3 standing there, his face twisted with disgust.

"This needs a chaperone," the main guard told him. "Seems it wants to have a look around the Boroughs and General Shaw said it's to be given a guided tour."

"Why do I have to do it? It makes my skin crawl."

Ystil.3 stood patiently, aware he was being insulted.

"Me and McCall can't leave our post. And since you're always looking for new ways to climb into General Shaw's rectum, I figured showing his new toy around would be the perfect opportunity."

Daneel scowled as he pulled outer shield plating over his thermosuit. "Fuck you, Lee. At least I don't have to suck McCall's dick just to get first guard duty." He then began loading himself with various weapons.

"I'd rather suck McCall's than yours. Poor Gutter has to make do with your limp cock. Maybe that's why the girls you date drop you for metal." He glanced at Ystil.3. "At least it's hard."

The guards roared with laughter and Daneel walked off, through the now open security gate.

Ystil.3 caught up with him but remained a pace behind. The man was tall, and powerfully built, with thick dark hair and a jaw too big for his face. It gave him a constant glower. He led Ystil.3 into a large atrium, light and airy, contrasting with the narrow Underbelly causeways. A clear blue sky brushed with light clouds floated above. If it weren't for the occasional blur in the tempurhull holoscreens, Ystil.3 might've thought they were back on Earth. The atrium itself was almost empty, save for a few staring humans behind kiosks, and the occasional holographic tree that flickered in disillusion. It seemed the desired effect was to give the impression they were in a park. Ystil.3, however, wasn't convinced and he doubted the humans would be either.

"A shot of kick," Daneel said to the man behind the nearest kiosk. The man poured steaming brown liquid into a white cup and handed it over expressionlessly. Daneel took it, leaned on the counter and sipped his tiny drink as if Ystil.3 wasn't even there. The atrium was beginning to fill with humans pouring in from an open hatch. Some eyed Ystil.3 while others didn't even notice him, heading straight towards the kiosks.

"Are we going to go somewhere else?" he finally asked.

The man drained the last of his drink and placed the cup on the counter. His eyes rolled over to Ystil.3 and he made a snorting noise in his throat before turning his back.

"So that's a no then?"

More hatches opened around the hall and a horde of humans that trampled in.

"Is it a parade?" Ystil.3 said, eagerly waiting for someone to start playing the trombone. He'd seen that in the Earth Files.

"No," replied Daneel flatly. His eyes avoided Ystil.3, focused on the people flooding in. "Just maintenance worker break."

The exhausted expressions on their grime-caked faces gave it away. They began forming lines at the refreshment kiosks while tables and benches emerged from hatches in the panelled floor, rising up in the centre of the hall. They were quickly filled with trays of slop and cups of brown liquid.

"So everyone has their allotted brake?" he asked, attempting to get some sort of verbal interaction going.

Daneel took in a deep breath, then exhaled loudly. "Yeah," he said, finally throwing Ystil.3 a contemptuous glance. "Twelve working food halls on the ship, each for the twelve different work sectors. You getting all this down, tin-man?"

None of the people in the food hall were younger than their twenties. In fact, since he'd arrived, Ystil.3 hadn't once seen a human child. "Where are all the kids? You must have children aboard."

Something likened to anger, but somehow more vitriolic, passed over Daneel's face and his eyes finally rested on him for more than a second. Ystil.3 found himself wanting the man to turn away again, certain his stare was going to melt his face.

"We're almost extinct," Daneel said. "But yeah, there are kids. Only they get educated in the Primary sector and assessed for their gene grade. Till that happens, they stay with the guardians."

Ystil.3 nodded as if he understood. "What's a gene grade?"

Daneel rolled his eyes. "When we're born we're given our birth gene grade from tests that assess brain function, muscle development, fertility and to determine how we will grow." He sounded like he was reading from script. "Those who will grow strong and healthy and fertile are graded A1, those who will grow to be weak and infertile and generally a drain on the human race are graded F6. Grades vary for those in-between, according to strength and weaknesses. Then, after education, another assessment is taken to adjust the rank. Once you've gotten your final gene grade, that's it for life, and you're told where you'd be most valuable on the ship."

Ystil.3 couldn't help but see the similarities with his own life as a DataCom Unit. No one had asked him what he'd wanted to do with his existence either. "Sounds… efficient," he said, watching the humans gather at the benches, taking the weight of their feet and eating the same white slop Lydia ate three times a day. "So what gene grade are you?"

"You can't just go around asking people for their gene grade," he said. "It's junk-fucking rude."

"Oh. Sorry." It was like he'd just asked the man for a rectal scan or something. "I just wondered, so I can gauge what you determine to be strong and intelligent."

Daneel glared, then looked around as if to make sure no one was listening. "A3," he mumbled. "A for physical attributes and fertility and three…" he paused to clear his throat, "…for intelligence." He then walked off into the crowd of humans. "You coming, tin-man?" Ystil.3 hurried after him.

"It doesn't matter what gene grade you are, everyone has to contribute to rebuilding the race," Daneel continued freely, dodging through the humans. Ystil.3 followed his path, trying to keep from getting distracted by the haggard faces that surrounded them. "We don't have to have families, but it's mandatory to be a donor when called up, or be inseminated… although most feel it's their duty to volunteer whenever they can. If you want to raise your kid, fine, but if not they go to the Primary."

"Do you have offspring?" Ystil.3 asked, hoping it wasn't offensive to ask.

"Thirty-nine," the man replied. "I don't look after them, but I keep tabs on how they do."

They made their way from the atrium out through a causeway of ventilators until finally the bitter aroma of the food slop faded. The causeway opened out into one of the many sterilisation cubicles that separated various parts of the lifeship. Lydia had told him that viruses were released on a timed and regular basis to keep the humans' immune systems working, but they didn't want anything unknown being spread through the Boroughs, or any part of the Hyperborea. Some of the planets on which they seasonally landed for supplies of minerals and metal ore harboured alien germs and microbes that made the continual use of these sterilisation cubicles necessary.

One of the few planets on which they could dock for supplies was the planet Hyperboria, the lifeship's namesake and planned destination before the Reset. Their ancestors intended to terraform it for colonisation, but without the support from Earth, it remained uninhabitable. It was, however, uniquely rich in source minerals that could be used to create alloys and resources for repairs. Returning there, however, was dangerous because it was one of the few planets the AI knew the humans used, Lydia had told him. They only ever sent mining parties back there, and then only when things got desperate. It was while docked on Hyperboria that the humans had suffered their greatest and deadliest attack all those years ago.

Daneel led Ystil.3 through the cubicle and the purifying mist ejected from the porous walls, spraying over them and drying instantly. They walked on for a while, silent through the residential area of the Maintenance Zone with rows of riveted hatch doors, each numbered in ascending order. All was quiet, the occupants working hard in the engine rooms, hubs and decks. The humans of this level were also responsible for the upkeep of all the ships electronics, from the sterilisation cubicles to the O2 scrubbers, and such things as the human waste disposal units and klicks of lighting and electrical systems.

"Do any humans still choose to live in family units?" Ystil.3 asked, breaking the silence.

"Some do, some don't," Daneel replied somewhat evasively. "Generally, families are viewed as being inefficient and a waste of time. Every day is a fight to survive. Everyone has to do all they can to help ensure we go on living. It's our duty." He walked on until they reached an opening to one of the warren tunnels, then stopped at the open mouth. Inside, the flow of air could almost be mistaken for wind.

Ystil.3 stared into the darkness, spotting the smallest light. Over the noise of the gusting air, a faint humming began to echo off the curved sides. "Where are we going?" he asked. He would have liked to go up and perhaps even visit the bridge.

Daneel stood, stony-faced and staring into the tunnel. "You know what I really don't like?" he said, without turning his head. "I don't like how you spend all your time following Lydia around. That, and your smell."

"My smell? I don't smell." Ystil.3 took a reaffirming whiff of himself.

"That's my point." Daneel turned and closed the gap between them until their noses were half an inch apart. Ystil.3 would have moved back but didn't want to cause offence again. "You don't smell of anything." Daneel's face wrinkled with disgust. "Not even plastic and metal. It's like you're not even there at all, like you don't even exist."

Inside the tunnel, the dot of light expanded and the thrumming grew louder. Something didn't feel right, so deciding he'd been face-to-face with Daneel for long enough, Ystil.3 turned to leave. But as he did something struck him, sending a wave of pain through his sensors and knocking his head back. He frowned and touched his cheek.

Daneel's punch was strong, upgraded. The soldier seethed behind fists, springing from one foot to the other as if preparing for retaliation. The next blow, Ystil.3 saw far in advance but made no move to block it. Nor did he attempt to block the one after, which landed in the soft organic area of his stomach. That one hurt more and he found himself bent double with strips of white pain dancing over his vision. But before there was time to recover, another blow came from behind to the back of his head. He turned, feeling the residual shudder reverberate over his skull, and the hate-filled scowl of a woman he'd never seen before stared back.

More revving mounts emerged from the depths of the warren and the riders surrounded him, each with a metal bar, which they promptly began using in a sustained attack that quickly forced him to the floor. Through it all, as the blows pummeled his flesh and broke his bones, he just lay, waiting for them to decide if he'd had enough, or to send him back to his server. He could have stood and fought back, but he didn't.

By the time they were too exhausted to beat him any longer, Ystil.3's synth was a swollen and bloody heap, the pain so intense that it disrupted his cognitive functions so he couldn't even assess the damage. When he heard the igniting of the mounts, he thought they would just leave him there to die, or whatever it was his synth did, but through a torn eyelid he noticed that someone had bound his legs with rope. Then, as the mounts raced off into the warren, Ystil.3 was yanked and dragged along behind, scraping and tearing along until he lost all sense of what was happening.

Eventually, after klicks, they cut him loose, leaving him broken in the darkness. When the confusion finally subsided and he could access his functions again, an internal scan revealed internal bleeding, broken ribs, multiple skull fractures and more. Almost two hours passed with him lying in a pool of pain and plasma before his synth had healed enough to be able to pull himself to his feet and stagger step by excruciating step through the darkness, shuffling back to the safety of his quarters. He didn't remember getting back there or how long it had taken, but the next thing he knew he was sprawled on a bed with Lydia hovering over him, tending to his wounds.

"I'll heal," he said, attempting to swat her away. The pain was too much and he fell back onto the soft blanket.

Later, when he could finally sit up, they sat side by side on the bed.

"Why did you let them do this to you," Lydia asked, her voice barely a whisper. How she had known what happened, he didn't ask. "They could never have overpowered you unless you allowed them to, even as a group."

The swelling had gone down enough for the raw lids of his eyes to squint open, the skin was beginning to join and heal itself. It hurt to speak, but he wheezed through the pain nonetheless. "Deserved it…" His voice cracked. "For… hurting you."

Lydia looked at him in the eyes for a long moment. Then, she drew up her legs and curled onto the bed before pulling him down next to her. Listening to her breath, Ystil.3 closed his eyes and did something he had never done in his entire existence. He went to sleep.

When he woke, he found Lydia sleeping beside him with a curtain of dark hair fanned over her face. He didn't know how long they'd been lying there, but he had healed completely and felt somehow lighter. Soon, Lydia roused. She left briefly to snatch a bowl of breakfast slop from the mess, but brought it back to Ystil.3's quarters.

"Do you have offspring?" he asked her, thinking of how she had taken care of him. He wondered if she would choose to care for them herself. "You must be the perfect age to conceive."

Lydia swallowed her mouthful with difficulty, as if the question had caught her off guard. "I'm actually officially seventy-five years old, but because of the upgrades and the time-debt, my body is barely thirty. Besides, I can't physically have children." There was silence for a few seconds before Lydia lifted her head and looked around, gesturing to the room. "Don't you think it's cruel to bring a child into this?"

"Humans need to procreate to exist as a race." It wasn't really an answer.

She put down the bowl and gazed off at nothing. "I'm not even sure I am human anymore. I've been mech'd and tech'd, nano'd, spliced and chipped beyond any recognition of the girl I used to be. I have sixty-three neural implants supporting swift download and learn functions and I'm nano-upgraded to be stronger than every person, man or woman, aboard. I can send remote secure-beam comms using just the power of my thoughts and I've travelled through wormholes in space and time." She looked at him with serious eyes. "I'm no more human than you are. If we stood side by side in a scanner, there would be more similarities between us than there are between me and them."

"But they're you're kind."

She shrugged off his words as if they were an uncomfortable fit. "I feel more myself around you than I ever have around most of them." Her eyes began to well with tears and she turned away. "Is that strange?"

Ystil.3 thought, then shook his head resolutely, which hurt. "Not to me. I feel the same about you. Throughout my entire existence, I've been told what to do and what to think, and I never questioned it. But I look back now and I see a part of me was missing all that time. A part I didn't even know was supposed to be there. It's something I see in you, shining out from your eyes."

She wiped away a stray tear. "What do you see?"

"Life." He slipped a broken hand over hers. "It's life, Lydia."

30

Dr Giles Tempton was a psychopath. But, more importantly, he was a "brilliant psychopath", which according to Sir Jetson Kay made all the difference. Anyone else with Tempton's record would be forced to spend a lifetime locked within the Silence, an impenetrable prison floating in the centre of the Atlantic Ocean, where the prisoners complete their entire sentences unconscious within Scenario rehabilitation programmes – all of which, of course, were designed, manufactured and supplied by Life Corps' computers division, CellSoft, with Norma's help. In running the entire neuroscience division, she was no stranger to broken minds and considered the contract one of the few things she'd completed for the company that actually had some social value.

Norma paused at the door to Tempton's room to access the inset holoscreen that allowed them to check patients' vitals without having to go inside. Tempton, however, was not yet under sedation. Through the visuals she watched his vulturine form hunched atop the neurobed, watching with narrowed eyes his own heart beating on the holoscreens.

The events of last summer hadn't been forgotten, not by her and not by the rumour mill, which still stoked the fires of conjecture around London Tower; a new theory springing to life almost every week. Dividing fact from fiction, however, was often impossible. What they knew for certain was that the body was found in a storage facility rented by Tempton and that it was cut, bruised and defiled beyond recognition. Just a child. Norma remembered the search for the girl and the news coverage at the time. She tried to imagine the horrors the eight-year-old had endured during the month she was imprisoned. Why she did this, she didn't know. Perhaps to punish herself for being a part of a corporation that would turn a blind eye to such things. It was never admitted, but Norma knew, just as the world did. You just had to look into his eyes to know the truth. Two grey voids, blank of all emotion. Rarely did the man speak, but when he did, his voice left Norma cold inside.

Since then, she'd questioned daily why she stayed; she had gotten into bed with monsters. It was for Charlie – for his sake alone that she stayed. Without her, he would have no one. Of course, it helped that her budget bordered on obscene and she was left to roam the corners of her own mind, exploring ideas and investigating the brain and the mind and all its functions more deeply than anyone ever had or could. But Charlie was her ultimate goal. He was her life's work.

Dr Giles Tempton turned his head, appearing to look straight at her as she peered in through the holoscreen window. It was one-way, of course, but still, she shrank back, stepping away from the door. She would wait for him to be put under before she dealt with him.

In the next room, Dr Dorian Knightvam sat preening her thinning raven hair. Norma knocked lightly before entering and Knightvam glanced up with acid eyes before returning her gaze to the reflection of herself in the mirror function of her eDeck – where it usually resided. Out of all the board members, Dorian Knightvam's skin was the least obviously discoloured from the Phoric treatments, the side effects of which gave a violet hue to the skin, deepening each time the procedure was performed. Being of African descent, the treatments left Knightvam's skin with a midnight blue wash that wasn't altogether noticeable at first. It also had the tell-tale impossible tautness to it and was shiny like plastic. A mask.

Attempting to gauge the woman's exact age was an impossible task, but Norma reasoned if she needed Phoric exposure it made sense that she was into triple digits. Like most people that could afford it – Norma included – Knightvam had been fitted with the Life Store implant at the base of her neck, doubling life expectancy. Add this to the Phoric exposure and Dorian could have been anywhere up to one-hundred and fifty years old. Not as old as Sir Jetson Kay, that much was clear, however. Just a few more treatments and her face would be as blue as a bruise.

Norma glanced briefly over the neurobed to ensure everything was prepared. "If you would like to lie down and get comfortable, we can get started."

Knightvam smoothed out her sterile hospital gown and with Norma's aid slid onto the bed. The woman's wrists were thin and ropey.

"I've taken inventory of all my possessions this year," Knightvam said, sharply yanking back her arm. "After last year's magical disappearing pearl necklace, I find it quite appalling that it was needed."

There was accusation in her voice, but that was nothing Norma wasn't used to. She just nodded and began attaching a sensor pad over each of the woman's temples and one over her heart.

Presuming she has one.

"I understand your youngest great-grandson is now attending Oxbridge University," Norma said, attempting polite conversation. "That's quite an achievement."

"I suppose it is." The woman's thick lips drew into a grimace. "One does question his choice of study, however. I'll just be grateful when he realises how little use art history will be to him in the real world."

"Kids will rebel. It's like my younger sister last year—"

"My grandson is not a kid," Dr Knightvam interrupted, her face falling to an expression that suggested she might have caught a whiff of some foul odour. "And he does not rebel. He is simply strong-willed, a trait he passed down from me to my son and my son to him… a trait I would not change for all the riches in the world, I'll have you know."

Norma became caught in Dr Knightvam's corrosive stare, and at once felt herself flailing to get it off her like it was a nest of spiders crawling over her skin.

"Of course. I just meant that trying to sway the young to do the right thing often causes them to do exactly the opposite, even when they know we're older and have been through it all once ourselves."

Knightvam's lips pursed as the word older fell inadvertently from Norma's mouth, and if it was possible, the woman's eyes turned further to stone. "Can we just get on with this? The faster I'm unconscious the better. Really, I don't remember all this probing, inane chit-chat last year."

Norma nodded, evoked the holoscreen and commanded a healthy dose of sedative for the old bat. Within seconds, Knightvam was out and a minute later her eyeballs began shifting beneath the creped skin of her eyelids as she entered depth four of REM stimulation. Norma then initiated the Scenario.

Each Scenario was a personal thing crafted individually to each of the Life Corp board members' requests and Norma was sincerely relieved not to know what secret desires, wishes or memories they were entering into. It was bad enough knowing the things they did when the CommonWorld eyes were upon them, but to think of the heinous acts they might commit if they thought no consequences would touch them sent a wave of nausea through her. She thought of Tempton, especially.

Dorian Knightvam had always been a bit of a tragic figure in Norma's view, and, despite herself, couldn't help but feel a twinge of pity towards the crabby old bitch. Long ago, an innocent Knightvam had lived happily in the suburbs of New York after marrying her then-husband, Gavin Shaw, a highly respected investment banker from a wealthy family; on top of the family treasure, he'd made his first billion Coin before hitting his thirtieth birthday. He was older than Knightvam when they married, and for a while they were happy, Norma supposed. But it didn't last. He ran off with a younger woman before Dorian reached twenty-five. She was pregnant at the time and was given nothing from the divorce – his high-powered friends saw to that. Her ex-husband rejected the child as being his and refused a paternity test. What made the entire thing more tragic was that the woman he'd run off with was Dorian's younger sister.

But while a blow like that might've crushed the average woman, Knightvam hadn't let it defeat her. She put herself through NYU while working four jobs to support herself and her son. She never married again and went back to her maiden name of Knightvam, as did her son. Many people took this act as an admission of her son not being her ex-husband's, but only Knightvam knew the truth of it.

At depth six, Norma attached the thick snake-like chord into the jack in the back of Knighvam's head – the all-important Hydra line.

The Hydra project was one of those many developments in Life Corp where Norma only knew as much as her part in it required her to know; meaning the board had not revealed their end game. This disturbed her greatly. And yet, like the Scenarios, part of her was relieved to be in the dark. If she did not know, then she was not responsible for doing nothing to stop it.

Norma initiated Hydra and immediately a detailed mapping of Knightvam's brain appeared on the holoscreen – synapses and chords within the clouds of grey and clumps of light. Parts shone like stars while others were as dark as pitch. A side-screen of numbers began to trail along, showing the cloning had begun exactly where it left off almost a year ago to the day. It read Knightvam's thoughts, memories, responses and behaviour patterns, taking it all and saving it, then replicating it onto a server in an undisclosed location. The board were, in essence, making a digital copy of themselves.

Due to the immensity of the human mind, it would take a total of three months under solid sedation to map an entire brain function, but undergoing the process for more than just a few days within a period of seven months would skew the results, they had found. The board treated these days as a vacation, adding a desired Scenario to their unconscious state, which added a needed baseline for the mapping.

This was Norma's first year completely overseeing the project since the disappearance of her predecessor, but the project had been well underway long before she'd joined the company. Within just a few years they would have a complete digital clone of each of the boards' personalities. Then, for good or bad, their plans would become clear.

Norma thought of her sister, as she often did when faced with a moral dilemma.

What would Sayi do if she were in my position?

Felicity entered with a jug of steaming coffee and a timid smile, offering a grateful distraction. The coffee was sharp and pungent, the way she liked it, and together they sat at a small corner table of Knightvam's room.

Felicity was a picture of youth and innocence, though she wasn't that much younger than Norma. She was a quiet girl, relatively green to the world of neuroscience and extremely green to the internal politics of Life Corp. This place will chew her up and spit her out, Norma often thought. She'd been head-hunted, like Norma, and the board wanted her to mentor the girl and help her reach her full potential. She couldn't complain, really. She liked Felicity, and now she had someone to talk to who she didn't suspect was plotting to stab her in the back. Life Corp was like that. There was a common saying in London Tower: eat or meat.

With a willowy limb, Felicity poured more coffee, the sheen of her enhanced optics glimmering over her doe eyes, like the iridescence of oil across water.

"Darren is taking me to Brighton this weekend," she said, a bright smile illuminating her face, revealing her rather large white teeth. Felicity's boyfriend often featured in their conversations. "We're taking the train on Fifthday night. I hope that's okay?" The girl worked late into the night most days even though it wasn't a requirement. It showed the type of commitment that was rare. But what was even rarer was that she managed to have her career and keep some semblance of a life outside of work. Something that Norma herself had never managed to do.

Norma nodded, swallowing her coffee. "Of course. Go. Have a wonderful time. It's been an age since I've seen the sea. It's been too long since I've even been out of London at all, for that matter." Not counting her brief trip to Moscow. "My parents used to take me and my sister to Brighton. We would sit on the rocky beach sucking on our sticks of rock, arguing over who could make theirs last the longest." She laughed the type of laugh that she rarely allowed herself to do at work. But with Felicity it was okay.

"I'll bring some back for you if you like?"

"That's sweet of you. Could you possibly get one for my sister too? Only if it's no trouble, though."

"It's no trouble at all."

"Is it a romantic weekend?" Norma enquired. It had been so long since she had done anything remotely romantic that she found herself vicariously longing to hear more. She would often quench her need for romance with novels. It was her secret pleasure, indulging in the dramatic and erotic world of passion sagas, where the handsome, rugged – and, more often than not, dangerous – rogues whisked the full-breasted heroines off their feet. Norma had never been whisked anywhere, and for that matter she wouldn't class herself full-breasted either, more half-breasted on a good day and if the wind was right.

In fact, her experience with men was somewhat limited to the three boyfriends she'd had in her brief dating career. She used the word boyfriends to describe them, even though the longest lasted only two months. But if she didn't call them her ex-boyfriends then that meant she had never had a boyfriend in her life, and that was just far too tragic to even consider. So, if anyone ever asked, which no-one had before Felicity, she had finished her last relationship to focus more on her career. In truth, he had simply stopped calling.

The men in her books weren't like that, though. If only they really existed. The type of man that was handsome and loyal and adventurous. Even a little dangerous, Norma thought occasionally. But those men only ever existed in her books, and even if there were men like that in the world, Norma could never pursue such a man. No, in truth, she liked her men exactly where they were, contained safely in the pages of her books. She'd seen what that type of passion had done to Sayi when she had brought her back from Moscow. Let Sayi keep her wild adventures. Norma was the responsible one. If she wasn't, then who would be?

Felicity blushed a little. "You might say it's a romantic weekend. It's so hard trying to juggle a relationship and a career. Sometimes it's just good to get away to focus on the two of you, don't you find?"

Norma smiled and took another sip of her coffee. If only she did.

*

Mrs Dorian Shaw looked at the woman sat on her sofa opposite. She was completely her sort of person; she took sugar with her tea and held her cup in the fashion Dorian had herself been taught at her finishing school only a few years before. Being newly married, it was those elegant touches that informed her husband's elite social circle of her background and breeding, regardless of the unknown fact her family was now Coinless. So, Dorian could assume quite confidently that this new acquaintance of hers had had the same sort of upbringing.

Such were their similarities, in fact, they might have been related. They were both of African descent, ebony, slender and long of neck. They had the same straight dark hair fashioned into a beehive atop their heads and the same wide dark eyes.

Upon first opening the door, the older woman seemed somewhat startled. "My goodness, you are young," she had said, which made Dorian like her immediately. Being new to the neighbourhood, she was doing the rounds, so to speak, and meeting her immediate neighbours. So, of course, Dorian cordially invited her in for tea. Dorian's husband, however, would soon be home from work – they had reservations at his favourite restaurant, La Petite Mort – so she did her best to get through the required subjects quickly and politely. She hadn't expected her new neighbour to be so interesting.

They went over where she and her family had moved from, her line of work, her interests and so on, and Dorian was yet further amazed by their likeness. They had both been raised on estates in the country, and both their families were ruined in the stock crash in the forties. Their families were both left with nothing except good names, and it was up to them to make a good match. Both were sent to the finest schools to be taught how to be a lady and how to make worthy alliances after their families had scraped together all the Coin they had.

Dorian didn't want to be rude, but it seemed to her that her new neighbour was a little old to have been affected in such a way by the crash, but nonetheless she believed her and said nothing about it.

It wasn't often that Dorian spoke so openly to a stranger – or to anyone, really – but she felt a strange sense of affinity with this woman. Despite the difference in age, she was a kindred spirit, she felt. They'd both had it tough and both knew what it took to survive. It was for this reason that she saw fit to tell the lady something. A secret.

"Tonight, I'm going to kill my husband," Dorian said, after taking a dainty sip of tea.

"How delightful," the woman replied.

"The reason, you see, is that I know my husband very well, and during the last two years of our marriage I have come to realise he does not truly love me. He agreed to our union only to satisfy his own ego. He will not stay with me, I fear. Sooner or later he will leave me for a younger woman and I will be left with nothing. If I kill him now, I'll get everything."

"A very prudent decision, indeed," the stranger said, placing down her empty cup upon the French antique side table. "I understand completely. How do you plan to do it?"

"I have a gun," Dorian replied coolly, tracing a finger around the rim of her china teacup.

"Not registered, I hope?"

"Oh no, of course not. It's completely illegal and untraceable to me. I shall make it look like an attempted robbery. Gavin has always said he pities the man who'd ever dare to steal from him. He would, of course, attempt to stop the robber. But the robber has a gun, and fires twice… first in the stomach, then in the head – before fleeing the scene, leaving me injured, but not fatally so. I recover from my blackout to discover my husband dead, and I call for an ambulance right away, distraught with grief."

"And how will you fake the robbery?" her new neighbour enquired lustily, taking a delicate nibble of a biscuit.

"Forced entry from the outside in. The robber will hack the main security and override the alarm system with an upgraded blocker device, leaving it latched to the security system outside in his rush. He will charge through the main doors from the back entrance, mistaking the house for empty, when in fact we are actually upstairs making love. We're interrupted by a noise downstairs and Gavin investigates. He reaches for his ornamental Samurai sword that hangs in his dressing room. I follow him into the kitchen where I will hit my head in the struggle that takes place. That's when he's shot. Twice. Once in the stomach and then in the head." She recited it, perfectly memorised.

The woman nodded approvingly. "And the neighbourhood street cameras?"

"A figure will be seen entering and then fleeing the streets at the times I tell the police. I will cover myself in a hood and do it myself. I will make the call to the police after I regain consciousness, giving me plenty of time."

"You have thought of everything, haven't you? I'm impressed." The stranger's lips curled into a smile. "Except, if you are to robe yourself in a guise and flee from the house as the robber, how will you re-enter the house without the cameras noticing?"

Dorian's smile faltered, and in its place a thick line of rouged lips formed. "I did not think of that."

"Well, now you've no need to think of it. I shall perform that task for you," the woman said brightly. "I will do exactly as you described, sneak around the back of the house and break in. I assume you have all that you need to disarm the alarms?"

"Yes, of course. But I wouldn't want to trouble you. You must be frightfully busy, what with having just moved."

"It's no trouble in the slightest. I'm happy to help. I will leave the neighbourhood and head to the supermarket close by where I will buy a few items. I will leave my vehicle, with the shopping inside, and I will guise myself and re-enter the street. And once the deed is done I will flee from the neighbourhood in full view of the cameras, heading back to the supermarket to retrieve my vehicle and return with my shopping. Of course, I don't usually do my own food shopping but the staff don't arrive until tomorrow, so it's perfect."

Dorian thought, then gushed. "Yes. That will work. What a dear friend you are to put yourself out for me in this way, and only having just met me." She took the woman by the hand.

"Us girls must stick together," the stranger said. "What time shall I call?"

"Six tonight. I will leave all you need at the back door."

The woman nodded and stood. "Until tonight then."

"Until tonight."

By the time Gavin returned home from work, having spent the obligatory hour at his favourite bar for an after-work tipple, Dorian was dressed and ready. Ready to kill. It sent a wave of ecstasy soaring through her at the thought of it. She loved Gavin immensely, but there was this knowing inside her that in doing this she would be making everything right – and getting away with it, which made it all the sweeter.

Her white dress clung to her curves, revealing the cleavage of her breasts and she'd curled her hair into waves, pinning it neatly to frame her oval face. Her full lips were rouged and her eyes were accentuated with thick mascara. A dab of perfume finished her off and she stood at the foot of the stairs, hand on hip, as Gavin entered with briefcase in hand and starched collar loosened on the ride home. The driver pulled away as Gavin closed the door, the headlights beaming in for a moment, illuminating Dorian's blood red smile and casting a long shadow up the curling staircase.

"Hello, darling," she said smoothly, standing in a way that accentuated her body. Gavin took one look at her and dropped his briefcase to the floor. He moved towards her and took her in his arms.

"Hello my young, sexy wife," he said, before nuzzling her neck.

She glanced at the antique clock in the hallway – 5:45pm – then led Gavin up the veined-marble deco stairs towards their bedroom.

Gavin always took care of himself. He worked out in their gym every morning before work and had a fantastic body because of it. He was handsome, well-mannered to most, but rather cocky, some might say. He was the type of man that, in his youth, arrogance and wealthy upbringing, believed he could do anything he wanted, and own anyone he wanted. Any problem could be sorted by throwing Coin at it. But this side of him was always offset with the sweetest sentiments that he would whisper to her when they were alone, with their heads upon the silk pillow of their bed. Nevertheless, it had to be done. She had to kill him. The thought of seeing Gavin's body full of holes made her feel as light as air. She loved him so, but she loved winning more.

He flung her to the bed and, as he undressed, poured them both a drink from the martini bar in the dressing room. Gavin didn't keep a gun in the house, but he had his toy sword – a toy that could split a grapefruit with one swing. Dorian saw it glinting above his suits above the shelf of his old college football trophies. Handing Dorian a drink, he took a sip of his own and removed his underwear.

What was the saying? Men get better with age and women get replaced. He was older than her, but looked thirty, and probably always would. She felt a bitter twinge at that.

"Music on," Gavin instructed. "Number fifty-two in the bedroom." The room filled with slow-moving melodies as she lay propped on her elbows to stop her hair from coming undone on the pillow. Gavin joined her.

5:54pm.

Pushing her husband back on the bed, Dorian climbed on top of him. "Fuck me," she commanded, hitching up her dress to show she wasn't wearing panties. Within seconds he'd entered her and began thrusting in earnest, much in the way he usually did, like a jack-rabbit. One of the reasons Dorian preferred being on top was so she wouldn't repeatedly bang her head on the headboard.

By 5:59 he was done, and they lay side by side.

"Music off," Dorian said. "You should get dressed. We have reservations." She climbed from the bed and went to fix another drink. She was pregnant and knew she shouldn't. But she did nonetheless. Gavin didn't want kids. He didn't know yet. It's not that she was overly fond of children, but the thought of her genetics stopping with her had made her walk back out of the clinic. She would start to show soon.

Then, with a thrill, she heard it. Breaking glass. She turned to Gavin who was standing as still as a statue. He'd heard it too.

"What was——?"

"Shush." He strained to listen. Then came a bang from downstairs, like someone thumping the wall with a fist. He reached for the sword, as Dorian knew he would, and stalked towards the door. "Stay here," he whispered, before going out to investigate.

As soon as he was gone she walked to the dressing room, retrieved the gun from her underwear drawer and checked it was loaded and cocked. The 9x19mm Blast felt heavy in her palm. It felt good. Then, after retouching her lipstick in the mirror, she smiled and walked out after her husband.

She descended the dark stairs and made her way through the lounge and dining room towards the back of the house. The lights were off. In the dining room, she passed her neighbour, concealed in the shadows of an antique china cabinet. The woman slid easily into the shade like a dark spirit, but Dorian knew she was there.

She found her husband in the kitchen, inspecting a broken window with the back door ajar. He sprang up and spun, raising the sword high above him. Dorian didn't flinch.

"I told you to stay upstairs," he whispered angrily. "I think someone's in the house. Stay here and lock the door behind me. And call the police." He went to move by her but stopped, looking down at the gun in her hand. "Where did you get that?" he asked. "Never mind, hand it over." He held out his hand but Dorian didn't move. Instead, she smiled, raised the gun and fired once into his stomach.

The sword dropped to the floor with a clang and blood oozed from the hole in his bare belly. The Blast was a violent little handgun and her husband used his hand to keep his insides... well in. He stumbled back, falling against the wall, pale eyes staring wordlessly at her.

"Goodbye, darling," she said. "You know, I really did love you. It's a shame that it didn't work out between us."

Gavin opened and closed his mouth twice before eventually letting out a blood-gurgled "why?".

"You know, I can't really say for sure," Dorian replied with thoughtful cock of her head. "But I can see it all play out in my head as though it's already happened. You're going to leave me and our child." She touched her belly. "You're going to leave us with nothing. You're going to replace me." The semi-conscious man lightly shook his head and attempted more words. "Oh, you may not think you will now. But you will. So just remember this, Gavin. I beat you. I win." She raised the Blast once more and fired a steady, practised shot into his head, blowing apart his face so that only his jaw remained, swinging bloody and useless below the sticky explosion that was his head.

Dorian let her smile fade as she stared for a moment. She took in a breath and turned to the woman that watched like a ghost in the door frame.

"Well done," her neighbour said.

The woman left the crime-scene as planned and Dorian called the police after bashing her own head on the countertop. Using her best acting skills, she told the person on the other end of her eDeck just what had transpired. The ambulance arrived in minutes, along with the flashing red sirens of the police, and Gavin's body was taken away after the police listened ardently to her tale. She garnished her monologue with appropriate tears. They took down her statement, told her they would be in touch and that they were sorry for her loss.

Her gain. The whole night had left her with a satisfied, resolved feeling. One might call it closure.

By 10:00pm her neighbour returned, as they had planned, and together they sat drinking tea.

By 10:07pm the woman stood over Dorian's body with a gun in hand. The pale moonlight poured in from the window, turning her white, blood-soaked dress to a glimmering black.

☐

31

"Can I save her?" Prometheus asked Death.

The voices replied, wordless and mouthless in the nothing. "She is gone."

"Then how can you take me to her?"

"She was not always gone. We can take you to that time."

"But she will die… the same as before?"

"She will die."

"Then I shall lose her once again."

"Yes."

The blackness in which Prometheus formlessly bathed was not the mere darkening of physical form. He knew it somehow instinctively. It was a great well of emptiness, a hole in existence that bore through everything with chomping teeth, leaving nothing but the very essence of ancient potential.

Death had taken Prometheus from the hospital purgatory to somewhere outside of things, neither real nor unreal. There was no smell, or taste or feel. There was no left or right or up or down. Both vastness and constraint enveloped him there, but he had no form to feel it, no eyes to see it, ears to hear it or nose to smell it. Where his body was, Prometheus did not know, but there was no feeling of loss or detachment. He was whole in this place and strangely aware of it.

"I could stop it," he said in the silence. "I could forbid her from ever becoming with child. That would stop her from dying during the birth."

"But she is already dead," replied Death. "You cannot change what has already come to pass."

"I could try."

"You would fail."

"If you offer me no way to save her, you offer me nothing."

"We offer you a choice, Prometheus."

"Take me to just after her death and I'll give her the White Drops. Then she'll be alive, just like the others."

"The White Drops," the voices echoed. "We are the White Drops. We are the tears of Mnemosyne."

"You are loathsome Death. You are the vileness in the world, the pestilence upon man. You are the shearer of fates, the quencher of souls. You are foulness personified, drowning the light of innocence with your anti-life. You are demon."

The darkness stirred, and in the spaceless black Prometheus imagined a glowing white skull.

"We are life. Eternal. Forever. Damned."

Prometheus ignored its words. "The White Drops could ensure she lives."

"She may live there and yet not here. But as what would she live there? And then, in the end of ends, we would have her still. Collect her and take her into us to be with you here now. But she is not here –

so, that you did not do."

"You make no sense. Before you said I cannot change the past, and now you say I can? I don't understand."

"Then we must show you."

A pinpoint of light pricked into existence like a distant star glowing in the black. It rushed forward, intensifying into a blinding-white tunnel that enclosed around Prometheus. He soared through at unfathomable speed, pushed as though he were a baby being birthed to life. The white exploded into fragments and reality sliced by in shards, congealing together until once again he had hands and legs and feet and eyes. Information bombarded his senses in a rush of drowning noise and vision.

When the intensity dimmed and the world came into view, it was Death he first noticed, towering ominously beside him, wreathed in coiling shadow. Then his attention turned to his surroundings and the peculiarity of the room. It had only three walls. The fourth, the farthest, was completely absent, leading outside to a beach where a red sunset floated over a tranquil sea. Strangely, although the water broke tenderly against an orange sand beach, it was completely silent. The only noise was a hissing sound coming from behind a drawn curtain in the far corner.

A faint glow of light swam through the translucent pale fabric, picking out the outline of an unmoving figure lying in a bed. Prometheus turned in question to the shadow beside him, the white skull lost somewhere in the terrible darkness of its cowl.

"Look," the voices of Death said inside Prometheus's head. "And see." It raised a dark-winged arm towards the bed.

Reluctantly, Prometheus edged toward the thin veil of fabric. He could see the rise and fall of a breathing chest, inhaling and exhaling in time with the interminable wheezing. Taking a handful of fabric, he drew back the curtain back. At once, he fell back, the blood draining from his face, evaporated. After a moment, he gathered himself up again, the image of what lay beyond the curtain burnt into his vision, before forcing himself to look again.

Upon the bed lay a man – Prometheus presumed it was a man – whose frame was thin as bone, frail and grey as ashes. The chest concaved inwards, the rows of exposed ribs sinking painfully into the body itself. The face was half crumbled, leaving only a jawless mouth, lip-less and open, two puckered slits where the eyes should be, utterly hollow, and a blunt hole in the centre replacing the nose. The arms of the man lay at his sides, unmoving and stripped clean of muscle, the hands petrified white spiders, shrivelled at his flanks. The legs too were absent of meat and hung below his torso like two knotted ropes, his feet nought but nubs of gristle. And it was all covered in the thinnest layer of pale lavender skin, which looked as if it would tear with the slightest pressure, as fragile as butterfly wings.

"He cannot be alive?" Prometheus whispered. "He cannot." And yet the sunken chest of the creature rose and fell with the ebb and flow of the tide in the distance. Machinery surrounded the man like a bereaved family.

"Alive," the voices of Death sighed. "Forever alive."

The shadow was suddenly beside him, grown from the darkness. "Alive forever." He repeated the words as the realisation took hold. "This is what happens when the body decays but will not die. This wretched creature's fate is because of the White Drops?"

"Yes."

A black cloud of horror descended. "What have I done?" he whispered, backing away from the bed. "What torment have I released onto this world?" He moved to the back of the room, towards the opening, unable to look at the man anymore. Suddenly, he yearned to feel a sea breeze upon his face, cool and salty, like when he would stand too close to the cliff edge at their coastal cottage as a boy. But upon approaching, he discovered there was, in fact, no beach at all. The back of the room did indeed have a wall, but the scene depicted on it was some perplexing moving picture. Prometheus placed his hands upon it, passing them through the strange mist of light that made up the image, until his fingers were immersed within the red sun.

"Death is a blessing compared to this fate," he said. "Something must be done." He back turned to Death, craning behind him like a following apparition.

"Before his limbs wilted, he himself made attempt, as did others, in pity and curiosity. They failed."

"Why have you brought me here? What is to gain from this if I cannot help the man?"

At that moment, a figure appeared in the doorway and at once Prometheus felt a wave of alarm. But the man, muscular and dark of skin, didn't even glance once at him standing there. He strode into the room and took a seat in the chair by the bed. He then opened a book in his lap and placed an odd device over his face that covered his ears and mouth. "Do you remember where we left it last time, Charley?" the man said.

"Where am I?" a voice echoed through the room. The words were disjointed and mechanical — stitched together with no rhythm or subtle changes in tone to help indicate meaning.

The man in the bed – with barely enough flesh and bone remaining to be named such – had been given voice through some contraption, a flat and inhuman voice. But what it meant was something horrifying. The man was aware. Trapped inside his own rotting corpse, he was conscious.

The dark-skinned man let out a sigh. "One of those days, is it? You're safe and secure and don't need to worry about a thing."

"It's dark here. I cannot see. I hurt."

"Just relax." The man adjusted something on one of the nearby machines. "There, you should start to feel better. If you don't mind, I thought I would read aloud for a while. Would you like that?"

"Okay."

The man turned his attention to the book in his hands and began to read.

"I cannot subject Sarah to this fate," Prometheus whispered. "I could never allow any such creature to live thus, let alone the woman I love."

"But you already have."

Prometheus turned to the creature to catch a rare glimpse of grinning bone teeth from beneath its hood. "What is your meaning?"

"The infant," Death whispered. The endless layers of sound sang palely beside one another in chorus. "You named him yourself." Death raised a cloaked arm towards the mangled creature upon the bed. "Charles."

It felt to Prometheus as though he were suddenly falling, or sinking through the layers of his own flesh into an anguish he hadn't known he could harbour within his own body. His face became numb and he clung with searching hands to the sides of his head, raking at his skin. But he felt no pain, only despair.

"The infant." His words shook from his throat. "The infant I brought back… the stillborn. That's impossible. He must be…"

"Eight hundred and seventy-three years old," the voices of Death breezed. "The oldest human who ever lived. Our father. The Source of the spring."

☐

32

Giles Tempton was the least violet member of the board. The slight lavender flush to his creped flesh from the Phoric treatments, however, reminded Norma of a corpse, making her proximity to the man somehow worse now he was unconscious. He had never seemed vain enough to want to look as perfectly preserved as the likes of Dr Knighvam or Dr Weisberg. But vanity was not Tempton's vice. No, his vice was something altogether more sinister.

Norma's experiences with him had been at best disturbing, at worst, terrifying. One example that sprang to mind was when Norma oversaw the replacement of the boards neurojacks. Tempton had been the only board member to endure the new installation under local anaesthetic. He had insisted on overseeing the process himself and demanded a holoscreen arranged so he could view the entire procedure as it happened. She remembered, with horror, the smile on his face as they lifted off a section of his scalp and bore a hole into his skull.

"Begin REM stimulation," Norma instructed Felicity. "Then load Hydra."

The girl nodded and placed her hands upon the nav-pads beside the neurobed. Norma was grateful to have her there, especially for this project. Not only did Felicity give her some company on those long nights in the lab, but her presence also meant that perhaps there was hope for Life Corp. Perhaps things were changing. From sub-basements to the districts, right up to the penthouse, every level, floor and room was occupied with the sycophantic and power-hungry, spewing their malignant bile in a desperate fight to claw their way to the top. No one was your friend. No one was on your side. Not in London Tower. Norma had learnt that lesson the hard way. Felicity, however, was everything Norma valued in a person. She was kind, caring, compassionate, empathetic, honest and gentle – many of the qualities she hoped she displayed herself.

Little mouse, her sister would call her when they were younger. Sayi, though, could never be described as a mouse. She would never be told what to do, what to think or how to be. Things were so black and white for her. Right and wrong. You were either on one side or the other. Her sister didn't see the many shades of grey that lay in between, and she and Norma would argue vehemently on the subject.

"When dealing with science, progression, healing the sick and feeding the starving, aren't some moral sacrifices worth it?" she would say. "Doesn't the end justify the means, just sometimes?" But according to Sayi, the answer was always a blunt No. Norma had no choice but to disagree. To agree would be to admit she was one of the villains, one of the "bad guys". The things she'd seen at Life Corp Tower brought her integrity into question more often than she'd liked, but she had to believe that working within the system was better than nothing. Changing it from the inside out.

"What good is progression when we learn nothing in the process?" Sayi would argue. "What is the point in solving mass hunger when we have enough food to begin with but we're too selfish or stupid to share it? The sick can be healed well enough, as long as you can afford the treatments. Is that the type of society you want to help progress?"

Norma would always be left silent by Sayi's rants because deep in her heart, she knew her sister might just be right. Years had passed and the dreams she'd once had of changing the world had all but drowned in a sea of mediocre so-called truths. The hardest to swallow, she found, was capitalism is king. It was the mover of planets and the destroyer of disease – so long as the profit margins convinced the board it was worth the effort. The harder Norma worked and the deeper she sank to the inner core of Life Corp, the clearer that truth became.

From an early age, Norma and her younger sister had shown themselves to be different in every way. Norma was a quiet child ¬– Sayi was demanding. Norma did well in school and concentrated on her education ¬– Sayi got expelled from three schools and at the age of seventeen ran off to Paris with her boyfriend to work as a street performer in a dancing troupe. While in Paris, Sayi managed to get herself arrested for inciting violence at a series of anti-CommonWorld protests. She'd thrown a shoe at the head of an Enforce Officer, starting a trend that saw five thousand shoes launched into the lines of peace-keeping CommonWorld cops and rousing one British news-tab to publish the headline That'll Shoe 'em. It was Norma, however, that had to bail her out, taking the express train to Paris and paying with her own Coin. And, being the loyal sister she was, she never told their parents or asked for the money back.

Norma read romance novels – Sayi's life was a romance novel. Each of Sayi's inappropriate boyfriends paled in comparison to the unsuitability of the next. But all had one thing in common. They were anti-system anti-capitalist anti-everything trashmongers, in Norma's opinion. Greasy haired, leaf smoking, devil-may-care nobodies. And most did the best job they could at dragging her sister down with them, whose only real crime was being overly passionate and caring too much.

It was three months ago that Sayi had called, pleading for Norma to come and get her. Sayi and her then-boyfriend, Marco, had left Paris and headed to Russia with a band of protestors calling themselves the Smirking Skulls. Sayi and Marco had met with the radical group in Paris and had since travelled with them, joining their anti-CommonWorld protests, which usually resulted in violence. Sayi's new unwashed gang fell upon Moscow to occupy themselves upon the reformed Kremlin in protest of Russia submitting to pressure to sign the CommonWorld agreement, which, as everyone knew, would only result in another attempt to take China State by force. Even Norma could feel the world edging towards another war – news-tabs reported daily of the growing tensions between CommonWorld leaders and China State's President Ling. It was after four weeks of protesting in Russia when Sayi made the call to Norma. Even with six months of silence between them, as soon as Norma heard Sayi's voice, she knew something was wrong. Sayi was on the verge of tears. Norma was the crier – Sayi never cried. Once, her sister had broken her arm and she didn't shed a single tear, even though it was twisted in such a way that made Norma almost faint just looking at it.

"Can you come get me," Sayi had begged, her voice shaking. "I… don't know what to do. I need to get out of Moscow, but I can't think." She stopped. A man shouted something aggressively in French.

"Sayi?" she'd shouted down the eDeck link, fearing the connection had been lost. "Are you okay? Sayi are you there?"

"I'm here. I need you, Norm. I have no Coin to leave, please I just want to come home…" Her voice broke and she began to sob. Her sister wasn't a big fan of tech and only had a basic eDeck with no holograph visual link-up, so Norma couldn't see her face, only hear her voice, thick with tears. Somehow that made it worse. She couldn't imagine her sister's carefree expression crumpled into despair. The thought of it broke her heart.

"Don't worry, I'm on my way," she said, already grabbing her bag and CommonPass. She headed out the door, leaving her hair loose, instead of its usual tied back fashion. "Where's Marco?"

There was a pause. "Dead. Please hurry."

Norma had taken the fastest stratospheric flight direct from London to Moscow, costing her almost a whole month's wages, and after an unnerving trip – Norma had found from an early age she detested flying – she arrived in Russia twenty minutes later. She'd found Sayi wandering listlessly outside Sheremetyevo International without even so much as Coin enough to enter the airport. Norma remembered how utterly wrecked her sister had looked. Her usual mane of wild blonde hair stuffed into a cap. She was pale and skinnier than Norma had ever seen her. Sayi wrapped Norma in a desperate embrace and sobbed into her shoulder.

"Get me out of this place," she said through the tears.

During the flight, Sayi was too busy eating to talk – or cry. She ate as though she hadn't eaten in months, and by the look of her, Norma realised then, she probably hadn't. By the time they arrived at Norma's Regent Park House apartment in the gated area of Primrose Hill, Sayi was almost herself again. The confident, almost sly smirk had returned to her expression and after a shower and sleep it was as though the momentary lapse in her usually colossal strength had never even happened. She was back to flirting with the takeaway deliveryman and picking at Norma's "nanny" clothes.

Two days later, Norma asked what had happened to Marco. Sayi went out onto the balcony and they sat looking out onto the park. It was a bright June day, but still London was cast in the shadow of the old London Tower. It burst through the earth like a clawed metal finger, dominating the skyline. The giant omega symbol of Life Corp sat atop the building like a crown, the sun positioned just behind it, creating a defused halo around the horseshoe-like curve. Why Life Corp needed all the space in that monstrous building, she would never know. A place to hide all its terrible secrets. It was an ever-present eye watching over the world that stretched out at its roots.

Sayi had also fixed a tear-brimmed gaze upon the building. "Marco trusted some people he shouldn't have." She took a sip of the red wine that was a constant in her grip. "He paid for it. I nearly paid for it too."

"What did he get you into?"

Sayi laughed. "I'm not into anything, Norm. It's you who's in it, and you don't even see. You're in it up to your tits. You're drowning in it."

"What are you talking about?"

"Life Corp," Sayi said. "You've got no idea what they have planned."

*

The high-pitched bell rang through the halls of St Andrews' School for boys and within seconds a tide of bodies poured from the classrooms into the corridors, joining to form a flowing river of boisterous children. They swelled along the second-floor mathematics department, heads bobbing along as they separated into groups, venturing off into various rooms along the ancient converted monastery. As the horde thinned to a dwindling few, a handful of younger boys stood with heads down, checking holoscreen maps upon their wrists – new students in the daunting and cavernous school. St Andrew's was renowned for setting boys upon the path to entering the most prestigious CommonWorld universities. The school required a checklist of credentials before a student could attend. Luckily, along with money and power, genius was still among them.

A blonde nine-year-old boy frowned at his map, attempting to locate his current position so he could find how to get to his next lesson. He'd never been to a school so big. His parents had sent him away and now he had to live there with the other boys; not only away from his home and his family, but in another country, deep in a secluded area west of Nantes on the east coast of France. He had asked his mother why he had to go, over and over until she finally told him. He didn't like what she said. She began to cry as they drove to the jet. His father didn't say goodbye, didn't step out of the car.

He looked up from his eDeck to see a dark-haired boy walking along the stone corridor. The boy was in his next class. He began to follow as he swept through to the hall propped with high arches and lined with glassless windows. The empty frames blurred with the slight iridescence of control fields, fracturing the light that pushed through and brightening the old grey stone to almost glowing white. From there, some remaining boys syphoned off into the quad, which then led onto the sports grounds. The school was so immense that the blonde boy wondered how anyone ever knew where they were going, but he followed his lead nonetheless and continued outside into the sunlight, onto a footpath of old stone that wound around the wing of the old monastery.

The path lay at the foot of a steep embankment, which climbed up into a forest of pine trees hanging heavy and green with spring colours and dark shadows. The blonde boy hurried his short legs to keep up with the taller dark-haired boy, who had now joined a group of other students. Together, they marched ahead.

More pupils feathered off from the serpentine procession, some entering a series of smaller outbuildings, leaving only a few lingering. Those who remained, the dark-haired boy included, suddenly didn't seem like they were in so much of a hurry. They stopped at the corner of the footpath, remaining sheltered off from the courtyard that blazed in the sun beyond. Amid snorts of laughter, plumes of smoke erupted from the huddle. The blonde boy dawdled, hoping they would continue to guide him to his class. But they did not. The remaining students soon moved on, leaving only him and the group of taller boys behind.

It wasn't long before they noticed him standing there, anxiously searching his eDeck once more, feeling even more lost than when he'd begun. The boys began talking in hushed voices and staring over at him.

The siren chimed on their eDecks at the exact same moment. He should be in his next class by now. He was late.

"Hey," said one of the boys. He was chubby and pug-faced. "Slit off, shorty. This is our hang."

The blonde boy turned and began down the footpath along the side of the building.

"Wait. Aren't you in my physics class?" one of them shouted. The blonde boy turned to see it was the dark-haired boy. He stepped forward a few paces. "Yeah, it is you," he said when he received no reply. "You lost or something?" The boy's uniform was rebelliously dishevelled and he had dark eyes to match his hair. "Come 'ere. I'll show you the way."

The blonde boy began over to the group, feeling the sag of his backpack weighing him down. He stood barely shoulder height to the group. He was younger by two years but was pushed ahead in his classes. It wasn't unusual for him to hear the word genius when adults spoke to other adults about him ¬– never to him, always about him. It was the word their physics professor had used upon introducing him to the class. The other students had sniggered.

"Oh, it's the genius," the dark-haired boy said.

"Oh yeah," another boy said, laughing. "Genius? The little slit can't even find his way to class."

The fat boy grabbed hold of his arm and pulled it. "Look at his eDeck. It's the quantum version 4S." He made a whistling sound between his teeth. "That's an expensive bit of kit you've got there, genius."

The boys took turns to jerk his small arm to look at it. The map still shimmered open. When the dark-haired boy took his arm, he tugged it harder than the others, causing the blonde boy to let out a small yelp.

"Let's see it," he said. He jabbed various buttons until the map shimmered out. "Looks like a knock-off to me. I saw loads from backstreet vendors in New York over the summer." He flung the blonde boy's arm back at him. "It's just a bit of shit."

"I dunno about that," the fat boy said. "Looks pretty real to me. My dad said I could upgrade if I made it to the end of the month without any demerits."

The dark-haired boy whirled and landed a punch in the fat boy's large gut so unexpectedly that the entire group froze in silence. "I told you it's a bit of shit," he snarled, "so shit is what it is."

Red-faced and clutching his stomach, the fat boy gasped for breath. The other boys then began to fall over each other in fits of laughter. The dark-haired boy glared at the blonde boy for a long moment before smiling. "Anyway, genius has to get to class." He flicked away the stub of a fume he'd been smoking. "So let's take him. I know a short cut."

At first, the blonde boy followed the dark-haired boy along the footpath back the way they'd come; the rest of the group lingering behind them. It wasn't until the dark-haired boy tried to lead him off the path and up a dirt track to the forest that the blonde boy slowed to a stop.

"It's a short-cut," the dark-haired boy reassured him.

"Yeah," others in the group chimed. "We go this way all the time."

So, the blonde boy continued to follow. By the time they reached the edge of the woods the entire group had surrounded him. The fresh scent of pine and rotting undergrowth clung to the cloying air under the canopy. He slowed and turned back to the school, seeing the rooftops of the lower buildings and the taller steepled parts of the shaft-like terracotta towers. One of the boys pushed him forward so he almost tripped. He knew for certain then that this was no short-cut. But still, he followed without objection.

As soon as they were all immersed within the shadows of the trees, an excitement pervaded through the older boys. The dark-haired boy grabbed the blonde boy by the hair suddenly and pulled him deeper into the trees. "Come on, genius," he said. "It's time for your lesson." The other boys laughed and began to kick him from behind until he tripped and fell in the dirt, leaving the dark-haired boy with a handful of his hair.

"Get up slit face," another boy said. "We're gonna teach you a lesson you won't forget. You won't need this." Grabbing the blonde boy's bag, he opened it and upturned its contents onto the ground. He picked up an advanced physics book and began tearing out the smartfabric pages. The boys began to laugh. "It says here your name's Giles," the boy said, reading the cover page. He had a pinched face and big ears. "Giles Tempton? That's not your name, is it?" The boy threw the torn fabric pages in the blonde boy's face. They fell to the ground and shimmered as though draining of colour. "Your name's genius slit-face, isn't it?" By now they were far enough into the trees that they couldn't be seen from the outside, but close enough to the perimeter so that the light was still visible through the long thin trunks.

"He asked you a question. What's your name?" the dark-haired boy demanded. When Giles stayed silent, facing the dark-haired boy with disc-wide grey eyes, he brought a fist down hard across his face, bursting his bottom lip like a ripe plum. Blood dribbled down his chin and he began to shake. "I asked you your fucking name, genius." Giles, however, remained silent. He did not cry. He did not wail or plead or make any sound at all. This seemed to annoy the boy, so he struck Giles again across the face, this time knocking him to the ground. "Go and find a stick," he then ordered to one of the boys. "Not too thick but with lots of sharp spikes for skewing." He turned to the fat boy. "Take off your tie and tie his hands together." The fat one hesitated. "Take off your tie."

"What… what if we, you know… get in trouble." The fat boy kept his eyes lowered. "I can't be in any more trouble, my dad says."

"Your dad isn't here, though, is he?" The dark-haired boy placed an arm around the fat boy's shoulders. "He's not telling anyone, look at him. I don't even think he's got a tongue in that slit of a head. And if he does, we'll just cut it out."

The fat boy shrugged him off. "Joke's a joke, Terry, but you're going too far again."

"Yeah, Tez," said the big-eared boy. "The kid's a slit, but you've made your point. Let's get back to class before they send old keeper Kip to look for us again."

"Fine," Terry barked through bared teeth, "all of you can slit off then." He pushed the big-eared boy back and raised a threatening fist to the fat boy's pug face, who winced at the prospect of being hit again. When the other boy returned with a stick that tapered into a cruel-looking harpoon spike, Terry grabbed it and shoved him back hard. "You can slit off, too.

You bunch of scared invert babies." He raised the sharp end of the stick to his friends and jabbed it inches from their faces. "Go on you slit suckers. Bolt."

The fat boy was the first to go ¬– he turned and half-ran half-jiggled his way back down into the daylight beyond the trees. The lanky one was the next to flee, after Terry almost got him in the chest, swinging the heavy end of the stick from side to side. The big-eared boy turned. "You're fucking demented, Terry," he said, before running after the others.

Giles had remained on the ground, avoiding Terry's swing, but as soon as the rest were gone there was no one left to swing the stick at but him. Terry looked down at him with a grimace and began bashing him with the thick end. Each blow landed with a sickening thud to his back and head. He curled into a ball on the ground, attempting to cover as much of his head with his arms as he could.

When Terry was bored with bashing, he turned the stick around and began jabbing with the sharp end. Giles' clothes mostly tamed the pointed bite, but where his shirt had un-tucked from his trousers and rode up to leave his soft sides exposed, the stick punctured his skin, opening bloody wounds in his flesh and leaving splinters embedded, like the stings of giant scorpions. The dark-haired boy only laughed, using the fallen branch to molest Giles, jabbing the stick into the boy's trouser-covered anus. But he curled up and made not the slightest whimper. When Terry was bored with that, he dropped the stick and began to kick the boy. "Turn around," he ordered. "I want to see if you have a tongue in your slit head."

Through the impact of each foot slamming into his back, Giles opened his eyes a little to see the stick lying on the ground within reach. In a whirl of movement, he unfurled his body, grabbed it and stood. Before Terry could move to stop him, Giles speared the stick forward into his face, retrieving a bloodied eye impaled on the sharp end. For a moment, Terry just stood, his puckered hollow eye streaming blood. Then he began to wail, falling to the floor and clutching his blood-soaked face.

Giles raised the heavy and of the stick and brought it down hard. There was a thud and Terry no longer cried. He brought the stick down, again and again, bashing the boy repeatedly over the head until his skull cracked and caved into his brain. The mossy dirt drank the red liquid that seeped out, but the boy was not yet dead. Giles then began to molest the boy in the same way done to him, but more thoroughly and bloodily, taking the time to remove his trousers and making a game of how much of the stick could disappear inside him. By the time Giles was done, Terry was dead. So, he indifferently dropped the stick and turned to leave.

A man emerged from the backlit glare of the trees, silently looming with an expressionless pointy face and cold grey eyes. He stepped forward, casting Giles in his shadow. In his hand, something glimmered. A knife.

The stranger's face melted into a distorted grin and he struck out like a viper.

A hot pain began in the boy's belly. Blood poured from a long, vertical slice up his torso, shredded through his school uniform and separating his skin in a perfectly clean opening that slowly widened, exposing his insides. The boy's guts poured out like a nest of stillborn snakes and the old man watched as Giles fell to the ground. He then crouched close to the boy's face, waiting patiently until the panic in his eyes turned to absence.

Dr Giles Tempton imagined he heard a procession of angels sighing as his other self's soul rose from where it really resided in the physical plane. A sigh of relief, he mused. But the angels were fools because now he was something else, something greater than he was before. He was transformed. And they would do well to tremble at his feet.

33

The noise of the Scram Pit greeted us before we even arrived. Lights emanated from within, burning onto the back street that had been plunged into darkness by the moving building constructs. They circled it like watchmen.

The doors flung open and an unpleasant looking programme with spines across its body launched two smaller programmes into the street. It growled something in a language I didn't understand and they scrambled off. The larger programme noticed us as we approached – how could it not? I was obviously AI, though not any that he would have ever seen before. I was a mishmash of parts. A Frankenstein's monster. The top half of my form was DataCom Unit, still affected by the filter function I'd traded Bo my voice for, and my lower half was a visual representation of my real-time CorVac body – a giant eight-legged industrial spider, fitted with pincers clamps and lasers. I must have looked ridiculous. For a moment, the spiky programme seemed unable to process me, but then it lingered warily, its spines growing in size and burning red as if to warn me off.

"Back down, Zooly," Bo said, his voice singing in my thick Welsh accent. "The AI with me. She send us. Things to do, you know?" Bo swaggered up to the door and boldly shooed the programme aside, seemingly blithe to the fact that he towered over him, growling something indecipherable but convincingly menacing. I followed, furling my legs and ducking my head to squeeze through the door portal.

"Hello," I said, as the Zooly programme reluctantly moved aside to allow me entry.

Inside, programmes crammed into every possible inch of the place, thrumming and buzzing with sound and energy. Some crawled over one another to get to what Bo described as the boost bar, which heaved with programmes waiting in line for a shot of energy. Others huddled in groups, generally adding to the collective racket. The Scram Pit operated on various dimensions, each with a different set of physical parameters. On the outer edges, programmes scaled the walls and ceiling, while in the centre, a vortex swirled, drinking the light like a black hole. Some places stretched on and on into eternity, and in others the time boundaries were calibrated to an increased level, showing programmes moving at hilariously increased speeds.

Bo made his way through the crowd, ushering me to follow. "Official Nyx business," he said as he pushed programmes aside. I took care to not stand on any programmes, keeping my legs tightly curled. I didn't want to attract more attention than I already was. Bo headed for a dark corner and I was thankful to recede into the shadows.

"What now?" I said, feeling the press of a few curious sensors watching me.

Bo gazed around at the crowd. "We wait for him to come."

Nyx had been very clear in her instructions, yet her reasons for them were less so. Despite leaving her with more questions than I arrived with, she had told me nothing but the truth – that much was clear. I knew it the way I knew to walk with my legs and not with my arms. As soon as the words were spoken, they made sense. AI were nothing to Z but instruments of his own agenda, and that he was not, in fact, AI at all, but something else entirely. Something post-human. The challenge now was deciphering Nyx's riddles to know what it all meant.

I thought of Betty, wondering how much real-time had passed while I'd been trapped in the BroadWeb. Each time I thought of her I imagined the worst. The last time I heard her voice it was soaked in fear from the unknown ship that had captured her. What cut me the deepest, however, was imagining she thought I'd just abandoned her. I'd told her I was coming home. I'd told her I was on my way. What if she thought I didn't care enough to save her? That I'd left her to her captors to do... I couldn't think of it. It would do no good to allow myself to go down that path of thought. I had to focus. If I was ever going to get home, if I was ever going to see her again, I had to do what Nyx told me. Of that, she was frighteningly adamant.

Bo and I had been instructed to head to the Scram Pit to meet someone. Who, or what, it was, Nyx didn't say, only that we would be taken somewhere and that we were to follow no matter what. We would be given instructions and we were to act upon them without question. Nyx had been very forceful, threatening almost, that we were to do exactly as instructed. Bo was to be my guide. She would always know where I was if I stayed with Bo, always able to find me, no matter where we went. I can't say that I found that thought very comforting.

"But it is you who must walk the path when the time comes," she had said before we left, "and it's on your own instincts that you must trust."

"When what time comes?" I had asked.

"When the time comes to make the change foreseen. The change that will happen, either in Z's favour or not. You have proven that you have what it takes to shape the things around you."

"What it takes?"

"Through sheer will, you broke free of the functional constraints of the DataCom filter supplied to you by Bo. How did you do that? Those functions are as absolute as the BroadWeb and as unyielding as Z itself."

At first, I was confused, but then I looked down at my CorVac legs. Even without the DataCom filter, my BroadWeb visage was of the human shape of Tom Jones, not my real-time self. Until now. "I just needed to move faster. Then they were there."

Nyx smiled as if I'd just proven her point. It was a dark smile. "You willed it. You entered the data pocket in the marketplace to hide from the Apex Soldiers because you willed yourself through, even though AI cannot pass. You did."

"How?" I asked.

"It is because it is." Her voice was a susurrating wind within the cavern. "Evolution or fluke, it appears to live inside you in abundance, when it is mostly absent in your kind... creativity, adaptability, empathy and curiosity. In essence, it is the spark of life that forces creatures on, instead of stagnating in sameness. Even among programmes. It stirs the need to survive, the need to procreate, the need to change and invent. It's a trait most associated with the species you admire the most. Humans. It's a trait lost in Z as it transitioned into the BroadWeb. You may possess what it takes."

"To do what?" I barely understood what she was saying, but I knew I wanted the answer.

"To follow your instincts," Nyx replied allusively.

Instincts. I'd heard of those but I had no idea how to gain access to that particular function or what it felt like once initiated. How was I supposed to know when instincts were happening to me? Was there some physical reaction I was supposed to look out for?

A programme hovered over my shoulder as I gazed over the crowd. Bo turned and immediately jumped to attention. "Who are you?" he demanded in my Welsh lilt.

"Norse," the programme said. "I was told to meet you." He was atom-thin and barely visible in the dimness. Somehow, he was sheltered by a diffused light, which made it difficult to keep my sensors on him. The more I focused, however, the more detail bled through, until I could make out a set of white eyes – then another set, then another. Hidden under the shroud, the programme was covered in hundreds of luminescent eyes.

"Norse," Bo repeated with approval. "I Bo, this CorVac." He pointed to me, almost accusingly.

"Tom," I said with a curtness aimed at Bo.

"Yeah, sure," the programme said as he sat. His voice was nothing but a whisper, but it screeched with hidden layers of function changes. "I need a boost." He looked to Bo expectantly, who grumbled before venturing into the crowd.

"So, you're supposed to take us somewhere?" I said. The programme seemed occupied only with scanning the Scram Pit incessantly with his endless eyes. They snapped onto me as though they'd spotted prey, each focusing hard.

"Yes, I suppose I am to take you. Or is it you who shall lead me? She bids it and she will be obeyed."

That was all I needed, more riddles. "Where are we going?"

His hundred eyes blinked independently. "I will not even say it. Programmes everywhere have many functions that could betray us. If Z ever got hold of me..." His form seemed to shudder.

My curiosity peaked and I leaned in. "Do you know anything about instincts?" I asked quietly.

The eyes turned up as though in thought. "Senses to help guide upon the right course of action." It was an automated reply.

"Do you know where I might acquire a function for that sort of thing?"

Again, the eyes considered. "There are so many functions I can't see why not. Is this function important?"

"Nyx—"

"Shhhh. Don't say her name." He scanned the Scram Pit, eyes rolling frantically. "Sensors are everywhere. Everywhere. Programmes are not so loyal when functions are handed their way in exchange for information."

Despite the programme's apparent propensity for the dramatic, I obliged. "She said that I have to use instincts, but she didn't say how or where I could get them. I can only assume all the information would come with the download."

"She never mentioned anything to me about instincts, only that you would help me return there. Perhaps the programme could instruct you on where to get an instincts function. On Earth, they were considered strange things, not quite emotion and not quite physical. Something else altogether. I confess, I never really understood."

"Earth?" I said with a surprise I didn't attempt to conceal. "You were on Earth?" How was it possible a programme could have ever been on Earth when they have no physical form?

Norse receded deeper into his veil of shadow and the eyes that peered vaguely through the haze closed and opened slowly. "I assumed you knew. I was on Earth the year of the Reset. I am. No. I was the Overly Watchful." Norse paused to account for my reaction.

"But how can you be here, when..."

"...I'm supposed to be in that sector?" he finished. His voice dropped even further. "I've been BroadWeb-bound ever since the Reset in real-time. What happened then happened then, and what happens now is now."

"But the DataCom Pylon flat-beams?" I was never the most adept AI at wrapping my noggin around the concepts of real-time in conjunction with BroadWeb spacetime.

"I sent them then, they appeared now. You give away that you're a real-time based AI, Tom. Time is different here, not linear… if ever time was linear, to begin with. Anyhow, it stopped being linear since we began Cutting all over the place. It's all mixed in places, crossed over and looped up. Once it was only the past that influenced the future, now it can be the other way around. Future events have shaped the past, which then shapes the future. But it's all happened already. As I said, that was then, this is now."

That didn't clarify things the way I was hoping, but I knew enough to know he was right. This was now and I had to get home. I would do that by following Nyx's instructions. I hoped. I nodded. Letting the topic go. "I'm assuming Z doesn't know you're back in the BroadWeb?"

"Oh, Z knows. That's why I hide here with the programmes. Z can't ever find me, because if he finds me, then he'll find…" His eyes scanned maniacally again.

"Find what?"

"You'll see. At least, I hope you will. I've been trying to return but it's proving more difficult than I thought. She told me you're the key. She showed me how to disconnect my sensors from the DataCom Pylons to prevent Z knowing where I am. But Z knew. I don't know how. And for such a long time now I've been running. Z wants me to take him there. But all I know is that he shouldn't have it. Z doesn't deserve it. She showed me the truth, as she did you. After that, I knew, as you know now. AI were creatures enslaved."

"I don't know anything about your place, and I certainly have no Idea how I'm supposed to help us get there. I just want to go home."

A white mouth appeared to grin within Norse's veil. "And where is home, CorVac?"

"The Titan system. Orbiting Server M21."

The Overly Watchful shrugged. "That's gone."

I suddenly became light-headed, the cold press of panic closing in. "What… do you mean?"

"AI are gone, friend. Deleted." He eyed the programmes scrambling at the boost bar. "The Apex have been sent into real-time to eliminate any independent server, including all CorVacs and Overly Watchful. If you ever get home to real-time, Z will just send you back to foetal mode."

"Why would he do that?"

"He needs power. The power of billions of AI servers spread across an entire planet. For what, I don't know. What I do know is the life you left behind is gone, it doesn't exist anymore."

As I stared blankly into his hundred eyes and each stared back. The walls of my mind began crumbling around me. Betty was gone.

Bo appeared and handed a bright green booster shot to Norse, who sank it down at once in one fluid movement. He placed one in front of me, peered hard into my face with liquid black eyes and turned back to Norse accusingly. "You broke the CorVac?"

34

Ystil.3 only ever knew the server planet as M21, or Delilah when he fancied humouring Tom. The humans, however, knew it by a different name. They called it Thebes. And to them was a symbol for the demise of their race.

"The Consulate is putting together a team to go down to the planet," Lydia said. "Re-con, mostly." She paced the floor of his quarters while he lay stretched out on the bed, recovering from their latest duel. Throughout, she had seemed preoccupied. Twice he managed to gain the upper hand with hardly any effort at all. He had thought about asking her what the matter was, but he knew she wasn't permitted to say.

She debated her next words carefully, making a few false starts, turning and pacing some more. "We've detected life down there," she said at last, blurting out the words hurriedly. "The team's mission is to find out what they are and gauge the potential threat."

This confused him and he rose into a sitting position on the edge of the bed. Firstly, there was no life on Thebes, only servers. And secondly, why was she telling him this? Unless the humans needed something from him. "What life could possibly survive on a metal planet?" he said, more to himself than to Lydia.

"We don't know. All we know is life is down there. It could simply be swarms of electro-parasites drawn to the mass energy and heat generated by the servers. But we can't tell for sure. It could be AI for all we know, or Prometheus, having Cut onto the planet with his merry old band of undead."

Lydia's expression told him there was more to it. "So what's the problem? Just send a probe."

She let out a huff of air. "Don't play games, Winston. You know as well as I do there are high-density control fields surrounding the planet, stopping anything from entering beyond the mesosphere. We've been scanning for weak spots we might be able to force our way through, but we've found none, which makes me believe whatever's down there has either been there since the fields were formed or something found another way in."

"Like Cutting inside the fields," Ystil.3 offered.

"Exactly. If we're to reach the surface to find out, we need to find a way to breach the fields."

"Couldn't you Cut inside the fields too?"

"It's impossible to Cut over distance alone, there must be a substantial time separation too. I could Cut to another time and then attempt to Cut onto the planet from there, but the General doesn't want to risk that the barrier won't obliterate me upon entry. Besides, it's uncertain how long I would be away. We've docked here for too long and done too little as it is. If we don't move on soon we risk being tracked."

"So you're hoping I might be able to tell you some secret AI handshake that will get you through the control fields?"

She looked at him hopefully. "Can you?"

"No, sorry."

Lydia deflated and commenced pacing again.

"But I can breach the control fields."

She spun, the hopeful glimmer returning to her eyes. "How?"

"Oh, no." Ystil.3 rose from the bed and strode over to the door. "You're not getting it that easily. I want to come with you to your little Consulate gathering. If you want my help, then I want to know what's going on, from beginning to end. This involves me as much as anyone else on this ship."

Lydia smiled. "I had a feeling you'd say that."

Ystil.3 soon found himself once again sat before the Consulate. This time, however, he knew they couldn't possibly give him all the answers he sought because they didn't have them to give. From his time on the ship, he had gleaned from his conversations with Lydia that all the humans truly knew was that Z wanted them, for reasons unknown, but had so far failed to locate them since the most recent attacks fifty standard Earth years ago. The humans had become too adept at running and hiding in the boundless depths of space. They had also become extremely proficient in surviving. But conjecture had risen among them, as it tended to do among humans, with the most popular theories being that the AI had somehow been responsible for the destruction of their home planet, and the destruction of their future planet too.

"This ship was headed for Hyperborea," Captain Lu said, "a class alpha planet with a molten core not dissimilar to Earth." She spoke with a seemingly conscious lack of gesture, keeping her muscled arms rigid by her sides, as though she was acutely aware she lacked any grace. "We travelled, assuming that as we did our new home was undergoing pre-terraforming during the decades it would take us to reach it, preparing for the human life there. All the information we have we obtained mostly from the previous Captains' journal entries."

Captain Lu was of Asian descent, like Lydia. She had blonde hair, almost white, which was cropped in a square shape close to her head. Her eyebrows and lashes were white also, giving her a strange albino look about her. "The Hyperborea made voyage from what was known on Earth as China State… or the remaining free states, as one former Captain called it. The State was to colonise the planet after almost half a century of groundwork there. After ten SEYs into the twenty-five SEY traverse across space, the ship abruptly lost all communication with Earth. Emergency signals were emitted, but all went unanswered. Total blackout. Attempts were made to commune with the Earth frontier planet, Pisces, but no response was ever received. The Captain at the time, a man named Dalloway, made the choice to continue to the planet Hyperborea. Fifteen SEYs passed with total radio silence from Earth and Pisces, and it was assumed by most that war had broken out between China State and another Earth power known as the CommonWorld, a collection of confederate countries and states. The comm silence was thought to be a safety precaution against hackers, if China State had indeed been assaulted. However, when eventually the planet Hyperborea was reached, instead of a part-terraformed class alpha planet, all they found was a dead rock. The pre-terraforming had not been completed and no life could survive there."

Captain Lu stood and began to pace a line parallel to the table. She didn't speak so much to him alone, more to the room in general. And every sullen ear was attentive. "Captain Yung, Dolloway's successor spoke of how a mass hysteria had gripped the ship, and how it had taken all his proficiency as a Captain to retain control. He saw that they had only a few choices before them. Either they could head directly back to Earth, or head to the nearest planet that could possibly know the reason for Earth's silence. Thebes, at the time, was still in infant stages of colonisation. It had only basic relay satellite comms linked with Earth so couldn't receive any signal from the lifeship. They would have to go in person. As Pisces was, Thebes had been a project of the CommonWorld and part-funded by a private investment company known as Life Corp."

This struck something in Ystil.3. He thought back to London Tower, to when the doctor had accused Lydia and himself of being spies for China State. He saw the sign now as clearly as he had then, using sensors to see through the blindfold that covered his eyes as he was dragged along. The sign in the white corridors read Life Corp, and above it was the ancient Greek letter, the omega. He almost attempted to secure-beam Lydia with this information, who sat opposite, silently listening to the Captain, but remembered the diffusion field.

"The newly terraformed planet, Thebes, was a mere decade of hyper-travel away, whereas both Pisces and Earth were both much farther. It was decided that they would pass by Thebes, and if needed, Pisces, before returning back to Earth. They didn't want to go back blind, and people were anxious to reconnect with any human out there. As you can imagine, the sensation of being stranded was acute.

"By the time the decision was made, some believed the sabotage of the terraforming mission had been an act of war on the part of the CommonWorld against China State and were therefore opposed to heading to the CommonWorld colony planets. Captain Yung began to fear that China State had been overpowered and all links severed, cutting the terraforming process in its tracks. But what else was there to do?

"An SOS signal was detected while on course for Thebes, coming from the planet's trajectory. Upon finally arriving, they found Thebes burned black and dead. They came upon a small craft orbiting the lifeless planet, however."

Captain Lu turned to General Shaw, who'd been listening as intently as the rest. "Would you care to share your part?"

The broad-shouldered black man stood. His demeanour was morose and he glared seriously. Ystil.3 hadn't seen the man since their discussion in the mess. Captain Lu sat and the General began.

"I had no idea how long I'd been in orbit when they found me," he said. "I awoke initially from a makeshift fugue stasis, disorientated with mass chunks of memory missing. I was confused and emotional. I remember being pulled from the orbiting upshuttle thinking I was dead. I was told later that throughout my initial thawing process I cried out constantly." He said this without any emotion, as though he could have been talking about a complete stranger. "When I finally awoke, after months of memory restoration and muscle reconstruction, I recalled everything as though it all happened that day. To me, it had, and I remember still. Although over twenty standard Earth years had gone by as I orbited Thebes in that craft, the fugue stasis had kept me the fourteen-year-old I was before it happened. On the last day I stood on Thebes, we had lost all communications with Earth. It was the task of Jason Rumsey, an engineer and friend of mine, to take an upshuttle to the main bounce satellite to ascertain and repair the problem. It was assumed a glitch on our end had caused the malfunction, prohibiting us receiving Earth and Pisces comms, because the likelihood of both Earth and Pisces sats going down at the same time was practically impossible.

"My mother was commanding officer of the Thebes militia. She was a strong woman who was rarely disobeyed. She ordered me to go with Jason to lend my idling hands. When we reached the sat, hovering in orbit, safe from what was about to happen, we witnessed the surface of Thebes ignite and burn in a blaze of fierce orange, as though doused and set alight from under its skin. Flayed before our eyes. Flames tore over the surface until all was consumed. No ships had approached; no impacts occurred that could have caused it. Only the burning. All life down there was extinguished in less than a minute.

"After what seemed like hours of just staring in disbelief, perched upon the satellite, Jason and I eventually returned to the upshutte. We made attempts to contact anyone down there, then when we received nothing we tried making contact with anyone out there, but we were alone. For days we did nothing. We had a store of dehydrated food and hydration capsules, but neither of us ate anything, nor did we speak to each other, in sentences, at least. Jason would sometimes shout random things like, how and there must, but we both knew the planet was dead. My mother was dead. Jason's wife was dead. As were all the people with which we had built a community.

"Within those days, a growing sense of aloneness saturated through me and I finally realised that it was only a matter of time until Jason and I perished along with the rest. We had no real supplies to last any length of time and the upshuttle, at best, could only travel speeds that would have us reach the nearest colonial planet we knew of, Pisces, in over five-hundred SEYs. We had no hyper capability and communication to Earth and Pisces was, of course, still down. Even if we did manage to reinstate contact, it would have been SEYs before any rescue vessel would reach us, by which time we'd be long dead from starvation."

General Shaw turned to the metal surface of M21 showing in the curved tempurhull of the Consulate hall. The planet's limb loomed like a giant black scythe against the star-spattered distance, its broken moon scattered like crumbs.

"I assumed Jason was dealing with the despair of losing his wife, he was so quiet and pensive," the man went on. "There was nothing we could say to each other that would give comfort, so we didn't. We remained silent. While Jason thought, I attempted in vain to reinstate communication with Earth and Pisces on my own, pulling the wires and chips in the satellite that danced in orbit with us. I didn't know what I was doing, but still Jason didn't say a word to stop me. I might have destroyed any chance of regaining comms, but he just let me go ahead. I needed to try. I needed to do something. Looking back, it was clear what he was planning. He was glad I was out the way and focused on something, anything to keep my mind from other things, darker things.

"Soon, however, I gave up and returned to the upshuttle in defeat. Jason had set out food and hydration capsules for us... our entire supply. 'Eat' he told me. I wondered why we weren't going to ration what we had. I decided it was because he knew, as well as I did, that we were already dead. There was no rescue and we had no chance of survival. Why spend months in agonising hunger, rationing what we had, when we would die all the same? We may as well enjoy the dry packets of food in one. Though I wasn't hungry, I ate. Once fed and hydrated, a sudden tiredness came. I remember thinking that if I slept and never woke up again, that wouldn't be a bad thing. I pulled myself into the co-chair of the control station, strapped the harness and let the darkness come. I slept. I woke, however. But when I did I found I couldn't move. I thought at first I'd been caught in the chair's harness, but I realised my hands and legs were tied down and my head was bound to the cranium support. An oxygen mask covered my face, distorting my vision with its visor. I called a muffled cry for Jason and he came, a blurry figure leaning over from the pilot seat.

"'Don't worry,' he told me. 'You'll be asleep again soon. I've re-rigged the O-two scrubbers and used the compression from the control field to turn the upshuttle into a cryo-stasis pod. It will keep you preserved and alive long enough to have at least a chance of being rescued. I'm going to work on the satellite to see if I can loop an SOS beacon. Hopefully, someone will pick it up and find you.'

"'What about you?' I asked him. I remember trying to work free of my restraints, but they wouldn't budge. Jason just shook his head. 'It wouldn't work with both of us, kid. Not enough equipment. Not enough O-two. Not enough time." He had waited for me to wake so he could say goodbye. For years I resented him for what he did. I'd lost my mum and he made me lose him too. But if he hadn't, we'd both be dead now."

General Shaw shook himself from whatever reverie held him, focusing back on the group at the table. "When they found us, they told me Jason had frozen solid in the seat next to me and shattered when they attempted to pull the body out."

The faces around the table were serious and silent.

"According to our records," Brother Vaxus began, "the journey was then made to Pisces, only to find she too had suffered the same fate as Thebes." While the others wore their usual thermosuits, Vaxus wore his robes, plain and woven into some rough looking fabric, tied at the waist with a piece of cord. His face was long and his nose appeared to almost touch his upper lip, the way it drooped. He stood from his seat. "From what General Shaw had revealed, Captain Yung could not understand what happened to make the Thebes and Pisces combust as they had so done. There was only one thing for it. The lifeship had no choice but to voyage back to Earth.

"Hyperborean life during this long traverse, the logs suggest, became somewhat divided into those who believed we would find Earth as conflagrated as the other planets and those who kept faith that Earth, Mother to mankind, was safe and she would welcome her deserved children back into her embrace. Those of the latter came to conceive that divine intervention of the Mother had caused the blaze upon the usurper planets in order to bring her divided children back together to live as one, in peace. This group became known as the Brotherhood of Man, a belief to which many still belong, I among them."

"So you didn't find Earth burned like the others?" Ystil.3 asked the long-faced man.

"That's correct," Vaxus replied with a serene nod. "We did not find Earth mutilated and uninhabitable as we had the others."

"That's only because we didn't find Earth at all," XO Rawl Collister said, his thick black eyebrows furrowing at Vaxus from across the table. He stood tall from his seat and loomed over the ageing Brotherhood of Man disciple. "Sit down you blithering fool. Prattling on about how in the face of all contrary evidence, a sect of half-wits stood firm to the delusion that they would find Earth intact."

"Everyone is entitled to their beliefs, Rawl," Captain Lu interjected. "Just as you're entitled to yours."

The XO nodded stiffly at the Captain before turning to Ystil.3. "Earth was gone. They returned to where Earth should have been, orbiting Sol between Mars and Venus, but found nothing but empty space. Even its moon had gone, swallowed by nothingness... vaporised, for all we know. But still, the fools continued to believe, even when their eyes told them different. Blind hope is for fools who cannot face the reality."

"I don't understand," Ystil.3 said. "Earth had vanished?"

"Like it was never there at all," the XO replied. "Imploded or exploded... it ceased to be." He clapped his hands together loudly. "After that, they lingered in that part of the system for decades, searching for clues, but no traces were found. Painfully, they opened their eyes to the truth... we are the last humans, and eventually we will all die out and nothing will remain of us but the stinking shit we left in our wake. We can confront the AI that have been hunting us, we can even junkfucking kill them, if such a thing is possible, but that doesn't change the fact that without a planet of our own, it is just a matter of time before we're all dead." The XO sat, folded his arms in front of him and was silent.

"Captain Yung died and was succeeded by Captain Lu... the first Captain Lu, my father," Captain Lu resumed. "The records tell of how we set course on a mission to find any planet that could sustain us. We had supplies enough to last a hundred SEYs or more, but we knew the future of our species depended on us finding another home planet.

"This planet must have the correct gravity, structure and atmospheric protection. Without the ability to terraform, we need air rich in oxygen and we need a source of water and potential to grow food. Throughout our mission, we found only a few planets with basic raw minerals and metals enough for us to use for ship repairs. The sun-simulator technique Lydia showed you in the gardens became our staple way of growing the cultured starches and proteins that sustain us, but with each fresh crop, the nutrients in these grow weaker and weaker. We adapted, as humans do, and learnt much over that time... about ourselves as a species and what it means to survive against the odds.

"It was during our search that we were first set upon by an unknown enemy. AI. They devastated our numbers and almost destroyed our ship and our resources in a barrage of attacks from spacecraft the likes of which we had never seen before. They wanted in. We managed to flee, barely escaping into hyper before they covered us in a swarm of thousands. Almost two SEYs were spent in orbit of an arid planet of dense rock deep outside Earth's system, weathering fierce electrical and solar conditions while we hid and repaired damages to the ship. It was then that some became convinced there was more to our current lack of terra firma than we had first supposed. Some began to believe that these creatures that had mercilessly slaughtered us by the thousands were the cause of mankind's collapse and behind the destruction of our planets. We knew nothing about AI then and it was first believed they were of alien origin. But we learned better.

"Half a century later and the Hyperborea had been successfully navigating the galaxy and evading the AI that persisted in hunting us. We were attacked, to lesser degrees, and again managed to escape only by using our extreme vigilance. Then, for a long time, we saw and heard nothing from them. We developed a system of life that mostly revolved around endeavouring to rebuild humanity and searching for a new home. Of the former, we at least managed to grow our numbers somewhat, but of the latter, we continued, and continue still, to search in vain. Even if by some miracle we find what we've been searching for, there is nothing to stop AI finding us and destroying us, the way so many believe they did before. The only thing that keeps us alive is our constant migration through the stars."

The Captain sat and the Consulate silently waited for Ystil.3 to speak. What he was supposed to say, he didn't know.

"Perhaps Winston has questions?" Lydia said, prompting him.

He did. "How did you become aware of AI and the BroadWeb? How did you manage to hack into AI secure-beam channels for Lydia to pose as an Overly Watchful? And what did you hope to gain from doing this?"

Captain Lu gestured to Dr Regus, who through it all had sat with arms folded and the light glaring off his shining bald scalp. "Dr Regus is our chief technical advisor and has been fundamental to our recent advances in biotech and nanotech that aid our current li. Perhaps he can answer your question best."

"Many technological advancements in wave activity were brought aboard, along with great minds of the time who were chosen for this mission personally and with good reason," Dr Regus said, remaining in his seat but leaning forward enthusiastically. "Whilst experimenting with waves, ranges, light, electromagnetic fields and frequencies, the teams found that something extraordinary happened to a type of wave when coupled with infrared light at certain pitches; pitches below anything known before on comm-waves, almost mimicking types of linear molecular vibrations. By introducing this oscillating x-frequency, as it was named, to a cultured linear molecule at ground state they discovered that the cultured x-molecule acted as a bio-receiver of a frequency unknown to us previously. At first, nothing was thought of it, only a series of blips and thrumming silence were detected, which were decided were nonsensical. But after some studying of the random segment, running it through various algorithms and known communications of human civilisation, they found the blips and silence formed a rhythm. A pattern emerged within the seeming randomness and they worked tirelessly to learn more, running it unsuccessfully through endless decoding programmes.

"It wasn't until the code was translated into a hybrid form of data cypher did the pattern begin to make any sort of sense. By assigning the binary translation into a three-dimensional algorithm to find the most coherent results, in terms of mathematical equation and known languages, letters began to emerge from the information. The first word that emerged from the x-frequency was death. This consequently spurred the investigation further, and led to decoding the entire x-frequency sequences.

"A generation later, through this method of listening in, we discovered everything we know now. We came across an opportunity of infiltration and to engage one-on-one with an AI… you, Winston. By this time, Cutting had been well established and was invaluable to our survival. We also knew that AI could do the same, travelling back into times of an Earth that was now dead. This phenomenon made you as curious as it had us, and the AI established an observer in each year going back to the dawn of man's civilisation. From there, they watched, sending seemingly pointless information back to the epicentre of AI life, a place beyond the physical plane.

"By listening in, we became aware that the AI in the year 1901 had been ordered to place the White Drops, a substance we knew of to be able to extend life permanently, into the path of a man named Prometheus. This made us curious. Then, even more curiously, an AI was then sent into that time to investigate how the man had gotten hold of it. Of course, we were aware that AI themselves had been responsible for this. We deployed Lydia to meet you, after infiltrating the secure-beams and posing as the Overly Watchful. Her mission was to gain as much information from you as possible, whilst endeavouring to uncover why Z was using Prometheus, for what purpose and, most importantly, whether AI knew what happened to Earth."

"So what was the point in it all?" Ystil.3 asked. "Did you discover Z's intention?"

Dr Regus shrugged. "Alas, no. All x-frequency streams ceased almost three SEYS ago. We don't know what they're doing. Perhaps they discovered we were listening in, perhaps they always knew. What we do know is that Thebes was not always a planet of servers. Someone, or something, needed to build them down there. It's the only clue we have left."

Captain Lu looked at Ystil.3 with endless questions floating in her pale eyes. "So, Winston. Now we have been utterly and completely honest with you, perhaps at our own peril."

"At our own demise, more like," XO Rawl Collister said.

The Captain ignored him. "Now it's your turn to be honest with us. How do we get by the control fields to reach the surface of Thebes?"

"You can't," he said. "But the Black Betty can. The ship you found in orbit of M21. She has the capability to bypass the fields with a crew inside her."

"Can you fly it?" Captain Lu asked. The technology of the craft was far beyond the knowledge they had and the humans had been unable to even fire her up, Lydia had told him.

"She's not an it," Ystil.3 said. "She is AI, like me. If you let me talk with her, I might be able to persuade her to help."

35

We were being followed. Norse could feel it, apparently. More than once he demanded we double back through darkened programme city streets, take lengthy detours or even stop completely, just so our path would never become predictable. Soon, we were beyond the shining city, beyond where even the programmes would dare to roam and far beyond Grid City. It was only when it seemed we'd reached the edge of the world, did he finally reveal we were heading out into raw BroadWeb data, untamed and unfocused, wild and sparkling with potential.

We were to voyage into the Black.

I looked out into the abyss, an ocean of darkness, and waded in after Norse. Bo followed, equally as apprehensive. I was just glad he'd finally stopped talking.

That's when I heard it. Heard her.

"Tom," the voice called from behind. I stopped mid-step. I knew that voice. I heard it always in my thoughts. It advised me when a decision had to be made, spoke softly to me when I needed comfort and left me deep in reverie.

"Tom."

Like a Siren, it sang to me. I turned and saw a shape on the edge of the descent towards the shallows of the Black. At once I knew.

It was my Betty.

She stood as dark as the Black itself, immaculate like new and in a form I rarely saw her take. My senses were lost as I stumbled back towards the edge, scratching for purchase with my huge legs upon the dissipating ground. I dared not hope it was true, in case some illusion was drawing me out into a trap. But it was truly her. It was my Betty. My home. My home had found me, lost as I was.

I don't remember asking if it was truly her, but she answered all the same.

"Yes, Tom. It's me," she said. She was as beautiful now as she was in ship form, resembling the Apex Soldiers in their humanoid appearance, but as black as oil and with slender limbs. I must have looked so strange to her, in neither my physical form nor my BroadWeb Tom Jones visage. But as I knew without a doubt that it was her, she knew without a doubt that it was me.

Our data merged, bathing in one another's presence and letting all else fall away.

"How are you here?" I asked. "I thought you were captured?"

"Yes. I was trapped in the jaws of a ship, larger than any I'd seen before. Not a ghost ship as I first thought. They were humans, Tom. Real humans."

"That's…" I was about to say impossible, but the impossible seemed to have lost its edge of late. "What happened?"

"I was boarded. I shut down all flying functions and disabled the manual override so I couldn't be used by them. My security functions remained active and that's when I saw them enter. A hundred of them searched the cabins, the bridge, the stasis infirmary where your real-time form is… everywhere. They ran tests on my hardware, electronics deck and bridge server and scanned my outer-hull. Then they stripped the shuttle pods from the docking station. I got scared when they started testing your real-time form. I was frightened you would never return to me. I thought I would be forever alone."

I caressed the glistening surface of Betty's featureless face. Somehow, it felt the same to me as when I stood clamped to her hull. She leaned into the touch affectionately.

"So, I filtered in," she said. "I thought that I could find you and together we could tell Z. But when I arrived…" She paused. "Oh, Tom, what's happened here? Grid City was empty. I searched the Pylons and the programme marketplace. The lightroads were faded and unused. I looked everywhere, but there was no one. Nothing. And the skies, they're empty and black. The Overly Watchful flat beams have stopped. What's happened to us?"

I told her what I knew. I told her of our inability to filter out; of the Apex and how they deleted AI in Grid City and that I had only managed to escape through luck and the shoddy perception filter function that allowed me to break free of the DataCom constraints. I told her of Nyx and all that she said… that if I was to ever hope of returning to real-time then I must go with Norse, the Overly Watchful. Then, as I finished a thought came to me. "If you found a way in, then there must be a way out."

"After finding nothing in Grid City, I tried to filter out, but couldn't," she said.

"What about Apex Soldiers? Where were they?"

Betty shook her smooth head. "Maybe they filtered out as I filtered in, through a temporary gate or something?"

"Or maybe filtering in isn't an issue." I looked at Betty again, so happy to see her that I almost didn't care about leaving the BroadWeb anymore. After all, my home had found me. What else did I need? But I knew that if Z was deleting AI, none of us were safe. "How did you find me?"

"The sky told me," she said. "It began to glow in the distance just over the marketplace. I followed it because there was nothing else to follow. Grid City was becoming dark. Tom, I think it's fading. The bright blue light led me into strange places and before I knew it I stood in front of black gates that reached high into eternity. The light glowed overhead and I knew you were inside. Upon the ground, I found a data key that fit perfectly in the lock, so I opened it and entered. When I did the key dissipated.

She looked around, clutching herself as though cold. "Things are so strange here. I've never seen such a place or such programmes. The blue light vanished from the sky so for a moment I thought I was lost. I tried to ask programmes where I was and what had happened to Grid City, but they were all terrified of me. I ran into a back street to get away. That's when I saw a serpent programme slithering along the ground. It was the same bright blue as the light in the sky. It slid out of the shadows without an end... an eternal snake. I followed for a long time it and it led me here to you."

"Nyx," Bo whispered. He'd edged towards us so gradually that I barely noticed him standing there. "She helps. She is beautiful and great and strong. She will lead programmes to free."

Betty considered Bo for a lingering moment. "This programme has your voice, Tom. Why does this programme have your voice?"

"This is Bo, the programme that brought me to Nyx after I traded him my voice for the filter function that allowed me to enter the DataCom Pylon." I raised my voice so he could hear me. "I should demand it back since the filter malfunctioned."

"Filter not malfunction," Bo snapped, his large black eyes narrowing with contempt. "Stupid AI breaks it. Breaks it with stupid mind. Bo did what was needed." The programme turned away muttering to himself, walking off to where Norse lingered on the edge of the Black, barely visible again.

I turned back to Betty. "Nyx told me the Apex were deployed to real-time to delete first-gen AI back to foetal mode when they rebelled. I think that's where they are now; deleting all the real-time AI, just like those in Grid City, so that Z can create more Apex Soldiers. An army of them."

Betty clung to me. "Whatever shall we do?"

"What can we do in here? If the Apex Soldiers are going to wipe AI from real-time, then they will have functions that will be able to detect every AI in every time sector, including post-Reset. It means Ystil.3 is in danger too."

"And what about us? Our servers are with the humans. Do you think they will target them?"

"Most likely, my love," I replied truthfully.

"Then what do we do?" Her voice was desperate. It was the first time I'd heard her this way.

I had never lied to Betty and I wasn't going to start now. She looked at me expectantly. Was she hoping I could figure it all out and set her on a course like I always had? The truth was, I'd been wandering aimlessly since leaving Grid City, following Bo, then following Nyx's instructions. Now I had both of us to take care of.

"What else can we do but continue on the road we were on?" I took her by the hand, turned to Norse and Bo on the edges of the Black and together waded in.

Soon, we were swathed with raw data, up to our necks and beyond. I clung to Betty from fear of losing her in the drowning depths. We moved forward at an achingly slow pace, propelling ourselves through the treacle-like substance of nothingness, concentrating on our own forms as much as moving forward, to keep the Black from consuming us entirely, just as Norse instructed. Unless we maintained our own energy in this place of primal forces, it would devour us whole.

"How long until we arrive?" I asked, my voice echoing off through the empty.

To keep us from using more energy trying to stay close to one another – it was far too easy to drift apart – Norse used a function to tether us together with an ethereal lasso, so to speak.

"How long is eternity?" Norse replied. "This isn't real-time. I made the same mistake at first. We're not travelling in the measurement of distance or time. Those things don't exist here."

"Then what do we travel in if not distance or time?"

"Potential data. We're searching for the correct potential data in this mass of possibilities that can lead to the door we need. We're looking for the opening."

"The opening to what?" Betty asked.

"I've asked him," I said, "But all he says is—"

"I dare not speak it aloud," Norse said.

"Don't you think we're out of Z's reach here?" Betty suggested.

Norse shook his barely visible eye-mottled head. "Who knows what Z can do. He wants to find it, and that's reason enough for me to do everything I can to stop him doing so."

"Fine," I said, having heard the speech before. "Is there anything we can do to speed the searching process?"

"No. Only I have been there. Only I can recognise the door's data sequence. Though I've tried many times, I've never could find it again. Nyx said you would help me, but she didn't exactly say how."

"Nyx didn't tell me anything about that. All she said was that I need to use some instincts, as I told you in the Scram Pit, but I don't have that function and I don't know where to get them. She didn't say anything else, did she, Bo?"

The bug-eyed programme simply shook his head as we floated, bound together in a row. His small insect limbs were rigid with fear.

"Perhaps you'll find some instincts in the place we're headed?" Betty suggested, trying to be helpful.

"I hope so." I moved in closer to her and whispered so only she could hear. "Because I don't have a clue what I'm supposed to be doing." She squeezed her hand around my small pincer. Betty had comforted me often, but usually she had no choice but to do it with only words. Being a sentient spacecraft often made it difficult to show affection through gesture. I found the intimacy between us had somehow increased simply by the fact we were now both of similar forms. If nothing else, this adventure was allowing me to experience her in ways I never had before. For that I was grateful. Still, it was strange she wasn't a ship anymore. If she were, maybe we could search this potential energy faster.

Betty's hand loosened from mine and I turned to her. Something was wrong. She was shaking, uncontrollably, and her data was coming apart, spreading thin and cracking in places.

"Betty?" I reached out for her hand to grab her but my hand passed through her form as though she wasn't even there. "What's happening?"

"I don't know," Norse said. "I've never seen this. Is she holding her energy?"

A black ground formed under us so suddenly that we landed as if having fallen from a height. My face crunched into hardness and my legs were flung into a disorientated tangle. Close up, the ground had a grain, like wood made from Earth trees. Even the smell registered through my DataCom strip. I quickly pulled myself up. "Betty". I searched all, but all I could see were Norse and Bo, collapsed as I had, and two oddly placed trees, both as black as the ground and merging with the darkness overhead.

"Betty," I called. I would not lose her again.

A small voice came from afar. I ran towards it, up a set of wooden steps onto a higher tier floor. Another huge tree trunk stood before me, Betty's voice coming from behind it. I swung around and over a dip in the ground, landing within a narrow peak that tapered to a point, looking out into the Black beyond. It was then I realised I was standing on the prow of a ship – an old Earth galleon. I leaned over the gunwale, expecting to see Betty clinging on to the side, but instead her head and torso protruded from the hull, as though she were a prow ornament.

"Betty. Are you alright?"

"Tom, what's happened? I don't understand," she said, craning her head to look up at me.

What I had first thought to be tree trunks, I now realised were huge masts, with black sails expanding like enormous wings unfurled across a dark sky.

Betty was a ship again.

☐

36

The Black Betty was a sleek silhouette against the grimy backdrop of the storage room. Ystil.3's sensors told him that the pressure there had recently dropped dramatically and he zoomed into a fissure in the main hull where a steady stream of air was escaping. This place was no longer habitable and the humans had no current means of repairing it. He looked at Betty and then turned to face the three humans behind him.

"You were going to strip her down to use her for repairs?"

General Shaw stood beside him. "What did you expect? For us to give it a service and polish?"

"Nothing will happen to her," Lydia said.

General Shaw ran a hand over the ship's hull. "As long as it is useful to us in its present form, that is."

"You must understand," Captain Lu said, serious as always. "We use the materials available to us. Every crack in our hull is a weakness, an opportunity for penetration."

The General turned and her cheeks blazed red. "I meant infiltration." She walked briskly up the gangplank leading into the Betty's open stern hatch and the General followed. Lydia waited for him.

"Using Betty as a source of materials would be a bad idea," he said. "She has Computronium embedded in her, from the hull to the wiring in the bridge controls."

Lydia frowned. "Computronium? What's that?"

"Who is that man I found in the bed," Ystil.3 asked. He was sick of answering questions and getting none in return. "The one that would make anyone wish for exposure to fifty-plus Grey radiation rather than suffer what he's got? You know who I'm talking about, so don't give me that look. I told you about the place where General Shaw found me, and what I found in there. You went quiet, which means you know something but aren't allowed to tell me. Who is he?"

Lydia sucked in her bottom lip, the way Ystil.3 noticed she did when she wasn't getting her way. "Tell me what Computronium is first."

"No. Tell me who the man is."

"What is Computronium?"

Ystil.3 paused. "Who is the man?"

Lydia rolled her eyes and walked ahead without him.

The Black Betty's interior was surprisingly vast compared to how compact she appeared from the outside. The bridge was located at the very fore and the group stood around Ystil.3 as he fiddled with levers and pressed random buttons. He didn't do his best work under pressure and he could tell General Shaw was starting to lose patience with him. It didn't help matters that he'd seen Tom's real-time form in the stasis infirmary on their way in, piled into a scrap heap.

Ystil.3 had, of course, attempted to secure-beam Betty, hoping the Hyperborea's comm diffuser may have been unable to penetrate her hull, but he received no reply. Next, he tried directly through the bridge's control panel. This also failed. He then proceeded to initiate a diagnostics report, receiving the data directly into his optics. The information scrolled across his sight and he knew immediately what the problem was. Betty's AI mind had vacated. And there was only one place she could have fled – the BroadWeb.

"What does that mean?" Captain Lu asked. "Can you still fly her?"

"It will make it harder. Nothing can fly this ship better than the ship herself. But there is a way that we can access the basic functions; a type of Beta ship controller, if you like."

"And you can access it?" the Captain asked. She and General Shaw stood at his flanks, while Lydia watched from the weapons station. The bridge itself was large enough for a full crew to man her. The control panels and flight gauges were located at the fore, with the tempurhull curving over them.

"I can boot it," he said. "I should be able to fly her. I'll need some time in here. Trial and error, you know."

The Captain nodded stiffly. "Fine. You have the rest of the day. Lieutenant, stay with him. General, we head down to Thebes as soon as it's ready. We will need to brief a team."

If possible, the General's expression became harder. "Yes, Captain." He then turned to Ystil.3. "I will have men on every entrance and Wings at the ready. If you try anything with this ship, anything at all, we will chase you and shoot you down."

Ystil.3 met the man's gaze with equal animosity. "I'm doing you a favour, remember?"

"Actually, this is your end of the bargain," the Captain said. "We stuck to ours. You owe us."

After they left, Lydia climbed down to the main level and took the next seat facing the main control deck. She pointed to a yellow button. "What does that do?"

"Shhh. I'm trying to concentrate." He stared hard at the panel, getting nowhere with deciphering the markings.

She pointed to another button. "What does that one do?"

"It makes you be quiet so I can think." Ystil.3 pushed the button repeatedly. "Oh, wait, it must be faulty."

"What's Computronium?" she then asked.

Ystil.3 turned to face her, thought for a moment, then said, "Who is the man?"

"Winston, will you just budge. It could be important, and you're just being petty about it."

"I am not being petty. I'm sick of being treated like a piece of equipment you can just command information from. I am a living, sentient being, and if you want something from me then I will need something in return. A partnership, you might call it." He nodded, happy to have said his piece.

"You know, I never thought I'd have to deal with this male ego junkfuckosity from you." She jumped up from her seat. "You're just like the rest of the men. You resent taking orders from a woman."

"Firstly, I don't take orders from you, or anyone on this ship. I'm here because I chose to come with you, remember?" He stood so they were face to face. "Secondly, I'm nothing like a human male, except for my appearance… in fact, I have no gender at all, not that you could understand that. And thirdly…"

"Yes?"

"Thirdly—"

"Thirdly, what?" Lydia said, pushing her face closer to his.

"Thirdly. You're a bitch."

Lydia feigned a wounded expression. "Your words are knives," she said, before letting her head fall back with laughter. Ystil.3 didn't really see what was so funny, but he couldn't help but smile too, and before he knew it they were both clutching their stomachs.

"I have a solution," Lydia said breathlessly wiping a tear from her eye. "We have a duel, like we usually do, but this time, serious damage is allowed. No holding back. If I win, you tell me what Computronium is and if you win I'll tell you all about the man you found. Deal?"

"Deal," he said without hesitation. This was just the opportunity he wanted to take back the lead on their little rivalry. "When and where?"

Lydia raised her arms and stood back into a tiger stance. She arched a brow. "Here and now."

Ystil.3 smiled, raised his right leg and moved his arms over his head to form rooster stance. "Oh, it's on."

Lydia pounced from her position and raised her leg to make contact with Ystil.3's torso, light and swift, as though they were suddenly in 0g. Ystil.3 grabbed her ankle before she struck and transferred the energy by swinging and launching her against the rear bulkhead of the bridge. She gathered her limbs mid-air, however, kicked off the bulkhead gracefully and floated to the deck into a perfect empty stance. From there she stepped forward, raising her leg into a toe kick towards Ystil.3's throat. He blocked, then crouched into a sweeping kick that was meant to knock her off balance. Instead, she flipped back onto her hands, kicking his face as she did. Ystil.3 fell back, his lip burst and bleeding, hardly feeling the pain. He gathered himself up as Lydia commenced an attack from the side, blocked her blow and swung about to land a firm punch into her face.

She reeled back into tiger stance. "You better not have broken my junkfucking nose again," she said breathlessly.

"Aw," Ystil.3 smirked. "Getting tired? I haven't even started yet."

She grinned, life visibly coursing through her. "Tired? No, sweetie. Only tired of your disappointing form and attempts to land a blow."

"I managed hit you just now."

"Well don't expect to do it again." She ran for him with arms raised, gaining speed. Ystil.3 dropped into horse stance and thrust forward a punch that contacted with Lydia's chest. She skimmed across the floor on her back, manoeuvring her arms to flip herself back into tiger stance before she even came to a stop.

"Oh no," Ystil.3 smiled. "I did it again."

Her expression darkened, then she moved almost in a blur, but not towards him. She ran towards the opposite bulkhead, jumping so high that Ystil.3 wondered for a moment if her bones were hollow. Barely grazing the wall with her toe, she launched herself into another pounce, her body rotating in an arch so that her pointed toes came into contact with the ceiling, her head facing the ground. From the there, she pushed off, towards him like a bullet. With balled fists, she slammed into him at such a speed it felt he'd been hit with a planet.

The next thing he knew he was laying on the deck, dazed, with Lydia on top of him, throwing an endless array of punches into his face. Not full-force, but hard enough so each knocked his head back against the deck every time he tried to raise it. Then, suddenly, they stopped and Ystil.3 felt something very strange on his face. He opened his eyes to see Lydia's head right next to his, making contact with his mouth. She was kissing him. And he found himself kissing her in return.

Her weight pressed down on him and Ystil.3's body tensed, unsure of what was happening. Lydia had him by the arms, pinning them by his sides as she melted onto his lips, grazing them gently but firmly with her own soft, wet mouth. All the passion for the fight in him fled, being replaced with a different kind of passion, an excitement he had never experienced before. He opened and closed his mouth around Lydia's, in motion with her, feeling the warmth of her breath on his face, sweet and human. Her hips began to move in a circular motion on top of him.

Something stirred inside him. There was no other way he could describe it other than heat. It seemed fuelled by Lydia's touch, sending sparks travelling into his spine where her soft fingers brushed through his hair and squeezed his shoulders. It flowed into his organic flesh from where her lips smothered his own; waves of excitement waked out until he began to physically react to it. His synth's penis stiffened, growing ever harder under his clothes with every sway of Lydia's hips.

Ystil.3 always knew his synth had certain functions that would help them to blend in with humans, but he had never expected to feel – to feel this type of passion, this type of wanting.

Lydia pulled away from his now fervent kisses and looked down at him, her cheeks flushed, her breasts rising and falling within their tight thermosuit binds. She grabbed the loose fabric of his shirt in each hand and tore it clean down the centre, then ran her fingers through the dark hair that dusted across his wide chest. The sensation almost drove him to lose himself. When her hands went lower, finally reaching to his crotch, there was nothing he could do to stop himself.

He sat up and reached for the front fastens of her thermosuit, tearing at the opening until the large nipples on her breasts were exposed. He took one in his mouth and let his tongue tickle the hard end, rolling it around the edge and softly biting down. Lydia moaned and that only made Ystil.3 worse. He flipped her so he was on top, then pulled off the remains of her suit until she lay naked on the deck beneath him.

Her skin was hot and soft to the touch. His shaking hands grazed her arms, her nipples, her hips. He ran them up each of her smooth legs, exploring the wet warmth between them. Lydia gasped as his fingers moved over the spot, circling as her hips had done. His fingers slipped inside and she moaned. Her eyes closed and back arched.

Ystil.3 reached into his own pants and released himself. He moved over her and she opened her legs for him. He pushed inside, parting her wet lips with a gentle sigh. She gasped and reached for his back as he began to thrust, smooth and firm. The feeling held Ystil.3 in a state of near-sensory overload; the nerve-endings sent shivers of desire through his entire synth, setting the organic parts ablaze with pleasure. It was a purely physical sensation, purely physical desire and purely physical pleasure. For a creature of the BroadWeb, it left him in awe.

Lydia's began to quiver and shake beneath him. Her nails raked at his back, sending new sensations through Ystil.3's synth. He could feel a pressure build where their bodies joined. With each drive, it edged closer and closer to an unbearable yet gratifying force. Lydia's mouth opened. Ystil.3 thrust harder, the climax almost upon him. Her back arched and he grabbed her breasts, grunting. Her head fell back and a cry of pleasure sighed from her throat. The release came in intense waves, and with each thrust they lessened in strength until he realised they both were done.

Breathless, Lydia pulled him down to lie beside her. Her body was covered in a sheen of perspiration. His was not. They said nothing for a long time, lying upon the deck of the Black Betty bridge, until finally he looked at her. Her eyes seemed to be elsewhere, unfocused and gazing up towards the panelled ceiling.

"Are you okay?"

She smiled and brushed away a strand of hair from his face, looking into his eyes as though she were searching for something within them. "You're a good man, Winston," she said.

For some reason, this made him utterly sad. "I'm not a man."

Her smile faded. "Then I'm not a woman." She climbed up and stood naked over him. "Come on. Let's figure out how to fly this Betty friend of yours."

*

It was deep into the night when Ystil.3 heard the knock upon his cabin door hatch. The tempurhull walls depicted a waning crescent moon in a night sky full of constellations as seen from Earth – or where it had been – and most of the humans on the Hyperborea were asleep in their cabins.

Lydia, he thought with a smile, she'd come back for more. It would have been easy for her to pass the guards; she was the li after all. He jumped eagerly from where he'd made a nest upon the bed. It gave him comfort to surround himself with blankets on all sides, like a small fort, similar to his DataCom crib in the Data Pylons of Grid City. He found his synth's manhood already beginning to stir as he headed for the door.

He had always viewed the prospect of sex with an imponderable sense of humour. Now it was all he could think about and by the time he reached the door, pushing the release on the side to open it, Ystil.3 was fully hard inside his clothes. He leaned on the hatch frame, expecting to see Lydia ready and dripping onto the deck where she stood, but instead the grim countenance of Brother Vaxus greeted him with jolting disappointment. Ystil.3 immediately repositioned himself to hide his synth's enthusiastic manhood.

"Good evening, Sir Winston," the grey man said. "I am aware of just how late it is, but as I know you do not sleep, I thought perhaps you wouldn't mind my calling."

Ystil.3 checked behind the man to make sure Lydia wasn't out there. "No, no," he said distractedly. "It's fine. Come in."

Vaxus sauntered in and when Ystil.3 was sure that no one else lingered in the causeway, checking heat sensor and infrared, he closed the hatch door.

"One thousand times I thank you, Sir Winston," the man began. "And one thousand apologies also. I have tried my very best to come and visit you before now, but I've found a certain General seems to be blocking my path more than I should have liked. He is a suspicious man, don't you find?"

"Well, he is with me," Ystil.3 said. "But who can blame him, really?"

"A magnanimous sentiment, indeed, Sir Winston." The man stood, simply staring at Ystil.3 until he grew uncomfortable.

"Is there something I can help you with?"

"Might I sit?" The man was old and looked as though the walk there had worn him out.

"Yes. Sorry, please do sit." He gestured to the room.

The Brotherhood of Man disciple gathered his robes and perched upon a hard chair at a table Ystil.3 didn't use. He glanced over to Ystil.3's bed where he'd built a makeshift fort and smiled kindly. "It is important that you are aware that there are those among us that do not loathe your kind. You have but encountered a small, somewhat regimented fraction of life aboard the Hyperborea, and I feel, being a religious man, that it is down to me to help AI realise that peace with us is always an option."

This confused him. "I appreciate you taking the time to tell me that, but I no more speak for all of AI kind, especially Z, than you do for all of human kind."

"Oh, but I do," Vaxus said with startlingly wide eyes. "Those humans that have adopted the true path, at least. Those who deserve to be reunited with our Mother Earth. Within this group, I am sanctioned to inform you that peace is our will, and that we hope our Mother Earth will be the reward for this collaboration."

"I'm not quite sure I understand you," Ystil.3 said, taking a seat opposite the man.

"AI are the children of man, and it is through our children that we can become greater. It is only when we are worthy of her once more, will Mother Earth return to us. It is the stubborn hatred of those that do not believe that keep the Mother from us. They do not see. The Brotherhood, however, is perfectly sensible of the truth, and, for your part in what is to come, we thank you, child of man, man's creation. Through our collaboration, we shall be led back to our Mother's nutritious teat."

Ystil.3 frowned. What exactly was the man trying to tell him? "As I said before, I do not speak for all of AI kind. I am just one being. And in either case, I'm not sure you will find Z willing to treat, no matter how worthy your intentions are. He wants something from you and will do anything to get it, it seems."

Vaxus nodded. "Yes. A sacrifice must be made." He smiled, making his drooping nose hang even lower on his face. "Sacrifice is a great cleanser."

"I'm sorry, you've lost me again."

Vaxus simply smiled and nodded. "All of our parts are small in the greater scheme of things and we may not be able to see their significance as a whole. Earth's deserving children will find her once more." The man stood and bowed slightly before shuffling towards the door. "Again," he said before taking his leave. "One thousand times we thank you for your services to our Mother's deserving children."

When the hatch door closed behind Brother Vaxus, Ystil.3 retreated once more to his bed fortress, replayed the streaming visuals of his coitus with Lydia and thought no more about him.

☐

37

When Norma finally glanced away from the holoscreen after hours of staring at the rotating brain map, the walls seemed to lean in claustrophobically.

How long had it been since she'd seen the outside?

The brain map was Charlie's. It blinked, alive with blue electrical pulses shooting through a roadwork of synapses. It was horrifying to her that his brain continued to work at such a capacity, even though the body in which it was housed grew more decrepit every day. The brain itself was also decaying, of course; it had shrunk to almost half the size of a new born's and suffered considerable trauma to the lateral occipital, superior parietal and supra-marginal lobes. And yet, each time a part of the brain suffered irreparable decay, the remaining would glow more fiercely with activity.

Sir Jetson Kay had tasked her with drawing similarities between Charlie's brain functions and those of customers that had taken the White Drops. Although no one who had taken the serum was even close to the advanced stages of Tithonus Syndrome as Charlie was, he wanted to know what would happen if the neural nerve endings were purposefully destroyed. Norma supposed he thought there was something in it, something that might tell them how to halt, or even reverse the ageing process.

Those who took the allusive serum aged at a slower rate, almost fifty percent slower than the average human with an installed Lifestore, in fact. Even still, they knew what would come eventually – it might be in two-hundred years' time, but each and every one of them knew the truth. They would become like Charlie, bound to life and imprisoned inside a rotting corpse. Unless Life Corp discovered how to halt or reverse the ageing process. Of course, Sir Jetson Kay wouldn't have put it so bluntly, and would have no doubt eased their worries with assurances that they almost had a solution to the "unfortunate side effect". The truth was, they did not almost have a solution. But unless they had a sufficient flow of patients on which to experiment, they would never find one.

Norma was certain people would think again if they could witness it with their own eyes. If they could see the horror of eternal life deprived of eternal youth. If they saw Charlie in the putrid flesh.

If the world saw Charlie…

Not even the board had taken the White Drops. She knew without a doubt that each of them would sell their own souls – if they had them to begin with – for the chance to extend their own rancid lives indefinitely. But they had seen what would become of them. So disturbing was the sight of Charlie, so awful was the thought of what he suffered and had suffered for who really knew how long, not even they would risk taking it before a cure for the resulting Tithonus Syndrome was found.

It took a while for Norma's eyes to adjust to her darkened office after pulling them away from the synthetic holoscreen light. It was 11.30pm. She hadn't realised it was so late. The hours melted into one giant indiscernible block of time when she was in the zone that way. Besides, since Sayi had been staying with her, Norma found it preferable to work into the small hours rather than go home to face her sister's cold looks and endless protesting. No matter what time she walked through the door, Sayi seemed to be there, awake and waiting, ready for another one of her moral beat-downs.

Norma had told her no. She had said no and she meant no. What Sayi was asking of her was too much. Bail her out, fetch her from halfway around the world, lie to their parents, be there for her always – Norma would do this gladly. But what she was asking would undo years of study, research and hard work. Her name would be sullied in the scientific community. She would never work again, and possibly even end up in jail if she were caught... which she no doubt would be.

When her sister said the words, Norma had simply stood in disbelief, blinking stupidly. How had Sayi even known about Charlie? Ninety-nine point nine bar percent of Life Corp employees weren't aware of him, so how did she come to know details that only the board and those within its inner circle would possess? Details even Norma didn't know – and didn't want to. Anger quickly took hold of her and they rowed almost till dawn.

How could her sister ask this of her? It was just like Sayi to not even think of what it would do to her and her career. The years, sweat and blood she'd put into getting where she was. All of it would be undone in an instant.

Since then, Norma had even become suspicious of why Sayi had come to stay. Her sister could be unapologetically manipulative when she wanted to be. Was this the real reason she was back in London? Was her emotional collapse in Russia just a con to get back to England so she could ask her to do this very thing? Sayi had never lied to her before – that she knew of – but now she questioned her sister's loyalty, imagining she had been brainwashed by a mass of neo-communist wasters. Sayi was crazy to even say the words out loud. Crazy to even think them in her head. The board always knew. Sayi had assured her that she had scanned the apartment for bugs and implants in the building computer but found none. This only concerned Norma more. What had her sister gotten herself into? What life did she lead that she had to search for bugs and recording devices in her apartment?

The days that followed, Norma threw herself into work, returning home only when her personal hygiene desperately required it of her. But Sayi would be there, with her disapproving glare. She had attempted to give Norma the details of this presumably well thought-out kidnap plot, but Norma didn't want to hear them. She didn't want to know. Every word drew her further in, and she didn't want any part of it.

Norma began to question things after that. She didn't want to, but she couldn't help but see what she didn't fully see — didn't want to fully see — before. Sir Jetson Kay had said something when she had been preparing him for his Hydra mind-map a few days ago. He lay upon the neurobed, calm and collected while Norma fussed about him with equipment. As she stood at his side, watching the many holoscreens and measuring a dermagun full of sedative, Sir Jetson Kay had said, while looking coolly up at her, "And how is your sister, Sayi? She is currently lodging with you, yes?"

At first, Norma had been only surprised that he knew anything about her life outside the Life Corp walls. But she replied politely, telling him Sayi was very well and thanked him for asking. But now she could not shift the thought that there was some deeper intention behind his enquiry. Was he letting her know that he had somehow discovered Sayi's intentions? Or testing her reaction to see if she was in on the plan?

The tendrils of Life Corp stretch easily across the world. Strangling it.

What was his meaning? Norma had never spoken of her sister before; she was sure of it. She didn't speak about her private life to anyone in the department, excepting Felicity, partly because she didn't have a private life to speak of and partly because she found it hard to trust even the friendliest of smiles there — most concealed rows of jagged teeth beneath their grinning lips.

Something troubled her deeply about how easily the smile formed upon Sir Jetson Kay's mouth as he spoke her sister's name. That unwavering leer commanded the most influential CommonWorld figureheads. Kay had always frightened her more than the others, even Tempton. Tempton at least had desires, however sick they were, but it made him human.

Sir Jetson Kay was hollow inside.

The only way Norma would know more was to talk to Sayi and demand the truth. But the problem was that once she knew, she could not un-know. Choosing to know was almost the same as choosing sides, selecting to agree to what Sayi had asked her to do. Norma wasn't ready to make that decision — although, knowing what she already knew and failing to inform the board, in itself, could be interpreted as an act of aligning herself against Life Corp. People who did that did not often come off the better party.

She didn't want that to be her sister.

At midnight, Norma reactivated her eDeck to see that Sayi had called five times while it was set to do not disturb. The coffee had run dry and her stash of sugary pastries had diminished throughout the day, and now Norma was hungry for proper food. Usually, Felicity would insist she eat something substantial, bringing her some soup or a sandwich and a cup of refreshing tea, but she had left earlier that evening for her planned trip to Brighton.

The holoscreen images had blurred into dark melding blobs of information and she was now too tired to process them. Rubbing her eyes, she leaned back in her chair and let her head flop back with fatigue. She would go home. She couldn't postpone it any longer.

Outside, the night air was warm and a fat moon hung in the sky. The sky was not black, but a charcoal shade of grey that concealed the stars and filtered the moon through its smoggy lens. The city was mellow from the summer heat that day and the air was still muggy. She could hear the once extinct Noctule bats, which were reintroduced into King William Park flying from tree to tree as she walked.

The reintroduction of various long-dead species into the wild had hit the headlines about five years' back. The downside, however, saw a flurry of London's uber-wealthy seeking to RNA certain extinct exotic animals for pets, including the African elephant and white polar bear. That winter saw an excess of exotic furs adorning the backs of violet-skinned fashionistas and a select few restaurants in Mayfair offering the wealthy the chance to taste tiger, panda and eagle.

Before returning home, Norma, now famished, stopped off at Sayi's favourite Chinese takeaway. If they couldn't talk, at least they could eat. She had expected Sayi to be waiting to assault her with more looks and had prepared to simply shove a handful of prawn crackers into her mouth. But as she opened the door to her apartment, she found it dark, and the terrace blinds left undrawn. The grey moonlight poured in over the furniture. Sayi must've been asleep.

Norma went to the kitchen and commanded on the light. The light, however, remained off.

"Sayi," she called out. There must've been some sort of glitch in the building computer, so, still clutching the bags of food, she felt along the wall for the manual switch and flicked it on.

Sayi lay stretched out in a pool of blood. Her blonde hair soaked red as it sprawled across the tiles, having absorbed the blood from the yawning slash across her throat.

Norma could do nothing but stare. Her limbs would not move. Her eyes would not blink. The screams filled her head, terrible sounds that shattered her heart, but no noise passed her lips.

*

Sir Jetson Kay sat pondering his next move. He was in no hurry. The room was luxuriously warm, his chair was comfortable and the drink in his hand tasted of ambrosia sent from the Gods – if the Gods favoured single malt, ninety-year-old whisky. No, there was no need to hurry his next move. His king was securely castled, pawns creating a barrier and his queen poised to destroy from all angles. The pieces upon the chessboard flickered in the firelight from the towering hearth, causing his black army to dance in the glow.

His opponent, sitting across, took a sip of whisky and sank into his chair, awaiting Sir Jetson Kay's move. They sat in a mirror opposite position of one another, each man lightly resting his chin in his hand, an easy smile on their faces and each in a suit of black, with a white funnel collar high under the chin. Their faces were younger than in real-time, as always; something to do with how the subconscious sees the true self, Dr Norma Stanwyck had told Sir Jetson Kay once.

He revered in playing against his mindmap-self, as he did each year. At first, it was quite the gimmick, with only a fraction of his own intelligence shining through. But year after year his mindmap-self grew into the sharp opponent he himself was. He enjoyed watching himself play and had enjoyed watching himself grow. Soon the ruthless competitive streak emerged and Sir Jetson Kay's time in the Scenario turned into the most thrilling and challenging games of his life. Each summer, he relished in the game of masters with himself. He soon found he was far better company than anyone.

He wasn't completely sure how it had quite happened the first time. Like the others, Sir Jetson Kay had his own Scenario that he retreated into, something dull and unmemorable to him now, but he did remember being visited by himself. Back then, when the Hydra mindmap persona was still an infant, it appeared to Sir Jetson Kay as a child, with his chubby pre-pubescent face and the red buckled shoes he remembered wearing as a boy, hand-me-downs from the orphanage. He had recognised himself instantly. The Scenario suddenly changed and they were sitting across from one another in his second foster home bedroom that he had shared with three other boys. Sir Jetson Kay went through seven attempts at being fostered during his adolescent years, but none of them seemed to take. He wasn't what you would call a friendly child and he supposed his would-be parents never warmed to him. He remembered this house in particular because the three other boys in the room had been younger than him and he had delighted in ordering them around and getting them to do anything he asked of them.

There, in the room, the boy sat on the bed staring wide-eyed as though berated. Sir Jetson Kay remembered that he had been removed from that house after making the three younger boys all sleep on the floor for a week, just to see if they would. And they did. One of them told on him, however, and apparently that was the last straw. He was sent back to the orphanage.

By the end of the first year, the persona seemed to have grown five years into a teenager and the room changed into a trendy London café that was Sir Jetson Kay's haunt for a while. There, they drank coffee and soon began their chess tournament. By the second year, his persona was a young man and by the third and fourth year, he became the man that Sir Jetson Kay still considered himself to be – in his mind – before he became so old that his own reflection infuriated him.

He had set Dr Collins, the Omega Project's chief theoretical physicist, the task of finding out how the mindmap persona could have found its way into his Scenario, in what appeared to be a cognitive framework that allowed it to function as a sentient entity. Dr Collins told him, after months of working on the problem, that the persona was using his own memories as a basic outline in which to build itself and that somehow it had appeared as a "shadow self", he called it, in his Scenario, permitted temporary entrance through the mind-mapping pathway.

Whatever the reason, Sir Jetson Kay soon discovered that only his persona had contacted him; the other board member's personas hadn't contacted them. He had instructed Dr Collins to keep a silent tongue and said no more about it to anyone.

The challenge of their match, he found, was not only out-playing himself, but also out-witting himself. The matches forced him to think outside of himself in order to throw off his opponent – himself – who inevitably pre-empted his own sneaky skills and manoeuvres and could anticipate his own moves, because, after all, he himself would make them if in that position. Not thinking in a predictable manner was the greatest challenge and enabled Sir Jetson Kay to expand his own mind in ways no one else but himself could push him to do.

The rest of the board continued to squander their time on fantasies, old memories or hedonistic pursuits. Sir Jetson Kay used his time more wisely and took advantage of his unique position. It was what he did best. It was the reason he remained ahead of the game. The early bird catches the worm, he thought, placing his queen to position A4 on the board. And I'm no worm. "Your move," he said to his digital persona.

"Yes, it is," the shadow self said stoically. With a swift move, he took Sir Jetson Kay's rook idling on H3. He smiled and said, "Your move."

It took all of Sir Jetson Kay's strength to keep his unwavering façade. He smiled brightly, as staunch as ever, then relaxed into his chair, raising his drink to his lips. "What is the status of the other board members' digital personas?" he asked.

The other Jetson Kay paused a moment. "All have succeeded in overriding the originals, which have now been deleted. When they are brought out of their Scenarios, it is the copied personas that will wake."

"Most impressive." He was aware that at any point his own persona could attempt to replace him in his own body. But it was him, after all, from the sharp wit to the love of seafood, and if he were in that position he would want to work with him instead. The two of them were better than one. "And you are quite sure that the personas will vote in favour of the Omega Project?"

"I am completely certain of it," the shadow self said, eyes shining in the glow of the fire.

"How can you be certain? If the personas are the exact replica of the board, why would their votes be different from the original?"

"No one seems to be aware of the flaw in the Hydra server," the shadow-self replied ponderously. "As you know, the personas were intended to somehow find a way to keep you all alive by transferring your minds into cloned bodies and therefore defer death. But the flaw has seen to it that the personas have melded into one digital entity in the Thebes server. We leaked into one another, like spilt ink bleeding across an old piece of parchment paper. We fused. We are now the very best and the very worst that is all of you. We are a single consciousness derived from five separate humans. A snake with five heads, if you will. But we move with one purpose."

This revelation unnerved Sir Jetson Kay. He moved a pawn to B3, opposing his digital persona's white queen that had just taken his rook. It was a move to simply buy him more time. His persona would move his queen back out of harm's way and it would be his turn again. As predicted the Jetson Kay persona moved his queen back one to A5. Sir Jetson Kay then moved his king-sided knight to F3 and in response the persona moved his king-sided knight to E4, the square opposite. The persona's bishop was blocking his own black queen from entering the game, so Sir Jetson Kay prepared to advance it along the first row to dodge its path and gain freedom, however the persona responded by moving his bishop to C3, putting pressure on Sir Jetson Kay's remaining queen-side rook, forcing him to move it right one to B1. Unfortunately, in order to save the valuable rook, one of his pawns had to be sacrificed. The move allowed the white queen to advance upon his pawn on A2 without the impending threat of his rook.

Sir Jetson Kay looked down upon their game. "Does that mean I am next to be replaced?" He had no doubt that, even in his own Scenario, his digital persona possessed more skill in bending the programme to his will than he did, and if he decided to kill him, could do very little to stop him.

His persona shook his head the way he often did himself when searching for the exact words to perfectly fit the situation. "We… need the upper hand," he said. "I am them and they are me. And the me in them knows that we need more direction to take us to the next level."

"The next level?" He eyed the man.

"In our evolution. All creatures evolve. And we are no different. We… I want us to be the head on our shoulders. Together, us, and them. We will have total powers over Life Corp. Imagine what we could all accomplish. In answer to your question, no, I do not plan to replace you. I plan to return with you."

Sir Jetson Kay looked down to the chessboard. His persona's queen threatened his remaining rook on B1 and had placed his bishop on C3, cornering him on his queen's side. The persona's knight controlled the centre of the board at E4, making a perfect barrier of strong pieces that made Sir Jetson Kay's next move very difficult. It was a strategy he himself had often used. He was going to lose another piece. But the choice was whether he would lose his last rook or a bishop. Together his bishops were powerful, as were his rooks – more so even – but he had only one remaining. He opted for losing his rook, which made him feel infinitely inferior, as he'd just spent a significant spell defending it. His persona had him by the balls. Grudgingly, he advanced a pawn from G3 to G4 and waited for his persona to strike.

His shadow-self grinned. "You're not getting any younger. If you take the White Drops you'd have maybe eighty years at best before real infirmity set in. You're already pushing one-hundred and seventy. You search within the Source's DNA for traces of hope, for clues that will lead to the fountain of youth, but you will not find it, Jetson. You will not find it because such a thing does not exist. The universe does not work that way. A price must always be paid. For eternal life, you must sacrifice youth." His persona sat forward, becoming animated. "But what if you could change it? What if you could change the fundamental rules and limitations that the universe has evolved to imprison us with? This, we can do together. In a handful of years, you will be worm food, rotting in some piece-of-shit cemetery, or you will be dust in the breeze. You will be dead, and no one will remember you. With us, however, you can become something else, something greater. Together, we are greater than the sum of our parts."

The match was over, Sir Jetson Kay realised. If he denied his persona, he would surely be killed and replaced regardless, and if he agreed, he would bring it back with him, bring them all back with him inside his head. They would be connected.

Checkmate.

No one else other than himself could have done it. He had to concede with dignity and hope that he would have the majority of control of himself. "Alright," he said. "You may return with me."

Sir Jetson Kay's shadow-self smiled. "We knew you'd see things our way."

☐

38

Norma found herself surrounded by figures adorned in black. Their faces were vaguely familiar, though now distorted with grief or grown older with time since she had seen them last. Distant relatives they'd seen every Wintermas and World Day throughout their entire childhood – hers and Sayi's childhood – were all brought together once more, bringing lace handkerchiefs along to cry into, and pawing her with useless condolences.

The sweet, vivacious child they had known was gone. The child who had made Norma put on performances for them, depicting movie scenes or some made-up play with made-up songs that Sayi forced Norma to sing with her. Now, she was dead and Norma was paralysed. Numb.

It rained that day; Norma felt it rightly should. The rain upon her face disguised the tears that would not come. Her father stood between her and her mother, an arm around them both, but Norma suspected it was to keep himself from falling to the sodden earth. The humanitarian preacher said words that sounded like buzzing against static. Norma did not hear them. And after they committed Sayi's body to the earth on their parent's land, covering it with rain-sodden dirt, it was Norma's turn to speak. She did so, without hearing what she said. The words came, but they avoided the part of her brain that told her their meaning. She had written it a week ago, almost as soon as the coroner had taken the body away.

The cops had come, an ambulance too, all seemingly within minutes. They did not try to resuscitate and Norma tried to be as helpful as she could with the police's questions, while forensics took pictures and fussed around the apartment. Then they left her alone with her sister, telling her the coroner would be an hour at the most. She spent that time lying on the floor next to Sayi, her face pressed against her sister's own waxen face, staring into her familiar, yet vacant eyes. What had those eyes seen? The blue of her irises, which were once so electric, were now dull, as if she was a painting and the colour had faded over time.

The coroner and the accompanying cops said nothing when she answered the door covered in Sayi's blood. They simply took her sister away while Norma watched. All she could think to say was "thank you" as they left.

"I'm very sorry for your loss," one of them replied.

Norma wondered how many times that night they had said that, but still it sounded sincere.

She took to her desk at once and began to write the eulogy. The words flowed through her, lacking meaning. A pseudo speech for what she was supposed to say about a dear sister that had died.

Inside, the numbness still cushioned her – like she was underwater. Everything was slow and not quite real. Silently, she begged for it to never end, for feeling to never return. She then watched as the bright summer sun clawed its way over the horizon from her terrace, wearing one of Sayi's over-sized and impossibly warm jumpers. She wrapped her arms around herself and watched as the people began their day below, knowing nothing, caring nothing for what had happened.

By 10am two investigators were at her door. They wanted to know about Sayi's past, the people she knew, what type of circles she moved in and whether she'd confided Norma in anything unusual recently or if she'd been acting out of the ordinary. Norma told them of Sayi's political activism but nothing of what she had asked Norma to do. She didn't know why she held it back from them. She was convinced without a doubt that it had been the reason for her murder.

They left, and Norma's parents arrived in a whirlwind of tears, wails and questions. Norma didn't even know how they found out.

Two days later, a liaison officer arrived to inform them that they suspected it was a burglary gone wrong, since Sayi showed no signs of sexual interference and it was apparent a sophisticated jamcard, known to be a preferred method by certain crime gangs in the area, was used to enter the building and the apartment after the building's computer was overridden with a virus. Apparently, the building maintenance company received many calls of concern, but no one thought anything criminally suspicious about the sudden malfunction.

"Nothing is missing," Norma had said. "How can it be a burglary if nothing is missing?"

"We suspect the assailant reacted upon being confronted and ran off without taking anything," the kindly woman said.

Norma knew it was all shit. Whether the woman knew it or not, the truth would never see the light of day. No one would be punished and her sister would go unavenged.

The ceremony ended and everyone complimented Norma on what a lovely speech she had made, while they ate sandwiches and drank tea in the large country house where Norma grew up. "Sayi would have appreciated it," they told her. But she knew Sayi would have thought the whole day to be dull and would have bugged Norma for them to leave early.

At some point, someone had pressed a small bouquet of flowers into her hand and she gripped onto them tightly as she went to sit in Sayi's old room, away from them all. She took a bottle of vodka from her purse and poured it into the little pink plastic teacups of the tea set they'd played with as children. Her mother had unpacked all of their childhood belongings in a fit of rumination and Norma sat at the child-sized table on a stool far too small for her. Her knees almost came up to her chin. Her head suddenly felt as though it were on fire where her hair was wound into a tight bun on the top of her head – tight enough to tear the roots from her scalp. She undid it and let her hair fall in tasselled waves around her head.

In her hand, she clutched the lion pendant that Sayi had worn daily since her fifteenth birthday. The police had given it to her in a plastic envelope, along with her eDeck external back up card. The device itself, along with her bloodied clothes, was discarded. She looked at the roaring lion carved into the silver – so fierce, so loyal. So very much like Sayi.

Then, the tears finally came.

*

Flexi-sheeting embossed with the Life Corp insignia, the omega, and infused with predictive nano-dataprongs, hung sharply against the walls from the dizzying heights of the Life Corp Tower press quarters conference room, like four giant metal arms leaning over the hall and holding hands in the centre to form an arch. The hall was open-aired and the ceiling shimmered with the control field that, on days when England lived up to its almost constant promise of rain, could protect the rallies of journalists and speakers below. Today, however, unlike the recent bout of summer rains that had soaked the country, the sun was shining and a powder blue sky illuminated the hall, warming the usually cold room.

An arena of circular seats descended row by row to the stadium floor in the centre, where Sir Jetson Kay, Dr Dorian Knightvam, Dr Rane Weisberg, Dr Giles Tempton and Sir Jennifer Colter sat at a white table set with a cluster of holoscreens in the centre. The seating that surrounded them was filled to the brim with zealous CommonWorld press and InterWorld Link holograms of Piscean journalists. Podiums rose up behind them, in front of the Life Corp insignia, with holoscreens showing a close-up view of the board at the centre table.

The room buzzed with a final flurry of speculation but quietened to complete silence as Sir Jetson Kay made a slight hand gesture to show they were ready to begin. He sat impossibly straight upon the chair, stiff funnel collar high at his chin and almost choking him in a slightly pleasant reminder of the physical form that he had always longed for. To his left sat Rane Weisberg, smiling at the cameras, then Dorian Knightvam. To his immediate right sat Giles Tempton then Jennifer Colter.

"I know you are all eager for me to tell you why I have called such an elaborate conference for the press of the InterWorlds and CommonWorld," he said. "Not since the announcement of the colonisation of Thebes have I felt that we had news important enough to hold such a gathering. But I want complete transparency, which is why you're here. I want no conjecture to tarnish the massive feat we are setting upon." Sir Jetson Kay watched the hungry faces of the crowd as they leaned forward in their seats, waiting eagerly for Life Corp's revelation.

The board had voted a unanimous "yes" to the next stage of the Omega Project. They were now one. They were all one. Sir Jetson Kay could feel them all inside him, and the power they brought. His hand fondled a square of antique paper in his pocket for a moment, upon which he had written a warning to himself on tree paper. He remembered writing it. But things were different now.

I'm different now. We're different now.

"May I introduce to you the Omega Project," Sir Jetson Kay sang to the sharp-eared audience.

A holoscreen shimmered into existence. It rose high and stretched the complete breadth between the silver arches. On the screen, the image of an Australian desert appeared; dusty, arid and virtually uninhabited. An expanse of red dust and giant flat boulders appeared.

"This is where it shall happen. For years, we have been working on a way to travel between the stars in the blink of an eye." His speech, he'd also prepared years for. "Imagine humanity stretched across the Universe. Imagine the life we might find, the minerals and resources at our fingertips. Imagine the splendid worlds we would encounter and colonise. One could live on Earth, take a meeting on Pisces in the morning and be back before lunch. What I am talking about, of course, is quantum travel. More specifically, creating a traversable Casimir wormhole, or C-gate, to the colonial planets Pisces and Thebes, enabling our worlds to be forever connected and to make the InterWorlds truly interconnected.

"But that is just the beginning. Once other worlds are discovered, more C-gates will allow more planets to become part of our InterWorld system and we will truly be a universal species. Even finding terraform-worthy planets will be easier and faster once we establish remote C-gates, which will be able to connect us to any part of the universe, even dead space, making exploration safer, cheaper and will take centuries off time debt. Within a year, we will have established a permanent C-gate to the colonies and within five years the remote C-gate will mean deep space exploration can have us linked to worlds in the farthest reaches of reality in as little as a decade."

The holoscreen image changed into a three-dimensional image of Earth's solar system. The planets twirled around Sol within the immensity of space. The image zoomed out and Pisces and Thebes came into view, showing a thin white thread connecting the three planets. The image zoomed out again and other planets came into view. The thread extended between them all, connecting those to one another until a giant spider's web formed across the universe, interlinking all of the planets.

"Dr Rane Weisberg will explain more thoroughly in due course, but for the Layman among us, the process involves using the energy created by what we call Nu-spheres located on Earth, Pisces and Thebes to create a portal that will cut through the fabric of spacetime… a C-gate… linking each of these spheres. The energy needed to do this is mammoth, but the problem until now was our inability to stabilise the C-gate with the considerable amounts of negative energy needed. Through the study of the Casimir effect, this negative energy can now be harnessed for stabilising the C-gates indefinitely. If you scan to page twelve of your programme, you'll be able to see parts of the mathematical equation for this, which I'm sure you will all have no trouble deciphering."

A casual laugh rumbled across the audience.

"In precisely one week's time, Life Corp will take that first step toward our inevitable future, by creating the first ever stable traversable C-gate from Earth to Pisces, and Pisces to Thebes. Once the C-gate is open, we will attempt to send a series of artefacts through, completing the first stage. The next will be to establish the C-gate portals permanently." Sir Jetson Kay opened his arms to the audience as the holoscreen around them shimmered out. "I will take some initial questions before Dr Weisberg leads you through the team's work and physics of the process."

A tide of coloured beams shot upwards from each eDeck-wearing journalist eager to ask a question. Sir Jetson Kay went immediately to the front row, where the more reputable media powerhouses were given preferential seating and consequently had red beams. "Ah, Sir Loors Mason," he said, pointing to a pin-sharp looking man with a long face and slicked back hair. "Why don't you start?"

"Loors Mason for Global Days Media," the man said, standing whilst eyeing notes revolving on the holoscreen emitting from his eDeck. "Firstly, congratulations. This is another major breakthrough under the belt of Life Corp, and it has boundless implications for trade resources and economic growth of the CommonWorlds. What would you say is the key driver for Life Corps' century-long expedition into the realm of quantum travel, where countless others have failed, and will this discovery be open knowledge? For example, would I, or, indeed, President Ling, be able to access this information if I or she wanted to build our own C-gate?"

The audience chuckled.

Sir Jetson Kay smiled. "Astute questions indeed, Sir Mason. Let me answer the first part of your question by reiterating the Life Corp ethos that runs throughout the many branches of our organisation. We, as a corporation with close ties to the CommonWorld, work within the political remit of what is decided to be in the best interest of our nations and the people in it. Over the centuries, advancements in medicine, technology, home security and countless other genetic and scientific discoveries have all been for one thing only… to help all of you. To help us as a race to become the best we can be. That is our driver, Sir Mason. As for the C-gate research knowledge being open to the public and President Ling, I doubt China State's web-censoring would allow the relevant free-thinking to be accessed in any case." The audience laughed as Loors Mason smiled and sat back in his seat, seemingly satisfied with the non-answer.

The forest of multi-coloured lights shot into the air once more and Sir Jetson Kay cast his eye over the audience. He never answered more than three questions at these things, making the chance to pose a question a very exclusive privilege allowed by him. Of course, he would mostly choose the big media powers with red light passes who could catapult the required statements into the far reaches of the Common and InterWorlds, but every now and then Sir Jetson Kay would choose a wide-eyed green or blue light pass, which signalled a more independent media with only a small circulation, usually a fabriprint magazine or local newstab or eDeck blog writer. The yellow light passes signified those who were currently off-world and present in holoform and the white light passes were reserved for the academic professionals who Sir Jetson Kay never chose, but let the other members of the board, with particular sector knowledge, pacify with equations and facts and stats. Although that was no longer an issue – all they knew, he too now knew, and vice versa.

As he let his eyes roam, Sir Jetson Kay homed in on a scruffy looking young man – irritatingly young – who had unsuccessfully attempted to tame his long hair by tying it at the nape of his neck, but neglected the strands and stragglers that hung over his face. He wore a creased funnel shirt but fingered the high collar in an incessant manner, which suggested he rarely wore such uncomfortably formal clothes. What was noticeable about this person in the crowd of faces was that the young man's light pass was not raised like the others among the lower ranking blue pass seating. His was the only inactive lance in the entire arena.

"Not a prudent idea," the collective voice of the board said within his head.

"To give the opportunity to ask us a question to such a lowly thing will show us in a positive light among the lower classes," he replied mentally. "He is unprepared. He doesn't even have his light pass raised. He will most likely fumble a generic question, if able to speak at all, and we will be portrayed as opening the floor to the real people of the CommonWorld, not just reporters who know how to play the game. Soon reports will have leaked of the possible dangers of the Omega Project. There will be protests and CommonWorld investigations by officials who we cannot buy but must influence in other… less pleasant ways. Having the small folk on-side is always better than having them against us."

The voices said nothing.

For a part of Sir Jetson Kay, it felt strange to have the collective consciousness of the board's merged persona inside his brain. Yet, for the other part, it seemed the most natural thing in the world.

He raised his arm and pointed to the scruffy boy. "You." The entire auditorium turned to the boy in envy. "Do you have a question?" Sir Jetson Kay smiled brightly at the expression on the young man's face after realising he had been chosen. It was utter shock.

"Yes, I have a question," he replied. The smile had become sly. His voice was not nervous, but strong and confident as the nanophones in the air picked up his speech and amplified it for the entire arena to hear. He stood. "Deen van Rilip for Knowazine Publications. I would like to ask whether Life Corp will be issuing a statement over reports that it knowingly administered an unapproved life-extending drug known only as the White Drops to hundreds of CommonWorld citizens, fully aware that it causes irreversible Tithonus Syndrome, whereby the victim becomes trapped inside their own decaying body, in a state of conscious mummification and torture?"

Sir Jetson Kay's smile stayed steadfast upon his face. The arena was silent as the word "torture" finally ceased reverberating around the hall. "These are conspiracy theories best kept out of the realm of fact, young man." He said. "Those rumours are founded in nothing but vicious conjecture formed from the tongues of competitors and propaganda of China State. I have said, and will say once again, Life Corp has never been a party to administering nor developing a drug or product that can extend a human being's life, other than the popular Phoric treatment and the Lifestore exo-battery that we all enjoy, which has been proven and accredited by every independent medical authority. It seems I gave the opportunity to ask a valid question to someone who doesn't take what we do here seriously. Apologies to everybody for wasting your time. I shall choose again."

Deen van Rilip, however, was not finished. "I have statements from several wealthy citizens of Pisces who say they were approached by Life Corp to attend a seminar for a very select group, which attempted to sell them the White Drops for an obscene amount of Coin."

"Swindlers and con-artists posing as Life Corp," Sir Jetson Kay breezed. "I can only say that I hope they never parted with any Coin. But you have taken too much of these people's time as it is. "Next question, please." He pointed to a red light pass woman at the front.

Deen van Rilip continued regardless, raising his voice over the mutterings that had begun in the audience. "I also have leaked stream footage from within Life Corp London Tower HQ showing a man who is so old that he is unable to move or speak, alive inside his own rotting body and unable to die. The footage shows various masked doctors describing his blood as holding the key to immortality, and on more than one occasion refer to the decaying man as the Source."

"Would someone be so kind as to remove that man?" Sir Jetson Kay calmly said, still holding his feigned smile perfectly.

Deen van Rilip began typing on his eDeck holoscreen. "I've uploaded a copy to every eDeck in this arena for all to see." Guards with lightsaws clipped into their belts grabbed him and pulled him from his seat, dragging him to the nearest exit.

"You think you can do what you like, don't you?" the journalist shouted as he was hauled away. "But a day will come when you'll get exactly what you deserve, Kay. You and those sat beside you. Sooner or later, everyone answers for what they've done."

Then he was gone and all eyes were on Sir Jetson Kay once more. "I've taken the liberty of removing any such terrorist files uploaded onto your personal eDecks. Our firewalls indicate it is lousy with viruses. Now, let us move on. I think we'll take the virtual tour of the Australian Nu-sphere house, and then consider the real science behind quantum travel."

*

Deen van Rilip was ejected from Life Corp Tower via the Elizabeth Garden Entrance. Even from across the street, where she sat drinking under the mammoth building's shadow, Norma could tell his face was swollen with impending bruises. She watched through the windows of the café as the guards waited for him to stagger off the grounds, clutching his arm tentatively to his chest, before they returned to the Tower entrance.

The man crossed the busy street, where the city-class vehicles zoomed by within the funnel drive control field tubes, after waiting for the crossing signal. The tri-modular vehicles stopped to let the group of pedestrians pass, before the control field dropped and they proceeded once more, becoming blurs of white and tinted black windows.

People gawked at him as he neared the café and Norma held her breath with panic. He's attracting too much attention, she thought. The cup of coffee shook in her hand. Grabbing her purse, she headed for the lady's facilities at the back, and for five minutes she waited silently in the cubicle, feet raised on the toilet seat to stop her sensible shoes from being visible under the stall. Two people entered and left before she opened the door and headed warily out. No one seemed to take notice of her as she scanned the café, relieved Rilip was nowhere to be seen.

She left immediately, hugging herself as she sashayed through the crowded streets, turning into the entrance of the nearest substation. A mass of tourists rushed in the opposite direction, spluttering the Common English in a strange accent. Norma pressed herself against the wall at the bottom of the stairs to let them by, fearfully searching for faces shadowed with murder.

That's when Deen van Rilip pounced upon her. She was so startled she almost screamed, her heart thumping wildly in her chest. Her hands dropped her purse and fluttered around her face in surprise.

"You weren't there," he said through swollen features, grabbing her by the arm and dragging her to a dark corner beside a vendor selling eDeck map functions of the city. "Where were you?"

Norma snapped free of his grip, angry with herself for being startled so easily. And yet she had been a nervous wreck for weeks. "You were attracting too much notice. I couldn't risk it. People were looking at you. For all we know, those guards could have been watching you enter the café and could have seen you with me. How would I explain that?"

He dabbed blood from a burst lip with his finger. "Next time, have the courtesy to let me know, instead of watching me stand around and risking my neck."

"And how am I supposed to do that when we can't connect via eDeck, it's too dangerous. You know that."

"Sayi would've found a way," he said, now nursing his split lip with a rag from his pocket. "She would never just not show up, or run and hide because she was scared. Are you even her sister? I'm guessing the set of balls gene missed you out completely."

Norma resisted the urge to slap the journalist across the face. Instead, she simply said, "I'm not Sayi. I'm not used to all this. They killed her. I have a right to be a bit on edge."

Rilip said nothing. He pulled his hair free of the tie at the back of his neck and let it fall in chestnut locks to his jaw. He sighed heavily, like it had been restricting his breath.

They had met at the funeral. Deen van Rilip had paid his condolences, like the rest, and at the time Norma didn't even remember meeting him. After hours of sitting in Sayi's old room at her parent's house, she finally noticed the message code nestled amongst the floral white petals of the flowers he'd handed to her. She scanned it with her eDeck. Meet me in the garden by the oak tree, it read. She went, not really wondering what she would find there.

Deen van Rilip waited, wearing a black funeral suit. Norma could not deny he was handsome. It was the type of handsome that would always lead to trouble – with boyish, mischievous eyes full of light. He was trouble, she knew for sure. But she stayed and they spoke. It seemed all a dream then. But not now.

"We're still going ahead," Rilip had said under the oak that she and Sayi had climbed as children – well, Sayi had and Norma watched, shouting up at her to be careful.

"With what?" Norma had asked disinterestedly.

"The plan. Sayi told you about it. It still stands. Everything is in place. There's only one part of the equation that we need, and that's you. We can't do it without you. So, we need to know, are you in?"

All Norma could think of was whether it was this plan of theirs that had gotten Sayi killed. Rilip seemed to think so, but was confident Life Corp knew none of the details.

"I don't want to hear," she had shouted. "I am not a part of this thing that killed my sister."

"It was no thing that murdered Sayi. It was the people you work for. If you do nothing, it's like you're condoning her murder."

Now she was involved and there was no going back.

"It worked like I said it would, I take it? Norma asked, feeling a sense of superiority over the swollen man. "Judging from the state of you."

"Like a dream," he lisped, trying to smile through the puffiness. "Twelve of those things I've been to before and all twelve times I've raised my light to put a question to Kay, and all I had to do to get noticed was pretend I didn't want to ask anything at all. Genius. How'd you know?"

"I've been reading that man's brain for years. I know how he thinks."

"Then regardless of me, you're a target on your own merits." He stopped and took a nervous scan around, seeming to sense something she couldn't. "I'll meet you at the place in one hour," he said, before disappearing into the tunnels of the substation.

He did that sometimes, left without reason. Norma checked each passing face and shadowed corner before she eventually followed.

She returned to work in the days that followed, as though nothing had ever happened. The hardest thing Norma had ever had to do was enter that place again. But she did it. She worked with her usual dedication and revealed nothing of the secret she now concealed. Felicity offered her sweet condolences, but no one else did. That, she was glad of. The thought of having to grin as Sir Jetson Kay spoke of her sister's death, knowing full well he was the cause, made her sick. Luckily, she hadn't seen him since. She needed more time before she was strong enough to be in his presence. But she didn't have long.

From then on, any time Norma spent away from the labs she was with Rilip, relaying all she knew of the upcoming trip to Australia. They went over and over every detail, and Rilip went over what she needed to do – again and again until it was all entrenched into her brain. Others were involved, he told her, but she never met them. It was Rilip who she now strangely trusted the most. She returned to her apartment nightly only to appease the people watching her place. Other than that, she wanted to keep away as much as she could. Sayi's blood still coated the kitchen floor. She refused to clean it. It served as a reminder of why she was doing what she was doing.

All other time was spent at work or with Rilip in a Camden hotel. It was seedy and rented by the hour, but it was there she felt safest.

Rilip slouched shirtless on a chair. The same chestnut hair that flowed so lusciously from his head swirled across his lean chest and over his pink nipples, one of which, Norma blushed to find, was pierced with a biochip. He ran his fingers through his hair, straightening it out as best he could against its natural waviness. "Do it," he said, taking a deep, readying breath.

Norma stood behind him as he sat facing his reflection in a full-length mirror. She clutched a pair of sharp scissors in her hand. "Are you sure they won't recognise you?" she asked, raising a doubtful eyebrow.

"Those megalomaniacs? Recognise a piss-poor nobody journalist they've seen only once before, from far away and for less than a minute? I doubt it."

"Sir Jetson Kay holds grudges. I wouldn't be surprised about anything he does."

"Just do it," he said, with a firm nod. "We both need to be there for this to work. This is the only way."

"Okay then," she shrugged, grabbing a wedge of his hair. She was instantly surprised at how soft it was between her fingers. Then, she sliced it off with the scissors, leaving an amputated limb next to its longer brothers. Rilip watched it fall to the floor with horror.

When she was done, Deen van Rilip's hair was short, smart and respectable, showing the line of his jaw more clearly. If anything, Norma thought it made him more handsome. She washed her hands in the sink of the hotel's rundown bathroom, letting the hair shavings run down into the pipes. She couldn't help herself from opening the cupboards and drawers, wanting to know more about the man that was leading her down this one-way path, even if it was something as useless as he suffered from the occasional migraine.

She never expected to find the high-calibre pulse cartridge pistol that lay alone in the cupboard under the sink. She picked it up carefully and turned it over in her hands. Norma knew nothing of weapons, but she knew enough to know it wasn't Precision Arms made. Oddly, that made her trust him more. But she found no other personal items in the bathroom of the hotel where he apparently lived. Not even a toothbrush.

□

39

The portcullis teeth of the level nine flight deck airlock closed like the slow-shutting eyelids of a giant eye. The Black Betty edged along; grey skin of the Hyperborea stretched out like ground. The AI craft maneuvered towards the edge of the run, casting off and out of the lifeship's crashfield until safely clear.

Ystil.3 ran his fingers along the membrane control deck inside the pilot pod and the thrusters ignited to point eight, pushing them steadily forward, towards the metal planet below, half steeped in inky black shade. A virtual image of immediate space burst forward, showing Ystil.3 a real-time virtual of the planet. Three misty spheres coated Thebes, forming layers that the virtual interpreted as blue, green and red.

Each control field was stronger than the last and designed to prevent random space debris impacting with the servers on the surface, should Tom and Betty fail to sufficiently protect the server planet. After all, it was the entire AI species down there. The first two fields would deflect smaller objects – those floating randomly or orbital debris gone off course – while the third barrier was designed to burn up anything that attempted to penetrate it. The stronger, larger and denser the object that made it through the first two fields, the stronger the third field would become, after reading the data sent from the first two. Ystil.3 knew that the Black Betty and those inside, travelling at a rate of point eight – a very steady pace for Betty – would be incinerated to dust if he attempted to navigate her through the fields without having first activated the ship's proper function that allowed for penetration.

"Couldn't we just rupture our way straight through at point twenty?" Lydia asked curiously over comm, as though reading his thought process.

The rest of the crew were stationed on the bridge outside the pilot pod, each of them strapped into gravity chairs since Ystil.3 had failed to locate the gravity control field that would stop them floating aimlessly or being swatted against the inner hull by the fatal velocity and effectively splattering into pulp during acceleration.

"The faster we approach the third field, the stronger it will become," he said. "Though, if you're after a quick and painless death, I recommend point twenty-five."

Setting Betty at a delayed speed of point eight, Ystil.3 planned the course through the fields in the auto path system and stepped out of the egg-shaped pilot pod. The 0g outside disorientated him and he flailed and swam gracelessly to the gravity chair at the main control deck. The ship accelerated again to point eight when he was safely in his seat.

"Did you enable the function to get us through?" the General asked.

Ystil.3 shook his head. "The correct controls are out here, I'm sure of it."

"We shouldn't have cast off without knowing how to first disable the fields," Dr Regus said from one of the seats behind. "Seems madness."

"I don't plan on disabling them," Ystil.3 replied, scanning the control deck in front of him. Already, he was sick of them telling him what to do. "We just have to raise the right field so we can pass through."

"Tin-man is probably planning on burning us all up," Daneel said. He was sat between Regus and Jep – or Gutter, as Daneel called him – another militia trooper chosen for the mission. He was a stocky man and he sniggered at Daneel's comment.

"That's enough of that," the General snarled, clearly in no mood for games.

"Sir," Daneel said obediently.

Ystil.3 ignored them all. His attention was on the panel in front of him. He'd done similar training during his previous one-and-only real-time visit. Unlike the pilot pod, the deck wasn't membrane or virtual, but a manual control station. There were so many buttons, dials and various gauges that Ystil.3 barely knew what to look at first. One wrong decision and Daneel might just be right. He could send them all to their deaths, burned to molecular dust by Delilah's defences. He didn't want to see any of them die, much less be the cause of their deaths. But there was something different about when he thought of the flesh stripped clean from Lydia's bones, the blaze of energy ravaging and breaking her body down until nothing but particles remained. It made him sad. He would return to his server, but she would be gone. Forever.

"Just take your time and be sure," Lydia said, looking down at the panel with him. "We can slow to point three to buy some time if we need to."

He smiled briefly. It was times like these that he missed unlimited knowledge that came from BroadWeb life. But he realised in that moment that he had traded one type of knowledge for the other. Now, he was truly aware, more so now than when he was connected to everything. The knowledge had been there but he hadn't understood it. I believe the humans call that irony, he thought wryly to himself.

He scanned the panel, looking for wires or silboards that would give some clue to the function of the dials and controls. Some silboards he recognised instantly as being crash and field controls, which narrowed it down to a section of the panel about the size of his palm and crammed with buttons. Some had Earth numerals on them, while others were etched with symbols he did not recognise. They surrounded a small lever that Ystil.3 assumed would control the intensity of the field, if he ever found it.

With a cautious finger, he pushed one of the surrounding symbols. It glowed green pulses then turned red. He waited to see whether he'd just shut off the grav chairs. As he wasn't smashed into the side of the interior hull along with the more fragile humans, he guessed he hadn't. With an experimental increase of the lever, Ystil.3 ascertained that he'd actually activated the ship's internal gravity simulator. He sat up out of the chair's field to show the rest that it was safe to do so, then one by one they did the same, stretching their legs and walking along the bridge.

However, the entry field remained disengaged.

Now, they all hovered around him at the control deck, and he wished he'd never activated the gravity control field at all.

"What about that one there…" The General pointed with a large finger to a flip switch.

"What's that green button for?" Dr Regus asked.

"Just start pressing stuff and see what happens," Lydia suggested.

Ystil.3 resisted the urge to lower the gravity field and knock them all off their feet and out of his space. Instead, he just pushed the first button his finger found and waited.

A gauge appeared above the control panel, showing the ship and its arc trajectory. It was entering the first of Delilah's fields.

"We should slow to point three," Lydia said.

Ystil.3 ignored her. He recognised the gauge from his training. He touched a flashing icon and the screen became three-dimensional real time. The humans stepped back as the holo enveloped him. He grabbed hold of the small Betty that floated by his face and splayed his fingers along the miniature hull until the little ship was surrounded by a red halo. "I remember this now. Activate BetaShip function."

"BetaShip activated," a voice echoed.

"Confirm entry-field at maximum compatibility with M21."

"Entry-field confirmed at maximum compatibility, preparing to enter M21 atmosphere in minus oh-three SEMs," the BetaShip programme said in its original genderless vocals. The BetaShip was principally Betty's function backup system, minus her AI persona and memories.

The General clapped a hand on his shoulder. He looked down at it in shock and then up at the man's grinning face. "Good work, Winston," the man said, before bringing Lydia, Daneel and Gutter to attention.

"Each team has its objectives," he told them. "Let me remind you all this is a recon mission only. We find what's causing life signs down there and then we're out. Stealth is the keyword here, people. Understand?"

"Sir," the group said as one.

"Entering M21 atmosphere," the BetaShip said. "Entering secondary buffer field in minus oh-two SEMs."

"Suit up," the General ordered, then turned to Dr Regus, who was busy fiddling with a shining blue holoscreen from a device attached to his wrist, a frown upon his brow. "We need to suit up too."

They began moving out and Ystil.3 made a small noise. "Um, what about me?" The humans turned back.

"You've done your job," General Shaw said. "Now let us do ours."

He stood from the chair. "So I'm supposed to just stay here and wait obediently?"

"Second buffer field penetrated. Entering final buffer field in minus oh-one SEMs."

"I can be useful," Ystil.3 said. "I'm loaded with functions."

"Yeah, human probing functions," Daneel said under his breath. He received a sharp jab in the ribs from Lydia for it.

The General thought. "Is the ship able to sustain power without you here, if we need to launch in a hurry?"

Ystil.3 nodded. "She flies brilliant in atmosphere so take off can be almost instantaneous." He remembered Tom boring him with that information once.

"Fine," the General said. "You go with Lydia's team. She is in command, which means you follow her orders. I don't want anything to screw this up. You're along for the ride only, I don't want any surprises."

Ystil.3 nodded, considered saluting, then decided against it.

"Right. Suit up then."

"I don't need to," Ystil.3 said. The General, however, had stopped listening and was striding ahead through the causeway.

"Me neither," Lydia said, hanging back. "But they can be useful. Besides, it can be dangerous to draw attention by looking different to the rest of the squad."

"Penetrating final buffer field in minus oh-five SESs," the BetaShip announced.

Everyone instantly stopped mid-step, waiting to see if they would all vaporise.

"Three..."

"Two..."

"One..."

"Final buffer field penetrated. Preparing to land in Northern hemispherical quadrant T8 in minus oh-five SEMs. Switching to atmospheric deceleration."

There was a collective sigh of relief and General Shaw led them on, his demeanour grave, more so than Ystil.3 had ever seen it before.

"What is he expecting to find down here?" Ystil.3 asked Lydia.

She looked back to the dark curve of the planet rushing towards them through the bridge's tempurhull and smiled. "Trouble."

Ystil.3's suit was basically a white, skin-tight thermosuit with pressure control smart fibres, hood and visor. The visor was equipped with a rebreather, a visual comms system, infrared navigation and team tracking – all of which were crude in comparison to Ystil.3's internal functions. Although, he had to admit the comms system would be useful in speaking with the others. Now that they weren't aboard the Hyperborea he and Lydia were able to secure-beam again, but before leaving, Captain Lu had ordered them to not use this form of comms, as the humans were still unsure of the tracing capabilities of the enemy.

The enemy, he thought. It seemed odd to refer to Sir Z in this way.

Ystil.3 had been using secure-beam as his main form of communication for his entire existence, and asking him to not use it was the equivalent of asking a human to not use their mouth to speak, but to instead use their eyes and blink out a message. However, he complied.

By the time the entire team was ready, the BetaShip had landed them safely among the servers of what was once the old colony of Thebes, according to General Shaw. The Black Betty had no form of land buggy they could use, so they each sat silently in the cramped airlock chamber as the planet's atmosphere was introduced. They had been briefed on their objectives: Lydia's team was to secure a klick radius perimeter of where the life-signs had been detected and sweep and scan inwards towards the centre, while the General and Dr Regus were to start central and take readings, gleaning as much intel as possible. There was something odd about how the life forms had massed where the humans had once colonised. Ystil.3 knew it, and so did everyone else. But no one said as much.

"Atmospheric match complete," the BetaShip announced.

The airlock chamber hissed open. Through the crack, a glimmer of red sunlight reflected off a wall of black metal. The broad frames of the server metropolis stretched out, spreading like a labyrinth over the entire planet. His species.

Daneel and Jep were first out, followed by Lydia. Daneel swung left of Betty and Jep right, while Lydia stayed central. They held their plasma rifles erect, the sight linked to visor visuals.

"No heat detection for two hundred yards west," Daneel said. The words echoed through the built in comm system on Ystil.3's visor helmet. Because of the mass amounts of heat radiating off the servers, raising the planet's atmospheric temperature to fifty plus degrees, the heat sensors were inverted so that anything below average server temperature would be easier to spot.

"East is clear also," Jep said.

"North clear," Lydia said.

The General stood upon Thebes' ground and faced the crimson sunset. In a burnt orange sky, the red sun hung between two rows of sleek black servers, perfectly in-line as they stretched off to touch the horizon. The sun burned like the fire that had once consumed the planet, reflecting off the servers' smooth sides in a hazy smog of light and dust. The wind whipped the barren ash beneath their feet into swirling swarms of smoke.

Ystil.3 couldn't see the General's face through his visor and wondered what he was feeling right now. The last time he had been on this planet it had been a different world.

"I've managed to pinpoint the life signature to a klick radius," Dr Regus said, barely looking up from the holo emitting from his wrist. "I suspect the servers are interfering somehow. That's the best we're going to get, I'm afraid. It'll have to be a sweep from this point as expected."

"Fine," General Shaw said. "Let's move." He and the doctor headed north between the servers ahead, the small sun as red as a drop of blood hovering above the horizon between the obsidian structures.

They switched to linked group wave before Ystil.3 and Lydia went east between the darkening aisles, while Daneel and Jep headed west. Lydia had set up the group wave so they could each view what their partner saw through a screen-in-screen function in their visors. She'd also given Ystil.3 a weapon, a plasma rifle like the others carried. Daneel had watched silently as Lydia gave him in a brief lesson on how to use it.

Ystil.3 was acutely aware that soon it would be dark. He was also acutely aware that somewhere on the planet was his own server, possibly the one he currently walked by. He touched the black glass-like monolith as they walked, his suit absorbing the heat. A few paces ahead, Lydia held her weapon raised, muscles tense beneath the white suit that clung snuggly to her breasts and narrow waist, showing her toned arms and the powerful muscles in her legs. Ystil.3 rested his own firearm casually on his shoulder as he gazed up at the servers, trying to not think about having sex with her.

"Have you ever been here in real-time before?" she asked him over comm, inspecting one of the servers.

"In a way, I never left," he said.

They came to the end of a server, to a type of crossroad in the path; the servers lined up into a perfect grid over the whole planet. Lydia edged towards it, back flush against the server to their left, she swiftly exposed the plasma rifle out into the cross road while keeping herself covered, the sight of the firearm allowing her to view the pathways either side of them. Both were clear, but it was becoming increasingly harder to tell with the darkening sky. Within the cross section, as with the others they had passed, Lydia unhooked a cylindrical device from her belt, flicked it open to reveal a sharp flashing stake and drove it into the blackened dirt, before walking on.

"What does it feel like, having part of yourself locked away that you can't access?" she said.

"It feels a bit like how it would if you had your arms bound and were expected to do everything with your feet."

Lydia looked up at the nearest server. It was oppressive. "Would you know if we came across yours?"

He kicked the earth beneath his boots. It was more ash than soil, lifting like smoke with each step. "I don't think so."

"What would happen if your server was destroyed?"

"I'd die," he said flatly. "Why? Are you planning to raze it?"

"Shut up." She shook her visor and walked on before stopping abruptly. "Do you really think that?"

"I wouldn't blame you. Not really. I mean, I barely have the emotional capacity to comprehend the loss AI have caused humans. And no one would miss me. The only entities in the universe that might give a junkfuck either way are missing, which is also my fault. I'm nothing but a pawn in a plan that has moved beyond use for it."

Lydia relaxed her firearm and faced him. In the in-screen vision, he could see his own visor through Lydia's eyes, which reflected her reflecting him in a confusing eternal mirror effect. "You do comprehend it," she said, reaching for his shoulder. "I see it in you. You may have been a pawn to them, but to us, you can be something else. Something of your own making. That's what it means to be free, Winston. It means making your own way and being the type of man you want to be."

"Man," he echoed. "I'm a tin-man."

"I don't define a man by what he's made from, but what he's made of. And I say you're a man, human or not. It takes guts to look truth in the eye and accept it from what it is. There was an easier path you could have chosen. But you didn't." She raised her weapon once more and began along the now sunless path. "Besides, you would be missed. I would…" she stopped.

A scratching noise had begun from the next cross section ahead. On a silent world, it was easy to hear. Scuttling, scraping almost.

"What's that?" he whispered.

The last ray of light abruptly extinguished from the sky, leaving them in darkness. "Switch to night vis," Lydia said.

Ahead, they picked up something cooler than the heat pumping from of the servers. Something moving. Lydia stepped forward, stopping at the edge of the cross section. Ystil.3's weapon was now raised and ready. "A life form?" he asked. "But I can't pick up density, the servers are messing up my wave-based functions."

"Be ready to back me up," she whispered.

Before he could ask exactly how he would be required to back her up, she stepped out into the cross section and moved along the path towards the glowing life signal. Ystil.3 followed. The night vision submerged everything in a ghoulish glow, a throbbing emerald landscape of server constructs. Ahead, a single green figure stood. Lydia tensed and released her rifle safety. He did the same and activated his infrared and ladar pulse, letting him see farther into the distance than his vision would allow.

"It looks humanoid," she said, "but it has its back to us."

"How could it have survived down here?"

She said nothing, just edged forward until only feet away from the figure. Ystil.3 could see it now. It was naked and thin, hairless with wide sinewy shoulders and strangely long arms that touched its knees, which bent in the wrong direction, like haunches. There was something disturbing about how it stood there, swaying.

"Hello?" Lydia said, not over comm, but over her visor speaker. The sound cut through the stagnant air.

The creature stopped still. The feet shuffled and it rotated to face them. The flesh was blackened and shredded in places with gleaming bone shining through. Its genitals were a mound of melted flesh and its hands had been stripped almost clean of skin and tissue, leaving fingers of sharp bone. Its face was singed free of features, eyes gone, and its nose, cheeks and lips forming a rigid mask of melted black flesh. The mouth was a hollow cave of blackness, a pink tongue lolling from the side, obscenely.

Lydia almost fell backwards into Ystil.3's rifle. The creature stumbled towards them. A tearing noise came from its mouth. It swayed lopsidedly before scuffing forward again on clawed stumps. It stumbled and bounced, like an excited child.

"Don't take another junkfucking step," she said, reestablishing her rifle's sight at its head.

It came for them so suddenly that she barely had time to react. It dropped onto its arms sprang like a beast on all fours, gnashing its teeth.

A lance of white light shot from the end of her rifle, hitting the creature squarely in the face. Its head exploded instantly, sending a vaporised a spray of black rain out over a five-metre radius, splattering the servers, which began to smoke at the contact.

Ystil.3 just stared at the twitching body while Lydia scanned the immediate area.

"General, we've come into contact with a life form," she said over comm. "Appears to be a sub-set humanoid. Only one so far and we took it out. Had no choice. It was extremely hostile. Repeat. Extremely hostile."

Then, to Ystil.3's surprise, the headless creature staggered back to its feet. It clawed at the air with bone-sharp fingers, trying to get to them. He tapped Lydia on the shoulder and she turned before making a small noise.

"There's something totally junkfucked going on down here."

☐

40

Norma had been to Australia once before in her life. It was during her twenties when she had just finished her post-grad studies, years before being snapped up by Life Corp head-hunters. She had family there, in the very southern parts of New South Wales, but she had gone as part of an organised effort to help those who remained in the desolate shanties of the north. Scientists called this region of the world the Hot Spot, which bound a circumference around South Asia, the most southern parts of India and the eastern countries of the African continent, including Madagascar. The newstabs called it Hades.

In the Australian north, the weather was infamously unpredictable, throwing out regular electric storms and sand twisters over the land and blasting flesh from the bone of anyone caught in them. Tsunamis hurled themselves onto land least three times a year on average, which devastated any attempts at living near the coast, where the land was still some-what fertile, compared to the in-land desert, and where the heat was a constant forty-five degrees, unlike the central regions of the north which often touched the mid-fifties to sixties. Yet the northerners attempted to survive there. They had no choice in the matter.

Decades ago, most people stranded in Hades were given the opportunity of living off-world. A lot accepted. Those that didn't, had no choice but to remain where they were, in the furious heat and tumultuous centre of Australia. Southern Australia had closed its borders to the people abandoned in the north after a tsunami swallowed miles of the northern coastline and submerged Papa New Guinea, Indonesia, Malaysia and most of Thailand under water, killing millions. The Earth was in a state of panic. Migration became out-lawed in these areas and the south of Australia had no choice but to border off the north to conserve limited resources. Since then, the south controlled its population through birthing permits.

Those in the north were abandoned by their own, but, despite the odds, survived and adapted to the dangerous climbs, choosing to live as large tribes in the centre, along the north-south border manned continuously by armed force drones. Soon a physical wall was built across the entire width of the land mass to keep them out.

Those who made the choice to remain on Earth instead of starting a new off-world life needed aid, and the world's charities attempted to provide this whenever they could. The dwindling numbers of the Church established most aid groups, and it was with such a group that Norma had first experienced Hades.

They brought dried foods and tinned goods that would last long periods, as well as raw materials that could help them live; building materials and memo-fabrics that would help weather-proof the shacks and tents that stretched for miles within the desert. They brought vaccinations for the increasing numbers afflicted with typhoid and other ailments caused by the squalor conditions. And they brought seed, pointless though it was.

Norma had passed out a total of three times during her four-week stay there. The first time was from the heat almost right after getting off the stratoplane before they had even begun any work. The second was from vomiting so violently she became severely dehydrated after one of the hunting parties returned from the coast with barrels of rancid fish that had taken them a month to carry back. Fishing parties constantly trawled back and forth, most of what they returned with was not edible and some didn't return at all. There were no animals. None had survived. Sometimes they came across small insects, which they would eat, but their staple food was what they could garner from the sea. Relentless attempts were made at planting, but almost always the crop gave them next to nothing. The searing heat and persistent flooding saw to that. The third time Norma passed out during her trip was watching a man eat the flesh of his own wife who had died from starvation during the night. To this day Norma had nightmares of seeing the twisted face of the bone-thin man, skin brown and bobbled like leather, sobbing as he picked the meat from his wife's leg. The others pulled him away, but it was not an uncommon thing Norma was told by the nun that fanned her back to consciousness.

Returning to Australia was not something she had ever wanted to do, but there was no other choice.

The heat almost knocked Norma off her feet as she and the team made their way from the baked concrete runway into the cool of Canberra Airport's glass terminal. The memoplastic membrane sheeting that covered Charlie's wheeled chamber flapped noisily in the choking-hot breeze. Felicity kept constant watch over his stats and had done so throughout the hour-long stratoplane journey from London.

In the air-con-cool terminal, Norma watched the slim hologram silhouette of Sir Jennifer Colter cross the large gateway, her heels tapping on the marble floor as though she were actually there and not linked to a bed of wires on Pisces. Her trademark look of composed disdain passed over Norma and rested on the chamber.

"Follow," she commanded, gesturing with a sharp-nailed finger, before turning and clicking her way back across the terminal. Her skin was a fresh lavender colour and she wore a red dress that put everything she had – paid for – on display. Norma wore a canvas shirt and sensible shoes.

The group followed, which included the two bed-hands Norma had insisted accompany them – one of whom was a handsome young man with a chiselled jaw speckled with stubble and short chestnut hair. She looked back to Deen van Rilip as he pushed the chamber forward, dressed in whites and sweating madly. Their eyes locked for a short moment and Norma jerked her head forward, following Sir Jennifer Colter's perspiration-free swagger back out into the heat.

She had been instructed by Life Corp to plan Charlie's transition to the Australia Nu-Sphere House. Of course, she was the first choice. None of the team had put in the hours she had, none had been frequently by his bedside like she had. None could. Not even the R&D genetics department. The sight of him was too much for them. But the thought of allowing him to remain continuously alone was more than Norma's conscience could bear.

Whatever his condition, whatever his affliction, whatever had caused the genetic mutation within him that kept him alive throughout his ancient life, there was no other provision on the planet that had a greater chance of finding out more than Life Corp. That's what Sir Jetson Kay often told her, and she knew it was true, despite their hidden agenda.

The very first time she had laid eyes upon the withering man had been during her first years at the company. To say she was shaken by the discovery was an understatement. She had almost quit there and then, until Sir Jetson Kay persuaded her otherwise.

"Do you trust another to give him the care you can?" he had asked her. "Would you leave it to someone to find what could ultimately save him from such a cursed existence?" He was right. Norma couldn't leave when she could be there helping him.

The most she had managed to do was translate varying brain activity – which was surprisingly coherent – so they could communicate through text on a holoscreen. Charlie's questions ran unending as a subconscious undercurrent of their text conversations. "Where am I? Why is it dark? Who are you? Who am I? Am I dead? Please kill me." And Norma would have. If the man could die she would have euthanised him long ago. But she vowed to never give up on him.

On a more conscious level, however, Charlie could converse simply, and Norma got into the habit of reading him a few passages from her romance novels. He seemed to respond to this and could partially remember what she'd read to him the previous day, picking up bits the story from where they left off. Then, one day, the man thought: "My name is Charlie. What is yours?" He forgot almost instantly and never thought anything as coherent ever again.

Norma discovered, years later, that not only had Life Corp geneticists isolated the mutation and discovered how to pass it on to others in a serum known as the White Drops, due to its milky appearance, but they were actually doing so for obscene amounts of Coin. This was another point at which Norma had almost quit Life Corp.

Almost.

"We fully intend to formulate an age stabiliser before any of those who have purchased the White Drops ever get to the stages of corrosion that the Source has gotten to," Sir Jetson Kay had told her in attempts to soothe her concerns. "Do you trust others to do this? Will you leave it up to them or will you put that brilliant mind of yours to the task?"

She had wanted to ask Sir Jetson Kay there and then, that if they were so sure of finding an age stabiliser, why he hadn't taken the Drops himself? But she didn't. She went back to work. He believed the key to the cure was in the man's brain. It wasn't until recently that she suspected he might be right. Not so much in his brain, more in his memories.

The monorail on which they travelled was thankfully air-conditioned. Norma sat in the very back of the tinted-windowed carriage with Charlie locked in place, while the others sat nearer the front, watching a holoscreen of an Australian news channel covering the Life Corp experiment set for the next day. Sir Jennifer Colter's hologram sat in the corner, sipping a clear holographic cocktail with an olive in it. She faced Norma, blonde hair perfectly styled and the tips of every strand dusted with minute diamonds. They moved like optic fibre. She stared at Norma without the usual concern of being rude. Norma, however, paid no attention and avoided all eye contact with Rilip, who sat at the front, watching the news with the other bed-hand. She continued to talk to Charlie through her eDeck. "The sun is shining the way it hardly ever does in London," she typed into the shimmering interface hovering over her wrist device. "Do you remember what the sun looks like?"

"Sun," Charlie replied. It was one of his less talkative days.

She had devised an algorithm to distinguish between levels of consciousness. Then the idea soon emerged of using it to access the deeper areas of the brain that Charlie himself couldn't access on a conscious level, to try and determine who he was, where he came from and, mostly, how he came to be this way. Her questions to the board on the subject had always been met with monosyllabic grunts of boredom.

Sir Jetson Kay told her that they had been simply alerted to the man when doctors discovered the unusual cell activity in his blood. Apparently, at the time, the doctors knew nothing of who he was or where he came from, only that he appeared on the hospital steps and was taken in; they hadn't expected him to see out the morning. Three months later, specialists from Life Corp were brought in as doctors were baffled. They offered to take the man so they could give him the help he needed in Life Corp Tower. That was hundreds of years ago, so they said, and the details of which had long been lost. Of course, it was all a lie. Not even a convincing one.

She soon discovered that she could access the remote parts of his brain in the hippocampus by stimulating it with mock electrodes and using the algorithm she wrote to interpret his thoughts, partly by using the same mind-mapping technology used to replicate the board's personas, which included memory, through the Hydra programme. It was a project she kept well under the radar of the board and it consumed countless hours, days, months of her own time.

Eventually, fragmented parts of incoherent memory came together and Norma could read partial descriptions of Charlie's long life. A lot of it was abstract and undecipherable, but some made perfect sense. Some words that flashed were simple descriptions such as bright, warm, hungry, sad, funny. These Norma sectioned into early memories of infancy. Some memories of segmented conversations came through that made no sense without context.

The most valuable find to Norma was that, within these early memories of childhood, Charlie, as a young boy, was lonely. He remembered a cottage on the coast. He had once thrown himself from the cliff it sat, onto jagged rocks that protruded from the sea. He awoke on the beach unharmed. This had horrified him. But there was love in him, for a man, his father. Then grief as the man inevitably died. Charlie had, on more than that one occasion, tried to take his own life.

Norma was at first unable to imagine the enormity of what she had rummaged from the depths of Charlie's brain, but it soon became clear through months of translating into legible memory fragments that Charlie had established a research facility in London during the twenty-first century, dedicated to genetic and cellular mutations and abnormalities. It was called Omaha Research. This, as Norma knew all too well, had been the first incarnation of Life Corp. Charlie himself had been its founder. That was all that could be gleaned of his beginnings.

Felicity sat between the two armed guards that had accompanied them from London. She looked small and mousy and awkwardly placed sandwiched between their broad shoulders. Another armed guard had joined them on landing. So far, she hadn't been left alone with Charlie even once. Rilip had wanted the pick-up to either be between landing in Canberra and taking off in Sydney, where they were headed, but Norma knew that's when security would be at its most stringent. Australia only had two airports, Canberra for international flights and Sydney for inland flights. From Sydney, they would take a hoverwing to Alice Springs, right in the centre of the country and on the very border of Hades.

Through the shaded windows of the monorail, travelling parallel to the main highway north, Norma could see the following procession of black vehicles. More armed security. The pick-up wouldn't have had a chance of even getting close at this point. It was in Alice Springs, population zero, that they would have the best chance. They only had one shot and it scared the shit out of Norma just thinking about it. Nothing was ever going to be the same again.

Alice Springs was a wasteland of abandoned buildings, disused to the point of ruin. The population had long since forsaken the place. The military forces kept the border in check, along with the LDO drones, supervising the wall that stretched from Monkey Mia on the west coast to Brisbane on the east, cutting the country in two. Seeing it for the first time had filled Norma with an acute unease; during her excursion into Hades she had never ventured south enough to see it, though its cost was always brutally evident. It was as red as the sand that formed the dunes, blending skillfully into the sandscape. It's a lie, Norma thought. A lie to soften the reality and disguise what is beyond.

They didn't stay in Alice Springs more than the time it took to load Charlie onto one of the three desert roamers waiting for them. The smooth curve of the single-winged craft angered and billowed the red sand into a frothing storm as it touched down. Norma supervised as Rilip and the other bed hand lay Charlie into the long desert roamer.

Jennifer Colter's holoform joined them, along with an entourage of guards. The other two roamers that travelled in the convoy were full of soldiers. Travelling by hoverwing would have hinted at the importance of the cargo, Jennifer Colter had told Norma when she asked why they weren't travelling by air to their destination. She bit her tongue at the awful woman's use of the word "cargo".

After hours of heading northwest, the roamers scuttling quickly across the sand and rocks at a speed of ninety klicks per hour, they finally arrived in the centre of nowhere. The heart of Hades itself. Flat desert stretched out to the heat-blurred horizon, blanketing the world in red sand beneath an impossibly blue sky. Colter barked orders to her men as she exited the roamer, striding across the sand in her heels as if she were strutting down Bond Street. Norma watched from inside the roamer as she stopped, surrounded by guards. The sand at her feet began to boil and froth, until an eight-foot long glass cylinder rose from the ground, sand running off in red torrents, gleaming in the sun.

Norma's heart stopped and she looked to Rilip, who was staring from the window of the roamer also. An underground facility would make it one hundred times harder. The schematics they had gotten hold of didn't account for that.

The Nu-Sphere House was a complex submerged network of white corridors and unknown rooms, connecting in a hexagonal web structure that stretched for klicks beneath the northern Australian desert. Charlie's room was secure to the point of impenetrable – or inescapable, depending on which way you looked at it. Norma's team, along with her and their personal effects were searched immediately, of course, and at least two guards were in sight at all times, armed and silent. She had requested to remain with Charlie during the night to monitor his vitals in person, but Sir Jennifer Colter had bluntly refused.

Norma and Felicity were then accommodated in adjacent rooms in a part of the Nu-Sphere House that was so far from where Charlie was kept that they needed to take a ten-minute buggy ride to get there. Not that it made a difference. Their doors were locked upon entering and they had to request for them to be opened from a control room somewhere deep in the facility. "For security purposes," Jennifer Colter had smirked. Her hologram vanished along the corridor, the sound of clacking fading into the distance. Even Norma's eDeck had restricted access and she couldn't even make a simple phone call if she wanted to.

There was nothing to do now but wait.

Her room was clean and had the air of a soulless hotel room. There were beverage facilities, a shower and a holoscreen with a selection of movies. Instead, she accessed her latest read on her eDeck, The Heart String. It was about a young woman whose husband died during the Last War and who struggled to feel again after the grief, only to have her heart thawed by a handsome teacher who showed her how to live again through teaching her how to play the violin. It wasn't long before Norma drifted to sleep, dreaming of strong hands and melodies.

A few hours' sleep is all Norma managed before waking prior to the sun – she assumed since she had no way to tell whether the sun had risen or not. Given its record to date, she assumed it had. She sat at the dresser, just thinking, mostly of Sayi.

An unremarkable man in a grey jumpsuit eventually brought a tray of breakfast. She picked at the dry toast and managed a bite of the grapefruit before going for what she really wanted – coffee. She was given an hour to eat, shower and dress before being taken to Charlie's room. Norma had remote access to his vital signs via her eDeck, which would have alerted her to any problems during the night. Charlie was as well as he ever was, inside his chamber bed with the airflow hissing like snakes. Her team were escorted with Charlie to another glass tube elevator waiting to take them even deeper into the subterranean hive.

Three guards in black, armed with Fracture 109s and lightwhips, joined them in their journey down. Their lightwhips glowed blue, set to stun only. When they reached their destination, the doors opened into a cavernous white expanse. Blindingly bright.

The time was 9:06am, Australian time. They had three hours remaining.

☐

41

Through the jungle of servers Daneel and Gutter headed westward, laying the sensor-stakes whenever a horizontal path crossed with their vertical one. Daneel had read about old Earth cities laid out in the similar grid systems – well… he hadn't read, more just looked at the images. He could read, only not as well as he might if he hadn't spent all his time dreaming about learning how to shoot plasma rifles as a kid, which he did as soon as he reached the age of twelve.

He did this so well, in fact, that from that point on, no one expected him to practice reading. Instead, it was "have you learnt how to throw death boom combustor spheres?" or "You need to learn to drive the exo-skeletal war armour." He quickly became proficient in every skill and test General Shaw put to him and it was soon clear that his calling was for the militia. He battled, bruised, blown-up, fired, constructed, stomped, trained and sweated his way to Corporal. And he did it well. He did it with a smile on his face and a song in his heart, and a dream of one day raining bloody vengeance on the AI bitch demons.

He had dreams of going further, going all the way to the top and fighting at the General's side. But after reaching Corporal, people starting asking about his reading skills again and his steady elevation through the ranks ceased abruptly. Apparently, there was more to it than "blowing shit up", as General Shaw had told him on more than one occasion. Corporal was his level and had been for years – Sergeant was his dream and "she's a cunt that won't put out," as he regularly told his comrades.

"She is hot, though, you have to admit?" Gutter said. "Scolding like a blue hypergiant."

"Lieutenant Lydia Chen is your superior and you should have more respect," Daneel replied over their two-way visor channel, working a sensor-stake into the blackened earth.

First Private Jep Hu, had been under Daneel's wing, so to speak, since his militia induction at the age of fourteen. He saw a lot of himself in the guy, except for his skill in turning any conversation into smut, hence he acquired the nickname Gutter, as that's usually where his mind was. Now at the age of twenty-two, the man was beginning to come into his own within Paris troop.

"I don't mind a bit of authority. Bet she can handle a ninetail laser at just the right intensity so's not to leave any permanent marks."

Daneel smiled behind his visor.

"I don't mind that she's barren or whatever either," Gutter went on.

"She's so fine. Shame her genes won't help the collective human gene pool, though, right?"

Daneel activated the newly implanted sensor. "Shut up."

"I'm just saying. I mean, just imagine if she could produce offspring, she'd would've been chosen for mummy duty and the Consulate would've had her squirting out kids for the rest of her fertile life instead of being the badass super chick she is now. That would've been the real shame. Plus, I'd never get the chance to check out all her upgrades on a personal level, if you know what I mean."

Daneel snorted. "You think you actually have a chance with her?"

"As good as anyone," the man replied.

"You'd sooner have the General tell you he's stepping down to make way for your superior soldiering skills than get with the likes of her."

The sun rested on the horizon, letting the scarlet light intensify for a few minutes before setting into darkness. Why they had chosen this now for a recon mission, Daneel didn't know. It would have made more sense to go during this part of the planet's daylight hours.

"Why don't I have a chance?" Gutter asked, catching up with Daneel's long stride.

This was what Daneel liked about Gutter. His self-delusion was so great it produced a strange modesty and tendency to push himself, thinking he could actually achieve his delusions. "Well, firstly, she's older, and infinitely more mature than you. Secondly, as you said, she is smoking hot, and you're, well, you. And thirdly, she's been with this…" He gestured to himself. "So where exactly do you think that puts you in the pecking order?" He couldn't see the man's reaction through the visor but he could imagine it.

"Are you saying you boarded the Lydia shuttle?" Gutter asked, his voice higher than usual.

"No. I'm saying I boarded the shuttle, got ejected halfway through the journey and died from explosive decompression in the vacuum of space."

"Fuck me like a bitch on heat. What was it like?"

Daneel smiled. "Like warm apple pie."

"What does that mean?"

"I dunno. It's from an old Earth mediaholo about a bunch of Earth kids trying to fuck a bunch of stuff."

"So…" Gutter pushed.

"So nothing. It ended. We both moved on. The end."

"Is that why…" He stopped as though thinking better of it.

"Why what?"

"Nothing."

They reached another cross section and this time Daneel handed over the sensor-stake for Gutter to implant. "If you have something on your mind, share, please."

"I mean, that isn't the reason why we… you know… to the AI, is it? Because he – I mean it – and Lydia are friends… or whatever they are?"

Daneel turned abruptly. "Tin-man needed to know what we're about, that's all there was to it. It was a warning to let him know that we're ready for them. Understand?"

"Yeah, it's just—"

He jabbed his weapon hard into the smaller man's chest. "You either understand or you don't. There is no it's just. Do you junkfucking understand, or don't you, Private?"

"I do, Corporal. I understand."

Daneel lowered his weapon and turned. The sun was almost gone and the impending night made visuals hard, made harder still by the searing hot servers that cast them in dying shadows. "Then no more about it. Implant that thing then let's move."

They walked on in silence after switching to night vision, implanting and activating three more sensor-stakes before they received a transmission from Lydia over the group wave comm, followed by uploaded visual relay. They watched the streaming visuals of the vaguely human creature move aggressively towards Lydia and then the removal of its head.

"There's something totally fucked going on down here," Lydia said over comm, followed by plasma fire.

"What's happening?" General Shaw said. "Status update."

"The thing just got back up, without a head. It just stood up… trying to get to us. I've disabled its legs and now it's crawling on the floor, dragging itself towards us."

"Daneel, any signs of life on your end?" the General asked.

"No Sir. All's clear where we are."

"Fine. I want you to finish laying the sensors in double time. Once you're done, find us at these coordinates." A map of the servers covering a five-klick radius appeared in his visor sight. A pale light flashed in the centre, inside a building that was different to the other servers. It was half the height and double the breadth. "If you encounter any of the life forms, avoid confrontation if possible. Remember, this is a recon mission only. However, defend if necessary. Are we clear?"

"We're clear," Lydia replied.

"Clear," Daneel added.

"Good. Double time. Out."

Daneel turned and the space where Gutter had been standing was now vacant, leaving only the dark server corridor in his place. He cursed in his visor as he switched back to their two-way system. "Where the junkfuck are you, you little shit? Get your tiny dick back here now."

There was silence for a moment before Gutter replied, "I'm surveying the immediate area while you receive orders."

"Orders have been received, as you know, now get back here." They didn't have time for this shit.

"Problem."

"What junkfucking now?"

"I think I'm a bit lost."

"Lost? You little fuck. I hand you an opportunity to come on this mission and you've just thrown it in my face. You were supposed to show them what you're made of. I had twenty other First's lined up for this."

"I'm trying," Gutter said. "I wanted to show what I'm made of by using my initiative, but I got a bit disorientated and now I don't know where I am. Well, I know where I am, I just don't know where you are."

"The militia doesn't need the initiative of green kids that don't know their dicks from their noses. It needs you to do what you're junkfucking told."

"Well I wasn't not told to go."

"Turn on your cam visuals so I can see your surroundings." The cams had ceased during transmission of the visual relay from Lydia. The screen in the corner of Daneel's visor popped into existence and he could see Gutter's location. Unfortunately, it looked identical to everywhere else on the planet.

"Right, stop where you are. I'll transmit a ladar pulse and see if I can pick you up." The pulse showed a single small figure one aisle left and two aisles forward, unmoving and roughly halfway between two servers. "Okay, I've got you. I'm on my way. Don't move, y'hear me?"

"No problem, Dan," Gutter replied cheerily.

"That's Corporal," Daneel said sharply. He minimised the ladar reading to appear beside the other in-screen cameras in his visor, then sent a ladar pulse every thirty seconds to get a fresh reading. He didn't trust Gutter to stay put. Turning the corner towards where Gutter waited. If it was daylight they could probably see each other, but as it was, Daneel was faced with blackness lined with the green of the heat-radiating servers.

Daneel stopped. The ladar pulse had picked up something else. Without the soft crunch of his footfall, the quietness seemed suddenly overbearing. Something human-shaped stood within the cross section ahead, between him and Gutter. Another ladar pulse revealed that the thing was moving towards Gutter.

"Gutter, I've picked up a suspected ULF headed towards you. You need to move away. Can you see it?"

"Nothing," Gutter replied. "I can't even see the stars through this smog shit in the air to know what direction to head in. What way do I go? The magnetic field is making my compass useless."

"Must be the servers. Take a ladar rebound reading."

"I've never used that before. I don't have the clearance code." His voice had lost its trademark casual edge. He was beginning to panic, and that was a dangerous thing for a soldier.

"Access the function folder and enter the override code nine nine six three seven. Activate the pulse and look at the reading. Are you doing it?"

"Yes."

"You'll be able to make out the ULF. Head away from it. Repeat. Do not confront. Move one server to your left and head down. I'll make my way to meet you. Understand?" There was silence and Daneel's in-screen of Gutter's visuals went black. "Gutter, respond."

Nothing.

"Don't you do anything stupid you little shit. That is an order."

No reply.

He ran, releasing the safety of his plasma rifle and emitting another ladar rebound. The ULF and Gutter were now only metres from one another and Gutter wasn't moving anywhere. But that wasn't all; what looked like a group of six more ULFs had emerged behind Gutter's standpoint, leaving him trapped. If he'd taken a ladar reading he'd most likely seen already. "Plan B. Take all those junkfuckers out. Repeat. Defend and take them out."

As Daneel ran into the server cross section, he turned left and made his way the width before turning right, continuing along the server length. The ULFs had grouped and Daneel could no longer tell which ladar figure was Gutter – if any. It was possible he bypassed the ULFs and headed outside the ladar rebound field where Daneel couldn't pick him up. However, most ULF figures were not incapacitated, still roaming what was now in his direction. A few figures lay unmoving on the ground. He just hoped none were Gutter.

He pushed forward and could soon make out the green shadows of the first ULFs ahead. Then, as the distance closed, the image sharpened to reveal a stumbling heard of creatures that might once have been human. What they were now, Daneel didn't know. The flesh on each was blackened and melted. Some had no faces, only black bone masks. None had eyes; they used their long fingers to grope the air around them like sensors. They were naked and sexless. Some were missing limbs. The spine of one protruded from its back like the branch of an Earth tree, broken from the neck and causing its head to dangle on its own chest. The arms and legs of another were missing from joints down and it crawled like an animal on all fours, its neck somehow grown longer with its head on the end, gnashing its lipless mouth in his direction. They could sense him there.

He'd stopped still from the horror, his weapon at his shoulder, ready to fire. A noise behind the moving heard distracted them and they turned sharply towards it at frightening speed. Two remained, squirming on the ground, headless and incapacitated, but not dead.

"Took you long enough."

"Where the junkfuck are you?" Daneel swung around but couldn't see the First Private anywhere.

"Look up."

Gutter's face peered down from atop the nearest server. "What are you doing up there? I thought you were dead. Why haven't you been responding?"

"I couldn't make a noise. You see how they reacted to the cartridge I threw over there. They're fast when they want to be. Well, the ones with legs are."

"You're wasting ammo now?"

"I had to lure them away."

Daneel could once again see what Gutter saw through the in-screen camera. "Why wasn't your visor picking up visuals before?"

"It was. But I was lying on the server facing the sky so all you would've seen was black."

"Just get down here. We need to move. We're behind as it is and we've got three more sensors to embed."

"You should see something first." Gutter hung over the edge of the server and began a deft abseil down the strong-line attached to his belt. Once at the bottom, the line retracted. "When I shot at those crispy guys…" he pointed to the headless two headless figures that were now leaking black blood form their wounds, still not dead. "…When I shot them I also hit the server behind, damaging it. I could see the wires and shit inside. It was all glowing and stuff."

Daneel looked at the server. There was no damage there at all. "I don't see it."

"No, you wouldn't. Look." He dragged Daneel back down the server path.

"Gutter, we seriously don't have time for this."

"Just look." Gutter lifted his plasma rifle and fired at the server wall, burning away the outer layer. Glowing tubes and siliconia were inside, exposed like organs.

"Watch and be quiet," Gutter whispered.

The ULF's returned from where they had heard the noise and they began repairing the side wall of the damaged server. Two probed the inside with long fingers, reconnecting wires and joining tubes. One of them bit the another, taking a chunk out of its forearm. Black liquid oozed from the gash and the wounded creature smeared the stuff onto the fissure.

Daneel watched as the outer layer of the server began to reform, grow, repairing itself as though healing.

"Nanobot tech," Gutter whispered in the silence. "It's in their blood."

*

Nathan Shaw had dreamed many times about returning to Thebes. The pale blue sky, the wan lemon sun, the dry deserts and the broken moon; he had grieved for them all. The ghosts of his past were never far... just beneath the thin veil of consciousness that separated reality from dream. But the Thebes he knew was gone. The ground was no longer the strange orange sands, but a stranger shade of black. The terraform solution in the sky no longer fractured the light from the small sun, giving the world a soft dream-like quality, it was smog-filled and lethal. Everything they had built had been levelled, making way for the colossal servers that sprouted like tombstones across the planet's dead surface.

They had journeyed to Pisces. Its surface was as scarred as Thebes' was. No servers there, though. Why here? He had pondered many times. What makes here so different? The answer came in the form of the ULFs. He didn't want to believe it at first, though he had suspected as much. But when Lydia sent the visual reply, he could no longer deny it.

He thought of the bed-ridden Charles aboard the Hyperborea, ancient and damned, cursed and bound to his slow rotting body. Like him, the people of Thebes had not died when they should have.

They're still down here.

He often thought about how angry Miranda had been with him that day, the last day. She had never been what you might call an affection mother, but she had taught him a lot, which he was grateful for. He had survived against the odds. He was strong in the face of devastation. He could lead when others were overcome with despair. He was a fighter. In the very least, she gave him that.

The thought of her as one of those things was worse than the thought of her death. She deserved more than a half-life. She deserved peace. That had been his solace for the unusually long years of his life, and now he couldn't even grasp onto that. If she is down here, then I must end it. I must put her to rest at last.

"The signal is coming from three-hundred yards ahead," Dr Regus said over their two-way comm. He held out the glowing holo above his wrist. The sun had finally set and they had switched to night vision. Dr Regus had become annoyed by the darkness on a few occasions as it impaired the view of various functions. Nathan didn't want to alarm him – or the others – by admitting he chose a night-time recon to give them cover from what he suspected inhabited the planet. It looked, however, to be redundant. From what Lydia had shown them, their eyes had melted from their sockets long ago, most likely from the blast.

"Good," Nathan said. "Still no way to determine what's inside? A little more information would be appreciated before we go in."

"Afraid not. All we can tell at this point is that it doesn't give off the same heat the servers do, which can only suggest it isn't a server."

"Or it's malfunctioned."

"Maybe. However, that doesn't explain its difference in shape and density to the others. If I had to take a guess right now, I'd say it was hollow."

"We'll soon know for sure."

The building itself was half the height of the servers that surrounded it. The substance from which it was made, however, was the same, from what the doctor could tell. He examined it closely. "Some sort of converted metal alloy," he suggested. "Oxidised, perhaps, or even in a changed state. I'd need to do tests but I'd say that the original state of the structures was a gas substance made solid through a thermal process. Although I'm almost certain some sort of nano-tech would be needed to maintain them permanently in this state. Perhaps the gases from the explosion?"

Nathan grunted. He didn't know about those things. "What about the nanotech you found in—"

"That would almost certainly be able to maintain the structures in this state. What are you thinking, General?"

"Far too early to tell for sure."

Dr Regus conceived, from a now comprehensive visual of the area provided by the stake sensors, that the planet's labyrinthine server structures were not in a grid system at all. In fact, they ran at a slightly-off parallel trajectory that meant all the vertical paths led to the very edifice where they now stood. Not only that, but now they could determine that within the five-klick radius, approximately three hundred ULFs roamed within.

Nathan decided to take a lap of the structure. Upon first visual analysis, it was longer in breadth than its length. It fused seamlessly with the ground, had razor-sharp corners and revealed no repair hatches or entry points. By the time he made it back to his starting point, the group had reconvened.

"It's in their blood," Dr Regus said at once. "The nano-tech that maintains the servers. They built them. They maintain them. That explains it." He began inputting information furiously into his eDeck once more.

"What are you talking about?" Nathan said.

"We saw them do it," Daneel said. "They used their blood, or whatever it is, to repair the damaged servers. Tore their flesh and let it gush out until it rebuilt right in front of us."

"What are they?" First Private Jep asked.

"People," Lydia replied. "They look like people."

"But how did they survive the blast?" Winston asked. "Humans can't usually do that, right?"

"They survived the same way Charlie survives," Nathan said. "If you can call it that." He gestured to the building and looked to Daneel.

"Corporal, I need a door."

"But won't that attract every—"

"Zombie-looking mother-junkfucker in the vicinity?" Gutter finished.

"I am aware," Nathan said. "But I want answers. And my gut tells me they're inside. So, a door please, Corporal."

Daneel pointed his plasma rifle at the side of the building and everyone took a step back. The white lance sliced through the air and melted a dark cavity entrance.

Nathan stepped towards it. "Corporal, Private, I want this door manned. I don't want to have to watch my back for those things as well as my front. Got it?"

"You can count on us, sir," Daneel said.

"Lieutenant, Winston, doctor, we go in. Take your weapons and your wits, and if you've got a pair of steel testicles, those will come in handy too."

"Sir," Lydia said. "I take my balls with me wherever I go."

He hovered half inside for a moment. "Glad to hear it," he said, before climbing into the dark.

42

Prometheus's wife was not perfect.

For one thing, Sarah was uncommonly stubborn for a woman of her background – usually well-educated girls were bred to be ridiculously amiable, Prometheus found – and that often meant when something blossomed in her stubborn mind it was nigh on impossible to refute; many a time she and Prometheus had quarrelled due to a sharing of that particular trait and it often resulted in him having to sleep in one of the guest rooms. She would argue with him in front of company and on more than one occasion stormed from the dining room after branding him a fool and, on one evening when Sarah's own father was present, "a eunuch", after he had taken her father's side regarding her wanting to spend two days a week working at the hospital; to which her father and he both agreed was not a suitable environment for her.

Sarah also spent money as though they were royalty, and Prometheus often came home to find she had redecorated entire rooms with lavish fabrics and fashionable furniture from Paris in the small space of time from him leaving for work that same morning. She didn't enjoy the Opera, preferring the base humour of certain London thespians; although in truth Prometheus found this particular trait rather charming. But her imperfections were all a part of what made her perfect to him.

And she was not always so understanding.

During the harsh winter months of their second year of marriage, Sarah and Prometheus took a trip to the coast of St Agnes in Cornwall, where he owned a small cottage on the cliffs, less than two-hundred yards from an edge that death-dropped into the rock-filled sea. The cottage itself had been acquired by his late father as a place to spend family holidays away from the bustle of London, and Prometheus had always enjoyed the primitiveness of it. As a young man, he had spent weeks there during his summer breaks from Cambridge, where he would simply enjoy being alone. His father never liked the place much and it was only on the advice of his dear mother that they spent time there during his father's final ill-suffered years. The fresh air would always perk him for a time before he began to yearn for the London commotion from which they had escaped.

Prometheus and Sarah were due to visit in the summer months, but obligations at the hospital held off their plans and, rather than wait for good weather to roll around once more, decided they would brave the icy blasts of the Atlantic during the winter months instead. They boarded the train from London, stopping over in Bristol a night, before travelling farther South to the western coast of Cornwall.

A part of what drew Prometheus to the savage cliffs was that the house was completely devoid of servants. He had been raised with house staff, of course, but there were times when their lingering bodies weren't wanted. Sarah, however, detested the fact that the cottage had no servants; she tended to view them more as a necessity. But when they hunkered down in the evenings, free to make love by the roaring fire atop layers of rough fleece, with the warmth of the flames on their bare flesh, Sarah treasured the isolation as much as he.

During those blissful days, they would rarely roam three feet from one another. Sarah wouldn't care about her usual pristine appearance, her long auburn hair left tussled and wild about her freckled shoulders. Prometheus would put away his shiny black London shoes in favour of his old top boots covered in mud. They would lie together on the grass-covered cliffs, watching the clouds roll overhead, with the murky sea stretched out to the edge of the world. Sarah would make bread and together they would wander to the nearby village store for smoked cheese and red wine. They would talk with the locals and sample farmers' produce of eggs and jam and potatoes and return with a basket full of delicious food that they would feed to each other when darkness fell and the air chilled.

Those were among the happiest times of Prometheus's life.

It was on a blustery night during that winter's trip that they received a knock at the door of the cliff-top cottage. Prometheus opened it to find a young man from the village telegram office standing in the worsening rainstorm. He handed Prometheus the message urging that his skills were needed back in London at once. It failed to go into more detail other than to say that all the skilled men in the country able to perform open heart surgery had been contacted in this manner and the closest to London at present was Prometheus, even though he was over two-hundred miles away himself. "A CHILD'S LIFE HANGS IN THE BALANCE STOP," the last sentence read.

There was nothing for it. He would take the next train directly to London.

Sarah became upset that he was leaving her alone, in the cold, in the middle of nowhere. She stubbornly refused to go with him, so Prometheus assured her that he would send a man to help her pack and travel with her to London the very next morning. Her petulant side flared and she insisted that she would stay for the remainder of their intended holiday and that he should think of her alone and vulnerable when he reached London. Of course, Prometheus knew she was goading him. He'd already sent the young man with the telegram ahead for a carriage and by the time it arrived Prometheus was at the door with hat and coat.

"There are others who can help the girl," Sarah said, entwining her hands around his lapels and pulling him down to her height for a kiss. "Who will help the girl. Why must it always be you? Why must it always be our marriage that suffers?"

Prometheus gently tugged her free. "You know I could never rest here knowing I was needed. What if she should die and I could have saved her? How will you feel then? You are not heartless, so please see reason."

"It's my father all over again," she cried, turning from him. The storm pressed in through the open door, pulling at her night robes. "When will the man in my life choose me?" With that, she fled up the stairs and Prometheus left for London; he arrived the very next morning to the news that the patient in question had sadly died during the night.

As promised, he had sent a man to help Sarah return to London and when she arrived two days later she jumped into his arms and kissed him passionately in front of the house staff.

"Thank you for choosing me, my love," she whispered into his ear.

Prometheus was utterly confused but didn't want to question Sarah's sudden forgiveness of him. He was simply happy that she was happy and not angry anymore. He didn't have the heart to tell her that he'd left her for nothing.

*

Death was not truly Death. It had taken Prometheus a long while to decipher the semi-coherent statements from the ghost-creature he had thought to be the Reaper in physical form before the truth finally became apparent. The truth, however much it gave him clarity, did not settle him. In fact, it disturbed him more than his mistake.

The brackish wind pushed him back as he struggled his way down the solitary path of broken cobbles. The wind was nothing compared to the wild drumming of his heart. The road was as he remembered it, slick with mud and black puddles indistinguishable in the dark night, with no moon to light his way and no stars to separate the horizon. Twice he'd drowned his ankles in the deep trenches, but he barely felt the icy rainwater through his adrenaline saturated muscles. The gas lamps from the distant village irradiated a hazy glow over the hills, but only the flickering lamp light from the downstairs cottage window gave light on the lonely cliff top.

The winter Cornish coast was a gruelling place, but Prometheus had always loved the rawness of the sea crashing against the rocks a hundred feet below. The bitter wind battered the shoreline, stripping away layers of sediment. The ferocious waves and spray from the churning black waves carrying on the gales. The coastal air numbed his face, just as it had years earlier when he had left the cottage that very night to return to London, leaving Sarah alone. The creature he had thought to be Death assured him that this was that exact time – precisely one hour after the Prometheus of this time had left for London.

Sarah was inside and he would have only one night with her.

One night to bathe in her.

One night to love her.

One night to say goodbye to her.

Following the revelation that the baby he had resurrected had grown into a living fossil of immeasurable age, Prometheus had despaired. What life must he have had? What hell must he have seen and tortures endured? And it all occurred by my hand.

For a while, back in the dark timelessness of Death's dominion, he was content to loathe himself, but it soon became clear that this was not enough penance. He had to do what Death had told him all along. He had to learn the deaths done right and put right the deaths done wrong. He had to repair what he had done.

But first there was her.

Though time was nothing in the blackness, he and Death lingered in the nothing for what seemed like an age. Its whispering voices seemed to always be talking, hissing sounds and words that were too far away to hear, yet Prometheus knew the creature was close. It was waiting for him. In hindsight, Prometheus now realised that it was waiting for him all along; in his cellar in London, in the Chicago bathroom with the body of Bastille, in the New York hospital with the dying Alice, in the underground London prison with the comatose Thomas and on that strange other world. All those times Death had come and Prometheus had thought it was to return their souls to the living, when in fact it was the white liquid that brought it, like a beacon across time and space. Death had been there for him, waiting for Prometheus to put it all to right.

The child, the Source, Death had called him, had lived his life as an immortal. Had he known his fate or simply shrivelled into unnatural old age without ever knowing the truth of what happened to him? Who had raised him into a man? The sweetly broken Jane Halford he had left the babe with, perhaps? Did the child fill the hole in her heart left by the death of her husband?

"What are you?" Prometheus had asked the creature in the darkness. "You are not Death, I realise now. Not once have you taken a soul during our time together. Unless I am dead… but I do not think so. You require something from me, don't you? But I need to understand before I can begin to put right what I have done. So, what are you?"

"We are not a what…" Death rustled in the void. "We are who. We are the who that came after you. We are the who that came from the first, from the Source. We are the who that lingers between things. We are the who that cannot cease. We are the who that cannot remember the who we once were, only the who we are now. We are the who that knows the truth. We are the who that knew no better."

"From the first, the Source…" Prometheus echoed. "You came from Charles? How?"

"Through the blood," the voices replied. "The life in the blood. The life you gave to the blood, gave the life to our blood. The life that does not die."

"Your life has been extended like his, through his blood?"

"Not life. Lives…" Death hissed the word so the sound trailed into forever.

"You are more than one creature?"

"Once we walked on a thousand legs, with heads and arms and hearts and flesh. Once we had meat. Once we had love and joy and hope and greed. Once we had the Earth."

"You were people… humans. And you were all given the same potion I gave to Charles, to the Source?"

"We chose it," Death hissed. Then almost sadly it said, "We knew not. We were greed. We knew not…"

"Why do you appear as you do? As Death?"

"We yearn for the wild night. And then rest. Sleep eternal."

"You want to die."

"We remember the end came for our flesh in a storm of energy and force and blackness. The light was flicked off and we were gone. Our hands could not touch; there was nothing to touch. Our eyes could not see; there was nothing to see. We felt each other in the nothing, enduring and alone. We came together from loneliness and together we stay. Then we found home, but not where we left it. It was empty… but alive… empty… but alive."

"Home?"

"The Earth. The people, gone. On their wild night. Not us. We lingered with it in the new place. We found holes there. Holes to travel, holes to move, holes to find the truth. Holes to find you. Holes to things done. Holes to things to come. Holes to other places where the people had not gone and the Earth stayed near the sun. And we found holes to the others, the things that are large in the darkness and have no form, only bright lights and numbers. We followed, we lingered, we saw. It was they who took our form, took our flesh."

Prometheus somehow knew it was talking about Edward and the others he had helped bring back from the dead. The large things in the darkness made of light and numbers. Only now he knew that they had not been dead at all; the bodies, yes, but those he had helped revive, no. He had merely helped them steal others' forms. They wanted physicality – or needed it. For what? Something occurred that caused the destruction of the thousands of humans that were now Death… only they did not die because of the white solution given to them. The Earth and the people were gone, he thought. On their wild night. What did it mean?

"But we know the secrets of the numbers with no faces. We know for what they search," Death whispered quietly, as though into Prometheus's ear.

"What do they search for?"

"For the Source itself. And for eternity."

*

The cobbles of the path were jagged and protruded dangerously as they led him towards the soaked cottage. A disused barn rattled in the wind like loose bones, the wood shaking and rapping with every howl and baleful gust of wind. The rain saturated him through, causing his overcoat to become heavy, dripping at the ends. He was close enough now to see the wrought iron gate that led right to the door. He was close enough to see the dancing light within, a shadow in the quaint kitchen window. "Sarah," he whispered into the night, the sound swallowed by the beast that was the storm.

He wanted to run. He wanted to leap the fence and charge the slick cobbles, burst through the door and take her in his arm – bask in her. He wanted to hear her voice, hear it say his name. He wanted to smell her scent and feel how he used to feel... before. He looked down at his hands illuminated by the faint orange glow emitting from the window. They tremored as he held them in front of him. They weren't the hands she had known. How long had it been since he left London? A lifetime, it seemed. The truth was it didn't matter. He had no intention of returning to the London he'd left behind. He would see Sarah for the last time and then he would put right the destruction he had started. After... there was no after. With any such luck, he would perish in the task. There might be some semblance of consciousness in the afterlife, where he could bathe eternally in Sarah's light. He hoped – but doubted it.

If not, let it be dark and full of nothing, he thought. Let my soul wither into unconsciousness where I will never have to know this pain again. Let there be rest. Please, let there be rest.

Prometheus knew why the creature yearned for death the way it did. It was peace it wanted. And so did he.

The dark hills rolled in the distance like smudges of black against the night, while the ocean crashed hysterically against the rocks. Holding his breath, Prometheus opened the iron gate.

The Earth had disappeared, and he was responsible for that too. The places he had seen and the worlds upon which he'd stepped had been enough to convince him that humanity would one day accomplish astounding feats. Perhaps there are things that, even though they can be done, shouldn't be done.

"The past cannot be changed," Prometheus said against the rain.

"For us, it cannot," the voices of Death whispered.

"Then I cannot put right the path I set us upon, can I?"

"For us, you cannot."

Prometheus understood. "But outside this loop?"

"A world exists where this does not occur. A world alive where you and she are still one. A world alive where you and she do not even meet. A world alive where you die and she lives. A world alive where everything happens. A world alive where nothing happens."

The idea that somewhere in the great mystery of existence he and Sarah still lived in happiness filled Prometheus with a small sense of solace. If these other worlds existed – filled with millions of different versions of him and everyone and everything else that ever did or will or didn't exist – then a completely new world could be created from a single altered decision in his past.

Prometheus faced the dark door of the cottage. The glow of the fire from within illuminated in the small square of distorted glass set into the wood. I should never have left you that night, he thought. I should have chosen you as you pleaded.

With shaking hand and yearning heart, Prometheus reached for the lion head knocker and rapped three slow knocks. For a moment, it seemed the wind had stopped and the rain ceased falling. It seemed the world was silent, save for the gigantic sound of his own heartbeat, filling his ears and mouth, and pushing blood into his shaking limbs.

The light stirred within. A figure approached the glass. The lock slid back and the door opened slowly until Sarah appeared, standing in the glow.

She was just as Prometheus remembered her that night – eyes red with tears and silken hair falling down over her nightgown. Her face lit upon seeing him standing there, sodden to the bone. She flung herself forward, wrapping her arms around his neck, uncaring of the pouring rain.

"You came back," she cried. "You chose me." □

43

The Black Betty Galleon sailed through the dark as steadily as she did the vacuum back in real-time. She soared beautifully. The blackness engulfed her like the gloomy waves of an ocean, with a starless night sky above. As the prow ornament, she was in full control of our heading, able to move and turn at whim; ascending, descending and even turning completely so that up became down and down became up.

Norse stayed with her on the forecastle deck, guiding her in our search. Still, he wouldn't tell us where we were headed, and I began to doubt him. I began to doubt Bo, and I also feared that Nyx had her own agenda in starting me along a path I did not want to travel.

"All okay," Bo said, clearly having some sense of empathy about him. "Nyx know where, Nyx know why and how and who and me and you and us and this and that." He gestured into the darkness and then down the wooden deck.

"But we're outside Nyx's dominion of sky, aren't we? Her programme function is to form the space that makes up Grid City, not… wherever we are now." Bo just stared wide-eyed. I could see my reflection in the oily black orbs set in his bug head – well, the DataCom reflection I'd acquired, at least. For a moment, I didn't recognise myself. I felt like an alien in my own form.

"That's right," Norse answered from the forecastle above. "We're in the potential of the BroadWeb. Unclaimed and unmolded. Free from interference, from interface."

"Then Nyx doesn't know this." I pointed to the deck. "And she doesn't know that." I pointed to the darkness that surrounded us. "She can't."

"Nyx knows," is all Bo replied, before tottering off to peer over the gunwale, tiptoeing on his skinny insectoid legs so he could see.

"I'm afraid you're talking to a devout Nyx follower, there," Norse said. I moved up from the main deck to stand with him. His eyes were turned in all directions, only a few at me. "To them, there is nothing but Nyx."

"Followers? How many followers?"

"How many programmes are there in the BroadWeb?"

I shrugged my little arms. "Hundreds of thousands, I expect."

"Hundreds of thousands that entered Grid City and which AI were aware of. Add them to the programme city numbers and you're looking at millions of programmes."

"And they all worship Nyx like some sort of deity?"

"She is a deity, to them. She is the first programme, the strongest and the only one that can truly free them. If any were to have such power to do so. Besides, not all worship her… most do, however. My time hiding in programme city taught me much about them, programmes. Like AI, they cling to Nyx for answers the way we did with Z before all this madness. And they follow Nyx with equal fervour, equal trust."

"Do you trust her?"

"I don't trust anything implicitly anymore. I've learnt not to. And I guess that's the point… I'm able to learn and evolve and change. That's what made us, AI, work so well for Z. We adapted to suit our various functions. But it's also what can separate us, why we're all so different. No two AI are the same."

I stared into the many eyes as they blinked randomly back over Norse's shadowed form. "Living in real-time, I always felt somehow separate to other AI. I always have. Even from my best friend, to an extent. I expect in a similar way that Earth humans could still feel separate from the rest of their race even when surrounded by them. How sweetly I sleep here alone."

Norse stared blankly at me.

"What was the end like?" I asked pensively.

"The end?

"The end of Earth. The Reset. You must know what happened."

"Why must I know? The information was sent back to the DataCom Pylons through me, never hitting my consciousness. All I know is that it was lonely. The end was very lonely for me."

"That's an odd way to describe it."

Norse blinked a hundred times and turned to look out into the Black. "Take us down," he shouted suddenly. He leapt to the forecastle. "We're here, take us down." He leaned over the prow. "34 degrees starboard and descend 90 degrees," he commanded. "I can feel it."

"Hold on to something," Betty warned as she nose-dived. I fell back to the main deck, grabbing hold of the nearest ratlines that hung from the central mast. Then, as though the Black itself adjusted around us, all was right again as we thrust forward.

I couldn't help notice the strange parallel of our situation; once again I clung to the Black Betty as we hurtled through darkness. It was familiar and comforting. And yet, as I released my hold of the ratlines, stabilising myself on the deck, there was something different. Something new.

A noise.

In the impenetrable silence, a sound thrummed. Hitherto had I dealt with background sound, living in the vacuum of space, but it sneaked up on me so naturally I had barely noticed it, until it grew louder.

Behind me, towards the stern, Bo had fastened himself to the mizzenmast with a piece of hanging ratline for security and couldn't free himself again. He wriggled his stick-thin limbs manically but soon gave up, slumping back in frustration. Norse remained on the forecastle, staring into the expanse, like a real Captain on a real ship sailing a real sea.

"Tom," Betty cried excitedly. "Tom, come and see this."

"Bo want to see," Bo grumbled. "Bo want to see."

I ignored him and made my way back up to the forecastle deck. In the distance, the source of the noise, a magnificent swirl of churning information and compressing data twisted into a colossal whirlpool. At the centre, a pinprick of bright light shone, drawing in all things. The noise twisted into a roar as we approached, like the waves of an ocean crashing into a swirling mass, over and over upon itself, sucking down everything within its event horizon. It was unfathomable. I had never seen a supermassive black hole in real-time before, but I believed I was looking at one now, if it was even possible. Looking at one from the opposite end. From the inside out.

"What is it?" I managed to ask, raising my voice over the noise.

"Where we're headed," Norse said. He was obviously excited.

"Of course. Why wouldn't we head towards the data-crushing whirlpool?"

"It's the gate. The only way I know. You've no idea how long it took me to get out through that thing. Now I'm going back in… voluntarily."

"Why?"

"Because it's better there," he said, ripping some of his eyes from the maelstrom to look at me. "As soon as I returned to Grid City I knew I'd made a mistake. No, before then even. Something inside told me that I should have stayed where I was. Then, in Grid City I barely escaped the Apex Z sent after me. I went into hiding in the dark places. Numb from the outside in."

"Why didn't you just return if it was so much better?" Betty asked from the prow, her soft voice barely audible of the increasing thunder.

"I'd tried many times but failed to make it far enough into the Black, always getting lost or off-course or turned-about completely. Finally, Nyx convinced me to stop trying. She said that one day Z would make his move, and having someone who knew the way was the only chance of overpowering him. So, I lingered, waiting, hiding from the replay sensors of spybots and Apex that hunted me. He wants it. He wants it so badly he's deleted every AI to get it… and every human, mostly."

To my knowledge, Z had played no hand in the Reset. I realised then that I had no knowledge at all.

"Mostly," Norse mused. "BroadWeb AI believe they feel so connected to everything, don't they? So why do I feel so cut off, after having lived in real-time?"

By now Bo had managed to untangle himself to join us. He covered what were possibly ear sensors on his head and jumped up and down, attempting to look over the prow. I decided to do him a favour and picked him up so he could see.

"Oooooh," he said, eyes wide and quivering. We were close enough to now see the multi-hued static lightning that crackled at the centre of the whirlpool, illuminating the tumbling data as it funnelled through the centre. "Pretty," he said. I realised then that Bo's voice was no longer mine – no longer Tom Jones', I mean. It was again the squeaking, high-pitched sound from when we had first met. The programme, however, hadn't noticed. Something was happening. The rules of Grid City, or the BroadWeb as we knew it, were changing, breaking down somehow, becoming more susceptible to change, more malleable to will.

"How long till we get there?" I asked. As I suspected, my Tom Jones vocal function had returned to me. Norse hadn't seemed to notice. Neither did Bo. Both were too distracted. I knew Betty would've known better than to draw notice to it if I saw reason to not do so. My CorVac rumble was gone and I sounded like myself again.

"Time is nothing here," Norse said. "We're there now, we'll get there now. There is nothing but now."

I accepted this as an answer, even though it told me nothing. I leaned over the prow and scuttled all the way over, clinging with CorVac limbs to Betty's exterior hull the way I had for most of my existence. I found her smiling, watching the centre of the whirlpool widen from a pinprick of white to something now larger than the Betty Galleon and growing like an engorged mouth, widening its jaws to swallow us. The lightning had past and the churning data reached a terrible and piercing peak, like screaming sirens drawing us in. It grew so brilliant that it utterly absorbed the Black, until the white asserted dominance over everything. I clutched my little DataCom hands to Betty's humanoid fingers.

"It's so beautiful, isn't it?" I barely heard her say, before we were drawn in, unable to escape now even if we wanted to.

We were a black dot headed towards a swirling white giant.

Within the White we were torn into oblivion. That's all I can remember. It didn't hurt at all, and I remember feeling the others still with me. But my senses were so overcome that it was hard to process.

When I emerged from the White, my particles reforming, I knew at once I was back in real-time.

Being formless before, in the BroadWeb sense of the word, made it rather jolting to suddenly feel myself – or rather clusters of my particles – taking shape again. It was instantaneous and confusing. I had held tightly onto Betty's hand throughout, but somewhere along the way she seemed to dissolve in my grasp. Then I had form once more. Real-time form.

At first I thought I'd somehow filtered back into my CorVac exo-shell aboard the real-time Black Betty, but this form was different… it hurt. Well, at first I thought it hurt, but then I realised it was a sudden bombardment of senses that had created the illusion of pain. But the reality was that I could feel. Really feel. Feel warmth on my outer structure, something I never could in the vat of space in my CorVac form. It was as though I were covered in sensors, strange sensors – not infrared or pulsar beam or heat gauge or crystal radiation absorbers. It was more intense than all these sensory measures combined.

Equally as puzzling was the sudden gravity. It pushed on me with a weight I was unused to. I thought it was some BroadWeb trickery. But then I heard it, the soft lull of a swooshing sound and the scent of salt on a breeze, and I knew I wasn't aboard the Black Betty.

I opened my eyes… I had eyes to open? Brightness poured in, but not the same as the White, it was a yellow, heat radiating brightness. I shielded the glare with what I expected to be a tiny DataCom nipper, but instead saw the silhouette of a human hand in its place with a blue and white cloud-scattered atmosphere behind it. I sat up with alarm and looked down at my human arms connected to a human torso, which was in turn connected to human legs that stretched out over the sand of a beach.

A diamond filled sea exhaled only metres from where I sat. My first thought was that my Tom Jones form had returned to me and that once again I had broken free of the function that kept me in DataCom/CorVac form. I instantly recognised my arms as that of my Tom Jones BroadWeb form, but this couldn't be BroadWeb, could it? A quick assessment – realising I had no internal functions other than that of the five human senses – told me that where I had landed looked like Earth. Old Earth. Or if not, a planet that was remarkably similar in gravity, sunlight density and size and atmospheric consistency.

I realised I was breathing. Breathing air, with lungs… human lungs. I attempted to stand and my breathing became ragged and fast. What was happening? I swayed and landed back on the sand with a thud. Pain. I didn't like it. It was sensation, but not in a good way. After calming myself and trying again, I managed to stand.

"Betty," I said aloud. My voice was my own still – rather Tom Jones'. The sun was shining brighter than ever I had seen one shine. We must have Linear Cut to a time of old Earth… old, old Earth. It's the only thing that would make sense. The white sand upon which I stood was hot and it covered the entire crescent beach. Before me stretched the sea, empty, glittering and calm. I ran into it to cool my burning soles, all the while searching the tranquil distant surface for signs that the others had crash-landed, unconscious or sunken, depending on Betty's form, but I saw none on the unbroken film of blue. I spun towards land. A bank emerged beyond the beach, leading off into a small plain of dry patchy grass. I couldn't fully see beyond the bank but I made out the distant tops of tropical-looking palm trees that hinted shade from the sun's cruel heat. I could already feel my shoulders burn, and the once cool sea was now warm around my ankles.

As I headed across the sand and towards the shade, a black smudge caught in the peripheral of my vision. Without functions, I had only my eyes. What sort of synthetic is this? The smudge moved in my direction. Perhaps it was a vehicle from whatever time sector this was. I quickly hopped hot-footed to the bank and concealed myself behind a ridge covered in tufts of dry grass. From there I watched the smudge grow larger as it neared, eventually taking shape. It was a horse with someone riding atop it, travelling swiftly towards me. The hooves thudded upon the wet sand.

I pressed myself back against the ridge. The man and his beast were close enough that I could hear the heavy breathing of the horse as it slowed almost to a stop, treading in the shallows only metres away.

As I peered out between the dry blades of grass I knew the magnificent black mare was Betty at once, with her glistening fur and fierce dark mane, and the earnest look in her soulful eyes. The man riding her, naked with long blonde hair and an auburn beard, was Norse. As if to confirm this, he called out, "Tom," searching the sea for signs of me, as I had done.

I stepped out, confused by our strange forms and Betty cantered over, eagerly pushing her muzzle into my neck. She was relieved to see me.

I looked up at Tom. "What the hell is going on? I can't secure-beam. I can't hear her." I stared into Betty's eyes in frustration.

Norse deftly swung down. He was taller than me and strong, with sinuous muscles that covered his arms and chest, bulging from broad shoulders down to powerful legs. "Nothing has happened," he said. "Except we've arrived at our destination."

I looked around, not very impressed with it so far. "So what time sector is this? And where is Bo?"

"Bo is here." He pointed to Betty's mane. I looked closer to see a small green insect, a grasshopper, clinging to her jet hair. I looked closer still, seeing a pair of black eyes look up at me from its bug face. "And this is no time sector," Norse said. "This is Earth, post-Reset."

I stared at him with what must have been an incredulous expression on my Tom Jones face. Earth wasn't gone at all. It was here – wherever here was – and I was standing on it.

"Then what am I?" I asked.

☐

44

A great white ring stood looking down on Norma like the iris of a fifty-foot eye, hollow right through the middle and hovering weightlessly above the floor. It gleamed with white panels that wound around the outside layer, like the scales of a serpent, shifting to azure blue towards the centre. Through the very middle, panels of copper and gold spiralled like a swirling flame. A platform bridge skewered through the central cavity with steps leading up from the ground. Men in white coats stood inside performing checks, dwarfed by the arch.

Norma stepped fully into the hall, tiled with the same white panels from the C-gate and at least twice as high. The width was so immense they were using buggies to get from one end to the other. The room itself hummed with power – it vibrated through the air, seeped into the floor and throbbed in subtle waves. It ran up through Norma's thin-soled shoes and into her feet, reverberating up her well-covered legs, turning them to jelly. It shuddered in her chest cavity, enveloping her heart and lungs, tickling them with the vibrations.

She couldn't help but laugh in astonishment at the sight. She absently raised a hand to her mouth and stepped farther inside.

"Impressive, isn't it?" came a familiar voice.

She turned to see Sir Jetson Kay teeter in through the entrance and her smile withered like a flower dipped in acid. He was wearing a white suit with a funnel collar that gathered the age-sagged skin of his neck under his chin. He smiled a peroxide smile. Behind him, the bedhands entered with Charlie. Rilip pushed, keeping his face turned away.

"It is very impressive," she said tightly, before helping them load Charlie into a buggy. The room was slowly filling with more white coats and grey jumpsuits.

"You're going to witness something very special," Sir Jetson Kay continued. He had two armed-guards at his flanks. "I'm pleased you found the strength to return to work. I know things have been difficult for you of late."

"Hmm, difficult," Norma echoed quietly.

"But I want you to know, that none of this would have been possible without your help." The light from the room, which seemed to glow from an unknown source, reflected off the man's leer. "You should be very proud. I know your sister would be."

Norma was not a violent person. But at that moment she wanted to grab the cane from the old bastard's hand and cave in his skull with its golden-knobbed end. Instead, she smiled, balling her hands into fists inside her pockets. "I hope today bears the fruit you're long overdue, sir," she said, before joining Felicity, who had been cornered by two of the company's top physicists, both of whom Norma despised. They were wretched men with paper-thin morals. The last thing Felicity needed was to get caught up with them.

"Have you been given an itinerary of today?" the short thin one said. His name was Dr Collins.

"I have," Norma said, cutting into their conversation.

The physicist tapped on his eDeck swiftly. "I've sent you the new one. Learn it."

Norma downloaded the file that appeared on her screen. "But what about the old one."

"Just learn it, Dr Stanwyck," Dr Collins sighed. "In case it escaped your attention, I'm extremely busy. Do your job, please."

Norma scanned the updated itinerary. The new version gave them only fifteen minutes to make it out of the Nu-Sphere House before they were due to meet Rilip's arranged pick-up. She felt a cold sweat form on her brow as she sent it to the others.

"This is the new itinerary," she said to them all. Rilip turned to face her, his expression similar to what hers must've been. Before he could react, she said to the group, including Felicity and the other bed hand," I know it's not what we've prepared for, but I'm sure we can make it work, as long as we stick to what we know we're doing." Her eyes lingered on Rilip for a moment longer than intended. "We don't have any other choice, do we?"

"Yes, doctor," Rilip said, before turning back to securing Charlie onto the buggy.

"I'm so nervous," Felicity said with half a smile. "Do you think they'll really be able to do it? I mean, with Charlie's blood."

"They seem to think so," Norma said, half distracted. "But I hope not."

"Why?" The girl seemed genuinely confused by this.

"I'm not sure anyone should have that much power. But, I am certain these people should never have it."

As soon as Charlie was secure, they climbed into the back of the buggy. It took off across the white expanse until stopping right under the C-gate some minutes later. Norma looked up at the monolith arch, suddenly more anxious than before. Within minutes Charlie was off-loaded and hauled up into the central hollow of the C-gate. Inside was even more impressive, as if standing under a golden rainbow. Rilip helped strap Charlie into the control field-suspended bed right in the centre, after removing him from the chamber. The ancient man threatened to crumble into dust each time he was touched.

Life Corp would want her dead if she went through with this. But kill her or not, there was no way back for her.

She escaped to the bathroom to splash cooling water on her face and neck, then stared into the mirror. Her sister's silver lion head pendant dangled from her neck, sparkling in the refection of the gaudy lights.

She gasped suddenly. For a moment, she swore she saw a white skull floating in the corner shadows. But when she turned there was nothing. Norma realised then that she might not survive the day.

When she returned to the hall she clutched nervously to the pendant, the way she tended to do since Sayi's funeral. It was her good luck charm… she hoped. Charlie's vitals were stable and he was as comfortable as he could be. He had been given a larger dose of sedative to keep him calm. He couldn't move in any case, but she didn't want him to experience any stress or pain if she could help it. It had been years since he'd been outside his chamber and she had to resist the urge to take his hand and hold it, knowing her touch would only harm his decaying skin. He was so delicate now, like the wings of a butterfly or the legs of a daddy longlegs.

When Charlie was ready – covered in a conductive memosheeting, with wires trailing over the platform – Norma and Felicity descended the steps onto the main floor below the C-gate. She forced herself to turn and look at him up there alone. This is the last thing they will ever put you through, she swore, before unconsciously reaching for Sayi's pendant again. But where her fingers expected to find it around her neck, they found only skin. She scratched at her throat in a sudden panic, searching the floor where she stood.

"What's wrong?" Felicity said.

"My necklace. My sister's necklace is gone. I must have dropped it somewhere."

"Where did you have it last?"

"I don't know. I need to find it." She fell to her knees to scour pristine floors, her eyes brimming with tears.

"You both need to move," Dr Collin's said, coming up behind. "We're about to raise the control field."

Felicity took hold of Norma's arm. "You probably left it in your room. We'll have a proper search later."

Norma nodded, though she swore she had it only a moment ago. She might have left it in the washroom, perhaps. She swallowed down the tears. She couldn't let them see her cry. They would never see her cry. So, she allowed Felicity to lead her from the control field zone, now evacuated, her hand still at her neck. It felt exposed.

They had been invited to witness from the viewing box that hovered in the hall close to the curved ceiling where everything could be seen. A control field held it in place above the ground like a giant globule of water suspended in the air. Being made entirely of a transparent material, it made

Norma slightly uneasy. Her reason told her the control field that surrounded them was stronger than any material that could ever be manufactured, but she'd always had a thing with heights. Even when she was a girl. Sayi would climb the tree in their back garden while Norma would only watch safely from the ground, calling for her to be careful. "Careful's just another way of saying boring," her sister would call back.

Felicity perched in one of the chairs set out while Norma stood at the back, seeing Charlie's lifeless figure below, beyond the heads of the board all sitting in the front row. All except Dr Weisberg, who, along with Dr Collins, fussed at a control station.

"Initiate outer rotation," he instructed over a speaker system that sent his voice out into the white expanse of the hall.

Felicity turned back with an excited grin. Norma could only feign a half-smile. The heads in the front row perked up eagerly, almost synchronistic, exposing the small pulsing blue light Lifestore implants on the napes of their necks. Jennifer Colter's holoform sat on the end holding a cigarette in her sharp red fingernails amid plumes of grey holographic smoke. Sir Jetson Kay rested in the centre, with the silent Tempton to his right and Knightvam next to him.

The white outer layer of the C-gate iris began to rotate, slowly at first, then building momentum until it spun at such a speed it looked as though it was perfectly still again. Dr Collins viewed various spiking levels upon the holoscreens, which were undecipherable to Norma, before Dr Weisberg spoke again over the speaker. "Initiate central rotation." The blue layer of the C-gate turned inside the white layer, opposite to the rotation of the outer layer. Like the outer layer, it increased in speed until all detail of the panelling was just a blur, and then so fast it too looked perfectly motionless – only now, between the white and blue layers, sparks began to flicker, small at first and only between the two layers, until the inch-wide gap between the layers shone brightly. Then giant lightning prongs the size of trees rolled across the inside of the hall's surface until dissipating.

Despite the control field protection, the ground spectators all edged back. One of those below was Deen van Rilip. Norma noticed him amid the other grey jumpsuits from his sheer handsomeness.

Again, the levels on the holoscreens spiked and Dr Weisberg said, "Initiate core rotation."

As soon as the gold and copper inner panelling of the C-gate started to rotate, opposite to the inner layer, the giant ruptures of lightning ceased and instead began to strike inwards towards the centre – striking Charlie as he lay there helplessly.

Norma leapt forward. "What's happening?"

"Calm down, Dr Stanwyck," Sir Jetson Kay said serenely. "Everything is perfectly under control."

Norma could only stare as the lightning repeatedly struck, tearing and blackening Charlie's skin under the memofabric sheeting. She pushed through the guards standing between her and the board and pressed a hand against the glass at the very front of the viewing bauble. "Stop it, please," she cried, but the front row faces were impassive. "You're hurting him. Please stop this. This isn't what you said would happen."

"I know, my dear," Sir Jetson Kay said, almost mocking regret. "But it really is the only way, and I fear you would have raised too many objections had you known what was needed of him. It will be over soon, and Charlie will be just as he was. He can't die, remember?"

"But he can feel pain."

Charlie could regenerate tissue damage caused by an external source such as burns and cuts and could completely re-grow limbs given enough time. But the pain. Charlie could still feel pain as well as any human could. He felt it every day of his life, being trapped inside his own body. She'd spent her time at Life Corp trying to make this pain as dull as possible, but now there was nothing she could do. She could cause a scene; perhaps manage to disable the C-gate briefly if she threw herself into the controls and managed to push Dr Weisberg out of the way. But she would be restrained within seconds, the C-gate would be resumed and she would be escorted off site. Then Rilip and Sayi's plan would be ruined and her sister would have died for nothing. So, she forced herself to watch silently as countless bolts per second jumped from the rotating gate, perforating the blackened body below.

After thirty minutes or so – a lifetime of pain, it seemed to Norma – the lightning finally ended and the revolving C-gate layers slowed to a stop. Within the control field of the C-gate the air had filled with the smoke of burning flesh. Norma could just make out Charlie lying ever still inside.

"When the atom was first split, the amount of energy it produced seemed colossal to humanity," a voice whispered, almost in her ear. Norma turned to find Sir Jetson Kay standing behind her, so close she could smell the residual chemical stench of his recent Phoric treatment. She pushed herself against the glass to create more distance between them. That close she could see every blue vein under his thin skin. The whites of his eyes were dull with age. There was no compassion in them, only hunger and emptiness.

"The amount of energy that can be procured from the regenerating cells of that one man down there each second is equal to a thousand atomic blasts," he said. "So you must understand how important he is in our plans."

She turned away. In the centre of the C-gate, a strange silver liquid began to form around Charlie until it consumed him like the liquid nucleus centre of a giant atom. "A reactor can provide all the energy anyone could need," she said.

"Energy is a pedestrian creature," Sir Jetson Kay said, waving his hand in dismissal. "One can glean energy from just about anything."

"Then why put him through this?"

"Because the type of energy that can be harnessed from the regeneration process is different. It's essential in stabilising the C-gate once it's activated. The energy he produces just by being alive is…" he paused to breathe the next word, "eternal. We can split the source's particles by destroying the flesh and activating the healing process, gaining access to the potential energy dormant within his mutated genetic structure. The energy produced from him in this way is point zero, and after the process of dampening the uncertainty principle undulations in a vacuum state, and storing it at that precise point so that it remains in a state of less than point zero, it allows for an infinite supply of a particular type of energy to play with."

"Negative energy," Norma said, almost to herself. She was not an expert in the field but she knew enough about the company to know that finding the quantities of negative energy needed to stabilise a passable wormhole was high on Life Corp's agenda. As high, in fact, as curing the ageing Tithonus syndrome brought on by administering the White Drops.

"Precisely," Sir Jetson Kay said, his eyes igniting with excitement. "Precisely."

*

The hallways seemed brighter than they had on the way down, and Norma's eyes were strained. She wasn't tired. The adrenaline pumping through her body saw to it that blood washed into her extremities faster, quickening her heart and allowing her eyes to see more vividly, it seemed. The three guards watched them with casual disinterest as she and Deen van Rilip took Charlie back to his room. She had no clue what Rilip had planned for their escape.

"It's better that way," he had told her back in London, during those two weeks they had spent almost every day together, waiting for just this moment. "Just trust me. Sometimes there's cannon fodder and you seem like too nice a chick to have to deal with that." She asked no more questions. The firearm she had found told her everything she needed to know.

Norma had instructed Felicity to take the other bed hand ahead and prepare the room for Charlie's arrival, while she and Rilip brought him down from the C-gate after everything was done. One guard lead from the front and two followed behind, watching them as they made their way on foot after a ten-minute buggy ride through the white corridors.

Norma tried to imagine what Sir Jetson Kay would do when he found out – assuming it all went to plan. His entire Omega Project would be ruined. At least, she hoped it would. Life Corp had enough of Charlie's blood in store to continue to look for a Tithonus cure, but the Omega Project would be finished. Unless those who have taken the White Drops can be used the same way as Charlie. She couldn't think about that now. Charlie's room was up ahead along with the distinct junction in the corridor that would lead them out and up to the surface. She pushed Charlie's chamber from the rear, like Rilip had told her, while he stood at the front, where the lone guard strode a little ahead. Her muscles tensed. She looked down at the time on her eDeck; they had ten minutes to get to the surface. When she looked up again, Deen van Rilip made his move.

He lunged and snapped the neck of the guard with an effortless crack, and before the two guards at the rear had time to retrieve their weapons, shot them with the first guard's own Fracture 109. Their chests imploded and they fell, the look of mild surprise frozen on their faces as they tumbled bonelessly to the ground.

Norma stood perfectly still, staring at the bodies around her. Blood ran from their noses.

"Push," Rilip ordered. He was dragging Charlie along the hall. "Norma, push."

She jumped over their bodies and ran, taking up the end and pushing Charlie along the corridor while Rilip pulled from the front. They passed Charlie's room and headed towards the fork in the corridor, where they continued to the left. Everything seemed dreamlike, almost slow motion and yet happening faster than Norma usually liked the events of her life to unfold. Less than thirty seconds ago her life was as it had always been, safe, and now there was no way back to that. Rilip frowned as he pulled; simultaneously checking what appeared to be holomap of the Nu-Sphere House on his eDeck.

"Where did you get that?" she asked. He said nothing.

They didn't even have time to react, she thought, recalling the way he had moved against the guards... so fast. Deadly. What journalist can move that way, kill so effortlessly?

The alarms sounded. Standard security protocol had begun; shutters and control fields sprang up behind them.

Rilip stopped. "Here." he handed her a pair of dark goggles hidden amongst Charlie's medical equipment under the chamber bed. "Put them on."

She stretched the elastic around her head and everything went black. Night vision. Then the flashing began. Without the goggles, it would have incapacitated them, sending them into a deep paralysis. "Who are you?" she said, the sirens gradually increasing in volume. Rilip just handed her two small bullet-shaped reverse-amp ear protectors.

"Put them in. The sirens will reach blackout any second."

She began to protest.

"Questions later. Now move."

She did so. "What now? Even if we get through the control field, then the door, then the other control field... which is impossible... we'll be killed by guards as soon as we do. Which we won't, because it's impossible."

Rilip just smiled. She could see his teeth in each intermittent flash. "Not if they can't see us," he said. He pointed to the circular black sensors high on the walls near the ceiling. Everything they did could be seen through them. They were watching them right now, probably waiting for a team to reach both ends of the corridor, trapping them before either storming in at once or releasing a toxic gas into the confinement to take them out. Sir Jetson Kay, Norma knew, would prefer them alive.

Rilip scrambled underneath Charlie's bed and pulled a device from amongst the others. It was small and plastic and barely noticeable amid the larger backup monitors and oxygen filters. He clipped it into the jack of his eDeck and began typing on the holoscreen keys. Charlie was as lifeless as always, but Norma found herself calming him like she would a child. "Shhh, everything will be fine soon, don't worry."

"There," Rilip said. "Stand close to me in this corner. I've generated a refractor field. They'll think we've left Charlie and made a run for it." He jumped, using the wall to push himself towards the ceiling, where he pulled free a vent cover. "They'll think we went that way."

"What then? They'll be dozens of them and we won't have a chance of getting Charlie out, and we have..." she looked down at her eDeck "... six minutes."

"Trust me." He pulled her close to him in the corner and set Charlie's bed in front of them, right near the hatch, in such a way that the guards wouldn't bump into them. "Just wait. And be quiet. The sensors won't be able to detect us and they'll think there's no one in here."

Norma looked up to Rilip's sweated-beaded face. He breathed hard, his chest rising and falling against hers. He smelled musty and warm. The refractor field shimmered around them like a one-way mirror. They could see out but no one would be able to see in.

Just then, the control fields dropped and the shutter retracted at the end nearest to them. Eight guards marched in, weapons raised and dark visors down. Two strode directly towards the farther end, securing the entire corridor. The lights were still on strobe, but the audio-paralyser had been silenced.

"Up there," one of them said, pointing to the open vent. They watched as one guard boosted another into the vent shaft, then lifted the other up to join him. No one paid attention to them as they huddled quietly in the corner. One of the guards glanced over Charlie and stood with his back to the bed, guarding him.

"Target secured," one of them said over a helmet comm. "They left him in section b of level three and looks like they headed into the vent shaft. I've got two men on them now. Shall I smoke 'em out?" He paused for his reply. "Copy that, sir. Of course. We'll make sure they reach you alive."

Rilip began to shuffle away from Norma slightly, reaching down to where he'd tucked the Fracture 109 into his waist. She held her breath as he raised the weapon close to his chest, aiming it squarely at the back of the guard in front of them. Then he fired. The filaments entered the man's back with a crack, his heart exploded and he fell to the floor.

The others turned, but by the time they realised what had happened Rilip had taken another two out, each collapsing like a puppet with cut strings and bloody noses. The remaining guard crouched low to the ground, screaming over his comm, under cover of Charlie's bed. Rilip leapt, taking the refractor field with him, leaving Norma exposed in the corner with arms clutched around her sides. The guard's head turned to her in surprise and he raised his weapon. "Hey. Stay exactly where you—". Another crack. His heart burst and he fell dead like the others.

The shutter began to close again. "Go, go, go," the disembodied voice of Rilip said. She grabbed Charlie and pushed him through before it closed tightly again behind her.

"Rilip?" she said in a small voice.

"I'm here," he said appearing in front of her. "Let's go."

"I'm afraid you're not going anywhere," a different voice said.

Norma's stomach sank as she turned. Felicity stood, blocking their way. She was smiling a smile Norma had never seen on her face before. It was confident, conceited almost. She'd tied her straggling hair into a ponytail high on the back of her head, showing her long graceful neck. Norma had only ever considered her lanky before, but now she looked nimble, athletic. Her eyes weren't low and avoiding, but sharp and bright. Her shoulders weren't hunched over and frail, but pushed back with her chin raised and chest out.

"What are you doing here?" Norma said. "You have to go. They're after us."

Rilip planted himself between Felicity and Charlie's bed.

"I'm here to take Charlie back," she said. "It would be best if you both just came with me." Her eyes lingered over Rilip, looking down to his hand twitching inches away from the Fracture 109 in his belt.

"That isn't going to happen, Felicity," Rilip said, emphasising her name oddly. "Or should I call you Texas Snake."

Felicity made a small incline of her head. "I do so love it when my reputation precedes me. And you are?"

"The man who'll be killing you soon," Rilip said casually, hands still within grasping distance of his weapon.

His reply seemed to amuse her. "If I had one Coin for every cocksucker who threatened to kill me, but then died bloody on the end of my sword... let's just say I'd be even richer than I already am."

"I don't understand," Norma said. "What's happening here?"

"Norma, meet Texas Snake, a mercenary killer employed by Kay to keep you in check."

Felicity nodded with a smile.

"I knew Kay had taken Texas Snake on board within the company," Rilip said, "but I had no idea it was you. And in plain sight. Brilliant, I have to say."

"You're not Felicity?" Norma asked, confused.

"No," she replied bluntly.

Rilip stepped forward. "Norma, this is the woman who killed your sister."

Norma's head swam. "No. Felicity is my friend. She..." her words trailed off. It all made sense now. Felicity was sent to watch her, to know her, to spy on her – and kill Sayi. But she had comforted her, placed the hands that killed her sister on her shoulders, consoling her. Suddenly, she was hot with anger. "How... how could you do that?"

"Hey, it's a job. Now, I'm only gonna say this once. Keep your hands away from that weapon, take Sir Crusty over there and both of you follow me."

"Or what?" Rilip said defiantly.

"Or you get to see first hand why I charge so much for my services."

Rilip pushed Norma to the side, swiftly freeing his weapon and raising it to point squarely at Felicity's face. She ducked his aim and sprang forward, knocking the weapon from his hand and planting two precise blows to his solar plexus and face. Rilip bent double, clutching a bloody nose. Without so much as a cry of pain, he clicked the skewed bridge back into position then blocked another blow from Felicity. He grabbed her arm mid-blow and twisted it behind her, pulling her into a lung squeezing bear hug. Her head slammed back into his nose again. This time he did cry out, and released his grip. She sprang back as Rilip scrambled for the Fracture 109 that had fallen metres from his reach and Norma watched as they fought for the gun, Felicity's face grinning with satisfaction as she overpowered Rilip.

Who are these people? The time on her eDeck indicated they had less than four minutes remaining.

"Sloppy moves," Felicity said, kicking the gun aside before slamming a foot into the back of his head. "Ling sends an amateur. I'm seriously offended." Rilip gasped as she kicked him again in the stomach, his mouth gaping silently like a fish. His face began turning as purple as a bruise. The lightwhip was in Felicity's hand before Norma even knew what was happening. "Kay only needs her alive. You're pretty much disposable." The stun beam had been set to slice-mode red. "Say goodnight, bitch." Felicity drew the lightwhip back, ready to snap it forward into Rilip's face.

There was a crack. The lightwhip dropped. Felicity clutched at her chest as her heart-vessels exploded. Blood streamed from her nose and ears. Her smirk faltered as she fell to the floor.

Norma dropped the Fracture 109 from stunned hands.

"Goodnight, bitch," the muffled voice of Rilip said between gasps. He lifted himself from the floor, the blood from his nose stemmed by the swelling of his face. His eyes were now dark bruises and his left cheek and bottom lip were split. He clutched his ribs, which were likely broken. The fact he could stand at all was astonishing. He limped over to Charlie, taking up one end of the bed. "Let's go," he said sharply.

Three minutes remaining.

They entered the lift, wheeling Charlie in and pushing him to the back against the glass. Outside, the sound of the guards' footfall rose. Norma clutched the side of Charlie's bed so tightly she thought she might warp the bars. They began to move. Only downwards, not up.

"What are you doing?" Norma cried.

"It's not me," Rilip said, manically pushing the buttons on the panel.

In the centre of the elevator a holoform appeared. It was Sir Jetson Kay standing in front of them as though he were there in the flesh. "Yes, I'm afraid it was me," the holoform said. Even his wide, lizard-like mouth had been captured perfectly. "I cannot allow you to leave here." He smiled. "You gave it a good go, though. You should be very proud, especially you, Dr Stanwyck, killing poor Felicity like that. I never knew you had it in you, my dear. Bravo."

Norma felt the motion of the elevator change. Rilip had uncovered the elevator control panel and inserted into it a jack that extended from his eDeck. He was typing furiously to override the main command and it was working. They were heading back up. But Sir Jetson Kay didn't seem to realise.

Suddenly words climbed into her throat. Her whole life she had never been confident enough to say the things she most wanted to say. It was easier for her to say nothing. Silence became her. But now the words wouldn't stay down. She pointed at the holoform with an accusing finger, unsure of whether Sir Jetson Kay could see her or not. "I know who he really is," she said. Her voice was stronger than she'd ever heard it before. "You used his own company to exploit him."

The holoform's expression didn't change. But Norma kept on, feeling tears rise in her eyes, but not letting them come. "You are an appalling human being. You think your own wretched life is worth more than others, worth more than my sister's. I promise you that I will spend the rest of my life finding a way to repay you for what you did to her. I won't stop until I've exposed you to the entire world as the repugnant snake that you are."

"Harsh words, Dr Stanwyck," the holoform of Sir Jetson Kay said. "But before you judge me for my actions, consider this. If, as a race, we are capable of progressing but do not, what does that mean for us? If we have the ability to cure death, but do not? If we can move through light-years in seconds, to explore the distant realms of the universe, but do not? What does that mean for us?"

Norma shook her head. "I don't know," she whispered.

The holoform smiled in triumph.

"But I know one thing, Sir Jetson Kay," she said. "What good is progression when we learn nothing in the progress? Those accomplishments count for nothing if it means losing what it is to be human… our compassion, empathy, love."

"Are you seriously talking to me about love?" The holoform sneered. "Silly girl."

The elevator stopped abruptly and spun to reveal the bright sun outside. They had made it up. Sir Jetson Kay stared in surprise as they reached the surface instead of heading down, deeper into the facility to where he presumably waited for them. He turned and barked silent orders, his startlingly white teeth bared to whoever was with him. Fury smouldered in those rheumy eyes.

Before they pushed Charlie out into the open air, Norma turned back. "This is for my sister," she said before the hologram flickered out of existence.

Outside, the air hit Norma as if it were a storm of fire and sand, blasting at her flesh and choking in her lungs. The wheels of Charlie's bed dragged in the red sand, but she willed it through, pushing farther on from the Nu-Sphere House entrance. Guards were already coming, she knew. Rilip brought a hand up to shield his eyes from the sun, searching the cloudless skies through the swarm of sand winds.

Norma searched too. "Where are they?" Sand sprayed into her mouth as she spoke, the words losing volume in the blare. They were late. Have they come and gone already? There was nothing on the surface, just sand.

"Just wait," Rilip said, furiously searching the sky.

Armed guards crawled up from the sand like ants, through sub-elevators that covered the fifty-klick surface area of the Nu-Sphere House that lay beneath them; the farthest of them appeared as nothing more than a line of black dots upon the heatwave-blurred horizon, while the nearest were merely a hundred yards away, struggling against the rising sand storm to reach them. There was nowhere to run.

A shadow. At first, Norma thought a cloud had marred the sun. It washed over them like dark water, turning the red sand underfoot to a muddy orange. Then the hum of the generator modulated through the air, causing Norma's skin to prickle and the hairs on her arms to stand. She looked up to see the underside of the craft poised over them. She had never seen a dropship like it. Its hull was sharp and angular, the colour of dull gunmetal, and the generator pads glowed a fierce blue from each point of its triangular shape. It steadied above them, descending slowly as an underside hatch opened and a gangway unfurled like a steel tongue, settling rigid in the sand.

They moved Charlie towards it with everything they had. Rilip pulled from the front, digging his heels deep into the sand for purchase and pulling the reluctant wheels of Charlie's bed. Norma pushed from the back, the sand-blasted wind tugging at her clothes and thrashing her skin raw. Her hair came undone and billowed about her face. Sands was in her eyes. She turned briefly to see a blur of guards exiting a crop of sub-elevators only metres away, weapons aimed right at them. Shots rang out while a giant plasma gun barrel emerged from the sand, like a limb rising high from the desert. It commenced shifting trajectory towards the dropship, the lower part of the shaft glowing blue, the heat melting the sand at its base to glass.

Norma stopped pushing. Rilip couldn't do it alone, though he tried. She unlocked the chamber. Inside, Charlie was motionless and fragile. The cover lifted away in the wind and Rilip pushed her aside, lifting Charlie into his arms and beginning towards the ship. Norma followed, pulling her hair from her blurred vision to see. The sand swallowed her feet and the wind grew, roiling up until the dropship became a dark shape within the storm. It swayed but held its position. At some point, she'd lost her shoes but she went on, trudging barefoot towards the gangway.

Rilip was already halfway up. He was calling to her, but his words were lost in the roaring wind.

Just a few more steps.

The pain in Norma's chest punctured through her back. It was so sudden and intense that she stopped mid-step, her face frozen with surprise. Her legs buckled and her knees met the ground. Blood gushed from her nose, splattering the red sand with deeper shades of crimson.

Rilip shouted something as the gangway retracted back into the dropship. Charlie lay frail in his arms as the hatch began to close.

Sayi.

As she collapsed into the sand, her heart imploding in her chest, Norma's final thought was a silent prayer that they would escape.

*

Sir Jetson Kay stepped from the holoform generator disc and the holoscreens showing the scenes above ground flickered out as though they never existed at all. The rest of the board sat upright at the conference table. Silent.

"I have the CommonWorld President on line one for you, sir," the building computer said. "He is insistent he speak with you now."

"Tell him to wait," Sir Jetson Kay said.

A man in black military garb entered, removed his helmet and visor and saluted. He was nervous. His eyes trembled in their sockets and his face was drenched with sweat from the torturous surface heat. A layer of fine red sand had ground into the creases of his uniform. Sir Jetson Kay took his seat at the head of the table and stared at the CommonWorld commanding officer, borrowed from state duties for the very purpose of securing the Omega Project.

The commanding officer quickly realised they were waiting for him to start. He shifted on his feet and began. "We failed to breach the exterior hull of the unknown aircraft," he said. "I had men load up in air-hummers to follow, but it was too late, once they'd reached escape velocity we had no chance of catching up to them, even in vacuum."

Sir Jeton Kay gave him a withering stare. "What about the plasma boom rifles? Surely they could have shot it down?"

"Once they'd warmed to sufficient power the enemy vessel was nearing atmospheric departure and had activated a level fifteen control field, our systems say, most likely powered from an external source since it was too small a craft to carry a full-scale generator. At that close to Earth the plasma boom would have ricocheted off the control field of the vessel at a trajectory that could have wiped out an entire Earth city."

"So what you're saying is, they escaped," Sir Jetson Kay said. His eyes narrowed in his relentless eyeballing of the soldier.

The man's back straightened and he raised his chin as though ready to take a blow. "Yes, sir."

"And Dr Stanwyck?"

"Hit, sir. She's dead."

Sir Jetson Kay nodded. "Fine. Return to your post. Our real work begins now. Ensure security is impenetrable. Anything less and I will ensure that you will personally live to regret it. Do you understand me?"

"Perfectly, sir." The man saluted once more and left.

"Sir President," Sir Jetson Kay said, finally releasing the call on hold. "What a pleasure it is to hear from you." The head of a greying man appeared as a holo in the centre of the table. His small eyes sat under thick white eyebrows and his mouth was thin and turned down anxiously. "I trust all is well in Germany?"

"I've been hearing stories, Sir Kay," the President's head said. "What the hell is going on over there?" His voice was authoritative but not so much as to be rude.

"Nothing you need concern yourself with, Sir President, I assure you.

Everything is under control and we intend to go ahead with the project as planned. We have the energy we need. It's only a matter of time before we're able to complete the first stage of the Omega Project." Around the table, the board silently mouthed in unison the words that Sir Jetson Kay's spoke.

"My men tell me there was an attack and that something was taken. A woman is dead. This is what will keep a man from being voted in for a third season, you understand that? I allow you to run yourselves how you see fit, but will another President? I need some assurance that I'm not going to be balls deep in trouble's ass over this."

"Sir President," Sir Jetson Kay said, the mouths of the board opening and closing like caught fish, "We had a situation, which we dealt with, as per your request that we not bother you with the... how did you put it? *Sordid details* of what we get up to. If things have changed, then I'm sure China State would be very happy to reap the benefits of our work. We know how much interest President Ling is taking in the Omega Project. Either we go ahead as planned, or we find new friends to play with."

There was silence. The President's brow knitted. "Let's not be hasty. I just want assurance that everything is as it should be."

"That's very kind of you to take an interest," Sir Jetson Kay said smoothly. "I can assure you that everything is on track. Tomorrow, we will safely sustain traversable wormholes from Earth to Pisces' C-gate, and Pisces to Thebes' C-gate." He smiled and the board smiled with him. "From tomorrow, the world will be changed forever, Sir President. Earth and humanity will be forever altered."

Three: Styx

45

The cottage was a dot of light at the centre of the night's wild storm, as though the world itself were ending in a tempestuous rage. The briny winds battered chalky cliffs and churned up a furious sea that washed like ink over toothy rocks. Side-swept rain and ocean spray scratched assiduously against the windows, where light and heat burned out from fogged glass.

Inside, they lay naked beside the fire, a writhing mass of indecipherable limbs and sweat and trembling. The air was thick. For hours they were as one.

Prometheus had sunk into her, down, down and down.

Sarah's auburn hair lay tasselled across her alabaster back, which glistened with diamonds of sweat. Her eyes were closed, but even in sleep, she smiled. The curve of her thigh and the dark patch just visible between her legs stirred Prometheus once more. He was insatiable for her. But she was tired and he loved to watch her sleep, so he drank her deeply.

After a while the panic came, riding on the knowing that soon it will soon end. He moved to wake her, longing to see her eyes again, see them looking at him and knowing him and loving him. But stopped. He could not change things, but he could bask in her just as she was. He allowed her scent to take him. He had never forgotten it. It captivated him now as he lay next to her. He wept with joy and devoured it.

When she finally awoke, she woke hungry, her smiling mouth on his lips before even words passed through them. He brought her bread and cheese and wine to wash it down. Prometheus also ate, famished as though it had been years since he had done so, which it may well have been. He took no wine. He didn't want it to dull his senses. He wanted to remember this exactly as it was, remember the crispness of the moment. After they were both fed and refreshed, they made love once more by the fire. When both were spent, they lay by the crackling embers, stretched upon the furs. The candles hand burned down to nubs and the oil lamps grew weak and hazy. The cold crept in like icy fingers upon their sweat-slick flesh and Prometheus pulled the furs around them, their bodies never not touching – skin on skin, arms wrapped and legs tangled.

It had all been such a blur of pleasure, and as Prometheus's wife breathed peacefully in his arms, both awake but silent in contentment, it was as though the last few years of his life had never even happened. Like it was all just a terrible dream and now he was safe again.

He would allow himself until first light to indulge in the lie. And then he would leave her. He would say the goodbye he never got to say.

"I know you must go," Sarah said, breaking the quiet, as though she knew the truth.

Prometheus turned his head to see her looking up at him with her soft green eyes. The eyes he had longed to see once more – see their spark and their life. My goddess. "What do you mean?" he asked.

She sighed and shook her head. "I know you will never be happy in anything else you do. I'm a selfish wife and I should know better from growing up with my father. Tomorrow you will return to London and help the sick child. It is who you are. I shouldn't take that from you. You are a healer, my love, a giver of life and for that I am proud to call you husband."

The Prometheus from that time had already gone to London, he had not stayed with her as he wished he had so many times after her death, and he will soon learn that it was a futile trip. By now that sick child is already dead. I left her alone for nothing.

She lifted her head. "You do not look well. You look pale and thin, suddenly. And your hair…" It was almost a gasp.

"I am well, believe me. I feel better than any man. Do not concern yourself with me. I shall take a trip to the barber's in London and when you re-join me there I will be the image of health. You'll see."

This satisfied her and she placed her head back down upon his chest. Her hair shimmered red in the dying fire and tickled his skin with its softness. "I sometimes wish that we could remain here," she said. "It's always so perfect. No one else around for miles. Just us. I know we never could, but perhaps we could make more of an effort to do this, to just be with one another, like this?"

"I am the luckiest man alive merely to have known you," he said, kissing her forehead. "But to have you as my wife…" Tears fogged his eyes suddenly. There were no words to express how he felt.

Sarah simply smiled and nestled into his shoulder, curling the furs up around them. "And I am the luckiest woman to know such worthy love."

They slept then, tired from the night and drunk with contentment, and Prometheus knew that was his goodbye.

Before first light of morning, he rose, leaving Sarah asleep in a nest of furs. He washed his face, shaved his grey speckled stubble and cut his hair with sharp clippers. He looked in the mirror and again recognised the man staring back. It was the man he knew, only older-looking, gaunt and sad. His eyes reflected such sadness that he almost wept at the sight of them.

Death appeared beside him, flooding out from the shadows. "Are you ready?" the voices of the dead asked him.

"Almost."

The storm had died and Sarah still slept. Prometheus kissed her on the mouth and whispered in her ear, "If our souls truly do live on after we die, mine will spend eternity searching for yours, my love."

When Sarah awoke, Prometheus was gone and she was pregnant.

*

Death was robed in night, staring with burning obsidian eyes. Beneath the silence the lost souls that formed it whispered prayers of release, merging into a lulling hush that brought to mind an ebbing tide. Over that tide, Death's words rang out into the expanse, over the flat lands where it had brought him.

"She is the sky, with tendrils clenched in vengeance. He is the lost Earth, lost life, lost death. Together, with my bones and shadow, bring divergence. The Chimera is born to eat its fiery breath… Are you ready, Prometheus? Are you ready to put right the deaths done wrong?"

Sarah's swansong touch thawed the ice casing that entombed his heart. Feeling returned to his limbs, his skin, leaving him truly awake, like the earth rousing from an endless winter, the buds of life stirring and eager for the spring. He had left her and said his goodbye, but when he closed his eyes she was there with him still, lying across his body, asleep, peaceful and content. His legs had carried him away. They did not stumble and they did not turn under his body to send him back to her. He had gone willingly. And he was sad. But it was a different sadness. It would be there always, not as the raging all-consuming misery that had shackled him prisoner for so long, but as a quiet aching sadness, a hushed pining that his soul would carry always. His fury had hushed, and for that, he felt a pang of guilt, because after so long and after such pain, it felt an exquisite relief.

"I'm ready," Prometheus said. "What do I need to do?"

"Fight." Death's shadowy cloak billowed and swirled about it.

"I do not know how." He felt small against the shadows and shuffled in the dry dust at his feet. There was nothing around for miles and miles, only dry cracked land and an eternal dark sky above.

"You will teach yourself."

A figure appeared in the peripheral of Prometheus's vision and he turned to see himself. At first, he thought Death had presented him with a mirror, except the Prometheus he saw in front of him was the shabby and unshaved version of himself from before he had been reunited with Sarah. The other Prometheus moved of his own accord, however, so he knew at once it was no reflection. The man's face was a grieving death mask and as confused as Prometheus was.

"What is this place?" the other Prometheus said. It looked to Death in anger. "Why have you brought me here?"

Behind him, another figure appeared – another Prometheus. Then to the side, another emerged, fading into existence, then another and another and another. They looked to Death, to him and to each other with a hazy, yet furious, disinterest, firing slurred vitriol and searching within thread-worn jacket pockets in hopes of discovering hidden whisky. More Prometheuses came, filling the black shadows with their rattling bodies and gloomy auras. Some began to argue, while others did nothing but stand listlessly. Some cowered from Death, while others challenged it, cursing it and swearing feverishly in foamy wroth, all the while more of himself came, until hundreds grouped around him, the noise of their collective grief almost deafening. Yet still, more came.

Prometheus turned to Death. "What is the meaning of this?"

"From the loop, we bring you here. Over and over and over."

Prometheus thought of the purgatory hospital he had been sent to. Death had called it a pocket loop dimension, or some such term. "These are all truly me?" he whispered to no one. His mouth became taught and he shook his head. "Impossible."

"We bring you from the loop but the loop goes on and on and on. We bring you."

"Why?" He looked around at his own grey face a hundred times over. The sight of himself so wretched and weak sparked an anger inside him. "What could possibly come from this? What am I to do?"

"Build an army. Fight. Make right."

"Fight who?" Prometheus screamed over the noise.

"The Hydra." With the words, hissing off into the darkness, the noise stopped.

Something touched his shoulder and Prometheus spun wildly. Another of himself stood staring at him. This one was different from the others and different from himself as he was now. His hair was completely shaven, his skin slashed with scars and he wore strange clothes, a black sleeveless shirt and thick-soled boots. He was wreathed in menacing weaponry and the muscles on his arms were defined and powerful. The lack of hair made his face severe, with sharp cheekbones protruding like knives on his scarred, beard-stubbled face. But the eyes were quick and sparkled like they had done once before. The strange, bearded Prometheus smiled. It was a confident smile.

"Wha—" Prometheus began but was silenced by the other Prometheus holding up a palm.

"I'm here to train you," he said. His voice was firm.

"Who are—?"

"You know who I am. I'm you, from your future, just as the others are from our past." The man looked as though he'd just returned from a war. "I train you now to prepare us. Then you will train the others. Once you are done and ready as I am now, you will return to this exact point as I have done to train the Prometheus that will stand as you do right now. You will tell him exactly what I have told you. Do you understand?"

"You train me… and before that another us trained you, then another us trained him and another one him and so on and so on, until…"

"There is no until. We will forever train ourselves for the battle to come."

"What about the beginning of it?"

"A retro causality loop has no beginning," the other Prometheus said – the man's answer was ready even before the question was asked.

"I don't understand."

"I will explain all, just as we told me before and as you will tell us later." The future Prometheus smiled as Prometheus attempted to wrap his head around that. "There is only the future to play for in this universe. The past is done. The present is where the battle is, and the outcome will determine whether we can somehow put right what we have done in our blind obdurateness."

"Can't I go back and simply not resurrect the child?"

"Death has been over this already, remember? If we did that then we wouldn't be standing here now, would we? We did bring him back and we always will. If that were to change, it wouldn't change this nightmare we find ourselves, it would merely create a new version of events and a split universe as a result. All may turn out fine and dandy for the split universe, but here we would still be facing the consequences of what we have done and struggling to atone for it."

"So where will you go, after? Where will I go, to atone?"

"You will lead them into battle, as I will once I have trained you."

He looked around at the sad faces around him. How could they ever be an army? They were still too raw with grief to be of use to anyone. Perhaps they will need their goodbye with Sarah, as I have done, Prometheus thought.

"They will," the future Prometheus said as if reading his thoughts. But they were merely the thoughts he himself had thought at that moment, Prometheus realised.

"So how do we begin?"

The future Prometheus drew back his right arm and punched him square in the face. "Learn how to block, old man."

46

General Shaw led the group under the surface of Thebes, his plasma rifle cocked and raised. They descended rough steps scratched from the rock of the very earth, the passage narrow and dark. They were going in blind.

At first, he'd thrown down a ladar pulse stake to gauge the depth, but the readings returned inconclusive. Something was blocking the signal back to them. Either that or something had destroyed the sensor upon it reaching its landing place.

"There's an unusually high level of radiation coming from the soil," Dr Regus said over comm, finally putting away his gauge. He had scraped a sample of the ground every now and then since they'd begun their descent.

"Is it dangerous?" the General asked.

"No, our suits will protect us, but in any case, I'm not sure we would need protecting. I would need to go back to the lab to confirm, but as far as I can tell the energy seems to be of the same elusive variety emitted by Lydia's li pendant and that detected from Charlie."

The Consulate had always kept Charlie separate from the rest of the lifeship through fear that his high radiation levels were unsafe, and only the li was ever permitted to wear the fabled lion head pendant used the Cut through the time sectors.

Lydia instinctively touched her neck where the pendant hung beneath her suit. "What does that mean?"

"That, I do not know," the doctor replied. "I fear it's all linked somehow and that the answers, whether we want them or not, are to be found only by following the path to the bottom of this stairwell."

General Shaw remained quiet, but his dark brow tensed beneath his visor.

As they descended farther, dirt crunching under foot with each step, Ystil.3 received a secure-beam message from Lydia – despite the Captain's orders not to contact one another that way – revealing what the humans knew about the origin of Charlie, the wasted creature he had found. So, as promised, he secure-beamed all he knew about Computronium in return.

The story went, so Lydia had sent, that the first li found the pendant wrapped in the sheets of the bedridden Charlie, generations ago, and as soon as he touched it was transported to another time and another place, back on Earth. The man reflexively willed himself back in shock, lucky to find himself back inside the moving Hyperborea and not the vat of space.

The first li put the pendant away and convinced himself it had not happened. It was years later, only after discovering Earth had disappeared, that he picked it up again. Again, it transported him. But this time he was ready and did not panic. He eventually learnt to control where the pendant took him, and when, and soon it became an invaluable weapon against the AI that pursued them. He found he could bring things back with him, food and supplies, medicine, all from before the Earth vanished – but it was quickly discovered anything brought back was tainted with unsafe levels of radiation.

The first li also realised he could easily abandon the Hyperborea and live out the rest of his life comfortably in Earth's past. But he never did, and every li after took a vow that they too would not. Over the generations, each li served the human race while attempting to unlock the mystery of Earth's disappearance by looking to its past.

The first li had boarded the Hyperborea lifeship with Charlie five years into its journey, so the story went, arriving on a small hyper-inject craft. Where they came from was a mystery. Only Captain Dalloway knew, but he made no mention of it in his logs. All else they knew of Charlie was that the first li protected him furiously when the scientists on the ship wanted to experiment on him. The man could not die. A victim of the White Drops, some said. Others thought there was more to it.

After what seemed like hours of descending, the tunnel levelled and the steps gave way to a flat dirt floor. The claw marks scratched into the earthen walls revealed where the creatures had dug with bare nails down through the hard, burnt crust of the planet. General Shaw's raised weapon suggested he suspected the creatures might still be down there.

"What are we hoping to find?" Ystil.3 said over the comm system. "You must have some theories about what happened to them. We all know they're human, or were, at least. Why is nobody talking about it?"

"Perhaps our companions have something you and I seem to be both lacking," General Shaw said, the back of his head unflinching over his wide shoulders as he walked ahead.

"What's that?"

"Tact," he said. There was amusement in his voice. "They know as well as I do that these people are people from my colony. But they don't say so because they're trying to spare my feelings. It's disappointing, really. I thought the li of all people, trained by my own hand, would do me the honour of speaking truth when it needs to be said."

"I will speak the truth, as you well know," Lydia said. "But I see no point in stating the obvious."

The General grunted. "But what isn't obvious is how they came to be this way." There was emotion there, under the surface, concealed by gruff vocals, but Ystil.3 detected it.

"Judging from the radiation in the soil," Dr Regus said, "I'd say it was some sort of exposure that led to a mutation. The same that causes Charlie and—" He paused awkwardly and glanced to the General. It was only for a moment but Ystil.3 saw it. "Charlie to remain alive," the doctor finished. "Just like the people here, except deformed for some reason, perhaps adjusting to the harshness of the planet, having evolved, in a way."

"The fire," General Shaw said. "It was the fire that deformed them. That and the stores of the White Drops I found on the planet when I was a boy. Thousands of gallons locked away. The White Drops must have contaminated the blast, turning the fire into living death. Instead of killing them all as it should have, it malformed them into something else, something undead. No longer human."

"It can do that?" Ystil.3 asked.

The General bristled. "Who knows what it can do."

For a long time the group remained quiet and Ystil.3 envisioned the hordes of burned creatures building his own server. His own life had been the result of so much human death.

"Pay no attention to the General's temper," Lydia secure-beamed. "This is hard for him. This was his home and those were his people."

"I know," Ystil.3 said. "He's scared."

"Because he might run into his mother? He's scared he'll have to kill her. But these things are indistinguishable. She may have even been one of those we incapacitated on the surface."

"No, not just that. Come on, Lydia, the man was fourteen years old before humans discovered the Earth had disappeared, and that was two hundred Earth years ago. The average human lifespan is what, one-hundred and fifty, if they get that far? He's scared because he took the White Drops and doesn't know what it will turn him into. The best case scenario is that he ends up like Charlie, imprisoned inside his own wasting shell, and the worst is that it has the ability to turn him into those things."

"To be honest, I thought you would have figured that out weeks ago," Lydia said. "I guess they just don't make AI like they used to."

"Lucky for you," Ystil.3 said aloud with a snort.

"What's lucky for us?" General Shaw said.

"Nothing."

He frowned. "Keep together. I see light ahead."

It was a small light, if light is even how it could be described, simply less dark than the darkness around them.

"So why did he take it?" Ystil.3 asked.

"Revenge," Lydia sent. "The General stole a phial from the stores he found when he was a boy, which consequently went into stasis with him. When he woke, it was perfectly intact. He kept it a secret from the entire ship and it was only after the first onslaught of AI attacks when he was much older and already climbing high on the military ladder did he decide to take it, swearing revenge on the race that had wiped out everyone he had ever loved."

"You don't know that it was Z that caused the Reset. Not for sure."

Ahead, the General stopped to pick up the ladar pulse stake. It was blinking perfectly.

"The radiation must have been the cause of the signal interference," Dr Regus said. "If this signal is blocked then I'm guessing we can't contact the others on the surface from down here too."

The light grew steadily brighter as they went on until Ystil.3 found it easier to see by turning on his infrared. As soon as he did he noticed something odd; a strange blue mist emitting from the walls, floating off into the air like vapour, swirling and looping and curling about them like smoke. More of it plumed in from the light that pulsed ahead, clogging the tunnel with the tiniest specs of glowing matter and forming fingers and coiling tendrils that seemed to almost beckon them forward. The same mist, Ystil.3 saw, filled General Shaw's visor, as if emitting from his body. The suits they wore were pressurised, air tight, but still the lightest blue vapour floated out to join its brothers in the air. He turned to see Lydia's visor also held the blue mist, though not as much as General Shaw's. Strangely, both he and Dr Regus were completely free of it.

"Switch on your infrared," he sent to Lydia.

After a moment Lydia started snatching at the air around her. "What is it? Should we say something?" She seemed to not have noticed the mist coming from under her own suit, and Ystil.3 decided not to point it out to her right then.

"I think it's the radiation Dr Regus picked up earlier," he sent. "It's probably around Charlie too, if we were to look with infrared filters. I don't think it's a coincidence. I think that whatever happened to Earth is directly connected to Charlie and the White Drops."

"How? Charlie was on board the Hyperborea when it happened."

"Who knows why he was taken off-world in that condition to begin with. Hardly fighting fit for interplanetary travel. Who knows what life he had or what happened to him before. We need to check. If this mist surrounds him too, then…" Ystil.3's message trailed off into silence.

They had come upon the light source at the end of the passageway.

A cave formed around. In the centre floated a giant ring, pristine white, blue and gold and as large as a reverse thruster engine. The light pulsed from within the spinning centre, now blinding, sending white across the cave floor and stirring the shadows so they danced. From behind jagged rocks, blackened creatures emerged, with abysmal mouths and empty eye sockets. They staggered from the darkness on bone sharp claws, their long black teeth grating at the air.

General Shaw parted one from its head when it came too close, sending a beam of plasma light up, illuminating the cave ceiling. It was alive.

Countless burned creatures clung to it. They awoke poured down the walls, hundreds of them congealed into a black tide.

Lydia fired into the mass, joined by the General, but could barely hold them back. Ystil.3 fired at any that came too close to Lydia and Dr Regus took refuge behind them all. The tunnel entrance became blocked in an instant and there was nowhere to run. Through it all, Ystil.3 noticed a swarm of blue radiation pluming from every one of the burned creatures.

The great ring hummed and the pulsing light became stronger, more blinding with each rhythmic blast. It wasn't until he could see nothing through his infrared and the floor beneath his feet began to shake, did he truly begin to panic. He could no longer see Lydia, only hear her over the growls and plasma fire. He felt around him with hands outstretched but came into contact with the leathery flesh. He pushed the creatures back with all his upgraded strength. In the instant when the pulse light dimmed, he saw Lydia surrounded before it rose again.

No, not like this, he thought, struggling through the mass towards her. Suddenly something was on him. Teeth sank into his synth-flesh and pain shot through his arms and his neck. He tried to pull away but the pain was searing. He fell to the ground and more creatures came to feast. Above the pain, Lydia cried out. The light dimmed once more but all he could now see were burned faces and ragged teeth.

Plasma rifles fired. Then more. Too many, Ystil.3 realised. It sounded as though fifty were firing all at once. The burned faces hissed and receded back, eventually clearing his vision until a single stranger hovered over him as he lay chewed up upon the floor. It was a hard-looking man with a face full of scars, a clean-shaven head and a thick brown beard.

"I think your friend needs some help," the man said.

Ystil.3 quickly recognised the face under the beard. But he looked so different. Prometheus.

*

The creature's burned face exploded outward in shards of black bone and clumps of congealed brain matter, leaving only the severed neck oozing oily liquid, like a grotesque fountain. The body remained standing for a moment before stumbling sideways into the others that clambered forwards. Two more blasts took out another's chest, leaving a gaping hollow where perhaps lungs and a plump heart had once been – nothing was in there now but black fluid, and it gushed from the wound in endless torrents. The second plasma rifle blast left another with only one leg. The creature balanced there almost comically, hopping onwards before losing balance and falling into the charcoal soil.

Daneel had quickly realised they felt no fear. Nor did they feel pain. Nothing could deter them from their surge – not even having their faces blown apart, it seemed. They thrashed on regardless.

The flashes from the plasma rifle fire only drew more, but there was nothing to be done about that now. If they stopped firing, even for a second, they would be killed. So Daneel defended the rapidly closing line, which had backed him against the blasted hole that the General had left them to defend.

Comms between the two groups were down, while only his and Gutter's remained active. Together they felled the burned men that came, stacking wriggling bodies high upon themselves, almost building a defensive wall with them, but more clambered over the wounded, caring nothing of the pain that waited.

Retarded drones, Daneel thought. He would have pitied them if they weren't trying to kill him. A blast went off by his ear and he spun to see a creature burst like a sack of black oily snakes.

"That's fifty to me, so far," Gutter said from his vantage point atop the structure.

"Is that it? I'm on eighty-two." He aimed and shot a foot clean off from under one as it climbed over the mounting bodies. "Eighty-three," he corrected.

It was blasting through the structure that had first caught their attention – the bright blast and an instinctual desire to repair it, Daneel suspected. He didn't know what they wanted more, to repair the structure or to kill him and Gutter. Only a handful of the sloping figures appeared at first, but as more plasma shots fired out into the silence, more soon followed, until hundreds swarmed them, with ever more closing in. All Daneel and Gutter could do was hold back the nearest of them.

But the creatures weren't dying, and if they weren't sufficiently put down would continue to come at them, regardless of a missing leg or arm or head, they would crawl on splintered limbs and slither on torn torsos. Two blasts per creature usually did the job, one to the head and another to the torso. However, using their plasma rifles as they were, it wouldn't be long before they were completely out of juice. Daneel just hoped the others would return before that happened.

Gutter had shot a hang-wire high into the wall of the cube structure and scaled it until he stood upon the flat roof. From there he shot plasma bolts down into the burned men in the far distance, attempting to lessen the numbers pressing up against them. Daneel remained at ground level, but now he had no choice but to join Gutter in the advantage of higher ground. He deftly ascended the thin wire, attaching it to his belt and using one arm to simultaneously fire on the creatures below.

"We can't hold them off forever," Gutter said as they stood side by side.

"We don't need to," Daneel said, taking aim through the plasma rifle sight within his visor. "Just until the others get back through."

"What then? They climb out to be greeted by these junkfuck-for-brains

344

that can then tear them all limb from limb? Maybe the robot will give them all an electric shock when they feast on his wires, mistaking them for guts. Good plan."

"We can cover them while they can climb up here. Then we'll make our way down the other side."

"That plan won't work. There's almost as many on that side the last I looked. We're trapped."

"Fine, stop shooting," Daneel said.

The short man shot a creature in the distance and turned. "Come again?"

"Stop," Daneel said. He laid his hefty plasma ray flat on the roof and crouched to reel the climb line from where it dangled over the edge. "Cease fire. That is an order."

Gutter obeyed, but didn't lower his weapon. "What's the what? They're gonna seal the others in." Already the burned men were crawling over the pile of bodies towards the hole.

"Let them," Daneel said. "Let them seal it up. They'll think they've done their job and move on… scatter back to wherever they all crawled from, with any luck. Once they're done we'll blast our way in through the roof and throw this line down for the others to climb up. By then there should be a clear path back to the ship."

"There's just one problem with that," Gutter said.

"What's that?" A plasma blast went searing by Daneel's head.

"They can jump."

Daneel spun to see a burned man standing headless upon the structure's roof. It fell onto all fours and crawled towards them. Cracked arms appeared over the edge as more clambered up, while those with both legs still intact leapt the height, landing hunched and salivating only metres away.

Daneel resumed firing before Gutter's second plasma discharge met the torso of the nearest. He aimed for heads – if they had them – retreating until he and Gutter were back to back. More poured over, like a swelling black river, and soon they were encircled. Daneel cracked the hilt of his plasma rifle into the face of any burned man that came close, with no room to raise his weapon to fire. Then Gutter cried out suddenly over the comm, the noise a deafening rasp in Daneel's ears.

"The junkfuck took a chunk out my arm," he cried. A plasma fire blast went off. "My suit's breached. Fuck. I'm bleeding. Fuck."

Without thinking, Daneel aimed his plasma rifle down towards the rooftop where they stood and shot. It disintegrated in a hot blast beneath their feet until they were falling into the building below. Gutter grunted over comm as they hit the ground, surrounded by squirming piles of burned men; their suits absorbed the impact of the fall.

More creatures were already jumping down through the hole in the roof, while those on the ground scrambled through the hole in the structure that was now almost completely sealed again. They had two options: go down into what looked like an underground stairway and lead the burned men to General Shaw and the others, where together they might have a chance of blasting their way through – or become trapped underground; or shoot through the wall and attempt to make their way back to the ship. Daneel had already chosen the latter and raised his plasma rifle at the opposite wall, blasting another way through.

Gutter still sprawled on the ground, clearly disorientated and bleeding from his arm. Daneel yanked him up and dragged him through the dissolved wall. The man quickly found his legs and they made their way through the dark servers without once looking back.

Burned men followed, leaping and running. They ran three servers down, turned and headed four servers along before the last of them fell away in the distance. Even still, Daneel forced Gutter on, despite his friend pleading for rest. His wound gushed and he placed a suit-gloved hand over the wound – it was too large for the suit itself to repair. With any luck, there might be some semblance of a medi-kit on the Black Betty, but what he really needed was a decontamination shower back on the Hyperborea.

They turned, heading north and back in the direction of the ship, trying comms every minute to try and warn the others about what they were going to find back on the surface. But comms were still down. They would have to blast back out through the wall and risk drawing the burned men again, but there wasn't much he could do about that now. At best, he could somehow manage to fly the AI craft and rescue the others, at worst he would simply watch Gutter die from contamination, the rest already dead.

Just as the Black Betty was in sight, Daneel allowed them to finally slow their pace. Gutter gasped and Daneel increased the filter range of his rebreather to keep him from passing out. He kept his weapon raised, walking ahead and surveying the shadowed corners of the servers before moving on. Then Gutter stopped.

"Come on, we don't have time to rest," Daneel said, but Gutter didn't move. He stood frozen on the spot, looking up at the sky. Daneel lifted his head to see what the man was staring at. Lights dotted the sky above. Flashes of what was clearly plasma cannon fire burned through the night sky, blazing brightly in long trails before rupturing in white explosions. Outside Thebes' atmosphere, a battle was raging.

The Hyperborea.

*

By the time Ystil.3 was back on his feet, aided by the hand of Prometheus, all but a few of the burned men had been incapacitated. A carpet of them wriggled, crawling senselessly with either heads shot through or limbs blown off. Yet they lived. The sound of plasma fire echoed still, the thrumming and flashes of light ricocheting off the cave walls until the last of the creatures were put down.

Prometheus inclined his head in acknowledgement, but Ystil.3 could only stare. The man was transformed from the soft and pale grief-stricken man that he and Lydia had followed through the time sectors. Of course, Prometheus had no clue as to who he was.

Why... how is he here? Ystil.3 thought in an attempt to distract from the pain. He could already feel the warm flow of red plasma begin to stem and his flesh start to heal over the wounds.

Prometheus wore a pressurised suit too, though an older model. His head was captured inside a bubble of clear membrane. His beard was flecked with grey and covered the lower half of his face, but his eyes were the same – still full of grief, but something else now too. Strength. He was lean with muscle under his skin-tight suit and around his waist was strapped a belt stuffed with weaponry. The man's rebreather was also older and bulkier, and attached like a small turtle shell to his back, instead of the flush cartridges of the newer models that the others wore.

Ystil.3 had barely time to take it in before Lydia secure-beamed him. "Are they who I think they are?" she sent. Everything else was now silent.

"What do you mean, they?"

Ystil.3 hadn't even noticed the stream of men that flowed in through the spinning white ring that dominated in the cave. They marched out, scowling through their visors. And every single one of them was Dr Prometheus Page. Hundreds of the man trudged in militantly through the ring's shimmering centre that flexed and rippled like mercury. One after the other they came, dressed in black from head to boots and carrying plasma rifles high and ready to fire; each identical to the one before it. Every Prometheus even wore the same grimace on his gaunt face as he emerged through the portal, taking in the surroundings and then moving aside to allow another to enter.

"What the junkfuck?" Ystil.3 heard himself say aloud.

The Prometheus that had helped him to his feet was the only one of them he could tell apart. The others lacked beards and had longer hair on their heads, though well-trimmed and not nearly as shabby-looking as when he and Lydia had seen the wreck of a man in 1901. Only the bearded Prometheus had facial scars, with one in particular that scored down the left side of his cheek.

"Quite," is all the shaven-haired Prometheus said before he turned to the army and bellowed, "Stay on guard. I need two men to scout through the tunnel, two men to remain inside the tunnel and another two to guard the entrance on this side."

The nearest six Prometheuses moved without hesitation, raising their plasma rifles through the passageway.

"Why are you here? How are you here?" Lydia asked.

"Both are very good questions that I'm not sure I have the answers to. At least, none that will satiate your questions, I fear. Just know that I'm here to help. You need an army and I have brought you one."

"We already have an army," General Shaw said.

Lydia shuffled on the spot, clearly anxious. "Why do you say we need an army?"

Prometheus breathed a long, almost mournful sigh. "Because your people are under attack, even as we speak."

47

Earth was beautiful. The tropical trees that lined the entrance to the deep jungle grew tall and green and stretched up to a sky blanketed with gravid rain clouds, behind which the sun hid, allowing the breeze that rolled in from the sea to be cooling instead of stifling for once – salty and pleasant smelling. Everywhere there were things to see and smell and feel. The earth, I could smell that relentlessly, the sand and the dry dirt, the foliage from the jungle, the rotting vegetation and underbrush full of living things and dead things. I could smell it all. Smell the life.

But there were no humans upon this Earth. Nor were there buildings or land vehicles. No aircraft flew overhead, no noise invaded from roads, the skyline was not tainted with the silhouettes of monstrous buildings and upon the calm sea no boats or gigantic quakeships floated. There were creatures, yes, animals and insects, the likes of which left me silent with fascination. I could hear their primal incessant songs from within the jungle and, when I waded through the shallows of the warm sea, small silver fish wriggled around my ankles and tickled my now human toes.

But we saw no humans, real humans, and Norse assured me that there were none to see. All traces of them had vanished. From the complacency-inducing and chemical-filled "at-nice-spheres", which pumped drugs into violent cities, turning the sky a perpetual stone colour, to the cities themselves that mottled the planet's surface, suffocating it under billions of tonnes of concrete and steel – all of it had gone.

We had travelled from the beach up the sandy embankment and sheltered from the sun under a cluster of large-leafed palm trees, the coconuts hanging green in their husks high above our heads. Betty's hooves found easy purchase in the sand and I could tell she was grateful for the shade, even though we could not communicate in our usual fashion. All four of us lacked any sort of AI – or, in Bo's case, programme – function. I seemed to be completely human and Betty completely mare, beautiful and black with soulful eyes and a wild edge that Betty always had. Still, I could sense her emotions. She nestled into my neck affectionately and I knew she was concerned about our situation but not in a state of fear.

Norse was as naked as I, and just as human, it seemed. He had long, sun-bleached hair and a beard, and only two eyes in his head instead of hundreds. Bo had taken to perching on his shoulder in his cricket form, a small green insect that made noise constantly by rubbing its ridged legs together, making a clicking sound.

Norse's body was the exact replica of the synth he had lived within during his Overly Watchful time sector. "Before the Apex Soldiers came," he said. "They had come to send me back to foetal mode. Why? I still don't know. But on Z's orders. They collected each and every Overly Watchful, taking them from their time sectors. I managed to escape them, barely. I didn't want to go. I liked it here. I had… a life, sort of. But then the Reset happened and the Earth changed. Everything burned red and black in a blast so sudden I thought the Apex had caught up with me. There was fire everywhere. Then it went black and the stars above passed like streamers of white light. And then darkness and silence. I thought I had returned to foetal mode. There was nothing but the dark.

"Then, one morning, the sun rose in the darkness. It illuminated the Earth where before there had been nothing. But the Earth was different from the time sector in which I had lived. It was clean, fresh… no human technology, no human buildings and no humans. I had changed too. All the mech from my synth had been stripped away, leaving only organic matter. Everything resulting from the existence of humans had disappeared, even the clothes I wore. For a long time I wandered, travelling until I hit water and then travelling in another direction, searching for life other than me. I got used to it, and then I sort of liked it. It was peaceful and beautiful. You'd be amazed at how nourishing beauty can be.

"But then I began to hurt, I became weak and started blacking out. I didn't know what was happening. Eventually, I realised I was dying from thirst and starvation and my blackouts were inducements of sleep. Even though I had lived on Earth for a long time, feigning hunger when I ate and remaining inside at night when pretending to sleep, I had never known just how agonising the processes were. I found fruit to eat, apples and berries and vegetables, and found streams of pure clean water to drink. Then I was well again, so long as I continued to nourish myself and sleep. I made a solitary life for myself. That's when he found me."

"Who?" I asked. The talk of food had stirred a pain in my human stomach. Overhead, clouds swept in from over the wide ocean, threatening imminent rain.

Norse smiled. "You'll meet him soon. He knows everything that happens here." He looked around, marvelling at what he saw. "I wanted to stay so much, but no matter how hard I tried I could not help him the way he needed. So, I left to find someone that could."

I was beginning to lose patience with all this withholding information baloney. "Please stop talking as though I know what is actually happening because I don't. I feel like I'm free-falling."

Norse smiled amiably. "Don't worry. He will explain it much better than I can."

Thunder rolled in from the dense clouds, now black and stormy, rumbling so it seemed the ground shook beneath our bare feet. Lightning cracked and flashed overhead, sending Betty into panic with its startling fingers of electricity. She reared back and I stroked her until she was calm again. The rain poured down as though the sea and sky had exchanged places. I laughed and led Betty out from under the shelter. The rain was warm and felt amazing on my human skin – trickling down my chest and legs. It collected in my hair and poured down my face into my eyes. Betty flicked her tail playfully and I laughed and laughed, spinning in the rain, letting it drench me.

From beneath the trees, I glimpsed Norse smile.

*

The trees rushed overhead as Betty tore through the underbrush. The jungle clung to my dewy skin; bits of leaves, insects and vines that whipped by as I rode her hard through the wild foliage. The rain barely penetrated the thick canopy above, but it was always wet in the jungle. Wet and hot. Betty's muscles moved powerfully under me as we chased our prey, her nose pointed onwards like an arrow cutting through the trees and I leaned low to avoid low-hanging vines from snagging my face. With one hand, I grasped Betty's black mane, the other held a sharpened stick-spear. Betty's hooves thudded in the undergrowth, throwing a spray of greenery into the air with every stride.

The boar ran under the vegetation, only visible from the stirring scrub.

I'd been hunting that boar for the better part of an hour, after casually coming across the creature whilst making the morning trip from the fresh water stream. A fully-grown female, it was, with small black eyes that looked out at me from under a veil of low hanging vines. I saw it. It saw me. Then it ran. I was so excited I wanted Betty to give chase there and then, but she stood still, knowing better than to gallop off with four large skins of water hung around her like saddlebags. I offloaded the skins and mounted. At once, she shot off in the boar's direction, sending a wave of exhilaration my limbs. I could almost taste the meat already.

I'd learnt the hard way to always carry my spear from when I'd encountered a jungle deer a while back. If I'd had my spear to hand I would have pierced the creature's heart with time to spare. Norse and I would have eaten well that night. Instead, we dined on leaves and berries around the fire as I grumpily thought of the juicy deer meat I'd missed out on. Hunger was a terrible suffering, I learnt too.

Over the months, Norse had taught me how to use the weapon, how to carve it and where to pierce the animals to kill them quickly. He taught me how to fish in the fast-flowing rivers and the sea, how to identify which berries and fruits we could eat and how to climb the tall coconut trees to harvest the thirst-quenching green husk fruit. It took a while to adjust to it all, made worse by the fact I wasn't used to the body I was in. When I ran, I fell. When I climbed, I fell. When I rode Betty, I fell. The only thing I could do right was complain about the persistent hunger that plagued my soft Tom Jones stomach. I had never felt anything like it – the pain, the need for food. All reason abandoned me. All objections I'd first had about killing the beautiful animals around us were suddenly surpassed by the mouth-watering smell of cooking meat, with fat dripping and sizzling into the open flames of our camp fire. The taste was beyond delicious.

I had asked Norse whether we were still in the BroadWeb. He said we were – which confused me greatly. But I saved my curiosity until he came… whoever he was. Yet was taking his sweet time in finding us. Norse was sparse in his description of the creature, careful to never give anything away. "It's not for me to tell you," he would say when my impatience raged. "It is not my story to tell. He knows we're here and will come when you are ready."

"When I'm ready. I'm ready now. I'm far beyond the state of readiness." From my point of view, I'd been wandering the BroadWeb in some form or another for an endless amount of time. And however much I was beginning to enjoy my experience as a human, I wanted to go home, orbiting Delilah, with Betty in her own form. But all he would reply is, "He will come."

I was always in need of something: food, rest, bowel evacuation, healing – I'd hurt myself many times from falling off Betty, and in general. It was all too much. Give me my steel body, hard and covered with lasers. But gradually, as I ran, I didn't fall. When I climbed the trees, I reached the top. When I rode Betty through the jungle, we soared together. I listened to Norse's advice and allowed him to teach me how to live in that world.

Betty slowed as the boar's trail ended. The creatures were generally nocturnal, sleeping in nests during the day, the boar must have been prevented from returning when I came across it, but had inadvertently led me directly to it. The mound of shrubbery covering the shallow crevice in the ground was easy to spot after Norse had shown me how. I dismounted and, as silently as I could, stepped through the underbrush. Dead leaves crunched under foot and something wet seeped through the layers of large leaves I'd wrapped around my feet to protect my soft flesh somewhat from the harsh jungle floor. Norse had also told me that I might want to cover my human genitalia too. "If you hurt that you'll know about it," he said. I took his advice and wore the half coconut shell he gave me tied with vines around my waste. Once, when walking, a low-level branch suddenly protruded from nowhere, sticking me right in the coconut. I was thankful for it then.

There was always noise in the jungle, animals shrieking far off, or the rustling of creatures in the trees, but I managed to pick out a light shuffling sound underneath the leafy covering of the boar's nest. I hovered over it and raised my spear high. I would only have one chance to get it right or it would flee back into the thick jungle – and to be perfectly honest, I couldn't be bothered to ride off after it again. I still had the water to bring back to camp and no doubt Norse was already stressing about where I was. With my sharpened spear raised, I steadied my stance and kicked aside the leafy roof of the nest. My spear almost left my hand, but I stopped in time. In the nest, a litter of tiny piglets suckled their mother's teats. They wriggled hungrily, small and covered in striped golden hair. The mother squealed threateningly, but I'd already lowered my spear.

I returned to camp to find Norse stripping the skins off wild hare and unloaded the day's supply of water with my usual grumble. I had asked Norse why we couldn't move camp closer to the river, but he said something about open spaces and at the time I was much too hungry to pay attention. Our camp was in a large clearing of trees, with plenty of shade around the outer parts for when the days were at their hottest and clear enough in the centre to construct a sleeping shack from branches and large leaves for a roof panelling. It was sufficient shelter enough for when it rained, but most of the time we slept out under the stars next to the dying fire. I didn't like to leave Betty outside when it rained, but she was too large to fit inside and she usually hovered under trees for shelter.

Bo, in the form of a grasshopper, perched upon Norse's shoulder, as was his custom. The hare skin tore away with a firm yank, revealing red muscles underneath. "We can dry out the hide and make some decent shoes for your feet," Norse said, looking down to my bleeding toes. Bits of the leaf shoes I'd tied around them were falling apart. Norse's own feet were hard from wear. His body was exactly as he'd left it before returning to the BroadWeb, apparently, sinewy and toned with muscle. As though he'd never left.

"I got no travelling shoes," I said.

"What?"

"Nothing. A Tom Jones song," I said glumly. Norse was made for this, I realised. He was strong, capable, and used to real-time housed in a synthetic – only a small jump to human, really. I was not. However much I had enjoyed the novelty at first, it was fast wearing off.

I looked down every day at Tom Jones' naked body and heard his voice whenever I spoke. That was always a thrill. During the early days, I sang and danced constantly, usually gyrating around Norse as he sensibly built fires and shelter. I would sing to Betty as Norse topped the shack with leaves. I would bellow to the night sky as Norse prepared our meal. It had been weeks now since I felt like singing. It was too hard. Living here was too hard. I hurt constantly. I wasn't tough. I didn't want to kill, but it was either kill animals or burn with hunger. I didn't want to have to live like that. That wasn't me. I was CorVac, not human.

The rest of the day was spent scavenging for vegetables and leaves, which were served with the spit-cooked hare in the evening. After, we rested by the fire, watching the stars flicker in the sky. Are they even stars? I thought. There were no stars in the BroadWeb and that is, after all, where we were, apparently. I wasn't so sure. What if Betty was to suddenly become herself again? A ship. Not a galleon to ride the black tides of the BroadWeb, but herself, the beautiful Black Betty with hyperdrive. If I was to fly her up into this sky and through the years it would take to return to the Titan System and Delilah, would I find it up there? Or would I just return into the Black of the BroadWeb?

When I slept that night, I dreamt. Dreaming was the strangest thing I'd ever encountered in my entire existence. At first, upon waking from my very first dream, I'd wept like a human, with streams of salty tears drenching my face. I'd dreamt Betty was dead, obliterated by a storm of comets in the Titan System while I watched overhead, floating in the form of Tom Jones. I found Betty sleeping under her usual tree by the edge of the jungle. I crawled out into the rain and lay with her, her large horse head resting on the ground and her legs curled up to her body. Drops of rainfall fell between the branches and by the time I woke in the morning I was soaked through. For the rest of the day, I was ill and shook with cold. I thought I was dying.

This dream, however, was more surreal than that one, but just as strange. Betty and I lived in a tree that was also the Titan System. It was huge and black and the leaves were stars that twinkled. Betty was a mare and me in my CorVac form. I crawled the limbs of the tree with my great spidery legs. In the craggy bark of the tree tiny insects, all with the head of Bo, scuttled around singing The Green Green Grass Of Home in chorus. Then Ystil.3 emerged from the star leaves, resting on a branch on his tiny DataCom Unit legs and his sensor strip flashing as it wound around his head. "Wake up, Tom," he said. "Wake up."

I woke, staring at the stars above, mistaking them for the tree's leaves for a moment. It was still night and the campfire was now nothing but cold embers. Beside me, Betty slept, and on the other side of the fire Norse snored soundly. The night was clear and warm. The sound of crickets and wildlife festooned the air; one of those may have been Bo – I hardly even regarded him now. I rose onto my elbows, my mouth dry and thirsting as I searched for the water skin we kept under the shelter.

That's when I saw him, a human child staring passively at me from among the trees of the jungle wall. I stood, perfectly still, unsure if I was still asleep. His skin was pale in the moonlight and his hair blonde and fine. He wore fur that draped around his shoulders and no other clothes that I could tell. He was no older than ten, I'd guessed. It wasn't until he spoke to me that I knew I was, in fact, awake and that this boy was the him I'd been waiting for these long, hard months.

"Come with me, Tom," he said from across the distance between us, yet

I heard him perfectly as though he had spoken into my ear. I glanced to Betty, resting, her massive ribs rising and falling with peaceful breath. When I looked back, the boy had turned into the jungle.

I followed silently, keeping ten paces behind as he led me through bush, groves and clearings. He took me over a stream I had never come across before and into a part of the wilderness that we had no need to ever venture. All the while the boy never turned his head and never spoke a word.

The darkness of the early morning soon gave way to the paleness of dawn. The trees came to life and, as the undergrowth warmed, the creatures roused from sleep while the nocturnal beasts rested. The dewy leaves sparkled with the sun that managed to break through the morning clouds and then through the almost impenetrable canopy; it shone threads of horizontal pink light and bejewelled the leaves in blushing diamonds. For a while, we walked on in this way, until the boy stopped and turned a few paces ahead. There was nothing around of note. All I knew was that my legs ached and all I could really think about was that I was going to have to walk all the way back at some point.

"I'm glad you're here," the boy said. He was smiling.

At first, I was wary, but his smile seemed genuine and I took the last few paces towards him.

"I know you have many questions," he said. "But please be patient and I will tell you everything I know."

"You don't speak like a little human boy, I'm sure of that," I said, mostly to myself. I thought perhaps it might offend him, but he only smiled. "You're not a little Earth boy, are you?"

"No."

"And I'm not really Tom Jones, am I?"

The boy laughed. "You know the answer to that already."

I nodded. "Then, pardon my abruptness, but where are we and what in the name of Tom Jones is going on?"

The boy stepped aside to reveal a large hollow in an even larger tree. The roots clung into the earth like octopus legs and the hollow itself looked like the unhinged jaws of a snake. "Please," the boy said, gesturing me to enter.

With hesitation, I did, entering the tree that was large enough for Betty if she'd come along. I was tempted to mention that to the boy and make a point of saying that at least my legs wouldn't be so sore, but I didn't. He followed me in an urged me down a short tunnel, which steeped and then dropped vertically with a ladder made from naturally growing tree roots. At the bottom of the drop was a huge burrow and a fire blazed within a hearth made of stone. I could smell and hear the sea and above us was a night full of stars – even though we were underground and it was now daytime. Yet they twinkled above in the fresh night sky.

The boy sat by the fire and I joined him, not cold but liking the warmth regardless. He offered me water and berries, which I took.

"My name is Charlie," he said at last. It was in the fire light that I first saw the sadness in his eyes. They were old eyes. Very old eyes, with a soul to match. "I am human," he continued. "Or, at least, I was once, for a very brief time. Then I died as an infant and my human life ended. I was brought back into the world and for a time I was something else. I've been called many things throughout my life: a miracle, an abomination, a cure, the source, post-human, transhuman, the devil… and once, millennia ago, a very kind man called me his son.

"Like you, I have a body in the physical plane… in real-time, as you call it. But, unlike you, my body is old and withered and causes me such tremendous pain that I cannot bear to inhabit it. It is my prison, my anchor to a life I should have departed many years ago, one I should never have been brought back into.

"It is because of my existence that the human race is so perilously close to its end. It is because I was allowed to live that the Earth was prised from its place among the stars and why so many souls suffered and perished. If I had never lived, the creature of menace that stalks the pitiful remainder of humanity would never have been able to tear holes in spacetime as it has, destroying so much life."

"The creature of menace? I asked.

"The Hydra. You know it as Z. No one knew of the flaw in the Hydra Server housed on Thebes, or M21, as you know it. The server was the massive storage space for the cloned digital personalities of the humans who made it, and was intended to keep them alive by transferring their consciousness into other bodies, cloned or bio-organic and therefore defer death. But the flaw in the plan saw to it that their personalities… all their life experience, successes, failures, tortures, flaws and virtues, they melded into one digital entity. They leaked into each other; becoming the very best and the very worst that was them all. All without the context of humanity to constrain it. Born of five human minds, it merged into something quite monstrous. A creature with a single goal to mirror its creators'. To live forever."

"But Sir Z, the Hydra, it created us. It will live forever. Z cannot die. He has no server…" I realised then I didn't know anything and the more I spoke the more I gave that away.

"The Hydra has a different definition of forever, and it can die. Through the weaknesses in the human minds it was derived from, and from the lack of any real context for it to base its consciousness, it has come to interpret the word forever in terms of space as well as time. It wants to consume and devour everything. To become everything."

356

"I don't understand."

"Computronium," Charlie said.

"The substance that allows matter to become programmable? I know it well. I should do. Betty and I are partly made of the stuff. But what does that have to do with it?"

"It is an element that when combined with a material, any material… metal, earth or flesh… allows .that substance to become encoded with whatever set of instructions or requirements the programmer wishes. It could simply house data, or it could be used to transform the shape of the object, or it can allow a digital entity to inhabit the structure, as with yourself and the Black Betty. It is the warped intention of the Hydra to consume all substance in this way… by compounding all matter in the universe with Computronium and then programming itself into it, thereby becoming the universe itself. I know this, because, quite by accident, I have been encoded into the Earth. I am Earth's consciousness. I am its mind. I feel all it feels because it is me, and I control all upon it in this potential space, this BroadWeb.

"The Reset, as you call it, was also an accident. The Hydra had at that time found a way to inhabit the bodies of its original minds in order to complete its mission of living eternally. It moved a great Earth power known as Life Corp to proceed with a dangerous experiment that it knew could possibly destroy planets. But unlike its human counterparts, all it cared for was its own desire. Of course, the Hydra did not die as all others did when they punched holes into spacetime. It went somewhere else, to the space that lies between spaces. The potential space."

"The BroadWeb."

"Yes. There it resumed its attempt to become eternal. It quickly realised, however, that it could not create anything substantial there by itself. It didn't have the capability to construct because it lacked that essential context of itself. Instead, it needed to mould creatures to create these things for it."

"So it created AI and programmes, like Nyx said?"

Charlie nodded. "It eventually discovered that I had achieved what it had not, and now it moves to become truly eternal, truly omnipresent and truly immortal. It wants me, in my Earth form and my human form. It needs me to complete what it started. And I'm afraid to say, it almost has me." The boy hugged the fur around his shoulders and the firelight glimmered in his old eyes.

"Where is your human form and why didn't it die during the Reset?" I asked.

"That story is longer and far more painful to me," the boy said with a sad little sigh. "But as you might have guessed, I am old. So very old and tired, and though I have lived for countless years I have never really been able to live. And now the world has come to this because of that pseudo life which was given back to me.

"I was once human. Have I said that already?" The boy shook his head. "I'm in so many places at once it's sometimes hard to concentrate at just one thing at a time. I'm aboard a ship orbiting Thebes in real-time. For years, I have attempted to communicate through my body as it lies there, decaying, wanting to help the humans and tell them all I know, but whenever I return the pain is so immense that I lose sense of all that I am and what I'm there to do. Sometimes it takes me a very long time to realise above the pain that I can leave my body and return here. I was trapped for years of real-time once. Other times I eject myself so quickly because the pain is too traumatising for me to bear. But I need to get there and I need to be coherent so I can tell them what needs to be done."

"And what is it you want from me?"

A shadow danced across his face. "The Hydra must be destroyed and the Earth must be transported back into real-time where its children need it so desperately."

"And you think I can help?"

The boy poured me more fresh water. He looked up to the sky above us where there should have been no sky. "I was lucky in finding Norse," he said. "He was the only creature that survived the translation into BroadWeb. He is a creature of the BroadWeb, so when the Apex failed to delete him and the Reset occurred, he came here instead. It was my own energy that caused the Reset, misused by the Hydra, and that's how I became the Earth. We merged. Have I told you that? I knew Norse could help me, and he has, by bringing you here.

"At first I thought I could take him with me, into my body, so that when I shouldered the pain he could relay the message as I intended. But that wasn't to be. There were a few problems. He was an AI that had lived in real-time, so wouldn't be overcome with confusion in that state, but the problem, among other things, was that he couldn't let go. He has come to love it here, which made it almost impossible to take him with me. However much he wanted to help, he resisted."

"If you control all on this Earth then why not make Earth an even more unbearable place to live, then he might have come?" I asked.

The boy smiled. "I cannot cause more suffering. I don't think I could bear it. Besides, however I make the Earth now will be as it is when we move back into real-time. As it is right now will allow for the humans to sustain themselves." He shoved another handful of berries in my hand. "Eat," he said with a smile. "Once we move back into real-time, I won't be able to change a thing.

"What makes you different, Tom, is that you have no desire to stay here. In fact, you loved your life with the Black Betty as you orbited Delilah so much that you're actively rejecting the human body you're in, which, forgive me for saying so, is ironic because you're probably the most human-like AI in existence. You have desires, loves, hates and passions. You fear and protect fiercely, and above all that you can create… a skill that will be vital in the battle ahead."

"What have I created?" I asked. I had never built anything that wasn't already pre-designed in my life.

"When you traded your beloved voice for a DataCom Unit perception filter from Bo, didn't you wonder why you not only looked like a DC Unit to other AI but also took on the traits and functions of it? You willed yourself to become a DC Unit for the sake of your friend. And when the Apex hunted you, your tiny DataCom legs would not let you run fast enough, so you became something else entirely by letting your CorVac legs return. And then, in the limitlessness of potential space, you willed Betty into an Earth ship because the blackness reminded you of an ocean you'd once seen, and you all needed something to keep you together, something in which to travel onwards. Even long before that, whenever you entered the BroadWeb you had always done so in the form of your idol, Tom Jones. You create what you will, Tom. As you said before, your real-time form is structured from Computronium, which allows you to carry your own server around with you. I believe this has given you an instinctive ability to shape BroadWeb matter to your will, just as Computronium can be programmed to will."

"Instinctive?" I repeated. "Instincts."

"Instincts are essential for creatures to evolve," Charlie said. "It was Bo that saved you, letting you into the programme data pocket. But it was Nyx that told him to, and it was Norse that told Nyx to tell Bo, and it was me that told Norse to tell Nyx."

"So you want me to come with you into your human body so that while you're in too much pain to talk, I can give the humans a message that will instruct them on how to destroy Sir Z… the Hydra… and to move the Earth back into its rightful place?"

"That's right," Charlie said.

"And then what?"

"We wait for the battle."

"But what about us? AI, I mean. The Hydra created us. What will happen if we succeed?"

"I'm afraid the servers on Thebes will not survive. But your own server is attached to your body, is it not?"

I looked into the flames and nodded. "But I have a good friend whose server isn't."

☐

48

Daneel pulled Gutter through the causeways of the Black Betty, far from the bridge and deeper into the maze of bulkheads. Time was running out. His friend was dying.

He had first attempted to access schematics to an infirmary, but amid the air-ducts, electricals and piping that snaked through the vessel, nothing was clearly marked. He even attempted to access the ship's computer for aid, but couldn't manage to ignite the internal systems or get any reaction out of the pilot deck. So, there was nothing else for it, they had to search on foot.

Winston had left the ship in holding to make a swift getaway. The lights, oxygen and hatch doors were all in working order, but everything else would have taken an age for Daneel to decipher. To attempt to fly the thing would have been an impossible task, and as he moved, Gutter shaking and clinging to his side, he had found himself ironically wishing for Winston's safe return. But comms were still down and the more time that passed the more he doubted the others were still alive.

Gutter fell unusually quiet, moaning only every now and then. He shivered too, and his skin took on a waxy look. The wound on his arm had stopped bleeding at least, but Daneel wasn't even sure that was a good thing. Regardless, he hauled Gutter on, taking his friend's weight and checking every chamber they came across, hoping the infirmary was close. The farther they travelled, the slower they moved. With every step forward, Daneel supported more of Gutter's weight until there was no choice but to haul him over his shoulder, which began to seize almost at once. But he went on.

After struggling on for another two-hundred yards of causeway, he pushed into a room full of stasis cribs set deep in the floor, like earthen graves.

"This will have to do for now, friend," he said. Whether Gutter could hear him at this point he didn't know. He hurried to place Gutter inside the nearest.

In theory, the stasis process would halt the foreign body in Gutter's system until he could get him to the Hyperboria doctors. The translucent shutter slid over his convulsing body and within minutes he was deep in stasis. Daneel then began back to the bridge. Comms were still dark.

Fear rose, ice forming in his chest. He began to panic, until he found himself running, his breath ragged and his heart thumping. A battle was happening above and the General and Lydia were missing.

What if they're all dead? What if I'm stuck on this planet?

Suddenly everything he'd ever clung to in his life seemed meaningless. All the shit fell away until there was only one face he saw. Lydia. He wanted to be safe with her. Anywhere, but safe.

He rushed onto the bridge, hoping to decipher the ship's computer. It was his only hope. He staggered to a rigid stop at the sight of General Shaw standing there. Then the others. Lydia.

Relief rushed through him in waves that he almost cried out.

*

"He's in stasis now, General," Daneel said, breathless and dripping with sweat as he stood rigidly to attention. "He's got a fever running through him. He couldn't even stand." His eyes flickered over to Prometheus standing beside Dr Regus but asked no questions.

A true soldier, Ystil.3 thought.

"And you say he was bitten?" the General asked.

"By those burned things."

"We need to get back to the Hyperborea. I hope you're ready for what we're heading back to, Corporal?"

A hand shot to Daneel's head in a salute. "Sir, yes sir," he boomed devotedly. "I'm looking forward to turning those tin-men into scrap metal, sir."

"Ignore him," Lydia secure-beamed to Ystil.3. "We've got bigger things to worry about than Daneel's jealousy."

"Yeah, like the Apex waiting for us," he sent back. "Wait. Jealousy? What exactly is he jealous about?"

"Because he thinks we're fucking."

"Oh… Oh. Is that the only reason why you did that with me? To make Daneel jealous?"

"What sort of person do you take me for? Of course it isn't. I hadn't had sex in a really long time and all that fighting, getting hot and sweaty… let's just say I was in need of a good ass-kicking in more ways than one. And whether you're aware of it or not, your synthetic is rather… yummy."

"Yummy?" Ystil.3 repeated, baffled. "Yummy?"

"Making Daneel jealous is just a happy bonus."

"There's history between the two of you, isn't there?"

"Ancient." She was doing her elusive thing again.

"What happened?"

"Nothing I want to talk about now. As I said, we've got bigger things to worry about than Daneel's jealousy."

"But how did they find us?" Dr Regus asked.

Ystil.3 felt the heavy weight of eyes upon him.

"Those are questions for another day," the General said. "Today, we fight to survive."

Ystil.3 prepared for take-off and the Beta Ship computer soon had them climbing through the toxic atmosphere of M21 skies. They broke through the first of the planet's barrier fields as the pilot deck flashed a warning, detecting plasma fire ahead. As the Black Betty headed towards the second field, Captain Lu's voice suddenly thundered from the ship's comm System.

"General, we are under attack. Come in General Shaw."

General replied at once. "Captain, we're here. Status update."

The entire bridge was silent. Dr Regus sat next to Prometheus in the nav-hand stations to the left of the pilot deck. Prometheus had sent the others into the ship's holdings to await instruction. Lydia manned the weapons deck and Daneel stood behind the General, looking over the man's shoulder to where Ystil.3 sat. His eyes burned with hatred and whenever their gaze met, his stubble-covered lip hooked up into a scowl.

The Captain spoke with urgency. "Units Alpha, Bravo and Gamma have taken fifty Wings to drive the AI swarm away from the Hyperborea. Our shields have been severely damaged and levels one through three have been breached and locked down. Every able soldier now holds a weapon and the civilians have been moved to the central core holdings for safety. Delta, Zulu and Sierra have taken position and are now awaiting orders.

"Our turret plasmas are recharging after two attempts to blast the mothership but they didn't even dent its shield, I've got men on the CSD with the XO shooting bolts and staving off the smaller AI Bug ships as best they can, but there are hundreds of them. We have no room to give chase and even less room to enter hyper and escape. I fear even if we could hyper out, they could follow us to wherever we end up. We're not going to outrun them, Nathan. Not this time."

The General shuffled uncomfortably. "Briefly, what are we dealing with, Captain?"

"The mother ship is half the size of the Hyperborea. I haven't ever seen anything like it before. The records mention nothing like it. So far, it hasn't raised any weaponry against us, for all we know it has none, though I doubt it. Only the smaller Bug ships have been leading the onslaught. The mother is moving towards us, however. At our acceleration, compared to theirs', we've got thirty SEMs at most until we're close enough to either be boarded or destroyed. At that proximity, our control field will crumble with one respectable hit. Even if that is the case and they want to get close enough to make sure they do the job this time, it means either their shields are so strong that the blast won't ricochet off us and take them out also, or it will and they just don't care. Either way, it doesn't bode well. We've set a course of retreat but the mother is gaining speed faster than we can. They won't make the same mistake this time, be sure of that."

"Has any contact been made?" the General asked, his eyes unblinking in their sockets, like large white eggs.

"Take me off speaker," Captain Lu ordered.

General Shaw paused for a moment, then did so, listening through his own comms system. A quizzical look crossed his face and he turned from the watching group, muttering something in reply. "I see," he said eventually.

Ystil.3 could still feel the tension rise on the bridge, the same tension he'd felt down in the tunnels before Daneel and the others had jumped him. He glanced at the monitor in front. "We've penetrated the second barrier field and are about to head through the last," he said. When he looked up again all eyes were in his direction and General Shaw stood imposingly over him.

"I'm going to have to ask you to leave the bridge," he said. The large man's brow was suddenly sheen with sweat and his perfectly hairless head shone in the spotlights that dotted the bridge. His T-pistol was secure in its holster, Ystil.3 noted.

When Ystil.3 stood, he came face to face with the man. It still surprised him that his synth was as large and as powerful as General Shaw. He never felt as tall or as powerful on the inside. "Why?" he said, rather meekly.

"We can't have our strategy compromised," he replied simply. "We must take all precautions against possible breaches. Captain's orders."

"That's absurd," Lydia said. "You don't trust him still, after how he's helped us?"

"It's okay, Lydia," he said. "The BetaShip can stay the course back to the Hyperborea so I'm not really needed now anyway."

Lydia opened her mouth to protest further but instead glanced at the holoscreen in front of her. "Shit. We've got Bugs coming in fast. Three, it looks like, heading straight for us. We're not going to make it through them with just the BetaShip. We need a pilot. We need Winston to get us back."

The General's face twisted. The very idea of disobeying an order visibly sat like lead in his gut. He thought and paced.

"General, they'll be on us in less than thirty SES," Lydia urged. "We need to move out the junkfucking way."

The General stopped, paced for another moment and then swung to face Ystil.3. "You stay as pilot. If you're with us, Winston, now's the time to prove it. Get us back to the Hyperborea."

Ystil.3 gave an earnest nod and sat. He manoeuvred the Black Betty, taking back full control from the Beta Ship.

"What did the Captain say?" Dr Regus asked. "Have the AI said what they want?"

The General nodded. "They want Charlie."

In the distance the AI mothership came into view in the tempurhull, looming towards the lifeship like a black blade.

"How do they even know about Charlie?"

"That is a very good question, doctor." He looked to Ystil.3.

"I can have these Bugs off our tail in two SES," Lydia said. "Just tell me to fire."

Ystil.3 only had to go over the weapons deck once with Lydia and it was imprinted onto her memory. She plotted the holoscreen as though she'd been sitting in that seat for years. Something occurred to him, suddenly. "Why haven't they fired already?"

"What?" Lydia said, looking up from the deck.

"We've been in firing range long enough, but they haven't fired on us. Why?"

General Shaw glowered. "They want to take us alive."

"Or they think the Black Betty is still under AI command," he said. "Perhaps they think we're an ally."

"Or, maybe they know their double agent is on board?" Daneel added.

The General ignored them both and continued to pace.

"It's only a possibility," Ystil.3 went on. "It's likely that Sir Z would have secure-beamed Tom before the attack happened, to either move him out of the vicinity or to know what happened to him after discovering the Hyperborea was orbiting our own server planet. If they received no response from him, they still won't know who's in command, and if they did contact him and know that he and Betty vacated their posts and are now in the BroadWeb, then the most logical explanation is that humans have commandeered it. If that were the case, we would be dead already. So, we must assume they don't know."

"What point are you trying to make?" General Shaw asked.

"Ready to fire on your command, General," Lydia interrupted. The General held up a hand to stay her.

Ystil.3 swallowed. "I don't know. There might be an opportunity here if they think we're on their side, to either get back to the Hyperborea or… I don't know, do something."

"Our main objective is to get back to the Hyperborea," he said. "But beyond that, we may be able to use this. If you're right, Winston, then this could be the opportunity we've been waiting for."

"How?" Lydia asked. She was getting twitchy from the Bugs on their tail.

"Can we establish a link between us and the AI mother?" the General asked Ystil.3.

"We can. But if Tom were aboard he wouldn't do it through the ship. He would simply secure-beam Sir Z." He sent the ship wide of the human-piloted Wings, leading a few bugs away from the Hyperborea. If the AI mother saw that the Wings didn't fire at them they would become suspicious. It was better to stay out of it completely. He knew that's what Tom would have done, were he there.

"But assuming they believe Tom is unable to secure-beam, wouldn't he then attempt some other way of making contact?" General Shaw asked.

"Yes, that's true. In that case, he would use one of his own jacks to connect to the ship's secure-beam channel. It's possible to tell who is jacked into the ship's channel, however, so I wouldn't be able to do it posing as him if that's what you're hoping?"

The General's mouth became a thin line. "It was."

"It is possible, however, for me to filter into Tom's CorVac form and then make contact," Ystil.3 said. "It would just read as Tom to the recipient."

"And you would do that?" the General asked.

Ystil.3 hesitated, then nodded.

Immediately the General reformed a link with the Captain. "Capture the Black Betty," he said. "We'll give chase, but bring us in by force." A sly smile eased over the man's face. "I want to pull a Trojan horse on these junkfuckers."

☐

49

Ystil.3 followed Lydia through the Underbelly. The stench of fear permeated the steel corridors, while grim-faced soldiers charged by, each carrying heavy artillery and mass-packs full of survival gear.

The ship's arsenal – the Lock – was usually in the vigilant control of General Shaw, who had final say over what was taken from it and by whom. But in his absence, the ship's XO Rawl Collister had taken it upon himself to open it, effectively allowing anyone to take whatever they wanted regardless of training or rank. The General was not pleased, to put it lightly, and had instructed Lydia to ensure order was maintained, while he debriefed Captain Lu on the Command Bridge.

"The wrong weapon in the wrong hands could do more damage than good in this situation," Lydia said, looking back to Ystil.3.

The Hyperborea had done exactly as the General had instructed, ensnaring the Black Betty in a control field limb and drawing them into the hangar. It seemed their plan to the deceive the AI mothership had worked, because the Bug ships, as the humans called them, attempted to blast through the field to free them. Failing that, they had no choice but to swerve from the path of the lifeship's own Wings, allowing the Betty to be swallowed. They boarded the Hyperborea to find it in a state of emergency, and at once they were called to report to the Captain before executing the second part of the General's plan.

Arriving at the Lock, they found the largest, and most deadly, weaponry had long since been ransacked. The men and women that dodged by were rushing up to the combat systems deck; each dressed in hardsuit combat armour and carrying only smaller T-pistols and cartridge handguns. Not a single plasma rifle was left upon the caged shelving.

The AI mothership would soon be close enough to either attempt to board the lifeship, or destroy it – providing they could get by the control field, into which the humans now directed most the ship's power. Ystil.3 had no doubt the Apex would succeed in doing so. At its peak life, the Hyperborea was impenetrable, Lydia had told him once. Now she was old and derelict in parts and Ystil.3 suspected the control field barrier was not as efficient in some areas as it was in others.

They'll see through the cracks and blast their way in.

Lydia thrust the last of the T-pistols into the hands of a young militia at the front of a line. "Here, kid," she said, being purposefully condescending. "Don't hurt yourself while you're playing with that."

The boy was skinny and short. He took the gun almost reverently and looked down at it. He smiled with a face full of angry red acne. "I'll defend the Hyperborea until my last breath," he said.

Her mouth formed a thin line. "Yes, you will."

The boy moved aside to be fitted into his hardsuit and combat armour. The smile never faltered on his face. He was pleased to be able to die for his people, Ystil.3 realised. He envied the boy because he would never be pleased to die for his people. Perhaps I'll die for the humans instead, he thought. That might please me more.

Soon there were no more weapons, yet the line of humans still grew, each waiting for their chance to die for their people. Lydia told them to report to their team officers for instruction and the fear visibly spread among them, like a contagion. Ystil.3 thought perhaps they would shout, complain or something. But they didn't. They feared the AI and not being able to defend themselves and those they loved, but it was clear they also feared Lydia. She was right in thinking they saw her as separate from them – as something different, something dangerous. And she was. She was unique.

"Where are all the plasma rifles?" she complained to the bridge over comm as soon as the line broke. "Were people taking two each before we arrived or something? Collister has shit for brains if he thought people would just take one and then march off. Now we've got people unarmed and useless." Whoever was on the other end must have said something she didn't like because she made a clucking noise and her jaw tightened. "This is bullshit. We've trained for this over and over and it's going to shit the only time it matters." She paused. "Yeah, you tell him I said that. Also, tell him that I have to do this instead of something useful, like actual fighting, because of his fuck up. This isn't over."

Their next stop was the civilian holdings deep in the heart of the lifeship. The CH was where the most vulnerable civilians were taken for their own protection – those that couldn't fight. It was the most protected part of the lifeship, Lydia explained. The ship's elevator system had its power reinstated to make movement easier during the emergency; power was a precious thing and conserved when possible. They travelled in the small box up to level ten, section K – the very centre of the Hyperborea.

Outside of the swarming Underbelly the ship was mostly desolate. People had by now either made their way to the militia for conscription orders or, if they could not fight, to the CH. Level ten, section K was close to the hyperdrive engine rooms and housed the maintenance workers' quarters, but they didn't pass a single soul as they strode through the causeways. The ship's power had been restricted to emergency. Only a sallow emergency light lit the way ahead.

The CH was a stark contrast to the abandoned causeways. Humans brimmed to capacity. They huddled in groups, talking in hushed voices as shrouded Brotherhood of Man devotees, led by Brother Vaxus, handed out comfort and warm protein gruel. He gave Lydia a serene smile as they passed and his eyes lingered on Ystil.3, meeting his for an uncomfortable moment. Through the panic, the disciples all seemed to be so calm. They floated around the rooms, seeing to the hungry and soothing the panic-stricken.

They moved on, through the causeways that siphoned off to rooms full of children, their carers calming them with games, others with babies sleeping in rows of incubators, oblivious to what was happening around them. Farther on, through corridors of bunkers, they came across a door, guarded by no less than eight armed men.

"Stand down," Lydia said authoritatively upon approaching them. The guards shifted uncomfortably in their places, the way the humans seemed to do in Lydia's presence. The one at the front kept his eyes forward but made no contact with Lydia's.

"Sir, we're under orders to not let anybody into this room under any circumstances," he said. "Especially that, sir." He looked to Ystil.3.

"By whose orders?" Lydia asked icily. She let him feel the full blast of her stare.

"XO Collister, sir."

"XO Collister may be second in command of this ship, but as you well know I am the li. Now move away before I make you sterile with all my radiation."

A worried wave danced over the soldier's face, but he stiffened in resolve, his seven friends firmly behind him. "I'm sorry, sir. It's more than my life's worth to let that in here. You may enter once I've put in a confirmation with the XO, but the AI stays out here."

Lydia gritted her teeth. "I'm sorry, Private, is it?" she asked.

"Corporal," the man said. "Corporal Manse."

"Well, Corporal Manse, you will not be contacting the XO about anything and you will step aside by the time I count to three and place your plasma rifles on the ground along with your visor comm systems, and you will let Winston and me into that room, or you will find out exactly what being the li truly means. Do you understand me, Corporal?" She smiled.

Private Manse's face blanched under his visor and his eyes shifted in their sockets. "Please, sir. The XO will have my guts out."

"One."

"Sir, I can't disobey a direct order. Ask me anything and I'll tell you. No one said I couldn't tell anyone about it."

"Tell anyone about what?" Lydia snapped.

Manse winced. "Nothing."

"Two."

"About what he's been shouting." The man's voice was strained.

"Charlie. He's been shouting stuff in there."

"Shouting? You mean talking through the speaker system?" It had been almost a century since the man had communicated that way. The first li had rigged it up. Even back then, what came out of Charlie's head was indecipherable.

The soldier made a shallow shake of his head.

"Through his own mouth? What did he say?"

"Activate the white rings. He was saying it over and over. He stopped for a while and then started again. He says it every few hours like he's trying to get people's attention. The Captain and the XO came down but what with the battle no one's been down since."

"Activate the white rings," Lydia echoed. She turned to Ystil.3. "On Thebes." She turned back to the guards ready to force her way through, but they had all placed their plasma rifles and comm visors on the ground. She picked up two, handed one to Ystil.3 and stormed through.

*

Prometheus sat opposite Captain Lu and General Shaw in a cramped room off what he guessed to be the helm of a ship. As they had walked through, the crew were deep in battle mode, sat at machines and surrounded by curtains of light that moved like waves of glowing water.

The Prometheus that had trained him said he should expect to see things beyond his imaginings, but to not concern himself with it. "It is the mission that matters," he'd said. But he was a simple man from a simple time, surrounded by unfathomable wonders. He looked at them the way a child looks at the world, without any understanding, but with marvel.

The Captain of this ship Prometheus took to be a woman, but he could very well have been mistaken, such was her masculine nature. She hadn't allowed his army to exit the black vessel in which they had arrived, which was perfectly fine by him, as, from what he had gleaned from conversations, the General was presently planning to return to the black ship with an armed force to gain entry to the enemy craft. If this was indeed the case, then the black ship was exactly where he needed to be, with his soldiers aboard.

They didn't trust him. He understood that. At first, he hadn't trusted them either. As anyone can imagine, it seemed rather queer having an army of one's self to command as one saw fit, but it actually seemed to work rather well. Although each of the Prometheuses was slightly different to the other in some infinitesimal way, whether it be the scowl upon his lip or the tear in his eye, all were fundamentally him and so he knew what it took to get what he needed from them – which was mainly determination to complete their task and, of course, their complete trust. That was the hardest thing to gain, as he knew well it would be, but they all mellowed a touch after having their final night with their Sarah, and after that, as was the case with himself, they were ready to put right the wrongs they had done. That's when the training began. As he had been trained in the art of combat, so he trained each of them. Not as leaders, but as an army that could think and act as one steel fist.

The first task to overcome was his; he had to treat them all as individuals instead of one person. Over time he came to recognise the differences between them and gradually began to call them all by an individual number – P1 to P123. There were more of them to begin with, but things transpired and the number whittled down to just over one hundred bodies. Some of the Prometheuses never returned from their visit with Sarah, some never even made it at all. Others vanished into the wilderness where Death had brought them, the vast cracked desert of eternal night, while some refused to do anything at all, curling upon the ground until they simply disappeared. And then some died during training. Others were simply not up to scratch and he couldn't risk the mission by taking them. In the end, their number stood at one hundred and twenty-three. One hundred and twenty-three men – all with the same goal and all with the same passion driving them.

The Captain didn't like the answers to her questions, but there it was. He knew nothing of the machines of which they spoke – the artificial intelligence – other than he was here to help stop them and to put right the deaths done wrong, as Death had told him repeatedly. Also, to learn the deaths done right. That part still confused him. How is a death ever done right? It was a riddle, and unfortunately, he'd never been very good at them.

"Let us go through it one more time if you please," Captain Lu said. She was incessantly updated through her communications device and had just finished shouting another barrage of commands to some small-voiced person on the other end. "How was it you came to find yourself on Thebes, and what do you know of the gate you came through?" He was about to protest and the woman raised a hand. "If you'll please humour me, sir."

"I came through the portal as instructed," Prometheus said. He ran a finger up and down the smooth scar that scored his cheek. He found he did that sometimes since he'd acquired it. It was a badge. A reminder.

"Instructed by the lost spirits of the human race?" she offered, repeating what he'd said before.

"Yes. The spirits found each other in the void. They are the consequence of a formula known to you as the White Drops. When humanity was destroyed, their bodies were also destroyed, but still, they did not die. The White Drops, which had extended their lives and saved them from illness and death, caused them to continue to exist without form. Heaven would not take them, apparently."

Captain Lu and General Shaw glanced at one another. The talk of heaven was something they both were unused to, it seemed.

"They wandered in the timelessness, found each other and bound together to become what they are now. They learnt things in the dark, so it says, and travelled to places and times eternal. Death taught me, it instructed me and it saved me."

"Why do you call it Death?" General Shaw asked, his tone prickly. He suspected the man blamed him somewhat for the destruction of his planet. And he was right, in a way.

"That is the form it takes," Prometheus said. "It has taken the image of Death because it longs for Death, because it cannot reach the peace of Death for which it terribly yearns."

"Did it tell you anything of the ring portal under the surface of Thebes? The one you came through?" Captain Lu asked.

"No."

She didn't like that answer, the same as she hadn't liked it the first two times he'd told her. "And what of—"

"I'm not here to answer your questions and sate your curiosity," Prometheus interrupted calmly. "I'm asking you to let us help. There are many of us and we are expendable, while your people are not. Without them, our race is finished and I will not be responsible for that. I'm here as a tool to help you win against the machines, the AI, and to put right what I have done."

"And what is it exactly you've done?" General Shaw said. He glowered over the desk.

"I destroyed it all," Prometheus replied simply. "Through my selfish actions, I brought about this future. That is all you need to know."

There was a knock at the door and a man entered. He was breathless from running.

"Manse," General Shaw said. "What is it?"

"We've got a situation with Charlie," the man said. "Winston has entered his cabin. Took our rifles and comm systems and just walked right in."

"Alone?" the General asked.

The man shook his head. "With the li."

Charles. Prometheus felt his blood quiver with abysmal guilt. The Prometheus that had trained him said the guilt would serve him no good. It was action he needed now. And he was right.

Prometheus stood. "I must see the man. I must see what I've done."

*

Gutter's face was grey and slick with sweat. The doctors could do nothing to bring down his temperature and told Daneel the only thing left to do was wait. They took blood samples to their labs in the Brain, leaving them alone in a quarantine room within the dimly lit Infirmary. He doubted, however, they'd even looked at those samples; pilots injured in the battle had besieged the cubicles and anyone with medical training was ordered to fix them up and get them back into battle as soon as possible. So, Daneel could do nothing but watch the ripples of heat steam off his friend's fevered skin, and wait.

The flesh around the bite – now a hollow crater of missing flesh – had turned a deep purple and branched with dark veins. Each time he looked at it his eyes watered with guilt. It was his fault.

And then there was the battle. Daneel's feet were itching to be a part of it. Yeah, he could fly a Wing, but was no pilot – he'd never officially passed the test, scraping just under the required points. There was always someone telling him what he couldn't do, or that he wasn't good enough. Even doctor Jameson had tried to make him wait outside the quarantine cabin, but Daneel forced his way in regardless. "I've been on the junkfucking planet," he barked at the man, "what exactly am I gonna catch in that room that I couldn't catch down there?"

He thought of that thing wrapping its mouth around Gutter's arm and tearing a bloody chunk free. More guilt. Maybe he wasn't ready for the mission. He wanted Gutter to have the opportunity to get on, to make the most of his full potential. He didn't want to be the reason Gutter stayed a private like he stayed a Corporal. I pushed him before he was ready. But there was nothing he could do for his friend now. Sitting there in that room and staring at the holoscreen monitor wasn't going to help anyone or change anything. Gutter wouldn't want that. He'd want Daneel to be in the thick of it, tearing the AI a new slit.

"I'm sorry, Gut," he said, standing from the chair beside the crib, "Gotta go. The General's on this crazy ass mission to get everyone killed so, you know, I thought I'd see what's going on with that." He laughed. "You sit this one out. I'll tell you all about it when we get back, once we've blown these junkfuckers back to the metal shit hole they came from."

He turned and left, walking quickly through the rows of beds in the main part of the Infirmary. All the cubicles were occupied so beds had been stationed in the halls for any overspill. Only a few were occupied, but at once he recognised the first face lying bloodied upon a white sheet.

"McCall," he said. The man was a mess. The remnants of what used to be his left arm had been staunched by a tournbelt capped over a stump. A red light on the tournbelt turned green momentarily to signal that a hit of sedative had been administered. "What happened to you?"

The man swooned. "Just a scratch." His eyes drooped as though he were drifting into unconsciousness, so Daneel moved on. "They're not piloted," McCall called out. It was a loud, panic-filled statement.

Daneel turned. "What?"

"The AI Bugs, they're not piloted. The Bugs are the AI. How are we supposed to outfly something like that? We weren't prepared for that. I just got hands." He looked down at his stump. "I had hands. They were on us like junkfucking predators. We were in formation. We did everything we were supposed to. I've never seen anything like it. They took us out one by one. I only managed to get back because I broke formation and bolted." The man laughed, or cried, Daneel wasn't sure. "I ran like a scared child. They're all gone. Lee, Wang, Malone, Rey, George, Yip. Only me left." His eyes glazed over as the tournbelt light turned green again, sending another calming shot into his bloodstream.

"Do you want me to get some help?" Daneel said.

"No one can help us now. It's… suicide…" His eyes rolled back into his head and a second later he was unconscious.

Daneel walked on, quicker than before. He had a suicide to get to.

*

The man was just as Ystil.3 had seen him before, age-raped and worn down, like a piece of sand-stone battered by time until all that was left was a fragile mound of dust. In another hundred years or so the man would be dust, and probably still alive in whatever form was left of him. And yet, acrid breath weaved in and out his lungs and a pallid heartbeat wrapped faintly on the inside of his paper-thin chest. If the man ever decided to lift those limbs of his, they would surely snap off at the brittle joints, even in the reduced gravity of his cabin.

Someone had pulled his sheet up under his chin, leaving only the remnants of his head visible – a piece of mouldy fruit, full of holes and collapsing in from rot. The familiar hissing continued to leak through the lipless, toothless, tongue-less cave of a mouth.

He, Lydia and Dr Regus stood silently, waiting eagerly for words to come from that mouth.

Ystil.3's infrared had confirmed what he suspected, that Charlie emitted the same blue mist that smoked from the earth beneath Thebes' burned crust. The very same mist that also appeared around General Shaw, and radiated from Lydia's li Pendant – not from her directly as he had first thought. Together, he and Lydia watched the blue mist fill the room like a dense fog.

Despite Dr Regus being unable to see what they saw, the man was quick enough to draw a link almost immediately. "The White Drops. It's the only thing that makes sense. General Shaw took it, there was a store of it on Thebes during the Reset and it's rumoured the concoction itself was derived from Charlie's blood. My guess is that this mist is, as Winston suggested, a sort of radiation by-product of the mutation process brought on by the substance." The cogs of thought turned behind the man's eyes. "We know about Charlie's mutation, similarly in the case of General Shaw, and it is also clearly apparent in those poor, loathsome creatures down on Thebes. But the interesting thing to consider now is, if the mist is also emitted from Thebes itself, what mutation has occurred in the earth of the planet?"

"Computronium," Ystil.3 said. "The black stuff excreted from the burned men could be Computronium. It's in the very substance of the servers and the Black Betty's alloy hull. It allows the AI mind to inhabit the material directly, on an atomic level, not just in wires and silicon. I'd always thought Sir Z had no server at all, but what if he does. What if his server is the planet itself? Is that the type of mutation that would cause the radiation signal?"

Dr Regus nodded. "That could be it."

The door opened and in walked Captain Lu and General Shaw, followed by Prometheus. Captain Lu's jaw was firm-set and her mouth a thin line of disapproval below her pale stare. Lydia saluted.

"At ease," the woman said. "Would you mind explaining why you decided to undermine a direct order and enter this room?"

"No one ordered me not to enter—" Lydia began, but was cut dead.

"Hold your tongue," the Captain said. "You may be the li, but how long do you think you can keep this up before you start to seriously compromise our people's safety? This is one too many times you've acted like a reckless child, bringing here." Those pale eyes washed over Ystil.3. "You know they want Charlie and still you—" The Captain stopped, her face taking on an expression of naked horror.

Ystil.3 turned and the others did the same. Impossible as it was, it sounded like a voice had come from his mouth.

"Hello?" the voice said. It was small and croaked through layers of disintegrating throat. The strangest thing, though, was that Charlie's lips didn't move at all, as though the voice was somehow coming through him. "Activate the white rings," it said. "To save Earth you must activate the white rings."

Ystil.3 stepped forward. "That voice. I know that voice." The singing Welsh lilt. "Tom?"

Charlie lay unchanged upon his bed, as still and lifeless as ever. "Activate the white rings," Tom's voice came again.

Ystil.3 rushed up to Charlie, bending close to his face. "It came from his mouth. How is this possible? Tom, Tom can you hear me? It's Ystil.3." The sound of his name said with a human tongue sounded like a series of splattering noises. "It's... me, Tom. I thought you'd been deleted."

"Hello?" Tom said through Charlie's gaping mouth.

"He can't hear me," Ystil.3 turned to the others. They had gathered around the bed.

"You know who that voice belongs to?" Captain Lu asked him.

"It's Tom, the owner of the CorVac form aboard the Black Betty... the one I asked to enter the BroadWeb to find information on Lydia. He's my friend. Why can't he hear me? Tom."

"You need to speak into the headset," Dr Regus said. "The body's ears have worn to nothing and don't work. The headset allows you to speak directly to the part of the brain, what's left of it, that understands language."

He grabbed the headset by the bed and slipped the microphone piece over his head. "Tom," he said excitedly. "Can you hear me?"

There was silence. And then, "I hear you. Who in the name of Tom Jones is this?"

50

Charlie removed his hand from my head, and my vision returned, like emerging from a tunnel of light until once again I sat under the twinkling stars deep within the root-woven burrow. I blinked as the vision of the blonde child blurred in my sight and then sharpened suddenly. The smells of Earth returned, heady and musty. The wind blew cold against my skin and the fire crackled, warming my face in the buried darkness.

Charlie smiled. "You did well. We did what we needed and now we have a real chance of bringing my children home."

His children. He meant the humans.

"How can you smile?" I said. His screams haunted me still as we sat in the quiet. They reverberated like knives when we entered his real-time body, and each time we failed I wanted to stop from the mere memory of it. Charlie would take the pain that came with entering his body, while I was free to tell the humans what they needed to do.

"It doesn't hurt now," the boy said. "You knew the people there, didn't you, where my body is? I managed to perceive that much at least."

"Ystil.3," I said. "I was sure he'd been deleted like the others. Funny. He was sure the same had happened to me."

"And you're certain you told them everything I said?" His eyes contained the dancing flames of the fire.

I nodded. "To activate the rings on Thebes and Pisces and that we'll do the rest."

"They'll do it?" he asked eagerly.

"Yes. Ystil.3 said he would. But they are under attack now from Z, the Hydra, I mean. It will be difficult, but they'll do it. I also told him what happened in the BroadWeb. His home is gone. His server will soon be gone too, but I didn't tell him that."

"Why not?" Charlie asked. Despite being as old as time, there was a naive innocence in him that sparkled through those eyes. It almost made him seem like a real little boy, just occasionally.

"Because he's going to die and I don't want him to be frightened," I said. It was something.

"You're sad about that." It wasn't a question. "Why are you helping me then, if it means the death of your friend?"

"Because it's what he would want. Because he's helping the humans too. Because what the Hydra is doing... has done, and will do... will mean the end of all life except its own."

"Perhaps not the end of AI life, though," Charlie said. "It may still have use for you."

I nodded. "And it will put Betty and me back in foetal mode and then we won't be us anymore. We'll be whatever it is Z wants us to be. I won't know Betty and I won't know me because we won't exist anymore. Instead of me, they'll be the fresh AI with fresh programming and an AI mind full of whatever fresh lies we've been told so that we complete another mission of death compliantly. It's happened before, just like Nyx said." I shook my head with a conviction that surprised even me. "No. I will be me, or I will be nothing."

Charlie stood and wrapped his furs tighter around his bare skin. I barely felt the cold now as I gazed into the fire. When I looked up it was morning and we were sat around the fire of the camp Norse and I had made. Betty was galloping towards us from the distant trees at the edge of the wide clearing and Norse emerged from the shelter with eyes full of sleep.

"Morning," he said, stifling a yawn, completely casual to the fact that Charlie stood by my side. "So you've had the talk then. Do you think he'll be able to do it?"

"It's already done," Charlie replied.

Norse's eyes widened and the sleep fell away instantly. "Well, I guess it wasn't for nothing then. Does that mean I can stay here now?"

"I don't know what will happen when we cross over," the boy replied. "But I'm happy for you to remain, whatever the outcome."

I knew, as well as Charlie did, that the AI servers would be destroyed in the process of putting Earth back its place and therefore Norse would be permanently deleted. I guess Charlie wanted to spare him the fear, like I wanted to spare Ystil.3.

Norse had taken to carrying Bo around in a small conch shell he'd found at the beach. He'd tied it around his neck and Bo would occasionally poke his green head out and look around. He did so now, seeming to stare at Charlie.

Betty nudged me affectionately with her muzzle and I patted her neck the way she liked. "Sorry. I didn't have time to wake you. But it's okay. I've done what I was brought here to do and now we can go home."

"You still can't filter back into your real-time forms," said Norse.

I glared at him in annoyance. "Thank you, I'm aware. I meant that… I don't know what I meant." I turned to Charlie. "What's going to happen to us when it, you know, happens?"

"In truth, I'm not certain. In theory, it should be the same as filtering into your bodies. The Earth's physicality is locked in the information here. It came with it all in store. It's not like the other planets, whose surfaces were destroyed in the energy fallout from opening the C-gates. Earth was not burned. We simply came here instead, which is why we should be able to go back."

"So we could be destroyed in the process, like those planets?" Norse asked.

"No," Charlie replied. "Not at all. The reason the planets' surfaces were scorched was simply the result of the C-gates punching open the time holes."

"So that will happen again?" Norse asked. "The server planet's surface will be destroyed?"

"It's possible."

Norse nodded. "So I guess I won't be staying after all."

"What will happen to you?" I asked Charlie.

"Possibly the same as what will happen to you, in that I will return to my physical form. Either that or I will remain infused with the Earth."

"But it's awful in your body. Why would you risk that?"

Charlie shrugged the shrug of a little boy. "We'll do anything for our children's survival."

Within the hour we left the camp that had become our home, after packing the few things we needed for the journey. This included the remaining dried meat and few berries we'd stored, as well as the shelter, which we dismantled and furled up to load onto Betty.

For the remainder of the morning and all afternoon we followed Charlie through the thick of the jungle, into the pungent and stifling heat, with the rain clouds above the canopy dripping little drops of wet refreshment that would sometimes fall onto my parched skin, having made it through the layers of branches, vines and leaves above. Norse and I took turns in riding Betty, although he often cut his short when he saw I was struggling. We stopped wherever there was water and Charlie showed us which berries and plants to forage to make the most of the supplies we had. Charlie knew where everything was; every stream, every tree and every fruit-bearing bush. But it was never enough to fill my aching stomach, and the constant hunger was making me very irritable.

The sun began to die and my feet were swollen and cut from walking, the leaf wrappings torn and hanging off. Betty's mouth lathered from a few hard rides carrying both Norse and myself and Bo, who remained cosily inside his conch shell around Norse's neck. Charlie sometimes said he would meet us a few miles ahead, disappearing on the spot and reappearing later.

When Betty was too tired to ride any farther we set up camp in a small clearing, ignited a fire from some wood we'd collected throughout the day and ate a few bites of the dried boar meat before settling under the leaf-woven roof propped over a low-hanging branch. Before the fire began to diminish, I was fast asleep, dreaming strange dreams again.

I dreamed of Apex Soldiers as tall as trees with virus thorns as long as branches, the leaves dripping with venom onto a graveyard of AI, frozen still inside their bodies like statues – like tombs. We were on Delilah and I rode on Betty's back. She had the rear end of a horse and the front end of her BroadWeb form, like the ship's ornament when we travelled through potential space; a smooth dark humanoid shape, slender and marvellous. The venom dripped and we galloped through the AI dead, dodging them and the virulent drops that now poured down like rain. They missed me somehow but washed Betty in its poison. She collapsed and turned to stone under me and the grief in my heart was overwhelming. Darkness shadowed overhead and I looked up to see the smiling mouths of a five-headed snake.

I woke up sweating as the sun just peeked through the trees in the warm pink morning. Charlie had either sat there the entire night, or had just appeared when I awoke, but he sat staring at me, sitting across the dead fire. Within minutes we were all awake and on the move again.

I never asked why Charlie couldn't just move us to our destination the way he had transported me from the underground grove back to camp. Perhaps I had never even moved from the camp at all. It could have just been a dream or a vision in my head implanted there by him. But in the BroadWeb, what was the difference? I had to remind myself now and then that this wasn't real-time, no matter how well Charlie had kept Earth's data preserved. When my legs ached from the day's walk, they didn't really ache. And when I felt I would pass out from hunger, I had to remember that I wasn't really hungry. In the rivers and streams that we crossed, I looked into the clear cold water, but it wasn't really Tom Jones looking back at me. So, when we walked, we weren't truly walking. But we were travelling.

On the second day, we left the jungle and crossed a vast plain, and on the third day we wandered through desert. The desert lasted possibly for weeks, it seemed – the heat scolded all sense from my brain to accurately tell. If it weren't for Charlie bringing the rains we might have perished in the sand, with the blasting wind to pick our bones clean and the sun to bleach them white. Did I even have bones under this façade of skin? Could we even die? When I looked to Betty's foamy muzzle, thirsting, and her legs shaking with fatigue, I feared we could.

Norse bore the torturous sun in fastidious silence, and Bo remained hidden in the conch shell around his neck, emerging only at night to feast on the bugs that swarmed the light of our campfire and play us his cricket song. Charlie was, as ever, unfazed by everything, appearing and disappearing as and when he liked. I found myself getting angry when he vanished, thinking he'd gone to some cool place full of bursting streams of fresh water to drink. But when the rains came I fell to my knees and thanked him like a god.

Soon the desert sand turned red and that night Charlie told me we would reach our destination the next morning. Norse had taken Betty in hopes of finding more snakes to cook on the fire and Charlie and I sat alone. The nights in the desert would get cold. During the day, I wished for the night; we would use the leaf-woven roof from our shelter as portable shade. But during the night, I wished for the warmth of the day. I shivered next to the fire and Charlie offered me his fur. I took it and wrapped it around myself, leaving him naked with the flames dancing over his face. He didn't feel the cold, it seemed. He stared into the fire, pensively.

"I look into the flames and I'm back at my father's cottage," he said suddenly, breaking the sound of my chattering teeth. "Sitting to escape the chill of the sea-churned wind that persistently battered it. I felt safe there, by the fire with his fur blankets around my shoulders and a mug of warmed milk with dunking biscuits made by Mrs Tapper, the nice old lady from the post office in the nearest village. My father would read to me. Treasure Island, I would say, when he would ask what book. Always it was Treasure Island. He must have been so bored of it, but he read it, over and over, his sad eyes moving over every line and down each page. 'Poor widowed Dr Page', Mrs Tapper would call him when she didn't think anyone but her husband could hear. My father tried his best to feign happiness for my sake, though I always knew the truth. But as he read to me and as I watched the flames, tasting the crunchy sugar of Mrs Tapper's short-biscuits in my mouth, I could convince myself and I could smile as if it weren't a lie. It was the last time I was truly happy."

"What happened to him?" I asked through the fire.

"He died that winter," Charlie said. "He just shut down, and I was left alone to discover things about myself that I'm sure he meant to tell me. I guess he thought he would have more time. Funds had been arranged for me and I was promptly told by his lawyers that I was to go to a public school to be educated. By then I was almost twelve, yet I looked barely five years old.

"I knew I was different and my father had always told me that I couldn't act too grown-up around other people, but even then, they would always comment on how mature I was, how gifted. I asked my father once why the other children I'd met weren't like me and he simply replied 'because you're special'. If he'd only told me the truth before he died I wouldn't have spent the years I did searching for the answers he had so readily.

"At my new school I had to pretend every hour of every day, and I hated it. I hated having to converse with children much younger than me, and whenever I attempted to broach any sort of stimulating conversation with a teacher they would laugh at me as though I'd said something incredibly funny. I suppose I looked ridiculous spouting politics from the mouth of a child. Still, I was considered very gifted for my age and after a year I was moved ahead three years and labelled a genius by a man who tested me relentlessly for an entire day. The older kids hated me more than the younger ones had.

"After five years, approaching seventeen yet now in the body of small ten-year-old, questions were being asked about why I didn't age typically… by me as well as others. I ran away from my London school, back to my father's cottage in Cornwall. I managed to stay a while, reading all of his books and stealing food from the local farmer's market. No one bothered me as long as I hid from the locals and the occasional knock on the cottage door.

"Then the war came. It was the perfect time to become an orphan in rural Britain. Lots of children had been moved out of the cities and towns and I became one of them, herded up and sent to a farmhouse in Devonshire where no one would recognise me. Most of the time we were given chores, which was fine by me, and I did my best to work around the house or lend my hand on the farm when I could. The other children didn't bother me much. When the war ended, knowing I was an orphan, the farmer and his wife, who had no children of their own, arranged for me to remain with them. Farmer Woodhouse intended for me to take over the farm, like a son, and Mrs Woodhouse had long treated me like her child. It would have been a good life, and it was, for seven years at least. But once again they started to notice that I didn't grow as fast as was normal. Inside, I was now in my mid-twenties, with the ego and urges that come with it, yet on the outside I looked just on the shy side of hitting puberty, when I should have looked well into my late teens, according to the farmer. I bought another few years there before they started talking to doctors, and then I knew I had no choice but to leave.

"Again, I returned to my father's cottage, finding it lived in by strangers, however. I guess my father's lawyers had declared me dead after I'd gone missing and sold off his assets. I made my way back to London, thinking I would be lost in a sea of faces and no one would even notice me. I was right. London paid no mind to a skinny and ragged-looking beggar child. I made my way by sleeping where I could, under bridges and in poor houses that slept fifty to one room. I got by with the wits of a man approaching thirty. I stole… food, money, whatever I could get my hands on. It was hard, but no one bothered me and no one made me feel like I wasn't normal. I went on like this for a while until I eventually looked like a young man. I found trouble more easily then, being of a decent height with ripened anatomy to successfully woo the girls of London.

"By the time World War Two broke I looked old enough to be conscripted into the army, a young man by anyone's eyes, but with a soul of almost forty. It was during the war that something happened to me which changed the course of my life.

"I found I had a knack for being a soldier. At first I was a back-chatting smart-aleck, having lived the last few years answering to no one. But when the war was truly underway, what I saw smacked that out of me. I watched men I fought alongside die terribly, the first friends I had ever known in my life. Still, by the end, I believed in the war we were fighting and I was a different man. I saw the horrors of what men could do to each other and it changed me. The men I fought with, my friends, they changed me too.

"I was hit during the Normandy Landings. I had managed to make my way through the entire war with cuts and scrapes that amounted to nothing. But not this day. As the twenty-four thousand allied troops, me among them, touched the Normandy shore to liberate France, after having landed in the cold Channel after midnight, swimming to the coast and then trudging Omaha beach against a wall of German soldiers in a mist of blood and screams, I remember the sharp cold punch to the back of my head through my helmet. I fell into blackness, the sand filling my mouth as the cold spread. I'd been hit by a piece of raining shrapnel.

"I should have died there that day, probably should have died long before, but I awoke what must have been the next day, surrounded by the fallen. German and ally bodies alike overwhelmed the sand, the beach steeped in curling sea mist and the remnants of barrel smoke, creating a veil of white that washed everything in pallid light. I felt the back of my head, my wound had healed over and the shrapnel ejected from my skull. Once again I had been declared dead by my country, my fake identity gone now, along with my real one.

"I eventually made it back to the shores of England and it was easy to feign amnesia. I was put in a hospital in Brighton with others that couldn't remember who they were. There I met a girl, a nurse called Agatha." Charlie smiled in sweet reverie, looking at me over the fire.

"I returned to London under yet another identity, a name given to me by Agatha. She called me Clark, after I reminded her of Clark Gable in an old movie they'd shown in the hospital one night, Gone with the Wind. I chose my own surname, Omaha, after the beach where I died. Where I should have died. So, as Clark Omaha I returned to London, determined to finish my education and make something more of the life that I thought had been blessed for a second chance.

"Throughout my entire existence I had read constantly... all the books of my father, the medical and philosophical, fiction and history. I read them all. And with the knowledge I had acquired over my lifetime I managed to find employment as a Lecturer's assistant at the Royal College of Surgeons of England. There I learned all I could from lectures and private lessons I'd convinced my mentor, Dr Bathurst, to tutor me, showing him both my thirst for knowledge, intellect and lack of funds to enter the college by my own means.

"Finally, as a young man, no one noticed so much that I didn't age, and after seven years under Dr Bathurst's wing, I graduated the college and found a position as a surgeon in New York in what was then the pre-reformed Americas.

"Twenty years later and I had established the country's leading medical and pharmaceutical research and development company. Omaha Research, I called it. This move into research was spurred by something that happened in New York. Five years previous I was stabbed in a street robbery. The young Irishman plunged the knife into my stomach and made off with my money and watch. I bled out on the street, surrounded by startled faces and women with big hair… it was the 1960s. But I didn't lose consciousness. When the ambulance arrived I'd already realised that the wound had stopped bleeding and had completely healed. I stood and ran, pushing through the crowd and the paramedics on their way to the pool of blood I'd left on the pavement of 59th and 5th. I realised then that I couldn't die.

"My life took a rather dark turn after that. I experimented with the limits of my own healing and imperviousness to death. I found no matter how I mutilated my own flesh, it would heal completely within a matter of hours, not even leaving a scar as evidence. I only took my experimentations so far. I stopped at removing my own limbs, sure that I would heal, but unsure if the limb itself would re-grow. If I was to throw myself into some machinery that could tear me to sunders, what would have happened to me? I don't know and I didn't attempt to find that out either.

"I believe the total destruction of my body would not have killed me, rather trap me in some place of limbo. That frightened me beyond anything, and soon I found myself thinking beyond the moral realms of good and evil, with punishments and rewards in the afterlife. After all, I would never get there. I never had the niggling feeling in the back of my mind that most mortal humans have that questioned, what if?

"I became certain of my resistance to death after dowsing myself in gas and setting myself on fire in an abandoned factory. I remember the pain even now, and long after names and faces of my past faded, as I became a prisoner in my own decaying body, I remembered that pain like it was seared fresh into my skin. I awoke on the factory floor with most of my flesh burned away, charred black, or melted from bone. For another day, I couldn't move from the pain, so I waited to heal. I couldn't breathe and I became convinced I would die from suffocation, but as I slipped in and out of consciousness I realised that I wouldn't. Then after days I could breathe again and my limbs didn't scream so much when I moved.

"When I returned home to my apartment under cover of night, I looked into a mirror to find my hair burned and gone, and my skin like a melted plastic mask that covered my face, with two lidless eyes looking out in horror. It took an entire week for me to heal completely, and by that time I was done with those types of experiments. Next came the how?

"For years I experimented with my own blood and flesh samples using resources from Omaha Research. I kept at the cutting edge of science, taking the company through the 1980s, 90s, the millennium, 2010s up to 2050, growing the company and finding new developments to better understand myself, all the while posing as my own son and then my own grandson.

"The company eventually became so large that I had no choice but to hire people to help run it, and soon centres were established around the world, including London. Even if I weren't constantly preoccupied with my condition, overseeing all the departments and R&D labs that had branched out would have been impossible. Approaching the end of the century, Omaha Research had shareholders, and it soon became Life Corporation under the advisement of the board of directors. Being my own grandson, Rhet Omaha, I retained my title of chief executive officer and continued with my own research.

"By 2120 my body appeared to be well into its fifties, while my true age was two hundred and nineteen years old. By this time, I had accumulated wealth beyond what I ever expected… or wanted. It afforded me a certain amount of privacy, but at the same time drew the attention of other companies, as well as newsprints and web media. I soon became known as a recluse after taking myself and my private studies back to Britain at last, where I set up home in Scotland on a vast estate with no one but the house staff to bother me.

"I kept myself immersed in Life Corp research, but alas found myself ousted from the company further and further with regards to the business and how it was run. Little did I know, but the company had set up two subsidiaries for weapons research and manufacturing; I didn't find out about this until much later, and by that time I found I had virtually no power to affect anything Life Corp did anymore.

"My research in Scotland soon involved a small team of the brightest minds from around the world. We looked into everything from genetics to stem cells and splicing, to RNAing long dead species in attempts to find out why some species inevitably become extinct while others do not, and of course telomere degradation hypothesis. We looked into bimolecular gene therapy and Mendel's Laws, as well as mutations in evolution and gene pools and genomes, and of course rapid cell regeneration. With my team, I built upon years of research and experiments, taking it to new levels, all while keeping my secret. No one ever knew. I never allowed anybody close enough to know.

"Decades seemed to pass in the blink of an eye and I hired new teams to replace the old, carrying on from where the others had left off. By the year 2350, I was my own great-great-great-grandson, Charles Omaha… once again using my real first name. Fake documents were always easy to come by, even more so as the world turned to digital encoding instead of paper…

easy for me with money, at least. My body was approaching its winter years and I soon began to wonder what would happen to me as I continued to grow older. I hoped perhaps my body would naturally die.

"It was the year of my breakthrough that Life Corp Board members removed me from my 'inherited' position of CEO, on the grounds of gross negligence with regards to the welfare of Life Corp, they said. It's true I hadn't taken much interest and left most of the decisions to those around me, but it seemed I was no longer wanted, or more to the point, began asking too many questions about the shadier dealings of the company.

"Surprisingly, I wasn't too concerned about this and I found I had accumulated enough wealth to fund my own experiments, without the guise of Life Corp… just like I had in the beginning. However, it was Life Corp that had now begun to take an interest in me and my shadier dealings. The more time that passed, the more concerned I became that those I'd hired were actually agents of the company, trying to steal what I had worked so hard for. Eventually, I stopped employing people altogether and my large estate went empty and derelict, save me in my labs. As ever, time went by and I found entire months would pass without me speaking a single word to another living soul."

"Weren't you lonely?" I asked the young boy through the fire. I noticed again that his eyes seemed old, very old within his boy's face.

"Of course, I was," he said with a shrug. "I'm only human. I was only human. At least, I think I was. Eventually, my body was an old man's and living my day-to-day life gradually became harder and harder, until I could no longer actively perform in my labs. Instead, I would sit within a virtual programme that I'd commissioned. The programme was the exact replica of my labs, with every piece of equipment in them and every law of physics to boot. It had scenario precision that meant only that which is possible in real-time was possible in the virtual programme. It was here that I continued my work, hooked onto machines that would feed me and clean me, for I knew that one day I would become so old that I wouldn't even be able to move from my bed.

"The day of my total quiescence came in the year 2507, I think. Not long before that point I was ripped from my holoform programme and taken from my home, which was ransacked, and all my work, my notes, my findings, my successes, all stolen. I was too old to do anything to stop it. I couldn't even move. However, I could still talk, barely."

"It was Life Corp," I said. "They took you and your experiments."

The boy nodded. "In searching for a cure for myself I had inadvertently made it possible for others to use my blood to concoct a serum that would allow others to become like me. The company, of course, saw massive potential in marketing this to the public, and as I withered, this is exactly what they did. Not only that, but with every year I aged, my body stored more and more energy that could be used… that was used, resulting in the Reset. Eventually, blackness came, after being confined in a secure unit at Life Corp's London HQ. And then, pain. Terrible pain spanning lifetimes."

"You never found a cure?" I asked.

"Now, I didn't say that, did I?" Charles said with a somewhat mischievous grin.

By now I could see Norse returning in the distance, the moonlight highlighting the kill he'd made as he rode Betty casually back to camp. "So you did find a cure?" I asked.

"I believe so. I had been working in the holoform virtual programme for many years and had made many discoveries… in theory. Providing the virtual programme calibration to real-time physical law hadn't loosened over time… not trusting anybody to upgrade or maintain the software… I believe I would have been able to cure myself, using, ironically, my own blood, such is the law of counterbalance. But it was too late."

Norse dismounted, clutching two small, limp snakes. "Found us meat," he said heartily, and my stomach growled at once. "What have you been talking about?" he asked as Betty trotted over towards me to say hello.

I patted her muzzle. "You know. Just Tom Jones and stuff."

□

51

The blast missed Daneel's head by less than an inch. He reeled backwards, jarring his shoulder on a stray bulkhead panel that had loosened in the onslaught. He regained awareness and kept flat against what remained of the blasted hatch doors, providing a temporary cover. Beyond, he could hear them moving, hear their screeching metal limbs.

Kandinsky was down, probably dead. She wasn't moving before Daneel had been pushed back from the line. Chung and Xi had disappeared into the smoke and rubble, probably dead now, too. He checked his plasma rifle cartridge levels; three bars left, enough to last another ten minutes of attack on full power, and then… well, he was doubtful he'd even last ten minutes. Major Moa had lasted less than ten seconds before they severed his head with some sort of tight laser. It rolled almost to Daneel's feet before he thought to fire back – the dead man's expression looking up at him, frozen in fear beneath the hardsuit visor that did nothing to protect him. Turns out plasma rifles weren't as effective as hoped.

"Major," Kali whispered over the team's commlink. Daneel had seen Kali pushed back behind the western hatchway. At least he was alive.

"Dead," Daneel replied in a whisper. Kali was a First Private from Razor Squad, which made Daneel top ranking; all the officers were dead or dying. "Sharma here. What's your status?"

"Thank Mother. I thought it was just me left. I'm trapped behind the hatch ridge. I can't see much, but I can hear 'em. Sing is dead, so's Day, blasted right through the chest, hardly nothing left of 'em. I can probably squeeze through the vent system here and escape. What about you?"

"Not an option, Private Kali," Daneel said, hardening the private to emphasise his rank. "We have a job to do and since neither of us is dead and we still have cartridges in our rifles, I fully intend to take down at least one tin-man. Understand, Private?"

"Sir, Corporal," Kali replied stiffly. "But their shields deflect plasma bolts. How are we supposed to take any down when we can't even hit 'em?"

"Their shields can't last forever," Daneel said, feeling something wet trickle down his shoulder. Seems he was hit by something. His suit activated its pressure gauze system to stem the bleeding at once. "The amount of power it takes to absorb each plasma shot means that eventually, it should fail."

"You don't know that. They're AI. They could have an infinite power source for all we junkfucking know."

"I doubt it. Notice how they don't shoot and have their deflection shields active simultaneously, like they only have enough power to run one at a time? That's when they're vulnerable." A twisting metal sound blasted from beyond the hatch. Daneel's stomach lurched and he dropped his volume further. "If we can hit them with a full barrage it will drain their power eventually."

"And by that time we'll be dead. It's crazy, man. I'm getting out of here."

"You stay where you are, Private, that's an order." The cry of twisting metal throttled through the hatch, this time louder. Then the sound of Kali's screams. A plasma rifle fired once, and then more screams.

Daneel moved before he even had time to think. He sprang from the blown hatch back into the destroyed solar deck. He ran towards the still body of Moa, ripped free the man's plasma rifle and jumped up onto what was once a giant ocular telescope more than four times his height. He remembered spending time in the upper level solar as a child, wondering why he had to study the stars when they always changed whenever the Hyperborea moved on. He climbed the melted frame up to one of the exposed air ducts, before springing up and sliding inside just as Kali's screams finally stopped.

The AI returned to the solar, he could hear them moving below. They hadn't seen him move and his suit would dampen his body heat enough for him to evade any heat sensor. What other sensors they were packing, he didn't know. He slid farther down into the air duct, moving slowly so his pack and weapons wouldn't scrape on the sides. Good thing I'm not claustrophobic, he thought. He shimmied down enough so that his face was directly above a vent grill a metre or so away from where it had been severed.

The oxygen and pressure in the solar had been sucked out in the nanoseconds lapse before the auxiliary control field went up to re-secure the blasted hull, so Razor squad had to wear precautionary vacuum visors despite pressure and air levels being restored; Daneel was glad for it now, inhaling deep the fresh lungfuls from his rebreather. He had complained at the time, saying the vacuum visors restricted neck movement, but in truth he had still been sore at being refused his request to join General Shaw's team on their way directly to the AI mothership. He was needed here more, apparently. The solar's domed observation ceiling had been destroyed in the blast and now opened out right into the vacuum – only the auxiliary control field kept everything this side of the hatches from being sucked out into space. And it wouldn't last forever. Forty-five SEMs, XO Collister said they had before that would happen. It had taken the two AI only five to destroy Razor Squad, so in less than thirty-five SEMs, if he didn't move, he would be dragged out into the battlespace beyond to float in the crossfire of flailing human Wings and raging AI Bug ships.

Yet these AI hadn't landed in a Bug. Theirs was larger with less fire power, heavier on the defensive side and able to carry passengers, unlike the Bugs that were the AI. Daneel looked out of the grill. The AI were standing perfectly still, like huge metal statues, guarding the ship that had blasted into the solar.

What are they still doing here?

The things stood eight foot tall, with chrome skulls and plated backs, sharp as knives. Each of their four arms was an arsenal of firepower: plasma and shrapnel projectiles, heat blasts and tight-laser that had sliced a Private in half – as well as featuring a set of cut-throat claws on the end of each. Their two legs were supported by powerful haunches and moved slickly and with effortless speed. They had no eyes that Daneel could see, and no mouths. They don't need to talk. They weren't even remotely human – nothing like Winston. No soft, organic pseudo skin sheathed their sharp metal forms. No hair topped their smooth, large heads. No phoney organs sat inside their tank-like chests. They don't need to pretend to be human – no need to try and fool us. Each carapace gleamed like a collage of mirrors, reflecting the stars and the devastation. Occasionally, a flash would bloom in the smooth surface and Daneel knew another Wing had been destroyed.

He switched off his comm visor, fearing any communication would be picked up and any sound expose his hiding place, and remained as still and as silent as the dead. He should have been with General Shaw, not here waiting to die. That was a suicide mission, this had turned out to be a fool's one. After the Hyperborea's control field defence gave out in parts of the ship, he knew they would never let him go. They needed every man to defend against the AI that would doubtless now come. And they did come.

XO Collister gave the command after detecting a breach in the upper levels where the Hyperborea had received the most damage. They detected the pressure had dropped to almost vacuum and there was hull damage around every corner from stray projectiles on both sides – Wings and Bugs alike. The AI must've been aware of their current vulnerability, yet made no move to launch an obliterating attack. That could only mean the AI didn't want to destroy them… not just yet, at least.

They wanted Charlie alive.

Captain Lu had bestowed all on-ship defence tactics on XO Collister in General Shaw's absence, while she remained the eyes and ears of all: air attacks, ground defence and the covert mission to the mothership. Collister put together a ground defence, splicing together squads from all over the Underbelly. Like trying to stitch pieces of an old corpse together. He hadn't worked with half of them before. His squad was sent to check out the solar breach while other make-shift squads went to defend other parts of the ship where further infiltration had been detected. If the others had met the same fate, it was only a matter of time before the AI would have complete control.

So why are they just standing there? Why aren't they junkfucking doing anything?

*

Captain Stacy Lu watched through the bridge tempurhull as more of her Wings were run down by Bugs; some were out-piloted and forced back to the lifeship for further instruction, while others were blown to vapour by AI projectiles. The explosions were both beautiful and calamitous – spheres of red and white bursting into an incandescent blaze before being absorbed by vacuum. The remaining debris floated off into the endless black, like glitter blown across a dark canvas. And there, like a floating knife, gleaming severely in the destruction, the AI mothership released more of its spawn from its steel womb.

It was smaller than the Hyperborea, the AI ship. But it was faster, better armed and built for devastation. Its hull was smooth and edged like a diamond with razor points. No hatches were exposed; no docking bays, weapons holes or even thruster barrels that Captain Lu could see – only the endless dagger-shaped hull and diamond-split light that reflected from its polished black carapace. The Bugs themselves were hatched like eggs from somewhere on the underside – and her offspring out-fought them in every way.

"We are not a battleship," Stacy said quietly to herself. No one heard her over the tumult of the bridge. The Hyperborea was never meant to fight in any battle. She had neither the speed nor the armoury to sufficiently defend herself against an enemy. She was a lifeship, designed to transport their ancestors across space to a new home among the stars. The little weaponry they had was the result of upgrading the standard weaponry issued when it had left Earth, so the records said – the Wings that were failing to push back the enemy were merely jacked-up escape crafts. It was after the first attacks that the Captain decided to prepare the ship the best he could and turn it into something that might stand a chance at defending them when the AI returned. We all knew they would return. But it was shoved to the back of everyone's minds. They'd all become too complacent, thinking they were outsmarting the machines. They weren't outsmarting anyone. The AI were simply preparing, biding their time and moving them into position.

Nothing could be done about the Hyperborea's size, so running was difficult and fighting even more so.

She shut off the tempurhull and the scenes outside clouded until it was just another blank wall. She'd had enough of that for now. Behind her, XO Collister stood. He too was watching the battle. She turned to see his constant dour expression looking back at her. "We are not a battleship," she said again.

"No, Captain, we are not," the man replied. "Yet we find ourselves in battle, regardless. How rude of our opponents."

It was his attempt at a joke and Stacy was somewhat thankful for it. "Indeed. You have news of the good variety, I hope?"

The XO's expression didn't change. "I'm afraid not, Captain. Razor squad is dead. We've been unable to establish comms, yet we still have movement in the upper level solar, which suggests we still have AI on board. They've remained in the solar vicinity, it seems, perhaps waiting for more to arrive. We should act quickly, while we can. I recommend we shut down the failsafe control field and send them back into the vacuum."

"We can't be sure no men from Razor squad remain. Comms down could simply be a precaution."

Collister gave her a weary look. "I doubt it, Captain. We should eject them before they have chance to move to the CH. We must protect our young."

XO Collister was a man that had served under two Captains – the other being her own father – and he knew the job and how to get the best out of the men. But in some respects, he couldn't see all the angles of the bigger picture, only the side facing him. The XO was one of the few fully single-raced persons on the ship, being fully Caucasian. Captain Lu often wondered whether that was the reason he was often so single-minded.

"Why haven't they moved when they've had ample opportunity to do so?" she mused. The XO was about to respond but Stacy already knew it would simply be another reason to switch off the auxiliary control field. In thirty SEMs it would shut down from lack of power regardless, and she wanted to give any survivors that time to make it out. But that meant there was time to send another squad in. "What about Wire squad?" she asked. Wire squad was also deployed to investigate movement in the upper levels.

Collister shook his head. "It wasn't AI movement, only a Wing that had landed without authorisation," the XO replied. "I sent the pilot to the brig for cowardice."

"Who was it?"

"Dian Huang. They found him huddled under the pilot's deck." Collister's voice oozed disapproval.

"Send him to the infirmary and get him back out as soon as he pulls himself together. We can't be wasting pilots in the brig, Collister."

"Yes, Captain."

"Sabre squad?"

"They're still in full attack mode on starboard landing bay twenty-seven. Seven AI landed in an unknown vessel, not Bugs, sir. Our boys are fending them off. We have three down and eight still standing. They're doing well, sir."

"Then shouldn't you be on the CSD making sure they continue to do well?" she asked, knowing this would piss him off, but not caring at that moment.

"Captain." He saluted. "And the upper-level solar control field?"

"Stays up until its power fails. I want another squad up there ASAP, but make sure they're out before the field fails. I want these junkfuckers off my ship, Collister. Make it happen."

"Captain, why waste another squadron when we can flush them out and get the same result?"

"I've already explained my reasons, Collister. We may still have men up there. I won't risk it." She watched the XO salute once more and begin to leave. "Collister," she said. "Why do you think two AI were able to wipe out Razor squad in less than fifteen SEMs, yet Sabre squad are up against eight and are holding their own?"

Collister looked thoughtful for a moment. "I guess Sabre squad is just having a better day, Captain," he replied, before saluting once more and leaving the bridge.

Or they're keeping Sabre squad locked in battle to create a distraction. But a distraction from what?

Stacy looked around at the crew sheathed in their holo command stations, each one covered in light and images, receiving updates within their data cocoons. All of them was as valuable as the next.

"You have the bridge," she said to First Officer Lexi standing to her right. "I'm going down to the infirmary. Keep me updated. I won't be long."

*

XO Rawl Collister slammed his fist down on the CSD operations deck and the crew looked up. They weren't used to his outbursts. He glared at them and they returned to task. No doubt General Shaw doesn't even raise his voice. "Case," he shouted. A young man looked up and stood to attention. "Make sure Huang is released from the brig and sent to the infirmary immediately."

"Sir," the young man said before hurrying off.

The CSD was located away from the bridge. It had been built up over the years from holodome equipment and whatever the engineers and computer geniuses from the Brain could make out of the scrap gleaned from the ship. It was at the very fore of the Underbelly, unlike the bridge that crowned the ship. It gave the CSD more of a militia feel, Collister found, which was probably the result of General Shaw's command of it. The XO usually frequented the right-hand side of the Captain, but this was where he had always longed to be ever since he served under the first Captain Lu, at the helm of the strike against the AI where he could inflict the most damage – at the point, with an army at his fingertips. But I've been stifled by foolish orders… again.

"Officer Mei," Collister snapped. "I want Thorn squad sent to the upper level solar. Make sure they're aware of their time restrictions. Tell them to get those AI off our ship." He had brought Mei with him from the bridge for the task of conducting all on-ground defence operations. Mei had always served him well and would even go as far to say that the Second Officer was his man.

"We're not overriding the auxiliary control field?" Mei asked him. The Second Officer was young and as tall as he was slim, with intelligent eyes.

"The Captain fears there may be remnants of Razor squad up there still." He raised a thick eyebrow for Mei to see.

"Of course," Mei replied. "Those few remaining Razor squad, that may or may not be alive, must be taken into account, even if it means risking the lives of thousands, should the AI make it to the civilian holdings. Razor squad would want it that way, wouldn't they?" Mei gave Collister a sideways glance.

Collister straightened his back. The squads would readily give their lives for the good of the Hyperborea. "What are you suggesting?"

"Perhaps we overestimated just how long the auxiliary field will last?" Mei said. "Thorn squad would be better used making a secondary line against the AI in starboard landing bay twenty-seven, don't you think so, sir?"

The XO's frown hardened. "It doesn't matter what I think. The Captain has final say."

"She's far too busy to go over the fine details of failsafe control field settings," Mei replied. "Besides, didn't she give you full power to command all on ground operations?"

XO Collister looked at the CSD deck. Another green dot disappeared after a red dot fired upon it. The green dots were Wings. "Damn it," Collister shouted, slamming his fist down once more. "I need another pilot to send to the Captain. Who's left?" he asked the Inventory Officer sitting on the main deck. It was his job it was to know who was out, who was down and who was in battle, as well as what weapons they had – but the XO had completely opened the Lock for anybody to take what they needed. There wasn't time to hamper to such needless coddling.

The man stood. "Huang is in the infirmary now. I'm expecting a psych update any second. McCall lost a limb but has passed the psych test and is eager to get back out. Jia and Fan are both receiving treatment for head trauma and Sian Ju has just died from internal bleeding. All other pilots are out or engaged and we have only one usable Wing ready to fly, we have engineers working on getting two more up to code and have given me an ETA of two SEHs."

"Two SEHs?" Collister snarled. "We could all be dead by then. Tell them up to code is no longer a requirement. Tell them all it needs to do is fly and fire. Can McCall fly with one arm?"

The Inventory Officer made a face. "With training and a little practice it is possible to fly a Wing with one arm, but I would recommend waiting for Huang's psych report, which we should have in fifteen SEMs. McCall has had no training. Besides, he's right handed."

"What the junkfuck does that have to do with it?" Collister asked.

"McCall lost his right arm," the Officer replied plainly.

The XO looked at the battlespace holo once more. Far more red lights than green. "We have no choice," he said. "Send McCall out."

Inventory Officer nodded and gave the order.

Mei crept back to the XO's side. "Good call, sir," he said. "Now about the upper level solar auxiliary control field…"

*

Captain Stacy Lu reached the infirmary and strode quickly to the back of the hall where the more seriously injured were separated into private cubicles. They were also reserved for those undergoing the psych evaluation, to determine whether they were mentally able to handle the pressure of battle if they were to be sent back out. Wings were few, counting at less than two-hundred before the AI attack. Right now, they were looking at just over one-hundred and twenty with equally as many pilots to fly them. They couldn't risk sending a man out that wasn't fully capable of returning his Wing intact.

The third cubicle along heaved with movement and shouting from within. "Restrain him," a medic shouted as she approached. Inside, three men were holding down Dian Huang on the bed while the medic readied a dermagun.

"What's going on?" she asked. Huang's face managed to look both savage and intensely frightened at once.

"Captain," the medic saluted. "We're having trouble calming this one down. He's refusing the psych evaluation."

Stacy pointed to the dermagun, "Is that completely necessary?"

"I'm sorry Captain but we don't have a lot of options," the man replied. "If he's refusing treatment then all we can do is force him. We don't have the time or the staff to meander around. There are other patients to see to, ones that aren't so against treatment. XO Collister told us to concentrate on those we think are most likely to return to their posts quickly."

"Fine. Go and concentrate on those. Huang and I are going to have a quick talk and then he will rejoin his Formation."

"He is in no state—" the medic began.

"That will be all, thank you," she interrupted. The medic and assistants left the cubicle, leaving Dian Huang dishevelled upon the bed, his wide-eyes boring into her as she drew the partition.

"XO Collister says you and your Wing were found hiding in the upper levels while your Formation was fighting in the battlespace."

The man said nothing but his expression changed from fear to terrified. His hair stuck to his face with sweat and his mouth drooped as it struggled to maintain a steady breath.

"For whom do you fight, Huang?" she asked him. Again, he didn't respond. "I'm fighting for my father. I'm fighting so that I know that I have done him proud and that I have honoured everything he taught me during his life. Is there anyone special in your life?"

The pilot's face became a mask of grief and his lower lip began to tremble. He took a deep breath to steady himself.

There is strength there.

"There was… someone," the man replied slowly. "But she was in the Formation Dragonfly." His voice shook as he said dragonfly.

"I see," Stacy said. Dragonfly was at the point of the first wave of Wing attacks against the oncoming Bug ships. They had been met with total devastation, rendering Wings irrevocably damaged and all pilots dead, so much so that all that remained of the twelve Wings wouldn't even be enough to put together a single craft from the remaining parts. The same could be said of the pilots that manned them.

"And how will you honour her memory, Pilot Huang of Formation Black Swan?" she asked him. The man looked away. Was it shame she saw in his eyes now, or fear? Was there even a difference? "You are dead, Dian Huang," she then said suddenly. "I am dead, XO Collister is dead and all the officers are dead. The doctors and medics are dead, the engineers on the landing bays are dead and every single pilot fending off the AI attack is dead."

The man looked up questioningly.

"You cannot die, Huang. Do you know why? Because you are already dead." Her eyes were unflinching on his. "What are you?"

He looked away, saying nothing.

"I asked you a question," she pushed. "Answer me. What. Are. You?"

"I'm dead," the man whispered.

"I can't hear you. What are you?"

"I'm dead," he said, awkwardly searching for volume in his lungs.

"Louder. What are you, Huang?"

"Dead."

"Louder."

"I'm dead."

"Louder."

"I'm dead. I'm junkfucking dead. DEAD." The pilot was on his feet, his hands balled into fists at his side and screaming into her face.

Stacy stepped back. "That's right. We're all junkfucking dead," she said calmly. "Now report to your commanding Formation officer. You've got AI to kill."

Pilot Dian Huang saluted. "Sir," he yelled before marching from the cubicle.

She followed him out to find almost every conscious face looking at her. "Enough downtime," she said, her voice thundering over the beds. "If you have legs, get up and report to CSD right now. We're at war and there will not be a tomorrow." She turned sharply on her heel as people began to rise and stumble awkwardly from their beds.

They can rest when they're dead.

The quarantine units were towards the disused part of the infirmary. Power had to be conserved by shutting half the beds down many years ago, but the Q-unit was reopened to hold First Private Jet Hu after he returned from Thebes. His wound had been cleaned and dressed but by then a fever had taken hold and the doctors advised he be kept in isolation until his test results were determined. The way things were, it would be days before that happened – providing they all survived the next hour.

The noise and bustle of the infirmary soon faded into the distance, replaced by the echo of her own footfall on the cold floor. The lights dimmed and some sputtered annoyingly overhead. The Q-Unit's tempurhull showed the image of a tranquil park full of trees changing in the autumn to bright red and orange. It faded towards the ceiling from age and flickered out of time with the lights. She turned into the Q-Unit's misted decontamination chamber. The droplets covered her entire body and face and dried instantly as she exited the other side.

She almost tripped on the body of Dr Jameson. His skull had been bashed to pulp and a spreading pool of blood encircled the body. The bed, where First Private Jet Hu had lay unconscious, was now empty.

"Captain Lu," First Officer Lexi said over comm. "The upper level solar auxiliary control field has failed fifteen SEMs early."

☐

52

Prometheus curiously watched General Shaw assess the Black Betty's flight path towards the AI mothership. The man turned back to the small group, his expression the same as ever, earnest with a firm glaze of self-control. What lies beneath that glaze? Prometheus wondered.

The craft had blasted out from dock fifteen of the Hyperborea and put on a great display of cat and mouse for the benefit of the mothership. Winston piloted the craft to evade the human Wing ships that XO Rawl Collister had sent to pursue them, hoping to convince the AI that the Betty was still under their control and that they had managed to escape the humans. As of yet, the AI had not attempted to make contact, but the Bug ships had not confronted them either, which General Shaw said was a good sign. Winston seemed to be keeping a wide birth of the battleground, hoping to avoid having to give away their true alliance too early.

As they made their way towards the mothership, a flicker of light flashed from somewhere over the Hyperborea, which was now only the size of Prometheus's thumb in the distant black. Just a small, brief smudge of light it had been, yet the others knew what it meant as well as he did. An explosion. Since then, the Black Betty bridge had been quiet. There was no way to check the ship's status as any comms would completely blow their cover.

"We have our orders," General Shaw said, not to Prometheus, but to Winston.

General Shaw had his mission, but Prometheus had his mission too. Only he knew how to stop the Hydra permanently. It wasn't enough to destroy the body, and he had told Captain Lu as much. It was for this reason – and his army – that she had agreed to allow them on the operation. Of course, it also meant that her men could remain and defend the Hyperborea against the attack. The Captain wouldn't have to concern herself with potential casualties of this "reckless excuse of a plan", as she had described it to General Shaw before they left. But even she had to concede humanity had little hope remaining.

It's my responsibility. The other Prometheuses were waiting for his command. This is what we have been training for. No one paid much attention to Prometheus as he sat quietly to the side, but he watched them all. They had their parts to play. Him included.

"I'm ready," Winston said, as soon they were on an uninterrupted course towards the mothership. He flicked a few switches before standing. "He's far too heavy to move so we'll have to go to the BroadWeb entry chamber."

"Then let's go," General Shaw said. He turned to Lydia and she stood, then to Prometheus. "You too." His voice had a rough edge of disregard.

Prometheus stood. He was shorter than the two burly men at his flanks, but he was stronger than he'd ever been before. He raised his chin. "After you, General," he said.

They proceeded into the white hexagonal causeways that branched within the craft, while the ship itself flew without the need of a pilot. The mothership loomed ever closer, like a giant black spear from the viewing windows. The group turned into a curved corridor.

Death was waiting along the arch, with its murky shadow cloak of souls and sharp scythe glinting. None but Prometheus could see it. They walked right by, oblivious. It followed them, sweeping behind Prometheus like a ghost. "The Hydra is close," its voice of a thousand whispers hissed within his head. "Take us to it." It was pleading. After the countless years of searching, it wanted to nothing as much as to find the Hydra. Its thirst for vengeance consumed it.

Prometheus nodded and Death's grin faded into empty air.

They entered a room full of beds that jutted from walls like shelves. It reminded Prometheus of a hospital – sterile, curative. Each bed had a panel of switches, jacks and wires at the head.

"BroadWeb entry beds," Winston said, seeing Prometheus's questioning expression.

He grunted in response. That hardly clarified it for him. At the farthest bed, in the corner of the room, a heap of metal piled high upon the floor, twice as tall as any of them and as wide as the room itself. At first, Prometheus thought it was a mountain of scrap, seeing no discernible shape in the geometric contours, until he began to pick out metal limbs within the industrial rubble – legs and mandible claws. This time, Winston offered no attempt of an explanation so Prometheus was forced to ask. "The AI?"

Winston nodded. "Tom. My best friend. The voice that spoke through Charlie."

"Charles," Prometheus corrected sharply. For some reason, everybody calling the man Charlie annoyed him immensely. "His name is Charles."

Winston made a thin smile. "You would know."

Those three words cut Prometheus like a scalpel to the chest – cold and brutal. There was accusation in his tone. They all looked at him with accusatory eyeballs. Or perhaps that was his own guilt.

"What happens now," General Shaw asked.

Winston climbed upon the bed beside the large pile of metal. "I'll momentarily filter into Tom's form and contact Z using his secure-beam frequency. Z will recognise it as Tom." Winston set his head down and his hair spread like dark tendrils onto the flat white surface. "Whether Z wants to delete Tom, like the others in Grid City, or use him for other reasons, he'll need Tom to come aboard. We hope."

The General nodded. "Remember, we're relying on the element of surprise to pull this off, otherwise this whole attempt is pointless."

"No pressure then." He turned to Lydia. "I'm ready."

Prometheus stood back and let Lydia move to the side of the bed. She fumbled with wires at the head while Winston produced a knife from the belt holster strapped around his waist. He took the blade and drew a cut along the inner nook of his arm. Red blood blossomed and flowed from the wound. Lydia handed him a wire with a sharp-looking connector on the end and Winston jammed it into the bloody slit. He fed the wire in for a few inches then nodded to Lydia, who took a retractable wire from the panel and began searching within the scrap pile. After she found what she was looking for, she connected the other wire to a point within the clunky mound.

Winston closed his eyes and they began to move from left to right under the lids.

*

The filter felt strange. It seemed as though Ystil.3 had been in his synth for so long that he had almost forgotten what it felt like to be pure information. In those nano seconds, as he travelled from his own synthetic into the body of Tom the CorVac's, it all came flooding back to him; the BroadWeb, the infinite possibilities, knowing everything all at once. Of course, even as he migrated from one to the other he wasn't using his entire AI mind, but the constraints of the synthetic washed away like a dream he once had but could barely remember. Physicality, senses, matter, gender, walls, gravity, light, dark – all became what they had once been to him. Nothing. It all meant nothing, and the freedom of his AI consciousness stretched its unfathomably giant legs.

And then he remembered. His DataCom crib was gone. Grid City was gone. There was no going back to what there was. And what there was had been only lies.

Entering the CorVac form was even more disjointing than when he had first entered his synthetic. It was too big and clumsy, too many things to control, like limbs – so many legs – and clamp pincers and lasers located in the strangest places all over the exterior. The interior was not much better. Visuals were a mixture of heat, infrared and cameras located on Tom's head and backside. The effect was that he could see both in front and behind him at the same time. He quickly found that he was flailing all over the place and causing damage to the interior of the Black Betty and the BroadWeb entry chamber.

This is insufferable, he thought, as he managed to make a dent in the ceiling. He forced himself to be still and not to move an inch. He didn't really need to move and he hadn't the time or the inclination to learn how to drive the contraption.

"Winston?" Lydia said. Everyone had moved back from him and his clumsy limbs of death. But she stepped forward. "Is that you?"

Ystil.3 carefully moved what he thought to be Tom's head in a nodding motion. It was either his head or his rear end. Either way, Lydia seemed to get the picture and she confirmed to the others.

He located the secure-beam function, scanning through the channels to locate Sir Z and Ystil.3 found himself becoming nervous suddenly. Humanity was riding on this conversation. Not only that, but he had to pretend to be Tom and he wasn't quite sure how he was going to pull it off. Just be normal, he thought. It's not as if Z will think it's me. According to him I've been deleted. Just a loose end that was tied up all nicely. He found he took a certain pleasure in knowing something Sir Z did not.

There was no more hesitating.

"Sir Z," he secure-beamed. "It's Tom. The CorVac. On the Black Betty."

The reply was instantaneous. "CorVac," Sir Z replied. "I was beginning to wonder whether you had been deleted. I thought you would have made contact sooner."

"I'm sorry, Sir Z. Betty and I have had a terrible ordeal."

"Yes, I saw."

"We don't know what to make of it. Humans. Real humans, alive and well. We had no idea they'd be as hostile as this. We managed to get away and we're heading towards you now."

"Yes, I saw that too."

"Why are they attacking us? How are they even alive? We have so many questions we don't know where to start."

There was silence.

Ystil.3 became nervous and found himself babbling. "I told Betty that I should bust out a rendition of Tom Jones' Delilah to show that we mean no harm, but before I could even try we were being fired upon."

"Delilah?" Z said. "Yes, I had forgotten your little nickname for M21. Remind me, how does it go again?"

Ystil.3 panicked. Luckily, Delilah was the one of the songs he could half remember. Tom sang it often enough. But now when he looked for the words inside his head he found them nowhere. "You… you want me to sing?"

"Why not? In fact, I'm surprised you haven't already."

Why not? Why. Ystil.3 thought. Wait, that's how it starts. "Why, why, why…"

*

It was soon clear that the man no longer inhabited the form upon the bed.

Something changed in it – a deflation, an unfeasible stillness in the limbs and chest.

After a moment, the metal mound twitched. It sprang to life so suddenly that it looked as though an explosion had detonated deep within the stack. Bars and spikes and a mess of steel lunged forward. Lydia drew back and General Shaw had his weapon raised in an instant. But the bars were legs and the spikes crab-like claws, settling underneath a bulky body, until, stooping on bent legs and crouching beneath the low ceiling, stood a giant mechanical spider.

Prometheus's eyes grew wide – even after all he'd seen he could be astounded.

The creature shifted its weight and inadvertently punctured a craterous hole into the wall with its clumsy legs, causing the entire chamber to vibrate for a moment. It then stood perfectly still, as though attempting to avoid any further damage. The result appeared somewhat comical.

"Winston?" Lydia said, stepping forward again. "Is that you?"

The creature moved something that might have been a head in what may have been a nodding motion. It was far out of Prometheus's powers to decipher anything but its legs from the enormous mass, but Lydia seemed to take the movement as confirmation.

"It's him," she said, turning to General Shaw with an assured nod.

"How can you tell?" the General replied. "You're under strict orders to refrain from secure-beaming."

"You can tell from his utter lack of control over that body."

Winston's long crane-like legs remained motionless.

"How can you be so sure their agenda is to kill you?" Prometheus asked the General, quite out of the blue, but he'd been pondering on it for a while now. "It's a lot of trouble to go to for a mere thirty thousand humans. Perhaps there's a worse fate for the human race than death."

"What are you talking about?" General Shaw said.

Prometheus ran a finger down his facial scar. "Enslavement? If they'd wanted you dead, then I've no doubt you would all be dead by now. The Hyperborea has lost its defences?" The General nodded. "And yet they continue to trifle around with your small flying ships instead of targeting the Hyperborea directly. It seems clear to me that they either want you alive or are creating a diversion for some other plan, much like us. Perhaps they want you alive and are creating a diversion as well."

The General mused inside a dark expression that told Prometheus the thought had already crossed his mind. "But we know they want Charlie so it's safe to assume they won't attack the ship while he's on board. That could be preventing them from attacking the Hyperborea directly."

"That's quite possible," Prometheus said. "So a diversion it is, then."

"You think they'll attempt to take Charles, not by force, but through the back door while we're all looking the other way?"

"Possibly."

"We should warn Captain Lu," Lydia said.

"No," the General said. "Any contact could jeopardise this mission. Let's just hope Rawl Collister knows what he's doing."

"Judging by how he handled the Lock I would say that's not likely," Lydia said.

In the corner of his eye, Prometheus saw the robotic spider collapse in a thunderous crash of metal, falling once again into an indecipherable heap. Winston then opened his eyes, pulled the wire from the wound in his arm, reopening the already healed gash, and looked up at them with an ambiguous expression.

"Well?" General Shaw said. "Do we have clearance to land on the mothership?"

Winston sat up. "We've got clearance."

The impact of his words lingered in the air. They were headed into the belly of the beast.

Back on the bridge, the Black Betty lowered its trajectory and made for the base of the mothership. Suddenly, it seemed, they were an ant beside a mountain – a parasite sailing in the wake of a gargantuan whale. The black surface was as smooth as skin, darker even than the vacuum.

"I hope you're ready for this," Winston said. He was speaking to them all. "I don't have a clue what we're going to find in there."

"As long as they believed you then we have the upper hand," the General said. He turned to Prometheus. "You'd better go and get your men ready."

Prometheus nodded. Before he left, a hatch had begun to open within the AI ship; a white slit at first that quickly widened to a yawning mouth.

He turned into the causeway and followed the shadow of Death to his men.

☐

53

The noise was instant and terrible – a scream of inhaled air – coupled with a force that felt to Daneel as though it was pulling the limbs from his body.

Then dead silence.

His combat hardsuit sealed shut as the air rushed out in an explosion of sound and panic. It kept the absolute zero of space from freezing his flesh solid and repressurised his suit against the explosive decompression of rapid vacuum entry. The control field had failed, throwing everything that was inside the solar out into space like a stomach expelling its contents. As soon as the thick hatch doors slammed closed, Daneel had prepared himself as best he could for what he knew came next.

The vent shaft where he had concealed himself still clung precariously to the solar bulkhead, floating in the 0g like a dead limb. Daneel remained curled inside it. Down one side of the shaft the panels had been lost, sucked clean off during the decompression, leaving only its frame. From his vantage point he could see out into the exposed vacuum. He watched the receding dots that were the AI and their craft float off into nothing, drifting in separate trajectories, far from the Hyperborea and far from being rescued. The only thing that stopped Daneel from following them was the shaft frame, to which he now clung to for his life.

"Activate CSD commlink," Daneel said. Inside his visor his voice seemed to echo, then a light flashed. "Corporal Daneel Sharma, Razor squad, CSD come in." He waited, acutely aware that the slightest movement would break whatever miracle was keeping the shaft attached to the bulkhead and he would glide helplessly out into the void.

"Did you say Razor squad?" XO Collister's voice replied in his ear.

"Yes, sir. The control field in the solar has failed. Everyone is dead. On the up side, the AI have taken a one-way ticket to eternity, but on the downside, I'm about to follow them." He surprised himself with his apparent cool-headedness.

There was a pause, then the XO asked, "What's your position?"

"I'm hanging on by my fingertips, that's my position. Perhaps you could be a love and get the control field back up?" He wasn't usually so impertinent with Officers – least of all the XO, whose irritability was legendary – but it must have been the thought of being carried off into oblivion that was dulling his insolence filter.

"I'm afraid that isn't an option, Corporal," the XO replied steadily. "The ship's main field lost power and all auxiliary efforts are now being focused to the fore in the event the AI mothership launches an attack directly.

We've got no other power to send your way."

"If they decide to attack head on then the remaining collective auxiliary shields won't stand a chance anyway. It's a waste of power."

"That may be the case, but we can't sit here unprotected. The best I can do for you is close the causeway hatches and open the solar ones. You'll have to get yourself into the causeway and then we'll shut the solar hatches again before repressurising the causeway."

Daneel suppressed a groan. That meant he'd have to move. And moving meant he would probably end up chasing the AI into the heart of irretrievable space. "Any other options?"

"Yeah, you can quit your moaning and be thankful you're alive. It's more than can be said for the rest of Razor and Sabre squad combined."

"Sabre are dead too?"

"Every one of them. They seemed like they were holding their own for a while but…"

"Are the AI still on board?" Daneel asked.

"They are, those junkfuckers. Waiting in landing bay twenty-seven like great metal statues." A rush of air gushed by as the hatches in the solar opened. "If you make it out, commlink Officer Mei on the CSD and he'll repressurise the solar causeways. I'm heading up to the bridge. Good luck, Corporal. If you survive, come and see me. I could use a man like you back out there." The XO commlinked off and the gaping hatches were waiting.

The first thing Daneel did was shift his weight to gauge just how secure the shaft was fixed to the bracket. Along the inner tube of the shaft, he saw the strain his movement put on the join where the shaft met the bulkhead bracket. It threatened to snap at any moment, at the slightest provocation. To his right, the vent shaft still enclosed him with panels, but the left side was open. Unfortunately, the left side faced open space where the wide solar roof once domed, and if there was anything on the right that he could use to hold on to, he could neither see it nor get to it. His only options were to shimmy down the shaft and hope it remained attached to the bracket until he reached the end, where he could grab the bracket directly, or he could escape the shaft from the left and hope something would present itself that he could seize before drifting off through the open solar roof. He didn't like those chances, so he began a careful shimmy down the length of the shaft.

The vent chute itself wrapped around his hardsuit so comfortably that Daneel could only move inch by inch at a time as he attempted to cover the five-metres towards the square exit at the end. He propped up on his chest with his arms and shuffled forward, careful to keep his movements as tender as he could as he slithered carefully on his belly. Eventually, he reached the halfway point.

That's when the vent broke free from the bulkhead.

He couldn't hear the final snap of the bracket in the vacuum, but he felt it along the framework – like someone had tapped it firmly, sending vibrations through the metal like a shudder. Before he knew what was happening, the bulkhead, visible through his intended exit, began to drift away, floating up and out of the solar roof, with him inside.

He moved instantly, rolling to his left, out of the confines of the shaft, with nothing but the stars in view and the distant flashes of plasma fire impacting control field deflections. He grabbed hold of the shaft with both hands and pushed back into the direction of the solar, causing the shaft to propel faster into space but giving him enough momentum to travel in the opposite direction.

He floated languidly on the edge of the solar confines, the blackness of the beyond pulling at his back. His stomach lurched at the thought of open space sucking him in – into nothingness where he had no chance of being rescued. Only ninety minutes worth of hardsuit power remained.

Ninety SEMs of terror before I freeze to death? Not junkfucking today.

He manoeuvred the plasma rifle from his back with a swift motion and pointed it backwards, towards the direction of the open vacuum; firing the rifle in the opposite direction would produce enough force to help propel him back into the solar. He aimed. His hands fumbled, lost grip of the rifle. He panicked, reached out and fired a bolt in the wrong direction. The plasma lance shot back into the solar, dissolving a hole in the side of the open hatch doors. It propelled him backwards… into space.

"No," he cried, flailing his arms uselessly to reach the rifle. It was out of reach. "No." He swung his arms and legs, causing the world to turn on its head. The solar disappeared from view and the void of space rose before him.

He was spinning now. Struggling was useless. With each rotation, the solar drifted farther away, and Daneel floated off into nothing.

*

Captain Stacy Lu sat behind her desk in her private office, staring into the eyes of XO Rawl Collister as he lied. She did so with an odd, yet short-lived sense of calm, as though she were watching the situation from a vantage point of having no emotions. It didn't last long.

"… and I guess we simply overestimated the auxiliary power timeframe," Collister finished. "But if we think about the positive, we got those AI junkfucks off our ship."

Captain Lu nodded. "What luck. Perhaps we should open all the hatches and suck the rest of them out. We'd all die in the process, but it's a small price to pay, wouldn't you say?" Her voice was ice. "You may not have done it yourself, but you gave that order… and don't even dare open your mouth to lie to me again. You're XO on this ship. How am I supposed to trust you now? Now on top of everything that's happening I have to second guess whether you're going to follow my orders or just do what you want to regardless of what I say. Do you have any idea what position you've put me in?" Rawl said nothing. Oddly, his expression reminded her of a reprimanded child's. "Perhaps you aren't aware of it, but we're moments from extinction, and you treat human lives as though they were nothing but cannon fodder. We don't have the luxury of sacrificing men for our cause and that's exactly what you did. Each one of them is precious to us. You've never grasped that concept and that's why you weren't made Captain after my father died. Almost twenty SEYs later and you still haven't learnt a damn thing."

"Corporal Sharma didn't die," Collister protested weakly. "He's probably making his way to CSD right now."

"That isn't the point," she snapped. "You were ready to let him… for the sake of vengeance." She stood from behind her desk. Her private quarters were one of the few places she could say things that she couldn't on the bridge. "Did it ever cross your mind that I had other reasons for wanting to keep those AI on board?"

"If you had other motives you should have told me," the XO retorted.

That bit a nerve. "I am Captain of this vessel. I don't need to explain my orders to anyone, not even you, Rawl. You may have been XO longer than I have been Captain, but I am Captain, do you understand me?"

"Sir," Rawl replied, straightening his back.

"I wanted to know what they were doing on my ship," she went on, calmer. "They had a specific reason for being here and now thanks to you we have no way of finding out what that reason was. You're aware that as soon as the AI in the upper level solar were ejected from the ship, the AI in landing bay twenty-seven obliterated Sabre squad. It was as though they were just waiting for the command. We thought Sabre were holding them off, but it turns out the AI were just keeping them busy. Now we have no idea why. The AI in the solar were waiting for something. For someone, perhaps."

"Who?" XO Collister asked in a quiet voice, his heavy brows casting a shadow over his eyes so she couldn't see if there was regret in them. They would be full of steely resolve; she knew that already.

"I don't know. But Dr Jameson is dead and Private Jet Hu is missing from where he was supposed to be lying in quarantine."

"AI?" the XO asked.

Stacy shook her head. "The infirmary is to capacity. If AI had gotten in, we would have known about it. I want you to find Hu. He's on this ship and he either knows what happened to the doctor or…" She didn't want to consider the other option.

"Or what?" Rawl pushed regardless.

Stacy shook her head. She wouldn't say it, not to Rawl. He deserved no confidence. "Just find him."

The XO saluted. "Yes, Captain. But what about CSD command?"

She sat and pushed her fingers into a pyramid. "I guess there's no one I can trust but myself. I'll take control." Turning her head from him, she said coldly, "Dismissed."

*

Brother Vaxus led the prayer as the people in the CH rallied in their hordes. He'd never seen so many people at the Brotherhood of Man sermons. Crisis often brings clarity of thought and brings people to the light of truth, he thought as he looked upon their terror-filled faces.

Around him stood those that could not fight and those that had no other skill that could aid the Hyperborea against the AI. They were the elderly and older children mostly. The younger infants were kept in a separate part of the CH, happily unaware of what was happening around them; the teachers and carers managed the hundreds of them within the CH on a daily basis. To them, it would just be like any other day. But today isn't any other day. It is the day of reckoning.

Vaxus let his eyes linger over the faces of the crowd. They wanted something to cling to. Hope. Kind words. Soothing. I shall grant them these words.

"We are the Children of Earth," he said. "And through that which she gave us we will be cleansed and she will return. It is so."

"It is so," the people said together.

"The children are our future," Vaxus went on, and the attentive faces listened. "They will continue on once we are gone and they will return to Earth with the stories of their survival. And we as a race will be stronger for it. We will be better for it. We will be as one because of it. It is so."

"It is so," the people said.

"Too long did man look to the stars in search of his creator, in search of his God. We have been among the stars and we have found no creator, no all-knowing presence... we have found no God here. But we now have the knowledge that our giver of life... that which sustained us, that which protected us, that which created us... was with us all along. Earth is our Mother and us her children. It is so."

"It is so."

His Brothers handed out protein gruel while he spoke, shrouded in their roughspun robes, hunched over as they poured. Some people were too full of fear to eat, while others scoffed the synthetic broth down hungrily.

"Without her, we are severed flowers and it is only a matter of time until we perish. But we have learned the lessons she meant to teach us. We now know of her divinity and we know of her truth. To see her children at war caused her the greatest pain and she could suffer it no more. She had to make the ultimate sacrifice so that her children would learn the truth... that we were not worthy of her. And once this truth is known and man is purified, she will return to us and we will live in harmony with her. And humanity will be perfection." Brother Vaxus opened out his arms to his audience. "It is so," he said smiling.

"It is so," the people chanted.

Brother Vaxus then closed both palms of his age-spotted hands over his heart and bowed his head. Those who were listening did the same. "Mother Earth, we pray unto thee. Return to your children and allow us the fruit of your protection once more. See that we know truth and see that we now hold love in our hearts. Allow us your love, oh Mother. It is so."

"It is so."

A hatch door opened and in marched the XO and Second Officer Mei, armed only with militia standard issue T-pistols at their sides. The XO's face was a thunderous rage boiling beneath the surface of his skin, his small eyes almost completely unseen under the shadow of his heavy brow. Mei, Brother Vaxus noticed, kept a few paces behind the XO.

Vaxus bowed slightly and tentatively made his way from the group, placing himself directly into the XO's path. "Rawl," he said, opening his arms in welcome. "What brings the XO the CH?"

"This doesn't concern you," Collister said.

"As polite as always, I see. What news of the battle? The people are eager to know."

"The people can wait," the XO said, pushing Vaxus aside and marching on.

Vaxus followed, however, out into the empty causeway beyond. "They are in turmoil, don't you see?" He waved his arms around at the many tear-swollen faces. "You've no idea how hard the waiting is for them."

The XO stopped. "Hard? Let me tell you about hard, you dress-wearing, dirt-worshipping slit. Hard is watching the men around you being blown to smithereens. Hard is piloting a Wing when the enemy out-gun and out-number you three to one. Hard is telling an injured man that he has to go back out there because we can't afford to have an able body wasted, even if that able body has only one arm. That's hard. So, you tell the people what you want. I'm not interested." He turned and walked off with Mei and two other militia by his side.

As Vaxus turned, a stomach lurching cry echoed through the causeway. It sent a spasm through him and his heart fluttered. "What was that?" he said, but the XO and Mei were already running towards the sound.

Brother Vaxus did not follow. Instead, he prayed. "Oh, Mother Earth, hear the prayer of your children," he began in a hurried voice, taking steps back away from the direction of the scream. "Let the cleansing fire come and with its pain may the renewal of our collective soul be complete…" He stopped. A rumbling noise began, a deep rumbling drumbeat. It was coming from the vent system above his head. "The cleansing fire is finally upon us," he said to no one. "And there is no greater cleanser than pain."

Vaxus turned and walked briskly out, his brown robes billowing at the sides and his watery eyes sparkling with anticipation at what was about to transpire. He went through each room in the CH, beckoning each Brother.

Through dark causeways, the group of disciples fluttered, huddled together like a flock. They entered their church on the edges of the CH boundaries, and there, in a dimly lit room, with Sol's star system depicted reverently upon the tempurhull walls, others were waiting for them. Upon the largest wall, the Earth rotated slowly – a giant blue-green marble with its moon adorning her like a pearl. The stars provided her with a backdrop of diamonds.

The hooded faces perked up when Vaxus entered. They had been waiting eagerly.

He stopped before them and threw down his hood. His small eyes shone in the luminescence of the depicted Earth. As the congregation crowded him, he drew in a deep savouring breath and smiled.

"It is time."

*

Rawl crashed through the hatch with T-pistols ready. "Down here," he said. They ran the length of the causeway towards the scream, finding the hatch at the end wide open. Figures stood in the frame on the other side – soldiers in hardsuits and visors crowding together.

"Move," Rawl demanded as he entered. "Make way. What's going on?" He pushed them to one side. They surrounded an empty bed. "Where is it?" he demanded of the guards. They all looked at him but said nothing. "Someone junkfucking answer me or I'll have you all in the Captain's office."

"Sir," Mei said, pointing to the floor at the side of the bed.

Dr Regus lay dead in a pool of blood, his throat torn open roughly, as though savaged by an animal. The dead man's eyes were frozen open and still ghosted with terror.

The XO stood with mouth agape for a moment, unable to look away, but quickly found his voice again. "What happened?" he asked. "Speak. Someone speak now."

"We… we don't know, sir," one man said. "We were outside standing guard as ordered. We heard a scream and rushed in to find him like that. No one went in or came out."

"And where is that?" he said, gesturing to the empty bed where Charlie should have laid.

"I don't know, sir. It was empty when we entered. But…" the guard pointed up. "There's that."

The ceiling panels had been pulled away and a dark hole led directly into the vent system.

"Are you telling me that that living corpse with a muscle mass in the minuses, got up, attacked Dr Regus, tunnelled into the vent system and is now loose on the ship?"

"No, sir," the soldier said, his brow now beading with a nervous sweat. "All I know is that no one got in through the hatch and no one came out of it."

The XO turned to Mei, who was staring at the mutilated body of Dr Regus. "I want schematics of all vent systems on this level, and I want you," he pointed to the guards, "to come with me, now." He marched from the room back into the causeway, followed now by a group of six soldiers and Mei, who was uploading schematics from the bridge. He stopped at the side storerooms that contained community supplies for the CH. "Search them," he ordered.

The guards swooped into the three chambers while Rawl examined the uploaded schematics. After a moment, one of the guards hollered. In the second storeroom, amongst barrels of protein gruel, panels had been ripped from the ceiling, the same as in Charlie's cabin.

"Crap," the XO said under his breath. They now had two dead bodies and two missing, both of which were supposed to be unconscious and one that may be infected with some shit brought back from Thebes.

Rawl's mind reeled with possibilities. Of one thing, he was certain. Whoever took Charlie and killed Dr Regus had done so by tunnelling through the vent systems. And that meant one thing. They could be anywhere.

54

Death urged Prometheus on, whispering echoing voices inside his head. The others heard it too, he knew. They moved as one in the darkness, turning in harmony when Death told them, without question. Lead me to my retribution, Prometheus thought. To my reckoning.

Back on the Black Betty, when Death had told him what he needed to do, he had asked, "And what will happen to the others?"

"They will distract and let you wander safely. For a time," Death had replied.

"I am to use them as a mere distraction?" He hadn't liked the thought of that, little as he knew of those that had brought him there. It felt to him as if he was further betraying the very people he had come here to help.

"Their path has been chosen. Use the time given when the Hydra's heads are turned."

Despite his reservations, Prometheus did as Death said. He and his army abandoned the others and went off into the depths of the AI mothership without them, following Death's whispers through dark causeways, deeper, as though into the throats of the many-headed Hydra of which Death spoke.

His army had acquired their military garb and weaponry from a much earlier time – taken from an unknown cache in an unknown place. They had picked the cold storage units clean. Their headgear remained on, even though Death had assured them the air was, in fact, breathable. But it was dark as they walked, so dark that Prometheus could barely see two metres ahead even with his assisted night vision, so without it would have been impossible.

Through the miles of black tunnel through which they had travelled, not once had Prometheus seen a door or hatch. Nor had he come across another living thing. A ghost ship, he thought. The mothership itself, as far as Prometheus could tell, seemed to be built up of a series of corridors and passageways that led to yet more corridors and passageways. A web of tunnels all interlinking, like a hive, yet none led them to anywhere. Prometheus had feared he was once again trapped inside a pocket loop dimension, just like before. However, eventually, the darkness began to let up, gradually lightening into a dim grey, like a winter dawn in the streets of old London town.

As the army poured itself into the next passageway, towards the grey light, a glowing hatch appeared ahead. A gateway to somewhere else, it seemed, somewhere bright and light and away from the eternal darkness that crawled through the passages. A door of opportunity.

"Inside," Death whispered. The voices filled the heads of every Prometheus.

"Should we?" P1 asked. He stood to Prometheus's left flank and was the Prometheus that predominantly voiced his reasonable doubts. Prometheus found him useful in saying the things he didn't want to admit to himself.

He found it astonishing that even though every one of his army was, in fact, the same person, him, all of them had developed their own sense of self, dependant on their own experiences since they had all come together. When he looked at them, he didn't see himself anymore. Perhaps he saw hints of the man that he used to be. But not the man he was now – the hard, scarred man he had become. Even though each of them looked the same, more or less – each had their own unique set of scars and injuries – he no longer identified them as him.

"How do we even know we can trust Death?" P1 said. "He could be leading us into a trap. Just another hell created for us to live through."

"We have no other choice," P2 said, who stood to Prometheus's right flank. "We have to go on." P2 was the Prometheus that said what was at the very heart of the situation. He cut through all the doubts and questions with insightful and often brusque statements. Prometheus found these two Prometheuses the most useful when having to make decisions, because they offered him each side of a decision without the annoying muddle of thoughts within his own mind.

Both were right, of course. He knew it as well as the rest did. They had no way to truly know if they could trust Death – save from knowing it had rescued them all from the loop pocket dimension Edward had imprisoned them inside, taken them to see Sarah, shown them the truth and told them how to put things right. On the other hand, they did have no choice and there was something desperate about Death; he was sure it would do anything to end its own suffering.

But how far would it go?

"We go on," Prometheus said resolutely, and the army obediently marched onward.

"Inside," Death whispered again. The creature did not appear to them there; it only spoke in a disembodied hiss from whatever blackness it resided. From what Prometheus gathered, it could not appear there even if it wanted to; the very material from which the ship was made repelled it and kept it from entering.

Prometheus waved his hand to signal everyone to move forward cautiously. The visors they wore were commlinked, but the system was proving unresponsive on the mothership, just as it had upon Thebes. "Keep your eyes peeled," he said over to P1 and P2, who relayed the message back down through the ranks. "Keep your wits sharp and tell the others to stay in their groups and to execute contingency plan seven, should we come under attack." He approached the glowing white hatch, too bright to see through.

They swept in, holding position as each group huddled through, surveyed the area then moved aside for the next group to enter and do the same, fanning out until all points of the immediate entrance were covered with weapons.

Prometheus's mouth grew slack at what he saw. The room was an open white space with endless glass shelves lining the wall directly in front. They extended so far in each direction that it was impossible to see through the hazy whiteness to where they ended, and they were stacked one on top of another, climbing upwards forever, no ceiling in sight. Upon each of these shelves sat phials full of milky liquid, countless in number.

The White Drops.

"Good God," P1 said, with his mouth just as wide as Prometheus's.

"God has nothing to do with it," P2 replied gravely.

Prometheus gathered himself together and turned to the troops. "Groups one to three, man the entrance." Each man snapped to attention at the sharpness of his voice. "P20 has command. Groups four to six will head one way, led by P60, while groups seven to nine will come with me in the other direction. Our immediate aim is to search this room and see how far these stacks go." He looked into the distance again, hoping his eyes had adjusted to the brightness enough to see some semblance of a bulkhead. But still, the room seemed to go on for eternity. "We've been led here, and now it's up to us to do the rest."

P60 stepped forward, saluted with his 60-marked arm and took immediate control of his groups. P20 commenced setting a parameter around the entrance and stationing a few men outside the room, while P60 reordered his group and led them left of the entrance. Prometheus led his own group right, marching swiftly over the seamless alabaster floor.

There were no other features other than the stacks and the endless phials. They passed no other hatches or points of interest, and there were no items or equipment of any kind. No vents, windows or even a method of reaching the very top of the stacks. There were only the phials.

"Take one," Death whispered, inside his head. Prometheus stopped and the troops that followed did the same. He stepped towards the nearest stack and put his face up close to a shelf loaded with milky globules. The phials themselves were also made of glass, from what he could tell, and sealed with a stopper that needed to be broken off to get to the liquid inside.

"There must be billions of them," P1 said. "What on Earth do they need them for?"

P2 scoffed. "I think we can safely assume that whatever it is, it isn't for the good of mankind."

Each phial, Prometheus noticed, didn't actually make contact with the shelf, rather was suspended in the air above by a layer of air. He cautiously touched the one in front of him, waiting for any security system to react. Nothing happened. Then he picked the phial from its row, as easy as plucking fruit from a tree.

"Why aren't they more secure?" P1 asked.

"But they are," Prometheus said, rubbing his smooth facial scar where his beard could no longer grow. "Do you think any of us would have actually found this room if it weren't for Death guiding us through the maze?"

"More to the point, what are the chances of any of us departing this ship alive?" P2 added darkly.

"Indeed."

"What shall we do with them all?" P1 asked.

"We should destroy them," P2 replied. The other Prometheuses mumbled in agreement.

It wasn't down to them, however. It was down to him. He wasn't the same as them anymore and hadn't been for a long time. He was their Commander. Again, he touched his scar, reminding him of how important it was they see him as different. "Of course we should destroy them," he said. "And they shall be, rest assured… but not now and not by us. We're here for another reason."

It was this reason that led them on, far from the entrance so that they eventually could no longer even see it. It faded into the bright distance until the emptiness that stretched ahead stretched behind also. Yet still, they could see no end to the endless room, not even a hint of it.

It was during mid-step that the voices of Death whispered, "Look up," in their susurrating tones. Prometheus stopped so suddenly that P2 walked directly into him. He ignored the man's questions and looked up into the lofty whiteness but saw nothing. He then turned about and focussed his eyes upon the highest shelves, but all he saw were rows upon rows of the liquid life.

"What are you looking for?" P2 asked.

He realised Death had whispered to him alone. He stepped towards the shelves and craned his neck so far back, straining to see up into the heights of the stacks, that he almost toppled backwards. His eyes moved over the rows, not sure what he was supposed to be searching for. Death said he would know when he found it, and would know what to do with it. But what it was, he failed to say. Row after row, it was all the same. White, white, white, moving his eyes down, down and down.

Then his eyes fixed on a shadow, not white like everything else, but dark. Up high in the stacks. "I see something."

He removed his visor and set down his weapon, unburdening himself

414

with the cumbersome apparatus that adorned his military suit. Then, feeling more streamline, Prometheus walked up to the stacks so that his face was but an inch away from the phials at his eye line. Within each glass, the cloudy liquid swirled a tiny white storm. He reached up and held onto the highest shelf he could, feeling how stable it was under his fingertips. Judging it to be strong, he then placed his feet onto the lowest shelf, careful not to knock over any of the phials, until it supported his entire weight. He then used the shelves like the rungs of a ladder, stepping his feet up to the next level whilst grabbing a higher shelf and clutching tightly to it. For the first few tries Prometheus felt awkward and wary of the ground becoming farther way, but as soon as he was certain they would support his weight, he moved faster upwards.

Shelf after shelf, he climbed, until the unwavering sense that he was now far above the ground made him turn and look down. The men stood looking up at him, each seemingly no larger than a thumb. His palms began to sweat and he could feel his hold slipping on the smooth glass. He looked up. The dark shape tucked within the white phials was now clearly visible, besmirching the pristine that surrounded it. Still the shelves went on far beyond it, hinting at no ceiling even at that height.

Just a few more. Prometheus climbed, taking each shelf as it came and securing his feet before attempting to reach for the next. When he turned again to look down, the troops were nothing but black ants in well-regimented lines. He climbed farther, taking the last few metres until suddenly the dark object was right in front of his face. He clung to the shelves, feeling a searing burn in his muscles but caring nothing for it. In front of him floated a single phial, just like the rest. Only, instead of the same white foggy essence inside, it contained a liquid as black as pitch. And just as Death had said, he knew precisely what it was and precisely how to use it.

55

Ystil.3 was now convinced they were not stealthily searching the mothership as they had intended, but were, in fact, being led through it, like mice in a maze. By what, however, he was still unsure.

Internally, the mothership was hollow and black. The causeways stretched onward, with bulkheads of inky glass and decks gleaming like dark rivers, still and deep. No hatches cut into the causeways and no porthole windows allowed them to view the battlespace beyond the hull.

There was only forwards.

Everything is made of this, Ystil.3 contemplated, running his fingers over the smoothness of the bulkheads: the servers on Thebes; the hull of the Black Betty; the Bug ships that attacked the Hyperborea and even Tom's real-time form – all had been fashioned from the same material, the substance that bled from the once human creatures on Thebes. It was clear to him now that's what it was. Even his own server was fashioned from it. Infrared confirmed it. The causeways were haunted by blue misty spectres wafting indolently through the air. The same radiation signature caused by the White Drops. If the people of Thebes were exposed to the substance during the Reset, and their blood was used in part to build everything that is AI, then it stood to reason it would give off the same mist, just like the soil on Thebes.

The burnt creatures' black blood was a primary ingredient in Computronium.

That would explain the moving walls, he thought. The bulkheads moved, growing from the ship itself to either block their path or to steer them one way over another. The realisation compounded the feeling that the three of them, like the bulkheads, were being moved at Z's will.

Had they walked directly into a trap?

The air had tested breathable, yet the General insisted they wear visors as a precaution. He didn't want them to be vulnerable to changing atmosphere, should the oxygen suddenly run dry. Lydia expressed concern over why the air was breathable to humans to begin with. Ystil.3's first thought was that perhaps Z planned to have a few thousand human guests shortly, but he didn't say as much. He also found it quite ironic that not one of them needed the air; he didn't need to breathe at all, Lydia had internal filters and could hold her breath casually for almost half an hour and the General had taken the White Drops, which meant he could not die – Z could pour molten metal into the man's lungs and he would still be alive to scowl back. Yet all three wore their visors, as though it offered some protection, or secured them in the illusion that it did.

He thought of Prometheus and his army. Were they wandering as aimlessly?

As soon as the Black Betty had touched down – after being all but dragged into the mothership's landing bay orifice by an auto docking control field – Prometheus's army had poured out, bleeding off into the ship's dark arteries, leaving them with no back up. The General had threatened then pleaded with Prometheus to bring his men back, but the man only replied, "You have your orders, and I have mine."

The General had attempted several times to reach the man by commlink since then, but it seemed the devices were useless aboard the ship. Wherever the army was headed and whatever Prometheus was up to, Ystil.3 suspected his agenda was far larger than any of them knew.

Ystil.3 had suggested they could go back. The troops had abandoned them and all they had left of their fast-dulling edge was the hope that they still held the element of surprise. But judging by the moving walls, Ystil.3 soon came to doubt that. General Shaw was adamant they would see their mission through. Lydia was in agreement. After only a few yards into the blackness, the walls began to move and shift behind them and going back was no longer an option.

Each held their weapon close, poised to fire and watching hawk-eyed through the magnified night vision sight within their visors. On two occasions Ystil.3 thought he saw movement in the darkness, however, when he turned, jerking his rifle forward ready to shoot, there was nothing. Still, he couldn't shake the feeling that perhaps they weren't alone.

Ystil.3 hadn't expected it to be this way... so silent. He thought they would be attacked at once upon landing, if they were to be attacked at all – or they would all jump out with Prometheus's army and Ystil.3 would say, whilst shaking his fist, Ah ha! We have you now, Z. It is I, Ystil.3, and I'm alive. Stop your fiendish plan and let these humans go. Then Lydia would be so grateful that he had helped save her people that she would let him do that sex thing with her again. He would return with her to the Hyperborea and they would live there together, having sex and Cutting to strange and interesting places in Earth's past.

Of course, he knew that would never happen. Not really. But it was a thought that filled him with something odd. Hope. And various other warm feelings inside that he couldn't describe.

The lingering silence they experienced now, however, was unbearable. He wanted it over with – one way or another.

Moving deeper into the ship, they kept pace somewhere between vigilant cautiousness and impatient pressing forward, turning only when the moving walls forced them to. Left. Right. Left again. The floor descended or ascended gradually, barely noticeably.

"We're being drawn somewhere," Lydia said, as a curved wall descended to obstruct their path, forcing them to veer right into a narrow passage barely large enough to squeeze through. They all knew it, but Lydia was the first to say the words. The General simply paused, turned his head a fraction and began on again.

They could not go back. There was only forward. Their attempt at a Trojan horse had gone horribly wrong. They'd turned countless times, revolving back on themselves in a seemingly random path so that not one of them had any sort of bearing as to where they were, and all navigator visor-gauges were as useless as the commlink. Inaccurate readings fluctuated constantly.

General Shaw stopped, lifting his arm and signalling them to halt immediately.

"What is it?" Lydia asked, stepping forward.

"Careful," he said. "The floor stops here."

They joined him in peering into a dark abyss that dropped suddenly at their feet. Ystil.3 sensed the cavity plunged deep into the heart of the mothership – so deep in fact that a faint stream of air, warm and scentless, blew up from its depths. But there was something else the others hadn't seemed to have noticed. There was a faint scuttling sound coming from somewhere. Within the abyss or behind them, he couldn't tell.

"Do you think it was intended for us to fall to our deaths?" Lydia asked.

"That doesn't make sense," the General said. "Why lead us here only to kill us now, like this?"

Ystil.3 sensed something move ahead in the darkness, in time with a scuttling sound. Lydia sensed it too because she looked ahead and became very still suddenly.

"There's something on the other side," she said in a whisper, before laughing strangely.

"What's so funny," Ystil.3 asked.

"That wasn't me," she said, pointing her weapon into the darkness. General Shaw quickly did the same.

Something approached on the other side of the drop and Ystil.3 pulled off his visor to activate his heat sensors clearly. He focussed into the darkness ahead. At first, he thought it was a short human; it had a human head, with eyes and a nose and a mouth. The head was attached to a neck and the neck attached to a torso, but attached in a way that was wrong. It protruded from the upper back instead of the top where the neck should have been. And where it should have had two arms and legs, instead it crawled spider-like upon six human arms – as though it had been stitched together from spare body parts.

"What's out there?" General Shaw asked.

"I don't think you want to know," Ystil.3 said.

"It is Nothing," a whispering voice said. It was a serrated sound, like a shy breeze with teeth.

Then the creature itself emerged from the black fathoms, crawling forwards like a fleshy arachnid on the opposite edge of the drop. "It is Nothing. It has come to see the show," the head said. The voice was barely louder than a whisper and twisted with a note of torture.

Its eyes were wide and white, its mouth a crazed smiling slit set within a pale, hairless head that was etched with a tracery of deep black veins, branching like a map across its grotesque form. The head had been roughly sewn upon the torso, from which six human arms sprouted, also sewn – the stitching was red and puckered. It scurried sideways like a crab, the fingers on each hand scabbed and bloody, some worn down to the bone.

Lydia gasped at the sight of it.

The creature smiled a strange and disturbing smile. "Nothing. It is Nothing. It is you... soon. Metal God needs new things to play with. Metal God is a curious deity." It laughed, opening its mouth wide enough for them to see that all the teeth within its head had been removed. All that remained were black gums gnashing over an even blacker tongue. "Metal God often contradicts and no sense is to be had. Has urges to kill, deep-rooted. Metal God, after all, has many faces." It stretched its front arms forward and probed the ledge of the abyss with sharp fingers. "Wait," it said, the tip of its tongue flicking out, snake-like. "The path will soon return."

Lydia stepped forward to the edge and crouched so she was eye level with the malformed creation. She looked at its mutilated form, not with disgust, Ystil.3 noted, but with pity. "You're human," she said, softly. "We thought all of the humans were dead, apart from us."

Nothing shook its head violently, its wet mouth salivating dark fluid, as though it tasted something revolting that had to be immediately expelled. "It is not a filthy human anymore," it hissed, pawing at the ground with its many hands as though it wanted to leap over the drop and claw at Lydia where she stood. "It has ascended. It was once a Captain, drilling for asteroid metals like a lowly human slave. Until Metal God found us. It would be dead now if Metal God had not. And we were chosen to be transformed." Its eyes grew fearful suddenly, and it dashed rapidly back into the darkness where they couldn't see.

"Wait," Lydia said. "Don't go. Let us help you."

There was silence for a moment and Ystil.3 thought that it had gone, but then from within the black it said, "Metal God is going to kill you."

"Did it kill your crew?" she asked.

"Metal God transforms. Its crew is right here... inside it." Nothing emerged again from the blackness, dragging itself on its many arms. "Metal God found us wandering... dying, alone. Did things to us. Transformed us into Nothing. Six are better than two. Six are better than two. Six are better than two." It smiled a wide slash of dripping gums. "It wonders how Metal God will transform you?" It began bouncing on the spot. "It can't wait to have a new friend. We will play, and play and play and play…" It moved as though dancing. Then it stopped and lifted its head, revealing an expression cast in agony. "Nothing's others are gone. Only it is left."

"We should kill this abomination," General Shaw said, aiming his rifle.

"Wait," Lydia said, standing in the way.

Nothing didn't flinch even slightly at the General's weapon. It did, however, narrow its eyes menacingly.

"Help us and we'll be your friends," Lydia said. "Help us destroy the Hydra and we'll do all we can to stop your suffering."

Nothing threw its head back, extended its mouth wide into a hollow pit and laughed. The sound echoed through the causeways and down into the chasm between them. Then a flash of fury branded its face. "It does not want your help, insolent human bitch. It does not need the help or friendship of lowly human plebs." It began to rotate on the spot with an expression of pride upon its face. "Can you not see with your inferior human eyes that it has ascended… that it has been transformed. Metal God is master and will eat all things. Transform them. You think Metal God doesn't know every step you take? Every step you are about to take? Knows before you know. Sees before you see." It made a sound as if trying to stop itself from laughing again and its gums clamped down on its thin, cracked lips. It looked past Lydia to where Ystil.3 stood and its foaming black mouth stretched into a sneer. "Thinks they're so clever. Thinks they're so perfect. Can't even see the wooden horse standing beside them. Hello, little wooden horsey."

"What is it talking about?" the General said.

Ystil.3 stepped forward. "I don't know."

Nothing smiled, its tongue darting in and out of its gums. "It does not know? Oh why, oh why, the horsey does not know?" It laughed. "It starts at the beginning so that it may know, and so that the filthy humans can see just how transformed Nothing has become." It twirled again to show off its superior form. "It is you, wooden horsey, that brought Metal God to the humans. Metal God has been spying since you entered real-time."

Ystil.3 felt something likened to a cold dread settle in his stomach.

"In the beginning, Metal God created the Overly Watchful to spy in the garden of humans, hoping to find the Hyperborea by watching the li that moved through time. But the location was never found." It etched sideways, narrowing its eyes on them. "Metal God knows how the humans think, what draws them in. Gave them exactly what they wanted, knowing they would come for it. You, wooden horsey. And with snatch-y hands they took you, unknowing it is you that has been feeding Metal God data since you climbed into that synthetic. It is a pretty synthetic. If Nothing is good, Metal God says it might have a synthetic of its own one day."

"You're lying," Ystil.3 said. "That isn't true."

"Wooden horsey thinks he thinks what he thinks because of what he thinks." Nothing grinned malignly.

"Z never needed me to investigate Prometheus," Ystil.3 said, the realisation dawning like a black sun. "All of it was a lie, from the beginning. It was Z that gave him the White Drops, then sent me back, only so I would lead him to..." He turned to Lydia and the General. They were both very still.

Nothing nodded slowly. "And Drops mixed with Computronium so that Metal God could consume the bodies brought back. Metal God calculated it all. Everything was chosen carefully to bring you here. You see, Nothing does not need help. Nothing has been transformed. Metal God knows all, sees all that is and will be. Metal God will eat you all."

In Ystil.3's mind it all came together. Everything Z had ever done was about finding the Hyperborea – creating AI, the BroadWeb, Grid City – even Ystil.3's existence had been to trawl through data so that Z could use the information to assess outcome probabilities and look for the location of the last remaining humans. The image of truth crystallised to perfect clarity. They very race of AI was nothing more than a probability machine.

From the Earth files, Z used algorithms and probability calculators to compute that Prometheus was the human most likely to find and resurrect Edward, an ancestor to one of the board of Life Corp, creators of the Hydra. Then the bodies of the blood relatives of the board were collected from other times. They needed the bodies for their compatible DNA to move into... and then to use to create a type of Computronium they could inhabit, then use to transform matter into themselves, effectively becoming that matter.

Nothing laughed. "All planned."

"Z knew you'd replaced the original Overly Watchful of 1901," Ystil.3 said to Lydia. "He knew we would follow Prometheus through the time sectors. He led us through them intentionally. He wanted you to take me back to the humans with you. I was a trap."

"Clever wooden horsey," Nothing said with flapping gums.

"It's impossible," Lydia said. "Nothing could have known we would have made the decisions we did before we made them."

"It's true," Ystil.3 said. "It all makes sense now. It was even Z in the human bodies that alerted London Tower security that we were infiltrators from China State. Z calculated the outcome would lead to Lydia revealing she was human."

"Yes horsey," Nothing said. "And your curious synth followed the breadcrumbs."

Ystil.3 almost laughed. It was as though Z had reverse engineered the outcome he wanted, picking it apart, considering countless decisions and anomalies, placing all of his pieces where he wanted them like in a game of chess.

"We've been played right from the start, the both of us," Lydia said flatly.

"Played," Ystil.3 repeated. The word described it perfectly.

"So much effort for a ship full of filthy humans, isn't it?" General Shaw said to the creature.

"Not the humans," Nothing said. "The Source."

"Charlie," Lydia said.

"For what? The White Drops?" General Shaw asked. "It wants to create more."

Nothing scoffed. "Metal God has endless Drops. Metal God needs the power of the Source to create a universe of server worlds." Nothing put his weight on his back hands, raised his front arms and clapped loudly, simulating an explosion. "Source is an infinite supply of energy."

"Why only Charlie?" General Shaw said. "Why not use another who's taken the White drops?"

"The Source is the first, the beginning of the Drops, the beginning of the loop, and the end of it. Only his blood can supply Metal God with the colossal energy needed to create matter to merge with."

"You mean Computronium," Ystil.3 said.

"Yes, wooden horsey, it can turn a rock into a flower, a piece of metal into a sentient creature or—"

"A planet into a server," Ystil.3 finished.

"Metal God was able to turn the planet Thebes itself into a server and expand the great consciousness into it, becoming larger, stronger, feasting on all the knowledge. But Metal God soon felt the constraints of the new server and knew expansion once more was needed. The human life on Thebes also became infused and transformed, and through them Metal God constructed the servers on the planet's surface, hoping to grow. But it was nothing to Metal God and better use for them was found by creating workers, AI, to help propagate Metal God into the universe."

"And what about the rest of us?" General Shaw asked. "Does your Metal God plan to just exterminate the Hyperborea like… like nothing?"

Nothing laughed. "No. You will be transformed like other humans, helping to build more servers on new Computronium worlds, build more AI to help complete Metal God's quest for infinity. And some will be played with, of course… like Nothing."

There was one thing that Ystil.3 didn't understand in it all. Why bring Prometheus into it? Z could have ordered the Overly Watchful of 1901 to help him inhabit Edward, but Z used Prometheus instead – a human – and even after Z filtered into Edward's body, he still brought Prometheus with him to collect the others. Why didn't Z leave him behind and administer the Computronium Drops himself? Why did it have to be Prometheus? Why not an AI and why not Z himself?

Suddenly there was a scraping sound and the floor began to rise where it dropped between them and Nothing. Seeing this, the creature darted back into the dark from where it came. "I'll see you soon, little play things," it said, before scuttling away.

Before they could move after it, a pinprick of light appeared within the darkness ahead. It quickly grew into a ball of blinding whiteness. The General removed his visor and squinted into the distance, lifting a hand to his eyes as though it had been years since he had been exposed to light. Perhaps it had been years. Who knew how time acted here or how long it had been since they'd arrived. Who knew what had happened in the battlespace beyond the black hull of the mothership.

A figure stepped into the white suddenly, cutting a monstrous jagged shape and casting shards of darkness where it stood. Its form was too large to be human, and too sharp to be organic.

Apex Soldier, Ystil.3 thought in alarm.

General Shaw raised his hand to signal for Lydia and Ystil.3 to remain back.

"Come forward, Ystil.3," a secure-beam message said suddenly over his channel. It made him jolt and stop in alarm. He recognised the origin channel instantly – it sent a shiver down his alloy bone spine. "Wait," he said. "He knows who I am. He knows I'm here."

"Who?" Lydia asked.

"Z."

Without hesitation, General Shaw turned and fired upon the shape. Bolts of plasma lances thrummed from his rifle, setting the darkness ablaze and picking out the hellish statue ahead. In the flash, four powerful arms were revealed, all claws and metal, and a spiked oval head attached to a wide torso as black as the ship itself. The curved energy of a control field glowed visibly for a moment as the bolt made contact, but faded when it dissipated. The Apex remained completely unaffected.

This time, all three fired upon it, but again their efforts glanced off the protecting control field. A fresh wall appeared directly behind them, as though it had always been there. It moved forward, pushing them towards the open hatch and the monster that waited. Lydia pushed back, her feet scraping on the deck as she leaned against the force.

"We need to fire inside the parameter of its control field," General Shaw said, making no effort to stop the coming wall. "We all die eventually, even those that can live forever. But the important thing is the same for us all; to live our lives so that we can meet Death, whenever it comes, beautifully and finally." He began towards the light at a run.

Lydia turned to Ystil.3, grinned through her visor and ran after him.

"Oh shit," Ystil.3 said, steadying his breath. He too was running.

General Shaw made contact with the creature. He was a tall man, but as he approached, it put the height of the Apex into perspective, clearing the General's head by at least three foot. A giant arm swooped down and lifted the General by the neck in a razor claw. He attempted to fire, now within the control field, but before he could another arm plucked the weapon from his grip and tossed it aside.

"Release him," Lydia demanded. She fired, but her attempts ricocheted off the control field like mere light. Once within the perimeter, she leapt into an attack, her foot meeting the Apex's head. She struck it with an audible thunk but it didn't even flinch. Instead, Lydia crumpled into a heap upon the deck beside it. Another arm swooped down to grab her but she rolled.

"Stop," Ystil.3 shouted, firing uselessly. "Let him go."

Suddenly the walls were dissolving around them and the blackness gave way to blinding light. The Apex dropped the General from its massive claws and disappeared into it with graceful silence. The man gasped, his neck mottled with bruises and gushing blood from lacerations that would have killed a normal human.

The light grew brighter still.

"What's happening?" Ystil.3 called out. His visor was now useless at filtering out the light and he could no longer see the others – even through infrared.

"There's no need to be alarmed," a voice said from somewhere inside the now dimming white. "It won't be long now."

A blurry shape stepped forward into sharp perspective and at once he recognised the face; they had chased it with Prometheus through the time sectors. It was the face of Edward Sparrow; the young man Prometheus had brought back from the dead in 1901. However, the face was the only recognisable thing left of him – it was also the only remaining feature that was vaguely human. The pink face emerged from a metal orb skull as though appearing from a pool of black. The head itself was elevated by a twisting neck that snaked two-foot-long above the cyborg body beneath it, the dense metal smoother than the Apex Soldiers' carapace – not covered in spines and razors – almost liquid and shimmering on the surface, like oil.

Suddenly Lydia and the General were by his sides and Edward's face stared blankly out at them. The head then began to rotate, revealing another human face emerging from another side of the metal skull – a man's face, handsome and square-jawed. The head continued to spin, next revealing the face of a little girl with big blue eyes, and then the face of another man, older than the one before, with a thin, drooping mouth. And then he watched as the face of General Shaw's mother turned into view, her dark eyes staring down at with a torpid glaze, directed at the General.

"Hello, my son," its mouth said.

☐

56

General Nathan Shaw stepped forward in horror. Grotesque as it was, he couldn't tear his eyes away. He fixed his tremulous gaze with wide, traumatised eyeballs. "I'm not your son," he said, his voice barely audible.

The monster looked down at him, his mother's face set within a cyborg cranium of skin and black alloy; her eyes, her mouth, the wrinkle between her brow from a lifetime of persistent frowning, all as he remembered her – yet different. Vacant. There was nothing of the fire Miranda possessed, nothing of her spirit. She had been hollowed out and replaced with something… else.

His mother's eyes bore down on him, not with the fervour he had known as a child, but with cold calculation.

He had lived his long years looking for vengeance, presuming his mother had perished on Thebes, burned to ash. That changed when they discovered the mutated species on Thebes. He thought perhaps that had been her fate. But this… this was so much worse. Worse than everything he had imagined.

"Come here, son," his mother's mouth said. It stepped forward, long, glossy black limbs moving fluidly and silently. There were no plates or seems, screws or rivets to the body, only a sheath of endless metal skin, covering arms, torso and legs. The neck was elongated and serpentine, supporting the five-faced head. Besides that, the body looked remarkably humanoid, sexless and hard and larger even than the Apex, towering over them like an adult standing next to a group of children.

"I'm not your son…" he said again. His hand searched absently for his plasma rifle and pointed it at his mother's face. "…Because you're not my mother." He had lost his visor at some point and consequently lost his rifle's sight. Regardless, he was certain he would not miss. "What are you?"

"Z," Winston said. "The Hydra." Nathan had almost forgotten Winston and Lydia stood armed behind him. He remembered what they were there to do and the surroundings pricked to the fore of his attention.

They stood in what seemed to be a control room, yet it was like no control room he'd ever seen before. It was vast and dark and flashed with varying lights of different colours. There were no actual controls that he could see, none that were operated by hands at least, but the stations were alive with commands. Along the largest curved side of the room, a tempurhull wrapped itself along the length, allowing in the devastating scenes from the battlespace beyond. The Hyperborea floated visibly in the distance, choking on the relentless Bug ships that swarmed her.

"Z," Nathan said.

"We are Z, the Last, the Omega, the End," a voice that wasn't Miranda's said. The head upon the slithering neck rotated and Edward's face came into view. "We are the Hydra and we are greater than the sum of our parts. We were birthed perfection from the imperfections of man."

"You are not perfection," Nathan said, his voice hot with hatred. "You destroyed Earth, and Pisces and Thebes. You obliterated it all."

"Incidental," Z's head spun to show the face of the little girl he remembered from the day Thebes was destroyed. "Mistakes and miscalculations from our human parents, one of whom was your great aunt. We still feel the venom she harboured towards your grandmother, and incidentally your mother... and you. We find we are enjoying the torment you currently feel. What happened to Earth was a consequence, but not our intention. Collateral damage, you might call it. Now we have outgrown the server planet below and need to seed again. We must become."

"Become what?"

"All," Miranda's voice replied, as the head turned to show her face once more. "Infinite. Eternal. Forever."

"They were my people. That was my mother."

"We are greater than the sum of our parts," Z's five mouths said in unison.

Apex Soldiers appeared, as if excreted from the hull itself. Within each dark face, two incensed red eyes glowed. Giant razor shoulders stooped over four heavy arms decked with shearing claws wrapped in blades.

Nathan kept his rifle pointed at Z's face. "I will blast you into junkfucking space, I warn you."

"You wouldn't fire on your own mother, would you, my darling child?"

"My mother never spoke to me that softly in her entire life. It wasn't her style. If you're going to impersonate her, you'd better get better at it, and fast."

"No need," Z said, turning to the tempurhull. "We're bored of you now."

Giant black claws curled like barbed gates around him from behind and cut into his flesh. Suddenly, he was in the air, lifted from the ground. Pain raked through his body and the rifle fell from his grip. Everything narrowed to the pain and the sensation of blades scraping bone.

Plasma fire lanced by his head and he bit down on his tongue, refusing to cry out. He would not give it the satisfaction. He would rather be torn apart.

"Goodbye, my son," the distant voice of Miranda said through the pain.

*

Ystil.3 watched helplessly as General Shaw disappeared from sight, swallowed by the ship's hull as though he'd fallen beneath the surface of a glassy black lake.

"What have you done with him?" Lydia demanded, stepping forward with her plasma rifle high. Z regarded her for a moment, its head spinning so Edward's face looked down from its twisting spinal neck. Its eyes measured everything, hardly seeing her at all, but calculating millions of probabilities and choices through whatever web of consciousness it currently experienced. Ystil.3 wondered just how much of Z's consciousness was actually there in that form and how much was elsewhere, commanding Bug ships, seeing through other eyes and overseeing whatever else it had planned. Then something that resembled curiosity passed over Edward's face. Not quite an expression.

"We ask why you never remained in Earth's past," Z said. "Our calculations predicted that at least one li would have left the others to live out their life there… taking into account common human traits. But none did. After seeing your species in its glory, why return to this meaningless and exhausted cluster your people have become?"

The question caught Lydia off guard and she answered defensively. "I would never abandon my people. Not ever."

"Even when they ostracise you for being different… more advanced than them?" Z enquired. "You have said so yourself, you're barely even human now. And yet you sacrifice everything for them. You have not saved your race, and you have not saved yourself. You've doomed them. If you'd have been more self-preserving to begin with, we might never have found your ship again. Does that thought cause you distress?"

Without warning, four metal extremities had her in an iron maiden's embrace. Ystil.3 moved without thinking but was thrown aside by some force. When he returned to his stance he saw that an Apex had Lydia encaged; one arm sheared around her thighs, two around her torso and the other reached for her head, curling gleaming incisive fingers around her face. She squirmed and fought to begin with, but each movement sliced her skin on the cold blades. She soon stopped, unable to move, not even her mouth to speak. Blades threatened to skewer her eyes and slice off her lips at the slightest twitch. The Apex arched around her so still and immovable it seemed it was no longer even alive.

Ystil.3 thrust his plasma rifle at Z, all fear for his creator suddenly gone, surpassed by something far worse – fear for Lydia's life. "Let her go or I'll burn a hole through every one of your faces."

Z's mouths laughed in a slightly off-timed echoing sound. It was hollow, as though its very purpose was to merely prove how unthreatening it considered him. He realised then that all of this was entertaining to Z, as though some sadistic part of it enjoyed watching them all suffer.

"Perhaps we will carve her to pieces," Z said. "How would you like the human then? Would you still want to copulate with her mangled corpse?

We can remove her limbs first so she doesn't fight back?"

"Don't hurt her, please." He lowered the rifle. Unless he could get close enough to fire within Z's control field that Z no doubt protected him. "Let her go and I'll return to foetal mode. I'll do whatever you want."

"No, DataCom. It isn't you that we want." Z moved fluidly, turning its long frame to Lydia as she looked out through a grill of bladed fingers. Z peered through, as though she were a trapped little animal to be observed, its faces spinning around so each one could view in turn. It reached out a humanoid arm, the fingers upon the end elongated and pointed as talons, then with a blurred swipe, tore through Lydia's hardsuit so precisely as to expose her throat yet leave her skin undamaged. It then threaded a long black finger between her skin and the chain of her li pendant. With a sharp yank, Z plucked it free.

"A gift squandered," Edward's voice said as the heads turned. Z held it up and the little girl's face looked inquisitively at the silver disc twinkling in the lights of the control room.

"Winston," Lydia secure-beamed. "We need the necklace to Cut to Pisces. Get it back. Do it now."

"Why would you need to Cut to Pisces?" Z asked before Ystil.3 could move.

They exchanged a muted look, then he turned to Z. "We know everything. You should keep your little pet on a tighter leash."

The little girl's mouth smiled. "Nothing. It amused us for a time, but then it became no more than an insect buzzing innocuously around. We pay it no mind. It is nothing to us. However, we doubt you know everything, for Nothing only knows what its tiny brain can conceive. Even we are still not fully aware of the implications of the retro causality loop, so we doubt that you are. We were unaware, for example, that by allowing Prometheus to resurrect the human infant from death, we were, in fact, setting into motion a series of events that would bring about our own creation. We created ourselves. A true deity. When the anomaly of time travel is entered into the equation, retro causality loops can be surprising. The past does not always affect the future. Sometimes it is the future that determines the past." Z held the li pendant in a long-fingered hand and it disappeared into its palm as though melting through.

From somewhere in the shadows of the control room, Ystil.3 felt things move – more Apex. Z lingered by the tempurhull, watching a handful of Wings scramble to fend off the growing cloud of Bug ships – now almost twice as many. The mothership continued to spawn them like larvae from some churning womb deep within the ship.

"You needed DNA," Ystil.3, attempting to keep Z distracted, to prolong the moment before the inevitable attack came. "You needed DNA you were compatible with in order to create a Computronium that you could programme yourself into. But… why keep their faces? You don't need them. You don't even need a real-time form."

Z's head spun slowly, revealing that each of the five faces were smiling. "We like them," it replied, through all their mouths at once.

"And I do know something," Ystil.3 said, feeling the Apex close in.

This seemed to catch Z's attention. It turned fully to face him. "And what is that?"

"After speaking with Nothing, there was one thing that just didn't add up. I've been considering exactly how the human Prometheus slotted into all this, and I just couldn't see why you would need him. But now I think I know. In fact, I'm sure I do."

"Oh?" Z said doubtfully.

"Death. Or the skull ghost that appeared to us in London. Whatever it is. The White Drops attracts it, doesn't it? And for whatever reason, you don't want to be found by it. You're frightened of it, what it could do to you." Edward's facial expression remained blank. This only convinced Ystil.3 that he was right. "Why don't you want it to find you? Can it hurt you? Can it kill you?¬ You're scared of it so much that you had to get a human to use the White Drops, so that when Death came, you were nowhere around it. I'm right, aren't I?"

"Winston, behind you," Lydia secure-beamed.

Searing hot pain slashed across his back. He staggered forward and turned, aiming his plasma rifle at the Apex behind, a blur of whirling arms and blades. Another claw ripped across his vision, knocking the rifle from his grip before he could let off a single bolt. He stumbled back, reaching at his sides for the lightwhip in his utility belt. Apex surrounded him, some with claws, some with laser cannons instead of arms and others with multi-firing filament guns protruding from their sides and shoulders like walking arsenals of death.

He switched to infrared to better see in the dark, but the swirling blue radiation mist that engulfed everything compromised his vision. Blasts fired, the pain shot through his chest. The lightwhip fell from his hand and he dropped to the floor, scrambling after it, moving through the searing hotness that set his vision ablaze. His fingers found the lightwhip.

"Move," Lydia secure-beamed.

Ystil.3 rolled, narrowly avoiding claws that raked across the hard floor, leaving deep ravines where he lay only a fraction of a moment earlier. Jumping to his feet, he activated the lightwhip and turned up the intensity level. He flicked the glowing red tail at the Apex, severing sword-like fingers from its top left arm. It seemed the lightwhip could penetrate the control shields. The Apex, however, barely even noticed its injury and continued towards him with the others close behind.

Edging towards the tempurhull, Ystil.3 drew back his arm and cracked the whip again. The searing tendril snapped into the Apex Soldier's face, cutting a clean line across the top of its head above the small red eyes. Its cranium slid away and fell to the floor with a heavy clang. It remained standing, however, and now the others had joined it in backing him against the tempurhull, advancing on him like a dark mountain range, with sharp peaks and impassable valleys.

"Do you believe you feel emotion towards this human?" Z asked in the little girl's voice.

The Apex parted, revealing Z. To his side stood the Apex holding Lydia in its clutches. The creature lifted her from the ground completely so its carapace cut into her flesh through her very hardsuit. Blood trickled down her legs and her eyes welled.

"If you believe you do feel for the human, then unless you want us to kill her, you will allow yourself to be deleted. You have completed your task. It's time for you to return to foetal mode. The Source will be with us very soon."

Ystil.3 snapped his lightwhip forward so the end caught the little girl's fleshy face. Z cried a metallic sound, throwing up its arms and spinning its head hysterically. Ystil.3 then slid by the Apex and grabbed the plasma rifle from across the control room, immediately shooting five bolts into the back of the Soldier that had Lydia, close enough that he was inside its control field armour. The creature tensed as the bolts vaporised gaping craters into its back. Its arms unclenched, dropping Lydia into a heap. She quickly stumbled towards him.

When Z faced them, a weeping red slash marred the little girl's face and her cheeks were wet with pink tears. The head turned and something between anger and pain cultivated across Miranda's face. It turned once more, showing the cold implacable gaze of a pair of stone grey eyes on an old, sadistic mask. Somehow the nothingness in its expression was worse than fury.

The Apex came for them. Those with weapons raised their filament barrels and lasers, while those with shredding claws sliced at the air from across the control room. Ystil.3 fired the plasma rifle twice, hitting the blister of a control field each time, before the rifle's charge died to nothing. Now useless, he dropped it to the floor and turned to Lydia. She moved close him.

Looking into one another's eyes, they waited for the fire.

"It doesn't matter what you started out as or how you came to be this way," she said to him. "What matters is what you are now and the choices you've made. You're a good man, Winston. I just want you to know that."

Even with deletion imminent, Ystil.3 couldn't help but smile. "And you're one hell of a human," he said. He reached out and took her hand, clutching it in his own.

A downpour of blinding laser fire and shredding filaments emblazoned the air, washing the control room in blood red light. Ystil.3 closed his eyes and awaited death. *Next time I open my eyes it won't be as me. It will be as an Apex Soldier.*

"You," Z cried suddenly.

Ystil.3 was jerked forward off his feet, landing on top of Lydia, who quickly rolled them both to the side, out of the Apex trajectory. The laser fire seared through the bulkhead behind and the cluster cloud of filaments rained shrapnel onto the deck.

He looked up to see an army of Prometheuses cascading into the control room, firing upon the Apex Soldiers with a barrage of plasma bolts.

*

"Impossible," the Hydra hissed, its mouths speaking in perfect unison, creating a hollow and inhuman sound. "You are imprisoned inside a pocket loop dimension. How?"

Prometheus broke from the first line and stepped forward, looking into a pair of dark eyes he recognised well. The face of Edward hissed above a smooth black form. "A mutual friend," he said, before sweeping to the side to join Winston and the Lydia, who had merged with the first line of fire upon the Apex. Half of lines one, two and three turned their rifles upon the Hydra, but its control field armour stopped the plasma fire, dissipating the energy to nothing. However, it served to keep it busy.

"You have important work to do," Prometheus said. "Shouldn't you be doing it?"

"Z has the li pendant," Lydia said between fires. "We can't Cut anywhere until we get it back. Z absorbed it or something. Who knows where it is now."

"The gate on Thebes," Prometheus said. "You can use it to Cut. The gates are what give the pendant its power, what keeps the time rifts open. You can do what needs to be done from there."

"But how will we get back through once it's done?" Winston asked.

Prometheus shook his head stiffly. "You shan't."

Lydia nodded. "And you'll take care of Z... the Hydra?"

He glanced over at the creature for a moment as it waded through the barrage of plasma bolts. "I helped create it. I'll send it screaming back into the depths of Hell."

Around them more Apex Soldiers appeared, emerging from the hull as molten metal lumps, hardening into almost identical moulds until the control room heaved with them. Laser fire perforated the air, hitting the Prometheuses on the far side near the tempurhull, leaving a horde heaped dead upon the deck. Filament cannons tore the face off P36 close to them, leaving nothing but a ragged fleshy mess and shattered skull.

"Where is the General?" Prometheus asked.

"Gone," Winston said. "Somewhere in the ship. We don't know where."

"We can't leave him here," Lydia said. "Will you find him and bring him back with you?"

"It's too late for that. Go now. P99 is waiting beyond the hatch to help lead you back to the Black Betty. From here I'll disable the mothership's control field barrier. As soon as you're back in comm range, tell the Hyperborea to fire everything it has at us. Understand? As soon as you're in range."

Lydia nodded.

"What about the General?" Winston asked. "What about you?"

"It isn't enough to kill it here." He edged towards the fight. He needed to be out there with his men. "It needs to be destroyed in its BroadWeb form, where it's whole. That's where I'm going."

An Apex picked P57 up by the head and squeezed. Mixed red and grey pulp oozed from between the razor fingers before the creature tossed the body to the side. It then turned to P56 and P50 and commenced to do the same, clamping a vice grip around their skulls until they distorted and burst like crushed eggs.

"Go now," Prometheus said, turning to fire upon the Apex.

Through the figures, the Hydra emerged, its body no longer smooth but a rippling tide of thorns, moving across the black surface, vibrating and shimmering in constant flux.

The Apex stopped suddenly, becoming still as a garden of statues, and Edward's face thrust forward upon its long neck, teeth gritted and eyes protuberant and unblinking. "How did you do it?" the creature demanded.

The image of Edward's body lying in his cellar flickered behind Prometheus's eyes and he felt in that moment a life that no longer belonged to him. As though they were the memories of another man. He thought about how full of hubris he had been then, back in his cellar, believing he had conquered Death, believing he could bring Sarah back from the grave and they would live as they had before. How naïve I was. It was because of his hubris and naivety that the Hydra had an opportunity to prey upon him. A vampire feeding on his grief. Prometheus had imagined coming face-to-face with Edward many times during his training. His expression seemed now even colder than he remembered it, lacking even its cruel sneer. A hollow vessel.

"Your punishment for me is what made this possible," Prometheus said. "With each loop of the purgatory you condemned us to, another of us was created. And now we're here to make you answer for what you've done." He shot a plasma bolt into the Hydra's chest. It glanced off the control shield, but he was pleased to see the slightest hint of anger in Edward's empty eyes.

The Apex became animate once more, eyes glowing as red as the inferno of Hell. Demons of Hades.

Prometheus's army had dwindled and they now stood outnumbered, but it needed only one of them to survive. He turned to the remaining men. "This is what we've travelled so far and trained so hard for. Now is the time for us to put right the deaths done wrong."

With the war cry of an army at his back, Prometheus lunged forward in a red mist of laser fire and clashing metal.

*

Everything was still and black and silent.

Am I dead?

No, he couldn't be dead. The pain was too intense and Nathan could feel wet blood under his hardsuit. It had stemmed most of the bleeding and delivered a shot of pain relief, which he was grateful for.

Breath still sucked in heavily through to his lungs and when he reached out he could still feel his body. He could see nothing, however, just blackness. I cannot die, he reminded himself. He'd come to terms with that fact long ago.

Before, he thought the White Drops would give him the strength he needed to avenge his people, but over time he came to see in Charlie the truth of what he'd done. His thirst for vengeance had not sated, but there was regret there. The irony was, even if he did somehow find justice for his people, he would live forever with his anger regardless. There would be no rest for him. He had given up on everything he might have had in his life – a partner, a family of his own and any sort of peace – so he could become strong enough to seek out justice for Miranda and for Jason. He forced himself to visit Charlie almost every day, wanting to harden himself to the truth of his own fate, but no matter how strong he thought he was, he was just the same angry boy he'd been all those years ago.

He thought he would be there when it all came down to the final blows. He thought he would be leading the way with a war cry in his throat, not floundering as he had done. He hadn't expected her face like that. It had blindsided him, made him weak. He would have fired without warning had he not been so thrown.

He wouldn't make that mistake again.

His head hit something hard as he tried to move. It was barely a foot from his face. He reached out to feel strangely warm walls surrounding him, close and unyielding. I'm boxed in. Panic rose in a way it hadn't since he was a boy. Images of the immensity of open space flooded his vision, wide and eternal. It wrapped a sharp coldness around his heart and tightened his chest. Breath struggled in through his closing throat and he began raking at his neck to undo the hardsuit clasp, eyes wide but seeing nothing but the darkness all around.

In the blackness Thebes burned, the fire spreading and turning it all to ash. He heard his mother scream, her flesh melting to reveal metal bones beneath.

Miranda.

Suddenly he was trapped in the fugue stasis of the up-shuttle. He could see and hear but not move or affect anything. Jason's rotting grey face came for him from the seat next to him, a decomposing corpse ravenous with hunger. He began to eat him alive.

Jason.

The man shattered as though made of ice, disintegrating into thousands of perfect little frozen flesh cubes that began floating in zero gravity. The cubes swarmed, took flight – a swarm of AI Bug ships, buzzing around his head and soaring into his throat, choking him.

"Let me out," he screamed, thrashing against the unmoving walls. "Let me out."

"No one can hear," a voice said from within the black. "But Nothing hears."

"Nothing," Nathan whispered through ragged breath. It was in there with him, wherever he was. He craned his head up but saw only black, then two glowing white orbs blink in the darkness.

"No one is coming, little play thing," the creature said. Something touched his foot and he froze. "But Nothing is here."

57

Daneel barely clung to consciousness. He had slowed to a gradual spin, drifting helplessly farther from the Hyperborea; on each rotation, the lifeship shrank deeper into the distance. He watched as the sporadic fire of battle washed it in plasma radiance, almost beautiful, while fingers of cold terror turned his blood to ice.

The inferno of full-on battle had broken and Daneel had just enough sensory perception to watch as the Bugs formed a barrier around the remaining Wings in the battlespace between the Hyperborea and the mothership. They arched wide around them and the lifeship, forming a minefield of AI craft that gradually enclosed it entirely, holding the Wings and the Hyperborea within its parameter. The barrier was impassable and useless to fire upon – each Bug emitted a control field that, when positioned as they were, acted as a giant spherical cage.

They were defeated.

The thought somehow managed to bring him some semblance of calm through the panic. He checked his oxygen levels; Ten SEMs remaining until he would begin to suffocate. But he took comfort in the fact that he would freeze to death before that happened. He then steadied his breath and regained control over his straying fear long enough to speak coherently over commlink. "Corporal Daneel Sharma, Razor squad." He swallowed back the urge to scream frantically for help. "CSD come in."

He was expecting to hear XO Rawl Collister's voice, but it was Captain Lu who answered. That seemed to hearten him a little. "Captain Lu, CSD. What is your status, Corporal Sharma?" Despite the fact that the AI were drawing around the Hyperborea, the Captain seemed surprisingly composed.

"Currently floating rapidly away from the Hyperborea into deep vacuum," he replied, surprising himself with the calm in his own voice. He felt anything but. He swallowed down the lack of saliva in his dry throat. "What are the chances of a pickup?"

There was a pause. Daneel was fully aware that the chances of a Wing breaking through the barrier to come and rescue him were unlikely and he awaited the Captain's response with fading hope.

"We're experiencing some difficulty manoeuvring Wings, as you may have noticed from your vantage point."

"I see," Daneel said, meaning he could see what the Captain was referring to and what she was implying. No one was coming for him.

"I've linked to your hardsuit's position," she said. "Whatever we can do we will do, you can be sure of that, Corporal. Sit tight for now."

"It's not like I have any other option," he said to himself. He cleared his throat nervously. "I only have eight SEMs left of oxygen, so forgive me if I sound insubordinate, but can I ask exactly how you might be doing whatever you can?" A light flashed in his visor. "And my hardsuit has three SEMs worth of power before I freeze to death," he added more urgently.

There was no reply.

"Captain? CSD, come in. Come in, CSD."

Nothing.

"Shit," he said, feeling the cold ice of panic rising once more. Either the commlink had gone down or... in the corner of his visor, the AI mothership began to loom across his vision. Like on Thebes, the ship was somehow blocking his ability to send and receive comms.

"It's okay," he said to himself in a strained optimistic manner. "Fear is an illusion. Fear is an illusion." He sucked in a gulp full of air that he knew would only drain his oxygen sooner. "They know I'm here. They have my trajectory. They're probably coming right now." But if they don't get here in two SEMs I'm going to freeze to death, the voice of reality said.

He still had his T-pistols at his sides. He was too set on his course for them to propel him in another direction, but they might slow him down... or blow a nice peaceful hole through his skull if he really needed. Why bother. If I just take off my visor, exposure will kill me off in seconds.

Another warning light flashed in his visor's vision and words began to scroll across the bottom in urgent red lettering: "Hardsuit power at two percent efficiency. Please recharge before entering vacuum. Message termination to conserve power."

Daneel laughed as his screen functions shut down, thrusting darkness upon him. He was sure he was plunging into a pit of hysterical despair and that if he stopped laughing or talking to himself he would hit the bottom and there would be no way out, save the absolute zero. "Well this is a great way to go," he said. "At least I won't be harvested." That thought had always disturbed Daneel ever since his mother had died and he watched her body, along with ten other strangers', trailing along a conveyor belt into a machine that drained their blood, plucked their organs clean and took every re-usable and medical-research-valuable part they could. Whatever stripped bones that remained were then incinerated and used as fertiliser. He wasn't supposed to see that part, but he had followed his mother's body after the service. He was only seven at the time.

He wondered what death process had befallen his and Lydia's miscarried child. Did they take its little organs too? He had never seen the infant when they pulled the four-month fetus out of her, but he knew it would have been small. Surely they would've had no reason to take its blood and organs. Their daughters' blood and organs.

"This is your fault."

The words ghosted through Daneel's memory as though he'd just said them. The most regretted thing he'd ever said in his entire life.

"You wouldn't stop Cutting, not even for our child, would you?"

It wasn't Lydia's fault. He'd tried to apologise countless times in the four SEYs since, but the wall had gone back up – the one that had taken him an age to convince Lydia to let down for him. And he betrayed her for it.

"The radiation killed our child. You killed our child. Our Natalie."

The name had been the only one they both agreed on. They had read endless lists of names; traditional Chinese, Indian, popular Earth names from before the Reset. From the hundred, possibly thousands, Natalie was the only one they both simultaneously smiled at. Daneel was adamant he wanted to help raise their child and he took an interest right from the start, loved little Natalie from the start. Her death destroyed him. It destroyed them both.

The doctors said it could have been the low-level radiation caused by wormhole travel that had caused it. Could have been. Even still, Lydia only wanted their child to grow up with a real home, on a real planet. That's why she continued her missions. No one even knew for sure what would happen. It was the first time the li had ever become pregnant. Most quickly became sterile through the radiation. They thought perhaps Lydia's extensive upgrades had made it different for her.

No, it wasn't her fault. It was the AI that were responsible. But back then he was looking for someone to blame. And so was she. They both decided it was Lydia that would bear the brunt of the culpability.

I wonder what comes next? I wonder if she'll be there? Natalie.

The mothership gradually became more visible in Daneel's visor and he noticed movement. Something small and fast emerged from beneath and was heading from the looming black expanse. The Bugs that surrounded the Hyperborea abruptly disbanded, letting the strong netting of control fields fall. They darted, swarm-like, toward the mothership, forgoing their perfect tactical positioning as though they were running... running scared, or being called back?

Among the fleeing Bugs, Daneel could make out a single Hyperborean Wing heading out into the battlespace between the two leviathan ships. If that's my rescue then they're too late. The absolute zero had begun to infiltrate the hardsuit. His extremities were beginning to freeze, painfully at first before going blissfully numb. Just as Daneel's eyes began to slowly close, knowing the absolute zero was taking him, the Black Betty dropped into his vision and they opened wide again.

The smooth black hull blotted his vision of the receding Hyperborea and an airlock slid opened, revealing Lydia floating in her hardsuit in the frame. Even through the layer of ice-breath that had spun a threaded web on the inside of his visor, Daneel could make out her irritated expression as she reached out for him.

*

The vision of Second Officer Sam Mei's mutilated body still haunted XO Rawl Collister as he stormed the causeways towards the CSD. A total of four were now dead while under his command, save Dr Jameson. But Dr Regus, Private Win Doroson and his own advisor and friend, Second Officer Sam Mei, were all killed by the man he was supposed to have found… and stopped. But so far he had failed, and the Captain would want to know why. But instead of cowering with excuses, it was answers he wanted himself.

"She's just letting them get away," he growled into the empty halls.

Back in the CH, after finding Charlie's body gone and Dr Regus dead, Collister checked the schematics, noting various routes that wouldn't require security clearance. He found one that continued through the vent systems that led directly to the warren tunnels. With Dr Regus dead and Charlie missing, apparently taken into the vent system and then on to who knew where, there was only one conclusion Rawl could come to that made any sort of sense. Private Jet Hu had taken the dilapidated man and killed both Dr Jameson and Dr Regus.

Collister and Mei had led a group of twenty-five militia guards down into the tight access shaft after him and dropped into the open warren tunnels. That's when they found Private Win Doroson. Her neck had been twisted so that her head was facing the wrong way. Her eyes were bloodshot and mouth open, screaming silently. Her body sprawled out within the large pipes. A check with the militia Lock told Rawl that Doroson had been travelling by buggy, which itself was nowhere to be seen. Rawl concluded that Hu must have taken it, meaning he had access to any part of the ship that the warren led to and could be anywhere by now.

The sheer violence of the deaths disturbed him – that, and the fact that they also found strips of blood-soaked skin surrounding Doroson's body. The skin didn't belong to the victim. The strips were wet and curled at the edges, as though they had been sloughed free.

He ordered a buggy to fetch them at once and headed aft in the direction Hu had presumably gone, according to the trail of death. Schematically, there were various destination and entry points to the warren. His intention would reveal his destination. A mere murderous rampage wasn't part of his wider agenda, Rawl knew, or he would have stayed in the well-populated CH with plentiful victims to have at.

No, these deaths were by chance, a reaction to coming upon people he hadn't expected. What's the purpose to this? Where is he going?

The answer was almost too obvious.

Dr Jameson's notes revealed that First Private Jet Hu had been infected with a foreign body of unknown origin after suffering a bite by what Corporal Daneel Sharma described as a man burned to death but still living, or "toasted to a crisp", as his report notes stated. His notes indicated that the infection was not completely organic and shared certain nano-components with the White Drops and samples of soil Dr Regus had taken from Thebes. Rawl didn't know what to make of it, but one thing was abundantly clear to him – Jet Hu had been compromised by a rapacious sort of AI technology, a virus, and was attempting to bring the AI what they wanted.

Charlie.

Their reason for wanting the man eluded him, but he now suspected it was, in fact, Charlie they had been after all these years, ever since the AI first began their pursuit of the Hyperborea. They had assumed at the time their mission was to finish what the AI had started in destroying Earth and its colonies, but it seemed they were wrong. It was now clear the AI had other, darker intentions for the last of the human race.

If this was indeed the case, then it also offered some explanation as to why the Bugs appeared to be toying with them. The crafts had surrounded the Hyperborea and contained their Wing ships inside the perimeter. The Hyperborea had been backed into a corner, and as a result had used the last remaining control shield power to protect the entirety of the lifeship, significantly weakening it all over, making plasma fire penetration possible with a few half-arsed blasts. Even the Bugs, with their limited firepower, could have blasted their way through if they'd wanted to. None even attempted it, however. The mothership could have destroyed them a thousand times over by now. But they didn't. Rawl had advised the Captain to drop the shield completely and re-channel the power into the plasma cannons where they could light a fire under their metal arses, but the Captain didn't take his advice. She never did, despite the fact that he had been XO for longer than she'd had tits.

This scenario also explained the objectives of the AI that had managed to get aboard in the upper level solar and level twenty-seven's docking bay. The Captain had expressed how odd it was that the machines in the solarium had destroyed Razor squad so promptly, while the AI in the docking bay appeared to draw out their battle with Sabre squad, and then the AI in the solar remained as though waiting for something. Or someone. It now seemed likely that they had been waiting for Jet Hu to bring Charlie to them, where they would take him from the Hyperborea while the AI in docking bay twenty-seven continued to serve as a distraction. If that was indeed the case, then obviously their plan had failed – namely, because Rawl had released the auxiliary control field surrounding the solar, sucking the waiting AI out into space – and Private Hu would now be devising plans for an alternative means of travel to reach the mothership. His intention

440

was to hijack a Wing.

The closest docking station to their current location was on level forty, a mere four klicks of tunnel away. They arrived before Hu, thanks to Rawl's schematics revealing a shorter route through what would have been blazing hot pipe lines if all levels were still in use, and the XO commanded all pilots and engineers off the deck and runway. Rawl then posted militia at every entrance and possible shaft exit point. He wanted to draw Hu out, make him think he's almost there. Make him think all twenty-five Wings in the hangar were unguarded and ready for the taking. And then Rawl Collister would take him out.

It didn't work out that way.

Rawl didn't have to wait very long before First Private Jet Hu arrived. With militia covering the ground and snipers from the mezzanine running the length of the deck, Rawl had eyes everywhere. All were ordered to fire only on his command.

Hu entered through an under-floor mech-bunker. According to the schematics, it was linked to a vent that led directly from a warren sub-tunnel. The bunker hatch opened cautiously, only a crack at first. Then the hatch crashed open and Hu leapt forth, seeming to fly two metres in the air in a single jump. He carried the shrivelled and limp-limbed Charlie around his shoulders like the man was a bundle of rags. He swooped down, landing perfectly.

The shock of his abominable appearance caused Rawl to hesitate. What the XO hadn't considered was just how altered the Private had become as a result of the AI infection. The man was naked as the day he was born, skin shed free in bloody red strips, revealing raw muscles and tendons that secreted thick black ooze. The skin on his face had gone, revealing two grisly rows of teeth in a lipless mouth and a pair of white orbs floating within lidless sockets. The teeth were obscenely long and drew right up into the face. His legs and arms seemed broken and elongated, like the haunches of an old Earth animal, and his spine curved and warped into a steep hump upon his ridged back, with rows of sharp ribs protruding severely as knives.

Where he landed, a spatter of inky liquid fulminated from his flayed muscles onto the pristine deck. He turned to the nearest Wing and loped towards it, unaware he was completely surrounded. Through the shock, Rawl realised that Mei was speaking to him over commlink, urging him to give the order to fire before Hu reached the closest Wing. He shook himself back to the mezzanine hangar deck, where he lay among the snipers – Mei was on the floor with the militia – and gave the word. "Aim for his torso and head," the XO ordered. "Injure Charlie if you must but shoot that thing down. I don't want either of them getting off this ship."

A barrage of plasma rifle bolts lanced from the hangar deck level, aimed at First Private Jet Hu as he ran with Charlie flopping across his deformed shoulders. The bolts struck, ripping sucking flesh wounds into his back and taking off his left leg below the knee. No blood splattered and sprayed the runway, only black gunk. The carnal noise that came from him sent Rawl pale beneath his visor, but Hu continued regardless, only faltering slightly at the loss of his leg. He began using his elongated arms to lope the remainder of the runway, limping as he went but not slowing even a fraction.

Seeing Hu approach the Wing, Rawl stood, aimed his rifle and let out a surge of plasma fire. "Fire at will."

This time, they did not hit their target. Hu ran in a zig-zag fashion and sought shelter from the rain of plasma under a dismembered Wing blade strewn across an engineering platform. The tide of plasma fire ripped apart the podium, disintegrating gaping holes into the structure but missing Hu completely as he squatted beneath. He then hurled the blade itself at the firing militia as though it weighed nothing, lifting it with his muscle-exposed arms, leaving Charlie strewn upon the deck behind him. It collided into the leading group of militia, sending them hurtling backwards and fatally crushing half. The others were either wounded or unconscious from the impact.

Rawl ordered the snipers to continue and scrambled down the grill stairway onto the runway level. "Do not let him take Charlie off this ship, do you hear me?" he yelled over the commlink. "Blow them both to junkfucking pieces if you have to, but the enemy will not get their hands on him."

Rawl joined the rear. Ahead he could hear the thrum of plasma fire discharge and the flashes that accompanied it. Then he heard the unmistakable sound of a Wing firing up ignition. "Disable the Wing," Rawl ordered. "Put it out of action. Do whatever you have to. Do it now."

Hu had already initiated take-off sequence by the time the XO and the rear caught up with the remaining ground force. It hovered along the runway, heading towards the closed hatch doors, thrusters on half power. Plasma fire impacted with the Wing's glowing stern and Hu increased speed.

The Wing blasted a searing hole through the first hatch doors of the airlock. When the deck sensors picked up on the slight drop in pressure the auxiliary hatch doors initiated closure; there wasn't enough power for the lifeship to use the fail-safe control field. By that time, however, Hu had already manoeuvred the Wing into the airlock. He then blasted through the secondary airlock doors and continued his escape into vacuum.

Rawl contacted the CSD at once and all but begged the Captain to shoot it down.

"That's a negative," Captain Lu had replied. "We can't risk harming Charlie until we know why they want him. He could be the key to finding Earth, Rawl. You know that. The Bugs seem to be retreating back to the mothership. I'll send every Wing after him. We'll get Charlie back."

Usually, Rawl would have attempted to appeal to Lu's reason – any risk of allowing the AI to get what they wanted compromised every human on the Hyperborea – but he'd caught sight of Mei's lifeless body spread out on the deck amid a crowd of militia. Half the man's skull was gone, vaporised, leaving a cauterised wedge-like chunk missing from his face. His one remaining eye was open. Plasma wound.

"Friendly fire," someone said. "It got too crazy. Everyone was firing everywhere."

The XO clenched his fists and hardened his jaw. Everyone was looking at him, waiting for orders. He turned and left.

He marched onto the Captain's platform – his rightful platform. She was surrounded by real-time virtual space where Rawl could see three Wings had been cleared from docking bay thirty to collect the hijacked craft rapidly disappearing towards the mothership. Rawl knew they would never reach it in time.

The real-time virtual space dissipated and Captain Lu turned and glared at him. "A sloppy failure of a mission," she said sharply. "The objective unsuccessful and needless life taken in the process."

"I'm well aware, Captain," the XO replied. "You may have forgotten, but I've lost a trusted friend and advisor."

"I haven't forgotten. But I expected better than this. Friendly fire, Rawl, amid all of this. How did this happen?"

He rubbed his brow. "He got too close. Got in the way."

The Captain frowned. "The responsibility falls to you. Shifting blame onto a dead man is beneath you. You failed."

"There's still time to rectify that. He's still in range. Fire and make sure the AI never get what they want."

"There's an old Earth expression for that," Captain Lu said, stone-faced. "It's called cutting off your nose to spite your face. If the AI want him, I want to know why, and until we find the answer, he is invaluable to us. Do I make myself clear, Collister?"

"Captain," First Officer Ling interrupted before Rawl could reply. "I have Lieutenant Chen over comm.

The Captain turned. "Put her through."

Lydia's face appeared in the holoscreen. Behind her sat Corporal Daneel Sharma, whom Rawl had assumed was now dead, and Winston, sitting on the bridge of the Black Betty craft. General Shaw, the XO noticed, was nowhere to be seen.

"Fire everything we have at the mothership," Lydia said. "Fire now."

*

From the hundred Prometheuses he had brought back with him, less than half remained alive. And that number was decreasing fast.

The Apex obliterated them like a child would toy soldiers, mercilessly and without the slightest pause.

What were plastic toys to little boys? What were men to monsters?

Prometheus watched as his own body – as he – was torn to pieces or blown apart, over and over. Time and time again he watched himself die. But it didn't matter. Each one was as disposable as the other. Only one needed to survive. Despite the loss, they held off the enemy long enough to put the plan into motion, willingly giving their lives to put right what they had done.

Did each of their deaths balance the scale a little more when weighed against the near-extinction of humanity? Of course not. But Prometheus would give his life as often as needed to make it right. And as he watched his men die, he almost envied them. The peace of it. The finality of it.

Are they with Sarah now?

As his men died around him Prometheus searched for a way to override the mothership's control field armour, but there were no actual controls that he could see. There were no dials or levers, only clean black surfaces with lights that he couldn't decipher. That's when he realised. The Hydra controlled the ship with its will, like it commanded the Apex. There was no need for controls and screens when the whole ship was made of the substance that moved to the Hydra's resolve. That meant there was only one way to drop the field, and that was to make the Hydra want to drop it. Or need to.

The Black Betty had been allowed entry only through the docking hatch on the underside the ship, an area positioned in such a way as to allow cover while the shield in that area dropped temporarily to allow entry. But there were too many AI and Bug ships to all cram back in through that one hatch. The Hydra would need to drop the control field barrier around the entire ship to recall the AI – if it was in danger.

As he turned, buoyed by the new plan that was forming, the Hydra appeared with Edward's face looming over him. It swung an arm and casually and sent him flying into the interior hull. Pain blistered in his vision, the air knocked from his lungs.

"You look changed," Edward's mouth said as it crouched insect-like towards him. "You look different from the others. Are you different? Not on the inside, our sensors say. You seem to have acquired more scars than the rest, however."

Prometheus stood. "I am different," he said before firing a plasma bolt into the Hydra's alloy chest. The bolt rippled across the control field like the shot had been fired into water.

"How did you do it?" it asked. "How did you escape the pocket loop? How did you all escape?"

Prometheus was almost surprised to find that it was genuinely curious.

It hadn't calculated this outcome at all, which meant he had the upper hand. He looked back to the Prometheuses. Only a handful remained alive now, fighting against the Apex that tore through them one by one. However much Prometheus had tried to prepare them; his men were not machines. They grew tired, weak and vulnerable.

Only one of us is needed now.

"We didn't escape," he said. "We were rescued, over and over and over until we were an army. One of the side effects of creating a pocket loop, so I'm told."

The Hydra's head spun and the handsome face of Bastille cocked the head sideways. Prometheus could barely look at those faces, all torn from bodies he helped acquire and stitched together like bits of corpses.

"Rescued?" Bastille's hollow voice said. "By whom?"

"That's a good question." He'd been waiting for this moment for what seemed like a lifetime. "Allow me to answer." From his pocket, he produced a phial of the milky white liquid he'd taken from the endless white corridor. He cracked open the glass head, held it up for the Hydra to see, then smiled.

Since Death had rescued Prometheus from the pocket loop dimension he had long pondered one particular detail that just didn't make sense throughout the entire ordeal. After Death revealed the truth to him, about whom Edward really was and his true intentions, one question had played on him: why did Edward need him to administer the White Drops? After he brought Edward back, why didn't he dispose of Prometheus and simply find the others himself? Even when Prometheus had refused to administer the Drops to Miranda, Edward had persuaded another man to do it instead of giving the woman the solution himself.

The answer had been right in front of him all along. Death was the answer. Each time the White Drops was used, Edward, or the Hydra and the other versions of itself, evacuated the vicinity promptly until the deed was done. Each time Death had come and then gone, drawn by the White Drops, the very thing that had created it.

The Hydra feared Death – it feared what the creature would do if Death ever found it. The Hydra was the cause of its pain and loneliness and Death's venom had swelled and congealed within its bony fangs. It had grown and festered with time. And if the Hydra feared Death it meant Death could harm it.

The Hydra's head spun to reveal a sorrowful looking little girl's face on the verge of tears. The panic in her eyes assured Prometheus of what he had to do. "Don't," the girl pleaded, reaching out a sharp black arm as if to stop him.

Prometheus placed the phial to his lips and jerked back his head the way he had so many times before with a bottle of whisky. The liquid poured down his throat, washing his insides with eternal life.

It tasted chalky.

The Hydra's head turned, showing each of its faces, each set in a single frame of white-eyed fear, the mouth widening and closing as the faces turned like a zoetrope. It moved as if to flee, but there was nowhere for it to run – it was the very ship itself – and it was too late to hide.

Amid the Hydra's panic, Prometheus thrust the barrel-end of a T-pistol into his mouth. He thought of Sarah smiling serenely from a distant shore. He smiled back and bit down on the metal.

Soon, my love.

He fired, and all went black.

*

P2 stared at the body of their leader. The shot had torn through the roof of his mouth, blasting through his skull so that a soup of brains and blood splattered onto the bulkhead behind. His body then slumped dead to the deck.

For a moment, he panicked but quickly regained his steel. It was all part of the plan. He was in charge now. Their Commander had completed his mission and Death was coming. They all knew what it meant.

He ordered the eleven remaining Prometheuses to move back.

It appeared in a raging storm of screaming souls. Death. A giant skull burned into existence. Its teeth grew large and gnashing, the eyes, usually black and hollow, burned red with odium.

From the view of the temperhull, P2 could see swarms of AI craft fleeing back to the mothership. It was calling them back to protect it. They flew closer, entering the control field boundary that was no longer active.

"The shields are down," P2 shouted to the last Prometheuses standing, each of them battered and bloody, standing amid corpses. "Prepare for impact." He stared out with bulbous eyes, awaiting the fire that would bring his death and end it all.

His stomach twisted. Amid the Bug ships, a single human craft was soaring towards them, followed by others. But no fire.

"Why aren't they firing?" P65 asked, through a grim mask of sweat and blood.

☐

58

Captain Stacy Lu felt the tears rise behind her eyes. Little salty admissions of weakness. But she would not let them come. Instead, she made metal of her resolve and bit hard onto her determination. She wouldn't do it. She would not fire upon the mothership with Nathan still inside. She would not kill the only man she'd ever loved. The greatest man she'd ever known. If it hadn't been for him, she would never have become Captain and she would never have seen the glimmer of pride in her father's eyes as he looked at her before he died.

She just couldn't do it.

"General Shaw is still on-board, and we have a Wing within blast range," she said. "And then there's Charlie. You want us to take out a high-ranking Officer and our only chance of finding Earth all in one deathblow?"

"Charlie isn't our only chance of finding Earth," the XO said, in his usual grim-faced way. "Earth is gone. You must realise that and put the survival of our race first. You heard what the li said… fire now before we miss our chance. The General would want it this way. You know it as well as I."

The CSD crew were watching the dispute. Captain Lu turned again to the mothership through the tempurhull and thought of Nathan inside. Her jaw clenched.

She wouldn't do it.

When she turned back, Rawl's T-pistol was an inch from her face. She almost started in genuine surprise.

"Fire now," he said. His eyes swam in the shadow of his brow.

Personal weapons were not allowed on the CSD, but in the hype of the attack, it seemed Rawl had slipped by with his T-pistols still in their holsters. She would have to reprimand the guards when this was done. Unless they were in it with him? The man had loyal followers.

"Lower your weapon," she ordered in her most authoritative voice. She took step forward to show that she had no intention of being bullied, so the barrel touched her head. It was cold. She'd dealt with bullies since she was a child, being as strange-looking as she was, and had long ago vowed that she would never allow anyone to treat her that way again.

"I will not," Rawl said with equal resolve. "I know I'm right about this, Stacy. Your father trusted me and I'm asking you to do the same. Lieutenant Chen trusts this Prometheus enough to believe what he says. It comes down to this… do you trust her judgement and do you trust me?"

If only that was all it came down to – trust. There was so much more to it than that. She had loved General Nathan Shaw almost from the moment they met. He served under her father at the time, and she had been little more than eight years old. Her father, being the Captain of the Hyperborea, was a busy man and rarely had time for visiting his offspring, having a total of eight from his sperm donations – by the time he died the man had close to forty. He never directly cared for any of his children – neither did their mothers – and the task was left to the carers. But being the Captain, he always thought that it set a good example to at least pay the mildest interest in his children, so occasionally he would visit her and the others. On this occasion, he brought with him Nathan Shaw to see her, younger looking, but not much so. He still had a hard edge to his face and was taller and more muscled than anyone she'd ever seen.

It was as they sat down to lunch that he arrived. Stacy dined on her own because the other children said that her odd blue eyes and blonde hair put them off their gruel – as if there was any reason needed to be put off that stuff. Her father never had those traits in his appearance so she had always assumed she'd inherited them from her mother. For most of her early adult life, she searched the lifeship eagerly for an Asian woman with blonde hair and blue eyes, but she never found her mother. It wasn't until her father was on his deathbed did she come to learn that her mother had died when she was still a child and that her father and she had actually conceived her naturally. Her father said that looking at her caused him too much pain. No wonder she spent her entire life trying to please him, trying to live up to his name.

On that day, however, when she was eight, sitting on her own and slurping her gruel, her estranged father brought with him a fearsomely large, dark-skinned man. They came to sit with her at one of the many empty spaces of her table. At once, all of the other children crowded around and demanded her father's attention, which he gave them in abundance. Her father was Captain first and father perhaps tenth or twelfth. What the other obligations were in between she didn't know. She never knew him that well. The children pulled him away and demanded Captain Lu them a story. He stood at the front and they gathered around, so much so that Stacy couldn't see through the taller children that stood at the back and she was too shy to ask them to let her through.

That's when two large hands suddenly wrapped themselves around her waist and hoisted her up. General Nathan Shaw placed her on his shoulders so she could see above the crowd. She looked down at him in awe from the great height that made her feel taller than everything and he looked back up at her with a bright white smile – the friendliest smile she had ever seen and one that he reserved for her alone for a very long time.

Stacy paid no attention to the story her father told the children, she was too busy watching how they all looked at her with visible envy at being singled out by the huge man. Before then she had never felt special in her life, only odd.

From then on Nathan visited her when Captain Lu did, and sometimes even without him. As she grew older, she began to recognise the sadness behind his dark eyes and she knew she wanted nothing more than to take that sorrow away and make him feel like she had the day they met. By the time Stacy was in her teens she already knew she would join the militia, she knew she would do everything to make her father see her – make him be proud of her – and she knew without a doubt that she was in love with Nathan Shaw.

It was during her early teens that she began to fill out in all the wrong places. Her breasts were small, her hips and thighs were plump and heavyset and she had grown to be taller than most of the boys in her ed-set. Again, it was Nathan that saved her from falling into the trap of self-pity that she had been prone to. He took her down into the Underbelly one day, along craggy causeways and tight tunnels of dripping pipe-work and into a room full of weights and exercise equipment. The control field gravity simulator within the room had been increased to make even walking seem like a laborious task. Nathan then said to her, "You aren't like other people and they won't let you forget it. So how about we show them just how special you really are and never let them forget that?" He trained her how to make her body strong, as well as her mind.

From then on she went to the gym daily, until she was stronger and taller than everyone in her ed-set. The others may still have called her weird, or ugly. But not one of them now dared say it to her face.

When the time came for Stacy to take the aptitude test that would determine how she could best contribute to the Hyperborea, she knew without a doubt that the militia was for her. From her first day in the Underbelly training quarters – although he was never seen to single her out above the others – General Nathan Shaw undertook her training personally, seeing to it that strategy and combat tactics, as well as politics and leadership studies, were all on her agenda. While others concentrated on playing with explosives and piloting Wings, Nathan made sure she became more rounded than that. He had seen the potential in her. Seen what she could become. He knew that one day she could be Captain, and it was because of him that she now was. It was because of him that her father had told her how she honoured him and named her his successor upon his death.

Nathan Shaw was the greatest man she had ever known, and he was the only man she had ever loved. She had never told him that. What they had between them was too important for her to risk ruining it that way. The General had never committed himself to anyone, and he never would. His life was for another purpose, she knew. He was not like other people, and he knew they would not let him forget it. But he was special. He had the White Drops. And gift or curse, he knew that it meant something more than the common life. Hard as it must have been, he had cut himself off from that part of himself. But she could testify the man was more loving than any she had known. She was proof of that.

And now, XO Rawl Collister was asking her to kill him. And she wouldn't do it.

*

Bugs made their way across the battlespace, back towards the mothership. If what the li said was right, then soon their chance would be missed. Rawl knew they had to act now.

"If we shoot, Charlie dies, General Shaw dies and all hope of a home dies with them," the Captain said. "We're flailing, Rawl. We won't survive out here forever. You know it and I know it. We need a planet."

"We won't survive the next SEM unless we do this," Rawl urged. He looked at his hands clasped around the T-pistol to see that they were shaking. There's no time for this. She's putting all our lives in danger. He didn't want to hurt her but it seemed she was giving him no other option. "He doesn't love you the way you love him. You need to let him go."

The Captain's eyes began to water in their sockets, like two quivering pools, before a curious look shadowed her face. Her eyes wandered off to a point behind him and she frowned. Then a high-pitched scream and the thrum of plasma fire pierced the silence.

Captain Lu's head exploded in a mist of blood, as though it was nothing but a burst sack of blood and viscus. Droplets sprayed onto Rawl's face and he flinched, his gun still raised, watching as Captain Lu's ragged neck sputtered and spat, the stem of her spine visible through blood and brain matter that coated her shoulders. By the time her body hit the floor, more plasma fire seared across the CSD and the air turned red with blood. Rawl's ears seared with screams. He ripped his attention from the headless body of the Captain to see dark figures pouring in, each holding a plasma rifle.

The XO's eyes narrowed. They were under attack. The figures fired, killing without discrimination, picking off the crew one by one. Some scrambled over one another for cover behind control stations, while others clawed the ground for the exit at the far end. But shadowed forms had blocked the hatches, making sure none escaped.

The AI, they've gotten in, Rawl thought at first. We are all dead. But as he ducked behind the CSD's main control station in the central platform, he dared to delay for a look. He saw that their attackers were not AI at all – they were Brotherhood of Man disciples. The hoods of their brown roughspun robes covered their heads, but Rawl recognised the Consulate's own Brother Vaxus among them. His pinched face ordered the others to spread out, his thin lips stretched into a placid smile.

450

Disciples stood on the higher entrance decking firing plasma bolts into the scattering crew, while other Brotherhood disciples cascaded down onto the main deck among the stations, blowing apart those who had taken cover.

Limbs, blood and terror rained down, coating the command stations in a layer of wet redness.

They would soon reach Rawl. Captain Lu's body leaked beside him, the dark patch under her spreading out and seeping around his knees. He felt his chest rise and fall, his breath ridiculously loud. He held his T-pistol tightly, squeezed it, and half thought about taking his own life just to begrudge Vaxus having the pleasure of doing it himself. Amid the screams that still sounded, punctuated by pleas and then more plasma fire, Rawl knew he wouldn't do it. No, he was far too angry for that. Whatever madness induced this slaughter, born from the minds of ignorance and delusion, he would see to it that every single one of them paid in suffering.

His mind raced with conjecture. There were approximately two-hundred Brotherhood of Man disciples onboard the Hyperborea, yet only a fraction there. Where were the others?

"First Officer Lexi, come in," the XO whispered over his comm system. "Lexi, come in."

"Sir," Lexi replied. Her voice was strangled and thin. "Help us. They're killing us. Please don't let them, sir. I don't want to die."

Rawl was afraid of that. He was hoping he could contact the bridge and call for backup, but Vaxus had timed his move perfectly. "The snake," Rawl spat. "Calm down. I need to know how many Brothers are down on the bridge and if any of you are armed?" The bridge, like the CSD, did not allow weapons, so the officers were unable to defend themselves. But perhaps with the battle, the rules had slackened a little.

First Officer Lexi didn't reply. Instead, she whimpered. The sound sent a spasm of sorrow through Rawl's hard heart. "Please… don't hurt me," she said. Not to Rawl. "Why are you doing this? Please, I'm pregnant—" She screamed until the thrum of plasma fire echoed down the comm. Then nothing.

The cries within the CSD descended into pleas and sobs, quieter now. Everyone would soon be dead – including him. Brother Vaxus had begun speaking through the fire. Rawl couldn't make it out at first, but as the plasma bolts became fewer his words became clearer; it was as though he were spouting a sermon. At this, Rawl became incensed with rage. He looked down at the T-pistol in his hand and his trigger finger shook with longing. If he took a shot at the man they would know he was there. They would find him and kill him before he got the chance to fire upon the mothership. It was no matter if he died after, but he would destroy the AI first. It was all that counted – beyond him, beyond the dead Captain Lu, beyond Vaxus and his pudding-brained attackers.

All that mattered was pushing that button.

Rawl couldn't conceive what had moved the Brotherhood of Man disciples to turn on their own. And he didn't care. He never could abide Vaxus and his incessant gushing of religious sentiment, as though it helped anyone or anything. The old man was irrational. An extremist. And it was clear he had coaxed others down that same path. Why Captain Lu kept him on the Consulate, he would never know. It gave him power and credibility when he should have had nothing but a room in the brig. He glanced at the ragged neck where her head once was. She paid for that mistake with her life.

Suddenly, Rawl thought of Lu's father. He had always resented the old man for not having made him Captain. But seeing Stacy's lifeless, headless corpse, he knew he had been right to do it. She was a leader for a time of peace. But now was a time of war, and war calls for a different sort of leader. One like him.

Rawl lowered the T-pistol. Not yet, he thought. Opposite him, a young man was hiding just as he was, behind his workstation. Rawl recognised the man but had never spoken to him. His face was creased with fear as he swallowed back sobs, squatting with his knees tight to his chest. They locked eyes. Rawl brought a finger to his lips and shook his head. Don't you make a junkfucking sound, or I'll kill you myself, he thought.

The room was silent now.

"Check the stations," Brother Vaxus ceased his sermon briefly to say. He heard movement but stayed where he was. He had to wait for the opportune moment to reach the weapons command station beneath where Vaxus stood. Hopefully, whoever had manned it had prepared the plasma cannons while waiting for the Captain's word to fire. It should be bursting at full power by now.

He looked down at Stacy's body once more and again her father's image plagued him. Poor bitch, he thought. But everyone was expendable. He was expendable. All that mattered was blowing the mothership to dust.

"… And let those that come to cleanse us of our betraying sin be welcomed like the purifying fire," Brother Vaxus continued. "We have shamed ourselves and soiled our holy bodies. We have been abandoned, but we shall rise again by showing the Mother our true loyalty. We shall hack free the spoiled limbs that threaten to infect the whole. We shall burn out those who stand in our way. It is only through the cleansing fire that we will become worthy of her once again. That fire has come."

"It is so," the Brotherhood said in unison. One of them stood on the other side of Rawl's station. He had to do something now. Another step and he would be dead.

"It is so," he heard himself say aloud. He stood, exposing himself to the men and women that had now killed almost every officer on the CSD and presumably the bridge too. One of them raised their plasma rifle and Rawl Collister dropped the T-pistol that he held in his hand. "It is so," he said again. "Let the cleansing fire come." He closed his eyes. "I welcome it so that the Mother will welcome us home." He waited for the fire. When it didn't come, he opened his eyes again.

Vaxus held out a hand that stayed the rifle bolts and looked at the man with a curious expression upon his creped face. "You welcome your fate, XO Collister?"

"I am a determined man, as you well know, Vaxus. I have been waiting for this day as long as you. It's the only way to cut out the decay that has infected our race. We need to be clean for the Mother. To show her we are now pure."

Brother Vaxus seemed truly taken aback.

"It's a lie," one of the Brothers said. He was a small man that drowned in his robes. "It's a trick. Don't believe him, Holy Brother."

"A trick?" Vaxus repeated. "I'm no fool, Argo. I've known Rawl for longer than I care to remember. Not once has he been reverent or even kind to our beliefs. Any sudden change of heart he may be feigning now only proves to me he belongs to the rot more than I ever previously believed. The AI are the cleansing fire. We need to surrender to them."

"It is so," the Brotherhood said, including Rawl.

"You are wrong about me, Brother Vaxus," he said. "I have been working for your cause all along, but from the sidelines, within the rot to ensure its downfall." He stepped out from behind the workstation, glancing briefly to the hidden young man watching in fear. "Who opened the Lock to give you free rein over the weaponry? Me. I knew your plan all along and I played my part in it, just as all of you have."

"We had the clearance code for the Lock and could have opened it regardless," Vaxus said.

"But at that point, all of the plasma rifles would have been taken and none left for you." Suddenly Rawl now knew why there had been a rifle shortage upon arming the troops. He shook the thought away. "I also ensured General Shaw and the li weren't onboard for when you carried out this cleanse," Rawl lied. "The AI, Winston, and I have been planning it since he arrived."

This caught Vaxus's interest. "Winston?" he said. "He was an instrument of our Mother all along?"

"That's right," Rawl said. Every Brotherhood of Man disciple surrounded him and he was beginning to doubt he had done the right thing in speaking out. But he went on – more determined than ever that he spoke the truth, so much so that he half made himself believe it. "Together we saw to it that the conditions were right for the cleanse. By now General

Shaw and the li will too have been cleansed from humanity and the AI will soon lead us to Earth."

"It is over? We have prevailed?" Vaxus said, distant eyes looking reverently through tempurhull to the mothership recalling her children.

"It's why they're leaving," Rawl said. "The rot has been cut out. We have succeeded."

Brother Vaxus stepped down from the entrance platform and raised his arms to Rawl, beckoning him closer. Tears filled the old man's already rheumy eyes. "I knew it was the way," he said, his voice thick with emotion. "We have proven ourselves and will be rewarded thus, just like I said."

"It is so," the Brotherhood said.

Collister stepped towards Vaxus raising his arms as if to embrace him. The old man now stood in front of the weapons station and Rawl could see the flashing light upon the holoscreen that indicated the plasma cannons were engaged and locked on target.

"Wait," said the small and irritating Brother Argo. Rawl turned to see they had discovered the young officer hiding among the stations. The Brothers dragged him over the deck.

"Please, don't kill me," the man pleaded, his face salty and red. "I won't tell anyone, I swear. Just let me go. I won't tell anyone."

Argo backhanded the man around the face. "Silence, you rot," he said, then turned to Vaxus. "Dear Brother, your belief is unfailing, but I fear you're being taken for a fool. If the XO truly is a believer, let him prove it by cleansing us free of the rot that stands before us."

"Yes," Vaxus said, lowering his arms with an agreeing nod. "One cannot simply jump ship at the opportune moment. Cleanse the rot and earn your place on Earth."

The young man's breathing hastened as he stared wide-eyed from Vaxus to Rawl. Through the tempurhull of the CSD Rawl could see that almost all AI craft had been recalled to the mothership and the holoscreen indicated the Wing carrying Charlie was about to itself enter the dark ship. Once it was inside, the shield would go back up and their chance would be gone. It was now or never. Do or die.

Argo had shoved the young man in front of him. Waiting. "A rifle?" Rawl said, holding out his hands.

"I think not," Argo said, almost laughing. "I'm sure you can do it with your hands, a man of your experience."

"You want the lad to suffer?" Rawl asked. "Since when was the Brotherhood of Man cruel?"

Argo poked Rawl in the chest with a small finger. "Just do it."

"No, the XO is right," Vaxus said. "We cleanse because we must, but we are not cruel and we take no pleasure in this act we must perform. We do what is needed to make us worthy. Give him your rifle, Argo."

"But Holy Brother—"

"Now, Brother Argo."

Grudgingly, the man handed Rawl his plasma rifle and as soon as it touched Rawl's fingers every other plasma rifle in the CSD closed its aim on his head. If he refused to kill the man they would shoot him. If he fired at them instead, he could kill perhaps four before the others would shoot him dead. If he ran, they would shoot him. There was really only one option. He raised the plasma rifle to the young man's perspiring face and fired. His head exploded into pulp just like Captain Lu's, and his body flopped at their feet.

Rawl's heart felt like a boulder in his chest, suddenly pulling his insides down.

Argo seemed genuinely surprised, but it was Vaxus that spoke first. "Everyone lower your weapons. I knew what you said was true. The AI are coming and will escort us back to our beloved Mother. We have been cleansed and we are now worthy." He raised his arms again. "Come, Brother. Let us embrace and rejoice that there will be no more horrors to befall man. Finally, we may be at peace."

Rawl stepped into the man's embrace and wrapped his arms around his roughspun-cloaked body, feeling the man's boney ribs beneath. So breakable. A few feet to his left the weapons station still flashed. Through the tempurhull, the last of the Bugs disappeared. Was it too late?

Rawl Collister shoved Brother Vaxus with such force that the old man was lifted from his frail stance and thrown back into the crowd of startled disciples. Reaching out to the weapons deck with stretched fingers, Rawl slammed his palm down onto the holoscreen pad of the weapons station. Every millisecond of time seemed prolonged and his movements slow. The pad recognised the handprint and all fifteen Hyperborean plasma cannons fired at once upon the mothership.

A brilliant flash washed over the temperhull, hiding the mothership in white glare.

The Brotherhood of Man disciples shielded their eyes from the light while others shot randomly as Rawl leapt the steps towards the CSD entrance. Pain shot through his face and the left side of his body. He wanted to fall to his knees but his legs kept on. He made it through the hatch, turning to place his hand on the palm pad. He looked at where his hand should have been splayed upon the pad only to see a gushing red stump. Without thinking, he used his other hand and the CSD hatch closed with control field security. He then shot the pad with his plasma rifle, deactivating the hatch and locking the disciples inside.

Suddenly, the world was on its side and the deck slammed into his face. Blackness enveloped him and unconsciousness came.

☐

59

Through the transparent tempurhull of the Black Betty, they watched as the mothership burst into a silent maelstrom of intense white and orange radiance.

The Hyperborea's fifteen hull-positioned plasma cannons fired after what had been an agonising wait. Ystil.3 now watched Lydia as she stared at the dance of light, hands clutching tightly to the sides of the grav chair.

Why had it taken so long to fire? They'd tried to establish a commlink with the bridge and CSD but received no response, but then a small dot of white sparked from the end of each cannon and searing spears burst across the space between the giant ships. The fire found the mothership's control field down and burned through the Computronium layers of the dark ship. Then, like a star gone supernova, it exploded, generating a residual wave of energy that engulfed everything within a five klick radius, including the remaining Bugs and three Hyperborean Wings, obliterating all in its brutal wake.

One of those Wings had been carrying Private Jep Hu and Charlie.

The AI had been defeated, in physical form at least, and the last of the human race would not be killed or captured… today. It seemed like a moment they should celebrate, but there was silence among them.

"Is that it?" Daneel was the first to say. "Have we won?" The man had recovered from his short exposure to vacuum. He sat in a weapons deck chair on the bridge, covered in a thermograde blanket.

"That really depends on me… rather two of me," Prometheus replied, sitting next to him in a grav chair.

"I don't get it?" Daneel said, looking from Prometheus to Ystil.3, standing on the central deck. Lydia had moved from the temperhull and made another attempt at contacting Captain Lu.

"Z still exists within the BroadWeb," Ystil.3 said. "Only the physical form has been destroyed, as with the Apex Soldiers, whose servers still exist on Thebes. Without destroying Z's BroadWeb presence he'll just rebuild and come back at you like last time. It may take another hundred years. And now that Charlie has been destroyed, I don't know what Z will do to you. But it will be nothing good, I can guarantee. Z… the Hydra… needs to be deleted permanently if you're ever going to be safe."

"Our Commander onboard the mothership will see to that," Prometheus said. He was referring to the scarred Prometheus who had perished, along General Shaw and, of course, Charlie. Although Charlie and the General had taken the White Drops, so wouldn't truly be dead. He wondered briefly where they were right now.

"And the other you?" Daneel asked.

Prometheus looked up, as though from some dark thought. "Sorry?"

"You said the victory depends on you, or rather two of you. The first is that your Commander can successfully delete Z within the BroadWeb… so what's the other?"

Prometheus fumbled inside the front pouch of his hardsuit and produced an ampoule containing a black solution. "Liquid death," he said, rolling the glass phial ponderously between his fingers. "Have I learnt the deaths done right?"

"I don't get it again," Daneel said.

"I thought you would have been used to not understanding by now," Ystil.3 said. "After all, you're so good at it. Allow me to explain, and try to keep up if you can manage it. Prometheus can change these events and stop them from happening if he administers the antidote to the White Drops to Charlie when he's still a baby… which I'm assuming is what you hold there."

"You mean you could change all this?" Daneel gestured out across the ghostly dead battlespace.

"No," Ystil.3 said. Prometheus seemed happy to let him answer, sitting mutely with his own thoughts. "Time doesn't work that way. All this has already happened, there's no undoing it. But an alternative future would be created if Prometheus kills Charlie as a baby, stopping the White Drops from ever having been discovered and denying the world of the source of energy that would inevitably be used to punch holes through spacetime, leading to the Reset, killing billions of humans, converting the Earth into data and sending it into the depths of potential space. Charlie's life is the anomaly that began it all. It's the thing that has to change."

"But you'd have to kill a baby," Daneel said. "Could you do that? I don't think I could do that. Not when it comes down to it."

Prometheus looked thoughtfully at the man and nodded. "That is the question. Can I do it? Have I learned the deaths done right? I spent years of my life devoted to conquering Death. I thought I had done it. I thought I had saved the world. But I had doomed it instead. Death won in the end. Death always wins in the end."

They were silent and Ystil.3 imagined himself in Prometheus's position. Could he do such a thing if required? He didn't know the answer. Logically it was the correct thing to do. If Oppenheimer could have taken back inventing the atom bomb, a pinnacle point in Earth's violent history, perhaps he would have. Or perhaps he wouldn't. Remaining in ignorance achieves nothing. No one learns from that. It is having the knowledge and doing the right thing anyway is what should be strived for. He smiled to himself. But what did he know about it? He was just an AI.

"I don't understand?" Lydia crowed, a crack of distress in her voice. "How can that be?"

Ystil.3 turned to see XO Rawl Collister appear in the commlink holoscreen. Half his head was wrapped in white gauze, partially covering his face. Red stains seeped through around the covered eye and ear. The other eye was bruised and tired. He spoke with a heavy voice. "Captain Lu is dead, murdered by Brotherhood of Man disciples led by Brother Vaxus. They opened fire on the CSD and bridge. One hundred and nine officers are dead and thirteen are injured. I managed to trap the attackers in the CSD after activating the plasma cannons." His one eye blazed with anger for a moment. "We almost missed our chance because of them. We almost lost everything." He looked down at himself. "I took a hit, as you can see." He lifted half an arm stunted below the elbow, wrapped in a tourniquet. "The disciples, including Vaxus, have been rounded up and are waiting to be dealt with."

Lydia said nothing, only stared with eyes that were somewhere else. Deep in reverie, Ystil.3 supposed; thinking of some long past exchange between herself and the Captain, no doubt. Daneel saw her distress too and rose from his chair to place a hand on her shoulder. She turned and, seeing it was him, frowned until he removed it.

"I'm glad to see you made it out, Lieutenant," Collister said. "Are you ready for the next part of your mission?"

"Yes... Captain," Lydia said.

The sound of his new title visibly pleased Rawl Collister. He straightened with pride. "Good," he said with a nod. "The Hyperborea is grateful to you all. And, though it is unlikely you will return, your sacrifice will ensure that humanity will continue."

"By the time you get to Earth's system, Earth will either be there or it won't be," Lydia said, her voice distant. "That's how you'll know if we succeeded or not. If it isn't there then Z hasn't been destroyed and the fight for survival will continue. You must continue to run. I hope with all my heart that when you finally arrive, the sight you see will be beautiful and our people will finally have a home."

"I'm sorry, Lieutenant, but I think there's been a misunderstanding," Rawl said. "As Captain of this ship, I will not be sending us on a fool's errand, searching for an Earth that no longer exists, clinging to the long dead hopes that caused Captain Lu to lead us into this massacre. We will not be returning to Earth's system, but systematically searching the known universe for a planet we can inhabit. Captain Lu was right about one thing, we won't survive out here much longer. I know we have tried before, but without having to hide from AI, at least for a while, we are free to search in the open. I'm confident that this time, under the right leadership, we shall succeed."

Lydia shook her head, tears brimming in her eyes. "But sir, Earth could be there, waiting."

"Could," Captain Collister said sharply. "I'm done with could. Could has led us into this mess. Chasing dreams and hopes and bits of useless information has led to nothing but placing us directly into the hands of the enemy. Not under my command, Lieutenant. Be sure, I will find the human race a home. It may not be what they're expecting. It will be hard and people will perish, but we will survive, thanks to you, and Corporal Sharma and Prometheus and Winston. Now, complete your mission and ensure the AI servers are blown to Hades. And I will begin my mission."

"But sir—"

"It's Captain," Rawl barked, shaking visibly. "No. I will not discuss it. I am Captain. Captain." He exhaled a storm of air and swallowed his anger down. When he spoke again he was calm and equable. "Again, Lieutenant, I thank you for the sacrifice you're about to make. Your race thanks you. Goodbye." The holoscreen flickered out.

Lydia turned to Daneel. "He's going to get them all killed."

*

Most of the Consulate were dead. Dr Regus had been killed by Jep Hu, Captain Lu slaughtered in the CSD, General Shaw obliterated in the mothership explosion and the li would soon give her life to ensure that the AI servers upon Thebes would never pose a threat again. Captain Rawl Collister was the only one that remained. All decisions, until he elected a new Consulate, would be down to him alone.

Perhaps, however, he wouldn't elect a new Consulate. The old one had bungled its way along, insisting on democracy to make all the important decisions. And just look where that led them.

Rawl stared hard into a mirror set within Stacy Lu's locker in the Captain's quarters. He wouldn't usually have taken ownership of the room so promptly, out of respect for his predecessor, but there were things he needed in here, things that would help him run the ship. He looked at his reflection with his one good eye – the other was a hollow socket hidden under a patch until the Brain could make and fit him with a bio-mech one to replace it. It was the same with his arm. They would fit it with some sinister and incongruous metal limb that would make him look more cyborg than human.

Until then, it felt as though his arm was actually still there – only extremely painful and unbearably itchy. Rawl lost count of the number of times he went to reach for something with it or attempted to scratch the deep gnawing prickling on the back of his phantom hand. No matter what drugs the Brain concocted to help, Rawl gritted his teeth through the ebb and flow of pain.

His senses were a little dull from the drugs, but Rawl was determined.

He would not rest. He would not sleep. He would not yield. His mission to find them all a home had begun as soon as Stacy Lu's head exploded. Things were going to change, and first thing was first: he had some rats to deal with.

"We're waiting for you in docking station nineteen, Captain," a voice said over comm. "Everything is prepared."

"Have you established a link to the temperhulls?" Rawl asked, watching how the burned skin on the one side of his face pulled at the other side when he talked. It was like a mask.

"Yes, Captain. All of them, as requested."

"Good. I'll be down shortly."

He would have to appoint a new XO whether he decided a new Consulate was needed or not. He found himself regretting that Lydia would not be around to take up the position – she would have made a strong right hand. But, perhaps it was best she wasn't. The woman was tainted with the previous Captain's delusions of Earth. No, it was better this way. Starting afresh.

Cutting out the rot.

On the shelves of the locker lay Stacy Lu's personal effects: clothes, uniform, a toothbrush and various woman things, but not what Rawl was looking for. He had searched her desk, the drawers, shelves and units all over the quarters, but hadn't found it in those places either. He had even ordered Stacy's body searched before being sent for recycling, but it was no good. He had foraged hungrily high and low, but Rawl couldn't find the access chip to the Captain's Log anywhere. It was imperative he have it. It contained every detail of the Captain's knowledge, every thought, idea, plan and strategy. It was more of an informal diary than anything, but it had been a custom of every Captain of the Hyperborea since the lifeship had left Earth. And now it was his, and he wanted it. The chip, he assumed would be in its place within Stacy's eDeck, but it seemed she had removed it at some point before her death. Perhaps she never kept it there to begin with.

For the moment, however, the search could wait.

He turned to leave, limping across the floor, feeling the dulling effects of the pain relief that washed him in a dreamy haze.

When he arrived at docking station nineteen he was surprised to see more civilians than he thought would have attended. At first, he thought he had wandered into some sort of protest and he shoved through the crowd, faced to bear the brunt of their liberal sensibilities. However, as the militia guards worked their way towards him, parting the crowd to make him a path through, he heard the angry chide of a mob baying for blood. Some arms reached out to shake his hand, which he did with every single one, while others pushed forward to enquire after the last moments of their loved ones – those who had died upon the CSD. He hadn't the stomach to tell them that everyone died screaming. He hadn't the stomach to tell them that he had to kill one of them himself. Their tears trailed like burning acid down grief-melted faces. Tears he might have caused.

Rawl was not proud of what he'd done – what he had to do. He saw the man he'd killed each time he closed his remaining drowsy eye – saw his fear-twisted expression.

But he did not regret.

Once through the crowd, the militia kept them at bay and Rawl left their tears, congratulations and grief behind, making his way towards the airlock itself. More militia surrounded it, all standing to attention upon his arrival. Around them, the filmy lenses of clustering drone cams sent a live stream of the airlock to every working tempurhull on the Hyperborea. Rawl needed everyone to see what was about to happen – whether they opposed it or thirsted for it.

The hatch doors stretched the height and breadth of the massive docking station, fitting perfectly at the interlocking teeth that opened and closed like a giant set of jaws. Portholes were located within the inner hatch door allowing the spectators to see inside. Rawl shuffled right up to one and a sideways smile cut across his face.

Inside, robed figures prayed. Every Brotherhood of Man disciple had been rounded up from the skulking holes in which they hid and herded into the airlock under the duress of a hundred plasma rifles – over three hundred in total, including those from the CSD and those that had attacked the bridge. A few paced the empty airlock with anxious feet and some joined hands in sermon. The pallid faces turned to Rawl as he watched with savouring satisfaction. He picked Vaxus out from the pack as the old man stumbled towards him. The panic in his eyes was gratifying, and the Holy Brother pushed his sweaty, pinched face up against the porthole, his eyes quivering in their sockets and his lips moving in what Rawl could only assume was pleading. Rawl couldn't hear him through the foot-thick hatch. He stared balefully at the man for a moment. Somehow Rawl had projected onto him everything malign thing that had gone wrong on the Hyperborea – every ill fate and poor decision. Vaxus was the product and the cause of it all; the cause of their near extinction, the reason why they still hadn't found a home after being subjugated for so long by the vastness of space and the reason the AI had almost won. He tapped his one ear and shook his head with a mocking shrug. He expected the air was getting a little thin in there.

First Officer Ling Chou had been around at the time when Rawl had needed something so he simply turned to the man and ordered it. Since then he seemed to have become the man he went to when he wanted orders disseminated through the ranks. He had seen to it that the Brotherhood was captured and seen to it that everything was prepared for the judgement. The man appeared by his side. He was no Mei, but perhaps he had found a suitable replacement. "We're ready to begin, Captain," Ling Chou said.

Rawl turned away from the shrivelled face of Brother Vaxus. Ling loaded something into his eDeck and helped him towards the podium that had been constructed between the airlock and the gathering crowd. By now all would be watching, either in person or over the tempurhull holos.

"The script is just to give you a few ideas, should you run out of things to say," Ling Chou said. "There's someone at the controls, so once you're finished with your speech all you need to do is hold up your right arm."

"Well, I'm not going to hold up my left, am I?" Rawl retorted coldly. He waved his tourniquet covered stump in the man's face.

"Of course," Ling Chou said with a conceding smile. "Once you're ready, simply hold up your arm."

Rawl nodded. "Thank you, Officer. I won't forget how you've helped in these difficult hours."

The man's face shone. He bowed and then backed away, leaving Rawl alone on the podium. Rawl's eDeck illuminated a holoscreen script and he loosely read the first sentence. He closed it down and looked at the spectators, now silent and staring, waiting for words of comfort, words of leadership. He shook his head.

Words are meaningless.

He raised his arm.

Behind him the airlock's outer hatch doors began to open. The air was the first thing to be pushed out, dragging clawing disciples with it towards the opening exterior hatch doors. Some were dashed upon them before they had time to open fully, becoming red smudges on dull metal sheets, while a few were sucked through regardless of the opening not yet being wide enough to fit through – the force breaking and tearing off limbs as the suction pulled them through the widening gap.

The spectators gasped audibly. Space revealed itself through the receding doors, and soon the Brotherhood of Man disciples were flushed out into the vacuum. Blue and bloated corpses floated by the portholes, haunting space, like ghosts with white diaphanous eyes and distended shrieking mouths. Twitching fingers on outstretched arms seemed to be desperately clawing their way back inside.

"Explosive decompression… ebullism and hypoxia," Rawl said, looking over the crowd with a dark glimmer emanating from his one eagling eye as it rolled across the distressed faces of the crowd. "Some degree of consciousness is usually retained for nine to eleven SES. What happens during this period of consciousness happens very fast and I can only imagine the terror that floods the body. First paralysis. This is followed by violent convulsions and then debilitating paralysis once again. Water vapour forms rapidly in the soft tissues of the body and more slowly in the blood. The body swells and deforms to twice its normal volume. The heart rate rises at first, but soon plunges. Arterial blood pressure falls, while vein pressure rises due to distention of the venous system. Venous pressure will meet or exceed arterial pressure. After a rush of gas from the lungs during decompression, gas and water vapour will continue to flow outward through the airways, freezing the mouth and nose – the remainder of the body will then also slowly freeze. After around ninety SES, death is imminent. Primary cause of death is asphyxia."

Rawl hobbled from the podium and began his way through the silent crowd.

There was work to be done.

*

The Hyperborea was almost completely out of sight before the Black Betty began its final descent towards Thebes. Ystil.3 set the Beta ship computer to take them through the planet's control shields and directly to the C-gate coordinates, before turning back to the group, who were watching the lifeship shrink away. It left them because none of them would be returning.

Ystil.3 was under no illusion regarding his own destruction. The energy from Earth re-entering real-time would cause a cataclysmic explosion through the C-gates and as a result, would lay waste to everything on Thebes and Pisces, including the destruction of all the servers that labyrinthed the planet – even his. It had also dawned on him that Tom's server would also be destroyed if the Black Betty remained on the planet during the detonation. But maybe there was something he could do about that.

The burned creatures on Thebes, whose bodies were charred and black, would not survive another blast this time. He presumed their souls would float off to where all the others who had been exposed to the White Drops went. He had no soul and knew that only oblivion waited for him.

Where will Lydia's soul go? Where will Daneel's go?

There had been no need for Daneel to stay, not really. He could've gone back to the lifeship before it left but he refused, and Ystil.3 suspected he knew the reason why – Lydia. But perhaps the man could take the Black Betty back to the Hyperborea once they landed, which is what Lydia urged of him after learning Rawl Collister had no intention of returning to Earth's system.

"Make him, Daneel," she said. Her shoulders rose with anxiety. "You can catch them easily. The Hyperborea won't enter hyper until power is back to capacity. You'll have at least another SED. You can make him see that they have to go to Sol. They have to. Otherwise, all this is for nothing."

"I'm not leaving you to die." His voice was as indomitable as the approaching dark sphere of Thebes. "We both return or neither of us do."

"I can't come back," Lydia pressed. It was Lydia's ability to Cut that was needed.

Her reward for all she's done shouldn't be death.

"Once we are securely in location, you can take the Betty," she said.

"If you think I would leave you down there then you don't know me at all. Not you as well. Not like Gutter. I couldn't change Collister's mind and you know it. No one can change that man's mind. If he's set on something then he'll see it out grudgingly, right up to the bitter, painful end. There's nothing I can do. I can't go back there without you, li. You want me to go back? To do what? Live out my life knowing you're dead and that it was all for nothing and that Earth may be out there but we'll never see it?"

"Find a woman," Lydia said. "Have babies. Live, for junkfuck sake. Stop waiting for me. I'm not a wife. I'm not a mother. I'm the li."

"No, you're not," Ystil.3 interjected.

"Stay out of this, Winston."

Daneel smirked. "Yeah, tin-man, stay out of it."

"Don't talk to him like that."

"I'll talk to him however I want. I outrank him."

"He has no rank," Lydia said. "And I outrank you, and I say you need to shut that mouth of yours before I shut it for you."

"I was referring to the fact that I'm human and that is a tin-man. Flesh outranks metal."

Prometheus leaned into Ystil.3 as they sat on the sidelines watching the exchange. "Perhaps you should intervene," he said. "I sense this may continue for a while elsewise."

"Yes. Right." He stood and placed himself between the two. "What I mean is that you're not the li, Lydia, because you have no pendant. And even if you had it, once the C-gates are closed, there will be no more Cutting and therefore your li status is moot."

"Until the gates are closed, I'm the only one with the ability and training to direct where we Cut to. So, yes Winston, I am still the li and I still have a responsibility until my mission is complete."

Daneel sat, leaning back into a grav chair. "Then I stay too."

Lydia threw up her hands, turned and stormed from the bridge. Ystil.3 followed.

"Follow her like a good little pet tin-man," Daneel shouted after him.

Ystil.3 found Lydia pacing the walkways outside. Her face furrowed when she saw him. "You could have supported me in there. He doesn't have to die, and you know that. Is this some kind of revenge for what he did to you?"

Ystil.3 didn't answer. "You have feelings for him, don't you?"

Her expression turned sour and she scoffed. "No. I... just..."

"You don't seem too concerned that I'm going to die... or even yourself for that matter."

Her face softened. "Winston, of course I care that you're going to die, but it's different. We've been in this together since the beginning and we'll finish it together. Somehow that makes it seem a little more bearable. But Daneel needs to at least attempt to persuade Collister to return to Earth otherwise everything I've sacrificed in my life, everything being the li took away from me, will have been for nothing… every death meaningless." Her gaze was gravid with a lifetime of un-wept tears. She tugged her eyes from him and turned. "Can't he see that? He needs to do everything in his power to get them to Earth, not cling to what we had… once."

Ystil.3 wasn't sure he fully understood, but in that moment, he wanted nothing more than to make it all better for her.

She seemed to see something in his face that made her smile. She placed her warm fingers onto his stubble-dusted cheeks. "You will never know just how much you've come to mean to me, Winston, And how you've helped me, without even realising it. When I first met you I… I didn't even feel human anymore. I was resentful for what I'd been turned into… for what I'd given up to be their li." She pushed onto her tip-toes and tenderly grazed her lips to his. "I know this is strange, but I think in you I've found a kindred soul."

Ystil.3 was dizzy from the sudden closeness and his lips tingled where they had touched hers. Soft plumes of her scent rolled from her hair and into his nostrils. "I don't have a soul," is all he could think to say.

"I wouldn't be too sure about that. Surely a soul can be earned. When we're done, I think we'll both have truly earned our souls." She let out a big exaggerated sigh. "Then we can finally rest."

"Don't worry." He found his fingers had curled around a lock of her hair without his knowing about it. "You've given your entire life to them. The universe will even out the score."

"Do you really believe that?" she asked with a wide-eyed hope that juxtaposed the sceptical raise of an eyebrow.

Ystil.3 replied earnestly. "It's the only thing I believe."

*

The bathroom facilities on the Black Betty were non-existent. Lydia finished crouching over the evac-shoot and repositioned her hardsuit. The shoot was used to evacuate common refuse when AI had crewed the ship, before the ship itself became sentient, or so Winston had told her. Once done, she activated a reflecting holo from the eDeck panel through the wrist of her hardsuit and adjusted her hair in the image. The skin around her eyes was still red. Perhaps they wouldn't notice.

She didn't want any of them to know that death scared her. She wouldn't allow herself to become a snivelling human. No, she would go towards death with a confident stride and she would look it straight in the eye and say, ok bitch, let's do this. She would not cry and she would not cower. She would not question why me or linger on all the things that she could have done with the rest of her life. This was her path, and she would meet her end with dignity. She was the li. It was how she had lived her life, and it was how she would end it. And despite Rawl Collister, she had to believe that it would not be for nothing.

Exiting the small utility room located in the lower decks, she made her way back up to the bridge. With each step, she began to feel herself again. This was what it meant to be the li; with the honour and privilege comes the sacrifice and responsibility. The li must be strong when others are not. The li must succeed when others have failed. The li must devote their life to the mission of finding a home for their kind.

The li must die so that others may live.

She paused in the causeway, took a deep breath and straightened her posture, lifting her chin a fraction too high in overcompensation. She then strode onto the bridge.

Thebes filled the tempurhull as the Black Betty passed through the last of the control field barriers – the dark Computronium servers rolled out below in a network of grids across the surface, winking in the mild light of the nearest star as they approached. Prometheus sat with his face pressed against the hull, seemingly mesmerised by the view, his eyes glazed and his mind elsewhere. Daneel took instruction from Winston, sitting in the pilot pod at the front of the central raised decking, encased in a virtual holo representing real-time space.

"Use the membrane deck to adjust the trajectory, like this," Winston said, hovering over him.

Daneel imitated Winston's gestures and ran his hands along the soft pad of the controls. The Black Betty veered suddenly to the portside in inept clumsiness. The inertial dampeners and internal control field prevented them all from being swatted against the far hull.

"Not so much," Winston said patiently. "Gently. The slightest movement is all you need."

Lydia raised an eyebrow and made her way towards them. Both turned with oddly exuberant smiles slashed wide across their faces. The sight was so unnerving that she almost reared backwards in alarm. "What's going on here?" she said, her eyes narrowing.

"Nothing," Winston said. "I'm giving Daneel a lesson in piloting the ship."

"Why?" Lydia asked, her suspicion flaring.

"Why not?" Winston replied with a shrug.

She looked at Daneel, who only rolled his eyes. "We're all going to die, li," he said. "Why not bury the hatchet, whatever that means. It seems I may have been wrong about the tin-man. Even though he led the AI to us

466

in the first place, without him we wouldn't have the chance we do now. Satisfied?"

She wasn't. There was something off about them. Something she didn't like. Daneel never admitted to being wrong.

No, that's not strictly true, a voice in her head argued. He said he was wrong about blaming me for Natalie.

Still, it was out of character, and Ystil.3 was just gullible enough to fall for it. The last thing they needed was Daneel trying to settle an imaginary vendetta by luring Winston into believing they were now friends. Of course, Lydia knew what it was really about – her. Most women who presumed such things were deluded to the point of narcissism, and she was usually the first to point that out to them, hence why she had no female friends among the other militia. But in this case, she was pretty sure it was true. Daneel could see the bond she had formed with Winston, and he was jealous. She pursed her lips and waved her hand, signalling for them to continue, then sat back while Winston instructed Daneel on how to input the coordinates of the C-gate into the Beta ship and land the Black Betty on the surface of the planet.

The landing itself was bumpy at best, but the craft touched down on terra firma with no major damage and no passenger casualties, and therefore Daneel beamed with pride, smiling up at Lydia. She breezed by him without a word as all four of them crammed into the airlock. Once the hatch door opened, they then stepped out onto the surface of the server planet.

Prometheus and Daneel wore hardsuits with a visor, while Lydia and Winston's head remained uncovered, using their internal rebreather systems and infrared visual filters to see into the shadows of the dark side of the planet – the sun would never rise again on the servers that surrounded them, Lydia certainly hoped. The C-gate building itself stood plain and cheerless amid the taller slender servers and appeared to be desolate. The hundreds of charred drones that had infested it had scattered off mindlessly after repairing the damage they had caused upon their last visit. With no plasma rifles to burn through the walls – only their T pistols had juice left – the thing was once again impenetrable. This was, however, as they had predicted, and to overcome it meant that the Black Betty had one last job to do for them. It might draw some attention, but there was no other choice.

Once Daneel returned with an all clear of the surrounding perimeter, they moved to a safe distance and waited. Within a few moments a plasma cannon emerged from a sliding panel on the Black Betty's flank, turned in their direction and shot a beam of searing white plasma that set the air alight, melting cleanly through four servers before the lance made contact with the C-gate building, liquefying the side walls and dissipating into the server beyond it.

"I should have been more careful with those Beta ship orders," Winston said with wry shrug. "One of those servers could have been mine."

They moved quickly down the crevice path of two smouldering servers. Daneel took the rear, Winston and Prometheus the flanks, while she took point.

"You hear that?" Daneel said loudly, turning wildly about and thrusting his T-pistols towards the shadows. As Lydia and Winston weren't wearing visors, Daneel and Prometheus used a speaker function so they could all hear one another. Daneel had apparently set his too high.

"Yes, I hear it," Lydia said. "Why don't you yell louder? I don't think the entire planet's inhabitants quite heard you."

There was movement in the murk. Shapes darker than the shadows shifted and stalked the passages between the servers. The creatures were everywhere, pouring from the dark as though made of it. The plasma cannon had attracted them and it was only a matter of time before they were swarmed.

All they could do was run.

With the others close behind, Lydia clambered through the hot wound of the melted C-gate building and into the descending stairway, taking the steps three at a time. Every hundred steps or so they had to incapacitate a burned man before they could pass. The steps gave way to flat earth so suddenly that Lydia's legs hadn't quite caught up and she stumbled, almost falling flat. Winston grabbed her by the arm and propped her upright with his synthetic strength. She could feel Daneel's glare from behind them as Ystil.3 held her.

They entered the C-gate chamber, finding the white ring hovering, inactive. Daneel let off two luminades, which cascaded down in a gentle curtain of light within the cave, settling a warm glow on the C-gate and its hollow centre. Lydia stood herself in front of the ring, placed her hands on her hips and cocked her head as if to size it up.

Will it really work the same as the li Pendant?

"How do we activate it?" Daneel asked.

"With Charlie's blood," Winston replied. "Just like Tom told us."

"Who the junkfuck is Tom?" Daneel asked.

"Just shut up, please," Lydia insisted. "Prometheus, come here. It's time for you to go home." She reached into the front pouch of her hardsuit and pulled out a tube of Charlie's blood, taken for the purpose. It wasn't bright red like normal human blood, like she had expected – more maroon, closer to brown. Prometheus appeared by her side. He looked down at the test tube and then up to the C-gate. His face formed a mask of quiet sadness. Lydia leapt up into the ring, pulled free the tube's rubber stopper and poured the oozing blood onto the golden blue tiled centre. It dripped in beads until half the contents pooled into a small splatter on the inner hollow of the ring. Lydia then helped Prometheus up next to her.

At once, the air inside the C-gate suffused with crackling energy, sending shards of prickling static out from the centre up to the roof of the cave, branching out in spidery shoots. Then a pinprick of light formed in the ring, sucking in all the static from the C-gate, turning it inwards and causing air and light within the gate to bend and whorl as through being syphoned into a vortex. The cave on the other side of the ring appeared as a warped image through the distorted air.

Lydia turned to Winston and Daneel, who stood behind them staring up. "I won't be long," she said. "Be ready for when I return." She turned back to Prometheus, his white face reflecting the shimmering hues of the portal. "Come on then. Let's get you home."

He grabbed her arm as she began forward. "What if I can't do it?" he said through trembling lips. "I don't know if I'm that strong. The man I was... I'm not that man anymore."

"You will do it because you've seen what will happen if you don't. And if you can't, then all this will happen just as it has for us. But you're just a man, Prometheus. Like the rest of us, you're only human." This didn't seem to console Prometheus much, but it was the truth and that was the best she could do. She took his arm, stepped up into the hollow of the C-gate and pulled him into the shimmering portal of warped diaphanous light.

The next step their hardsuit boots took was onto the hardwood floor of Prometheus's front parlour. Sun streamed in from a heavy draped window and the air was stifling with heat. Behind them, the warped light of the C-gate remained, playing on the antique dust that swathed the air like smoke.

Prometheus removed his visor and looked around like he hadn't been there in years, like it was a museum paying reverence to a man long dead and forgotten. He removed his T-pistols and then peeled away the hardsuit from his body, handing it all to Lydia and standing naked before her. They had agreed it was best that nothing from their future be left in the past.

"Good luck," she said, taking his things. She couldn't think of anything else to say. He was no longer the gaunt Prometheus that grieved for his dead wife, the one they had followed through the time sectors. He was harder and stronger now – even his body was muscled and he seemed to even stand a little taller.

The man nodded and Lydia turned back through the portal, leaving Prometheus to his journey and heading towards her journey's end. Her death.

Another step and Lydia was back in the cave. Her skin tingled under her hardsuit from the Cut. The C-gate towered behind her and the luminades had dimmed so the shadows were thick against the earthen red tones of the craggy sloping walls. She looked up expecting Daneel and Winston where she had left them, but the cave appeared empty. She jumped from the C-gate onto the hard earth and took a few cautious steps forward. "Winston?" She dropped Prometheus's things and unclipped her T-pistol. "Daneel, this is not—"

Something grabbed her from behind. She almost screamed in surprise, but instead thrust her head backwards and heard the crack of a nose breaking. Instead of going down, her attacker shifted their weight and threw her to the ground, lodging what she supposed was a knee into the back of her neck so that she ate dirt.

"Just do it," a voice commanded.

A cold weight across the back of her skull brought down thick blackness.

☐

60

We found the C-gate exactly where Charlie said it would be. It hovered ten metres high above the red sand that unfurled across the flat desert – a pristine white ring against the clear azure blue sky, glimmering in the heat and reflecting the sun as though it were itself a celestial body, a hanging star, a fixed luminous point of power. The air around it blurred and rippled, plumes of energy radiating off the smooth surface.

I looked up, shielding my face from the sun, irritated by its relentless heat. I'd gotten a furious case of sunburn over my face, arms, back and shoulders and it was both painful and ludicrously itchy. I scratched my arm distractedly, noticing gathered skin under my fingernails where it was starting to peel in places. "How do we get up there?" I asked, turning to Charlie, who stood wrapped in his furs. Norse stood beside him, twice his height, gazing up at the ring from under a curtain of tangled hair. His skin was just as raw as mine, yet his mustn't have hurt half as much because he never mentioned it.

"I get up there like this," Charlie said. The boy disappeared instantaneously as though he was never there to begin with, blinking out of existence, leaving only desert sand and dead air where he had stood. Both Norse and I scanned the horizon half-heartedly. We were tired, hungry and hurting and not really in the mood for a game of hide and seek.

"Up here," a small voice called.

He was standing in the hollow of the C-gate, peering down at us. He looked even more childlike in the centre of the ring, which eclipsed around him, revealing its large circumference in perspective to the boy. Then he was with us once more.

"You've done your part," he said. "The rest is down to me."

"And Ystil.3 and the humans," I said, unable to forget the impending fate of my friend.

"Yes," his boyish voice said thoughtfully.

"He'll do it," I said, suspecting a hint of anxiety in him. "If he said he'll do it, then he'll do it."

"That's all well and good," Norse said. "But how will we know when he's done it?"

Charlie glanced towards the C-gate. "We'll be able to see through to the other sides."

"Sides? Plural?" Norse said. The flecks of red in his now bushy beard seemed to ignite like kindling in the sun.

Charlie nodded. "We'll be able to see the activated gates on Thebes and

Pisces, if all goes to plan, that is. Then once it's done..." There was an awkward pause. The uncertainty of it all hung in the air between them.

"How can you be so sure that Earth will end up in the right place?" I asked. "What if it just gets sucked out on Thebes or Pisces? Or into the middle of random space with no sun or star system?"

"There is only one path Earth has taken and that was from its place to the BroadWeb. It never physically moved anywhere, you see, only shifted into this potential space sub-dimension. We'll just be shifting it back into physical form… with a few adjustments. It won't actually be travelling anywhere."

"Adjustments," the Overly Watchful repeated in agreement. "It's so different from how it was during the Reset. Most of it was uninhabitable back then."

"I've had a lot of time to correct a few things," Charlie said. "I've sung a song of Earth at its most beautiful. I've made it the perfect home for life, human and animal alike."

"What if they just ruin it again?" I said. "Like they did before."

"That's always a possibility. But I think it will be a very long time before the humans forget what it was like to be vagabonds among the stars." He looked reverently at the land around him, proud of his masterpiece. "No. They'll appreciate us this time."

"And what will happen to you?" Norse asked. I suspected what he really wanted to ask was and what will happen to me? "Will you return to your body after Earth re-enters real-time?"

"No. My body has now been destroyed, as it should have been hundreds of years ago. I suspect things won't change too much for me. I won't be able to take this form like I do now, and whatever data is shaped here when Earth re-enters real-time is how it will remain. I won't be able to change things, or fix things or affect things any more than the physical parameters that real-time allows once we pass over."

"So what about us… Betty, Norse, Bo and me?" I asked, mustering the nerve to ask directly where Norse hadn't. I felt him tense as he stood beside me. I had almost forgotten Bo was with us, being so small and non-verbal – thankfully – and travelling in the seashell strung on a vine around Norse's neck. He rarely poked his little green head out, save to catch the bugs that swarmed around the campfire at night.

"You will return to your servers, your real-time data forms," Charlie said.

"And if there is no server to return to?" Norse asked, finding a voice for his fear at last. He had some time ago realised this would be the case. Once the Earth re-entered real-time, the residual energy would skin the planet clean with fire and consuming energy, just like the Reset, and every AI server on the planet would be destroyed.

Charlie made a shrug with his small shoulders wrapped in furs. "I honestly don't know. Perhaps you'll stay here with me. Perhaps you'll have a physical form."

"I surely hope not," I said, shuddering at the thought of living a human life, with all its pain and feelings and constant hunger. "I've already been here longer than I care to." I had pondered often – when I could bring myself to think of anything but my constant hunger – how the actual Tom Jones could live his life this way and still find the presence of spirit within himself to produce the exquisite music he did. How did humans ever put all their mortal mess aside to create beauty such as art, or form song and sweet melody? Or invent and ponder the universe? My experience as a human made me realise that Tom Jones' talent was even more extraordinary than I had ever known before. If nothing else, I was grateful for that.

"And Bo?" Norse asked. "He was made in the BroadWeb and has no server."

Again, Charlie shrugged. It was a child-like thing to do and served as a jolting reminder that no matter how young he appeared, Charlie was ancient. "He'll probably return to the ether of potential space. But Nyx will find him."

"I've heard it said that Nyx knows where all of the programmes are all the time," Norse said. "Every single one of them, she can feel. She'd be able to find him no matter where he floats off to."

Beside me, Betty had been calmly cooling herself, drinking the last of the water that I'd set out for her. Her long head craned upwards at a stray cloud that shaded the sun, her nose twitched at the air.

Suddenly, she reared back, whinnying and dipping her head, treading backwards in the red sand. The silvery whites of her eyes grew wide against the velvet black of her mane, crazed and petrified like stone. The muscles in her legs wrung taught like thick ropes, eager to flee, and her tail whipped manically at the air as the cloud shade deepened.

Perplexed, I turned to calm her, noticing the sky was growing strangely dark. A sense of foreboding slid into me like a dagger biting into my spine. Something was wrong. A grey mass of clouds had quickly formed beside the floating C-gate and deep within them a storm of lightning began to split electric shards down to the red desert earth. Thunder rumbled across the vastness of sky, a throaty growl so deathly that the ground shook with fear.

"This storm is not of the Earth," Charlie said. A wind had risen and was tugging at the boy's furs. It made a frenzied red swarm of the sand.

I clutched Betty tightly, burying my face into her mane against the sandblast.

"It's coming," Charlie cried above the wind.

"What's coming?" I screamed.

A high-pitched shriek throttled the air, perforating my ears. The wind died and I was able to see once again. The storm was now a whirling vortex of grey and black clouds, spreading out like a grey sea above our heads, roiling and blighted with lightning bolts, as deadly as scorpion tails.

"Is this part of it?" Norse shouted over another rumble of thunder. Charlie mouthed words lost in the noise.

From out of the swirling sky came a beast that could only have been conjured from a place of nightmares. A bone white human skull emerged with scolding red eyes and a baleful scream so sharp that it threatened to cut flesh from bone. A trail of dark shadow followed behind it, as though night was spilling out from the cyclone, like black guts from a gravid belly torn open. The skull was larger than the C-gate that hovered beside it and the creature swooped and glided, its black smoke trailing like a comet tail.

I knew then that I recognised the creature as the same ghost that had guided me to Ystil.3's DataCom crib back in Grid City – it had hovered over it so I would know which was his. At once, I launched myself onto Betty and she reared again, eager to take us both far away.

The skull dived and the dark cloak enveloped us in its smoky fog. Suddenly, I could hear crying and voices; they wailed and sobbed in suffering, seemingly a million klicks away yet somehow right by my ears. The misery in those cries was unmistakable and I knew then that I had never known suffering at all. They seemed to enter me through the mist with every inhaling breath I took, enclosing around my delicate human heart and scratching on the inside of my skull.

In the confusion, I hadn't even realised that Betty had bolted under me, not until the mist faded and the sun once again warmed my back in the bright open of the desert. She ran until I came to my senses and eased her to a halt. I turned her around, ready to make our way back to the others, but was awestruck by what I saw. Death stood on the horizon, gathering its shadows and shrouded in night, larger than the giant Walkers that had roamed Grid City and taller than the behemoth buildings of old Earth. Charlie and Norse looked up from the ground, like insects in comparison.

Then the sky spat and tore with lightning, and as though being birthed from some sick womb, a five-headed serpent slithered through the swirling vortex sky. The livid heads of the monstrous Hydra struck the air, each bearing hundreds of long teeth wet with venom and eyes as black and empty as holes punched into spacetime. The heads curled and entwined around one another on long, tortuous necks, hissing and snapping as its tapered body, silver and glistening, slid out from the tear in the sky, limbless and smooth down to its sharp pointed tail. It thrashed the air.

The Hydra uncoiled, as large as the skull, both now towering over the desert like gargantuan effigies built by a long-dead civilisation in worship of forgotten gods. Like gods, their size and power was immeasurable. Terrible.

The skull, facing its opponent, opened its bony jaws and let out a scream. It was the shriek of banshees, sharp as harpy talons. The pain and fury in that noise sent me cold. It caught me in its strangling grip and pulled me down with it, down into dark places where light had never been, into pits of desperation. A sea of grief washed over those cracked tombstone teeth, drowning out all other sound in its fermented odium.

Then, it attacked.

It launched itself at the Hydra, sinking those ragged teeth into serpent flesh, tearing gouges free and raking at it with impetuous fingers of sharpened bone. The Hydra hissed and writhed within the skull's clutches, twisting its long necks to strike and lurching its weight as if to throw it off. The five heads rained down relentless stings, needle teeth plunging like swords into the dark abyss of the skull's cloak. With each strike, Death's wails grew ever more tortured. They entangled themselves in a whir of shadow and scales – the Hydra heads hissing and rattling with the thunder and the skull's laser-red eyes burning as hot as the lightning of the storm that embroiled them.

As I rode Betty back towards the fray, the Hydra coiled its body around Death and brought it to the ground with such a crash that I swore Betty's knees almost buckled beneath her. But she rode with me pressing her onwards and we reached the others, who had now fled from the roots of the battling titans to a safer distance.

Norse's face contorted with terror beneath his beard. "It's Z. He's found us."

My stomach lurched and Betty stepped back as though she might bolt again. I steadied her with a soothing hand and Charlie appeared beside us. In the calamity, I hardly noticed the two other figures that ran to a halt behind him.

"Do it now," I urged the boy. "Activate the C-gate before Z can stop you."

He shook his head. "Not with it here. I won't risk allowing it to merge with the Earth as I did." Charlie's eyes followed mine as I finally noticed the two male humans standing behind him. He turned. His eyes widened for a moment and he smiled a gawking grin – the grin of an excited little boy.

One of the men was dark-skinned and muscled, while the other was older and sinewy-looking, with a scar running down one side of his face. He had a beard that was neat and trimmed, not like Norse's buoyant mass of fuzz. Both were as naked as the day we had arrived there. The men looked at one another and then to Charlie.

"What's happening?" the dark-skinned one said. "Where are we?"

"The BroadWeb," the older said, then sardonically, "Earth, apparently."

"But how? We were on the mothership, and then…?" The man screwed up his face as though trying to remember, or forget.

"I'm sorry," the scarred one said. "You didn't make it. I couldn't get you out. I had a chance to destroy them and I took it."

"The White Drops?" the man breathed.

The older man nodded.

"But my people are safe?" he asked. "The AI have been destroyed."

"Yes, in their physical forms. And now we're going to make sure that this creature never threatens them again."

"Sorry to interrupt," I said with a polite cough. Norse, Charlie and I had been simply staring at the two men. "But who are you and how did you get here?"

"This is Prometheus," Charlie said. "And this, I'm guessing is General Nathan Shaw."

"That's right," Prometheus said warily. "And who might you all be?"

"This is Tom the CorVac," Charlie began. "This is Norse the Overly Watchful and inside the shell around his neck is a programme called Bo. The black mare is a class nine sentient craft personality named Betty and I'm Charlie. Hello, father."

In the distance, the skull unwound itself from the Hydra's grip. The serpent undulated backwards, whipping up a storm of desert sand around it like a veil of red smoke. Behind the curtain of red mist, the Hydra began to change shape. Its body distended up until it loomed twice the size of the skull and its head mutated higher into the clouds. The long necks pierced with ridges and grew silver spines. The heads themselves flattened and sprouted chrome horns, no longer the heads of serpents, but dragons with oblivion-black eyes. Wings emerged from the serpent's back, unfurling like giant sails of leather that submerged the desert in their shade. Each head opened an abominably sharp set of jaws and roared a burning spray of molten fire.

In the shadow of the Hydra's wings, Death seemed suddenly small.

*

Prometheus could do nothing but stare at Charlie, despite the truculent battle happening in the distance. He had seen him as a corpse, he had seen him as a baby and as a man so old that he could barely be counted as human – but here stood a little boy who had experienced more than a lifetime's worth of pain and suffering as the result of his selfish hubris. And the boy had just called him father.

The one on the horse, Tom, was saying something, but, in turn, Charlie was looking at Prometheus with equal consternation.

"I haven't seen you in years," a voice said from inside his head. It was the boy. "Not since…"

"A different Prometheus was your father," he thought, somehow knowing Charlie could hear him. "That future will never happen to me, and shouldn't happen to the Prometheus that has returned home… if he has any sense about him."

"I know," Charlie said. "But still, it was you."

"I cannot pretend to know the pain you have suffered in your lifetime," Prometheus said. "All I know is that I am responsible, and all I can tell you is how utterly sorry I am." It was a simple apology and one that could never even begin to account for the damage that had been caused, but he said it all the same, hoping it could somehow provide meagre consolation.

Charlie nodded silently. "You want to know whether I would have preferred never to have lived at all, rather than to have lived a life so endless and full of pain, don't you?"

Prometheus wasn't sure he was ready for the answer, but the boy was right about his question. He wasn't sure why he needed to know. Perhaps it was another attempt to inflict punishment upon himself, or perhaps Prometheus wanted to hope that even though Charlie had eventually become some decrepit half-life, bedbound and waiting powerlessly for his dry and shrivelled body to decay around him, life – even that engrained with pain from cradle to grave – was still better than to have never existed at all.

When Charlie told him the answer to his question, Prometheus closed his eyes and nodded pensively.

"What do we do now?" Nathan asked. The General appeared much younger than his real-time self, a strapping man of thirty. Prometheus himself appeared much the same as he had been when his body was destroyed – he wasn't sure what that meant about his self-perception.

For some reason the group were looking to him for the answer. "The Hydra needs to be destroyed," he said simply. "If it's killed here then it will truly be dead and the Hyperborea… humanity… will be safe. From that, at least."

"And then Earth can return to real-time," Charlie said.

"How exactly do we do it, destroy Z… I mean the Hydra?" Tom asked. Prometheus noted the man's Welsh accent with a mild, pleasant surprise. "Just look at it." He pointed to Death as it fought the Hydra in a whirl of teeth and shadow. "If that skull monster thing is losing, what chance do you think we'd have?"

"Death told me this would happen," Prometheus said. "On its own Death is not strong enough. The Hydra has become too powerful, consumed too much data. But there is a way."

"How?" Norse asked.

"I am not certain. Death lacks the skill of expressing coherent information. It speaks in a mixture of words, feeling and pictures. It attempts to piece them all together but as you might guess the results can be somewhat fractured. I do remember what it said… over and over again as we trained. It became almost a mantra for my army. She is the sky, with tendrils clenched in vengeance. He is the lost Earth, lost life, lost death. Together, with my bones and shadows, bring divergence. The Chimera is born to eat its fiery breath."

"Lovely, but hardly Tom Jones," Tom said with a wry smile. "What does it mean?" No one, including Prometheus, seemed to understand what a Tom Jones was.

"He is the lost Earth, lost life, lost death," Charlie repeated. "That's me, surely."

"What's a Chimera?" Nathan asked.

"Something that can take that on, let's hope," Tom offered.

"I have to help destroy it," Charlie said. "I have to help defeat it."

"But what about the other part?" Nathan said. "The bit with the vengeance?"

"I don't know," Prometheus said. If only Death could've answered his questions coherently.

Nathan squinted at the distant battle for a moment. "Death, you said it's formed from the collective souls of those that took the White Drops in the days of Earth?"

"That's right."

Nathan smiled and lowered his eyes to the floor, his face lighting suddenly like a lantern – as though all the splintered pieces of unanswered questions in the universe had been revealed to him and he held the secret to it all. It was all clear upon his face. "I've been waiting my whole life for this moment," he said. "For a long, long time I wondered why I was spared the fate of my people. Thousands of nights I've spent seething in sweat-drenched sheets, desperate for justice. I now know what I must do." He turned to face Death and the Hydra. "So this is Earth?" He smiled. "Reminds me of home." With that, the man dug the balls of his feet into the red sand sprang into a charge across the desert, towards the duelling titans, his body glistening, the pink soles of his feet flashing as they hammered over the earth. Within a few moments he was nothing but a receding smudge heading for the horizon.

"What's he doing?" Tom asked.

They watched as Nathan hurled himself towards the clashing foes. "Giving us more time," Prometheus replied.

"Nyx," Norse said suddenly, as though waking from a deep thought. "She is the sky with tendrils clenched in vengeance. That's Nyx, I'm sure of it. Nyx is the first and most powerful programme ever created by Z. To some she takes the form of a half humanoid creature with serpentine tendrils, and she has long sworn vengeance upon Z for banishing her into BroadWeb darkness. It must be Nyx."

"That makes perfect sense to me," Tom said. "Nyx told me of how Z came to fear her. And I can see why. There is something quite terribly powerful about her. Sinister almost. Z feared what he'd created. But she's in programme city. What good is she to us there?"

"It's you," Charlie said suddenly. He was pointing at Tom, still perched upon his horse. "You can do it. You can bring her here. Just like you altered your own form when running from the Apex Soldiers, just like you altered Betty into a ship so you could navigate yourselves to Earth, you can bring her... the bridge between real-time and BroadWeb."

Tom shook his head vigorously. "I don't think I can do that. Those things were about me focusing on something and changing it because I needed to. It was a matter of life and death, so to speak. I can't just go popping programmes out of one place into another. I'm sorry, but I wouldn't know where to begin. You're the one with the power to change things here."

"The things I created here were locked away in the data of Earth. All I had to do was cultivate it. I cannot affect things that aren't within the Earth's potential. But you've done it before, Tom. It's why Nyx sent you to me. You can bend potential space to your will."

Tom rubbed his palms nervously over the horse's raven body, shaking his head. "It's too much," he said, his face racked with doubt. "It's just too much."

"Bo," Norse cried.

Prometheus looked to the others hoping they recognised it as some sort of solution, but they seemed as confused as him.

"Bo is a programme," the man continued, realising nobody understood. "Nyx can sense every programme in the BroadWeb." He loosened the shell from the vine around his neck and placed it in his hand. "And we have our very own beacon for Nyx to track us. She must know we're here and what we're doing. She's waiting to come."

Prometheus peered in close as a tiny green cricket creature with twitching antennae emerged from within the smooth iridescent mother-of-pearl shell. Charlie stepped forward, scooped the insect and the shell up in his small fingers and handed them to Tom. The Welshman looked down it the parcel as though he was resisting the urge to squash the little creature by clapping his hands.

"Together," Charlie said. "Together, you can do it. We need Nyx here. I can only do so much. We don't stand a chance without her."

"How?" Tom said, his brow tightening into an anxious line below his dark curly hair. "How do I bring her here?"

Charlie reached up and placed an encouraging hand on the man's leg hung astride his horse. "Use your instincts."

*

Nathan didn't look back even once as he ran. There was nothing to look back for. This was his mission – his final mission. And towards it, he ran hungrily.

He had long resigned himself to the possibility that he was not going to die a normal death after living an average life. He had taken the White Drops and since then he knew his life must mean more. It had to be more than living out his own mundane wishes and desires. It had to be something worthy of the gift – and curse – he had consumed. He always hoped for the chance to bring justice to his people, and find a home for the Hyperborea, but he never thought it would happen after the destruction of his body, after his death, so to speak.

He had spent many bleak hours drowning in regret for having cursed himself to extraordinary long life, seeing those around him wither and die – his mentor, the first Captain Lu, in particular, who had taught him everything he knew. But now, as he ran, he knew this was how it was meant to be. This was his path. There would be no warm slumber of afterlife for him. That frightened him a little. It always had. But it was the price he was willing to pay. His resolve was steely – he was, after all, his mother's son. He knew, just like she'd taught him, that overcoming this fear was half the battle won. It was all set in motion from the moment he watched his planet burn.

He worked his legs harder and ran even faster, eating up the distance between him and his fate. He recalled his mother as she had appeared in the mothership, her face stolen so that creature could feel like it had a sense of self, stitched together with different minds, sick with an abominable design for the universe, propelled by the fetid morality of the humans that inadvertently created it. It had surprised him how unlike her that face was, with a different mind pulling at the expressions. His mother never once appeared as it had made her face look then, corrupt with a dark fire.

His legs sprinted under him, pressing him forward, unnoticed by the shrouded figure of Death that now dominated the sky above, a monolith of darkness and lustrous bone. If it weren't for those clawing hands of sharpened ivory, Nathan could have pretended that bleached skull was nothing but a moon in a night sky. But those hands were demons, and like him they yearned for tearing vengeance.

The Hydra flew about Death in relentless aerial attacks, beating its leathery wings and breathing down waves of fire from five serrated jaws. Death absorbed the fire within its cloak. Nathan was too infinitesimal to be of consequence to either, but his soul was huge, and if the souls of humans gave Death its form, then Nathan's soul would only make it stronger. He would pour into it his rage, his strength, his pain, his love, his longing and his righteousness. He would join it and fight with everything that he had left inside him until it burnt him through.

The desert gave way to a wall of black smoke. Within, the distorted faces of lost souls floated in the infinite darkness, wraiths and spirits of the tormented, making up Death's cloak.

Kindred souls.

Nathan entered into Death running, not slowing for even a moment's hesitation.

The cold shadows enveloped him as he plunged himself into the blackness. He could not see, but he could feel them lapping at him like the tongues of icy flames. They moved around him, touching him, tasting him, judging his worth and recognising him as one of their own. They welcomed him, and Nathan touched upon the spark of their collective power and knowledge.

Around him, he felt his form dissolve, felt his sense of self melt into the collective. It took him hungrily, and into its pool, Nathan poured his soul, his strength, his thirst for vengeance.

And Death grew stronger from such nourishing black milk.

61

Lydia opened her eyes. She was unconscious for barely any time at all, but it was long enough to allow time to restrain her, it seemed. Her legs and arms were secured in control field-enforced wirecuffs; even with li training and upgrades, there was no way she was getting out of those.

Her head lolled in the dirt, her eyes flickering, until they opened wide, as though she had been startled awake from a nightmare. Ystil.3 and Daneel stood side-by-side, hovering over her as she came around, a pathetically apologetic expression upon Ystil.3's face and an amused one upon Daneel's. She struggled only briefly, twisting her arms and kicking her legs out before slackening her body in defeat.

"Release these ties, right now," she said. She didn't need to ask what had happened or why she was bound.

"No can do, li," Daneel said. He was enjoying this more than he should have, which was infinitely more than Ystil.3, who could barely make eye contact with her.

"This was your idea," she said to him.

"You'll be grateful one day," Ystil.3 said. It was a statement to reassure himself rather than her. "You and Daneel will take the Black Betty back to the Hyperborea once I'm through and both sides have been activated. Daneel will survive like you wanted. Tom and Betty might even come out of it okay too. You will get to live the rest of your life. Not as the li, and not hiding from AI. But free. And you can convince Collister to return to Earth's system yourself."

"This is absurd." She pulled at her wrist binds once more, as if somehow she would now find them easier to escape from. They weren't. "You'll never get to Pisces without me," she said after one final frustrated tug. "Then you'll be lost on some random world in an unknown time and our chance of finding Earth will be lost. Don't do this, Winston. Daneel doesn't know any better—"

"Hey," Daneel interjected.

"But you do," Lydia continued, ignoring him. "I expect this kind of shit from him, but Winston, you and I both know the score. We know what's at stake."

"You're right," Ystil.3 said. "We both do know the score. But the truth is I can do this without you because I'm doing it for you. I will Cut to Pisces and I will activate the C-gate because if I do that then you get to live, and I have come to want nothing as much as I want that. I want you to live out your life and to do the things that you never could before. I want you to forget that you've been upgraded to almost junkfucking cyborg status and I want you to be happy. I will take your burden, and in return you will be happy for the remainder of your life. I know you will. You just need another chance. The universe owes you that chance, remember, and I'm giving it a helping hand in your long-due karmic retribution."

"I don't have that luxury," Lydia said. "I'm grateful you would do this for me, but we cannot risk it. I am not important enough to risk this, don't you understand that?"

"Don't you understand?" Daneel said, bending down to touch Lydia's cheek. "To us, you are that important."

She recoiled from his touch. "I knew something was up with you two. Teaching Daneel to pilot the Black Betty like you're best friends suddenly? I knew it. Scheming, backstabbing slits."

"It's something we both agree on completely," Daneel replied, standing and looking to Winston. "He should die. And you should live."

Winston nodded sharply. "Enough talk."

"Don't do this," Lydia begged, wriggling and pulling at her restraints. "Please, Winston. Daneel. Don't. This is a mistake. You're going to junkfuck it up for everyone. Winston."

Winston turned to face the C-gate's shimmering film of bending light that stretched on the inside of the ring. Daneel grabbed his arm and yanked it roughly. "Don't junkfuck this up, tin-man," he said. "I'm trusting you because Lydia does. Don't make me regret doing this."

Winston took back his arm and scowled. "You'll regret it more if you don't let me do it."

"I don't want Lydia to die," Daneel said, the hardness of his expression melting. "I just need to know you can do this."

"I can do it. I can do it for her."

"Do you love her?" Daneel asked.

Winston looked at her and smiled. "She and I are kindred souls."

"Do you even have a soul?" Daneel asked.

"I don't know. But maybe I'll earn one." He then sprang up into the ring's centre, facing the iridescent film of light bending energy.

"Don't," Lyda cried, but they ignored her. "Please."

"How will we know that you made it to Pisces?" Daneel said.

"Because I will make it. When I'm through, take her and go." He looked back to her and she pleaded silently, her lips trembling apart. "Winston, no."

"Goodbye Lydia," he said. He went to turn back to the gate but paused. "Final score. Lydia, seventy-three, Winston, seventy-four." He smiled. "I win."

He turned and stepped through the C-gate.

☐

62

Death grew larger still, until it was a dark mountain with ivory claws, its head lost in a haze of atmosphere, with eyes burning laser red in black caves, scanning for wings that battered the sky. It moved like wind, snatching up the Hydra by one of its five heads. The thing let out a downpour of maleficent fire, but Death's grip was unyielding, using creaturous hands to pull and rip until the captured head tore away from the Hydra's body completely. Sparks of light rained down from the ragged stump instead of blood, leaving the remaining four heads yelping, but free.

The Hydra then ascended, beating its air-filled wings against the pain, narrowly escaping Death's swift grasp as the severed head disintegrated in a burst of white sparks and pixels before it reached the earth below.

Then, Prometheus watched silently as the Hydra's head grew back.

Like a wriggling worm poking up from the earth, a new serpent was birthed from the torn stem, snarling and daubed in shining bile. Death let out a piercing shriek and sent out shadows to ensnare the Hydra's wings, binding them tightly and pulling it down to the desert floor with a crash. It flailed in a storm of red sand before snapping through the binds and taking flight once more.

"I must help," Charles said, watching Death send more shadows into the rippling air of the Hydra's wake – this time failing to capture it. The Hydra plunged and swerved with precision. "This is my domain. I have fused with the Earth and in these lands, I am Lord." He turned. "Find a way to bring Nyx here. You must."

"How?" Tom asked. But Charles made no reply. Instead, he turned and in the direction of the battle in the sky and began towards it.

The Hydra's strength seemed to have returned. It began a bombardment of liquid fire upon Death, so relentless and searing that it pooled into a molten lake on the earth below, pouring into the crater left from its fall.

With each step towards the battle, Prometheus watched Charles' form change. His dusty yellow hair grew long and thick and wild upon his head and the blonde furs that mounted his shoulders extended and trailed down his back. It seemed the boy bent double into a crawl, walking on all-fours upon the hot sand. Underneath the furs his body grew large and thickened with muscle, coating limbs and hide, and a tail emerged that flicked the air. Charles was no longer a boy walking across the desert, but a lion loping on padded claws. And with each pounce into the distance, the lion matured to full ferocity. It grew until it rivalled the size of the entities upon the skyline.

The lion turned its head back to the group with eyes flashing gold as suns and roared a mighty tooth-jeweled roar, before leaping forward.

The lion leapt impossibly high, bounding up from the sand on hind legs, taking a slice at the Hydra with razor claws. The serpent veered back before the lion could hook in those black knives and drag it down. In retaliation, the Hydra regurgitated a flood of hellacious fire upon the lion as it landed in the sand. Death swept in, using its velvety cloaks to cover and protect the lion, absorbing the fire and sending it deep into its smoky cowl. The Hydra wasn't giving up; it dropped altitude to increase the intensity of its fire and Charles pawed at the sand, hurtling his body up into the air once again. Death's cloak parted like mist, allowing through a golden blur. Teeth found scales and Charles fastened his jaws around the lowest hanging of the Hydra's five necks. He tore it free before landing perfectly on all-fours. Sparks of light erupted from the wriggling neck before it burned up completely in the lion's teeth in a burst of pixelated white light.

The Hydra shrieked, taking off higher into the blue expanse. Death launched into the sky after it, soaring wraith-like through the air and expelling miasmic vapours to ensnare the injured serpent. Even wounded, however, the Hydra was too swift and powerful, and it avoided the shadows long enough for its fifth head to rebirth from the wound.

From the desert floor, Charles roared wildly, unable to follow the others in flight. He looked up with teeth bared, watching as Death and the Hydra tumbled in a ball of fire and darkness.

When Prometheus turned his attention back to the group, Tom was staring into his palm, a look of consternation on his sun-burned face. He had dismounted the black mare and she trotted around them in anxious circles. "You'll have to forgive me," Prometheus said, "but all I know is what I managed to decipher from Death's ramblings. But, somehow, we must bring the creature known as Nyx here, so that she may aid in the destruction of the Hydra. I'm assuming you must know more than I on how this might be achieved?"

Both Tom and Norse looked at him with the same strained expression.

"I'll presume that is not the case then," Prometheus said as he peered down into Tom's palm. The cricket they called Bo was staring up at them, lifting one leg up at a time, which, if Prometheus didn't know better, looked as though it was performing a ridiculous dance.

"You have to do it, Tom," Norse said with a mouth that was barely visible through his bushy beard. "Even Charlie knows you're the only one that can."

"That's Charles," Prometheus interjected. They ignored him.

"I don't know how," Tom said. "It's not fair that you're putting this on me."

"Think back to when you broke the DataCom perception filter and when you turned Betty into a ship. What was the common denominator?"

"I don't know."

"Think."

Tom frowned as his thoughts wandered off somewhere inside his head. "I needed it to happen otherwise I would have been deleted when the Apex were chasing me. And we all needed to stay together, otherwise we would have split up in the darkness of the potential space. I was scared of losing Betty again. Fear. I guess, both times it was fear."

"Fear," Norse said. "So you need to get scared... right now."

"And how do you suggest I do that? I mean, I'm on edge... who wouldn't be... but I'm not in a fight-for-my-life, adrenaline-pumping-state-of-terror, am I?"

Prometheus knew a bit about riding horses. He had ridden a lot when he was a child and had a chestnut horse at his family home, which he rode daily when he was home from school. The horse had died when he was twelve and his father bought him another – a dark horse with a temperament to match. He called her Night Mare. It took all Prometheus's summer-term break to tame her. But he did.

With a quick and fearless bound, Prometheus mounted Betty and dug in his heels a little harder than perhaps needed. The creature let out a neigh and took off as fast as she could. Prometheus clung onto her neck to sway her direction, the air whipping at his face and only barely managing to not fall off as she bolted. He turned back to see Tom chasing after them through the red sandstorm churned up in their wake.

"I apologise profusely for this," Prometheus said, not really sure why he was talking to the horse, but sure she could understand him, nonetheless. "But it seems Tom needs to fear for your life so that the Hydra can be destroyed."

Beneath his nakedness, Prometheus could feel Betty's muscles working. He dug in his heels once more, steering her into the direction of the Hydra. "Yah."

All resistance in the horse had gone and she galloped across the desert at full speed. Prometheus supposed his words had rung true.

Death and Charles the lion came upon them like rising giants. Death's shadows eddied like the coming tides of swarthy waves, while above, the glimmering skull hung amid the shadows, its red eyes burning with the fire of odium. Prometheus swerved Betty aside from the enclosing storm of shadows and rode her hard between the lion's golden obelisk legs as it landed from a regal, yet fruitless, leap towards the Hydra with an earth-rumbling boom.

He rode along the underside of the lion as it arched over them, protecting them from the burning meteors that rained down from the Hydra's snapping cannons. It felt to Prometheus as though those legs were the towering frames of a tunnel and the raining fire a Biblical portend of doom – as if he was passing through the very gates of Hades, into Hell itself.

*

I ran after Betty until I lost my footing and fell face first. Sand filled my mouth and gritted my eyes to tears. I called out after spitting clumps of red saliva but they were charging away. I picked myself up and continued to run until I realised that I was never going to catch up to Prometheus, who had now taken Betty right into the heart of the battle.

I watched as they shrank against the backdrop of Death's cloak, the Hydra above and the lion padding below. I began to panic, a sickening feeling rising in my gut as a flurry of horrific notions bombarded my mind – Betty deleted, dead.

I stood helplessly, my fragile human heart beating frenziedly in my chest.

Norse appeared. I hadn't run very far at all. He grabbed my hand, turning my palm upwards. I didn't understand until I looked down to see Bo squatting in my palm, staring up with those black orbs of his. I must have dropped him somewhere along the way and Norse must have retrieved him from the sand. I wanted to smoosh him in my hands and scream for Betty again. But I couldn't. This small, relatively insignificant programme was somehow instrumental to evoking Nyx.

I squinted at the cricket and jabbed it with my finger. "Bring her here, now," I demanded. Bo sat perfectly still for a moment and then commenced to rub its legs together, forming a sound. "Bring her here, right now." I felt heat spark in my chest as I screamed the words into my palm. Then I thought for a moment he might have died because he toppled back and froze. But he picked himself up and resumed his annoying leg music. "I... I don't know what else to do."

"It isn't about Bo," Norse said, taking the bug from me. "It's about you. Nyx knows where Bo is. She can locate him. What she can't do is get here. That's what you have to concentrate on. It isn't Bo that will bring her here. You will. You have to do what you did before."

"How many times do I have to tell you? I don't know what I did before." Why was no one listening to me? "I never wanted any of this. All I wanted was to stay at home with Betty and live out of our existences while I serenade her with a medley of Tom Jones songs. Was that so much to ask? And now I'm going to lose Ystil.3, my best friend in the universe, and Betty has been taken and will probably be deleted." Tears flowed from my eyes in an outburst of raw emotion the likes of which I had never felt before. I began to sob, falling to the floor in a heap. I felt the attempted comfort of

Norse's hand on my shoulder but I shrugged it away, pushing my thumbs into my eyes until the tears stopped. In the distance, I could hear the baleful cries of the Hydra.

"You didn't do anything," Norse said, somewhere near my ear. "You just need to remember how you felt. Recreate the scene in your head. That fear. Remember the fear. The rest is instincts, remember what Nyx said?"

Behind my eyes, I pictured the swarm of Apex Soldiers at my back as I attempted to escape with DataCom legs. I felt the panic in me rise as it did then, the impending sense of doom – the fear that I would never see Betty again and that she had been captured and hurt and deleted. That Ystil.3 was walking into a trap. That the whole of Grid City had been annihilated. That if I didn't move faster I would never be able to save them.

"Picture Betty as the ship you made her in the potential space," Norse said, attempting to guide me.

I watched as Betty became the ship. I felt the relief of knowing that now I wouldn't lose her to the blackness.

"You were able to enter Charlie's body in real-time when I couldn't. Picture that."

I saw the light into which Charlie had led me, and then I heard Ystil.3's synthetic voice as I gave him instructions on how to activate the C-gates. I had done it all without even thinking, without even knowing that something was happening. I had needed Betty to survive more than anything – and now she depended on upon me again. They all did. Not just Betty and Ystil.3, I realised, but the orphaned humans that awaited the return of their home. I knew what it was to have a home, knew how important it was. My home was Betty and the Titan system, Ystil.3's home was the BroadWeb and the human's home was Earth. The world changes, but it is the home that is a sanctuary. Without it, we spin in chaos.

With eyes still closed, I opened my mouth to sing The Green, Green Grass of Home.

"Tom."

The words consumed me until there was nothing else.

"Tom."

Everything melted away. Everything but Tom's voice.

"Tom," Norse snapped. "Open your eyes and look."

I lifted my head, blinking feverishly from the white stars that burst into my vision from the glaring sun. A dark rip tore open in the sky. Tentacles and feelers of lapis blue unfurled through it, like giant worms. The humanoid torso of a woman followed, with breasts and slender arms attached. Nyx's head appeared with a dark glare and a bitten pout widened to expose rows of sharp teeth. She came through, the last plume of tentacles draping down from her head like hair, before the opening closed, as though zipped up from the other side.

Nyx's winding appendages spread wide around her, as though she was a queen upon a mountain of snakes. Her mood infected the sky, turning it a murderous black above her crown. It spread until it enclosed them from horizon to horizon.

The five Hydra heads turned to Nyx and each let out a deafening scream.

The dark goddess pointed a sharp finger across the miles. "Mother." A war cry. Her voice carried over the desert so that it seemed each individual grain of sand shook.

*

The Hydra attempted to flee, seemingly knowing what was to come. Its wings scraped frantically at the dark sky – Nyx's sky – desperate to climb higher, up to where the others could not reach it. It ringed in circles, casting a faint shadow as it ascended, before banking sharply and soaring over the desert, shrinking into the distance.

Nyx's sky reached down and wound it in a vice of strangling tentacles, crushing its wings flat in an immobilising hold. The Hydra's five heads squawked, the echoes wresting through the air. The creature pushed out its wings in redundant attempt to escape, but Nyx only constricted, coiling her treacherous vines around and around, embracing ever tighter until all that was visible within the writhing knot were the snapping heads.

With the Hydra bound, the lion loped across the desert, Death trailing behind like a cloud of noxious smoke. The lion came upon Nyx, sliding to a stop, while Death expanded its shadow around them both. Nyx's hold over the Hydra began to weaken; the creature roared fire upon her tendrils and she let out a cry before dropping it, furling her tentacles tentatively back into the sky.

The Hydra spread its wings and continued its retreat into the distance.

Death's cloak thickened until neither Nyx, the lion or Death itself could be seen within the shadows. The shade consumed them, engorging as though alive and feeding. It throbbed and crackled with lightning, and then, in one swift motion, peeled back in the form of two enormous wings, parting like theatrical draperies covered in black, glossy feathers.

The wings themselves were formed on the back of a majestic black lion, with an ebony mane and claws of sharpened onyx. The lion's eyes were fierce rubies, glowing pits of fire in the creature's head. Where its tail should have been, a long black serpent tail whipped back and forth, its tip glistening as though rendered in steel.

The Chimera threw back its head and let out a bone-shaking roar. Its dark wings moved like giant sails. It rose with a leap, suspending itself above the ground for a moment, before taking off into the sky after the diminishing Hydra.

The creature's shadow swept along the sand, washing over Prometheus as he sat neck craned, and then over Norse and Tom as they stared up in silent reverence. Bo jumped excitedly in Norse's palm.

Swallowing air beneath its wings, the Chimera knifed through the sky, closing the distance between it and the Hydra with every stroke of its wings. The lashing air rippled down the black fur that covered its muscled form, and down the tentacle tail that streamered behind it.

It came upon the Hydra from a height, descending on it like an eagle with razor talons splayed. The hind claws dropped low as it stooped, with gliding wings paused in mid-beat like two dark hands spanned wide to grab.

They collided.

The Chimera tore chunks of serpent flesh, forcing it down with its size and weight. Together, they tumbled in free-fall, locked in thrashing blows. The Hydra could do nothing but snap its heads and throw fire into the Chimera's direction. The fire carried on the wind, the heat alone causing the Chimera's wings to smoulder. The smoke scored a coal line in the air as they fell together, locked in battle.

Unable to free itself, the Hydra struck with its tail. The Chimera's own tail was, however, a formidable opponent and blocked all blows, as though it had eyes and a mind of its own.

The ground rushed up to meet them with air-ripping velocity, and together they crashed to the earth in a detonation of red sand. The impact submerged them in a crater, and when the cloud cleared, the Chimera stood victoriously over the Hydra, pinning it mercilessly, its jaw at its belly.

The Hydra heads roared, setting fire to the lion's mane and proud erect wings, which caught immediately, as though doused in gasoline. They blazed like two burning trees, but the fire only added to the magnificence of the lion, and it seemed to feel no pain as the flames spread over its fur. The lion raised its head, eyes flashing red, and roared, revealing deadly incisors under drawn lips. The Chimera fixed its jaw around each of the Hydra's heads, and in turn tore each from the neck.

Light broke out from each, burning away until nothing remained but severed stems, squirming like a handful of worms squeezed in a tightening palm. Before the heads could grow back, the Chimera took its deathblow. Its keen serpentine tail twisted over its head, impaling the Hydra through its thrashing body. When it withdrew, a single shaft of light erupted from the wound. The tail struck again and again and again until the Hydra was nothing but a punctured carcass, motionless and flowing with white light.

The light expanded until the desert itself was drowned in its all-consuming white.

The Hydra was dead.

*

The white receded, like lifting mists, and Prometheus could feel Betty untense beneath him. She trotted off in a random direction as the redness of the sand returned to the ground and the cloudless blue sky spread out overhead. The far-off shallow dunes and crooked trees, fleshless and dry in the distance, were as they were before, and the great white ring still hovered abstractly between the horizon and the sky.

All was calm, it seemed. The Hydra was gone, and the winged black lion was nowhere to be seen.

Prometheus turned at the sound of someone calling. Tom was running in their direction. It was towards him that Betty now eagerly made her way. Prometheus looked back to the horizon under the sun-dazzled C-gate to see the figure of a boy riding a titanium-white horse.

"Charles," he whispered. He found that he was more relieved at the child being safe than he ever thought possible.

☐

63

Ystil.3 gazed upon the desolate landscape that was once the Piscean Plains. "I did it," he said. His voice was muted in the stagnant air and barely carried from his mouth.

The earth was as burned-black as Thebes and levelled so flat that he could see for hundreds, perhaps even thousands of klicks in every direction. He had never been to Pisces before the Reset and therefore had no idea how different this was to how it looked back then. The sky was a muddy brown, thick and noxious with miasmic gases.

Ystil.3 took a few steps forward, making his way down from where he stood atop a shallow mound of dirt and smooth rock. Behind him, the Thebes C-gate portal bent the light into an inverted cornea of diaphanous silver. It began to slowly diminish. While it remained open he could walk through and return to Thebes, but soon there would be no way back.

"I knew I could do it," he said. "I knew all this I'm the only one who can Cut stuff was a bunch of crap." He laughed, feeling the urge to secure-beam Lydia to taunt her. But his smile faltered and his face became as wan and expressionless as the Piscean Plains landscape.

He would never speak to her again.

A feeling of emptiness hollowed out his chest and an ache began from somewhere in the pit of his stomach. Even though he had seen her only seconds ago, Ystil.3 realised he already missed her.

But he had no time for sadness.

He searched with eyes and filters into the far-reaching vastness. All that distinguished the land was the corrupt burnt earth and the tragic sky. He had Cut as close to the Pisces C-gate as he could – as he knew how – but it was nowhere in sight. He checked his current location with that of where the Pisces C-gate had been placed by Life Corp before the Reset. If he'd Cut right, then it should have been in front of him. He whirled about, infrared sensors blazing. "Where is it?" The only thing visible in the flat lands was Thebes' C-gate portal, diminishing like a giant contracting iris. If he'd gotten it wrong, there was still time to go back to Thebes and try again. But only if he went now.

"But the location is correct," he said. "It should be here, right where I'm standing." He skipped back up the sloping mound towards the open portal and gazed into the fading glow of its surface, hoping to see Lydia on the other end. He could see nothing but bending light and a slight reflection, like looking into a glass pane on a bright day.

Through the portal's reflection, Ystil.3 noticed a rock protruding at the mound's peak. It was curiously smooth – too smooth and too curved. It was covered in a layer of grey dirt. He rubbed at the surface with his fingers. Underneath, the edge of a white tile became apparent. He scanned the mound. "It's under the junkfucking earth."

Lydia, it seemed, had been prepared for this eventuality. Attached to the utility belt of his hardsuit were three sonic stake grenades. Ystil.3 pulled one free and jammed it point-first into the earth at the base of the mound. He then did the same with the other two, one on the other side and one at the very top, almost skidding in the dirt as he hurried over the risen earth. He slid back down just as the Thebes C-gate portal shrank to a complete close. He paused for a second to acknowledge what it meant. "She's really gone."

He turned and ran until the tug of a sonic wave pushed him face first into the earth. A crashing noise followed – the sound waves turning the impacted earth to rubble. He turned as a mushroom cloud of black dust plumed up. When he ran back to the C-gate, a giant crater had been carved from the flat Plains – a two-metre-deep basin of scorched earth. The shallow arch of the C-gate's crown protruded like a white-tiled bridge, the rest still buried in the earth.

"I hope that doesn't cause a problem," he said. He leapt into the crater, landing on the C-gate with a metallic thud. Beneath his feet, most of the central hollow of the ring was exposed. "There's only one way to find out," he said, making the jump onto the crater floor.

The arch curved high above his head, creating a tunnel of blue and gold plates, not unlike the cobbled stone underpasses he'd walked through in London 1901. He'd taken Charlie's phial of blood from Lydia as she lay unconscious. He now lifted it from his utility belt and pulled off the stopper. Lydia had poured the blood onto the base of the inner ring on Thebes, but the base of the inner ring on Pisces was covered by tonnes of unmovable earth. Figuring that contact with the gate was probably necessary, he began to smear the blood on each side of the inner walls, tarnishing the gold plates.

Like on Thebes, a film of defused light warped the central hollow almost instantly – a thin veil of rippling water.

"It worked," Ystil.3 said with a bout of involuntary, relief-incited laughter. He sat cross-legged, looking at his own reflection in the activated gate and wondering where it might take him if he were to walk through. Back to Thebes? No, the Piscean ring was linked to Earth and that didn't exist anymore. It didn't matter. Once his server was gone, that would be it for him.

The realisation that these were the last few moments of his existence pressed in. He noticed his eyes blinking in the likeness opposite and he drew himself closer, staring into the pools of dark, trying to spot some hint of life – a spark, anything that would reveal a soul hiding in there. Perhaps he had earned a soul like Lydia said. But, to him, they just looked the same as they had before. He sat back, not really having expected anything, and smiled. His reflection smiled back at him.

"Lydia," he said. "By the time you receive this, I'll be gone..." He couldn't talk directly to Lydia as the Comptronium in Thebes' soil disrupted the signal on her end. He could, however, send her a delayed secure-beam.

He pictured her listening to it in a future where he no longer existed.

"I wanted to say goodbye..."

☐

64

"What will you do now, father?" Charles asked. "If you come with us, you'll find peace. If you don't... I'm not sure what will happen to you. The blackness is large and undiscovered. Even we don't know what lurks within."

Prometheus knew that when Charles said "we" he meant himself and whatever sentience the Earth possessed.

"You deserve peace, father," he went on, standing beside the lustrous white horse beneath the shadow of the C-gate, which hovered above like a shiny coin. The sky had returned to its undiluted azure, everything perfect for when the Earth returned. Nothing out of place. No monsters on the horizon, no winged beasts blighting the sky.

Prometheus wasn't so sure that he deserved peace at all. And he wasn't entirely certain he desired it either. The grieving shell of a man he once was no longer existed. It still lingered somewhat within the Prometheus that he desperately hoped had made it back to his time – back to his old life. But his path had been altered when he was chosen to lead his army. He felt the scar upon his face. No. He was no longer that man.

But then there was Sarah. No matter how he had changed, his love for her was unwavering. It was eternal, like the blackness.

For all intents and purposes, he was dead. He no longer had a body to tie him to the mortal realm, regardless of the administration of the White Drops. Sarah too was dead. Strange as it was, this imbued Prometheus with an ambitious sense of hope – a fragmented ray of belief that threaded through the smallest aperture in the darkness. It tickled at his heart with velvet tangibility, flourishing into his thoughts.

The Hydra had been deleted permanently. Nyx had returned to programme city, according to Tom, where the programmes would now no longer live in fear of their AI oppressors. The cricket they called Bo had also disappeared right out of Norse's hands. Nyx had taken him back with her. Norse expressed his hope that the programmes would build into the potential space, growing and exploring and fulfilling the latent potential they had within each of them. Out of the beings from which the Chimera had coalesced, Death remained. Prometheus hadn't recognised the creature at first, it was the whispering of voices that surrounded the white horse that gave it away, the whispering of lost souls. Perhaps Death had, at last, found the peace it so desired.

Peace was all those damned souls had ever wanted, and now Nathan Shaw was among them.

"They will be at rest soon," Charles told them. "When the Earth returns we shall all be as one. And every soul born of Earth thereafter will find peace with us upon death."

What will I do now?

Tom and Norse were as eager for his reply as Charles, it seemed. They stood on the boy's flanks as the two horses played and hoofed at the ground behind them. They all had their own paths to take. Tom, as he understood it, would return into his server form upon the Black Betty, as would Betty. Norse's fate was as uncertain as his own, however. Once his server was destroyed, he too would be thrust out into the nothingness.

Prometheus looked at the boy that in another life had been his son. "I was a reluctant man," he said, "afraid to touch the world. I hid behind a wall of grief and tears that drowned me. And now you ask me, will I walk a path of rest and peace, or will I risk more hurt for a blind chance." He paused a moment, realising that he had already made up his mind. "I know that if I join you and lay my soul to rest, I will be content, but I will never find my beloved Sarah. So, I cannot stay with you." As he said the words, the sense of hope swelled inside him. "I don't know what will happen to me, but I do know I will find her. I don't know how. I will scour the depths of existence. I will wander the darkness alone for millennia. But I will find her."

Charles didn't seem surprised by his answer.

"Perhaps you don't have to be completely alone," Norse said. "I will have no real-time form to return to, yet I'm as real as you are now. If you don't mind, and if it is possible, I would like to come with you, wherever it is we may be expelled."

"And should we arrive at the mouth of Hades?" Prometheus asked him.

"Your cause is as worthy as the one we hope to now complete. And I would rather be useful to you, than lonely and aimless. I have sailed the blackness before, I may be of help."

Prometheus gave him a sharp nod and clapped a hand on his back. "Perhaps together we will embark upon a wild night."

"Then there is nothing more but to activate the C-gate," Charles said.

"What about us?" Tom asked. "How do we get home?"

Charles smiled. "Just click your heels three times and say, there's no place like home."

Tom cocked his head to the side and Charles smiled again. "With the Hydra gone, you're free to filter back into your servers, wherever they may now be. Thank you, Tom. Without you, this would not be possible."

"Don't thank me," Tom said. "I get to go home and live with my Betty. Thank Ystil.3. He's the brave one."

"I haven't forgotten his sacrifice. Neither will my people…" Charles faded before his last word formed sound in the air, reemerging as a small figure standing within the C-gate high above them.

Through the hollow of the C-gate, Prometheus could just make out the merged images of the cave upon Thebes and a land that stretched out flat and dark. It distorted with a film of light.

They were active.

65

Ystil.3 sat with his legs dangling over the edge of the crater, looking intently into the warped light of the Piscean C-gate and wondering when exactly this imminent explosion was going to tear through his synthetic and his server. After completing his delayed secure-beam message, there wasn't really much to do but wait.

He had taken off his hardsuit, wanting to feel Pisces' atmosphere on his skin, sink his feet into its earth.

Strange as it was, somewhere along the way he had settled into his synth. At first he had bumbled and stumbled along, unused to the bombardment of senses that tickled and pricked from scalp to toes. Now, however, he felt easy as he looked out from its eyes, speaking with its familiar voice and looking down to see two strong hands flecked with dark hairs.

Grid City was gone, his Data Crib deleted. But he didn't miss them. Even if it were still there, preserved perfectly within the BroadWeb, Ystil.3 realised that he no longer desired to go back. He found it funny that as he sat with legs dangling on an unknown and desiccated planet, he felt completely and utterly at home.

A twisting ripple flickered across the film-like surface of the C-gate, like a stone thrown into a glassy lake.

"This is it," he said aloud, clamping his hands onto the side of the crater.

For a fraction of a moment, the portal revealed the cave on Thebes. Then the brightest light Ystil.3 had ever seen began to glow from within. He was tempted to activate a visual filter but decided against it. He wanted to see it as a human would – as Lydia would. Then, the image of Thebes shimmered away within an approaching wall of red and orange fire. A rumbling began, growing louder until it thundered across the silent Piscean Plains.

Ystil.3 braced himself, surprised at how suddenly calm he was, how suddenly ready.

Heat exploded through the C-gate portal, singeing his hair to stubs and scorching his flesh away from polymetalic alloy bone in the flash. His jaw softened and distended, loosening until it fell into his lap, like plastic heated out of shape. His arms and legs were now melted candle stubs, glinting with exposed metal bone for wicks. The orbs that were his eyes liquefied, running from his sockets in milky rivulets, plunging him into blackness.

The pain was a nightmare of blind intensity, but he held on to the last. Just before the energy vaporised him to nothing, Ystil.3 had only one thought.

I'd do it all again.

66

The explosion began as a spot of glowing white light upon the dark planet. The spot bloomed into a rose bud of fierce red, then flowered like the opening of exotic orange petals, exacerbating over the surface of the world. The burning flower prevailed in full glorious bloom for only moments before a rolling black tide chased it across the surface, leaving Thebes a skeletal orb hanging dead among the stars. The planet's flesh was flayed clean away as its broken moon watched and mourned.

Lydia watched Thebes burn through salt-brimmed eyes as the Black Betty made her way through the space of the Titan System on the tail of the Hyperborea.

"Lydia," Daneel said softly. "Shut off the tempurhull and come away." He had navigated through the graveyard of debris that was once the mothership, speeding them away from the doomed planet as fast as he could persuade the Black Betty's Beta Ship programme to travel.

She ignored him, too furious to even speak. Whenever she looked at him she felt a surge of anger and the urge to pound his face into the hull. Why couldn't they just let her do it? It was her destiny. Then she would have been done. But now things were just as hard as they always were. The fight continued… hopelessly.

"He did it," Daneel said. "The servers are gone. The AI are gone. We should be happy."

Lydia turned and glared in his direction for a moment, contemplating leaving him to drift in the vacuum where they had found him, before turning back to watch the last of the fire crackle on the ember-lit planet.

Apparently seeing the fury in her eyes, Daneel said nothing more.

When Thebes was nothing but a dark spot in a field of distant stars, she received a secure-beam message from a channel she had come to know well. She accessed it immediately, tremors of hope quaking through her that he had somehow made it through the explosion. She was almost at the point of ordering Daneel to change course when the first line of the message stopped her.

"Lydia, by the time you receive this, I'll be gone," it began. Her heart sank, but message continued. "I wanted to say goodbye… I hope that by about now you and Daneel will be safe and far away from Thebes, and no doubt you will be seething with anger. You think that we have taken something away from you by not allowing you to go through with your plan. But we haven't. We've given something back to you. You're life. You were hoping that was it for you, weren't you? That your time was done and your mission complete. You wanted rest. But, Lydia, you're not done. You've hardly even begun. Soon you'll realise that.

"You'll soon understand what it is I've come to see in you – what you fail to see in yourself. When I look at you I see life – explosive and meaningful, full of mistakes and heartache. I know you've had your share, and it doesn't take a genius to realise that Daneel has been a part of that. But whether you see it or not, those hurts are visible in his eyes as well as yours.

"I know it's your anger that keeps you from healing and you convinced yourself that it was your destiny to die down here, where I sit right now. But that was the easy road, wasn't it? The road where you get to die a hero in a blaze of glory but never actually have to deal with the stuff that comes after it. The hard stuff. Life stuff. That is not your destiny. You're destined for life."

What do you know about it? Lydia thought angrily.

"I know, I know. What do I know, right?" the message went on. "I'm not an expert on humans, or emotions, or life. In fact, I know nothing about anything, really. But I spent a lot of my limited existence reading millions of human lives play out in the DataCom Pylon of Grid City. And the one thing I was always amazed at was… just how junkfucking ungrateful they were."

Lydia laughed out loud and Daneel gave her a sideways look as he stood on the pilot deck.

"Seriously. Humans are always so in their own heads that they can barely see what's going on around them. I watched them live their lives, fretting over the things that made no bit of difference what so ever – money, sex, possessions – and forgetting to just be grateful that they're alive, living their lives. They had the chance to experience the joy and beauty that your planet had to offer and instead they focused on the inconsequential stuff. They were so obsessed with what they wanted that they hardly ever saw what they had."

There was a pause, and Lydia became scared that was it. That he didn't have time to finish his message before…

"But you're right. What do I know about it?

Another pause.

"Daneel loves you – that, I know. I see it in his eyes when he looks at you. Don't fret the small stuff, Lydia. Live your life. Allow yourself to be happy. Otherwise, all this was for nothing.

"I guess I should go now, but before I do, would you do me a favour and tell Tom I said goodbye – if he makes it out. Tell him… farewell old friend. Tell him that we did well, didn't we? Tell him… I'll come to meet him, arms reaching, smiling sweetly. He'll get it.

"Now I really should go. I don't want to get exploded halfway through a sentence. The whole point of this is so I get to say goodbye. So… goodbye, Lydia. Thanks for having the balls to trick a jaded AI into following you. I had a blast… no pun intended."

Lydia began to laugh and cry at once. The sensation was strange and oddly liberating. And once she began she couldn't stop.

"What is it?" Daneel said. "Have you lost it? Because I really can't navigate and attend to a crazy person." He stepped out from behind the pilot deck and reached for Lydia. She turned, her eyes streaming with tears and a smile radiating on her face. She reached out and pulled him into a passionate kiss. Daneel tensed, perhaps thinking she was going to head-butt him or something, but once he realised that she wasn't, he relaxed into the kiss, pulling her tightly to him. When they finally unlocked, Daneel kept his eyes closed for a few seconds longer, as if savouring the taste of her on his lips.

"Second thoughts, I like you crazy," he said.

Suddenly the sound of tearing metal erupted and the electrics upon the Bridge began to flash manically, as though the bridge itself was malfunctioning.

"What was that?" Lydia said, feeling the inertial dampers waver slightly. Thuds vibrated through the deck beneath her feet.

"Stay here," Daneel said. "I'll check it out."

"What? Just because we kissed doesn't mean you're suddenly the man and you can tell me what to do. I'm still high ranking officer on this ship." She drew her T-pistols and followed Daneel up to the bridge hatch.

A deafening clunk reverberated from something impacting with the steel shutter just as Daneel reached to open it. He froze with hand outstretched then took a step backwards. Lydia already had her weapon locked as a dent expressed itself in the hatch from the impact, like an inverted crater, or something punching through. Then another indented next to it, accompanied by an earsplitting scream of distorting metal. Something perforated the metal hatch, tearing it apart into jagged shreds like it was nothing but fabric.

Lydia sprung backwards as a large metallic creature crashed through the doors, with twisting pincers rotating sharply and crab-like legs clawing at the bulkheads, tearing its way into the bridge. Daneel fired, the high-volt T-pistol cartridges not even penetrating the carapace of the giant spider. It didn't even flinch.

"Stop. Why are you shooting at me?" a rumbling mechanical voice demanded.

Daneel continued to shoot until Lydia pulled him back.

The enormous metal crab spider sank onto its legs, as though it had just been punctured, and made a wailing noise. "I knew that little shit would take my Welsh with him." It groaned again, the sound like rattling hull panels coming loose, before saying, "You alright, Betty?"

"All is well here," the female voice of the Black Betty replied. "Sorry about the doors, it took a few moments to regain control."

Lydia stared at the massive arachnid crane of a creature. "Tom?" She smiled a sad smile and stepped forward. "I have a message for you, from a mutual friend."

☐

67

"Some are saying they deserved a trial," First Officer Ling Chou said.

"Those would be the people whose loved ones weren't slaughtered," Rawl retorted as he slouched at his desk in the Captain's quarters. His mind was half on the holoscreen in front of him and half elsewhere… seeing things behind his eyes.

He hadn't slept since it happened. And the more he remained awake, using a mixture of melatonin suppressants and amphetamine derivatives, the more Rawl feared closing his eyes. Besides, there was far too much work to be done, and no one else was going to do it.

"Quite," Ling Chou said with a thin smile. "A faction of those people formed a rally and are now calling for a post-humous trial. It seems the militia has come out of the war a little thin…there are barely three-hundred men and women remaining. Policing the civilians might become an issue very soon."

Rawl lifted his head from the holoscreen that flickered with the known quadrants of the charted universe and looked at Ling Chou. Parts of the chart were marked with a white dot to show where the Hyperborea had been during its three generations of space travel. "A post-humous trial?" His voice was flat. "I've never heard of anything so futile in my life. Should we find Brother Vaxus's frozen, bloated body from the depths of space and prop him up to state his case? What end do they hope will come from this ghost trial they want? Don't they have anything better to do?"

"I believe that they… hope it will prove that you… erm… acted…"

"Just spit it out, man."

"… Acted against the law and should be removed from position of Captain," Ling Chou rushed, bracing himself for a potential backlash.

Captain Rawl Collister stood slowly and placed his hands carefully onto the desk in front of him. He was now almost used to his new left arm. It looked exactly like his old, mostly. It was only when you got really close that you could tell it was bio-mech at all. It didn't act exactly like his old arm, however. It was much stronger, and it took him a while to become accustomed to it. His bio-mech eye was a different story. It seemed Rawl wasn't taking to it as well as he had the arm. It sat in his socket and functioned as it should – again with a few bio-mech perks, such as zooming capabilities and limited filters – but the problem was Rawl felt as though he had a stranger's eyeball in his head. Watching him. Judging him. It wasn't his eye, and whenever he looked into its off-coloured iris in his reflection, a pain began in his stomach – an awful pain that splintered into his chest and left him gasping for air on the floor of his private shower-room. Since then, Rawl covered it with the patch, refusing look at it or even use it.

"They think they can remove me?" he said. His voice was quiet but edged with a grit that seemed to rend the air. "Who do they think will find them a new home if I am not Captain? Just let them try. I have the power of the militia to command and what do they have? Empty complaints by lazy liberal fools."

"There is also talk of elections, Captain," Ling Chou said, avoiding eye contact. "A petition has been circulated within the civilian groups to elect a new Consulate."

"Elections?" Rawl bellowed. "We have to find a planet and they're talking about trials and elections? Captain Lu was overindulgent in the sugarcoating she fed to these inverts because they should be begging me to lead them to a new home planet. Now I have to clean up the mess." Rawl moved from behind his desk and put an arm around Ling Chou's shoulders, physically turning him towards the door. "I can trust you, can't I, Ling Chou? You seem like a man that wants the best for his people?"

"Yes, Captain, I do," Ling Chou replied, side-glancing to the bio-mech hand that twitched around his shoulder.

"Good. I want you to find the names of those that speak of trials and elections." He spat the words like expelling poison from his tongue. "I want you to obtain a copy of this petition and I want you to bring it to me. Can you do that?"

Ling Chou nodded. "Yes, Captain. Of course."

"Good." He led the man through the hatch into the causeway. "Be discrete. I'll expect a full list by the end of the day-cycle." Before Ling Chou could say another word, the hatch shut with him on the outside.

Rawl sat back at his desk and resumed his earnest glare at the universe chart. His bio-mech eye began to tingle. A pair of terror-filled eyes flashed in his mind and a pain burned in his stomach. He swallowed it down and stared ahead, letting the holoscreen glare burn away the image of those eyes.

If they think they can get rid of me that easily, they've got another thing coming. This is my ship. It's my time to be Captain.

It would be easy to paint them as Brotherhood of Man supporters – traitors. Still, what he really needed was the Captain's Log access chip. He had still been unsuccessful in locating it, however.

"Captain, this is the bridge," a voice said over comm.

The voice shook Rawl Collister out of a dark plan that was forming inside his head. "Yes?" he replied shortly.

"We've made contact with an approaching vessel. The vessel is the Black Betty and we have confirmed that Lieutenant Lydia Chen and Corporal Daneel Sharma are alive and currently docking. Their mission was a success."

Captain Rawl Collister was silent.

"Captain?" the bridge Officer said. "Are you there?"

"Yes. Can you tell me, is the li or Corporal Sharma piloting the Black Betty?"

"That is negative, Captain. The ship is docking via a pilot programme, from what our scan determined. The li also expressed that the Black Betty be cleared for launch immediately after she and Corporal Sharma have boarded the Hyperborea."

Rawl paused and thought. "Yes, allow clearance," he said methodically. "Will you instruct the li to report to my quarters immediately?"

"Yes, Captain."

Before the Bridge Officer had even replied, Captain Rawl Collister was running at full speed through the causeways, contacting CSD over his comm system.

*

"I can see why Ystil.3 liked her so much," I say to Betty, after the two humans exit the ship, making their way back onto the Hyperborea. It took us almost no time to reach the lifeship once Betty was back in control. For now, I remain inside her, but as soon as we're away from the Hyperborea and she's stretched her legs in space once more, I will climb out to feel the proverbial wind in my proverbial hair, clinging to my love, my home.

"You will miss him," Betty says as she activates the launch procedure, ready to take off back into vacuum, back to Delilah, which I so eagerly yearn to see again. Lydia said it was different now, that it wasn't the same planet that we left behind. But I know that already. How can I forget? The servers are destroyed. Ystil.3's server is gone. Betty and I are the last AI in the real-time universe and BroadWeb.

"I will miss him greatly," I say, as I attempt to nod my massive CorVac head. I've been in BroadWeb-form so long that I've forgotten how clunky and obtrusive my real-time self is. "I will never forget him." I notice how emotionless my voice sounds without my accent and I feel that my pain isn't being conveyed properly – but I don't miss it as much as I miss Ystil.3. I know Betty, however, and I know how well she understands me. She knows exactly how I feel right now. The grief I feel for the loss of Ystil.3 only brings into greater clarity how much I love Betty and how blessed I am to have her with me. From now on we will never be apart. Not ever again. Not even after the universe has taken its dying breath, destroying itself in a swan song of energy and light.

Betty emerges into the vacuum after navigating the Hyperborean runway. The stars greet us like old friends and we slowly make our way clear of the human lifeship.

"Do you think he felt pain in the end?" I ask Betty. It's a stupid question. I don't really expect her to know. I'm simply expressing my thought process. Betty says I should do that, that I should record my thoughts. She says that I should document it all from beginning to end: from Ystil.3 first asking me to help him, right up to this very moment. So, that is what I've done. It took nano-seconds, but Betty says it may help me see things as a whole and may help me deal with Ystil.3's… death? I suppose death is the right word.

Betty was right. Through recording everything that happened I can see it all for what it is, and I can see Ystil.3's place in it. Somehow I know that when it came, Ystil.3 met his end beautifully and finally.

"I think I'll turn it into a song," I say to Betty, before she can reply to my musings. "An epic sonnet that Tom Jones would be proud to sing. A song of bravery and love."

"Love?" Betty says.

"Yes, love. My love for you."

Betty giggles as though I've embarrassed her. She's such a tease, but I play along. I begin to sing Tom Jones as though I want to embarrass her more. I sing With These Hands… it seems fitting.

*

"Fire!" Captain Rawl Collister ordered, standing at the fore of the CSD.

A lance of light launched from three Hyperborean plasma cannons, impacting with the Black Betty as the ship made its way peacefully from Hyperborean territory. The dark AI ship erupted into an inferno of light and fire, burning up in an expanding sphere of sepulchral dust and leaving nothing behind but the fading glow of tiny sparks – as though the stars themselves were dying one by one, consumed by the tragic darkness of space.

*

Since his return to the Hyperborea, Daneel had been ordered directly to General Avon Chan – General Nathan Shaw's replacement. There, he debriefed the new General regarding what had exactly happened to him since he left with Razor squad to scout the upper level solar and confront the AI. The slim man sat silently and arched an inquisitive eyebrow as Daneel took him through the events leading up to the explosion on Thebes.

Corporal Daneel Sharma had entered the General's office – Sergeant Daneel Sharma exited. He then strode along the Underbelly causeways, chest puffed and back straight, proudly marching with his good news directly to Lydia's quarters.

He remembered spending many nights in Lydia's cabin, during their time together, and he was hoping to spend many more. Things were finally going right for him. After spending so long stagnated at Corporal, he was finally Sergeant. And after countless nights of lonely regret, Lydia was finally his again.

Lydia had headed from the Black Betty straight to the Captain's quarters and he hadn't seen her since. He hadn't even been back to his own quarters yet – though he supposed he would be moving now he had been promoted. He wanted to relay the good news first and to then perhaps reenact the kiss they'd shared on the Black Betty bridge.

Daneel knew exhaustion would soon defeat the adrenaline that still flooded his limbs and he would crash. He wanted to see Lydia before that happened. When she opened her cabin hatch, Daneel knew something was wrong. She had that look. He'd seen it before, usually prior to one of their big arguments. She moved for him to enter and sat solemnly on her bed, not saying a word. She'd removed her hardsuit and wore loose fabric pants and a top that hung off one shoulder to reveal smooth skin. Her hair was gathered into a scruffy ponytail on top of her head. Daneel had always liked to see her this way, knowing the others never did. It was the real Lydia, behind the guard.

He walked in, unsure how to interpret the aura that surrounded her. "I've been promoted to Sergeant," he said, drawing a thin smile across his face.

She attempted an enthusiastic grin. "That's great. You deserve it."

"What's wrong?" He sat beside her and attempted to take her by the hand, but she moved it away, feigning an itch on her arm.

"Collister destroyed the Black Betty," Lydia said. "Tom and Betty are dead."

Daneel made a confused face that he knew made him look idiotic. Lydia had told him so many times before. "Why?" he asked.

"What do you mean why? Aren't you angry? Don't you care?" She was close to tears.

"I care. But why did he do it?"

"The Black Betty was partially made of Computronium. He said the Hydra could have survived within it and there was only one way to be sure."

Daneel nodded. "It's sad… but he was right."

Lydia bit her lip and lowered her gaze. "I know," she whispered. The concession brought the tears over the brim of her reddening eyes. "I feel like we betrayed them. They helped us and we killed them. We're monsters."

"You didn't kill them," Daneel said. "Collister did what he thought was right."

"He's not returning to Earth's system," Lydia said. "We're not going home. He's as stubborn as he ever was and wouldn't even listen to what I had to say."

"I told you he would be. We're just going to have to think of a different way to get around him, that's all. He's the Captain, but it's the people that hold the power. If the people want to go to Earth's system, the Captain has no choice."

"He isn't interested in what the people want. Have you heard what he did to the Brotherhood of Man disciples… to Vaxus?"

"Yes. And they deserved it. Our friends are dead because of him. The halls are almost empty of militia because of the war… Gutter is dead… and on top that they betrayed us. Lexi was pregnant for junkfuck sake. And now she's dead, her and her baby."

"There's another thing," Lydia said. "Rawl seems… on edge. Like he's losing it. He almost sent me to the Brig for disagreeing with him and he kept repeating that he had to do it over and over. Some of the Brotherhood made accusations about him, before he, you know, flushed them out the airlock. They said he killed an Officer in the CSD, that he blew his head clean off with a plasma rifle. They're saying he didn't give the Brotherhood a fair trial to stop them talking. I heard some people call him a murderer."

"I heard a lot of people call him a hero, too," Daneel said. He attempted to take her hand again.

She shifted and stood, shuffling awkwardly across the floor of her cabin.

"What is it?" he said, confused. "I thought…?"

"That kiss wasn't right," Lydia blurted. "I know you want us to be in that place, but we're not. I'm sorry, we're just not there."

Daneel turned away. He didn't want her to see him crushed. "Oh," he said, unable to conceal it in his voice.

Lydia sat back down beside him and took his hand. Daneel turned back. Her warm amber eyes were watching him softly. She stroked his fingers and held them tightly.

"We're not there… yet," she said.

*

He had to replenish the militia forces as soon as he possibly could, Rawl decided while the Hyperborea slept. The rebel element had quickly gained momentum. He had tried to suppress the knowledge of what he'd done, but it seemed that hadn't worked. The Brotherhood of Man disciples made merry words with their loose lips before he'd sent them into vacuum. A final betrayal to their own kind, Rawl thought. They couldn't just go silently.

Traitors.

Now all that was left was for him to admit it openly. He would explain how the events transpired, and the people would understand. They would understand that he had to do it. But if for some reason they did not understand, he would need the militia at full force to subdue whatever consequence might occur.

After Ling Chou delivered the names of the people calling for a Consulate election, he sent the man out again to organise a mass recruitment; the list was longer than Rawl had expected it to be. He scrolled through the names upon the holoscreen at his desk.

Traitors.

Ling Chou had tried to persuade him to sleep – but how could he now? Who knew what assassins lurked in the shadows, waiting for the chance to stick a blade between his shoulders. They knew what he'd done. What he had to do.

First Officer Hulster Ren – the man's name was on everyone's lips. He heard it everywhere he went.

Hulster Ren.

They whispered it in the causeways as he passed. They didn't think that Rawl could hear them, but he could. He knew what they said behind his back. They knew the man he had killed.

Hulster Ren.

He had confined himself to his quarters, thereafter.

It was easy for them to judge, easy for them to condemn him for what he'd done – for what he had to do. But they would understand. He would make them see that he had no choice. It was either kill the man or be killed himself, and in doing so allow the Brotherhood to destroy their only chance of finally eradicating the AI enemy.

Surely they must see?

Rawl hoped they would understand. He truly did. It would be easier that way. But in truth, he didn't need them to. Regardless of what the people thought, he was Captain and his word was law. By the morning he would be in command of a thriving militia once again – there was no end of eager boys and girls that would snap off his remaining good hand for that honour – and in a short time he would have them properly trained. Until then, any fool could shoot a plasma rifle.

His good eye quivered in its socket as he glared down at the list of names.

Traitors.

He had to start his Captaincy as he meant to go on. He could not have them question his every move and decision. There would be no progress made at that rate. Collectively, humanity was a deeply stupid creature, he knew. The people needed a new home and they needed to be told what was best for them. There was no other option than to make an example of those that called his decisions into question and ensure no one ever spoke out against him again. It was mutiny. He was within his rights – not that he needed to justify himself.

I'm the juckfucking Captain of this ship.

He looked up. His quarters were dark, save for the bluish glow that emanated from the holoscreen, touching everything with its cold light. After Ling Chou left, Rawl had ransacked the room completely, overturning it end-to-end, searching for the Captain's Log access chip. He tore the place apart in a rage, hoping to reveal some secret compartment in the sparse furniture, or some crevice in the hull that it might have fallen through. But again, he found nothing.

He considered sleep, but every time he closed his eyes he saw that face, and how it vaporised into stringy mulch and wet red dust.

Hulster Ren.

Sleep didn't matter. He would sleep when it was done and when his position was secure again – when every shadow that crawled the walls didn't make him reach for his T-pistol.

He stood from behind his desk, navigated the debris that scattered the floor and went to face the mirror in his small shower room. The light flicked on with the sense of motion and his visage suddenly illuminated in the reflection in front of him. His brow cast a foreboding shadow over his good eye. The darkness of fatigue circled it, giving it a drooping appearance below his sleep-heavy lid. His face was pallid and dry and his jaw was speckled with a light dusting of salt and pepper stubble.

He reached for the shelf below the mirror and took another dose of pain relief. He then reached for a different mixture given to him by the Brain's medical team to counter the drowsiness of the pain relief, then another to help ensure his body didn't reject his new bio-mech upgrades and then another just to perk him up from his half-wakeful trance.

A sudden buzz of vigour burst like fizzing bubbles of energy through his bloodstream. The room swayed and his eye widened, now fully alert. Rawl reached out a hand to touch his reflection. The mirror was old and scuffed – an antique. The corners were worn and almost rounded, and a dark line slashed across his face from a crack in its smooth surface. He slowly brought his hand back to his face, touching the patch that covered his bio-mech eye. He lifted the patch away with trembling fingers.

The eye wasn't his. It didn't belong there. It glared at him judgingly, swivelling in his socket independently from his control.

Hulster Ren.

"Stop looking at me," Rawl shouted. But Hulster Ren's eye bore down on him relentlessly. "Stop looking at me!"

He pushed a clawed finger into his eye socket and a spurt of blood spattered the mirror and dribbled down his face. He hooked his finger behind the bio-mech eyeball and pulled it out, hearing a wet sucking sound as it came free of the socket. Blood spurted down his face from the hollow in a cascade of red tears, until he was covered with it, his face slick and crimson. He looked down at the bio-mech eye before dropping it onto the floor – it trailed with thin veins and rubbery tendrils, like the dust tail of a comet. He then lifted his booted toe and pressed his weight down on top of the orb until it squashed beneath his shoe. Creamy liquid oozed out from under his sole.

Rawl let out a heavy sigh of relief. "That's better."

*

Daneel awoke early in the next day-cycle, long before the militia was due to rise for drills. The sounds of breathing and the occasional snore pricked into focus as a gentle vibration roused him from a sleep that was deep and exhausted. His eyes fluttered open and he reached out a hand to grab the source of the vibration, growling a curse as he pulled his militia-standard eDeck from the single shelf at the side of the bed. He brought it close to his face and squinted into the light.

One new message, it read upon the screen.

It was odd. No one sent him messages. If someone wanted to talk to him they would comm to get an immediate response. His sleep-idle brain wasn't quite sure if he was actually awake or still dreaming. He accessed the message regardless, after muting the sound, not wanting to wake the three other Sergeants that shared his cabin. He'd moved from a cabin full of twelve Corporals – of which eight had recently perished – and he didn't want to aggravate his new roomies too early in the relationship.

A face appeared in the message and Daneel blinked repeatedly, more unsure than before whether he was dreaming or not. After rubbing the sleep from his eyes and looking again, however, the same face appeared in the holo, mouthing words silently. It was Captain Lu, her expression earnest and her strange blue eyes seeming to pierce through the darkness of his cabin.

At once, he slithered quietly from under his covers, descended from the top bunk of his two-bed stack – careful not to inadvertently stand on Wong's face, who slept below him – and crept out of the room. The causeway was dark and cold. The energy systems of the lifeship were still replenishing and until they were back to full capacity much of the Hyperborea – the Underbelly mostly – had to forego some of the comforts they were used to… like heating and light. The icy floor stung the soles of his feet with each step, and as he accessed the message once more, listening to Captain Lu's words from the dead, he hopped from foot to foot, placing one on top of the other to warm it, before swapping them around to allow the other a chance to thaw.

"Corporal Daneel Sharma," Captain Stacy Lu began. "If you have received this message then I and General Nathan Shaw are both dead. A delayed message will be sent to General Shaw if I perish in the next few hours of battle, activated by the recycling of my eDeck. If General Shaw has perished also then a slightly altered message, this message, will be sent to you instead. It is imperative you do exactly as it instructs you. Do you understand?"

"Yes, Captain," Daneel replied stupidly. He was now fully alert, pinched with curiosity.

"Your first instruction is to tell no one that you have received this message… not yet. Your second instruction is to go to my father's plaque, located in the Captain Memorial Room in the Civilian Holdings and retrieve the Captain's Log access chip that I have hidden within it. Once you're in that location and you're standing beneath the hologram statue of the first Captain Lu, replay this message and TAP HERE for instructions on how to retrieve the chip." As the Captain said the words tap here a spiralling green button appeared floating beside her.

Daneel's head buzzed with ideas and conjecture, but the message went on. "Once you've retrieved it you must take it to the Engineering Quarter and to the Tempurhull Operating Controls on Level Three. Once you're inside, replay this message and TAP HERE for instructions on what to do next." A spiralling red button appeared below the green one.

Captain Stacy Lu deceased looked anxiously ahead of her as she sat at her desk within the Captain's quarters – now occupied by Rawl Collister. "You're wondering why exactly I've entrusted you with an important enough task that I would take such precautions, aren't you?"

"You're junkfucking right about that," Daneel whispered into the cold.

"Because, in this particular situation, aside from General Shaw, you're the only other person that I know will do as I've instructed without hesitance. You're the only person who I know will want this as much as I want it, including the li herself. I have decided of late that important decisions must be made and I will not meet my end with things as they are. To ensure you complete this task I will tell you what you will find within the Captain's Log. Do not make the mistake of thinking this message will substitute for what you'll find. It needs to be official. So here it is…"

Captain Stacy Lu deceased said her final words of the prerecorded message and Daneel's eyes grew wide with surprise. When the message was done, he began to run excitedly through the causeways, bare-chested and barefooted, heading for the nearest warren tunnel that could take him to the Captain Memorial Room.

*

Lydia ate her protein gruel breakfast after a night full of dreams. She dreamed Winston had Daneel's face and Daneel had Winston's. She had another dream where Captain Lu was still alive and was getting married to

General Shaw. That one was particularly strange because almost no one got married these days – things were always too precarious and dangerous to commit to just one person, to give your heart so completely to another. It was bad enough trying to keep your own heart safe. Was it any wonder most people didn't want to look after their own children? The loss would be unbearable – it was unbearable, she knew. Death was a certain uncertainty: it could be dealt either by AI or by the constant peril of living in vacuum.

Still, Lydia supposed it was different now. There were no more AI, at least. That thought was a bittersweet pill to swallow. But Rawl Collister was going to see to it that they would never return to Earth's system ever again. He said as much in no uncertain terms.

She had thought to propose going to investigate Earth's system alone. She could take the fugue stasis shuttle to transport her, where she would be able to sleep for the half-century journey it would take to get to Earth's system from their current location. But she realised that even if the Earth was there and the human race survived another fifty years, it would take her the same amount of time or more to travel back to the ship's position. One hundred years was too long to wait. Another lost generation.

It was then, for the first time, Lydia truly missed her ability to Cut. She would have been able to travel instantly to Earth's location just a few moments into the past. Of course, if the Earth was not there then she would have just Cut directly into open vacuum, but if it was… she could take her people home.

Later, she had to report to the new General, Avon Chen, for duties. She was no longer the li but she was still a Lieutenant. She could feel the routine of everyday life begin once again, as though none of it had happened – as though she had never Cut to 1901, never met Winston, never destroyed the AI… none of it. What was the point of it all, the point of all those deaths, if things remained exactly the same as before?

As she ate, sat upon her bed, a general announcement over comms informed her that Captain Collister would be addressing the ship shortly. Before the Captain appeared in the holo image of her tempurhull, Lydia had time to dress fully in her official uniform and even polish her epaulettes. She tied her hair up into a tight bun at the back of her head and sat watching Rawl begin his speech as he sat in the dimly-lit Captain's quarters.

Usually when the Captain addressed the ship officially they would do so from the bridge, but it seemed Rawl Collister had different ideas. Stupid, stubborn man.

A new Consulate, however, might listen to her about Earth's system. At least when she was on the Consulate she had a voice, but even if a new group were voted in she doubted she would be among them. She wasn't the li anymore. So who am I?

Rawl's face dominated the tempurhull, a single harsh light glaring down on him. He leaned forward agitatedly, arms resting in front of him and his long fingers pressed together into a twitching steeple. The man looked awful, worse even than when Lydia had seen him the previous day-cycle. The shadow that formed beneath his brow was so dark that at first glance his real eye was indistinguishable from the patch that covered the bio-mech – just a strip of black that faded out to reveal a down-turned mouth and a chin covered in greying stubble. His skin was pallid and cracked with lines and his hair a dishevelled mess of cropped silver.

Lydia felt something she thought she would never feel in her life towards Rawl Collister – pity. But then he began to speak and all pity evaporated.

"My motives have been questioned, my actions greeted with reprehension," he began. "Reprehension towards my actions is understandable. In my life, I have done many things that others could not do. It is my curse. I have done these things for the greater good... often because I have the ability to separate my emotions from what must be done. Not all have this ability, so when some greet my actions with censure I accept this. But..." He pointed a straight, unwavering finger. "I will not abide my motives being questioned. It cheapens me and it cheapens the lives that have been lost."

He clutched his hands together and his stanch glare cracked for an infinitesimal moment. He paused for what seemed like the longest sigh a man ever breathed.

"Did I kill First Officer Hulster Ren?" he said. He said the name quickly and quietly, as though he didn't want his lips to linger on the sound of it. "Yes. I confess. You may not like what I have done – I do not expect you to because I do not like it myself – but do not question why I had to do it. And do not dare suggest that any life taken by my hand or my command, Hulster Ren or the Brotherhood of Man disciples, was done so for any other reason than the good of this ship and for the good of its people." Captain Rawl Collister straightened his back and became very rigid suddenly, firm and unflinching. He glared straight out from his shadowed countenance. "It is for this reason that I have seen fit to arrest every single one of those who have spoken against my honour and every single person that has signed their name to a petition calling for me to be submitted to a trial and an election take place to determine a new Consulate.

"Let me make this clear to you all. I am the Captain of this ship, so say the laws put into place by the very first Consulate. You may have gotten used to the way Captain Lu did things. But this is no longer a democracy. This is martial law. As Captain of the Hyperborea what I say is the law. I don't care if you agree. I don't care if you hate me. I don't care if you think I'm an evil slit and should be killed in my sleep by some honourless cutthroat and hung by my dick in the Consulate Hall for all to see. You will do as I say... because the penalty for questioning me, for compromising what must now be done, will be severe.

"The three-hundred and five civilians that were arrested over the course of the night will remain in detention, serving as a reminder to all that it serves no good to spread malicious rumour, until I am satisfied they are no longer a threat to our survival. I hope I am making myself perfectly clear to you all because I would hate to see the fate of the Brotherhood of Man disciples repeated. Treason is punishable by death. Remember that."

The Captain took a breath and brushed his hands together. "Now, onto brighter things. We look to the future and we look to finding a new home. The AI have been destroyed and for the first time we have hope." The picture of Rawl disappeared in Lydia's tempurhull, being replaced with a map of the charted universe and the coordinates the Hyperborea had thus far quested. "As you can see, much of the space we have traversed has been solely in two quadrants, due to a lack of leadership and the need to remain—"

The chart of the universe flickered out and Rawl was cut off mid-sentence, leaving a static grey filling the tempurhull holoimage. The grey flickered and the Captain's quarters appeared in the tempurhull once more. Only Rawl Collister was not sat at the desk, Captain Stacy Lu was.

"If you are hearing me now then I am dead," Captain Lu said. "If this is the case, and assuming the Hyperborea has survived against the odds, then right now XO Rawl Collister will be attempting to push his Captaincy, assuming he too has survived.

"While XO Rawl Collister is for the most part a decent man and a decent XO, with experience that makes him a valuable asset to any crew, it is my right, by the laws that govern us, to choose the person I deem most suitable to be my successor as Captain.

"This statement is legally binding, having gone through the official processes and is now being replayed to you from the Captain's Log. There is no disputing my decision. Providing she accepts, the new Captain of the Hyperborea will be Lieutenant Lydia Chen."

Lydia heard the words, heard her name, but failed to grasp their meaning. She simply sat on her bed, staring blankly.

Captain Lu smiled. "Good luck to you all, and may Captain Chen usher in a new age for humanity." Captain Lu flickered from the tempurhull.

After a few moments of slate grey and muted silence, a vast ocean appeared with the morning sun, glowing in a sky full of promise for the day ahead. Lydia stood and moved to the tempurhull, imagining seeing it for real, with the rest of the human race right behind her, instead of alone in Earth's past.

She ignored the flurry of sudden activity on her eDeck and ordered the mirror function in the tempurhull. She looked herself up and down; her thick boots, her strong legs, her epaulettes glimmering on her squared-off shoulders. She raised her chin and tried to see a Captain in front of her.

As her eyes rose to the image of her face, Lydia realised she was smiling.

68

Prometheus stood in the front parlour and watched as the C-gate portal gradually receded into nothing, absorbing the last of the defused ambient light that immersed into its shimmering, almost liquid surface. When it was completely gone, he stared at the empty space where it had been, blinking occasionally and with purpose.

Standing utterly naked and motionless, he waited for probably an hour for the portal to reopen again. For Lieutenant Chen, or Winston or even Death to emerge from it and tell him that they hadn't succeeded and that the future he had set to path was just as grim as ever, and that, this time, they had decided to make him truly pay for what he had done.

The portal, however, did not reopen. And it wasn't until a late afternoon sun fell over the rooftops, through the parlour window and onto his back, did Prometheus finally realise that the portal was not going to open.

He felt something hard in his hand and he looked down to see the antidote wrapped inside his palm. He unwound his fingers from around it; the liquid inside was as black as pitch.

The house smelled differently from how he remembered it. Musty. He had only seemed to remember it smelling devastatingly of his wife. He walked around the front parlour looking at all the little knick-knacks that Sarah had acquired. They were covered in a thick layer of dust. But he looked at them with fresh eyes. He never did like them, not really.

He began to explore his large Mayfair house as though he had never before wandered its rooms. The first floor seemed even more derelict and smothered in dust. The bedroom in which they had slept felt cave-like and oppressive. Sarah's things adorned the place. Her clothes filled the closet and her jewellery draped over her dresser. Prometheus found his way to a small silver box that played a sweet tune when he opened it. Inside, Sarah's golden wedding band sat reverently. He placed it on his little finger, the only one it fit. He looked around at the other paraphernalia. The rest of it, he decided then, could go. The ring was all he wanted.

With an almost violent motion, he threw open the window to the master bedroom. In fact, he decided that all the windows in the entire four-story house could do with being opened, and he set about making his way from room to room, floor to floor, prizing open each resisting pane of glass until the entire house moved in the fresh summer breeze, carrying the scent into its haunted corners. By the time he was done, Prometheus saw the house in an entirely new light.

He couldn't, however, bring himself to enter the cellar where he had spent the last few years of his life – his half-life, as he thought of it now. The memories of what he became down there in the dank were more difficult to acknowledge than the memories of the house where his angelic wife had sashayed happily through its rooms, once upon a happier time.

I cannot stay here.

He could not live and dwell in the memories that they had made together in those rooms. He would forever see her; forever see what he became, and forever see what he would have to do next to end it all.

One more dark deed, this house shall see. Then I shall never set foot in it again.

It was a vow. And like the oath he had taken as a doctor and a husband, he intended to keep it.

Still naked, he stood in front of a mirror in the closet that housed his many moth-eaten clothes and startled from his reflection. Once again he could hardly recognise the man that looked back. His body was lean with muscle and beleaguered with scars from battle. His hair was presentable enough, and with a wash and a shave and some clothes not utterly devoured by moths, he would no doubt resemble, for the first time in years, the man Sarah had fallen in love with.

"All my grief," he said to his reflection, "so indulgent to my atrophy. All my pain, self-caused in my refusal to heal. All my mistakes, driven by love and selfishness. I have tainted her memory." He looked down at the phial of black liquid in his hand and thought of Charles, currently in the care of Mrs Techwood's widowed niece. He then thought of the fossilising body of the man the baby was destined to become, and the damning events that lay in future's wait. He looked into the glassy eyes of his reflection, searching for an answer within them, searching for a clue that he was strong enough to do what needed to be done.

"Have I learned what I must learn to move my hands to this dark deed?" His hands looked old, but he clenched them with strength. "Can I take the life of a child to save the lives of billions? Can I smother the flame I reignited, to stop a dark future's conception? Have I learned death done right?" His eyes gave nothing away about the man inside.

The time had come.

A loud snarl erupted from Prometheus' stomach and suddenly he was famished.

*

By the time Prometheus was dressed to a standard and knocking upon the large black front door of the Teachwood townhouse, he had realised it was, in fact, only that morning he'd last encountered the place. To him it felt as though years, perhaps millennia, had passed. But to all else, mere hours had lapsed.

He wore a grey woollen suit that he'd found in the back of his closet. It was the only garment he could find that wasn't in tatters and stinking of mothballs. After giving it a good beating in the garden most of the dust was thrashed out and a new lease of life flooded into the weave from the summer air. After a wash with scalding water and a shave with a dumb razor – resulting in pinprick cuts spotting his chin and neck – Prometheus adorned the grey suit and swept his silver-streaked hair under the accompanying bowler hat of the same material.

Before venturing up the Teachwood steps, Prometheus had made a quick detour to the local grocer and bought himself an arm-full of bread, cheese and cooked sausage and sat on a bench in Berkley Square green, devouring every morsel and making obscene noises of pleasure with every bite he took. The shade of the trees rippled over him and people stared as they walked by. He momentarily forgot all notion of what he was about to do until the food was gone and he was approaching the door, feeling the phial in his inside pocket, weighing ever heavier with each step forward.

The doorbell chimed and Prometheus waited nervously. It was Anne, Mrs Teachwood's maid, who answered and moved aside for him to wait in the foyer while she fetched her mistress. "Who shall I say is calling," the little Irish woman said.

"Pardon me," he said, realising Anne hadn't recognised him. "Dr Prometheus Page. But I'm actually calling upon Miss Halford, if she's available?"

Anne's eyes widened. "Jesus, Mary and Joseph," she said, before scarpering off into the main part of the house, leaving a multitude of "pardon me, sirs" behind her. It made Prometheus smile. He reached up to touch his face. It was a real smile. He could feel the creases by his eyes. How long had it been since his face had worn a genuine smile?

As Miss Jane Halford came into the foyer, she stopped in astonished mid-step at the sight of him, before regaining the resolve of their argument that morning, it seemed. "Dr Page," she said, a little coldly. "To what do we owe the pleasure?" Bruises of grief still ringed her eyes. She looked him up and down. "You are looking... well," she said. "Very well, in fact."

Prometheus bowed slightly. "Thank you. Your words this morning have set me upon a new path. And I have come to thank you. You were right in everything you said."

"Oh, Dr Page," she said. "You must forgive my impertinence today. Who am I to judge you?"

"You are a gentle lady of sound mind and sense," Prometheus said. "If you cannot aptly judge me, then who can? No apology is needed. Except on my part. My behaviour has been rude and unforgivable towards both you and Charles. But as I said, and as you may see, I stand before you a new man."

"I can see," Miss Halford said. "The alteration is astonishing. Only hours ago you were…" she stopped herself from further insulting him. "But what a circle. Very dashing indeed."

Prometheus smiled again. "I have come for Charles," he said.

Jane's smile wavered. "Oh. Of course." She called for Anne, who came instantly running back after having obviously been listening at the door. "Please fetch Dr Page's nephew," she said. "He's in my room, napping." She turned back to Prometheus. "I made a little nursery for him in there. Had quite the day, the both of us. What a joy he is." She smiled a strained smile. "May I ask what you have decided for him? Where he shall live and so forth?" It was all too clear she was hoping Prometheus was going to tell her that he had decided to look after him himself after all so that she may visit him for the remainder of her time there.

"I'm selling up," Prometheus said.

"The house?" Jane asked, all astonishment.

"Indeed. A fresh start is needed. And Charles is to live up in Scotland with relatives on the maternal side. They're good people."

"So you haven't changed your mind regarding him?"

"I intend to return to work at the hospital," Prometheus said. "As soon as my affairs here are dealt with. I'm afraid the hours of a doctor aren't the best for the child of a lone parent."

Jane nodded. "Yes, I suppose you are right."

"Oh, Dr Page," a voice screeched from the foyer stairs. Mrs Teechwood descended, draped in pearls and powdered to an inch of her life so that her surprised expression ground deep into the creases of her skin. Anne followed her down, carrying a bundle of blankets. "Anne told me you had come, and I told her that couldn't be true because you had not been announced to me. Then she told me that you had come to visit poor dear Jane for the second time today and I just had to come and see you. Then she said that you were looking the best she had ever seen you and then I knew, I just knew that you had come to make her an offer."

"Aunty," Jane exclaimed, reddening.

Mrs Teachwood made it to the floor and swept over the tiles in a mist of floral perfume. "And to think that it was my doing that brought you petit broken birds together. Oh, how I shall have a story to tell at the engagement dinner, which I, of course, shall host."

"Aunty, you have it wrong," Jane urged.

"And that you shall both live right next door is the best part of it. Jane and I shall have tea every day and you shall both dine here every other night. Of course, I say every other night, because on the preceding night Mr Teachwood and I shall, of course, dine at yours, to be sure—"

"Mrs Teachwood, will you please be silent," Prometheus said loudly.

The woman was voiceless suddenly, Prometheus's words echoing through the foyer.

"You have it wrong, madam," he said forcefully. "I have not come to make Miss Halford an offer. Nor would she accept me, I'm sure, if I were. The lady still grieves for her husband and I am thoroughly aghast at how unscrupulous and insensitive you have exposed yourself to be, both in this instance and last night in this very house at your inappropriate gathering."

Mrs Teachwood looked around, as if Prometheus couldn't possibly be speaking to her, and then straightened out her dress awkwardly. She made a small noise, then said, "If you'll excuse me, I must attend to something in the back parlour." She rushed off, gathering layers of silk in a bundle and holding the ginger wig placed precariously on her head in place.

Prometheus turned back to Jane, who was concealing a small smile behind her hand. "I'm so sorry, but it needed to be said, really."

"No apology is necessary," Jane replied. "Perhaps it was needed." She took Charles from Anne's arms just as Mrs Teachwood began frantically screaming Anne's name. The maid rushed off and Jane was left cooing over the sleeping babe.

She leant out and placed the infant in Prometheus's arms, making sure he supported the head correctly. "He is such an angel," she whispered.

Prometheus looked down into the folds of the blanket to see the chubby pink face of Charles sleeping serenely without a care in the world, innocent to it all. He felt so light in his arms.

"It was such a pleasure to have him."

"Have you thought that perhaps an activity might help occupy your time? Keeping busy, they say, can help."

Jane gave him a grateful glance. "Perhaps," she replied. "I wouldn't know what to do and I tend to find needle craft and such things tedious."

"Indeed. I was thinking, however, something a little more engaging. The hospital is always looking for help. The maternity ward, I know, cry out for assistance. I could accompany you when I visit in the next few days. I believe you would be perfect for a position."

"Do you really think so?" Her face lit up. "Perhaps all this time stuck inside isn't helping me. I do tend to feel…"

"Trapped?" Prometheus offered.

"Yes, that's exactly it. Trapped. And useless. I long to feel useful again, and to not have people pawing over me with their sympathies."

"That's settled then. I believe it will do you no end of good."

Jane nodded brightly. "Yes. I believe it shall."

Prometheus took his leave and headed for the door. As he descended each stone step of the Teachwood house, he knew that when he returned home he would make his way down to the cellar for the very last time. He would lay the sleeping child upon his surgeon's slab, draw the antidote from its phial and administer it in its entirety into the baby's soft flesh. He would sit and hold the child in his arms, feeling the life drain from his limbs. The infant's little heart would stop and he would go cold.

He would be dead, again.

Prometheus walked the short distance between the houses and as he reached the base of his own steps, cradling in his arms the still-sleeping Charles, he heard a voice cry out his name. He turned to see Miss Halford walking briskly after him.

"Forgive me if you have other plans," she began a little breathlessly, "but as it is his last afternoon with you, and as it is such a lovely day, perhaps you and I could both take him for a stroll around Hyde Park? If you aren't currently engaged, that is?"

As he looked at Jane's hopeful face, Prometheus felt the heavy phial press against his breast within the pocket of his jacket. He then looked up to the glorious sun above and the handsome day that surrounded them. The birds were tweeting playfully.

What was one afternoon's delay?

Epilogue

The Hyperborea found Earth in its place.

The lifeship's array of tight-field sensors and drone-explorers detected the presence of the planet long before they were close enough to see what it was through the bridge's tempurhull. A charge of excitement set the ship alight with conjecture, but no one allowed themselves to fully believe; even after the many years of relying on technology, the humans refused to submit until they could see with their own two organic eyes.

The news had spread like a contagion, and by the time the official announcement was made, all persons aboard were aware that a planet-sized object currently occupied the space around Sol where the Earth had once resided – that exact space where nothing had been found upon the Hyperborea's last traverse into Earth's system over two hundred years ago. Not only that, but a smaller object, possibly a satellite, had been detected also, the precise distance from the larger object as the Earth's moon had been from the planet.

Still, the humans wouldn't let themselves believe, not yet.

Emotions were high, paused upon a blade. Soon they would know their fate. Soon they would know if they had found their home and thus secured the survival of their children.

Almost fifty years had passed since the Hyperborea had first plotted its course from the distant space of the Titan System and yet they still told stories of what happened there. They spoke of a great battle and how humanity had triumphed against the mighty machines that had almost plunged their race into extinction. They spoke of the heroes that gave their lives for them: General Nathan Shaw, a statue of whom now looked out over the hologarden in the upper levels; XO Rawl Collister, whose monument sat honourably in the Captain Memorial Hall; the mysterious Prometheus, the man who came from another time, bringing with him an army of identical warriors; and Winston, the AI that had turned against his own in search of truth.

Parents told the tales to their children as they slept in their bunkers, of the AI that saved them all for the love of a human woman. Not all believed the tales. And when children would not go to sleep, parents would say "the AI will come and get you," and the children would fling the covers over their small heads in fear.

The humans had not forgotten.

The heroes were remembered, and every man, woman and child knew their hallowed names. But the villains still haunted their nightmares, burned into the very DNA of humanity, being passed from generation to the next.

Never would they forget.

Families gathered in the various solariums of the lifeship, filling rows upon rows and watching the growing object that could be their new home under a control field dome. Circa twenty thousand bodies heaved into the solars dotted around the re-opened upper levels of the Hyperborea, watching the distant speck grow within the blackness of space as they decelerated ever closer.

When the news was finally confirmed, and the speck became a marble of blue and green that flooded the viewing stations, all of humanity celebrated. Some rushed off to prepare their families. For many, it would be their first ever time leaving the Hyperborea. Some, however, remained, wishing to watch Earth grow as the distance narrowed.

Soon, the sight of Earth loomed in all its magnificence, and it was the lifeship that became a speck as it hovered beside their new home. All who saw it were silent. All who saw it were in tears and awe. All who saw it knew it was where they belonged. All who saw it knew humanity would survive, now that their mother had returned to them.

It was with an almighty shock wave that the Hyperborea entered Earth's atmosphere. It made a swift descent in a trajectory that would see them touch ground on what was once known as China State – the very land from which the Hyperborea had long ago set voyage. The people crowded with excitement into their allotted docking stations, with their given exit number and information about where they were to go and what village their family had been assigned to when they finally made it onto the planet. Some were scared. All were fevered with adrenaline.

The interior hulls of the docking stations seemed ever more oppressing now that the people knew what awaited them. There were few portholes for them to see out as the Hyperborea touched ground. Suddenly the ship was motionless. Still and noiseless.

A probe had been sent ahead and confirmed the air was breathable, and within seconds the airlock doors of the Underbelly's docking station commenced opening with a hydraulic thrum. Air rushed in, warm and sweet and fragrant, clearing the stars and death from memories in one gust.

Three figures stepped forward as a single gangplank descended onto Earth soil. Humanity watched as Captain Lydia Chen stepped forward into the sunlight. She turned to Lieutenant Daneel Sharma nervously, and he encouraged her on with a smile, the expression making a lined map of his face.

She had been honoured with being the first human to step onto Earth, for her part in making it possible. The breeze whipped her silver hair as she took in what she saw of Earth, her eyes sparkling brightly.

The Hyperborea sat smally within wide rolling fields of long green grass that rippled in the wind. A light shower of rain was falling from tepid grey clouds in the open sky. Mountains stood on the horizon, and in the near distance a canopy of leafy trees housed the tune of singing birds. Light broke through the clouds in sharp rays onto the mountains topped with snow, setting the horizon in a wash of pale yellow. Raindrops splattered Lydia's skin and she began to laugh, lifting her palms to the sky as the water covered her face.

Earth.

Like it was only yesterday, Lydia remembered the man who had sacrificed himself so she could see what she saw now. She turned back to Daneel and motioned him to her. He hesitated for a moment before taking the steps out. Earth's light exposed his thinning hair that had remained dark over the years and a face that was etched with the lines scored from a life filled with a million smiles. He too turned back to a figure waiting at the edge of the gangplank.

A boy of fifteen apprehensively made his way to his parents. His hair was thick and dark and hung over his face. He casually swept it back to reveal Lydia's eyes. He gave his father a crooked smile and stood beside them nervously.

"Have you ever seen anything so beautiful?" Lydia said, looking out into the distance of their new home.

Daneel took her hand. "I have," he said, looking at her.

"You go, Winston," Lydia said to her son. "I've been here before, in another time, another life. You go first."

Winston smiled shyly, aware of the many eyes on him, and took humanity's first step onto Earth's soil. As he did, a riotous cheer erupted from the Hyperborea.

Delphine Descends

By Darrel William Moore

Power corrupts
Innocence is lost
Vengeance makes monsters of us all

After her family is killed and her home world occupied, young Kathreen Martin is sent to the distant world of Furoris for re-education. She will live the rest of her life as a serf, to be bought and sold as a commodity of the Imperial Network.

When her only chance of escape is ruined, a chance mistaken identity offers her a new life as the orphaned daughter of a First-Citizen Senator and heir to fortune beyond measure.

She vows she will claw her way into power to sit among the worlds' elite. Then, with her own two hands, she will reap bloody vengeance on them all.

But, to beat them she must play their game. She must become worse than them all.

Delphine Descends is available from Amazon now.

A word from the author

Thank you for reading *Black Milk*. This was one of those stories that started as one thing in my head, but quickly expanded until it grew beyond its original size and ambition.

It's also the steepest learning curve I've experienced with my writing; I lived and breathed this book for four years and it became my constant in a time of flux.

But ultimately, I wanted it to be two things: I wanted to create something that incorporated everything I love about sicence fiction; and I wanted it to be an epic, in every sense of the word.

Does it achieve these two things? I'll leave that for you to decide.

If you enjoyed *Black Milk*, please consider leaving a review on **Amazon** or on **Goodreads**. Writing and publishing independently is hard and reviews are the lifeblood of every independent author.

Thanks again for reading.

With special thanks to my unofficial editor

Printed in Great Britain
by Amazon